WITH THIS WOMAN

THE STORY FROM JESSE (BOOK 2)

JODI ELLEN MALPAS

Jodi Ellen Malpas

With This Woman was first published in 2023 by Jodi Ellen Malpas

ISBN eBook - 978-1-957597-04-1
ISBN Paperback - 978-1-957597-50-8
ISBN Hardback - 978-1-957597-03-4

Editing by - Marion Archer

Proofing by - Karen Lawson

Cover design by – Hang Le

PRAISE FOR JODI ELLEN MALPAS

"Malpas's sexy love scenes scorch the page, and her sensitive, multilayered hero and heroine will easily capture readers' hearts. A taut plot and a first-rate lineup of supporting characters make this a keeper." —*Publishers Weekly* on *Gentleman Sinner*

"This book is JEM at her best, the secrets, lies, enemies... and tongue it cheek humour. It's all there on every single page! I had no idea where this book was going or how the book would end. The journey was as captivating as it was enigmatic." - *Kindle and Koffee Book Blog on Wicked Truths*

"It's just twist after dark and delicious twist; a completely, unquestionably unpredictable ride from start to finish. This is the kind of book where every page is important, because there is just SO MUCH going on, and it's an intricate dance from loathe to love for this couple." - *Jeeves Reads Romance on The Brit*

"So it's safe to say, Jodi has once again completely smashed it with another sensation making it the best read of 2021! Hold on tight your about to be enthralled." - *Booksobsessive on The Enigma*

"A magnetic mutual attraction, a superalpha, and long-buried scars that are healed by love. Theo is irresistible." —*Booklist* on *Gentleman Sinner*

"Filled with raw emotions that ranged from the deepest rage to utter elation, Jodi Ellen Malpas wove together an incredible must-read tale that fans will certainly embrace." —Harlequin Junkie on *Gentleman Sinner*

"The characters are realistic and relatable and the tension ratchets up to an explosive conclusion. For anyone who enjoys *Sleeping with the Enemy*-style stories, this is a perfect choice."—Library Journal on *Leave Me Breathless*

"*The Controversial Princess*, told from Adeline's POV, is thick on plot, rich in character development with Kindle-melting sex and the perfect blend of twists and turns, shockers and villains!" —SueBee, Goodreads Reviewer

"*The Controversial Princess* is an all-consuming, scorching hot, modern royal romance with twists, turns and a jaw-dropping cliff-hanger that will leave you begging for more." —Mary Dube, *USA Today HEA*

"*The Controversial Princess* provided us with the romance our hearts needed, the passion our hearts craved, with jaw dropping twists and turns that kept us guessing and eagerly flipping the pages." —TotallyBooked Blog

"A brave, cutting-edge romance…This is a worthwhile read." —*Library Journal* on *The Forbidden*

"Unpredictable and addictive."—*Booklist* on The *Forbidden*

"*The Forbidden* proves that Jodi Ellen Malpas is not only one of the romance genre's most talented authors, but also one of the bravest. In this raw and honest portrayal of forbidden love, Jodi delivers a sexy and passionate love story with characters to root for. *The Forbidden* is easily my favorite read of 2017!"—Shelly Bell, author of At His Mercy, on *The Forbidden*

"*The Forbidden* is a gut-wrenching tale full of passion, angst, and heart! Not to be missed!"

—Harlequin Junkie on *The Forbidden*

“Every kiss, every sexy scene, every word between this pair owned a piece of my soul. I could read this book a hundred times and still react as if it was the first time. *The Protector* is a top 2016 fave for me.” —Audrey Carlan, #1 bestselling author of The Calendar Girl series on *The Protector*

“4.5 stars. Top Pick. Readers will love this book from the very beginning! The characters are so real and flawed that fans feel as if they’re alongside them. Malpas’ writing is also spot-on with emotions.”—RT Book Reviews on *The Protector*

“*With This Man* took this already epic love story to a whole new, unthinkable height of brilliance.” – Gi’s Spot Reviews

“Super steamy and emotionally intense.” –The Library Journal on *With This Man*

"Jodi Ellen Malpas delivers a new heart-wrenching, addicting read."—RT Book Reviews on *With This Man*

“We really don’t have enough words nor accolades for this book! It had everything and MORE with added ghosts from the past as well as a surprising suspense. But mostly, it was about a love that proves it can conquer anything and everything placed in its way. A beautiful addition to one of our favourite series!”—TotallyBooked Blog on *With This Man*

For Evelyn.
I cannot wait for all of the adventures we'll share.

With This Woman

JODI ELLEN
MALPAS

1

I DON'T KNOW how many times I've opened my eyes and quickly closed them again. I don't know how many hours or days have passed. I'm moving but not moving. Hearing but not hearing. Feeling but not feeling. My skin is sore, my head thumping. My darkness too comforting to leave. I'm too afraid to open my eyes, too much of a coward to face my wrongs.

Without the energy to fix my fuckups.

There are so many.

You're one fucked-up sorry state.

You need help.

But . . . I'm beyond help. Especially now—now she's gone too.

Everyone. *Gone.*

I melt back into the hard floor, feeling like I'm fading away. Wishing I could finally be spared the mercy of this agony. Never. Because I don't deserve respite. Every cruel, painful thing that's happened to me in my lifetime is justified. And offering me the hope of redemption before taking it away? Giving me Ava and taking her away? I had it coming.

I hear some yelling, but it seems far away, and I roll my jaw, feeling it scrape across the decking under my cheek. My mind bends and twists, my past playing on loop, ruthlessly reminding me, yet again, of the endless hole of misery that is my existence. But amid the horrors something shines through. Something good. It's hazy, barely detectable, but it's there, trying so hard to overpower the merciless evil.

Ava.

I pushed her away, screamed at her, scared her, made her question . . . everything. *I* made her run. *I* made her fight her feelings.

I made her leave me.

But she's not gone? Not gone, but not quite here either.

Because she can't find her way through the darkness to me. *I have to get to her . . .* but someone pulls me back, stopping me. I feel something press into my back, my brain rattling as my head is lifted, hands rubbing all over my face, through my hair, all over my naked chest. There's talking. Words that sound miles away. I can't decipher what they're saying. Can't make out the voices.

But then there's one I recognize, and it's begging me to open my eyes. Saying my name repeatedly, sounding distressed. A face appears through the darkness, and my heart races as I reach for her. She's too far away.

No!

My legs start moving, frantic and fast, trying to run to her and yet I get nowhere, watching her drift farther and farther away from me. Soon, she'll be out of reach completely. Soon, she'll give up trying to find me. Soon, she'll be gone forever.

Soon, all I'll have is this darkness and more regrets.

No hope to cling on to. I don't think I can shoulder anymore grief. I can't lose the only piece of relief and happiness I've found in years.

I'll never survive it.

Don't leave me!

Warmth penetrates my hand, and something seeps into me, something soothing. I still, concentrating on feeling it. It's familiar. Comforting.

And then it's gone, and I'm suddenly weightless. Moving. *Don't take me away from that feeling!* Something soft meets my back, and something softer meets my cheek.

It's back. That feeling is back, and as it rubs gently up and down my face, the darkness starts to fade again. Something subtle and delicate invades my nose, and something presses to my forehead. Lips. Soft, full lips. My arm shoots out, grappling at the lingering darkness, trying to seize the source. "Ava?" My eyes sting just trying to get them open, and the glare hurts, but I frantically search everywhere, looking for her.

And then I find her.

Her mouth moves, she's speaking, and yet awe is clouding my ability to hear her. A rush of memories takes me hostage—our row, the drink, her face a picture of shock and devastation. Disgust.

You're one fucked-up sorry state.

You need help.

I try to lift my head, but it's so heavy, so painful, and I slump back down, out of breath. Broken. My mouth is dry, words sticking to my tongue, but I force them out. "I'm so sorry. I'm sorry, I'm sorry, I'm sorry, I'm sorry, I'm sorry . . ."

She takes my hand and lifts it to her face. Her touch is like a sedative. My mind shuts down, the weight of my regrets too much, and I succumb to my exhaustion.

I have only enough energy to pray she wasn't a dream.

2

I'M WARM. So damn warm. I gingerly allow my eyes to peel open, the dusky light not quite dusky enough not to hurt. I look down my body, squinting, seeing blankets coating every inch of me. My sensitive skin feels tender under them. I'm sweating, suffocating, so I lethargically push the stifling material down my body in search of some air. How did I get here? With blankets and a pillow?

I reach up to my pounding head, putting pressure on my temple to try and dull the pain. "Fuck," I murmur. There's only one cure.

Vodka.

And I need it before my mind has a chance to kick in after it's fought through the fog, before it has a chance to remind me of where I am and why I'm here. What I've lost.

I swing my legs off the couch and scan the room in search of my savior..

And nearly stop breathing.

"Ava?" Her name falls past my lips, sounding like a desperate plea. She's here? I rub my eyes, certain my mind is playing tricks on me, certain the vodka is fucking me over. I'm dreaming. I'm still asleep. She can't be here. Why would she be?

I open my eyes, bracing myself for the disappointment, and slump back against the couch when I find her still curled up in the chair. I can do no more than watch her, waiting for my reality to catch up and take her away. For her to disappear.

Yet ten minutes later, she's still in the chair. Fast asleep. Peaceful.

Swallowing hard, I push my hands into the sofa, but quickly take my weight off them when pain shoots up my arm. I hiss and assess the swollen, purple mass, turning it over, gingerly flexing it. It's ugly. The reasons behind the injury are ugly. Everything in my life is ugly.

Except . . .

I divert my attention to the chair again. "Except you," I whisper, using my legs to get me up. Every bone in my body cracks until I'm standing; I'm feeling dizzy and lightheaded. And old. Jesus, I feel so fucking old.

I give myself a few moments to stabilize, drinking in as much oxygen as I can before I attempt to put one foot in front of the other. My steps are tentative. Every time a foot meets the floor, it sends shockwaves up my legs, through my torso, before exploding in my head. But I endure the punishment, accept it, take it all.

I make it to the chair and lower to my haunches, reaching for her hair. Her beautiful, dark, shiny hair. Her face looks a little blotchy. *Tears*. And yet every part of this woman is so alive and vivid. And every part of me is dull and dead. I could tarnish her beauty. Strip her of her sass. I could ruin her. Maybe I already have. "I love you," I whisper, as if in apology. As if those three words are an acceptable excuse for what I have done. I have nothing else. I love this woman with a crippling intensity. It's a love that sends me into a new kind of madness. A madness that's far more appealing than my past craziness. Through no fault of her own, Ava's become my crux. A reason for me to go on.

I exhale heavily, the silky strands of her hair sliding through my fingers, feeling soft against my sore skin. And suddenly, her eyes open. I fucking hate the torment I see in her stare as she slowly comes around. I did that. I caused that.

She blinks and shoots up from the chair, and I startle, my tired body not working fast enough to stop me falling back.

"Shit," she yelps.

I flinch at the harshness of her language, as well as the volume. "Watch your mouth," I croak, fighting my way to my feet and dropping onto the couch, fucking exhausted.

"You're awake."

Fuck me, she needs to turn her volume down. My eardrums feel like they could burst along with my head. There's no denying she's seen me at my absolute worst. But . . . she's here. For once, I haven't got to chase her down. Although she looks ready to bolt at any moment, her eyes wide and panicked, her body rigid as she backs up to a chair and lowers.

The silence is unbearable as she looks at me, her mind obviously racing. I can see the endless questions running circles, while endless excuses loop mine. Endless apologies. Endless regrets.

"How are you feeling?" she asks, breaking the awkward silence but somehow making the atmosphere even more uncomfortable. I breathe out, looking down at my mess of a hand. Black. Purple. Blue. Yellow. Every phase of bruising you could imagine adorns my swollen limb. And it hurts again. It really fucking hurts. *How am I feeling?* I swallow, and that hurts too. How could I possibly convey my regret? Apologize? Reassure her? I ponder that for too long, until Ava stands abruptly.

My knackered body responds without instruction, straightening, ready to stop her leaving. I can't let her walk away from me again. God knows where I'll end up next. "Where are you going?" I blurt, set to charge her down. Make her listen. Make her hear me. Just as soon as I find a way to explain myself.

"I thought you might need some water."

Water? I need something, and it isn't water. I need forgiveness. I need absolution. I need *her*. This distance between us, this hesitancy, isn't boding well. Neither is the fact that at this moment in our relationship, for the first time, she is both the strongest mentally *and* physically. But make no mistake, I've always been at this woman's mercy. Now more than ever. She left me, but she's back. What does that mean?

Ava goes to the kitchen, and I watch her the entire way until she disappears. Even in another room, her absence is excruciating. I can't fix this with my power over her. I can't use what I've always depended on. Our chemistry. Our attraction. The explosions we create when we're intimate. Things are too broken. *You must give her words*. But where the fuck will I find the right ones? And is she prepared to even listen?

In complete despair, I drop my heavy head into my hands, willing my brain to back me up and give me something. *Anything*.

Nothing.

It feels like the whole fucking world is against me.

Even myself.

As I stare down at the threads of the carpet, feeling like the worst kind of shit on every level, her bare feet appear. Her perfect bare feet. I lift my tired head to face her. Her eyes are swimming. Despair to match mine. I can't bear it, and in a knee-jerk move, I reach for the water, laying my hand over hers, desperate to feel her. For her to feel *me*.

She jumps out of her skin, startled, and my heart jumps out of my chest, pained. Cold water drenches my hand, spilling up over the glass, my shakes not helping. My shakes are the least of my worries, and they look like the most of Ava's. God, she thinks she knows, when she knows nothing. Absolutely nothing. This here, me now, it's just a smudge on the vast canvas of my fuck-ups. And look at her reaction. It's not natural for us to be this . . . distant.

"When did you last have a drink?" she asks quietly.

Of all the questions she must have, she asks that? *Ask me if I love you. If you mean the fucking world to me. If you're the difference between life and death.*

I take some water to wet my mouth and hopefully loosen my lips. "I don't know," I admit. Each sip, each bottle, went that little bit further to complete oblivion. It was the only way. Lose the memories. Lose the days. "What day is it?"

"Saturday."

"Saturday?" I choke, scanning the room for empty bottles, finding none. Did she clear them? Did she count each and every one of my sins as she tossed them in the bin? "Fuck," I breathe. I should be dead. And if I don't somehow fix this mess, I will be.

Find the words, Ward.

Except . . . nothing seems adequate, which leaves more silence, me playing mindlessly with my glass and Ava going back to the chair, meters away from me. If I could only hold her. If she would only let me touch her. I'd apologize with every inch of my skin on hers. Make her remember.

"Jesse, is there anything I can do?" she asks, sounding helpless.

I laugh on the inside, but there is not one scrap of humor, only despair. "There are lots of things you can do, Ava," I murmur, my eyes on the rippling water in my glass. "But I can't ask you to do any of them." Because it isn't fair. She deserves more than I'm capable of giving. For weeks, I agonized over what to tell her and how. For weeks I swayed from courageous to cowardice. And here we are, every reason for me to keep my mouth shut proving itself. She's had only a fraction of my unbearable tale. The rest? The rest will put the nail in the coffin for me. And it will kill her too. And yet, selfishly, I can't bear to tell her to leave before I do any more damage.

"Do you want a shower?" she asks.

A shower. A few weeks ago, such a question would've had me up out of my chair like a rocket and carrying her like a caveman to the bathroom. Today, I can hardly find the energy to pick *myself* up. She won't join me. She's merely caring for me. Out of guilt? Duty? Because she feels sorry for me?

Or because she loves me?

"Sure." I hiss my way up to my feet, mentally begging her to help me. She doesn't. "Shit." The blanket falls to a pile at my feet, my hands not fast enough to stop it. I look down my naked body. Limp. Flaccid. Useless like the rest of me. I struggle to reach down and hide myself. "I'm sorry," I say lamely, covering my body. *I'm sorry for everything.*

She looks insulted for a moment, and I very nearly blurt out that my condition has nothing to do with her and everything to do with being broken. Does she realize she's the medicine?

Ava sighs and leads on, and I follow, my feet dragging, my heart following. I'm even more fucked by the time we make it to my bathroom, out of breath, aching, feeling weaker.

"Would a bath be better?" she asks.

Undoubtedly. My legs won't hold me up for much longer. "I suppose."

As Ava draws me a bath, I rest against the wall for support, and I take in every inch of the space she designed. The vanity unit, where we finally came together. The shower, where I've cleaned her endlessly from the top of her beautiful head to the very tips of her perfect toes. The bath, the one I braved facing because she was in it with me. A bath before Ava crashed into my life was inconceivable. I could never have soaked, relaxed, not when every bath time with Rosie would have been at the forefront of my mind.

I swallow back the building lump and find Ava. She's staring at the vanity unit. Is she thinking all the things I'm thinking? Seeing us both in here, naked, together, smiling?

And loving, even if neither of us found the courage to speak the words?

I see her physically shaking herself back to life, clearly unable to face those thoughts. "There." She points to the full tub and makes a hasty exit.

"You're acting like a stranger," I call quietly, halting her escape. We're not strangers. Nowhere near strangers. We're one. A force. She's a salve to my cracked heart. She's my soul. My fucking *everything.*

"I feel like a stranger." Her voice is wobbly, riddled with emotion, and it echoes in the silence that follows. Her pain, mixed with my pain. It's toxic. We need to be rid of it, and yet, I have no clue how to start fixing it.

With the truth.

But the truth is too risky. I'm not prepared to make any moves that'll see this woman walking away from me again. Never. God have mercy on my soul, I have to do whatever it takes. *Anything.* I will protect her from the truth if it kills me.

"Please look at me, Ava," I whisper, begging, knowing our chances of surviving this will be so much better if she could just face me. See me. *Feel* me.

It takes too much courage of her part, and too much fear on mine, but she turns wearily. Looks at me. And her head starts to shake, tears brimming again. "I can't do this." She's gone from the bathroom faster than my brain can compute what's just happened.

"Ava," I yell, begging my legs not to fail me as I run after her, chasing her down the stairs, reaching for her endlessly, but I grab thin air each time, missing her. Thin air. That's what will become of me if she makes it out of this apartment.

Nothing.

Empty.

Dead.

I dig deep for some strength and seize her wrist, yanking her back. She's facing me in a second, and I stagger back from the force of her frantic shove. But I don't lose my grip. I *can't* lose my hold of her.

"No," she cries out, hysterical. "Don't touch me!" The state of her, the state *I've* made of her, crucifies me.

"Ava, don't do this." I try to get my face close to hers, force her to see me. "Stop."

Every muscle in her body seems to give, taking her down to the floor by my feet. "Please, don't," she begs. "Please, don't make this harder."

I look down at her, horrified. My God, what have I done? How have I managed to transform the fierce, sass-filled lady that I fell in love with into this? A shattered woman. A woman in despair. *Broken.*

Every reason for me to turn my back on my past, to bury it, is on her knees before me, sobbing her heart out.

I drop to the floor and grab her shuddering body, tugging her onto me, cradling her, hugging her, rocking her back and forth while praying into her hair.

"I'm sorry," I choke, tears starting to fall. I cry for her. Not for me. I deserve this pain. Ava does not. "I'm so, so sorry. I don't deserve it," I whisper, "but give me a chance. I *need* another chance."

"I don't know what to do," she sobs, hiding in my chest from our reality. She doesn't realize it, but she's doing it already. My trembles have calmed. My heart is steady. My delicate skin is relishing the friction of her all over me.

"Don't run away from me again," I order, though it's gentle, and she sniffles, breaking away from me. My scar tingles under her gaze as I take her face and force her to look at me. I need her eyes. No matter if they're full of hopelessness and not the fire I so love, I need them. Just to check she's really here. Just to check she's real. "I'm going to make this all right," I vow. "I'm going to make you remember, Ava."

Her look tells me she believes me. She should. I'll never let her down again. I've been in various levels of hell. This is up there with the worst of them.

"Can you make me remember the conventional way?" she asks, totally serious. It brings the first smile to my face in too long. There's nothing conventional about us. Never will be. I had my way, she had hers. And together, it worked. It'll work again.

"I'm making it my mission objective," I say with grit. "I'll do *anything*." My words seem to reach something inside of her, and her lips part as she scans my face. I hope she sees determination in my eyes, and I know she has when she falls into my chest and clings on like she needs me. As much as I need her. Even just a glimmer of hope would have charged me with resolve. This? How hard she's holding me, how deep she's snuggling? It's more than a glimmer. It's a lightning bolt. She's healing me. Healing *us*.

I exhale, sinking my face into her hair, my arse beginning to go numb, but my heart feeling everything there is to feel. So much fucking love.

"Your bath will get cold," she whispers.

"I'm comfy." It's a lie. My achy muscles are screaming.

"You need to eat as well. And that hand needs seeing to. Does it hurt?"

"Like hell." And eat? My stomach turns at the mere thought.

"Come on." She peels our skin apart as I moan my dismay. Yet I'm drained of the physical strength I need to keep her here. I should also be amenable to her clear desire to take care of me. It's backward, not us, and I hate it. But . . . I'll take anything I can get.

She offers her hand, looking down at me. It's admirable, but we both know she couldn't move me an inch, even when I'm useless. But I still accept, wincing my way up to standing, and let her unhurriedly lead the way to the bathroom, my eyes unmoving from our joined hands between us.

We enter, and I take it all in, wishing I could erase the horrid memories of this space, leaving only the amazing.

"In you get."

I find her pointing at the tub—the giant tub that's way too big for one person. The potential of soaking in it alone isn't the only strange notion I'm dealing with. "Are you making demands?" I ask, unsure whether I quite like it or hate it. The dynamics of our relationship are shifting too fast for me to get used to.

"Sounds like it." She's indifferent, in a smug kind of way.

Would it be too much to expect her to join me? It would be a major step in the right direction, a leap closer to our normal. "Will you get in with me?" I ask, sounding very unlike the Jesse Ward who met this young beauty only a few short weeks ago.

Her indifference turns on its head, and she moves away, now unsure. "I can't."

Bullshit. She can and she should. She simply *won't*. Injured, I try to explain, rather than enforce it, which is exactly how things would happen if I wasn't standing here with my tail between my legs feeling half dead. "Ava." I breathe out her name like a plea. "You're asking me not to touch you. That goes against all my instincts." She knows that. Is she punishing me? Every second without her attached to me in one way or another feels like the worst kind of torture.

"Jesse, please." She looks away, clearly unable to face the hurt in my eyes. "I need time."

Time for what? To decide whether she's staying in my life or not?

Time to decide if she's going to forgive me? Then why the hell is she here? "It's not natural, Ava. For me not to touch you, it's not right."

Her eyes dart to her feet, and she's silent. *God, what's going through that head of yours, lady?* If she'd tell me what to do, I'll do it. No questions asked. Anything.

Then do this, Jesse. Give her the time she's asking for and just be grateful she's even here.

Fuck. Can I do that? Abstaining is hard enough when she's not around, but when I can smell her? Smell the relief and the cure so close?

Ava finds it in herself to look at me, and it's a blatant effort to show me her stance. Adamant. It's ridiculous. We both know what will erase this pain. Me. Her. *Together*. She's hurting too, and the remedy—me—is standing here before her begging her to let me repair what I've broken.

It goes against the grain for us but, reluctantly, I do as she's asked, dropping my blanket and stepping into the tub. Alone. "It's not the same without you in here with me." I rest back and close my eyes, hoping my lack of vision will take the edge off how odd it feels to bathe alone. How much I hate it. Listening to her moving around. Knowing she's here.

She wets my hair, and her fingers massage gently across my sore scalp. I grit my teeth, forcing my hands to remain still and close to me. Then I feel her palms circling my body, soaping me up. Cleaning me. *If only.* My throat tightens, the strain to remain unmoving making my muscles ache more. Her hands spend extra time around the sight of my scar, slowing in their soft circles. She'll never clean that enough for it to be gone. My lungs start to scream, and I realize I'm holding my breath, bracing myself for her to question me on it again.

"You need a shave."

I exhale discreetly, feeling her touch move to my jaw, and I open an eye to find her taking in my overgrown face.

"You don't like it?" I ask, having a feel myself, stroking at the bristle.

"I like you however you come," she whispers, but my relief to hear that is clouded by the flicker of pain in her dark eyes. She said it. She didn't mean it. She wouldn't take me when I'm drunk. She wouldn't take me shouting insults at her, being a bastard.

You were good. In fact, you were the best I've had.

And I've had a lot.

I shy away from the sketchy memories, flinching, feeling her slap across my cheek as if she's just delivered it. Jesus Christ. "I'm not touching another drop again," I promise. I'll never forgive myself for being so fucking weak. For drowning my sorrows in alcohol. Never again.

"You sound confident."

"I am." I push myself up, taking her face. *Fuck.* I grit my teeth, flexing my injured hand. *Motherfucker.* I push back the agony and focus on what's important. Another agony. One that hurts more. Her distance. "I mean it, never again. I promise you." She has to believe me. "I'm not a raving alcoholic, Ava," I go on, needing her to know that, while at the same time ignoring the voices in my head calling me out. Telling me I'm deluded. "I admit I get carried away once I have a drink, and I find it hard to stop, but I can take it or leave it. I was in a bad place after you left me. I just wanted to numb the pain."

Jesus fucking Christ, are you hearing yourself, Ward?

Ava looks away. She's not sure whether to believe me, so I have no option but to prove myself. And I will. Every fucking day for the rest of my life.

"Why didn't you tell me sooner?" she asks. "Is this what you meant when you said I would cause more damage if I left?"

I look away, ashamed. I said so many things, many of which I'm sure I can't remember. I was desperate. "That was a shitty thing to say."

"It was."

"I just wanted you to stay," I whisper, looking at her again. Some things need to be said while looking someone in the eye, and this is one of them. "I was stunned when you told me that I had a nice hotel."

That moment. The realization. I still don't know if it was a blessing or a curse. Would she have given in to the potent chemistry we share if she had known in that moment exactly what The Manor was? Who *I* was? "Things got pretty intense, pretty quickly." I felt like my dead heart had been hit with high voltage. It was new, addictive, and I knew I had to explore it. Even if the object of my newfound desire tried to rebuff our connection. "I didn't know how to tell you. I didn't want you to run away again. You. Kept. Running. Away."

"I didn't get far though, did I?"

No, and she didn't want to either. I knew it. She knew it. Which made the whole tiresome pursuit a mix of frustrating, exciting, and fucking exhausting. "I was going to tell you," I assure her. God, if she knew of the war going on between my heart and head. "You weren't supposed to come to The Manor like that. I wasn't prepared, Ava."

Once again, she becomes thoughtful, and I will her to speak those thoughts. She doesn't. She probably finds it odd too—we've always talked with our bodies. Our chemistry. "Come on, you're pruning." She presents me with a towel and an expectant look, and with a lack of anything else to do, I do as I'm bid, stepping out and letting her dry me. It takes me back to the time she stood like a zombie before me, the morning after she drunkenly confessed her love. And then bloody forgot. Should I remind her?

She reaches my neck, and I smile at the concentration on her face. "A few weeks ago, I was nursing *your* hangover."

"I bet your head is banging a lot harder than mine was," she retorts quickly, and I recoil, offended. I don't know about that. She seemed on a mission herself that night. At least my binge was spread over five days. "Food and then the hospital."

"Hospital?" I blurt out, stunned. *What the fuck?* So she's having me sectioned? If I'm crazy, it's only because she's made me that way. Or is she talking rehab here? Therapy? *She's* my therapy. "I don't need a hospital, Ava." *I need you.*

"Your hand."

I frown as I take a peek, flexing it a little on a suppressed hiss. It looks like a fucking balloon. "It's fine."

"I don't think it is."

"Ava, I don't need to go to the hospital." I don't need a doctor poking at me, smelling the alcohol on me, assessing me, drawing conclusions.

"Don't go then." She leaves the bathroom, and I scowl at her back. The only problem my hand is giving me is the lack of ability to grab her and toss her on the bed. But I would certainly try, and I would sustain the pain, because it could never hurt as much as this.

I follow on heavy feet and fall to my back on the bed as she goes to the dressing room. I hear her rummaging around, and turn my face up to the ceiling, feeling annoyance that I have no right to feel creeping up on me. This is all so wrong.

"Here, put these on." A pile of clothes lands next to me, and I drop my head to the side on a sigh that I absolutely want her to hear. How long will she do this? Haven't we both suffered enough?

I make no attempt to dress, without the energy or the desire, my aching head refusing to help me out and give me any direction, other than what comes naturally when it comes to this woman, and I've already established that I can't throw my weight around, not that I have the strength, anyway. Gently does it. I'm not filled with confidence. I tried gently already, when we first met, and I got absolutely nowhere.

I feel something tap my ankle and look down my body to see Ava holding my boxers at my feet.

Oh?

I sit up, looking down at her. Why would she put herself there? At my feet. Her face level with my dick. My blood surges, and no amount of self-control would stop it. God, and I thought the pain couldn't get any worse.

I stand and she starts dragging my boxers up, and with her hand brushing my legs added to the already unbearable situation, my dick literally pings to life. So much so, it knocks the towel enough to loosen it around my waist.

It drops to the floor.

Ava freezes and stares at my raging hard-on for a few silent moments, and then in a delayed reaction, as if she's suddenly remembered she's resisting me, she startles, moving back. She looks up, her lips parted, her eyes alive. I know mine match. *Grab her. Show her.*

How long will she be able to keep up this fight? She still wants me. She wants me so badly, but forcing this is not the way forward. She'll reject me, if only to make a point to herself. It's like the time we met all over again, except this time, begrudgingly, I must do something other than making demands to win her over. "I'll go to the hospital," I say, pulling my boxers up. "If you want me to, I'll go." I'm playing fair. Fuck knows why, since she's always loved me playing dirty. But sexual manipulation, something she categorically loves, feels so wrong given the delicate situation.

"Agreeing to have your hand looked at won't make me fall to your feet in gratitude," she fires, looking insulted.

What? Was there any need for that? I'm being amenable, doing as I'm told, and she gives me her lip in return? "I'll let that slip," I grate, bristling terribly. *Rein it in, Ward.*

She doesn't take too kindly to my scorn. Never does. "I need to feed you." She leaves in a strop, and I start to wonder if her mood has anything to do with the high possibility that she was ready to jump me just then and *I* stopped it. She has questions, and she's told herself she won't submit until she has her answers. Which basically means we're never having sex again. I've seen the result of some truths being revealed. I'll be damned if I'll willingly put us through that again. So I have no choice but to find another way to give her what she wants and at the same time get what I need.

I pull on the sweats and T-shirt and trudge after her, inspecting my hand as I go. It really does look nasty. "Ouch," I mutter, scowling as I take the stairs, pushing aside how much it fucking hurts. I gaze around my penthouse, sensing her absence even though she's here, and walk into the kitchen, ready to apologize all over again. But I find it empty. "Ava?" I call, turning on the spot, listening, trying not to let panic get the better of me. But my voice rises naturally as I call her name repeatedly, my feet carrying my heavy body to the door. I grab the handle with my injured hand. "Fuck!" I bellow, the pain excruciating. I feel sick. I swap hands, yank the door open and head for the elevator, but a distant sound of a door closing stops me, and I look back, reversing my steps. A whooshing sound kicks in, and I follow it until I'm upstairs again, standing outside one of the spare bedrooms. The shower. Not *our* shower. More pain. Another kick in the gut.

I reach up to my face and drag my hands down my bristle, resting my forehead on the wood of the door. Why is she even here if she's just going to punish me like this?

I drag myself back downstairs and find my phone charging in the kitchen. I call Sam, and he answers fast, his tone soft. Concerned. "Please don't ask how I am," I say, my voice rough as I pace in front of the terrace doors, up and down. I look at the staircase again. Hear the shower.

"Mate, don't ever do that to me again," he warns, and I swallow, nodding. "I swear to fucking God, I'll kill you myself. You won't need vodka. How's Ava?"

My eyes are still on the stairs. "Distant," I say simply because that's exactly what she is. Here but not here. Caring but not caring.

"Give her time, man. It's a lot to take in."

"How did Kate take it?" I make my way to the kitchen to get more water, so fucking thirsty.

He's silent, and I frown. It actually makes my head bang. Just a frown. "Quite well." He sounds reluctant. Wary.

"What's going on?"

"Nothing?"

"Talk," I order, necking my water in one fell swoop. Has Kate said something to him I should know? Something to do with Ava? My heart starts to pound.

"I need a guest pass for The Manor," he blurts out fast, and the frown that was hurting doubles in size *and* pain.

"What?"

"Don't make me say it, Jesse."

It hits me like a boulder, and I rest my glass slowly down on the counter. "Fuck," I breathe. "For Kate?"

"Of course for Kate," he breathes. "For fuck's sake. But you can't mention anything to Ava."

"Are you serious?"

"Yes, very. And Drew took Victoria out for dinner last night to ask her if she wanted to explore—"

"Jesus Christ," I huff out my disbelief, traipsing back to the lounge, trying not to feel unreasonable resentment. Not that I'd want to take Ava into the rooms of The Manor, of course. Never. "Fine. It's not like I'm not keeping enough of my own secrets, is it? What's one more?" I collapse to the couch on a grunt.

"You need to be rid of those secrets."

"Are you fucking insane? Did you miss the fucking shitstorm that just happened?" I snort to myself. "She can barely look me in the eye, Sam. And you want me to add to the list of reasons for her to leave me for good?" Not a fucking chance in hell. I'll die first. Seeing Ava so obviously distraught is enough to protect her—and myself—from more pain. "Have fun at The Manor." I hang up and let my head drop back, closing my eyes.

I shouldn't have. *Faces*. So many faces from my past, the faces of people I love, pass through my mind like a reminder of all I have lost. Jacob. Rosie. Carmichael. I squeeze my eyes tighter, trying to suppress the memories from creeping forward.

"God, Jake, no!" The car hits him, hurling him fifty yards up the road, and I slow to a stop, suddenly paralyzed. The sound of his helpless body hitting the ground is chilling.

And that montage of memories blends and blurs into others.

Rosie. Her little smile. Her chubby little body slipping around in the shallow bath, bubbles everywhere.

Carmichael. The disappointment on his face when he walked into the bedroom as I fucked Sarah with nothing but anger fueling me.

Fuckup after fuckup.

The people I love. Alive. Until I ruined them. Killed them all. Slowly started to kill myself. Then past all the grief and darkness,

Ava appears. A light shining amid the ruins. But the light starts to dim, and I reach for her, begging her to stay. My hand wafts through mist.

No!

I jolt upright, scanning the room, disorientated, sweating, breathless.

I find Ava pulling the front door open. "You have a rhino ram-raid you?" someone asks as I try to shake the sleep and dreams away.

"Something like that," Ava replies, assessing the door too. What happened to the door? I get up to go find out, my muscles screaming again, my eyes refusing to focus properly.

"I can secure it for now, but it'll need replacing. I'll get it on order and let you know when it arrives."

"Thanks." Ava turns and stutters to a stop when she finds me behind her.

"What's going on?"

"John had a fight with your front door when you didn't open it."

John. God, I'd better brace myself for that blasting. "I should call him." I don't want to call him. Face him. Have strips ripped off me for being such a pathetic dickhead.

"How are you feeling?" she asks, assessing me up and down, her voice brittle.

Terrible. "Better." But what about her? Has she softened even a little? "You?"

"Fine." She lies. "Time to get you to the hospital. I'll get my bag." She starts to pass me, and my arm is moving before I can think better of it.

"Ava," I say quietly, racking my brain for what else to say. I don't know. All I know is my skin is on hers in this moment, and it feels good. And I cannot take my eyes off her profile as she stands motionless. Tense.

After the uncomfortable silence has stretched for too long, she looks up at me, her face a blanket of impassiveness. Then her eyes drop, she sighs, and she removes herself from my grip. "Shit," she blurts, and I flinch, making my muscles jolt. Jesus, will this pain ever go away? Every last piece of me is fucking killing.

"Watch your mouth, Ava," I growl, more annoyed with my body than her language. "What's up?"

"My car's at Kate's."

"We'll take mine." Why the fuck am I offering a way out of this predicament? I don't want to go to the hospital. I want to lock us away in my penthouse and never leave. The outside world is dangerous to our relationship.

"You can't drive one-handed."

"I know." I could actually. But . . . "You can drive." I grab my keys and throw them, wondering what the fuck I'm thinking. My Aston is a far cry from her little Mini. She'll never cope with the power.

Ava catches the bunch and stares down at them, looking nervous. My fears amplify. Never, not once in the time I've known Ava, has she driven us anywhere. Times are changing. But not too much, I hope. I need to find our normal again.

"Come on," I say, fighting the urge to take her hand and lead her out. The sooner we get this done, the quicker we'll be back in the safety of Lusso and we can get on with fixing this shit. I hope. I open the door for her and watch her walk out, thanking me too formally.

It's silent to the door.

We're silent the entire way down in the elevator.

Clive is silent as we pass through the lobby.

I see my car, the window no longer smashed. Fixed. Unlike its owner.

It's silent when we get in my Aston.

And silent for the first fifteen minutes of our journey, except for the roar of the engine. I can't bear it.

I cast constant looks across to her, taking pleasure amid the screaming quiet at the sight of her concentrating so hard. Anyone would think she's on a driving test. Her hands are positioned perfectly, and she's constantly checking her mirrors. Part of me is relieved she's such a careful driver, but there's slow and there's slow, and when my eyes catch a bicycle passing the passenger window, the rider looking at me with a shake of his head, I decide enough is enough. It'll be next week by the time we get to the hospital. Next week before I get her home and resume my mission.

"Ava, you're driving like Miss Daisy," I say, exasperated. "Will you put your foot down?"

The scowl she throws my way is epic, if brief, so she can get her attention back to the road. "Shut up," she mutters, but we pick up speed, and I smile at her profile.

"That's better. It's easier to handle if you're not pussyfooting around the power." I should heed my own advice and stop pussyfooting around Ava. And when I see her straining to keep her mouth in check, fighting her smile, I know she's thinking the same.

There's no denying, she's the one with all the power. Always has been.

Maybe one day I'll admit it.

One day when I'm confident she loves and needs me too much to even contemplate living without me.

I pray for the day. Although given my life, the destruction, the sacrifices, I'm not sure even praying to a god I don't know will help Ava's defenses to lower.

But regardless, I will pray.

3

Two hours. Two fucking hours of my life wasted sitting on my arse waiting to be seen. And, worse, to rub salt into my moody wounds, Ava's put herself opposite me. Not next to me. Not even one seat away from me. She's opposite me, with a good three meters of space between us, distracting herself with trashy magazines. On the plus side, I can see her, though she refuses to look at me. Stubborn woman.

I grumble under my breath, and she glances up for the first time. I purse my lips. Her eyes narrow a little. And she returns to her magazine. For fuck's sake. "Fuck this shit," I mutter, rising from the chair. "I'm done. We're leaving."

"What?" She's up fast, dropping the magazine. "You can't just go."

"Watch me." I head for the door. I've had enough. Two hours alone with Ava in private will serve us better than seeing a fucking doctor about my hand, which, by the way, is absolutely fine. I lift said hand to push my way out and on cue it throbs, protesting, having me withdraw from the door on a hissed curse.

"Jesse Ward?"

"He's here," Ava calls, and I look over my shoulder, seeing her hurrying toward me. "You're seeing a doctor," she says, all matter-of-fact, taking my good hand. "End of."

I recoil, and she cocks her head, challenging me to challenge her. Oh, would I love to challenge her. Throw her over my shoulder. Show her who's boss. And yet I'm distracted from going all caveman on her arse by the feel of her hand around mine.

"Come." She starts to lead me toward the room, and I follow obediently, a slave to her order, at the mercy of our physical connection.

I hear someone speak, but I have no clue what they're saying. I can't take my eyes of our hands. "Jesse," Ava prompts, and I look up at her. "Sit down."

"What?"

"The doctor asked you to sit down so she can take a look at your hand." She releases me. It's unbearable. I plonk myself in the chair and dump my hand on the padded arm. I am *not* behaving like a toddler.

"Oh, what have we done here?" the doctor asks, inspecting the swelling, cuts, and bruises, her eyes jumping between my hairy face and my unsightly hand.

"It's nothing," I grumble. "Doesn't hurt a bit." At that moment, she pokes it, and I inhale sharply, pulling my arm into my chest protectively.

She raises her brows casually, and I scowl. That was totally uncalled for.

"He's just being difficult," Ava pipes in, and I turn my unamused eyes her way. Where does she get her nerve? "Ignore him."

Fucking charming.

"I think we need to get it X-rayed." The doctor pulls off her gloves and pops them in a bin. "And go from there."

"It doesn't need X-raying." For fuck's sake. "Just tell me it's not broken, and we'll be on our way."

"I'm not leaving until you have it X-rayed." Ava gives me quite the cutting look. "How can they tell if it's broken if you won't let them X-ray it?"

"Your wife is right, Mr. Ward." The doctor goes to the door. "I'll let them know you're on your way to the X-ray department."

I don't protest further, because . . . wife. My *wife*. Not only does it sound good, but the fact the doctor clearly doesn't think I look too old to be with this young beauty thrills me. I chew my lip, peeking at Ava, just as she lets out a bark of laughter.

"Oh, we're not married."

She finds that funny? Laughable? Is she just here to make me feel even shitter than I already do?

Jesus, I can't believe I'm thinking this. *Wife*. It sounds fucking amazing. You'd think after my shambles of a first marriage and my psychotic ex-wife, I'd avoid it at all costs. Always thought I would.

But I never anticipated Ava O'Shea.

Or . . . Ava *Ward*.

I raise an eyebrow to myself. It would settle me in so many ways. Commitment. On *every* level. A contract we promise never to break. Both of us willing. Both of us devoted.

"We'd better get you that X-ray," Ava says quietly, leaving the room. I follow, staring at her back. I'd be an amazing husband for her. Attentive, passionate, and back to my usual easygoing self. She'll thank me for it.

You're running before you can walk, Ward.

Or . . . am I?

I spend the next half hour while being X-rayed wondering how I can convince Ava that marrying me is the best solution for both of us. Ava will get my vow never to touch a drop of drink again, because I won't need to if I have her for a lifetime, and I'll lose the fear of losing her. Perfect.

"It's not broken," the doctor says, staring up at the X-ray image. I scoff. No, perhaps my hand isn't broken but everything else is. "Just a bit of muscle damage. I'll leave the nurse to take it from here."

"Thanks," I mutter as the nurse moves in. No breaks. It's fine. I throw Ava a look, one I know she won't appreciate. What a waste of our time.

"Have you been resting it?" the nurse asks. "If it's been a few days since you incurred the injury, I would expect the swelling to have subsided by now." She checks each of the cuts before wrapping it in a bandage.

"No." *I was clenching a bottle of vodka with it.*

"You should have been, and it should be elevated."

I roll my eyes when Ava's eyebrows look like they could jump off her face, but I'm distracted from my soon-to-be wife's cockiness when the nurse sticks my arm in a sling. The bandage isn't enough? I'm not walking around with that thing hanging around my neck. It's bad enough feeling like an invalid. I don't want to look like one too.

"Are we done?" I ask, and she nods. "Thanks." I leave the room, Ava following me, and toss the stupid sling in the trash on my way out of the hospital.

"What are you doing?" I hear her call.

"I'm not wearing that thing."

"You bloody are!" she yells.

I've come to a hospital, seen a doctor, had an X-ray, and let them bandage me up. The sling is a step too far and fucking pointless. Like the doctor said, it's not broken, though that's a fucking miracle considering the abuse it's been subjected to *and* the fucking pain.

I stomp to the car, feeling at my pockets for the keys. No keys.

Ava arrives on the other side of my Aston, her expression fire. I mirror it. "Are you going to open the car?" I ask.

"No, not until you put this back on." The sling appears. She rummaged through a bin?

"I told you, Ava, I'm not wearing it."

"Why?"

"I don't need it."

"Yes, you do."

"No, I don't."

Her nostrils flare, and the fire rages harder. If I wasn't so agitated,

I might find it attractive. "Put the fucking sling on, Jesse," she yells, for the whole fucking car park to hear.

My mouth falls open in shock, surprise, disgust. "Watch your fucking mouth."

She snorts. It's condescending as fuck. "Fuck," she spits.

What? My pounding head pounds harder. "Mouth!" I bellow, shaking the ground with the volume of my yell. And my fucking head. Jesus. I clasp my temple, and pain radiates through my hand. "Fuck!" My eyes water, I clench my good fist, grit my teeth, circling on the spot, hissing and spitting. Not broken?

Something, another noise, filters through my cursing fit, and I glance up and find Ava chuckling on the other side of the car. I can't even appreciate the sparkle in her eyes. The flush of her cheeks. The face-splitting smile.

"Open the fucking car, Ava."

"How's your hand?" She snorts, her lips pressed so tightly together they're turning white. Then her cheeks balloon and she folds in half, falling apart. I can only watch her, part delighted, part fucking furious, her body jerking and shaking, the sounds she's making glorious. I discreetly adjust my jeans, hardly wanting to admit that her insolence turns me on.

She eventually returns to vertical. Good. I have her attention again. "Open."

"Sling," she retorts, throwing it at me. It lands on the roof, and I snatch it and toss it to the ground.

"Open!"

"You're a child sometimes, Jesse Ward. I am not opening the car until you put that sling on."

We both know I'm not putting that sling on. It's not about me thinking I don't need it anymore. It's something else now, and as I stare her down, seeing her head tilt, seeing her challenging me with her dark gaze, I realize she is one hundred percent asking for it. *I think.* "Three." I sound sure. I'm not. Am I making a massive mistake?

Ava looks disgusted, but that's standard. "You are *not* giving me the countdown."

Hear me, lady. "Two." I prop my arms on the roof, all casual, as she continues to stare at me like I've just landed from another planet. But I'm not so broken I can't see the faint sparkle past her disbelief. "One."

"You can get stuffed."

"Zero," I mouth, pacing around the front of my car, as she gasps, heading around the back, keeping her distance. "What are you doing?" I ask, changing direction. So does she. Fucking pointless. I'll catch her, even now when I'm running on half a tank.

"Nothing." She keeps her eyes on mine, wary, thrilled, annoyed.

"Come here." I make my demand purposely low, showing her exactly where I'm at. Hungry. Starving, in fact.

"No."

Fine. I break out in a sprint without warning, and she screeches, bombing off in the other direction, running between some parked cars before disappearing completely.

Fuck, where did she go? I slow, already pretty fucking knackered, my ego majorly dented, my body letting me down. Damn it. Turns out the tank's nearly empty. I catch my breath, scanning the car park for her. Nothing.

"Fuck it," I mutter, resorting to dirty tactics, bending over, bracing my hands lightly on my knees, heaving. I peek to my left, seeing an elderly couple heading my way, their old, wrinkled faces a picture of concern.

"Jesse!" Ava's voice sounds high and distraught. I'm a little bit sorry. Not much.

"Is he all right, love?" the old guy asks, just as I spot her feet in my field of vision.

"I don't—"

I move as fast as my body will allow, and she yelps as I lift her over my shoulder and stride away, enduring the pain in my hand. Because she's attached to me. Touching. Close.

"Don't mess with me, Ava." I smile at the old couple, who look rather alarmed. "You should know by now, I always win." With my busted hand holding her on my shoulder, I go in for the kill, feeling up her leg until I pass the hem of her dress. I inhale, warmth radiating throughout me. My bad hand instantly feels better. My heart instantly settles.

"My knickers are flashing," she whines, feeling back to try and pat down the skirt of her dress.

"No, they're not." Five minutes ago, my dick was the only part of me that *didn't* hurt or ache. Trust my unquenchable need for this woman to fix that.

When I reach the car, I reluctantly let her slide down my chest, our fronts compressed. I can feel her heart. Can she feel mine? It's pounding harder than it has in days. I can't bring myself to release her. The longer I hold her, the more chance there is of her remembering.

Her eyes level with mine, I gaze at her pensively. *Kiss her.* Show her. Remind her.

But she starts wriggling before I can put my plan into action. "We need to go to the supermarket," she says quietly, diverting her eyes, looking away from me. The supermarket? When the fuck have I ever been to a supermarket?

Just last week. To stock up on vodka.

My hand starts to throb again. My heartbeat dulls. My head bangs. I release Ava's squirming body on a tired exhale. "How can I fix things if you keep dodging my attempts?"

She sorts out her dress and gives me a pointed look. We've gone from hysterics to playful to downright awkward in the space of a few minutes. It's a roller coaster. I want off. "That's your problem, Jesse," she says, clipped, and I shrink a little under her condemning glare. "You want to fix things by distracting me with your touch instead of talking to me and giving me some answers. I can't let that happen again." The Aston doors unlock, and she falls into the driver's seat.

And that's your *problem, Jesse.*

She's not asked me any fucking questions to answer yet. Won't talk. Seems content enduring the screaming silence that keeps falling between us. So, where does that leave us? In no-man's land.

I fall into the seat, and Ava pulls off a lot faster than before. She's mad. With herself? I can't imagine having to resist something that I desperately want. What I *can* imagine is being deprived of something I desperately *need*. And there might be our problem.

She *wants* me.

I, on the other hand, *need* her.

The two are very different and put us on opposite ends of the desperation scale. That's not a good position for me to be in.

Who has the power, Ward?

Stupid fucking question.

4

I HATE SUPERMARKETS, but today more so. It's just another obstacle in my way, something to delay me getting Ava home. "There's a space." I point across the car park and get my arm smacked in thanks.

"That's a parent and child space." She sails past it, and I look back on a frown.

"So?"

Her eyes flick to me briefly. "So, I don't see any child in this lovely car of yours, do you?"

I don't mean to look at her stomach. It just . . . happens. "Did you find your pills?" I didn't mean to say that either. *Wife* sounded pretty fucking amazing. Mother to my children?

"No." The car stops. She must have found a space. I don't know.

"Did you miss any?" My wondering is just falling out of my mouth. I can't help it.

"My period came last Sunday evening." She jumps out, and I remain in my seat, my head spinning. Her period came. She was relieved. Which means she would have been worried. I don't know how I feel about that. Do I have weak swimmers? I wince when I bite down a little too hard on my lip. God, am I getting too old to reproduce? She's a twenty-six-year-old woman. Babies might not be on her agenda just yet, but they will be in the coming years. What if I can't give her babies? That'll be a good enough reason alone for her to leave me. My empty stomach flips, and I know straight away that it's anxiety. Am I *that* broken? And how many pills did she miss?

I blindly reach for the handle and get out, feeling . . . inadequate. Unsure. Fucking terrified. "Could you have parked any farther away?" I ask moodily as I pace around the car.

"At least I'm parked legally." She collects a trolley. Not a basket for a few things, but a whole, *big* trolley. Is that a good thing? Is she preparing to stay with me for a while? Like, forever? "Have you ever been to a supermarket?" she asks.

Only for emergency supplies. "Cathy does it." I trudge alongside her, my mind elsewhere. Should I get a sperm test? Have myself checked out? "I usually eat at The Manor." I peek out the corner of my eye to gage her reaction to the mention of my business. It's not a subject that's been broached yet. And by the look of her suddenly sharp expression, it's not one she's keen to get to. So, we're just going to pretend it doesn't exist? Sounds like a good plan to me. Like ignoring the endless fuckups of my past.

Ava collects all the boring things as we wander up and down the aisles, while I collect essentials. I pick up a jar of chocolate spread and dump it in the trolley as we pass the baby aisle, my eyes once again studying Ava. She doesn't give it a second glance. My shoulders drop. Hasn't she given having kids a single thought? Does she even want them? We've never talked about it, because why the fuck would we when we've known each other mere weeks? She's ambitious. Driven. I love that about her, despite it being irritating, if only because her aspirations feel more important than I am. And that, right or wrong, hurts. There's nothing in this world more important to me than she is. Nothing.

"Do you not have anything?" she asks, confusing me, until I realize that while I've been contemplating life-changing stuff, Ava's been practical and has spent that time considering my empty cupboards. It's a sign of the drastic difference in our headspace right now.

I claim the trolley when she pulls some milk from the fridge. I need something to do with my hands. At least, my good hand. I've been trudging up and down next to her for half an hour. I can't touch her. My hands are twitching. "Cathy's been away," I say as she takes the end of the trolley and leads us into the next aisle. The alcohol aisle.

I glance at the shelves, and I feel . . . nothing. It's the same nothingness I felt when she walked out of my office the very first time I met her. No urge to get to midday and have a drink, only an urge to see her again.

Ava stops suddenly, gasps, and spins around, crashing into the trolley. "Fuck," she yelps, and I flinch just as hard as she does, but for a very different reason. I keep telling myself that if I hear her curse enough, I might get used to it. It hasn't happened yet, and she swears like a fucking man.

"Ava, watch your mouth," I bark.

"We don't need this aisle." She forces me and the trolley back, away from temptation. She doesn't get me. I shouldn't be injured by that. I hardly understand myself these days.

"Ava, stop it," I warn gently, hating the panic on her face.

"I'm sorry." She looks like she could burst into tears at any moment. "I didn't realize where we were."

"For God's sake, woman, I'm not going to dive into the shelves and rip the caps off the bottles." I look down at her shin, which she's rubbing furiously. "Are you okay?"

"I'm fine." She *sounds* like she could burst into tears too, her voice broken. I felt the force of her shin hitting the trolley. She's in pain. I take the few steps needed to get to her and fall to my knees, taking her leg and kissing the spot. I feel terrible. She's hurt, and it's my fault *again*. I should wrap her up in cotton wool and never let her leave Lusso. It'll save her pain, and it'll save me guilt. And stress. "Better?" I look up, finding she's staring down at me. She hasn't tried to pull away. She hasn't told me to get off. "I'm sorry," I whisper, oblivious to where we are and who could be looking. "For everything, Ava." *For all you know, and for all that you do not. I'm sorry.*

She swallows, one, twice, looking a bit bewildered. "Okay."

Okay. It feels . . . inadequate, but what else did I expect? For her to fall into my arms and tell me everything will be fine? That she won't leave me again? That yes, she wants to be with me forever, be my wife, have my children, stay wrapped up in cotton wool and let me keep her safe from the world and my past?

Is all that too much to ask, especially when a man's life depends on it?

I sigh, dragging my heavy body, my heavy heart, and my heavy head up. I can't help but kiss her stomach as I pass. She would look wonderful pregnant. And I'd double wrap that cotton wool. But I'm terrified the Fates have decided I was too careless with Rosie. That I don't deserve the blessing of being a daddy again. I shy away from that thought—a thought that's never entered my head—because I never had reason to think it. I have reason now. I want to be able to give Ava everything she could ever want. Rosie could never be replaced, but to have that kind of love again? And share it with Ava? It's the ultimate.

I feel her studying me. I can't imagine how disgusted she'd be if she knew the whole truth. How fast and how far she'd run from me.

I'd never get her back.

She'll want the fairy tale when she's ready. The perfect, wholesome husband. Kids when the timing is just right. I divert my eyes, ashamed, and watch as Ava walks away, leaving me to follow. Can she see me as that man?

When we make it to the checkout, I make myself useful, packing the bags while Ava unloads the trolley, and never once does she look at me. I keep telling myself that if there was no chance for us, she wouldn't be here. I can't entertain the notion that she merely feels sorry for me. That she's here to help get me back on my feet before she exits my life for good.

She's not capable of such cruelty.

And I've felt her need more than once. I have to hope it soon overpowers her other need for answers.

5

I STARE AT THE DOCTOR, *his words resting on my skin, refusing to sink in. They're dead. I can hear Sarah next to me screaming her denial, outwardly rejecting the doctor's claim. I turn my eyes her way. Find her head shaking furiously. "We did this," I murmur. "This is our fault."*

"No," she whispers, her face a mess, makeup smeared and smudged down her cheeks. "Jesse, no."

"Yes," I say simply. I'm unable to console Sarah. I'm unable to hug her. Because nothing will be okay ever again. Why? Because she persisted. I fought. I fought with all I had, and then I caved.

And now they're dead.

The hole in my heart that Jake's death caused is growing. "I have to go," I say, my voice thick. I turn and walk out of the hospital in a haze of ruin, every inch of me in agony. Guilt. It'll never leave me. More guilt to add to the endless pot of it. More to mix with the remorse still sitting heavy in my stomach four years after I lost Jake. How the fuck has he been gone four years? Where did that time go?

I start to hyperventilate, my bleak future that Rosie made brighter now desolate again. Air. I need air. I stagger through the doors and start gasping for breath, having to brace my hands on my knees to support myself. I feel her hand on my back. Sarah's. I straighten and shrug it off. "Don't touch me," I warn. Every time she touches me, the guilt grows. Every time I look at her, my regret kills me. That will never change. "Don't ever touch me again, Sarah."

"Jesse, we only have each other now," she sobs. "We have to be here for each other."

"I don't want to be here at all." I can hardly talk through the ball of anguish in my throat, picking up my feet, forcing myself away. I make it to my car and scramble for my keys, juggling them in my shaking hands to find the right one, brushing at my cheeks in between.

I freeze when I hear the undeniable sound of a woman screaming.

Not Sarah.

I turn to find Lauren diving out of her parents' car, running at me full pelt, her face a picture of devastation. She crashes into me, flinging her arms around me, cuddling me like I know she's wanted to for years. And what do I do? I return it. Because what the fuck else can I do?

She shouldn't be embracing me. She should be kicking me, punching me, screaming at me.

I killed our daughter.

My eyes ping open on a loud inhale, my fingers clawing into the material of the couch, but I don't dive up in a panic, my exhausted body preventing me. "Jesus Christ," I whisper, finding Ava asleep on the chair, the room dark. She's still here.

My hurting heart settles a little.

Still here.

I've never in my life been so tired. I've been in pain. Felt grief. Tackled hate. All of it exhausted me, but never has plain fatigue made me feel this weak. I only laid down for a quick rest after we came home from shopping. What time is it?

Dragging myself to sit up, I bury my face in my hands, taking a few needed breaths, my lungs yelling, burning, reminding me I'm still alive. *And they are not.* Scrubbing down my cheeks, I let my eyes find Ava again. Everything inside is telling me to scoop her up and take her to bed. Be close to her. Feel her. And yet I know she'll refuse me, and I honestly don't know how much more pain and rejection I can take.

Tentatively, I rise to my feet and creep over to her, not wanting to wake her. I don't want to bring her back to our reality as it is now. Not if she's hurting like I'm hurting. I hunker down and let my gaze travel over every inch of her face. Even sleeping she looks tired. Drained.

Ready to give up?

"Please don't." I reach for her, taking advantage of her unconscious state. She won't let me touch her when she's awake. I realize she's afraid everything will vanish with the coming together of our bodies, all of our hurt and troubles. How can I convince her it's what we both need? "I love you," I whisper, my voice thick.

She stirs, and I gulp back the hope that those words brought her round. That she heard them. Is responding to them. She sits up, rubbing at her sleepy eyes, and then finds me before her. Kneeling. A slave.

My hand takes on a mind of its own and pushes a strand of hair from her eyes. "Hey," I say quietly. Will she let me take her to bed? Just to cuddle? Just to keep the demons at bay?

"What time is it?"

"Just gone midnight," I say as I lift a little and push my lips into her forehead, inhaling every bit of her into me. She allows it. She allows me to kiss her, and just as I'm about to gently coax her into my arms, my mobile rings, stopping me.

There is only one reason I'd get a call at this time, and it's pushed the building contentment away. "For fuck's sake," I mumble under my breath, grabbing my phone. "John," I breathe, bracing myself, knowing it'll be serious for him to call me at this low point in my life.

"We need you here."

My muscles lengthen everywhere, making me taller in an instant. "Why?"

"Immigration enforcement. They'll only talk to the owner," he says, as I flick a cautious look Ava's way. "I've told them you've been signed off by your doctor but—"

"No, it's fine." I can feel the tension creeping back into me, and I desperately don't want Ava to see that. She hates The Manor. Right now, I hate The Manor too.

"You sure?" John asks.

"Yeah, give me half an hour." I disconnect and search for where I kicked off my shoes earlier, locating them at the end of the couch. I head over and stuff my feet into them, feeling Ava watching my every move.

"What's the matter?" she asks with obvious worry in her tone. I can't look at her. Can't allow her to see the unrestrained rage building. The police. The Manor. Things in my way.

"Problem at The Manor," I say, heading for the door. "I won't be long." As soon as I'm in the elevator, I fall against the wall. "Fuck," I hiss, catching sight of myself in the mirror when the doors close.

I look gray. Empty.

Old.

I turn away from my reflection and stare at the wall until the doors open, and I pace to my car with my head down. "Mr. Ward," Clive calls, but I ignore him. I have no faith that I can be polite. I've not even moved forward and I'm already taking backward steps.

I slip into my car and start her up, taking the wheel and hissing. "Fuck," I breathe, my throbbing hand protesting. *I shouldn't be driving.* I gingerly flex it for a few moments and pull off fast, stress and frustration making my foot heavy on the pedal.

Nothing's changed there.

The circular driveway is heaving when I pull up. Members leaving. "Fucking hell," I breathe, swinging into a space by a white Mercedes van. I get out and spot Sam on the steps with Kate, and Drew emerging from the entrance, fastening his tie. No Victoria? Drew spots me and gives me a quick assessment. He must conclude I'm okay because he launches into a rant. "Great for business," he snaps, pulling and yanking at the material around his neck.

"Where's Victoria?"

He scowls. Obviously *that's* a sore subject. "What the fuck's going on?"

Kate sees me approaching, and her cheeks soon match the color of her hair. If I was in the mood, I'd smile. "Hey," she says, nowhere near her usual fiery self. "You look—"

"Like a bag of shit, I know." I exhale, coming to a stop, watching people leaving on mass.

"How are . . . things?" she asks, almost cautious.

I look at her tiredly. "Amazing."

She smiles, and it's small. "Give it time." She rubs at my arm. "She'll come round."

"She will?"

"Sure. I still love your crazy arse, so Ava has to."

I look at Kate. She doesn't look convinced. "Where are they?" I ask, walking on and entering the foyer.

"Bar," Sam answers, wary as fuck. "You okay?"

"Fucking ace," I mutter, arriving in the bar, where an army of men and women in uniforms are congregated. "Jesse Ward," I declare, and they all turn my way. I'm trying my fucking hardest not to be hostile. Trying and failing. What the fuck are they doing here?

A man approaches. "Kev Baxter," he declares. "Chief Immigration Officer."

"Excuse me?"

"I said—"

"That was a rhetorical question."

"Right," he says. "Perhaps only ask me serious questions going forward, yes? Since this is a serious situation."

"I don't know what the fuck the situation is."

"We have reason to believe you have illegal immigrants in your employment." He produces a piece of paper, and I snatch it out of his hand. "The warrant."

"The warrant for what?"

"To search the premises."

I baulk at him. "For people? You think I'm harboring illegal immigrants?"

"Just following some intelligence."

"You're not searching my premises," I assure him. Fuck me, I'll lose every fucking member I have.

He smiles, and it's a smug smile. I want to punch it off his face. "We've already conducted the search," he says, plucking the warrant from between my fingers. "We don't need your permission, Mr. Ward. Hence the warrant." He turns and points, and I look past him. I see Mario and Rosa sitting in the corner looking a little bewildered. "As an employer, you are obliged to check potential employees' papers." He faces me again. "Did you?"

My teeth grind. Someone's stirring shit. I turn to John, finding he's displaying utter disbelief. "Everyone who works for me is here legally," I say, fucking fuming. "If you'd contacted me instead of ram-raiding my establishment unannounced on one of the busiest nights of the week and scaring all of my members away, I would have saved you all this trouble."

"No trouble." He smiles. "Like I said, just acting on intelligence."

"Well, your intelligence is shit," I say as Sarah approaches with a file. The file I must need. I accept it when she hands it over and shove it in the officer's chest. "The papers for every foreign member of my staff."

His face undeniably drops as he takes the file, his eyes remaining on me as he backs up and lowers to a chair. He starts flicking through, and the further he flicks, the more his nostrils flare. I can't even begin to imagine the cost of such an operation. All for nothing.

"Now, if you don't mind." I sweep my arm out toward the door, smiling as smugly as he did not so long ago. "Unless, of course, you'd like to stay and play?"

I can see Sarah beside me, and I definitely see the subtle thrust forward of her boobs. And then her whip appears. For once, I smile at it.

"Thank you for your time, Mr. Ward," Baxter says, standing and tilting his head toward his army of officers.

"Welcome." I watch as they all file out and as soon as they have gone, I go straight to Rosa and Mario. "Are you okay?" I ask. Rosa nods, her eyes daunted, and Mario shakes his head, his arms going up in the air in exasperation.

"I come here for twenty years. Twenty! I work hard. I pay my taxes."

I try to smile through my straight lips. "I know, my friend." I give his shoulder a rub. "Get home, both of you. And take tomorrow off."

"No, Mr. Ward," Rosa says, waggling her finger at me. "I must work."

"No, you will take a day off," I insist. The woman doesn't *stop* working. "Paid," I add, stopping her from arguing, because that's the issue here. Money. "Go," I order harshly, and they're both up, passing me, Mario thanking me in Italian, Rosa in Spanish.

I close my eyes and breathe some calm into my lungs. "Someone's got it in for me," I say, hearing John's huff of unamused laughter. I turn and find his glasses have been removed and he's rubbing at his eyes. "Any offers?"

"Too fucking many," he rumbles, shaking his head. "And I want a key to your apartment."

"Why?"

"So I don't have to smash your door down again if you go AWOL."

"I won't be going AWOL." Not ever again.

"Get me a key," John grates, and I submit, holding my hands up.

"And me," Sarah adds.

"Why do *you* want a key?"

She looks indignant. "I had one to your rental."

Yes, but that was then. "I—" I'm just gonna cause an argument if I protest this, and I can't be fucking bothered. "Fine. I'll get Sam and Drew one while I'm at it too."

"Good. I'll take this back to the office." John slides the file off the table and heads out, leaving me with Sarah. I can feel her studying me, but I'm a little afraid to face her.

"What?" I ask, heading for the exit.

"How's Ava?"

I stop. I notice she doesn't ask how *I* am. I'm here, she can see me, and it's clear as fucking day that I'm not okay. My handling of the police. My short temper. And the fact I look like death warmed up. But she doesn't ask about me. No. She just wants to know if Ava's still around.

I turn slowly to look at her. She's been busy tonight. I can tell by the haphazard fastening of her bodice, her boobs not perfectly even, and her red lipstick is smudged away. "Did you let Ava in last Sunday?" I ask, my head tilting. I know John didn't. And *I* definitely didn't. Which leaves only Sarah. We're the only three who have remote access to the gates, the members have codes, and Ava doesn't know the code.

She looks injured. It's not a look Sarah carries well, her heavily worked-on face unable to stretch to accommodate the expression. "No, I would never do that. The gates have been playing up for a few weeks."

"Why didn't you tell me?"

"Because you were kind of busy with the interior designer, who, by the way, still hasn't produced an actual design."

"Don't start, Sarah."

"And while you've been busy trying to get in her fucking knickers and be all fucking crazy while you do, John and I have been run off our feet."

In her knickers? Wrong. I've been trying to get into her fucking heart. "That's what you think?" I ask, astounded. "All this madness just because I want to fuck her?"

"What else could you possibly want? She's in her twenties, Jesse."

"I'm not listening to this shit." I point a finger at her, seething. "Back the fuck off," I warn.

"I'm—"

"Just leave me the hell alone." I storm out and slam the doors of The Manor behind me. Then slam the door of my Aston once I'm in the driver's seat.

And hit the steering wheel.

"Fuck," I yell, heaving, my hand feeling like it could explode. I hate her sometimes. And I hate the guilt that's hitting me now. I have no more room for guilt. No space. I'm riddled with it.

I look up at the front of The Manor. The building is beautiful. The grounds immaculate. And yet all it's ever brought me is ugliness.

I wince and start the engine, pulling off, mulling over all of the people who could want to fuck with me. I laugh. Where the hell do I start?

I'm still reeling off names to myself when I pull up at Lusso. I have a list as long as my arm and zero brain capacity to analyze it. I enter the lobby and find Clive snoozing at his desk. I don't wake him, keen to get upstairs and put myself back within the reach of peace.

The doors of the elevator open, and I let myself in the penthouse, my eyes homing in on the couch, expecting to find her there snoozing. She's not. "Don't panic, don't panic," I whisper to myself, my eyes jumping around the space as I toss my keys on the table. I walk into the kitchen calmly, fighting the urge to run, and stop on the threshold of the empty space, willing my heart to calm the fuck down. "Ava?" I call, backing up, heading for the stairs. I left so abruptly. No explanation. No apology. Just left. Holding out on her again.

You'd think I'd fucking learn.

I dial her as I take the stairs in leaps, urgency feeding my weary limbs, and push my way into the bedroom. Empty bed. Her phone goes to voicemail, and I dial again as I jog to the bathroom. Empty. And I get her voicemail again. My jaw rolling, my stupid fucking heart speeding up, I charge into every bedroom, flicking on the lights, dialing her on repeat. By the time I make it to the farthest bedroom, I can hardly breathe, and I charge in, dialing her yet again.

I stagger to an abrupt halt past the threshold as her scent hits me. I don't need to turn on the lights. She's in here. My shoulders drop, like a release of pressure from my entire being leaves me. "Shit," I say on an exhale, taking a moment to regulate my out-of-control breathing. Once I've gathered myself, I tread carefully across the carpet to the bed, and then I just stand there. Stand there and stare at her looking all wrong in the spare bed. Enough is enough. She wants me. I need her. Why the fuck are we going through this process? Because Ava needs answers? Because she's trying to prove to herself that she can be sensible? Keep me at a distance while she figures out what she wants to do? It's bullshit. She knows what she wants, her heart is telling her but, God damn her, she's letting her head get in the way again.

"I love you," I whisper, and her eyes blink open immediately. She *is* hearing me. Those words are sinking deeply into her. I lower, lifting her into my arms, my body not letting me down, and carry her to our bedroom. She's a feather. Perfect in my arms, the perfect weight, the perfect fit against my chest.

"You sleep here." I place her down gently and strip out of my clothes, climbing in behind her. The moment her back meets my front, energy surges through me. A bolt of life. *Peace.* Hope when I feared it was lost. "We're going to be okay," I whisper, feeling her melt against me, her breathing easy. "I love you so fucking much, Ava. So it *has* to be okay."

She's silent. Unmoving. And when I rest my mouth over the back of her neck and her pulse starts beating against my lips, I register the rhythm.

She's asleep.

I lie there the entire night, just feeling her heart beating close to mine. Letting every pulse push a little bit more life into me.

6

By sunrise, I've not slept, but it's been the most peaceful night I've ever had. Watching her. Listening to her. Feeling her. Deciding what it is I have to do. This thing between us, the uncertainty, the awkwardness, the lack of contact, it needs to end. We can only get past this if Ava can find it in herself, allow herself, to accept the insane connection that knocked us both off balance in the first place.

I shift and crawl on top of her, swathing her with my body, dropping my face into her neck and kissing her awake. My lips haven't been on her body for so long. "Wake up, baby," I whisper. "Wake up and let me remind you of how incredible we are together."

She stirs, moaning, her body stretching beneath me, her lids flickering.

"Morning," I whisper, suppressing a groan when she unwittingly rolls her hips up at the tail end of her stretch. Her eyes open, and before she has the chance to commence the war between her heart and head, I lift, pulling her up to sit with me. I see the first signs of a sparkle in her eyes. The same sparkle I've seen every time we're intimate, kissing, or even simply touching. "I need to do this," I say, moving my hands to the hem of her top gingerly, slowly, taking my time. She doesn't fight me when I peel it over her head, but she's rigid, despite radiating want. I can smell it. Desperation. I dip and kiss her breastbone, licking my way up to her neck.

"Lace," I whisper, reaching to unfasten her bra, kissing her everywhere I can reach.

"Jesse, we need to talk."

"I need *you.*" I work my way across to her lips and take her mouth softly. Tenderly. Her whimpers are quiet, as if she's desperately trying to suppress her natural sounds of pleasure.

I feel her withdrawing. "Jesse, please."

"Baby," I murmur, resting my palm on her neck and applying pressure, keeping her close. "I do my talking this way." I can feel her loosening, softening, giving in to the power. "Let me show you."

She yields, letting me lay her down beneath us, and I kiss her. Slowly. Lovingly. I kiss her like a man should kiss a woman he adores, and there is no question I adore this woman. I leisurely trace my fingertip all over her body, needing to reacquaint myself with every curve, and she holds on to me with firm fingertips digging into my shoulders. I don't feel a thing. Nothing could get past this oblivion of pleasure. This is exactly what I mean. *Lost.* Both of us. *Peace.* For both of us.

Love.

And in this moment, I know, it's love for both of us.

I push into the mattress with my good hand, getting to my knees, and start pulling her knickers and shorts away. "You need reminding."

"This is not the conventional way," she says on an exhale, gazing up at me, her words contradicting her squirming. I smile to myself. There's nothing conventional about Ava and me. Not one thing.

"It's how I do things, Ava." I yank her up to me, our flesh slapping on impact, and I take her mouth hungrily. "We need to make friends."

She's with me. One hundred percent with me. I feel the remnants of her restraint snap and she's quickly grappling at my boxers, shoving them down. My gratitude leaves me on a deep moan, my dick breaking free, and I take us back down to the sheets, lying beside her, the perfect position to kiss her and feel her. Her foot is suddenly in the waist of my boxers, pushing them the rest of the way. I shift my feet, wriggling them to be free of the material, my tongue relentless in her mouth. Her hands are in my hair, her tongue matching the lazy swirling motions of mine. The devotion being communicated in this moment is inexplicable, and the emotion clogging my throat catches me by surprise. Jesus, I can't cry. I can't appear to be any weaker than I am. And yet feeling our love, even if it's not yet been spoken, is washing away the pain—both physical and emotional. Or is it just papering over the cracks?

I swallow and pull away, immediately sinking my face into her neck to buy myself some time, taking my hand to between her thighs and dragging it slowly up her body. "I've missed you, baby." I can hardly speak past the blockage in my throat. "I've missed you so much." She's been here, but she hasn't been here. But she's here now, in all of her beautiful, powerful, healing glory.

"I've missed you too." Her palm rests on the back of my head. It's a gesture of comfort, and I hate it. It feels so good, but I hate it. The dynamics of our relationship don't work this way. This isn't what I really need—her comfort. I need her to need *me*.

I take in air and put myself on top of her, my erection falling just perfectly into position, and I swallow, bracing myself. It might take a while. And in the meantime, I'll just look at her. Look at her and know I haven't completely lost her. "Thank you for coming back to me." I have to say it. She needs to know how grateful and relieved I am that she's accepted me. The Manor, the drink. Both could have ended this bliss.

Her hands framing my face, she silently traces my lip, eyes on mine, and I open, allowing her to slip her thumb into my mouth. I kiss the tip gently when she pulls it free, my happiness becoming overwhelming. I'm ready. I'm ready to do this—to feel and fall. I'm ready to hear and I'm ready to speak. I push into my forearms and lift my hips, holding my breath, watching her closely. And I sink in calmly and lazily. It's immediately too much, the friction, the pleasure, the injection of life. I hold still as her internal muscles welcome me, compressing and pulling. *Jesus*. Ava's eyes close, and I use the opportunity to gather myself, my head hanging limply, my eyes clenching shut, my breathing already going to shit. Fuck me, this is intense. The sensitivity, my crazy heart rate, my clammy skin. I need to take a second. Find some strength. How I'm feeling, overwhelmed and weak, has nothing to do with functioning on a half-empty tank and everything to do with pure, raw love. It's crippling.

I open my eyes, my purpose and strength found. "Look at me." I don't know if it's my hoarse demand or my dick kicking inside her, but she obeys on a broken cry. I make sure she's looking straight into my eyes before I speak. Emotion finds me again, taking over, ruling me. "I love you," I whisper, and the moment the words leave my mouth, I feel like the world has been lifted from my shoulders. But just as fast, a different weight is placed there. A heavier weight. Not the world. But the fucking universe. I blink away the sting in my eyes, trying so hard to keep myself in check while she's staring at me. I won't fuck up this time. I won't lose her. I *can't* lose her. I'm on a journey to redemption, and I'm fiercely ignoring the possibility that by confessing my love to her, I'm also condemning her.

She suddenly isn't holding me anymore, her arms on the bed, her eyes closed. "Don't, Jesse."

I flinch, injured, but this isn't what she thinks. My confession isn't an apology. It's not a token gesture. It's not an attempt to pacify her. "Ava, look at me." She obeys, and it's a comfort. So is the hope in her eyes. She wants to believe it. "I've been telling you how I feel the whole time."

"No, you haven't." Her words are soft. Unsure. "You were hijacking my phone and trying to control me."

I smile to myself. *Trying*. And she was *trying* to make me crazy. Thrived on it. But we always agreed on one thing, and as if speaking up, my dick pulses its presence. I roll my hips on a strangled moan. She wants words. "Ava, I've never felt like this before," I say quietly as I drive calmly into her, feeling her stiffen and heat beneath me. "I've been surrounded by naked women with no respect for themselves all of my life." I take each of her hands and pin her to the bed, ignoring the pain, raising slightly to get some leverage before pumping once, smooth and firm. Her body jacks, and she cries out my name.

Another purposeful drive. "You're not like them, Ava." Nothing like them, and that is only *one* of the reasons why I love her so fucking much.

I build up to consistent, constant thrusts as she cries out continuously. This, the effort, it should be draining me, but with each thrust, I feel more energy and purpose seeping into me. More love. "Jesus." I stop abruptly, staring down at her panting, wet face. "You're mine, and mine alone, baby," I say quietly, and her throat rolls from her swallow. "Just for my eyes." I scan her face, refreshing the mental pictures of her I have filed in every corner of my brain. "Just for my touch, and just for my pleasure." I draw back, and my dick sliding through the hot walls of her pussy has me gritting my teeth. "Just mine. Do you understand me?" I hit home on a grunt, and she's here for me. Absorbing. Taking it. Accepting it.

"What about you?" she asks. "Are you just mine?"

I smile on the inside. I'd be nothing at all, if I could only be hers. "Just yours, Ava," I assure her.

And now . . .

"Tell me you love me," I demand, retreating and plunging.

Her face is a picture. "What?"

"You heard me. Don't make me fuck it out of you, baby." I'm already fucking it out of her, and it's wonderful. "Ava, answer me." I stare down at her, my expression fixed, as she looks up at me, stunned. She can't be surprised. She knows. "Don't hold out on me." I continue to drive, retreat, and plunge, and Ava starts to shake.

"How did you know?" She slams her eyes closed on a yell of pleasure, and I growl, beginning to get frustrated, my moves becoming more brutal, a slow withdrawal, a hard smash back into her. I am *not* leaving her body until she says it. She needs to get it off her chest as much as I did, and I really fucking need to hear it.

"Damn it, Ava, look at me." I see with worrying certainty that she's getting emotional, caught between dealing with the intensity of this moment and dealing with how fucking meaningful it's become. Whether soft and slow or hard and fast, always so meaningful. She swallows, bracing herself, and then she opens her eyes. "I love you," I tell her again, my teeth clenched, my body vibrating as I pound into her once more.

"I love you too!"

I freeze, my lungs screaming, my chest rolling. *Finally*. But I never considered how I'd feel once she'd actually spoken those words while looking me in the eye. Sober. Words she was scared to say. A confession she was terrified to admit. Yes, I feel untold relief. But I also feel the guilt swell, and I wasn't prepared for that.

I must make sure she doesn't regret loving me.

Condemned.

"I love you so fucking much." I swallow, my throat tight. Will my fierce love save us? Or kill us? "I didn't think it was possible." I smile faintly, happiness and sadness at war inside of me, as I lift my hips and sink slowly into her. "Now, we make love." I drop my lips to hers, release her hands, and kiss her until my tongue aches and the urge to make her endless promises overcomes me. I find her eyes, but I don't voice my promises. In this moment, I don't need to. My devotion must be written all over my face, emblazoned across my sweaty skin. She is my be all and end all, and the way she's gazing at me as I make love to her, she knows I won't let her down.

"Together," I whisper, feeling my control slipping.

She nods, her hands on a mission across my back, her legs stiffening and relaxing constantly.

"Christ, Ava." My cock jerks, the blood pounding, and she whimpers as she comes, squeezing her eyes closed to deal with the intensity, every inch of her rigid.

"Eyes."

She gives me them immediately, and I groan, staring at her, my jaw tight, every muscle locked down, as her body absorbs my climax. "I love you." She murmurs the words, and it's the perfect end to a perfect moment. Reinforcement.

I kiss her gently. "I know you do, baby."

"How did you know?" she asks, and I smile. I saw it. Questioned it. Drove myself crazy wondering if I was reading too much into it. Even when she was drunk and spilled it.

"You told me when you were drunk after I showed you how to dance."

Her frown is adorable. So is the hint of embarrassment. "I don't remember."

I roll myself into her firmly, seeing her mind working overtime. She'll never remember. I've never seen a woman so wrecked. "I know you don't. It was so fucking frustrating."

She blinks, frowns, and I see with perfect clarity how she's piecing together the aftermath of that night. *Yes, I already tried and failed to fuck it out of you, baby.*

"You knew all along?" She sounds so accusing.

"You were drunk," I mutter. "I wanted to hear the words when you were of sound mind. Women get drunk all the time and confess their undying love to me." And some *don't* need drink. Coral, case in point.

"Do they?" she blurts. She doesn't like that thought. I have to stop my amusement from showing. She won't appreciate it. Or the women hounding me. God, I hope they've moved on.

"Yes, they do." Even when I'm shitfaced. Even when I'm a bastard. Even when I treat them like objects. I have to look away from Ava for a moment. I was a bastard to her. Drunk and cruel. "I wasn't sure if you still did after . . ." I pause a beat, not wanting to go back to last Sunday. Not ever again. "Well, after I had my little meltdown."

She's silent for a moment—an uncomfortable moment, and I kick myself for bringing up a time I'm sure we both want to forget.

"I love you," she more or less growls, looking angry. *I love you.* It sounds so good. She loves *me.* I rock my hips, and she sighs, taking my shoulders and pulling me down. And she hugs me. Fiercely. And I consider for a moment that it's not the memories of last Sunday bothering her, but the women I alluded to. Could she be possessive? The thought thrills me. Unreasonable, maybe, but thrilling. I smile and snuggle deeper, so fucking content.

"How old are you, Jesse?"

What does it matter? I love her. She loves me. End of. I lift and get her in my sights. I'd love to know how old she *thinks* I am. Right now, probably sixty. Although life has been injected into me again, so perhaps only forty. "I can't remember," I say over a pout, feigning thinking.

Mischief is suddenly all I can see in her eyes, and her twitching hand against me is a massive clue as to what comes next. "We were at thirty-three," she says with too much confidence for a woman who has a huge, obvious tell.

My grin is epic. God, I love that I know her so well. "We should start again."

"No," she blurts, horrified, taking things to a sneaky level by nuzzling my cheek, my nose, my neck. "We got to thirty-three."

Silly girl. "You're a rubbish liar, baby. I like this game. I think we should start again. I'm eighteen."

"Eighteen?" she gasps in disbelief.

Frighteningly, eighteen puts me closer to her age than my real fucking age. I feel sick. "Don't play games with me, Ava."

"Why won't you just tell me how old you are?"

"I'm thirty-one."

She deflates, annoyed. Did she honestly think I'd forget? Every second I've spent with this woman is etched on my brain. Bar last Sunday, although those hideous memories are slowly creeping back little by little. "How old are you?" she demands again, like her change in tone might get her somewhere.

"I just told you, I'm thirty-one."

"It's just a number," she says. "If you ask me anything in the future, I won't answer—not truthfully, anyway."

What is this crazy talk? "I already know everything I need to know about you," I fire, and she pouts. "I know how I feel, and *nothing* you could tell me will make me feel any different. I wish you felt the same." My past chooses now, this moment, this lovely, blissful reunion, to stomp its way across my memory, and I wince away from it, because I've already vowed to protect Ava from hurt, and my past is a sure-fire way to hurt her. So, yeah, she knows everything she needs to know, and that's the important thing. I love her. I won't drink. And The Manor is a piece of me that is, in a sense, no longer a piece of me.

"You said before that I might run a mile if I know," she says. "I'm not going anywhere."

"No, you're not," I laugh over the words. It's not my history of fucking that makes her a flight risk. *Jesus.* "Ava, you've found out the worst about me and not run a mile." Shameful. Utterly fucking shameful. "Well, you did, but you came back." I drop my lips to her forehead and close my eyes, mentally punching myself in the face. "Do you honestly think I'm bothered about my age?"

"Then why won't you tell me?"

"Because I like this game." *Or because it's a distraction from your other secrets, brother?* I frown as I burrow into Ava's neck, hiding as she hugs me, wrapping her limbs around me protectively.

"*I* don't," she retorts softly, and I remain hidden, waiting for Jake to muscle in on my moment some more, waiting for him to tell me that I'm making a mistake. I think I prefer my conscience taunting me. Somehow, with Jake provoking me, it's harder to ignore.

Because I'm your twin, dickhead. A piece of you.

I clench my eyes closed, willing him to leave me be.

"Are you okay?" Ava asks, as my damp body shakes.

"Yeah," I whisper, frowning, listening, waiting. I think I really do need to see someone about this. It's only mildly acceptable that the voice is my twin brother. Or could it simply be the guilt talking? I don't know, but I'm not so unreasonable to recognize that it's an issue. "What time is it?" I ask.

I wish I'd kept my mouth shut when Ava starts to break away. "I'll go check the time."

"No," I grunt, wrestling with her squirming form to keep her beneath me, not yet ready to face the world. "I'm comfy. It isn't that late."

"I'll be two seconds."

I huff my displeasure, grimacing as my cock slides free of her, and slump to my back, as Ava saunters off across the bedroom. I prop myself up on my elbows, my eyes nailed to her arse as she goes, until she disappears out of the door. I grin, wriggling up the bed to prop myself up against the headboard, glancing around our bedroom. *Home.* It feels right again. Ava here, in our bed, in our kitchen.

In my life.

Now all I have to do is ensure she never leaves.

"I've got twelve missed calls from you," she calls.

And bombarding her with calls when I'm having a mild panic attack probably won't help my cause. I find her at the door. I can't even muster the appreciation of her naked body. "I couldn't find you," I grumble. "I thought you had left." I'm sweating merely thinking about the feeling of fear as I jogged around the penthouse looking for her. "I had a hundred heart attacks in ten minutes, Ava." No joke. "Why were you in the other bedroom?"

"I didn't know how things stood."

"What does that mean?" What am I, a complete imbecile?

Her shoulders drop, as if she can't quite believe she's got to explain. She hasn't and, actually, I don't need to hear it, but before I can halt the impending annihilation, she goes on. "Jesse, the last time I saw you, you were a stranger who told me that I was a prick tease and had caused you untold damage. Forgive me for being a bit apprehensive."

I wince. Cringe. Fold with guilt. Ouch. *Fucking, ouch.* "I'm sorry," I murmur sullenly. "I didn't mean any of it." I give her sorry eyes, and she shakes her head a little.

"Right."

"Come here." I encourage her toward me, needing to get her close again. She climbs onto the bed and lies next to me. "You'll never see that man again."

"Will you never drink again?"

"No." Never. Ava is all I need. My eyes jaunt down the length of her body, my fingertip homing in on her hip. I smile when she shudders.

"Never?" she asks, breathless from the simple touch.

"Never, Ava. All I need is you, and for you to need me. Nothing else." It's that simple. She has to understand that, but when a few lines appear on her forehead, I fear she hasn't understood at all.

"You already made me need you," she whispers, almost reluctantly. "Then you destroyed me."

The stab of pain in my gut makes me flinch. Now would not be a good time to devalue her hurt and point out that I was pretty destroyed myself. "I'll never hurt you."

"You said that before." Her eyes scan mine, looking, waiting for my reaction. I won't disappoint. Another flinch. Here I am, vowing to keep her from harm, and I am the biggest risk of causing it.

"Ava," I say, getting my face close to hers, desperate for her to comprehend the depth of my devotion. "The thought of you in pain, emotionally or physically, is appalling to me. Completely unspeakable. I feel crazy just thinking about it. What I've done to you makes me want to plunge a knife straight through my own heart."

"That's a bit over the top, isn't it?"

She has no fucking clue. Not over the top at all. Justified. "It's the truth." And since I've found myself forced into speaking a few truths, let's get something else off my chest. "Just like I feel violent when I imagine another man lusting after you." Like her ex. Or Van Der Haus.

"You can't control *everything*."

I laugh on the inside. *Wanna bet?* It's pretty essential if I'm going to maintain a decent level of calm. She'll soon grasp that. *I hope.* "Where you're concerned, I'll try my best, Ava." *Or we're both in trouble.* "I already told you, I've waited too long for you." I need to shut the hell up. "You're my little piece of heaven." I can't, my need to express exactly how I feel about her running away with me, maybe assisted by panic. Panic that for me to maintain this bliss, I need Ava's compliance. And my Ava isn't very compliant. "Nothing will rob you from me. *Nothing*." I kiss her hard, surprising her, trying to find some calm in my self-created madness. "As long as I have you, I have purpose and reason. That is why I won't be drinking, and that is why I will do everything in my power to keep you safe. Understand?" God, how could she not? I can hear myself. I might sound passionate and determined, but I also sound like a fucking lunatic.

Handled with pure style, brother.

I can't even protest that claim. Style indeed. But Ava still nods, even if she looks slightly alarmed. And as if the world hates me, her eyes drop to my scar, reminding me that I'm going to need more than determination and patience to bat back her relentless enquiries about how it came to be there.

"How did you get this?" she asks.

"Inquisitive this morning, aren't you?"

"Yes."

"I already told you, I don't like talking about it."

"You're holding back on me." She looks up, pissed off, and like the coward I am, I look away, falling to my back and hiding my face from her accusing glare. She's soon on top of me, and for the first time in the history of our relationship, I can't get excited about that. She yanks my arm from my face. "Why won't you tell me about your scar?"

"Because, Ava, it's in my past where I want it to stay." There. Simple. "I don't want anything affecting my future."

"It won't," she argues. "It doesn't matter what you tell me. I'll still love you."

I slap on a smile, those words helping. She loves me. "I know. You already told me that when you were legless."

"So why won't you tell me?"

Because it's ugly and she'll be disgusted and disappointed in me. From here on out, I can't be anything less than a hero to her. Strong. Protective. Devoted. Dependable. Her *god.* So I go below the belt and take her thighs. She's solid above me in a heartbeat. "If it won't change how you feel about me, then there is little point in tarnishing your pretty little head with it, is there?"

Her scowl is beautiful. "I'm not going to tell you anything if you ask me."

"You already said that." I know everything I need to, anyway, and I can say with confidence, nothing could make me question my love for her. I sit up and distract her some more with a searing hot kiss.

"Did you ever find out how the gates came to be open?" she asks. "And the front door?"

I need to work on my distraction tactics. "What?" I ask, trying not to show my impatience.

"When I went to The Manor on Sunday," she says, her lips pursing. "The gates opened without me pressing the intercom and the front door was ajar."

"Oh." Doesn't she just want to forget last Sunday ever happened, because I'm sure as shit I do? "The gates malfunctioned, apparently." I can hear the hesitation in my voice. I'm skeptical, I admit. The gates have never malfunctioned. "Sarah had it sorted out." I kiss her again, keen to get back to where we were, but Ava pulls away, and I scowl, pissed off. Not only with her.

"That's very convenient. Did the manual front door malfunction too?" She tilts her head, and it is one hundred percent condescending.

"Sarcasm doesn't suit you, lady." But she has a valid point, although I refuse to burden Ava with Sarah's possible transgressions. I'm well aware of the friction between them, and I can't expect Ava to appreciate the situation, because she doesn't know the story. *For fuck's sake.* "What would you like to do today?"

I don't like her sudden awkwardness, or the fact she's eyeing me, like she could be weighing up what to say. Whatever it is, I'll do it. "Well, there's just one thing I have—"

My phone screeches, and I curl a lip at it. "For fuck's sake." I swear, if John hits me with more problems, I can't promise I won't pack our things and fuck off to another country. Somewhere quiet, where no one can spoil our bliss. I move Ava off me and get up, taking the call outside the bedroom. "John?"

"The immigration police have been in touch again."

"You're kidding?"

"You've known me for decades. Have I ever played jokes?"

"Didn't we sort it out last night?"

"We might have, had you not been so welcoming."

I roll my eyes. "It was early hours of the fucking morning. What did they expect, welcome drinks, canapes, and a show? They've seen all the paperwork for the staff in question." I sigh. "They're trying to warrant the money and time they've just tossed down the drain on a wasted raid." And at the same time, waste my fucking time. *Fuckers.*

"But for the sake of getting them off our backs, let's play nice, yeah?"

I grunt my answer.

"And what the fuck have you said to Sarah?" he asks. "She's been on the verge of tears since you left in the early hours."

I wince, and I hate myself for it. Guilt. Always the guilt. "She's sticking her nose where it's not wanted."

"She's worried about you."

I scoff. Worried? She should be happy for me. Happy I'm not spending my life in a constant state of drunkenness. Sarah's spent years mothering me, fussing over me, being the only consistent woman in my life. Now she's not, and *that's* what's bothering her. She's being possessive. She doesn't like not knowing where I am and what I'm doing. I'm ignoring the reasons why. I can't ignore the guilt, though. "Fucking hell," I breathe, slapping my palm into my face and pulling it down. Fuck, that hurt. *Stupid hand.* "I'll sort it."

"Make sure you do. I don't need to remind you that your manor runs like clockwork because of that woman. Including making sure all the correct paperwork is in place, you get me? Show some fucking gratitude."

"What, like letting her at me with her whip?" I ask, because we both know that's what she really wants. As well as my heart.

"Motherfucker," he rumbles, hanging up on me.

"Back to the real world," I say quietly, my head dropping back on my shoulders. This isn't how I wanted to start my day with Ava, and I'm pissed off about that. "Fuck it," I hiss, returning to the bedroom. "I've got to go to The Manor." I head into the bathroom and collect a towel from the pile, throwing it over the top of the glass pane, keen to get this out of the way so I can crack on with my new life.

"Is everything okay?" Ava calls.

"It will be, get ready." I flip on the shower and step into the stall, washing myself roughly, my mood low. Until I look up and see Ava standing naked in the doorway. And there she is. The cure to all the things. I flick my head, and she wanders over, joining me. But what's with that look of apprehension?

She claims the shower gel and sponge. She's going to wash me. Care for me. No. I claim them and turn her away from me, taking a moment to take in every wet, naked inch of her back before I start to soap her up. She's quiet, and I'm definitely not imagining her tenseness.

"Jesse?"

I forsake washing her and dip, kissing her shoulder before resuming cleaning, hoping it'll loosen her up. "Ava?" I whisper in return.

"I really don't want to go." She rushes over the words, tensing further, and I pause, staring at the back of her head.

The Manor. It's always going to be a problem for her, and that's a major problem for me, because it's not going anywhere. "Can I ask why?" Is it the memories? The women? The sex? All of it?

"Can you just give me some time to get used to it?"

I feel my whole being deflate, disappointed. I can't enforce this. I want to, but I can't drag her there, kicking and screaming. And I certainly don't want to argue with her over this. "I understand," I say reluctantly, pulling her back into my chest, kissing her hair. "You're not going to avoid it forever, are you?" How long does she need? "I still want my new bedroom designs."

"No," she says, and I smile. "Anyway, I'll have to go to oversee the work once we finalize the designs."

"Good." I can live with that. Besides, it's probably wise to keep Sarah and Ava apart for the meantime.

"What's going on at The Manor?" she asks.

I grab some shampoo—mine because she took hers when she left me—and start washing her hair, dragging my hands from her scalp to the very tips at her lower back. "The police turned up last night."

"Why?"

"It's just some idiot playing games." I am *not* mentioning how many potential someones there are. *Who the fuck was it?* "The police rang John this morning to arrange a few interviews. I can't get out of it." Her hair washed, I put Ava under the showerhead and rinse away the suds. "I'm sorry."

"It's fine," she says, her eyes darting across my chest. "Kate was at The Manor last night."

She knows? So why the fuck did Sam swear me to secrecy? I don't know, but I'm playing dumb. If Ava thinks I've kept that from her, it won't do me any favors. "I know, it was quite a surprise."

She looks at me, worried. "Was she okay?"

"Yes, she was fine." I drop a quick kiss on her nose and tap her butt. "Out you get."

She pouts, thinking, and I know those thoughts involve Kate and what she's gotten up to with Sam. Could it have been Mike, I wonder, my thoughts going back to the raid. He certainly hates me enough. But so does Freja. And Coral. And Van Der Haus. And—

"What's up?" Ava asks, frowning at my thinking face, snapping me back into the bathroom.

"Nothing." I quickly turn her and guide her into the bedroom, then go to the spare room and riffle through her things, locating her underwear. I take it back to the master and find Ava sitting on the edge of the bed when I get there. I kneel before her, holding the lace knickers and tapping her ankles, and she obliges, standing to let me shimmy them up her legs. I snap the waistband, smiling up at her, before giving each boob a moment of my mouth's time while she looks down at me on a raised, amused brow. But she doesn't contest me. Just lets me do my thing.

"Done?" she asks.

"Trying to get rid of me?"

"Never." She dips and kisses my forehead, and then lets me help her into her bra. I stand back, admiring her. *Always in lace.*

"Now are you done?" she asks, her head tilted.

"Until later, yes." I kiss her hard, leaving her breathless, and go to the dressing room to get ready, pulling on some old jeans.

When I exit, tugging my T-shirt over my head, she's splayed on her back on the bed, and I stop, groaning. Why? Why would she do that? Her eyes drop to me as I pout, backing out of the room, getting a safe distance away from her. Her restrained smile tells me she knows of the internal battle I'm having. *Temptress.*

I pull the bedroom door closed behind me, putting the wood between us, and take a few moments to compose myself.

Then I smile.

She loves me.

7

I GET out of my Aston slowly, looking up at the building, taking a moment to appreciate what I've long stopped appreciating. I've lived in a dense fog of misery for so long, everything distorted, everything hazy, and for the first time in a long time, I'm seeing things so very clearly. Most of all, Ava O'Shea.

I smile as I slip off my shades and make my way into the predictably quiet lobby. "Morning," I say to one of the housekeeping staff, getting a feather duster waved at me as I pass. "Hi, Pete," I call as I stride past the bar, seeing him loading the glass washer. "Sarah," I say more civilly than she deserves as she exits the spa area, sliding to a stop on her heels. I flash her a smile and get scowled at for my trouble.

"Someone's happy," she mutters.

"A confession of love will do that to a man," I say quietly to myself. From the right woman, of course. Unlike Coral or Freja Van Der Haus.

"What?" Sarah asks, falling into stride beside me, scurrying to keep up.

I frown, keeping up my pace. "What, what?"

"What did you say?"

"Nothing. What's the situation with the gates? Fixed?"

"They're being serviced later."

So there will be no more malfunctioning. Not of the gates, anyway. "Good." I take the handle of my office door and burst in, all smiles. And it drops like a rock when I find Coral on the couch. I did it, didn't I? I fucking jinxed myself.

"I'll leave you to it." Sarah smiles too, but hers is smug, and she nudges me in the back, sending me staggering farther into my office, then slams the door. My lip curls.

"Jesse," Coral says, sounding rather subdued.

"What?" I don't even scorn myself for being curt. I've never known a woman with such thick skin. My good day is fast slipping down the pan.

"Won't you even look at me?"

I send my eyes to my feet and walk across to my desk. Where the fuck is John, anyway? And that immigration officer? "What can I do for you, Coral?" I ask as I tap and hit at the keys of my laptop randomly. Keep it business. Keep it cold.

"It's—"

"Actually"—I slam the lid down and shoot up—"I don't want to hear it." I round the desk, and her eyes follow me as I make my way to the door and swing it open. "Out." This woman has caused me so much stress, triggered untold fucking headaches. I owe her nothing, especially not my time. "I said, out." I ensure I keep my eyes off her, not wanting anything to soften me, and tears might do that.

"But—"

"Out," I yell, frustration getting the better of me. But my energy levels are being tested as it is, and Coral is an additional drain. I'm done.

"Please, Jesse. I have nothing."

I can't make her problems my problems. I have too many of my own fucking problems, so I remain silent, standing my ground, refusing to give her eye contact, until she eventually relents and slowly stands. I step back, out of range, as she leaves my office. And when I close the door behind her, I fall against it and finally give my lungs the air they're screaming for. "God help me," I breathe, resting my head back, taking a few needed moments to collect myself. Every time I'm here, I feel like I'm running the fucking gauntlet. Fighting for my life. I groan and drag a palm down my face, and then jolt forward when someone tries to open the door behind me.

I hiss, the edge of the wood smacking me straight between my shoulder blades. "Ouch, you fucker."

John appears, scowling.

"Don't ask," I warn. "Where the fuck are the police, anyway?" Isn't that why he summoned me?

Suddenly, John's frown isn't a frown anymore. It's a sneer, and he steps to the side, revealing the cocky wanker of a Chief Immigration Officer, Kev Baxter. Good. Let's deal with this so I can get out of here. "Take a seat." I go to my desk and rummage through the files, searching for the one I need.

"I'm not here in an official capacity," he says, and I pause, looking up, finding him shifting uncomfortably on his feet. He smiles awkwardly and closes the door behind him. I flick my eyes to John, and he peeks over his glasses, eyebrows high.

Ohhhhhhh.

John said Baxter had more interviews to conduct. A way to get me back to The Manor? Turns out it's me interviewing him. Resting back in my chair, I get comfortable. So he fancies a piece of my manor, does he? *Come on, you dirty fucker. Say it. Ask me.* I might even make him beg. He was a professional cunt last night.

I motion to the chair, and he wanders over, lowering as he clears his throat, and I assess him, watch him, as he tries to find the pluck to speak. He's clean-cut. Looks a bit of a drip, to be honest. But it takes all kinds. The question is, can he afford it? I've met people who have balked at the membership fees and people who haven't batted an eyelid. I've also learned not to assume someone's financial situation. Some members are born with silver spoons in their mouths, Coral being an example. Some members are self-made, Drew, for instance. And some come into money by other means—a windfall or inheritance. That's Sam. So, yeah, it takes all kinds, and all kinds come with a variety of riches.

After a good minute of silence, uncomfortable for Kev Baxter, easy for me, I start to feel my patience fraying. I want to get back to Ava and resume all the love, hear her say it, feel her show me. I sigh. Let's move this along. "It's forty-five grand a year excluding food and beverages."

He doesn't bat an eyelid, instead smiling a little. "Negotiable?"

"No. Take it or leave it."

"I'll take it."

"You have to be endorsed. Know any members?"

"One. Steve Cooke."

The cop. He's cocky. Self-important. It figures. I bet he and Kev Baxter get along swimmingly.

"Everything okay?" Sarah asks as she breezes into the office, her eyes narrowing to slits on Kev Baxter's back.

I stand. "Mr. Baxter would like to join. He knows Steve Cooke," I say, rounding the desk and offering my hand, killing him with friendliness. "Sarah will give you a tour. I have somewhere I need to be."

Naturally, Sarah's first reaction is to scowl, because she knows where *somewhere* is. I ignore her, and she soon loses her irritation, the potential standing before her irresistible. She plasters a smile on her face, thrusts her tits out, and motions for Kev Baxter to follow. Poor guy has no idea what's coming to him.

"Have fun," I call, and Sarah laughs her way out of my office. He's going to be whipped like a bitch for the inconvenience he caused last night. "Right." I look to John, praying he's not going to stall my escape. "I'll be off, then."

"Sit down."

"What?"

"Sit the fuck down now, motherfucker."

Wisely, I lower my arse to the edge of my desk, sheepish, as John yanks out the chair Kev Baxter just vacated and lowers his big body into it. I wait. Cautious. Worried.

"Talk," he demands.

"About what?"

"Don't test me, Jesse." He leans forward, pulling his suit jacket together before resting back. "With the girl."

"She's a woman," I mutter. Why the fuck does everyone insist on pointing out the age gap? I'm over it. Kind of. They need to get over it too.

"The woman," he mimics, his bald head glimmering under the ceiling light. "What's happening with the woman?"

I grin, and I absolutely cannot help it. "She loves me."

"Fuck me, you should get an award for being so fucking bright." He pulls his shades off and rolls his eyes, and I pout, injured. "Of course she loves you."

"Yeah, but she's said it now." I'll skip over the fact that I fucked it out of her. "We're on the same page." Finally.

"Does this mean you'll stop acting like a crazy motherfucker?"

"Totally." I get to my feet and rest my hand on his shoulder. "I've no reason to be crazy because all twenty-six years of her loves all thirty-seven years of me."

"Oh, so you've finally shared that key bit of information with her, have you?"

What's with everyone taking away my smiles? "Not exactly."

"Fuck's sake," John breathes, shaking his head as he slips his wraparounds back on. "Tell the girl how old you are and be done with it." He pushes himself up from the chair. "If she loves you, it won't matter." He strides away. "Same as your motherfucking history, you deluded motherfucker." Stopping at the door, he looks back. "You told me you'd tell her everything once you were sure she wouldn't run."

I wilt, stepping back. "It's not that easy."

"It is. Talk. That's it." He gazes around the office. "Look what happened the last time you kept something from her. The girl deserves the truth."

"Woman."

"Whatever. Talk."

I shake my head. Talk about my history? My brother, my daughter, my uncle? Talk about the fact that I betrayed her when I stayed away for four days straight. "I can't hurt her again."

"Then you'll be living on the edge for eternity, and this new, amazing thing you're feeling won't ever be truly amazing because it's a fucking lie. Tell her before someone else does." He slams the door, and I flinch, not only at the deafening sound.

"Ouch," I murmur, reaching for my chest and rubbing at the sting. I have to stand by my decision. Protect her. It's simple. Protect her from everything, but especially protect her from me.

My face screws up, and I exhale, my earlier lightness lost. There's only one way to fix this despondency, and it's not here.

I snatch up my keys and leave.

8

On my drive home, I make detailed, elaborate plans for the rest of our day. It involves no clothes. No interference. And I'll tell her how much I love her every opportunity I get.

I jog through the foyer, seeing Clive wrestling with something under his desk. I should stop and help. Should.

I step in the elevator and answer my mobile when it rings, having to hold it at my ear with my shoulder so I can use my good hand to punch in the code. "What?" I say to Drew. My phone slips from my ear and hits the floor. "Fuck." I scoop it up and wedge it between my shoulder and my ear again, going back to the panel on the wall.

"Why the fuck is Sarah showing around the copper who was here last night?"

My mobile slips again, hitting the floor *again*. "Fuck it," I yell, yanking at the bandage around my hand and pulling it off, my hand throbbing. I stuff it in my jean pocket and pick up my phone gingerly as I enter the code. "He's a member, but probably not for long once Sarah's done with him."

"A member? Why the hell are you letting in people who've pissed us off?"

"Whose manor is it?" I ask. "And what happened with you and Victoria? I thought you were dating?"

"I don't date, Jesse."

"I believe you took her out to dinner."

"I took her out for dinner and asked her to join me at The Manor. It didn't go down too well."

I chuckle, and Drew hangs up, the moody fucker. I start pacing the small space as I'm carried to the penthouse, and I squeeze through the doors the moment the gap is big enough, locating my key on the ring as I hurry to the door. Bursting in, I slam it behind me and stand, scanning the room. "Honey, I'm home," I call, grinning to myself. I poke my head into the kitchen, check the terrace, and when I find both empty, I take the stairs three at a time, hoping I find her exactly where I left her. On the bed, drenched in lace.

I fall into the bedroom. The bed's empty.

The bathroom. Empty.

"Ava?" I yell, proceeding to check every other room, my nerves becoming more frayed by the second. I'm getting worked up, unable to reason with the dormant fear rising inside, John's words crowding my head. I force my legs to take me back to the bedroom and sit on the edge of the bed, gazing around. Listening. She's not here. I gulp down the giant lump in my throat, wiping at my forehead while I dig my phone out of my pocket, repeating the same mantra over and over. *Be cool. Be cool. Be cool.* But she's run too many times, and this feeling that descends every time she's not where I expect her to be is unstoppable. She never mentioned leaving the penthouse. She never said anything about having to go *anywhere*. Surely, given she knows how I react to her disappearing, she would have. I dial her, and the fact she answers first time completely escapes me. So does her chirpy tone.

"Where the fuck are you?" I yell, standing and circling the room.

There's a moment of silence before she retorts, "I'm with my brother," evidently pissed off. I can give no time to that either. "Calm down."

"Calm down?" I blurt, my voice high. "I get home and you've run out." And she's telling me to calm down?

"Fucking hell," she says quietly.

I'll give her *fucking hell.* "Watch your fucking mouth."

"I've not run out. I've come to meet my brother."

I recoil. She didn't mention meeting her brother. So she knew she had plans and didn't tell me?

"He's back from Australia," she goes on. "I was supposed to see him yesterday, but I got a little caught up elsewhere."

"I apologize for inconveniencing you." I need to get off my high fucking horse.

"Excuse me?"

I ignore her and get to what I need to know; how much time have I got to kill before I get her back? "How long will you be?"

"I said I would spend the day with him."

"Day?" I blurt. All fucking *day*? "Why didn't you tell me?"

"Your phone interrupted me," she says, almost tiredly, as I fight to get my breathing under control. "And you were sidetracked with problems at The Manor."

Sidetracked? I'm never sidetracked from Ava. It's fucking impossible, and there's half my problem. She's a constant on my mind, and I'm beginning to resent anything and everything that stops us being together. I never thought I could resent The Manor. Coral, yes. Freja, yes. Sarah, yes. But never The Manor. And now, her brother too. It hurts that while I seem to spend every moment away from her itching to get back, Ava's quite content to have a life detached from me. She's my be all and end all. Clearly, I'm not hers. "Where are you?" I ask, this time gently, falling to my back on the bed.

"I'm at a café."

Vague. What, does she think I'll track her down and drag her back? "Where?"

"It doesn't matter where." She's giving me nothing. Not risking it. "I'll be back at yours later."

Later. Fuck me, that sounds like a long fucking time. What the hell am I supposed to do with myself until *later*? This is dependency of a different kind. And so completely unhealthy too. *Fuck.* "Come back to me, Ava." I sound desperate. Can I help it? No.

"I will," she says, soft and pacifying. It works to an extent, but it won't bring her home any faster. I know I'm being a little unreasonable. But this feeling, the constant dread, the fear. It's as strong as my love. As uncontrollable.

"Ava?" I whisper.

"I'm here."

"I love you."

"I know you do, Jesse."

The phone goes dead, and I drop my arm to the mattress, closing my eyes, wondering if I can sleep until *later*. She didn't tell me she loves me in return. Does that mean she's changed her mind? Have I blown it? "Shit," I hiss, scrambling up and going to my dressing room, rushing into some running gear. I can't sit around here. I'll drive myself insane.

Too late, brother.

Like a man possessed, I scramble into my shorts, hopping around my dressing room like an idiot, before stuffing my feet into my trainers. I scan my drawers. For the life of me, I can't remember where my running shirts are kept. I feel myself getting more and more worked up by the second, so I abandon looking for one and hurry out. I walk up and down the elevator, back and forth, willing it to hurry the fuck up, and when the doors open, I'm out of the cart like a horse bolting, flying through the lobby, no stretching, my flexing, no preparing my recovering body. I just need to run.

I can hear Clive yelling after me. I don't stop. Can't stop.

The gate opening courtesy of a fellow resident is a blessing. The clear road outside so I can run straight over it is a blessing.

My damn fucking mind and thoughts are a curse.

I pick up my pace, hell-bent on banging them away, each pound of the pavement breaking down the clusterfuck in my head. Every store I sprint past seems to beckon me, the liquor shelf flashing. Run. Just run. Run off the anxiety. Run off the negativity. Just fucking run.

My head is burning by the time I make it to St. James's Park. My heart is burning with it through Regent's Park. My whole fucking body is flaming hot by Green Park. But I keep running, because focusing on the inferno within is a far better option than obsessing over whether I'm being dramatic. Questioning my choices. Questioning Ava's love and commitment to me. *Avoiding the drink.*

And there's my problem. I'm not being dramatic. Every fear, every worry, every wild, drastic action is warranted. I'm a man on the edge of rapture and ruin, and I'll do whatever the fuck it takes to keep myself on the lighter side. And, more importantly, keep Ava there with me.

I run.

I run, and I run, and I run.

My bare chest is drenched, my heart booming, but that's okay. At least I know I'm still alive. At least I know I'm still breathing.

Nothing could slow me down.

Until I get a fucking blister. I break down to a steady jog, hobbling like a dickhead, my face screwed up. A fucking blister. I find a wall and rest back against it, drinking in air urgently. I feel sick. I try to regulate my breathing, try to get hold of the nausea. "Fuck." I brace my hands on my knees and fold at the waist, heaving my guts up, retching. But there's nothing inside me to bring up. *Empty.*

I drag the back of my hand across my mouth and look up, blinking my vision clear. I don't even know where I am. I wince my way upright and glance around. I shouldn't have. A liquor store waves from down the road, enticing me that way. And this is the man I've become. One wobble, one doubt, one insignificant hint that Ava's gone, and I'm a fucking wreck. Useless. But, and it's fucked up on too many levels, it's got to be better than drowning in a bottle of vodka. Has to be. Or else why the fuck am I putting myself through this? And Ava. Why would I put *her* through his? Not that she knows what state I'm in now. She's having a merry old day with her long-lost brother while I'm here trying to fucking kill myself in an attempt to occupy my mind until I have her back in my arms, where I'm sane and she's safe.

Safe from what?

"Everything," I gasp, sniffing. "Every tiny little fucking thing." I swallow and reach down for my T-shirt to wipe my face. No T-shirt.

I'm beyond fucking help. I start pacing down the road, away from the liquor store, trying to talk some sense into myself. I've got her. She loves me. I've got to get past this, get my head on straight, or I'll fuck it all up, and that's going to lead me straight back to the bottle.

I never had these kind of withdrawal symptoms when I tried to abstain from alcohol.

But trying to abstain from Ava?

Fuck me.

It's brutal.

9

"AH, MR. WARD," the concierge says as I drag my knackered form through the lobby. I made it a few hundred yards walking before I broke back into a run. Desperate. And now, virtually crawling.

"Not now, Clive." I smack the elevator button, step in, and check the time, pulling up when I see endless missed calls from Freja Van Der Haus. If I had any breath left, I'd lose it. Jesus fucking Christ, what now? What could she possibly want now? I call her back, and she answers quickly. I don't speak.

"Jesse?"

"What do you want?" I ask, keeping it cold.

"I heard you were missing."

Missing? Is that what we're calling it? More like dying. "I'm not missing. So how can I help?"

"I was just checking in on you."

"Are you joking? The last few times I've seen you, you've threatened to tell your husband about me and casually pointed out that my interior designer is *his* interior designer."

"Are you still seeing her?"

I freeze. Is that why she's calling? She's heard through the grapevine that I've gone off the rails, more so than anyone is usually used to, and she's drawn her conclusion. Me and Ava are finished. "Why are you so interested in me and Ava, Freja?"

"Just curious," she says too casually for my liking.

"Right. Well, your curiosity is wasted here. Goodbye."

"Oh, before you go, you should know that Mikael knows about us."

I laugh under my breath. It's that or hit something, and my hand has been through enough. "Wonderful. How?"

"It came up during the divorce."

"What about the other men you fucked? Did they come up?"

"I'm just telling you out of courtesy."

Bullshit. "Thank you," I say through my teeth. "And have you shared anything else?"

"Is there anything else to share?"

"No."

"I'm still welcome at The Manor?"

It pains me. Fucking *pains* me. "Yes." *But do not come near me or Ava.* "Goodbye, Freja." I cut the call, my head drops, heavy and tired, and I watch as beads of sweat hit the elevator floor. Uncomplicated love. That's all I'm asking for. Is it too much to ask? And while we're speaking of wishes, a bit of forthcoming information from Ava would be nice. Information of her movements so I don't get home all excited, looking forward to getting my hands back on her, only to find she's not there.

Plodding to the front door, I let myself in and stand for a few quiet moments taking in my penthouse. It's plush. Expensive. Tasteful. All a man could ask for. Except it's not. It's missing something.

Tossing my key on the table, I go to the kitchen and down water until I fear I might bring it up. I could. I still feel nauseous, and my marathon run is only half the reason. I'm fucking ruined. Body and mind.

Music. I need some music.

I scan the countertops for the remote control, coming up empty, so I go to the lounge and kill a good ten minutes rootling down the side of the sofas, searching under cushions, scratching around the furniture. I start pulling open the drawers of the cabinet, one after the other, shutting them loudly. The silence is screaming. "Fuck it," I curse, getting panicky, yanking open the final drawer. I freeze, staring down at the two photographs I shoved inside not long after I moved in.

Jacob.

And Rosie.

My eyes burning, I slam it shut and run up the stairs, going to the bathroom and turning on the shower, my blister and my fucking hand throbbing. The rush of water eases the chaos in my mind. But not enough. "The terrace," I say, my memory saving me. I dash downstairs, slide open the doors and see one of the controls on the table by the lounger.

Where I lay, wasted.

When Ava found me.

And then left me.

I snatch it up and hit button after button urgently until the penthouse is booming. Massive Attack's *Angel*. I see her immediately. I see her the day we made love, proper love, after our date in Camden. Her face. Her awe. Swallowing, I go to the kitchen, downing some more water, before taking myself back to the bathroom, the music building. I walk into the shower in my shorts, sliding down the wall to my arse, and close my eyes, reliving that time all over again. And after that, each and every moment we've shared—the looks, the words, the touches.

Everything.

With those thoughts, the music, and the water showering down on me, I manage to find a sliver of calm in my chaos.

"Where have you been all my life, Ava?" I swivel deliberately and firmly. "Promise me something," I demand, executing another flawless grind, making her moan. She's struggling to keep her eyes open, but I see the question there. "You'll stay with me," I murmur, gazing at her, full of hope. She stares at me, caught between the untold plea-

sure we're sharing and bewilderment I just can't stand. And then she nods, and I groan as I pull her down and circle into her. "I need to hear the words," I mumble, increasing the pace and the friction. But she doesn't speak. She doesn't say what I need to hear. She encases my cheeks with her palms, scans my eyes, swallows as I watch her, and kisses me. Except, I don't melt into it, her lips feeling unfamiliar. Odd.

"Jesse," she says, but her voice is different.

It's not Ava. I jolt, ripping my mouth from hers, blinking, trying to find some sense amid the madness, and when I finally focus, I don't see Ava. I don't see the woman who's saving me.

I see the woman who nearly ended me.

"Lauren?" I murmur, bewildered, trying to scramble away. Get away before she tries to kill me again. What is she doing here? How did she find me? She should be locked up. She shouldn't be able to get to me.

"You don't get a happy ever after," she says, almost smiling. Taunting. "Not for what you did to your brother. To your uncle. To Sarah. To me. To our daughter. Don't you see, Jesse? You've killed or ruined everyone who's ever loved you. You don't deserve peace. And you will never have it."

I jerk, my head flying back with such force, my skull cracks on the tile behind me. The pain is nothing. I gulp down air endlessly, my eyes darting around the shower stall, trying to gather my bearings. "No," I breathe, smacking the ball of my hand into my temple repeatedly, my other hand instinctively and protectively lying across my scar. My knees come up, my head goes down, and I fight to keep my breathing in check. To breathe at all. *You don't deserve peace. And you will never have it.*

Fear and despondency rip through me unmercifully, my face screwing up, my eyes clenched shut. And then I hear something.

I look up, without the energy to even consider appearing okay.

There she is. My torment. My peace.

With a knowing, sympathetic smile, she joins me on the shower floor, not bothering to undress, straddling my thighs, wrapping me up in her safe, warm arms. Comforting me. "I love you," I whisper into her neck, feeling completely beaten, despite having her close again.

"I know." Her words are a sigh. Not tired. Not exasperated. More concerned. "How many laps did you do?"

"Three." Or was it four? I don't recall. I just ran.

"That's too much."

"I freaked out when you weren't here," I admit, way past putting on any form of front. She heard me on the phone. Feels my subsiding shakes now.

"I kind of got that."

I pinch her lightly on her hip. "You should have told me." I pout to myself. A fair warning, a mention, anything to give me some kind of heads-up that she wouldn't be here when I got home. Then perhaps I wouldn't currently be a useless mess of a man on the shower floor. *Perhaps*.

"I was always coming back. I can't be joined at your hip."

"I wish you bloody could," I say, snuggling deeper into her. My nostrils are suddenly burning, and I frown. "You've had a drink." I don't mean to sound so accusing. My issue with Ava drinking isn't the issue of my burning nostrils now. It has nothing to do with catching a whiff of my nemesis and feeling tempted. My issue is her safety. And perhaps the fact that people make stupid choices when they're under the influence.

"Have you eaten?" she blurts, tense. Avoiding my statement.

"I'm not hungry."

"You need to eat, Jesse. I'll make you something."

I couldn't stand if I wanted to. Every muscle has seized up. I'm far from my strongest right now. Haven't been since Ava walked into my office all those weeks ago. And yet in other ways I am. Strong enough to not drink. *If she's here.* I exhale wearily. That strength will vanish if Ava vanishes. It's a very real, very unhealthy problem. For both of us. "Soon, I'm comfy."

She doesn't argue for once, and I'm grateful. I need to stock up on a bit of energy and valor before she hits me with more challenges, and it's surprisingly nice being sopping wet and having a dead arse, so long as she's on me. Near me. Touching me. I sink my face deeper into her neck, ignoring the smell of wine. See how calm we are? How much peace is shrouding us? Don't tell me this isn't the cure for all things. I wouldn't believe you.

"I hate this song," Ava murmurs, and my bottom lip juts out a little.

That's a shame. "I love it." I want her to love it too. "Reminds me of you."

"It reminds me of a man I don't like."

Her straight-up counter has me clenching my eyes closed. "I'm sorry." What could I ever do to make it up to her? I nibble my lip, thinking. The answer is easy, and we both know it. I lick the column of her throat, and I feel her body flex on top of mine. I could move if . . . "My arse is dead."

"I'm comfy," she says, smiling against my cheek, and I smile with her, giving her a little dig in her tickle spot. "Stop." She wriggles and worms, laughing, and it's like rocket fuel to my dick. "I need to feed you."

Food? My stomach turns, my body rejecting the idea. My dick, however? "Yes, you do," I agree. "And I want *my* Ava, stripped naked and lying on *our* bed so I can binge on her." All week long. All month long. Fuck, forever, just nibbling, licking, sucking, kissing every inch of her. And when I'm done, I'll start all over again. And again. And again, and again, and again.

I rise, bringing Ava up with me. "I'm all for that," she says, hanging from my front. "But I need to feed my man. Food now, loving later."

She's got it all wrong. "Loving now, food later." I set her wet form on the vanity unit and take a moment to admire her there.

"Where's your bandage?" she whispers, her eyes on my battered hand as I take a towel and start to dry her off.

"It was getting in my way." An obstacle, like so many other things in this world hell-bent on holding me back. I wrap her in the towel and hurl her forward onto my mouth. The pain that shoots through my hand makes me flinch, and she doesn't miss it.

"Please, let me feed you." The imploring in her voice brings on a surge of guilt. She's worried, and I made that happen because of my fucked-up inability to hold myself the fuck together.

This guilt I *can* fix. "Okay." I relent easily. "Food now, loving later." I force a smile, rub my nose across hers and press my lips to her forehead, breathing her into me. She's cold. "Come on," I whisper, taking her under her arms. "You need some dry clothes." I engage to lift and get batted away. "Hey."

"Your hand." She points to the still-swollen limb. "It's never going to heal if you're hoofing me all over the place." She's off the unit before I can protest, and just as I'm about to enforce my demand to carry her, she starts stripping out of her dress and my brain turns to mush. Fuck me sideways, would you just look at her. She denies me closeness and then does shit like this?

I swoop in and toss her onto my shoulder, ignoring the pain my move causes. "I like hoofing you about." I fling her onto the bed. "Where's your stuff?"

"In the spare room."

I snarl at her, getting my point across, before plodding to the spare bedroom at the far end of the landing, dripping everywhere. "Fucking spare room," I mutter, snatching up all of her things until they're pilled in my arms and taking them back to where they should be. "There." I drop it all on the bed in a heap, and Ava starts rummaging through. She pulls out some knickers and a top. Knickers that aren't lace. *Seriously, lady?*

Moving in, I confiscate her knickers of choice and find a pair of *my* choice. They should be her choice too. "Always in lace," I say, smiling on the inside as she accepts and slips them on.

I peel my wet shorts down my legs and pull on some dry ones, feeling her watching my every move. I hope she's regretting her insistence on food now, loving later. I turn and find her pouting. *Definitely* regretting it. Silly woman. I collect her and take her down to the kitchen.

Dropping her to her bare feet, I sink my face into her wet hair and steal a kiss as she pushes her palms into my chest, trying to get away. Reluctantly, I release her and she turns off the music, going to the fridge. "What do you want?"

"I don't mind." I spot my peanut butter on the shelf and move in to seize it. "I'll have what you're having." Her bare neck glistening within range pulls my mouth there.

"Put that back," she orders, trying to claim my vice, her face screwed up in disgust. Not a chance. I dip out of her way, amused, and put myself on a stool, making fast work of getting into the jar. One generous scoop loads my finger, and I inhale, slipping it into my mouth on a victorious grin.

"You're a child." She turns back to fridge and pulls out some chicken. She's going to cook for me. Like a woman who wants to look after her man. I probably sound like a pig. Don't care.

"I'm a child because I like peanut butter?"

"No, you're a child because of the *way* you eat peanut butter." She places the tray of chicken on the worktop and pouts, thinking. "No one over the age of ten should finger-dip jars, and as I'm being kept in the dark over your age, I assume you're over ten." Her look is fierce but playful all at once. She loves our game too.

I ignore her dig about age. "Don't knock it until you've tried it." I take another scoop and offer it across the island as she faffs with the chicken, placing it in an oven dish. "Here."

She eyes my finger, unimpressed, not accepting, and I shrug and slowly work my way through my jar, watching her move around the kitchen, content. Both of us. Calm, settled, happy.

Safe from the outside world. But what about after she goes back to Kate's? I narrow an eye on the jar. *When* will she go back to Kate's? *Never*.

"Enjoying that?"

I look up, my finger in the jar, and find her sitting on the worktop studying me. "I can eat the stuff until I feel sick."

"Do you feel sick?" she asks, head cocked.

"No, not yet."

"Do you want to stop now before you do and save some room for the well-balanced meal I'm making you?"

Well-balanced? I don't need well-balanced food. I just need to *be* well balanced. "Why, baby," I coo, slowly placing the lid back on my vice. "Are you nagging me?"

"No." She snorts, horrified. "I'm asking you a question."

She's nagging. I quite like it. She's cooking me dinner, and she's nagging me. Both turn me on. But more than that, how easy this is, us in our home, just being normal, turns me on more. "I like your sweatshirt," I whisper, nibbling at my lip. I bet I can make her change her mind of the food versus loving matter. "I like black on you." It adds a sultry edge to her never-ending elegance.

"You do?" she asks, coy.

"I do."

"It's Monday tomorrow." Her shoulders straighten in an act of assertiveness.

I frown at her random statement, stowing away my palms by folding my arms. "And?"

"And . . . nothing. I was just wondering what you might have planned."

Oh. Her question wasn't random at all. It's Monday, therefore the start of a working week. I've only just got her back, and now I'm going to lose her to the demands of her job? And, more worryingly, clients. Has Van Der Haus been in touch with Ava? Should I be worried? "What have *you* got planned?" I ask, testing the waters.

"Work," she replies, all too vague for my liking. What work? What clients? And the anxiety returns. How am I going to deal with this? It's quite simple, really. I just need to ensure The Manor's renovation takes up all of Ava's time, make sure it's financially appealing for Peterson, and hope he disperses her other clients to other staff. Peterson will be easy to convince. Ava, however, is another matter entirely. How do I approach this?

"Don't even think about it," she says, snapping me from my plotting. I blink and look up, not liking the warning on her face. "I've important meetings to keep."

With whom? "Just one day?" *Until I figure out the solution that works for both of us.*

"No," she answers quickly. Too quickly. "You must have lots to catch up on at The Manor."

"I suppose so," I mutter, accepting that enforcing anything to do with Ava's work right now isn't going to do me any favors.

"Oh, Clive said there was a woman here earlier."

I still for a moment, frantically trying to find my poker face. A woman? "He did?"

"He said that she was trying to get up to the penthouse," she goes on, while I fight to keep my eyes from widening in worry as she studies me. *What the fuck?* "She wouldn't give her name and you didn't answer your phone when Clive tried to call you. Blond woman. Mature. Wavy hair."

"I'll have a word with him," I say quickly, looking past her to the oven. "Is my well-balanced meal ready yet?"

"Who was it?"

"No idea."

She's watching me too closely as she slips down and checks the veg. Christ, I'm breaking out in a sweat here. What the fuck is Clive playing at? Clive and I clearly need to have a few words about appropriate discourse with the lady of the house. I go to the drawer and collect some cutlery.

"You really don't have any idea?"

I cringe at the wall, my brain working too slowly. "Ava," I breathe, plastering on a smile as I go back to the island. *Think, think, think.* "I really have no idea." Blond woman. Mature. Wavy hair. *Freja Van Der Haus.* Why can't she just fuck off back to Denmark and take her ex-husband *and* my problems with her? "But I assure you, I will speak to Clive and see if I can establish who she was." I've bought myself some time, but how much? Freja will soon have it confirmed Ava and I are together. I could revoke her membership. Problem is, I don't know if she cares. When I spoke to her a couple of hours ago, she was apparently worried about me. But then she hit me with the news that Van Der Haus knows she's been in my bed.

Then she was asking questions about Ava. What? Was she checking we're still together before she enlightens her husband on that too? *Jesus fucking Christ.* "Now, feed your man."

Ava scowls, though it's playful, and relents with the interrogation—thank God—serving up the chicken. It smells divine, and I'm suddenly starving. And desperate to move the conversation along. I load my fork and dive right in, humming my approval. "How was your day with your brother?" How long do I have to share her with him? I remember Ava mentioning he was living the dream in Australia. Good. So he'll be fucking off to continue living the dream very soon.

"Fine." She joins me at the island and starts working her way through her food.

"Just fine?" I ask. "This is really good."

She smiles, though it's light. "We had a great day. We did Madame Tussauds and went to dinner at our favorite Chinese."

"Tussauds?"

"Yeah, it's our thing." She sounds almost embarrassed, studying her chicken as she cuts through it.

"It's nice to have a thing." If Jake were still alive, what would be our *thing*? I smile on the inside. Superbikes. That would be our thing. We didn't have a chance to have our thing. I swallow, flexing my aching hand. "You've eaten already?" I ask, and Ava stalls from shoveling another forkful in. "Are you eating for two?" I'm testing the waters on that front again, looking up at her. Her eyes bulge. She's *definitely* never considered motherhood.

"No," she says, before chewing and swallowing. "Stop worrying."

Worrying? Of all the things I have to be worried about, *that* isn't one of them. Nowhere close. Could she be? Because I sure as shit have never known her to tuck away food so ravenously, like she's not eaten for days. Her period came last week. *Not* pregnant.

So, again, am I broken? I ponder that while I hum and moan my way through the rest of my dinner, just so she knows how much I'm enjoying it. Enjoying *this*. Her here, me here, no one else here. How many pills did she miss? Perhaps none, because new packs kept appearing, so she obviously had reserves. Anyone would think she's passionate about *not* having kids. Again, I wouldn't know, since we haven't had that conversation. My eyes naturally drop to her stomach, my teeth going to town on my lip as I set my knife and fork down, watching her as she starts to clean up, fascinated by how at home she is. I feel content. Until I catch signs of her back getting straighter by the second as if she's building herself up to something. The questions are gaining momentum again in her mind. I slide off my stool and walk quietly across the kitchen where she's wiping down the worktop, and she turns around, inhaling, ready to fire her questions—

And bounces off my chest. "Oh!"

"Lose the sweatshirt."

She peeks up at me, and I ensure she sees nothing but sheer grit. I've indulged her. Let her feed me. It's been nice, enjoyable, but nothing takes me to the clouds like being physically close to her, and I absolutely cannot take any more interrogations today.

Without question or hesitation, she pulls the sweater off, and I inhale subtly as I drink her in, radiating coolness but falling to pieces on the inside. "You're impossibly beautiful," I whisper over the lump of appreciation in my throat. "And all mine." I drop to my knees, taking her lacy knickers and dragging them down as I go, tapping a foot in turn for her to lift. I can smell her arousal. Smell her need.

Smell her love.

I look up at her. "I think I'll let you come first. Then I'm going to rip you clean in half."

She gulps as I stroke up the backs of her legs, her chest pulsing. My mouth is watering, the sustenance I truly need to survive within licking distance. My fingertips kneed the backs of her thighs, my tongue darting out, licking my lips, before I pull her forward and dive into her welcoming pussy, kissing her there deeply and ravenously.

"Oh shit." She sinks her hands into my hair, pushing me farther into her, encouraging me, every bit of her trembling against my lips and tongue.

"Mouth," I warn, giving her no respite, sucking her hard in between firm rolls of my tongue. I introduce a finger, just one finger, inserting it slowly, feeling every inch of her hot walls draw it deeper, hearing her whimper. "Tell me when, Ava." Another finger. I suck air through my teeth, feeling her throbbing against my tongue.

"That's it." Her hips push forward, applying pressure, and she comes against me on a mumble of a few inaudible words, shaking like a leaf, heaving violently. I smile against her flesh, holding her snug to my mouth, slowing my swirling motions and slipping my fingers free, her muscles defiantly resisting.

"You're too good," she pants, and I peek up, gently thrusting, easing her down.

I free her from the pleasure of my mouth and slowly rise, nibbling my way over her chest as I pass. "I know. Aren't you lucky?" I lift her to my front. "Are you ready to be fucked good and proper, baby?"

Her smile. God, her smile. "Knock yourself out."

I intend to knock both of us out. But not in here. I've had her in the kitchen, more than once. But the gym? This is going to be fun. I kiss her hard and walk us out, moaning my approval at her keen tongue whipping through my mouth greedily. Lowering her to her feet, I encourage her backward until we're by my rowing machine. I let my lips leave hers and kiss my way to her ear. "Fancy a workout?"

"What did you have in mind?" she asks, shuddering as I lick the shell of her ear. I separate us and step back, removing my shorts and freeing my aching dick. I give her a moment to take me in, encouraged by the unadulterated need radiating back at me. She eventually makes it to my eyes, and I indicate behind her with a little flick of my head.

She turns, looks across my gym equipment, and I wait for the penny to drop. But when she faces me again, I can see she's clueless. *Come on, Ava.* I raise my brows, and her expression is riddled with a fleeting frown and unsure amusement, before realization descends. "Oh." She exhales, immediately squirming, as I move in and claim her, leading her to the rowing machine. Rowing has never been my thing. I have a feeling that's going to change.

I lower to the seat and smile when her eyes root to my imposing erection standing to attention. I pull her forward and get her into position, standing over me, my hand lifting to her breast and massaging gently.

She goes lax, her head dropping, her chest pumping.

"Ava," I breathe, tingling everywhere in anticipation. "You fucking kill me." She finds it in herself to look at me, and it's a look I'll never tire of. Surrender. "I love you." I take her hips gently, smiling to myself when she twitches. "I love how you flinch when I touch you here." I love how she flinches when I touch her *anywhere*. "I love how wet you are for me here." Completely saturated, begging. I slip a finger inside of her and my groan blends with her moan as I push high, the soft, spongy walls of her vagina welcoming me again. "I love how you taste." I lick her essence away and swallow it down, before encouraging her onto my lap, my cock slipping into her so fucking easily. Like she's used to me. Like her body accepts me willingly. Like it's all it knows. She whimpers, breathing into my face. "I love how it feels to be inside you." Nothing will ever beat it. "Wrap your legs around me," I order, shaking with the effort not to grind into her as she follows my instruction, circling me with her long, slender legs. "I. Love. You." I push my feet into the floor, gliding us up the runner to the end, anticipation for the buffer that'll stop us having me biting my lip. And then it happens, and I am far from prepared for it. I suck back air and close my eyes, gathering myself before I come. Jesus. My cheeks puff out, every muscle I have firming up to find some control, my cock spasming. I open my eyes. She's watching me. Watching me struggle. Watching me prepare for movement. And then she kisses me, and it both settles and stimulates me.

"I love you," she mumbles around my mouth, and despite her kiss being earth moving, I have to pull away, just to look into her eyes and see that love. And so she can see the appreciation in mine.

"I can't tell you how happy that makes me," I whisper, getting us moving up the runner. "Do you need me?"

We hit the top and exhale our pleasure in unison. "I need you." Her voice shakes.

"That makes me happy too. Again?"

"Please."

We hit the end, and my moan is broken, my hands flexing on her hips, the deepness of our connection mind spinning. I give us no time to gather ourselves before the next jolt, taking us back up the rail to the top, bracing myself.

"Oh," she gasps, her jaw tight, her body tighter.

"I know." Fuck, this is good. "More?"

"Yes," she says, eager, attacking my mouth ravenously, all control, if there was any left, now lost.

Which means my meticulous moves are no longer measured, my restraint gone. We hit the top, this time with power neither of us are prepared for, and I bark over a cough, as Ava gives up my lips for the sanctuary of my shoulder, crying out into my flesh, her face turning in and out of my neck repeatedly.

"Oh shit." My legs take on a mind of their own, sending us on another fast glide up the machine to the top. Every hit pushes her boobs harder into my chest and my dick deeper into her pussy. Stars start to pop into my vision. *Fuck.* My feet push into the floor once more, eager for that sharp smash of our bodies. She fists my hair, anchoring herself, her hot, breathy pants on my shoulder burning my skin.

Bang.

I gasp, feeling her biting at my flesh, squirming on top of me.

"Fuck, Ava," I yell, drifting back down to the bottom, her bites turning into clumsy kisses while we descend.

"Get your teeth back into my shoulder." I launch us back up the rail again, my dick twitches and swells, and I choke on a cough, sinking my face into her neck and clinging on to her. "Shit, I'm going to come." My legs turn to jelly as my climax builds. "You ready?"

"Yes," she yells, frantic, tightening every limb around me,

preparing. And then her walls squeeze my cock, and it completely sends me off the deep end in the best way. I push off my feet, sending us sailing up the runner.

Bang.

And again.

Bang.

And again.

Bang.

Fuck!

Ava cries and yells above me every time we smash back to the top, clawing at my back, biting, screaming into my shoulder. My orgasm hits me like a bulldozer, unforgiving and ruthless in its power, and Ava's body tightens, her teeth sinking deeper, her scream muffled. We're slick with sweat. Buried in each other's necks.

Breathless.

And it's fucking amazing, the tingles all over my skin relentless, the feel of her stuck to me tightly, depending on me to hold on to her.

Holy.

Fuck.

Ava's the first to move—eventually—pulling back, kissing my skin. I smile and look at the damage to my shoulder. A collection of red marks greets me. "You're a savage, lady." And it's fine by me. I kiss her and let my muscles loosen. "I'm going to take you to bed and sleep all night buried deep inside you." I hoist her into me and rise, making sure my softening dick remains exactly where it is. Warm. Happy. "Kiss me now." She obliges, but not before giving my hair a possessive tug. "Savage," I whisper, feeling her smile, satisfied.

By the time I've carried us to our bedroom, the blood is reloading in my dick. It's a vital sign. Proof if ever I needed it, for me and for Ava, that we're both where we should be.

I lower her to the bed, helping her to the pillow, our kiss smooth and calm. "Stay with me." I look at her beneath me, her skin still flush from her latest orgasm.

"I'm here," she whispers.

"Move in with me." I want this clarified before the start of a new week. I want all gray areas wiped out. I want understanding. Confirmation. It will benefit us both, especially if she insists on going to work. "I want you here when I go to sleep. And I want you here when I wake up." She stiffens against me as I trace the seam of her lips with my tongue. "Starting and ending my day with you is all I need." I'll deal with everything in between as it comes.

"Don't you think this is all a bit soon?" she asks.

No, it's too fucking late. I free her lips, not liking her response, for no other reason than Ava's silly head might be getting in the way of her heart again. After everything, especially the past day, I thought we'd got over that. "*You* obviously do."

"It's been two days."

Here we go. "Two days since what?" I can see what needs to happen here. I should have suggested this when she was sky-high on pleasure in the gym. *Idiot*. Haven't I learned? But . . . I can save this. I move, getting myself into position, smiling on the inside when she comprehends what's about to go down. *Yes, baby, I'm about to get my way.* I retreat, my eyes narrowing, and thrust forward purposefully. "I want this every morning and every night." My smile isn't containable, not when she's fighting with everything she has not to succumb to the insanity. "And maybe a bit in between," I murmur, grinding and driving deep. She wants that too. God damn her, why does she have to make hard work of every step in our relationship?

Her sparkling eyes try to narrow. And fail. It's an added bonus that she always fails to hide her desire for me. "You only want me for my body."

"You don't want this?" I plunge deeper, firmer, with more purpose, and she squirms, groaning, fighting the onslaught of pleasure.

"You don't play fair, Mr. Ward."

She loves how I play, so perhaps that's why she makes every step in our relationship hard work. Because she wants this. "Say yes," I demand, at the same time hammering into her fiercely. "Have I got to fuck some sense into you, Ava?" Because I absolutely will, and she'll love that too. There's only one outcome here. I know it. She knows it. Our bodies know it. But if she wants to extend the process, I'm game. Always game.

"No," she yells, breaking eye contact and grabbing the headboard, her mouth saying one thing, her body saying something else entirely. And she thinks avoiding my eyes might help? I take her nape and manipulate her head up, my lips twisting a little, dealing with the pain.

"Say it," I grate, pounding forward.

"No."

My God, she's really asking for it. And I'll relish every smash and drive until she backs down. I take in air, knowing I'm going to need it, and let loose, indulging in her defiance. It won't be the last time. "Fucking hell, say it, Ava!"

"No."

"Ava." My hips piston, my body instantly dripping, and she screams over and over, every high-pitched yell fueling me, along with the tightening of her muscles around my dick. It's coming. Her submission *and* her orgasm. I drop my mouth to hers and give her a kiss to match my frantic pace. "You like that?"

"Yes!" She moans, screams, moans and screams.

"You want this every day?"

"Yes!"

God, yes. She can keep putting her spanners in my works if that's how she wants to play it. I'll never get tired of removing them. "Say it then," I order, gripping her hair hard, plunging and retreating on constant yells.

"Yes," she screams, the sound piercing, and I grin on the inside, finally letting my body's demand for yet another release take me as Ava literally bursts. And it's not only her body that loses all control, but her fucking mouth. "Yes, yes, fucking hell, yes!"

I'm out of my mind, unable to see straight, but I can still fucking hear. "Watch your fucking mouth," I bark, punching the mattress, trying to gain some stability. *Fuck.* The pain. I clench my teeth and ride it, focusing on the end game, hissing with each breath I take, and though I'm expecting it, as ever, I'm far from ready. I sink into her, holding myself deep while holding my breath, and I'm gone, taken out by the pleasure, my moan long and strangled. *Crazy.* My limp head drops and hangs, beads of sweat trickling from every pore. "That wasn't so hard, was it?" I wheeze, still dizzy, tingling everywhere.

"I was under the influence." She's breathless, and I smile. Drunk on me. That's what she means. I kiss her softly and fall to my back, bringing Ava with me. "I can't be with you every second of the day," she says quietly, sounding a little worried.

"I know you can't," I breathe, semi accepting of that. "I wish you could."

"I have a job, a life."

And there's the problem. Dependence. Or in Ava's case, *in*dependence. "I want to be your life." I'm unable to keep the dejection from my tone.

"You are," she says, but she's wrong. She has a career. Friends. Family. A thirst for self-sufficiency, whereas I only have a thirst for her. I look down at the back of her head as she strokes over my chest delicately. I feel like I'm asking to have my cake and eat it. Everything Ava is, how she's wired, is why I fell for her so hard and fast. It's not fair for me to expect her to change that to appease me, I know that. So I must try my fucking hardest to give her what she wants and at the same time feed *my* need. Compromise. I can do that. But can she?

I chew on my lip thoughtfully, resting my head back, feeling her everywhere as her breathing becomes shallow and her body heavier on my chest. There's no question; if old ghosts weren't loitering on the peripheral on our existence, I might feel more confident that she truly means it when she says she'll never leave me. So until they all fuck off, I'm just going to have to suck up the anxiety, hide it, keep Ava away from my past, and make sure she sees nothing but strength and stability in me.

Piece of cake.

10

I SLEEP LIKE A BRICK. There's no point asking myself why. The answer is still in my arms come dawn, snuggled as deep as she can get, breathing lightly. I sigh, contented, and squeeze her closer. I could gently turn her over. Wake her up in the best possible way.

But I need to kick my *piece of cake* plan into action. So, and it fucking hurts, I carefully start peeling her body from mine, so tense, my dick protesting. But needs must . . .

Leaving Ava splayed on our bed, I find some boxers, yank them on, grab some cash and my phone, and hurry down the stairs and out of our penthouse. When I make it to the lobby, Clive is on the phone. He trips up over his words when he spots me exiting the elevator in my boxers, his old eyes wide and shocked. I put myself in front of his desk, a big, fat, cheesy grin on my face. Clive and I haven't exactly seen eye to eye since we met. I need to change that.

"Yes, sir," he says down the line. "Well, that's definitely doable, sir." He picks up a pen and pulls a pad toward him. "I'm ready to take the details, sir."

My shoulders drop. Can't he see I'm working against the clock here? I start drumming my fingers on the marble desk, my eyes on his writing hand, willing him to hurry the fuck up.

"Ah, indeed, sir. Let me run through that with you again, sir."

What? No. I reach over the counter, seize the phone from Clive, and put it back in the cradle.

"Mr. Ward," he splutters. "I was on a very imp—"

I slap a wedge of cash on the counter, holding it down with my fingertips, my way of telling Clive that the money isn't his just yet. "We need a chat," I inform him, and he glances up at me. "You mentioned there was a lady here looking for me yesterday."

"Not Ava, of course," he says. "Another lady. A bit older."

Mature, Ava said. "A bit older than me?"

He hums. "I suppose so. How old are you, Mr. Ward?"

"Blond?" I question, ignoring him.

"Yes, blond."

"Hmm." I look past him, my teeth going overtime on my lip. Showing up at The Manor is one thing. My home? Freja's done it before, so I shouldn't be surprised, but still. What the hell is she playing at? Is she hoping for visual confirmation that Ava's still in my home? In my life? I release the cash and pluck the pen from Clive's hand, scribbling my mobile number down. "Any more women turn up, besides Ava, you send them away and call me." I tap the wad of notes. "Okay?"

He smiles, bright and cheerful. I think Clive and I will get along just fine now. "Of course, Mr. Ward. Have a good day."

I nod on a sardonic huff of laughter and board the elevator. "I'll try," I say to myself, smacking in the code, my mind turning in circles. Van Der Haus. I wasn't his favorite person before he knew I'd fucked his wife. Now? And if he finds out I'm in love with the hot, young interior designer he has his eye on? How the fuck am I going to work my way around that? If it needs working around. Freja might not tell him about me and Ava. *Might* not. Fuck. Then why is she so fucking interested in our relationship?

I exit the elevator and call John. "I need a favor," I say, letting myself back into the penthouse, my eyes landing straight on the stairs, listening for any signs of life from the bedroom.

"No," John says, and I recoil.

"I haven't even asked."

"Don't care. I know I won't want to do it."

"You get out of bed on the wrong side?"

"I haven't even gotten out of bed yet, you irritating motherfucker. It's only just seven."

I close the door and head for the kitchen, my mind working overtime. What to do, what to do? "I'll buy you a bonsai tree."

"I have enough."

"I'll give you a pay rise."

"Don't insult me."

I sigh, dropping my arse to a stool. "Please, John." I'm at his mercy, and I will do anything, absolutely anything he wants, if he'll just help me out here. "I'm desperate."

"For what?"

"Sanity," I mumble, and he laughs. "It's not funny."

"How can I help with that, except smash you in your stupid face to try and slap some into you?"

"You can look after Ava for me."

"What now?"

"Take her to work, escort her on her lunch break, that kind of thing. Discreetly, of course. I don't want her thinking I'm having her babysat."

"Discreetly? When I'm driving her to work? Last time I checked, Jesse, I was a six-foot, two-inch Black man with a chest wider than the Thames and a bald head so shiny you could catch a glimpse of it from the fucking moon. Discreetly?"

"Yeah, well, the driving part she'll agree to. But—"

"You think she might oppose me tailing her every move? I can't imagine why."

My head finds my hands. "John, this is important."

"Why?"

"Because Freja Van Der Haus is sniffing around. She's called me, asked about Ava. She also turned up here yesterday. Thankfully Ava wasn't here, and the concierge wouldn't let her up, but it could have been very different. I can't risk her intercepting Ava and telling tales."

"But they're not tales."

My jaw tightens. My blood starts to sizzle dangerously. "I'm just trying to reduce the chances of Ava finding out shit I really don't want her to find out until I know how I'm going to handle it."

"Fuck, you don't half make hard work of your life," John says tiredly, and I laugh out loud. "Fine, I'll take her to work. Fine, I'll pick her up. But I draw the line at following her, so you'd better work out something more practical. And quickly. I've got shit to do."

It's something, and I'll take anything I can get. "Be here at eight?"

"Fuck you." He hangs up, but my sanity definitely isn't saved, because John is right. This isn't sustainable. Not to mention the fact that Ava's probably going to throw a fit of colossal proportions when she finds out the lengths I'm willing to go to keep my sanity while keeping her safe from all the people haunting me. Ironic that I'll probably send her insane in the process. I need to get hold of her diary. Or better still, hire a fucking hitman to get rid of all the fuckers who are trying to ruin me. I growl and go to the fridge, having a few scoops of peanut butter to calm me down. Then I put on the coffee machine and head up for a shower to execute part two of the plan.

I enter the bedroom and stop on the threshold, and for a split second, all of my woes melt away when I see her sprawled in my bed, beautifully unconscious and unaware. I sigh, leaning a shoulder on the doorframe and admiring the vision, not daring to get any closer. I'll be blindsided by the potential of morning loving. Of giving her a quick reminder of our perfection before I lose her for the day to the outside world. "Fuckers," I whisper, forcing my eyes away, my focus on the bathroom.

Leaving Ava sleeping and not ravaging her takes untold strength, but I need to be gone before she's ready and discovers John in the car park waiting for her. And I need to appear one hundred percent together when she finds me ready for my day at work, which will be spent kicking my heels around The Manor, begging for the time to pass by quickly.

I shower, shave, scrub my teeth, rinse with extra mouthwash and once again avoid her in our bed as I hurry to the dressing room. I pull out one of my best suits, a new white shirt, and finger through my selection of ties. Pink. I put myself together, fix my hair, slip on my Rolex, and get my feet into some tan Grensons.

Done.

As I'm fixing my tie in the full-length mirror, I smile at the man before me.

Hot. As. Fuck.

I grimace, flexing my fist, the mass of bruises and swelling clashing with my fine charcoal suit. "Motherfucker," I breathe, looking over my shoulder when I hear stirrings from the bedroom. And groan. "Agony," I grumble, and not about my hand. I exit the dressing room, keeping my eyes safely from the bed, and head downstairs to the kitchen. I see Ava's bag by the door and, naturally, my conniving mind starts whirling.

Snatching it up, I rummage through, as ever, astounded by the amount of crap one woman can keep in a handbag. I find her phone, go to the settings and change the ringtone for my number, smiling as I do. Then, without much thought, I rummage some more, scratching to the very bottom in search of . . . something.

I still when I hear the familiar crumple of a packet of pills, looking left and right and all around me, like I'm checking I'm not being caught in the act of complete psycho behavior.

Don't do it.

I look up to the ceiling for some guidance. For some reason. For anything that'll stop me. Her period came a week ago. *Not* pregnant. After my despicable stunt, that's a blessing. So why the fuck am I not seeing it as that?

A noise behind startles me and kicks my arse into action, and I drop her bag, shove her pills in my pocket, and scoot into the kitchen, quickly pouring myself a coffee and sitting down. *Fuck-up, Ward. Total fuck-up.*

Two seconds later, Ava falls into the kitchen, and my heart clatters before plummeting into my stomach. My eyes take a leisurely jaunt across her naked form, my dick punching against the fly of my trousers, wanting out. I have time. I'll make time if I have to.

"Morning," I say quietly, ridding my shaking hand of my coffee and standing. My voice is low. My body ready. She looks a little bewildered. And really fucking enchanted.

"Urh . . . morning." Her dark, delighted eyes take in my suit-clad form as I swoop in and lift her, crushing her naked front to me. Her cheeks are pink. Her eyes alive, despite being sleepy.

"Sleep well?"

She hums, happy, as I drag my mouth across hers.

"You see," I whisper, my voice getting deeper with every word I speak. "This is *exactly* why I want you here morning, noon, and night." I loosen my hold, and she slips down my front, already breathless, if still somewhat perplexed. I know what she's thinking. She's thinking this is a stark contrast to the man she found in the shower yesterday. On the outside, yes. On the inside, I'm hoping and praying I can eradicate all potential issues before John quits as Ava's chaperone. Or, more likely, Ava fires him.

And kills me.

I peek down her front, my lip lifting at the corner. She frowns. Takes a quick peek herself. Realizes she's butt naked in the kitchen.

"Shit," she blurts, and I flinch, slamming my eyes closed. I shouldn't have. When I open them, she's gone.

"Oh no," I mutter, going after her, taking the stairs three at a time, the sight of her smooth, pert arse within biting distance sending me cross-eyed. *Christ alive.* I seize her and turn us around, taking her back to the kitchen. "Watch your mouth." I plop her on the island, chuckling when she squeals at the coldness against her bare skin, and spread her naked legs wide open. "I want you to come down for breakfast every morning just like this."

"You're confident I'm going to be here every morning," she says, her voice breaking, her body tensing, as I drag my touch to between her legs. She's playing. It's cute. And really fucking annoying.

So she needs a reminder, and I am more than happy to deliver. She can sit here looking all coy, sounding all resolute, but her body doesn't lie, and her body is currently screaming for me. "I *am* confident," I say quietly, torturing her with light circles of my finger. "Because you said *yes*. Or was it . . ." I fake thoughtfulness, feign trying to recall something. "Oh, I remember. It was . . . *yes, yes, yes, fucking hell, yes*!" I smile darkly, starting to fuck her with my finger, watching in satisfaction as her dark eyes darken further, filling with a hunger that only I can feed.

"I was caught at a weak moment," she pants, wriggling and spreading her legs wider. *Wanton.*

"Do I need to remind you why it was a good decision?" I kiss her hard and up the ante, introducing another finger. When she fists the lapels of my perfectly pressed suit, I have my answer, her whimpers around my tongue enforcing it. Fuck, I've got to have her. Now. Here. I ease her down to the counter and start yanking at the belt on my trousers, watching her chest pumping as she waits for me. My cock bursts out of my trousers, weeping its happiness, and I waste no time putting it where it needs to be. I take her thighs and pull her onto me, and instant pleasure rips through my body.

Jesus.

"This is another reason," I wheeze, retreating and powering forward again. She screams, her head thrown back, her body bowing violently, her hands gripping the edge of the counter. She knows this is going to be hard. She's prepared. Good, because there's no fucking way I can hold myself back. I start pounding into her unforgivingly, my hips fast, my arse tense, my fingers clawing into the flesh of her thighs. I bark my curses, over and over, the blood rush to my head burning, the temperature of my body so high, I feel like I could burst into flames.

"Fuck, you feel perfect, baby." I reach for one of her bouncing boobs, molding it firmly, as she cries out with every brutal drive. "Remember yet?" I clench my teeth, my body out of control, as she accepts every merciless second. "Answer the question, Ava," I order frantically, seeing her holding her breath, searching for the orgasm she needs. "Now."

"Yes!"

"You're staying with me?" I don't ease up. Won't give it to her until she gives me what I want.

"Oh God," she wails, her head tossing from side to side constantly. "Oh God. Jesse!"

My name. Hearing her scream my name. I'm going to fucking come so hard. But . . . "Answer the fucking question, Ava."

"Yes," she bellows, her voice cracking, her back snapping into an arch.

And I let go, my hips rolling, and I come on a groan, losing all ability to hold my body upright, my legs like jelly. I fall forward, swathing her with my hot, heavy body, and that is what you call the perfect start to any man's day. But as a result, I'm fucking knackered. Shit, we're so fucking perfect together, I could weep.

"God, I fucking love you." I force my head up to see her. To see the shade of her cheeks and the drowsiness in her eyes.

"I know you do," she pants, still struggling to breathe properly, her sleepy eyes taking in my jawline. "You shaved."

"You want me to grow it back?"

"No, I like seeing all of you." Her palm on my face is more fire on my skin, and I turn my mouth onto it and kiss her softly. And now I really must get out of here. I drop my face to her tummy, breathing her into me, before reluctantly pulling free from the warmth and tucking myself in.

"I've got to go," I say, fixing myself. "Get out of my sight before I take you again." I pull her up, and her mouth so close gets me. I kiss her. I kiss her deep and hard, crying on the inside. "Now." Ripping myself away, I stand back, but Ava hovers, contemplative, looking at me in a way that suggests she wants more. So I narrow my eyes, silently warning her, begging her not to make this more painful. She eventually picks up her feet and sashays away with too much purpose in the sway of her naked hips. The little temptress. I sink my hands into my pockets where they're restrained, feeling something, and I'm about to pull it out when I remember what it is. *Fucking hell.* I leave the pills exactly where they are. Hidden.

I turn my body slowly, following her to the door, and she stops.

Looks over her shoulder. "Have a nice day," she purrs, stroking between her thighs and slowly licking away the remnants of our morning session.

Jesus, Lord above. "Fuck off, Ava."

Her smile is sultry and satisfied. Good for her. And I'd certainly be walking with a spring in my step, if my damn dick wasn't iron again. I blow out air and cup myself, rearranging my trousers. And then I smile. She loves me. Can't resist me. I pull out the pills, cringing, fighting with my conscience. *Put them back.* "You need help, Ward," I mumble, putting them back in the wrong place. My pocket.

I scoop up my keys and head out. Clive looks a little more awake when I pass through the lobby, and a tip of his hat accompanied by a cheesy grin tells me we're now on the same page. "Have a good day, Clive," I say cheerfully, slipping on my shades and breaking out into the morning sunshine. I come to a stop and breathe in the new week, determined to make it a good one. I can do this. It's eight . . . ish hours. I inwardly groan. Eight fucking hours. It's going to feel like eight years.

"You look like you've been mauled by a lion."

I turn and find John leaning against the bonnet of his Range Rover, looking over his glasses at me. I smile and peek over the top of mine. "It was a lioness, actually." I stride over, still with no spring in my step. "Thanks for doing this, big man."

"And what are *you* going to do?"

"What do you mean?"

His gold tooth is revealed when he snarls at me, and I back up a few steps, wary. "I mean, to sort this shit out so one, I don't have to babysit your girlfriend, and two, because you just need to sort this shit out."

"I don't know," I admit, a little stumped.

"So what's the deal with Freja Van Der Haus?"

"She told her husband I fucked her." I shake off a shudder. Freja knows Mikael dislikes me. She knows her husband hates The Manor, and now he knows she's been in my bed. Ava will be a red flag to a bull, and that flag will be billowing in the face of the bull if Mikael finds out I'm rather attached to the flag. "Now she's sniffing around trying to find out if Ava's still the object of my affections."

"And craziness," he mutters, prompting me to look at him tiredly.

"I refused to entertain her advances, and now I'm feeling a little vulnerable."

"Like she might tell Van Der Haus exactly how recently you fucked her."

"Yes." So, basically, I'm screwed either way.

He looks over his glasses at me, his nostrils flaring with anger. I can relate. "You said no more crazy shit. This is crazy. Just be honest with Ava."

I laugh hysterically as I break out in an anxious sweat, pointing back at Lusso. How many times do we need to go over this? "Tell her that I betrayed her? Tell her I lost my mind for a brief moment and accepted two women into my office after sinking a bottle of vodka?" I scoff. "That'll confirm everything she fears, and the possibility of losing her will become a dead certainty." I'm a fuck-up. And as if to confirm it, I stuff my hand in my pocket and feel the pill packet I just stole from the love of my life. The love of my life who I fucking betrayed. Just give me a gun and I'll put myself *and* everyone else out of their misery. "We've just got back on track. I'm not telling her," I affirm, marching toward my Aston. "I can't lose her, John. It'll be the end of me." I fall into the driver's seat, start the engine, and roar off toward the gates. Tell her? Give her all of the ammunition she needs to leave me for good? "What the fuck is wrong with people around here?" I yell, smacking the steering wheel a few times, cursing with every pound and every sharp pain through my fist. "Fuck." I sniff and roughly wipe at my welling eyes, frustration getting the better of me. The moment, the very fucking second I leave my paradise, my world is upended and my reality crashes down around me. I drop a gear and slam my foot down, my teeth grinding.

Think of Ava.

Just think of Ava.

So I do. All the way to The Manor, I run over every second of our time since I opened my eyes and found her asleep in the chair after my week-long trip to hell. Of each moment she fought me but didn't want to fight me. And the moment I spoke the words I've dreaded saying. And hearing her say them back. A lump springs into my throat, my knuckles turning white from the force of my grip.

She loves you. So maybe she won't leave you. And can you really carry on like this? Hiding your secrets? Hiding your daughter? Hiding your miserable story? Hiding me?

No, I can't go on like this. But the alternative is Ava getting beneath this exterior, and I refuse to be anything less than the man she needs me to be. The man I want to be. The man she's helping me to be. A few minor meltdowns aside.

And cheating on her aside.

"We weren't serious," I yell, giving the steering wheel another punch, heaving like an angry gorilla. It's a lie. It was *very* serious. For me, anyway. And that's exactly why I turned to the bottle. It's a fucked-up kind of compliment to Ava in a way. Because no woman in the history of Jesse Ward has sent him crazy. No woman has enchanted him. No woman has made him fall in love.

Until now.

And with my love, unfortunately for Ava, it seems there comes a whole heap of crazy.

11

The Manor is dead, the foyer silent, the bar empty, the summer room quiet. I don't see one soul as I walk to my office, calling John to check in. Or, more to the point, check he's still in one piece after collecting Ava from Lusso. "She's here, Jesse," he rumbles, unimpressed, before hanging up. And that's that. She's in his car, though I bet there was a pile of indignance that got in with her. Nevertheless, I feel like I'm winning.

I smile and put a call in to the maintenance guy at Lusso to order a new remote control for the gates before calling my new friend, the florist. "Jesse Ward," I say when she answers, pushing through the door of my office.

"Mr. Ward. Same again?"

"Yes, please."

"Same address on Bruton Street?"

"Of course."

"And what should the card say?"

I sit down at my desk, thinking for a moment. "You got a pen?" I ask, and she confirms. "It should say," I begin, reaching for my shoulder and rubbing at the place she sunk her teeth into me. "You're a savage and a tease. You drive me crazy. I love you. Sign it off J. Add a kiss too."

"You know, we're living for your calls, Mr. Ward," the florist says, and I frown. "My colleagues and I have a little bet going on about what swoony words will be delivered with each bunch."

I laugh a little. "Too cheesy?" I ask. I've never been cheesy, and I don't want to start now.

"Oh no, very romantic."

My pathetic chest swells, and I grin at thin air across my office. "Women love romantic, right?" Why the fuck am I looking for reassurance? I know what Ava likes. I don't need this woman to tell me.

"Right," she confirms. "I might have to look for an older man myself."

I choke on my tongue, balking. The cheeky fucker. "Charge it to my card." I hang up and get to my feet, feeling at my freshly shaven face. Older man? Is that what people see when they see Ava with me? Older man with a younger woman? The doctor thought she was my wife. I pout, just as Sarah walks in. She looks me up and down, and I jump in before she can comment on my crumpled form. "How old do I look?"

"So you're talking to me then?" She struts across to my desk and takes a seat, swinging one leather-clad leg over the other and pouting her pouty red lips.

I narrow an eye on her. "How old?"

"Now? Two hundred."

"Oh fuck off," I mutter, rounding my desk, heading straight back out. "At least I'm all natural." What am I, a bitch? I roll my eyes to myself and yank the door open. I'll go for a swim. Have a sauna. Maybe even smash a few balls over the net on the courts. I look up to the ceiling. Killing time. *Again.*

"Why are you so concerned about how old you loo—" Sarah stops abruptly, gasps, and then starts laughing. The sound stabs me in the back. "Good God, you're paranoid the young, hot interior designer will find a hotter, *younger* man."

I swing around, outraged. "There aren't many men in this world hotter than I am, no matter their fucking age."

Her smile is slap-worthy, and she shrugs, standing slowly from the chair. "Well, that's the risk you take when you start fucking a younger woman."

Fucking. She refuses to accept I'm capable of anything but emotionless fucking. "What, like the risk Carmichael took with you?" It's out before I can stop it, and I don't hold back there. "Because you were certainly on the lookout." Permanently. And I was her unlucky prey.

Sarah doesn't even flinch, the hard-faced bitch. She knows I'm being spiteful because I'm injured, even if every word I'm spitting at her is one hundred percent accurate.

"Carmichael spread himself as far as I did. You know that." Her nose lifts in an act of vigor. "You must be paranoid, or you wouldn't ask. Obviously, Ava hasn't given you the reassurance you need."

Oh, she's given me plenty of reassurance. I throw Sarah a dirty look and leave before she presses some more and figures out that Ava doesn't actually *know* how old her boyfriend is. I'm too mature to be a *boyfriend.* Regrettably, I'm not in my twenties like my . . . girlfriend? I roll my eyes.

"Where are you going?" Sarah calls. "I need to go over the schedule for the anniversary party with you."

I stop and look back, finding her waving a file.

"The guest numbers need confirming, and the party bags putting together. And the business bank manager will be here at four thirty to update and verify our identities."

"You want me to help put party bags together?"

"Just give me some time, will you? I've been doing this all on my own while you're off out there behaving like a crazy bastard." She gives me a pleading look. I hate that look. It's a guilt-inducing look. Damn her. She's always managed just fine without me, regardless of the workload. Why *now* does she desperately want me around?

It's a stupid question. Besides, I need to kill time.

Beaten, I trudge back to my desk, pulling my phone from my pocket when it rings. And with it, I manage to pull out Ava's contraceptive pills too. They hit the floor with a little ding, and I stare at them for way too long before I register my brain screaming at me to pick them the fuck up before Sarah does. I dip fast and swipe them from the floor, stuffing them back in my pocket, not daring to look at Sarah. Would she know what they are? Would she click?

Fuck it. My phone continues to ring, offering me the perfect distraction to buy time and compile some bullshit story about Ava leaving them in my car. Until I see who's calling me.

I heart jumps into my throat, and I reject Amalie's call and drop to my chair, tossing my mobile onto my desk as Sarah lowers warily on the other side. I peek up at her, my jaw rolling. "Okay?" she asks.

"Fine," I grunt, as my phone starts vibrating across the wood.

Sarah cranes her neck, and her lips form a straight line. I will her to keep her trap shut. I do not need a lecture on why I'm avoiding my sister's constant attempts to reach me. It rings off, and a moment later, a voicemail alert sounds. I reach for my phone and calmly clear the screen.

"It's your birthday a week today," Sarah says quietly.

"I don't do birthdays." Like I have to remind her. They're too hard. Too painful. And this year? Fuck, I'm dreading it. No alcohol to drown in. To help me pass the day as quickly and as pain free as possible. "So, the final numbers," I go on, looking up at her, sounding completely together. I'm not. Jake should be here. He deserves to be here. *It should have been me.*

"Jesse?"

I blink, jerk, and inhale. "Numbers," I croak, clearing my throat.

"Seven fifty." Sarah slides a spreadsheet across to me, eyeing me closely. I collect it and skim to the page I need, running my eyes down the list of names. "Remove Freja Van Der Haus," I order, tossing it back across my desk. Jesus, that might be a terrible move, but she can't be here if Ava is, and Ava is *definitely* going to be here. On my arm. All night. "And add Ava."

"What?"

"And make sure she's at my table."

"She's not been here since she found out what this place is and left you, and you want to bring her on the busiest night of the year?" She looks exasperated.

"Yes." She'll be fine. Everything will be fine. Just as soon as I've explained to Ava that The Manor anniversary event isn't a giant orgy. At least, not downstairs before ten thirty.

"And what do I tell Freja Van Der Haus?"

"No fucking idea."

"Helpful."

My phone starts dancing across my desk again, but this time it's John, thank God. I answer, not bothering to excuse myself from Sarah. "John?"

"I dropped her off to get her car."

I frown. "Why? You were supposed to take her to work."

"Well, she asked me to take her home to get her car."

"It's not her home," I bark, making Sarah's eyes widen and John curse his arse off at me. I compose myself. Not crazy. "Ava's moved in with me."

Sarah's eyes go rounder, and I glare at her, daring her to pass comment. But John can't see my warning look. "Does Ava know that?" he asks, flat and coolly.

"Fuck off. You're a shit chaperone." I hang up, well aware that I've just signed my death warrant and lost Ava's chaperone. "Next?" I ask Sarah expectantly.

She wisely goes back to her files, and over the next few hours, she puts me through my paces, reeling off information I'm sure I don't need to know. I should thank her, really. It's killing time, even if I'm not technically needed to chew over numbers and finalize the finer details of The Manor's anniversary party on Friday.

I'm distracted, more than once with a few texts from Ava, and I grin like an idiot as I open them and reply, getting a few tired, impatient sighs from Sarah each time I'm unfocused. Ava's thinking of me. Forget the fact I've made it pretty impossible for her *not* to think about me.

"And the private suites aren't open until ten thirty, agreed?" Sarah asks, and I blink, looking up at her.

"What?"

She shows her annoyance, her lips straight. She's not pissed off that I'm distracted from work. She's pissed off because of *what's* distracting me. "The rooms," she grates. "They don't open to members until after dinner around ten thirty."

"Why am I here?" I ask her, not giving her an answer. She doesn't need one. For years, she's run The Manor like clockwork without boring me to tears with the ins and outs.

"You tell me. You clearly struggle to be at The Manor since you met the new, *young* bit of stuff that you're currently fucking."

"I hate you sometimes."

"Just sometimes?" She rises from the chair slowly. I'd love nothing more than to slap the front she puts on right off her face. But, and it's ridiculous, I prefer this bitch to the needy, desperate woman who throws herself at me and spikes endless, untold guilt. "See you around, stud," she purrs, sashaying away. When she reaches the door, it flies open, narrowly missing Sarah's face. Such a shame.

"Watch where you're fucking going," she snaps, and Sam wisely backs up, hands raised in surrender.

"Sorry." He gives her a cheeky smile and strides to my desk, dumping himself messily in the chair Sarah just vacated.

"Come on in," I say flatly.

"Fuck you," he mutters, suddenly looking stressed, leaning across the desk. "You need to tell Ava how old you are before Kate cuts off my balls for the information."

I stare at him. Just stare at him, aware of Sarah still on the threshold of my office. The stupid fucking prick. I'm going to kill him.

"What?" Sarah asks, interested, and I close my eyes and breathe in through my nose, out through my mouth. Calm. Remain calm. "She doesn't know how old you are?" Her bark of laughter cuts through me.

"Oh shit," Sam murmurs.

I open my eyes, giving him a look to suggest he's dead meat.

"Oh my God," Sarah howls, clinging to the doorframe to hold herself up. "This is priceless."

I snarl at Sam, who shrinks farther in his chair, mouthing a sorry as John walks in. He looks at Sarah, who's still hysterical. Looks at me with a face like thunder. Looks at Sam who's sheepish.

"What?" he asks. "What the fuck's going on?"

"Jesse's little plaything doesn't know how old he is." Sarah's head gets tossed back, her laughter increasing. It's unbearable. And . . . *plaything?* I am out of my chair like a bullet, stalking across my office, ready to rip her sick head clean off her shoulders. Obviously, once I make it to her cackling form, I don't rip her head off. Wouldn't. Couldn't. And she knows it. "You'll keep your big fucking trap shut."

"Promise," she coos, pivoting and dancing happily away.

"How the fuck did Carmichael ever love that woman?" I ask when she's gone, my head in my hands.

"She wasn't this twisted back then," John says on a sigh, looking across at Sam. "I saw your car outside a certain flat this morning."

"We're friends," Sam grunts, turning his attention to me. "When the fuck are you going to put an end to this stupid game you've got going on with Ava?" he asks. "Man, I'm tired of dodging the bullets. So *you* must be fucking exhausted."

"Who's exhausted?" Drew asks, strolling in.

I throw up my hands, exasperated. "What is this, the new venue for your morning coffee club?"

"Would love one." Drew drops onto the couch and gets comfortable. "No sugar, an extra shot."

"Why aren't you at work?"

He gives me a sarcastic smile. "Just checking you're still alive. And sane." His eyebrows raise slowly. "And sober."

I roll my eyes and leave the boys, stomping to the spa, finding peace and quiet in the men's changing rooms. I sit on a bench and dial Ava, just needing a little hit to get me through the rest of the day. But a text comes in before I can connect. And my heart sinks. Sarah didn't waste any time letting Freja know.

> I just got a message from Sarah. Thanks for nothing.

I reply quickly.

> It's nothing personal. But it will be very personal if you want to make it. I can dig up dirt and make it yours, Freya. Now is the time to let things go.

I wait a good five minutes for her to retaliate, but I get nothing. It doesn't make me feel any better. But something will. I finally dial Ava.

"Hey," she chimes, sounding cheerful.

I feel anything but. "God, I miss you." This morning has been the longest morning ever. It doesn't bode well for our future together.

"Where are you?"

"At The Manor," I pretty much grumble, glancing around the empty changing rooms, Sarah's wicked cackle still echoing in my ears. "Everything is under control. I'm not needed here." Unless someone wants to rub me up the wrong way. "Do you need me?" I ask hopefully.

"Always," she whispers, and I sense the smile in her tone. She likes that I'm missing her.

"Now?" I'll watch her work. Take her to her appointments. Does she have any? And if so, with who?

"Jesse," she breathes, bursting my bubble. "I'm at work."

"I know." I drop my head into my hands. "What are you doing at this precise moment?" I wince before she's spoken, praying she's in the office and not out for any fancy lunch meetings with fancy Danish men.

"I'm on my way to a client, and I've just got here," she says. "So I'll have to sign off."

"Oh," I grumble, wanting so badly to ask who her meeting is with, but not wanting to risk raising suspicion. "Okay."

"I'll stay at yours tonight."

I frown into my palm. "I would hope so. You live there."

She's silent for a moment, and I fear she's rolling her eyes to herself. "I'll see you later."

"You will," I assert. "What time?" I need to know exactly how many hours I've got left to sustain his torture.

"Six-ish."

I smile. "Ish," I mimic. I hope there's not too much . . . ish about it. "I love you, lady."

"I know you do." She hangs up, and I stare at the wall of shiny wooden lockers, chewing my bottom lip. *My* place? I thought the debate over our living arrangements had been agreed. Obviously, I was mistaken.

I need to fix that.

But first I need to sweat. I stand and start ripping my suit off, grumbling and grunting as I do, my mind constantly wandering to who Ava has her appointment with. Fuck me, I'm itching to call Freja and pick her brain, but I think I've just well and truly burned my bridges there. "Fuck it." I stuff my feet into my trainers, pull on some shorts, grab a racket, and head to the courts to smack balls at thin air.

Then I'll swim.

Then I'll sweat in the sauna.

Then I might take my bike out for a few hours.

I shake my head to myself as I stalk through The Manor, thinking about what I used to do with my time pre-Ava. Sleep. Recover. Drink. Fuck.

Hide.

And repeat.

I get to the courts and flex my battered hand, trying to get a decent grip of the racket. The swelling has subsided, the purple fading to yellow, but I'm not exactly ready for Wimbledon. I switch my racket to my other hand and start to devise a plan that'll make the most of Ava's and my time together this evening. It involves constant contact. I'm aching for her, every moment away from her hurting me.

Dependency.

She's a different kind of addiction. Not as unhealthy, though. Not for me. But for Ava?

I grunt as I smash the ball over the net and check the time. One more hour down.

I swim one hundred lengths of the pool.

Another hour down.

I go to the sauna and sweat, but the silence beats me after just ten minutes, and I have to abandon that idea.

I head for the changing room and get in the shower, plotting my next time-killing exercise. A nice ride in the countryside. Then I'll go get Ava a key cut for my apartment. Then I'll go to the supermarket and stock up on chocolate spread and squirty cream. Then I'll go home. Get comfy on the couch and wait for the glorious moment she walks through the front door. When she gets home to me. My stomach turns at the prospect of enduring this every working day of the week. Weekends won't be a problem, of course, because she'll be attached to me.

I reach for a towel and rub at my face, turning toward the lockers. I find Sarah blocking my way. I'm never usually shy. I never usually feel exposed when naked in front of her. She's seen me more naked than dressed over the years, always the first to storm my private suite in the morning to kick out any women who had fallen into my bed. And yet now, I feel extremely uncomfortable.

I hold the bunched towel over my groin and get a raised brow. I ignore it and step out. "Do you mind?" I ask, shuffling awkwardly around her.

She laughs. "Juliette will be here in an hour."

"Who?"

"Your personal bank manager."

"What?"

"Annual verifications? I did tell you this morning."

Fuck. My plans go to shit in the blink of an eye. "How long will it take?"

"I don't know. It takes as long as it takes."

Ava said she'd be home at six. It's a forty-minute drive from The Manor to Lusso. It's completely doable, if the traffic is on my side.

But I can't risk it, especially at that time of day. If I'm not there when she gets home, she won't be able to get in. She'll leave.

I start dressing urgently, forgetting my earlier coyness, and dart out of the changing rooms.

"Oh my fucking God," Sarah yells. "Where the fuck are you going now? Jesse! We have a meeting!"

"I'll be back." I sprint through The Manor, leap down the steps, and dive into my car, pulling off fast, the back end of my Aston all over the place, the air dusty. I split my attention between my phone and the road, pulling up Google and searching for the nearest key cutter. A mile down the road would be too far, too much time lost. I locate one three miles from Lusso. "Fuck it." I put my foot down and overtake a tractor up ahead, driving like an idiot, distress, as ever, getting the better of me when I'm behind the wheel, but this time for an entirely different reason.

I arrive at my destination, park illegally, and dash into the store, slapping a key to my penthouse on the counter. "As quick as you can," I pant, checking my watch.

"Any particular color?" the shop assistant asks, and I frown, looking up to find him gesturing to a wall of keys in every shape and color known to man.

"Pink."

"Coming right up."

"And a few extra," I say, remembering John's demand.

Like a speed demon, I race through the streets to Lusso with my newly cut pink keys and run into the lobby. Clive looks up, his face alarmed by the disheveled man sprinting toward him. "Mr. Ward?" he says in question as I land at his desk, panting like a loser.

I slide a key across to him. "Make sure you give this to Ava when she gets home from work."

"Oh, you're giving her a key." He takes it, smiling.

"Of course I am. She lives here." I turn but think of something that I perhaps should have thought of before. Returning my attention to Clive, I find a smile for my new friend. "The CCTV files," I say, glancing at the bank of screens. I know my girl. She's cunning. She'll want to know who the mystery woman who turned up here is. "If Ava asks, don't give them to her."

"Oh?"

I raise my eyebrows. "You hear what I'm saying, don't you, Clive?"

"I think so, sir." He feigns some pathetic kind of thinking face, as if trying to figure out exactly what it is I mean. Crafty fucker.

"This shouldn't be an issue, since it's restricted to residents," I remind him.

He puckers his lips, holding up the key and looking at it, still thoughtful. "Ava isn't a resident?"

Oh, he's good. I narrow my eyes on him, dipping into my pocket and pulling out a few notes, leaning over and stuffing them into his blazer pocket.

He smiles, bright and satisfied, and pats his pocket. "You have a good day, Mr. Ward."

I shake my head, walking away. I'm being blackmailed by an old man. Today is getting shitter by the second.

12

I PUSH my way into my office and first note Sarah's furious face. Then the woman on the couch. My bank manager. An array of paperwork is fanned out on the coffee table before her. "Sorry I'm late," I say, joining Sarah on the opposite sofa, ignoring her questioning look. I've rejected all her calls while I've sat in bumper-to-bumper traffic, making me a whole hour late for our meeting.

"You remember Juliette?" Sarah says.

Nope, can't say I do. But that's not a surprise. I don't remember much about life before Ava, my days spent in a haze of drink. "How could I forget her?" I flash her a killer smile, expecting her to become flustered. She doesn't. Instead, she goes to her laptop. I look at Sarah out the corner of my eye. She looks away.

"I need some form of photographic ID. Your passport or driver's license." Juliette's fingers work fast across the keys of her laptop. She's not happy. Well, neither am I. I don't want to be here. I lift my arse and rootle through my pocket, pulling out my wallet and driver's license, tossing it on the table for her.

Picking it up, she inspects it closely, taking her time, keeping me waiting. She's proving a point. Then her eyes move to me. And back to the photo on the license. *Jesus, come on.* "It's me," I assure her, receiving a tight smile.

She says nothing and slides a piece of paper across to me. "I need your signature here."

"Sarah's a signatory on the account." I move the paper to my right toward Sarah, and she pushes it right back. I look at her in question.

"I've already signed it. Anything relating to the bank requires double authorization, and John's gone home to feed his trees."

I roll my eyes and scribble my signature where indicated. "Is that it?"

"I just need a copy." Juliette holds up my license, looking between me and Sarah.

"Sarah can scan one over to you." I get up. "It's been a pleasure," I say, with just enough sarcasm.

"Has it?" she mutters, not looking up.

My hackles rise. Okay, I was late. I apologized. Who the fuck does she think she is? I must be one of her best clients. "Would it be—"

"Juliette's husband recently joined The Manor," Sarah says, and I swing my eyes to her. *Oh?*

"*Ex*-husband," Juliette corrects Sarah, and I back off, her animosity now making perfect sense. "I'll be going." She stands, roughly gathers up the paperwork and pivots haughtily, stomping out. The door crashes against the wood behind her.

"Wow," I say, dropping down to the couch and placing my phone on the table. "That is one scorned woman. Who's her husband?"

"Steve Cooke."

"You're kidding?" I get up and get myself some water.

"Not kidding. We're keeping an eye on him at the moment."

"Why?"

"He's just a little . . . loose, if you know what I mean."

"You've had a complaint?"

"No, no complaints. Just my observations. Some women are more adventurous than others, let's just say that."

"Well as long as there's good communication between members, there shouldn't be a problem."

"Exactly."

My phone rings, and I down my water as I go to retrieve it but stall when I see who's calling me. I peek at Sarah. She peeks at me. It's uncomfortable as my mobile continues to ring, Amalie as persistent as ever, until it eventually shuts up.

Then the voicemail alert sounds.

I move fast, but Sarah moves faster, swiping up my mobile and holding it to her chest. It's a tactical move. She knows I won't touch her. "Give it to me," I say, my tone threatening. "Now."

She shakes her head and presses a few buttons, and Amalie's voice comes over the speaker. And with her voice comes the excruciating pain in my chest. I have to physically push my fist into my heart to try and stem it, massaging urgently, battling to keep my breathing in check. "Jesse," my sister says, her voice as wobbly as I'm feeling. "Please, I beg you. Call me back. I miss you so much. I need to know you're okay. Okay? Please. I love you."

I swallow repeatedly, over and over, walking aimlessly up and down my office. "Why the fuck would you do that?" I ask, seething.

"You need to talk to her."

And say what? Sorry? Ask how Mum and Dad are? Ask if they're still ashamed of me. Still hate me? Blame me? "Get the fuck out, Sarah. Just get the fuck out now." I hear my mobile drop to the coffee table and the sound of her leaving my office. No apology. No explanation for being such a cruel bitch. She meets John at the door, and he looks at her passing, his forehead a map of lines, his eyes following her down the corridor. But he doesn't ask. And she doesn't tell.

Neither will I. "I'm out of here." I edge past him, and he does something John rarely does. He places a hand on my shoulder and stops me. Physical force. His words or a look usually do the trick, so whatever John's about to say means he thinks I'm going to run away from it.

I don't look at him. Just feel the weight of his heavy hand and thick fingers wrapped over my shoulder. "This obsession isn't healthy," he says quietly.

"It's not an obsession."

"Fixation. Infatuation. Whatever. It isn't healthy."

For whom? Ava or me? I swallow and bat that thought away. "I don't expect you to understand."

"Try me."

"Fine." I shrug him off and face his imposing frame. "I dreaded every day, John," I grate, Sarah's stunt not helping me keep my temper in check. "Waking up. Knowing all I had to look forward to was an oblivion of alcohol and sex." He knows all this. I've said it more than once, not that I need to actually fucking say it. But if he wants to hear it again, I'll tell him. Remind him every fucking day if I have to. "And then by some fucking miracle, something stumbled into my office and offered me reprieve from my misery. A lifeline. And I am fucking terrified that that lifeline could vanish in the blink of an eye if she finds out about my shitty past. The people I've ruined. What I did when I walked away from her." My voice quivers more with every painful, truthful word, and my body trembles along with it, my jaw set to snap, my breathing shot. "I've fucked up so much in my life, and I know I'm close to fucking this up too. You hear me, John?"

"I hear you," he says flatly, his face impassive. But I see his concern. I pull out the keys I had cut and hold them up. "There will never be a repeat, I'm never touching a drop again, but if having a key to my apartment makes you feel better—"

"It does."

"There's one for Sam and Drew too. *Don't* give one to Sarah."

John reaches for the keys as I wait for some words, any comeback at all. I shouldn't be surprised that I get nothing but his vacant expression. He must know how serious this is. But why do I get the feeling that John still believes he needs a key? I don't want to answer that. I turn and walk away, my vision clouded by my regrets, my body heavy with guilt.

"If she truly loves you like you say she does," John calls, "she'll accept everything that's made you who you are. And she'll forgive you for that stupid moment you let yourself and her down."

I slow to a stop and face him. I let her down. "What I was before Ava was disgusting. I don't want her to know that man. I only want her to know the man I am *now*."

"The crazy motherfucker?"

"Better than the drunk. The careless bastard. The slag. The murdering motherfucker."

John flinches, as do I. "Stop it. Please, just stop blaming yourself."

I'll never stop blaming myself, that's simply something I have to live with. "I can't go back, John." Ironically, Ava's the only thing in my world that can stabilize me. I might be able to redeem myself. Be able to find some kind of absolution if I have something worth living for.

Be everything to someone instead of nothing to everyone.

13

I TRUDGE through the foyer feeling heavy, tired, and defeated. Clive looks so pleased with himself, so much so, I could gladly slap his smile away. "She asked if you'd asked me about that woman who showed up," he says, coming out from behind his desk and flanking me to the elevator. "Naturally, I said no."

"Got it, Clive." I smack the call button and step in when the doors open. It's just as I thought. She's a dog with a bone. Punching in the code, I glance back at Clive, finding him waiting on the outside of the elevator, that smile still stretched wide. What does he want, a pat on the back? And then I realize.

I sigh, pulling out a twenty. The conniving old fucker is going to rinse me dry. I slap it in his palm as the doors close and get a polite tip of his hat. Falling back against the wall, I look up at the ceiling, my hands deep in my pockets, my eyes heavy. I'm pissed off. Pissed off that the world has drained me dry, and all the plans I had for tonight with Ava feel like a mountain to climb.

When my phone rings, I reach into my pocket and turn it off, done for the day. Amalie's begging words have haunted me since I left The Manor. That and John's comments. I'm not fixated. Maybe infatuated. Definitely not obsessed. *Idiot*. I'm committed, that's all.

Committed to my reclamation. Committed to being everything Ava wants and needs.

I inhale as I pull out her pills from my pocket and shake my head at myself as I toss them into the little bin in the corner. Not obsessed at all. She does *not* need a man trying to trap her. I need to stop with that particular crazy.

The doors open, I use my shoulder blades to push myself away from the wall, and drag my feet to the front door, letting myself in. I smell her before I find her. And my heart turns in my chest, yelling its presence. I close the door, shut out the entire world.

When I reach the kitchen entrance, I find her on a stool. She looks tired too. Still beautiful but tired. I have to take a moment to absorb every inch of her, here in our kitchen. This is what I've been desperate for all day. To be back here. Just Ava and me. And yet it's temporary, because tomorrow I have to do today all over again.

"Are you okay?" she asks after a time of silence, her eyes worried as she watches my beaten, static form. I'm okay now. Again, temporary. I go to her, helping her stand from the stool, resisting kissing her to death, tasting her, breathing her in. I will. But first, I just need her all over me. I need to rest my tired mind and body for a while and bring myself back to life. I find the hem of her lovely black dress and inch it up before taking the backs of her thighs and picking her up. The sweet scent of her neck lures me in, my nose falling into her hair. God, she smells so good. *So* fucking good. Clean, pure, and mine.

I carry her up the stairs, the feeling of her arms wrapped around me, holding me, accepting me, settling me. I can hear her silent questions. Millions of them. I haven't the energy to dodge them right now, only energy to hold her and love her. Our bed comes into view, and not bothering to undress us, I crawl on with Ava beneath me, settling every inch of me over every inch of her.

And it's perfect. Like today was worth enduring if only to get to this point. My reward. My reward for surviving the day.

"Tell me how old you are," she whispers, and I close my eyes, nuzzling deeper.

"Thirty-two." But I feel three hundred right now.

"Tell me," she pushes, flicking her shoulder up, nudging me.

"Does it matter?"

"No," she whispers, sounding disheartened. She knows she's not winning this. "But I would like it if you told me."

"All you need to know is that I love you." It's the most important thing. Right now, my age is a mystery, and everyone likes a good mystery. It keeps them busy. Distracted. "How was your day?"

After a relenting sigh, she clings to me tighter, as if delivering a silent message that she really doesn't care how old I am. After Sarah's brutal words earlier, I'm not so sure. There are millions of men out there younger than I am. The novelty of my mystery age will only wear off if she finds out how old I actually am. So maybe she should never find out. "Stupidly busy, but very constructive," she says quietly. So that's why she's tired. Not because she's exhausted from missing me so much, or because she's been shirking demons all day, but because work has exhausted her. "And you need to stop sending flowers to my office," she adds scornfully.

I find the will to pull free from my hiding place and throw a dirty look at her. "No." Why would I do that? I want her to know that I think about her every second of the day. And, terribly, the flowers, the texts, the calls, the gifts, are my way of making sure too much time doesn't pass without her thinking about me. "Have a bath with me."

"I'd love to."

No counter. No resistance. No cheek. Good. I haven't the energy to fight her. Breaking away from her amazing warmth, I give her a little kiss. Only brief, only chaste, or we'll never make it to the bath, and I'm craving more of this closeness. Except naked. And wet. "You stay here," I order gently, and one corner of her mouth lifts. She likes this. Me looking after her, me taking the lead, she likes it. "I'll sort the bath." I get off the bed and shrug out of my jacket as I head for the bathroom, groaning at the size of the tub she had put in here. That's going to delay our soak considerably. I look over my shoulder and smile, reaching up and taking the knot of my tie, tugging it as I reverse my steps, conjuring up my plan to fill the time. It doesn't take long. Every second is quickly mapped out in my mind, and it is magnificent.

I find Ava sprawled on her back, still and relaxed, but the second she clocks me by the door, she visibly tenses and she's far from still, her chest rising and falling quickly as she studies me. I drop my tie on the chaise and move on to my shirt, unfastening each button slowly, relishing the longing in her eyes as she watches. I lose my shoes and socks, and as I straighten, I smile on the inside. "Enjoying the view?"

She blinks, coming back into the room. "Always."

"Always," I whisper. "Come here." I jerk my head a little, and she edges to the side of the bed, kicking off her shoes. "Leave the dress." I'll enjoy peeling it off but, honestly, I don't know how I feel about her wearing such figure-hugging outfits to work. You can see every perfect curve of her body, not leaving much to the imagination.

When she makes it to me, her eyes are swimming with love, lust, and hunger. "Turn around," I murmur, my skin burning, my heart thrashing. She takes her time, working us both up more, and the second I place my hands on her shoulders, she jolts. Yes. Contact. "I really like this dress." I drag my palms to her neck and move her hair over her shoulder, revealing the zipper. In no rush at all, loving the signs of her struggle, I pull it down, her head tilting constantly. Her shoulders high. Her breathing loud. I just can't help but make her struggle more, licking up her spine to her nape. "I love your back," I mumble against her flesh, feeling her shoulders roll. I move in close to her ear. "You have the softest skin." The warmest. The smoothest. She goes heavy against me, leaning back, seeking solace in my neck. I turn my head and catch her mouth, our tongues finding each other's immediately, dancing slowly, as I remove her dress. "Lace?" I ask, pulling back. She nods, and I thank her with another kiss, gentle and slow, my hands moving to her boobs and massaging them over the delicate fabric, my dick pulsing, preparing. "See what you do to me?" I push into her lower back, throbbing against her. Her eyes sparkle madly, and my heart clatters wildly. "I'll die loving you,

Ava," I whisper hoarsely, my thoughts falling out of my mouth, my mind lost to her, to this, to us. I roughly pull the cups of her bra out of my way and tickle her nipples with a light brush of my hands. Her lips part, her chest expands, her eyes beg me. "You and me." My hand falls down her front to her knickers, her arse pushing into my groin before rolling forward into my touch.

"Do I turn you on, Ava?" I ask, my eyes lasers on her profile, watching as she bites her lip, puffs out air, constantly clenches her eyes closed.

"You know you do." Her acceptance is like an injection of energy into my dick. I need to move this along before I come in my trousers.

"Wrap your arms around my neck," I order, and she does, immediately. "Are you wet for me?"

"Yes."

I take her knickers on each side and lick slowly behind her ear. "Only for me."

She convulses. "Only for you." This craving in her. This need. This undeniable desperation to have me all over her, worshipping her, making her lose her mind. I smile and yank at her knickers, ripping them clean off, and drop them before placing a hand lightly on her hip.

"What shall I do with this, Ava?" I ask. "Show me."

Her hand appears, and she takes mine, panting, and directs it to her inside thigh, guiding it up, up, up. I inhale when my palm meets the heat between her legs, slipping easily across her flesh. Her groan is loud and broken, her arse flying back to escape the torture of my touch, and her head turns into me, searching for some mouth action.

I give her contact, but not a kiss, just brushing my mouth over hers as she directs my hand over her pussy, biting my lip as she does, her body rigid. "Don't come," I order, and she stops dead in her tracks, pulling my touch away. Fuck, that's hot. Her submission. Her obedience. I lick her condition from my hand and find the clasp of her bra, unfastening it and turning her around. The look in her eyes could put me on my arse. I've never seen so much passion in a stare, so much love and adoration. The fact that it's coming from this woman and is directed at me is almost too much for my dark soul to cope with. "Promise me you'll never leave me," I order, my stupid fucking mouth running away from me again. But she's doing everything I'm asking of her right now. I'll push boundaries, milk it for everything I can.

"I'll never leave you," she assures me, looking slightly bewildered.

"Promise me," I grate through a tense jaw.

"I promise." There's no delay. No questioning. It's as if she knows it's what I need to hear. But does she truly mean it?

Claiming my wrists in turn, she unbuttons the cuffs and pushes my shirt away from my body. All I can do is watch her undress me, useless for a moment, awestruck. She rids me of my trousers, making a meal of feeling at my arse, and the second my dick is free, it juts out proudly. Ava inhales, staring, her hands roaming the planes of my chest. She's having a wonderful time admiring me, feeling me. I, on the other hand, am fast losing my mind.

"I can't wait anymore." I kick my trousers away urgently. "I need to be inside you." How I thought I could bathe with her before making love to her, I don't know. I must have momentarily lost my fucking mind. I seize her, haul her up to my body, and very nearly fall over when my dick skims the fire between her thighs. *Fucking hell.* She inhales sharply, and I find the nearest wall and thrust her up against it, my cock finding exactly where it needs to be. But I don't push into her, needing to gather myself and prepare for the relief about to find me. I might be a while. My legs feel unstable, my head is spinning. But before I'm given even a second to compose myself, Ava moves, and I'm inside her. Every inch of me wrapped in the soft walls of her pussy. I choke, tensing everywhere.

"Oh, you fucking kill me." I buck and pulse, my teeth grating. Jesus, this is unbearable and incredible. "Are you holding on to me?" I ask, her hands in my hair doing nothing to help me calm my greedy need. I find the will to slide free, leveling serious eyes on her.

"Yes." Everything tightens against me, her muscles, her hold. And her eyes darken. She knows what's coming.

I wedge each palm into the wall behind her—my right with care—and pull out slowly, her chest inflating as I do, taking in air, bracing herself. And I flex my hips, driving forward carefully, gaining momentum, working us up, getting ready for the attack. She moans, I growl, over and over, my head pushing into hers, my drives gathering speed.

"Kiss me."

She takes my mouth clumsily, her thighs locking tightly, her body lifting up the wall and dropping.

"Good God, woman," I bark. "What the hell do you do to me?" My hips are out of control, and apparently that's fine with Ava. "I've waited all day for this." I kiss her. Thrust hard. Kiss her harder. "It's been the longest fucking day of my life."

She hums, accepting it all, willing it on, begging for it. "You feel so good."

"I feel good?" If she could feel what I'm feeling, see what I'm seeing, taste what I'm tasting. "Fuck, Ava, you do serious things to me."

She screams my name, grappling at my back.

I increase my pace, now in my stride, ready for the finish line. "Ava." I thrust harder, hissing at the stabbing of her nails in my flesh. "Wherever I'm going from now on, I'm taking you with me, baby." I pound hard, gasping for air, my sweaty palms beginning to slide on the wall. "Shit," I bellow, and she screams. "You're going to come," I pant into her face, watching her struggle, fucking *loving* her battle to hold on.

"Hard!" she yells, and I wince when she sinks her teeth into my lip, but I endure the pain, the pleasure taking over every nerve ending and sending my big body into spasm, as she jerks, tenses, moans, scratches.

She comes with force, her face plummeting into my neck, her body racked with shakes, and I tip the edge with her, holding my breath and smashing home, exploding, releasing air on a bellow of her name. My legs fail me, and I fold to the floor, fucking knackered. Ava somehow finds it in herself to sit up, astride of my lap, rolling her hips, bleeding me dry of pleasure. I'm done for. Totally useless, my body splattered and splayed. But I can keep my eyes open and watch her grinding into me, quiet, thoughtful, a small, satisfied smile on her face.

"What are you thinking about?" I ask, my words labored.

"About how much I love you."

Music. Fucking music to my ears. "Do I still qualify as your god?"

"Always." Her hands work circles across my chest, feeling me everywhere she can, her walls still hugging me snuggly. "Am I still your temptress?"

"That, baby, you most certainly are." Her smile is pure gold. "God, I love your grin."

"Bath, god?" she asks, giving my nipples a little pinch.

Bath? We're having a bath? And there's a fine example of what this woman does to me. She makes me forget everything except her when I'm lost in her, which makes being lost in her a necessity. "Shit." *The bath.* "It's still running." I shoot up, taking Ava with me, neglecting to remember that my hand still hurts like a bitch. I suck back air, enduring the pain, irritated by the hindrance.

"Put me down." She wriggles, and because I'm a fucking dickhead, I grip her harder.

Motherfucker.

"Never." Half dead, I'd still hold on to her with everything I have. And I might need to. The thought is more than sobering, and not one for now.

"You could leave that bath running for a week and it wouldn't be full."

"I know." I step in with her wrapped around me and sink us into the water on a happy sigh. "The designer of all this Italian shit obviously has no regard for the environment or my carbon footprint."

"Says he with twelve superbikes," she huffs, coming to settle on my lap, her pussy still clinging to me as she studies me, her eyes roaming happily. And I'm more than happy to lie here and be the focus of her gaze. "I could look at you all day," she whispers, her finger dragging across my skin, her eyes following it, her head tilted thoughtfully. It's a vision I'll store away forever and call upon endlessly. The way she's looking at me. The contentment. The ends of her long, dark hair skimming the water, strands stuck to her wet breasts, her nipples erect, hard on soft, perfect mounds. And don't get me started on her eyes. I relax back and watch her closely as she works her touch across my body, finishing at my mouth. Her eyes flick up to mine, her smile demure. "I love your mouth." She slowly falls forward, kissing the corner, the center, the other corner. "I love your body." She pushes her front into mine and her tongue into my mouth. "I love your crazy mind too." I'm gone, consumed, absolutely blindsided by her, by now, by this kiss. Someone needs to love my crazy, and it's a good fucking job she does, since she spikes it.

"*You* make me crazy, Ava." I feel her hands circle my neck, holding me. "Just you." Our kiss deepens, tongues lapping lazily, bodies pushing closer. And then she's gone, leaving my mouth bare and lonely.

"Crazy," she whispers, and I smile.

"Ish." There's really no ish about it. I'm arguably certifiable these days. And here is my antidote, straddling my lap, naked. The cause and the cure. She's fully mine in this moment. Acquiescent. I need to take the opportunity while she's presenting me with it. "Let me wash you," I say, turning her around, getting her comfortable and snug between my legs, my mind racing with how best to approach this. I take a sponge and start gliding it across her skin. Demand it? Beg for it? "I need to talk to you about something," I say, cringing as I speak the words, hearing how unsure I sound.

"What?"

"The Manor." I look down at the back of her head, my lip getting a punishing chew. I'm nervous, and her body stiffening against me isn't helping. Neither is her silence. So I go on. "The anniversary party."

"What about it?" Her dismissiveness gets under my skin, however much I try to stop it.

I release my lip. "I still want you to come." And latch on to it again the moment I've spat out the words.

"You can't ask me to do that." She shakes her head as she speaks, and my hand goes limp, my hope sinking. I *can* ask, and I have. "You asked me to go before I knew," she goes on, her voice tight.

"Are you going to avoid my workplace forever?"

"I might do," she grumbles, and I roll my eyes dramatically. Just yesterday she said she *wasn't* going to avoid it forever.

"Don't be stupid, Ava." I take the sponge back to her skin to busy my hands and push my mouth to her head, giving her a pacifying kiss. "Will you please just think about it?"

"I'm making no promises." It's not a no. "And if you even think about trying to fuck some sense into me on this, I'm leaving."

Don't bite. She has a knack for firing loaded words. Words she knows will push my buttons. Words she doesn't mean. She's not leaving, and I'd fucking appreciate it if she didn't threaten it. But rather than warn her, I wrap her up in my limbs, a silent message that she's going nowhere. "I want the woman who keeps my heart beating with me." *Take that, baby. Deny me now, I dare you.*

She stills, and I smile to myself, letting her absorb my declaration as I carry on soaking her with the sponge, my heart, as if backing me up, thrumming into her back at a comfortable, steady pace.

"Did you speak to Clive?" she asks out of the blue, and I falter in my flow, the sponge stalling momentarily on her chest.

"About what?"

"The mystery woman."

God damn it, she's not going to let this go. "No, Ava, I didn't have time." I try not to sound bored. Or irritated. *Fail.* "I promise you I will. I'm just as curious as you are." *Dickhead.* Change the subject. "Now, are you hungry?" I lick her ear, breathing long, hot breaths, feeling her shudder.

"I'm not going to sleep until you tell me who that woman was."

Who said anything about sleeping? She sounds as impatient as I'm feeling. Doesn't she trust me? I flinch. She shouldn't. One of the reasons Ava resisted our connection was because she deemed me a danger to her heart. She, like Sarah, and perhaps thanks to Sarah's input, too, thought I was in it for one thing and one thing alone. Fucking. *You're not the kind of man to build dreams on.* Yes, there have been many women in the past. Yes, some of them are bold and brash and undoubtedly jealous. There are many things Ava doesn't need to or *should* know, and a hot list of my past fucks is one of those things. "How can I tell you if I don't know?" I ask tiredly, wishing she'd just drop it. Move on.

"You *do* know."

"I don't fucking know," I bark, frustrated. I immediately regret it, reining myself in. Ava jolts, startled, the water splashing around us, and I blink, shocked myself. This was supposed to be a lovely evening, just me and Ava, nothing in the outside world violating our peace. Until Ava let the outside world in. That, I can't control. Her questions. Her curiosity.

Fuck it. None of this is her fault. It's mine. All mine. "I'm so sorry, baby."

"Okay," she whispers, unsure, making me feel rotten to my core. I cannot take my frustration out on her. Can't be mad with her.

"My lovely lady is exhausted." I hold her close, my arms like a vise around her shoulders, my mouth busy around her ear, apologizing some more. "Takeout?"

"You have a fridge full of food. It's a waste."

No, time lost cooking will be a waste. "Can you be bothered to cook?"

She ponders that for a few moments. I hope she reaches the correct answer. "Takeout."

Good. "I'll go and order while you wash your hair." I get out of the tub, and it's surprisingly easy to leave her in there. A grilling will do that.

I leave the bathroom, get the shampoo and conditioner I bought, and take it to her. Her gratitude is endearing. "Wear lace," I whisper, kissing her on her forehead. Then I leave to order dinner.

14

I'M STUCK behind a pane of glass, walking up and down, feeling, searching for the end. But it's never-ending. A constant barrier.

I am on one side.

And everyone I love is on the other.

Jake.

Rosie.

Carmichael.

They're all there, within reach but not. The shield between me and them has no end. There's no way to get to them. I reach out and hit my hand. I call out to them and my voice ricochets back off the glass. I start thumping it, yelling, desperate to get to them. But my hits make no noise to get their attention. I'm invisible to them.

"It's just us now."

I follow the voice. Lauren is standing with me. On the same side as I am. She looks up at me and smiles, reaching for my arm. Touching me. I look at my bicep, at her thin fingers. At the wedding band. She still wears it.

"Just us," she muses, motioning to the glass, encouraging me to look.

"No," I whisper. There's another person with Jake, Rosie, and Carmichael. "No!"

Ava.

"No!" I lay into the glass, hitting it with everything I have, yelling, needing to get to the other side. The glass doesn't give. It remains steadfast, letting me see my loves but not touch them. Get to them.

Be with them.

15

I COULD BE LYING in a bath, I'm so wet. I can't move, my body pinned down. I peek out the corner of my eye, not wanting to disturb her, not wanting her to see me like this, sweating and haunted. She's dead to the world. And still clinging to me. I exhale and look up at the ceiling, fighting the dreams away. I can close the door, shut out the world and my past. But I'll never be able to shut it out of my mind. I'm exposed, vulnerable, unable to fight away thoughts if I'm unconscious. "Fucked up," I whisper, scrubbing a hand down my face as I splay my hand across Ava's back, feeling her.

And it's another day, with less than a great start.

I can change that. Turn things around. Start as I mean to go on. And perhaps in the process, completely knacker her out so she cries off work. Perfect solution.

Ever heard of codependency, brother?

"Yeah, you can fuck *right* off," I mutter, gently breaking away from Ava's warmth. And yet I smile, because as fucked up as it is, hearing my brother, it tells me of the kind of man he would have been.

Sarcastic. A joker.

Where the fuck has all that time gone? "We'll be thirty-eight on

Monday, bro," I say quietly, locating my running gear. "Thirty-fuck-ing-eight."

You're only as old as the woman you feel.

I break out in laughter, getting my foot caught in my shorts and hopping around, trying not to fall flat on my face. I fail, losing my footing and hitting the deck with a loud thwack. "Fuck it," I grunt as I land. I laugh again. And shut up the moment I detect stirrings in my bed. Quickly getting my shit together, I get up, pull my shorts up, a vest on, and swipe up my trainers from the floor. Then plonk myself on the end of the chaise to get my feet in them, shaking my head to myself.

Section me.

Just do it.

As I tie my laces, I spy Ava out the corner of my eye sitting up in the bed, watching me. And by the time I'm done, she's silently lowered back down to the sheets. Bless her. I stand and creep over, watching the rise and fall of her chest. I've watched this woman sleep no end of times. I know the pattern of her breathing. The form of her mouth. The flutter of her lashes when she's dreaming. Her attempts to fool me are an insult.

I kneel on the edge, silent. One of her eyes opens slowly, and my smile widens. The indignation is instant, and she throws her body onto her front, hiding under a pillow. I chuckle as I yank it away and flip her onto her back. "Good morning."

"Please don't make me," she says around an adorable pout.

I ignore her pleas and pull her up. "Up you get."

She moans and gripes, genuinely looking like she could burst into tears when I pass her gym kit over.

"I want sleepy sex," she whines. That's adorable too. But I need to run. And I need Ava. So I'm taking both. "Please."

I get her up and remove her knickers. "It'll do you good." *And me.*

"This is torture."

Torture? She knows nothing of torture. "I like having you with me," I say softly, helping her into her things, ignoring her persistent protests and moans.

I take us down in the elevator, smiling at her disgusted face the whole way. She isn't impressed, so when she voluntarily starts stretching in the car park, I'm pleasantly surprised. I join her, giving my hamstrings a good pull, aware of the admiring coming my way. She appreciates the view.

"Ready?" she asks, running off, her strides full of bounce. I shake my head as I go after her, wondering why the fucking hell she protests so hard all the time.

"Just think," I say, slowing my pace when I make it to her. "We can do this together every morning."

The quick, shocked inhale tells me what she thinks of that. But she'd do it. And, naturally, when we're done, she'll get a reward for indulging me. I glance down at her often, my pace half that of my usual speed, but my peace this morning is found from the company rather than the need to run until I feel like I might keel over.

"Hey," I say as we approach the point at which Ava gave up last time, seeing her looking back, her expression blank. Not strained. Not accomplished. Just vacant. Something's on her mind.

She looks up at me. "I'm fine."

Really? Because she doesn't look it, and that smile she just forced was lame. She starts to slow down, and the second an opening into the park appears, she diverts off the street and flops onto the grass on a loud huff. "I did better than last time," she pants as I stand over her. What a woman. It only proves that she can conquer anything if she puts her mind to it. My running route is no easy feat, and yet this time she knowingly took it on. Like she's knowingly taking *me* on. *Or not so knowingly.*

She is strength. Perfection. Determination. But, again, there's definitely something on her mind this morning. "You did, baby." I lower beside her and take a leg, rubbing some life back into it. Her moans are glorious. "I'm proud of you," I say, swapping for her other leg, working firmly into her flesh. I shouldn't be doing this. I should be leaving her to seize up so she can't move, therefore can't leave Lusso. "Give it a few days and you'll fly through it."

She doesn't contest that, busy enjoying my hands working her muscles until my fingertips are numb. I glance around, spotting a coffee house across the road. Perfect. Pulling her up, I flash her a note. "I came prepared." *With money and words.* "Coffee?"

She looks over her shoulder and sighs, then proceeds to toss her arms over my shoulders. I chuckle and lift her, forcing her to release me. "Come on." Holding her hand, I walk us across the road to the coffee house and lead her to the counter. "Do you want something to eat?"

"No," she says, adamant, ripping her eyes away from the pastries.

She's a case. I take her nape and pull her close, kissing her sweaty forehead, before giving the server our order. "Go and get a seat." Returning my attention to the counter, I ponder how best to approach The Manor anniversary this Friday, glancing over my shoulder every now and then, each time finding Ava lost in thought on the couch in the window. She said she'd think about it. Something tells me that's what's on her mind this morning, and I'm not sure I like her pensiveness.

"That's fourteen pounds twenty, sir."

"Thanks." I hand over a twenty and take the tray. "Keep the change." As I make my way to Ava, my concern increases. She's staring blankly out of the window, constantly squinting, sometimes wincing. She is. She's thinking about The Manor. Drawing conclusions, making assumptions.

"Dreaming?" I ask, setting the tray down, snapping her out of her thoughts. Her smile is tight as I cautiously unload our drinks, pushing a muffin toward her. She stares down at her cup as she stirs, absentmindedly fingering the muffin. I lower to my chair, my appetite dying with each second I watch her building some courage to speak.

"I'm not coming to the party," she eventually says, refusing to look at me. It's probably best, as I know she wouldn't appreciate my impatient glance at the ceiling. "I love you," she goes on, "but I can't do that."

She's wrong. It's not a case of *can't*, more *won't*. How the hell do I solve this if she won't meet me halfway? I know she's expecting some dark, seedy joint. It's kinky, filthy, yes, but it's as tasteful as a sex club could be. Comfortable. Safe. The happenings of The Manor won't feature in our relationship, but The Manor itself will. Is she going to refuse to ever step foot in the place again? Not only is that impossible if she's going to fulfil the new designs, but it's unrealistic if Ava and I are in a relationship.

I exhale, trying to wipe away my irritation, just managing to do that before she looks up at me nervously. "It's not going to be how you think it will be, Ava." Talk her through it. Be patient.

"How do you mean?" Her head tilts, curiosity rife on her pink face. This is good. Whatever she's convinced herself The Manor is, she's still inquisitive.

I ply my dry mouth with some coffee, ready to talk her through her worries, and, hopefully, settle them. "Has The Manor ever given you the impression of a seedy sex club?"

Her lips pout a little, and I smile on the inside. "No."

"Ava, there won't be people wandering around naked propositioning you," I explain, grimacing when my teeth automatically clench. God help anyone who even tries. "You won't be manhandled up the stairs to the communal room. There are rules."

"Rules?" she asks. Her frown is endearing. I need to remember that Ava is way younger than the average member. My world would never have featured in her life before she met me, not that she'll be a part of my world in that sense. I bet sex clubs have never even cost her a thought, let alone dating the owner of one.

"The only places people are permitted to remove their clothes is in the communal room or one of the private suites." Her frown smooths out. "The ground floor, spa, and sports facilities are run like any other exclusive resort. I don't run a brothel, Ava," I go on. "My members pay a lot of money to enjoy everything The Manor provides, not just the privilege to pursue their sexual preferences with likeminded people."

Her lip slips between her teeth, her mind spinning. *Come on, baby. Ask me.* "What's *your* sexual preference?" she asks, pensive, quiet, and I can't help but smirk. This isn't just about The Manor and what goes on there. This is about me. Just as I can't stand the thought of Ava amidst the sexual activities, she can't bear to imagine me there. She's nothing to worry about. I am off the menu. But we both know that's not always been the case, and that is part of the problem for her. Is she showing signs of possessiveness?

Interesting. I break off a piece of cake and slip it past my lips, relishing in her sudden squirming. I have one preference these days. "You."

She nods slowly, her lips twitching to smile. "Just me?"

"Just you, Ava." She needs to stop looking at me like that. We're not in a place where I can bend her over and fuck her until she believes nothing else.

"Good," she says happily, chomping into her muffin, her appetite obviously found. I shift in my chair, blood surging south. I don't think there's anything in this world that could turn me on more than Ava being possessive over me. But as I watch her, fighting to control my urge to jump her, thank her, tell her she can be as possessive as she likes, because I definitely will be, I realize she's not actually said she'll come.

"You'll come?" I ask, making sure I pose it as a question, watching her chew slowly. "Please?"

She huffs quietly, her eyes taking on a sparkle of life. "Only because I love you."

Those words make me grin like an idiot. They also fuel my raging hard-on. "Say it again."

"What?" she questions, smiling. "That I'll come?"

"Oh, you'll come all right." And scream until she loses her voice. *Fuck, yes.* Then, no work for Ava today. "No, tell me you love me again."

"I do. I love you."

"I know you do." And her love is life. "I love hearing you say it." Getting up, urgency replacing my satisfaction, I haul her up into my arms. My work here is done. But my work back at Lusso is yet to begin. *If* we make it to Lusso. "If you had kept running," I whisper, pushing her wet hair from her face, scanning her sparkling eyes, "we would be at home by now, and I would be lost inside you."

I kiss her hard and with purpose, a silent message of what to expect once I get her home. Fuck, it's going to be a long ride. I groan under my breath and dip, hoisting her up onto my shoulder and pacing urgently out of the café, and she yelps then laughs. A man up ahead watches, alarmed, as I carry her out, holding the door open for me. Good man.

I search for a cab and thank every god that ever existed when one rounds the corner up the street. I raise my arm, feeling Ava's palms wedged into my lower back, and open the door when it pulls up to the curb, lowering her in and nodding at the cabbie when he looks back, his eyebrows high. "St. Katherine Docks, please, mate." I drop to the seat next to her, keeping my eyes forward. It's the safest way. "And make it snappy." I give him a tight, telling smile, clearing my throat as I reach down and adjust myself.

The cabbie grins. Looks across to Ava. He should stop that immediately. "Yes, boss," he says, returning to the wheel and pulling off as fast as a black cab can manage.

I peek down at Ava's hands pushing into the leather of the seat, her fingers clawing. Restraining. I can feel her eyes on my profile. "Don't look at me," I warn, doing the unthinkable. Moving away. And I look out of the window, willing the cabbie to hurry the fuck up before I send his vehicle up in smoke. My foot starts tapping, every piece of me restless as I count down every mile back to Lusso, cursing every light that turns red, every car that pulls out, every bus that pulls over at a bus stop, stalling us.

By the time we make it to Lusso, I'm dizzy with impatience. I throw some money at the driver, seize Ava's hand, and haul her into the lobby, one gear off breaking out into a sprint.

"Morning, Clive," I say when he looks up, his old eyes startled, following us into the elevator. The doors aren't even closed before I have Ava against the wall, my kiss greedy, my hands frenzied. "I might have to fuck you *before* my run in future."

She whimpers, rubbing up against me, matching my mouth's pace and hunger. Good God, I'm delirious with desperation, my moves clumsy, my kiss haphazard, and her acceptance, her equal passion, is like adrenaline being pumped directly into my veins. She moans, groans, grapples at my back, as desperate and impatient as I am, as we eat each other alive. I vaguely hear the doors open and blindly walk us out, tripping up each other's feet as we go, awkward and chaotic. Relinquishing one hand from her hair, I feel around in my pocket for the key, pinning her against the door, still kissing her madly as I pat and smack at the wood, trying to locate the lock. *Come on, come on, come on.*

I get us in, kick the door closed, and get to work, tearing away her clothes, our hands colliding, our arms all tangled as she pulls at the material covering me.

Get inside her. Sate this mad urge. Cool the burn.

Ava rips my running vest up over my head, separating our mouths for a second before we reunite, our lips colliding, our tongues thrashing. I push her back into the wall. I need leverage. I need some weight behind me. I need an anchor for Ava. "On your knees," I growl, breaking our kiss, turning her away from me. "Put your hands on the wall." I shove my shorts down, toeing my trainers off, watching as she sinks to the floor and plants her palms onto the plaster. Waiting. Ready. Panting.

I blow out my cheeks, as ever in awe of what she does to me and, even better, what I do to her. I lower behind her, my eyes nailed to her arse as I take her hips, smiling when she twitches. I spread her legs. Look at my cock hovering on the threshold to heaven.

"Don't come until I say," I order, practically smelling her need for release. "Understand?"

She nods, solidifying, bracing herself. There's no need to ply her. No need to ease in gently. She's now more than accustomed to me. *Only me.* I breath in, swallow, and power forward on a broken growl, and the moment I'm buried balls deep, the urge for more friction takes over and my hips take on a mind of their own, thrusting brutally, yanking her onto me ferociously with each pound.

"Jesus, Jesse," she yells, shocked but accepting, absorbing every hit.

"You knew this would be hard, Ava. Don't you dare fucking come." I piston on, beads of sweat flying off my skin with the force of each bang. "Fuck." My fingers dig into her hips, my vision becomes blurred. "You," I grunt, smashing into her hard. "Fucking." *Bang*. "Drive." *Bang*. "Me." *Bang*. "Crazy." *Bang, bang, bang*.

My God, is there anywhere better in this world I could be? The feel of her gliding over my shaft, watching her head thrash, her grunts every time I hit home. I move my hands to her shoulders, my body locking down, hardening, preparing, the pressure rushing forward. My jaw aches. My head spins. It's there, coming hard, fast, ready to take me out. I look up at the ceiling, yelling. And then it happens, and I'm less than prepared for the onslaught of pleasure, the intensity, the shakes.

I have to stop moving, holding myself deep, gritting my teeth to deal with the sensitivity, hissing and using what remaining energy I have to hold Ava's ponytail, tugging her head back, moving my spare hand to her pussy and massaging her clit. "Come." I exhale over my demand, my look full of praise, her look full of wonder. And I kiss her, swallowing her moans, my spent body soaking up her trembles, my finger slowly circling her clit as I pulse inside of her, still seeping, still solid, until she eventually goes lax.

"You *are* a god," she breathes, and I smile into her mouth as she throws her arms back over my head, holding on. The move forces her chest forward, her nipples like bullets, her skin glistening.

"You're so lucky."

"You're an arrogant god."

I snort to myself. She loves this arrogant god. I suck back air, pulling free, and turn her around in my arms. It's been too long since I had her eyes, and when I find them, they are drowsy. Sparkling but drowsy. "Your arrogant god loves you so fucking much." My mouth homes in on her cheek, kissing, tasting the saltiness. "Your arrogant god wants to spend the rest of his life smothering you with his love and his body." Dreams aside, it's been the best possible start to our day, and you can be sure I'm starting as I mean to go on. I doubt so much about myself, but one thing I know I can give Ava is incomparable love and pleasure. She makes it so easy.

I stand us up, accommodating her demand for my mouth as she smothers me, nuzzling, humming her happiness. I just want to put her in our bed and carry on with this easy affection.

"What's the time?" she asks.

"I don't know." I dismiss her quickly as she backs up, me following, still kissing.

"Shit," she mumbles around my mouth, and I flinch.

"Hey, watch your fucking mouth."

I'm completely ignored, even shrugged off, and before I can blink and reprimand her, ask her what the fuck she's playing at, she's gone from my arms and leaping up the stairs.

"It's quarter to eight," she shouts, panicked, disappearing from view.

Oh.

Work.

I scowl at nothing before me, wondering how the fuck she goes from all consumed to all distracted. And, worse, by work. That one thing that I absolutely cannot stop her from doing. I won't try and kid myself that she works because she needs the money. She works because she loves her job, and that fucking sucks because it means convincing her she should let me support her, look after her, is a nonstarter.

"Fuck it," I grumble, trudging after her. Where the hell did she find the energy to run? I was hoping for complete exhaustion. I need to get creative. Convince her to skive off, and then work my arse off to prove that staying at home with me is a far more appealing option than going to fucking work. Think, Ward. *Think, think, think.*

I reach the bedroom, hearing the shower running, but before I put my plan into action, I grab her bag and retrieve her phone, quickly changing her ring tone again and checking the recent call history. I'm looking for one name in particular. And I find nothing. But he could have called her office. Emailed her.

I replace her mobile and creep to the bathroom door, groaning hard when I find her soaking wet under the spray, working up a lather in her hair. My aching dick, the insatiable bastard, pings to life and points the way. And I'm more than happy to let it guide me. There's only one way I can convince Ava to skive off work today.

I walk in quietly behind her and slide my hands across her wet, hot, slippery tummy. She stills for a moment, becoming taller, her shoulders pushing back.

Just. One. Touch.

I smile smugly as she wipes the suds from her face and peeks up at me. "Don't." Her voice is shaky, lacking any conviction. I, however, am full to the brim with it. I take her shoulders and kiss her hard. "I'm going to be late," she more or less whines.

"I want to make an appointment." I thrust my body into hers.

"To fuck me?" she asks. "No appointment necessary."

For the love of fucking *God*. "Mouth," I bark. "I already told you, I don't need to make an appointment to fuck you. I do that whenever and wherever I please." Like now. And in another hour's time. And then an hour after that too.

She inhales, a steely expression crossing her face. That's not a look I'm liking. "I've got to go." She dips, escaping, and I sag against the wall, pouting to myself as she dries herself, scrubs her teeth, and leaves, not looking back.

"Fucking work," I mutter, roughly washing my hair and soaping my body. "She doesn't need to work." I snatch a towel down and rub myself dry before tossing it in the wash basket. "She doesn't need to live by someone else's schedule, only mine." I dunk my finger in my pot of wax and head into the bedroom. "Why can't she do that?" I ask thin air, working the gunk between my fingers. Coming to a stop, I throw her a filthy glare as she happily applies makeup, making herself even more beautiful for others to appreciate. Mikael Van Der Haus? God damn it, my threat to Freja was very real, but does she care? Has she told Mikael about me and Ava?

I trudge into the dressing room and scan the row of suits, indecisive. Unsettled. So I go back to the bedroom, to the mirror where she's sitting, and lean in over her, poking and pulling at my hair, my cock virtually tickling her cheek. *Go on, baby. Resist me.* I smile on the inside, feeling her staring, seeing out the corner of my eye the wand of her mascara hanging limply in her grasp.

I can feel her frustration. Good. Maybe now she gets mine. Breathing in her patience, Ava goes back to applying her eye makeup. Playing hard to get? She's a treasure. We both know there is only so long she can participate in that game. I am set for the win.

I push a piece of hair to the right, peeking down, moving my leg just so and rubbing softly across her forearm. She stills and exhales, her hand dropping from her face, and I do a terrible job of hiding my amusement. My hair looks perfect. Rough and messy but perfect.

Finding her exasperated form in the reflection of the mirror, I lower to my arse behind her, her eyes following me down, and bundle her up in my arms, giving her what I hope is an irresistible pout, my face pushed close to hers.

"You're beautiful," I whisper, flexing forward, indicating my condition.

She arches her back, trying to escape the inevitable. "You are too." Her eyes are swimming. Her body calling.

"Don't go to work."

"Please, don't," she begs.

"Don't you want to fall into bed and let me pay special attention to you all day?" I ask, giving her puppy dog eyes.

"I *have* to work."

I nibble at her lobe, breathing into her ear, getting closer and closer to breaking her down. "I have to have *you*."

"Jesse, please." She squirms, and I sag.

It's depressing as fuck that she *wants* to work—more than she wants to be with me. "Are you denying me?"

"No," she sighs. "I'm delaying you." And she writhes again, fighting to escape my clutches, somehow managing to turn herself around. Before I know it, I'm on my back, and Ava is spread all over me. *Yes!* She goes straight for my mouth, and I give in to it, arms sprawled, my body relaxed, as I'm kissed like a woman kisses a man she loves. Complete heaven.

"I need to work, god."

Well, that ruins the moment. "Work me," I insist, rolling my naked hips upward. "I'll be a very grateful client." The *most* grateful.

She arches a lovely eyebrow. Her eye makeup is stunning, her dark eyes smokey, her lashes long and thick. Fucking beautiful. "You mean to say that instead of busting a gut keeping clients happy with drawings, plans, and schedules . . ." There's an edge of teasing in her voice. "I should just jump into bed with them?"

What the fuck? How the hell did she manage to conclude *that*? "Don't say things like that, Ava." Van Der Haus would love nothing more.

"It was a joke." She chuckles. Least funny joke ever. She shouldn't even speak about such things, no matter how figurative. I'll burst a fucking blood vessel.

I growl and spin her, blanketing her with my body. "Do you see me laughing?" I ask, and her lips straighten when she grasps that I'm deadly serious. Good. I can tolerate many things, but any talk of other men isn't, and never will be, one of those things. "Don't say things that'll make me crazy mad."

"I'm sorry," she whispers, looking guilty.

Yeah, me too. I'm sorry for being unable to control my possessiveness. Or my thoughts. Or, apparently, my fucking woman. I get up and walk to the dressing room, hoping to walk off some of the tension, my mind back to Ava, her working day, and who she might be meeting. Good God, this is horrific. Has she spoken to him? And again, does Van Der Haus know she's with me? Not *seeing* me. Not *dating* me. But *with* me. How the fuck can I find out without asking Freja? Perhaps I shouldn't have been so hasty and withdrawn her invite. Perhaps I should have made sure I kept her onside. Plied her for information. I pull on my navy suit trousers, laughing at my stupid self. And what would she have wanted in return? Stupid fucking question. I'm backed into a corner here. "Fuck it," I snap quietly, shrugging on a shirt, buttoning it up roughly, getting some socks and shoes on, and plucking a gray tie from the drawer. In the grand scheme of things, only having one woman on my back is quite an achievement given how many there could be. I flip my collar up and slip my tie around my neck, thoughtful as I knot it. Clive said mature, blond. That's half the women at The Manor, so what if it wasn't Freja who was sniffing around? But . . . who else?

I grab my jacket, slip it on, and head to the bedroom, growing increasingly worried about the day ahead. My cause isn't helped when I discover Ava, hair pinned up loosely, makeup perfect, her body encased in a beautiful red dress. She's a man magnet.

"I like your dress," I say quietly, reaching for my tie to straighten the knot as she turns, clearly delighted by what she finds.

"I like your suit."

I smile, appreciative of her appreciation, while she gathers what she needs and puts her bag on the bed. But not appreciative enough to stay home and binge on me. I tug my collar down, grumpy, as she ploughs through her handbag, her forehead heavy. I leave her to it and go to the bathroom, pulling my aftershave out of the cupboard and tipping some in my palm. I rub my hands together as I return to Ava. She's still digging through her bag.

"Lost something?" I ask, patting at my face.

"My pills," she mutters, slamming her bag down on a quiet curse. My hands still on my cheeks, my whole big body tense. Guilty. *Keep your mouth shut, Ward.* She didn't notice that yesterday? Does that mean she didn't take a pill yesterday?

"Again?" I ask, dragging my hands down my face. I need to sew my fucking mouth shut. Ava glances up, her cheeks turning pink. She's embarrassed. I need to get out of here sharpish before I clue her in on my guilt. "I'll see you later." I quickly kiss her cheek and make a speedy departure, reaching up and wiping my brow.

I take the stairs, looking back over my shoulder, hoping my unusually keen escape hasn't made me look as guilty as I am. Jesus Christ, I've tried to trap her. But is it trapping if she wants to be here? Listen to me. I'm disgraceful—I'm fully aware of that, and yet . . . I can't stop myself. This . . . compulsion. God, if anyone could only hear my thought process. The justifications. Problem is, time isn't on my side, and not only because I'm considerably older than the object of my affections. There are so many ghosts chasing me, and I know deep down they can't stay ghosts forever. Not to mention the fact that I'm actually quite worried I've pickled my reproductive system with too many years of binge drinking. Stealing her pills is fucking pointless if I'm infertile. I flinch. *Infertile.* She'll eventually want kids, and I may not be able to give them to her. And she'll leave.

I stare at the bin in the corner of the elevator. I could get them out. Pretend I found them . . . somewhere.

Could.

But . . .

16

I LEAVE the pills where they are and exit the elevator, marching to Clive's desk, getting his attention with a slap of my good palm on the marble. "Mr. Ward." He smiles, probably because he knows he's about to earn another nice tip.

"The CCTV we talked about," I say, reaching into my pocket and pulling out a note. "I'd like to see it." I slide the twenty across to him, keeping the tips of my fingers on the edge.

"Not a problem, sir."

Of course it's not. I release the note and lean over the desk as Clive huffs and tuts his way around the screen. "Technology," he mutters, clicking, scrolling, frowning. "Simple, they said."

I roll my eyes and glance down at my watch, keeping check of the time passing. The last thing I need is Ava strutting out the elevator and finding me mid-bribe of our concierge.

"Simple." He laughs. "Whatever happened to good old-fashioned watchmen?"

I glance at the elevator, getting twitchier, and am about ready to seize the controls and help him along when he sings, "Aha. Here we are."

Thank God. Leaning over the desk, I squint, trying to focus on the figure by the pedestrian gate. "You can't zoom in?" I ask, getting my face closer.

"I suppose there's some fancy gadget on here that'll give us a close-up."

But it might take until next year for him to find it. I look at the elevator again, listening. Fuck it. "Let me," I say, rounding his desk and hijacking the controls. "Watch and learn, Clive." I click a few buttons and zoom in on the gates, squinting, feeling Clive bend and get close too.

"It's a bit grainy, huh?"

"Yeah," I agree, biting my lip. Tall. Slim. Blond hair. Freja Van Der Haus. *I think.* Definitely not Coral. I exhale, straightening, looking over my shoulder to the elevator. "Remember our deal?" I ask Clive as he removes his hat and tucks the twenty inside.

"Remember," he confirms as I head out. "I also have a message for you from maintenance." He starts scratching around on his desk. "Something about the door."

"Talk to Ava," I shout back. "She's the lady of the house." I break out into the sunshine and slip on my shades, pulling my phone from my pocket to call the florist but falter when I see John. My surprise is real. I half expected him to quit his job and our friendship. "All right?" I call, pushing my key fob to open my Aston.

He looks over his glasses at me, his face deadpan. I'll take it as a yes, since he's not growled or threatened to pummel me. He hasn't even called me a motherfucker. It could be a great day. "I'm fine."

"Why don't you look it?"

"Sarah's got one of your keys."

My shoulders drop. "How?"

"Because when I gave one to Sam, she took one too and I wasn't about to wrestle her for it."

She's a fucking pain in my arse. "So how many people have a key to my home?"

"Including Cathy?" John asks. "Seven."

For fuck's sake. "I'll see you later."

"And how old are you today when she asks me?"

"Thirty-two." I go to my car, jumping in and pulling away before I'm caught in a potential crossfire. Because there might be one when Ava finds John waiting for her again. Or maybe not. She was fine yesterday. Accepting. But her car wasn't here yesterday.

I call the florist to order flowers, and my thumb hovers over Freja Van Der Haus's number, unable to decide whether I'll be jumping out of the frying pan and into the fire or defusing the situation. Fuck, I don't know, but after a mile of London traffic, I decide I've got no option but to call and ask if it was, indeed, her who came to Lusso. And maybe ask if she's opened her mouth to her husband about me and Ava. But she doesn't answer. No surprises there. Fuck me, I feel exposed, blind, uncertain.

As I navigate my way through the early morning traffic, I once again begin the tedious task of planning my day. I've made it to the edge of the city by the time I've concluded I'm pretty fucking screwed. Even if I was run off my feet, had endless tasks to fill my time, I'd still struggle. I need to get Ava back to The Manor and consume her working day with the extension. I'll pay handsomely. Eradicate any intervention from her money-mad boss. Everyone wins.

I nod agreeably to myself and glance at my dashboard when my phone rings. "Clive?" I say when I answer, tensing in my seat.

"Mr. Ward. I did as you asked."

"What did I ask?"

"To inform Ava of the new door, since she's lady of the house."

"Oh. Good." I frown at the road. "Is that all?"

"She asked me to tell you that she doesn't live here, sir."

My foot naturally gets heavier on the accelerator, my hackles rising. "She did, did she?" And there is my proof, if ever I needed it, that Ava is the most challenging thing this planet has ever seen. Her message was sent for one reason and one reason alone. To wind me up. Get a reaction. Make me crazy. "Thanks, Clive." I hang up, my grip on the wheel tightening, and I try in vain to cool my temper before ringing Ava to discuss this. But she beats me to it, her name flashing across my dashboard. I'd love to believe that my love's incoming call is because she misses me already. I am, however, not delusional. I hit the answer button on my steering wheel, my mouth opening to fire some facts at her, like, actually, she *does* live there.

But she beats me to it.

"Stop messing about with my phone," she yells, the sound level of her angry demand echoing around my car.

I stare at the road, flummoxed. "No," I bellow. "Reminds me of you. What do you mean, you don't fucking live there?"

"I'm not your fucking maid."

"Watch your fucking mouth."

"Fuck off."

My entire body goes into spasm, twitching behind the wheel of my car. "Mouth," I yell, swerving to overtake a bus. God, I could wring her beautiful, defiant, challenging neck.

"What's John doing here?" she asks, short and snappy. All this because of a fucking door? Too far. This is going way too far.

"Have you calmed down yet?" I ask, coming to a stop at a red light. I'm surprised I see it, since my entire vision is red right now.

"Answer me!" she screeches.

"Who the hell do you think you're talking to?"

"You! Are you listening? Why is John here?"

Calm. Breathe. Be the adult. "He's going to take you to work."

"I don't need a chauffeur, Jesse."

"He was in the area," I say. "I thought it would be easier than you trying to park."

"Well, at least tell me what's happening if it involves me," she hisses, and then the line goes dead, and I blink rapidly, still twitching as a result of her obscene language and overall over-the-top shitty approach to a trivial matter. I realize we both probably need a timeout from each other, but what I actually want to do is find her, haul her back to our bed, and reinforce a few things. "Fucking woman," I mutter, rubbing at my aching head as I pull off from the lights on a screech, flinging up a hand in exasperation. "I'm sure she's trying to set a world record for most curses from a woman in a lifetime." I take a corner a little too fast, the back end kicking out. I shouldn't be driving when I feel like this. An okay mood has me being reckless enough, without the added benefit of Ava's transgressions riling me. "Her fault," I mutter, slowing to a stop at another set of red lights. I start drumming my fingers on the wheel, looking over my bruised hand as I wonder how the hell I get rid of her foul mouth. How I stop her defiance.

I thought you loved her defiance, brother? Keeps you on your toes and all that.

"Sometimes," I agree. "I definitely hate her foul mouth, though."

Because you never swear, do you?

I breathe out my exasperation, not biting. How can I stop this horrible tense, stressful feeling inside? I reach up and rub into my chest. I really have fallen in love with the most difficult woman on the planet. "Typical," I mutter again, glancing to my left when I feel someone looking at me. I find a man on a scooter peering over his shades at me, watching me waffle on to myself. I roll my eyes and wave off his amusement, pulling out and passing a delivery truck. I dial Ava, now that I'm a little calmer. Hopefully she is too.

"Yes, dear?" she answers sweetly.

I scowl fiercely. She wants to thank her lucky stars she's out of reach. But there's later. She'll regret this. "Don't be sarcastic, Ava," I warn. "It doesn't suit you."

"You'll be pleased to know that I'm on my way to work with John. Would you like confirmation? John, make yourself known."

"S'all good, Jesse," he mumbles on a laugh.

All good? Is it?

"Happy?" Ava asks.

"Very." I narrow my eyes, my mind mentally planning my revenge. "Ever heard of a retribution fuck?"

"No, are you going to demonstrate?"

Yes, just as soon as I've finished plotting and deciding exactly what a retribution fuck will involve. "If you're lucky," I say quietly, all anger gone and craving setting in. "I'll see you at *home*." I cut the call, leaving Ava to look forward to what's coming her way. And so my day is pretty much mapped out. I'll be inventing the retribution fuck. I haven't nailed down the finer details just yet, but I can promise it's going to be biblical.

I smile and call Sam. "Fancy one of your girlie coffee dates later?" I ask when he answers. He laughs. "What's so funny?"

"You," he says over a sigh. "*You're* funny."

I recoil, indignant. "Why?"

"Never mind. Yes, let's do coffee. I need to talk to you about something."

My interest is piqued. "What?"

"Membership for The Manor."

"You have membership for The Manor."

"A friend," he says slowly.

"Who . . ." My eyes widen. "Wait. Kate?"

"You may pass go and collect two hundred."

"Fuck," I breathe. "So she had fun, huh?"

"Yeah, *we* had fun. But there's definitely something she's not telling me."

"Like?"

"I don't know. I'm not down with women and emotions, but I get the feeling she's been burned. Every other sentence alludes to us *not* getting serious."

"So you're taking her to The Manor?" I say over a laugh.

"Problem solved."

"And you're willing to share, are you?" I ask, smiling while Sam takes way too long to answer. Kate's young. Very attractive. Red hair, blue eyes, a firecracker personality. She'll go down a storm at The Manor, and Sam must have considered that.

"You know me, mate. Share the love."

I snort. He's as crazy as everyone claims *I* am. I'm surrounded by idiots. "Whatever. But who's paying, because I'm sure as shit bakers aren't falling into Britain's top earners."

"I expect mate's rates."

"Obviously. Talk to Sarah, she'll fix you up."

"Kate doesn't want Ava to know."

I don't need to ask why. "Not a problem." I can barely mention

The Manor without Ava's lips twisting. I'm certainly not going to volunteer further information, especially when it concerns her best friend. "So, that coffee?"

"Sure. Kate's heading to Brighton so I'm at a loose end. I'll talk to Drew."

"Call me."

"Yes, dear," he sings, hanging up, and as soon as he does, I go back to inventing the retribution fuck. I have a feeling it's going to be one of my favorites.

17

TO BE FAIR, the day passes reasonably fast, my time filled with anniversary party plans and Tuesday evening retribution plans. Sam and Drew ended up coming over to The Manor for that coffee, and Sarah utilized the muscle, having them shifting furniture around the summer room, ready for Friday.

Before I leave The Manor, I shoot up to my private suite and pull open a few drawers until I find what I'm looking for. I smile, smug, as I stuff the handcuffs into my pocket and leave, itching to get home.

Clive dives out from behind his desk when I pace into the lobby, walking with me to the elevator. "She arrived home ten minutes ago, Mr. Ward," he says as I hit the call button.

I smile down at him, thinking Clive loves playing not-so-private detective. "Mood?"

"Rushed." He pops his hat back on his head, and I frown. "She was in a rush, I think."

"Oh?" Interesting.

"She didn't stop to talk. Maybe she wanted to have your dinner ready by the time you got home, sir." He grins, and I laugh to myself as I step inside the elevator. Have dinner ready? I don't think so. Her independence won't allow it. "But then again," Clive muses, "she was very angry this morning."

"Wasn't she just."

"You got yourself a young pocket rocket there, sir." He chuckles. *Young*. "She'll keep you on your toes, that's for sure."

The doors start closing. "Or on the edge of insanity," I mumble, flicking Clive a pound coin. I just see a glimpse of his scowl as he catches it before the doors come together. *What the hell is she in such a rush for?*

When I reach the penthouse, I close the door quietly behind me, listening carefully, as I creep through the space, my eyes peeled. Not in the lounge. Not in the kitchen. *Definitely* no dinner waiting for me. *As if.* I still at the bottom of the stairs, hearing the distant running of water. "Well, this will make things easier," I say to myself, taking the knot of my tie and yanking at it as I climb the steps to heaven.

I strip out of my suit, leaving it in a messy pile by the bed, and drop the cuffs on top before removing my boxers and pacing to the bathroom. I hear the shower shut off, and when I reach the doorway, I find Ava frantically washing her naked, wet body. It's quite a sight. But, again, why's she in such a hurry?

She steps out, yanks a towel down, spins, and then yelps when she crashes into me.

"Surprised to see me?" I ask, towering over her.

She peeks up, wary. "A little."

"Thought so." I consider the merits of manhandling her to the bed, risk her fighting me, but no. Not now. Now, she's going to do what I ask, *when* I ask it. She's going to make up for her insubordination this morning. She's going to hand all the power back to me. "We have a small issue to resolve, and we're going to do it now."

"What if I say no?" Her voice is small. Unsure. Fucking pointless.

"You won't." I move closer, letting my jutting dick meet her stomach. Her breath hitches. *Go on, baby. Say no.* "Let's not play games, Ava. We both know you'll never say no to me." I drag a finger across her warm, wet skin, and she inhales, gripping the towel harder, her eyes fluttering closed. "Do you believe in fate, Ava?"

"No," she says, looking up at me, confused by my question.

"I do." I encase her pussy with my palm. "I believe that you're supposed to be here with me," I whisper, watching as her dark eyes smoke. "So you advising the concierge that you *don't* live here just fucks me off."

I tweak her nipple hard, making her grunt under her breath, and push my fingers into her. She immediately melts. "Oh, God." The towel is discarded, her hands flying up and gripping me. The column of her throat glows when her head drops back, and I'm there, spreading my attention across her flesh, fingering her meticulously.

"I'm going to fuck you until you scream, Ava." I seize her face, demanding her eyes. She looks startled, overcome, confused. "Go and kneel on the end of the bed," I demand. "Face the headboard."

I'm astonished when she goes straight to the bed, fulfilling my order without question or hesitation. *More* than astonished. But it does confirm, without question or doubt, that I can bend her to my will when she's in this state of mind. Make any command and she'll do it.

This state of mind needs to be a constant.

I collect the cuffs and move in behind her, mesmerized by the smooth planes of her back, her pert arse resting on her heels, her hair a jumble of waves held up messily. Her shoulder blades, sharp but veiled in soft, olive skin. Skin that, with just one touch, sends my mind to mush. Hair that, with one smell, short-circuits my brain. An arse that sways like a pendulum when she walks, subtle and smooth.

My cheeks blow out, my hand dragging down my face. I need to pull my shit together. Make the most of this moment. I place the cuffs carefully down on the covers as my chest meets her back, and I look up at the ceiling, pulling in air quietly before taking her hands and guiding them to her boobs.

She shakes. Her shoulders vibrate. I'm in full control here. In control of her pleasure. Of her body. Of her thoughts. I circle her palms slowly over her nipples, looking down at her, absorbing the ecstasy emblazoned all over her face. *Oh, baby. I've not even warmed up yet.* But her responses. Her reactions, they're holding me in good stead. She knows I'm in control too. And yet she still pushes her luck, thrusting her chest forward in an attempt to gain more friction on her nipples. I quietly scold her, withdrawing, denying her. Her muffled, dejected cry makes me smile. "Do you trust me?" I whisper in her ear.

"With my life." Again, no hesitation. No question.

"Have you ever been handcuffed, Ava?" I ask, taking her arms and pulling them back, putting the cuffs around her wrists. She fights the restraints on a gasp. "Keep your arms still." I lower her hands to her arse, my eyes on her shoulders. Apart from the face, it's the most telling place on a human. Many emotions that could be displayed on a face can be revealed through the movement of shoulders. Raised when in protective mode. Rolling back when preparing, bracing. Hunched in when stressed or shocked. Shaky when scared.

Ava's are low. Relaxed.

Accepting.

"Good girl," I breathe into her ear, feeling through her hair for the pins holding it up, smiling at the memory it spikes. Our first night together feels like years ago. And at the same time, so powerful, so perfect, the feelings are as strong now as they were then. I discard the grips and let the strands slip through my fingers, thinking Ava never will. Not now.

Love.

And, God, do I love this woman. I count all the ways I do as I draw a perfect line down her perfect back onto her perfect arse, hooking an arm underneath her and pushing her front to the bed. "Down you go," I whisper, taking a moment to appreciate her position. Bare. Inviting. "Do you realize how fucking amazing you look like this?" Totally fucking amazing. "I'm not going to take your arse." I smile at that memory too, pushing my groin forward, drinking in air when the tip of my dick nudges at her opening. I kiss her back. Smell her skin. Where has this feeling been? This all-consuming, mind-blanking, gut-wrenching contentment. I feel both hard done by and equally thankful. Because I could have gone a lifetime without this. I could have remained stagnant, lost, unfulfilled. But the fates chose otherwise. It must be a sign. It must mean something, because nothing in this world could be cruel enough to give me her, give me this feeling, only to take it all away.

But with that thought comes many unwelcome thoughts. The universe gave me Jacob. And it took him away. The universe gave me Carmichael. And took him away. It gave me Rosie. And it took her away.

I swallow, pushing my face into my shoulder.

No.

Not again.

Surely I'm deemed worthy of redemption. Surely I deserve this . . . this . . . this happiness. Surely, they can't take another person I love away.

The only reason I'll lose her is because of *me*. *My* wrongs. *My* fuckups.

My grasp of Ava naturally tightens, holding her, keeping her, refusing to allow her to be taken. She flinches, uncomfortable. "Don't move," I warn, fighting away the pollution invading my mind in this moment.

Focus.

I take a few needed breaths and ease into her slowly, just a little, readying both of us, so fucking furious with the world. With myself. "You want it all the way?" I ask, teeth clenched.

"Yes," she gasps.

God, woman, if you only knew of the demons I'm hiding from you. Would she run? Would she stay? The fact I can't answer that with any certainty infuriates me. I look up at the ceiling, begging for mercy as I retreat, slipping out of her. Her internal muscles are in overdrive, fighting to draw me back in, but I fight her with all I have, keeping her on the cusp of penetration. Keeping her on the edge of pleasure.

Increasing her desperation. Increasing her need.

But then she jerks back, sending me deep, and I gulp, blink, and my hand shoots out, thrashing her arse in warning. I need to do this at my pace. *My* way.

I need to maintain the control.

"Fuck!" Ava yells, jerking violently.

"Mouth." The word is garbled, broken, and I clench my eyes closed, calling on some restraint. "Don't move."

She pants, forcing herself into stillness, mumbling my name.

"I know." I breathe in and out, over and over, my hands on her hips absorbing her violent shakes. Or are those my shakes? Shit, I couldn't tell you. She's obeying me, keeping still, trying to please me, and that's a stimulant I've never had. Women have always bent to my will. Always strived to please me. But now, with this woman—a woman who is so precious to me—it's a whole new level of gratification.

"I can't do this." The distressed tone of her voice pulls at my heartstrings. She *can* do this. She *wants* to do this, but, like me, she's simply struggling with the formidable intensity, and we've just hit another level.

"You can do it, Ava," I say softly. "Remember who you're with." *Me.* She's with me. And I will move mountains to ensure she remains exactly here, stripping me of strength and sureness, but at the same time loading me with power and hope.

I press my lips together. *I'm her god.*

So let me take her to heaven.

I power forward, punching a glutaral scream from her. "What did I say you would do, Ava?" I drive into her again, and she goes limp, accepting me, breathy grunts leaving her on each assault of my hips. "Answer me." I spank her, waking her up from her delirious daze.

"Scream," she cries. "You said I would scream."

I advance hard. "Are you screaming?"

"Yes!"

My head falls back, my fingers flexing, my spine stretching. But my eyes remain focused on her body, watching it absorb me, watching it roll and prepare for the next attack. Over and over. Hit after hit. Drive after drive. "Is that good, baby?" I smack her arse, relishing the glow. "Where do you live, Ava?" Let's get to the whole fucking point of this exercise.

She mumbles and moans, her head turning into the covers, turning back out, her hands bunching in the cuffs, her hips rolling and retreating.

"Ava," I bark, slamming forward again. "Where the fuck do you live? Don't make me ask again."

She screams into the bed, frustrated. "Here! I live here!"

"Damn fucking right you do." She lived here before I slammed it out of her. She knew it. I knew it. Even the fucking concierge knew it. This is a game. A power play. I'm here for the win. I smack her right cheek again, feeling the sting on my palm, and then get ready to finish this, getting a firm hold of her and letting loose.

I watch as her shoulder blades close together, her face turning into the sheets, and I feel my shaft squeeze, impulsively trying to push back the onslaught of pleasure steaming forward.

Slap.

Pound.

Slap.

Pound.

I know the second she goes, her spine cracking violently, her scream thunderous. And with that, my body gives in, and I go with her. I bellow into thin air, unable to control my mouth, my body, my thoughts, as I mumble complete nonsense through my orgasm.

I'll get her pregnant. Marry her. Confess all my sins and fall to my knees to beg for her mercy.

Wrong fucking order, bro.

I shake my head harshly, blinking away the haze and the voices. *The cuffs.* I reach down and flip one off before falling onto her, my hips circling of their own volition, working us down, settling my arms over hers, our bodies rolling as we breathe in unison. "Friends?" I ask, spreading light kisses across her nape before moving to her ear and giving it a little bite.

"Where did that come from?" she asks, having to take in air with each word she gasps.

"Tell me we're friends," I order quietly, and she sighs.

"We're friends. Tell me where that came from."

She really doesn't want to know. I had planned on hard and fast. Shock and awe. But with my toxic, uncontrollable thoughts comes panic, and with panic comes irrepressible wildness. I drop a kiss on her ear and remove the other cuff, turning her over, swallowing when my sensitive, tingling, softening cock withdraws. I check her wrists. They're a little red. No blisters. No welts. Because she didn't fight me.

I secure her beneath me, my hands over hers on the pillow, and I gaze down at the aftermath of my retribution fuck displayed all over her face. Glistening eyes. Flushed cheeks. A damp brow. Wild hair. She's a beautiful mess.

"I like hearing you scream," I say around a smile. "And I like knowing that I'm the one making you scream."

She tries to look offended. It's sweet. "I have a sore throat."

Good. Hopefully talking will be uncomfortable and she'll think twice about arguing with me in future. "Are you hungry?"

"No."

I bet she was too busy to eat, to even think about eating, and that right there is another firm reason to resent her work. Self-neglect. "I'll go and get you some water and then we can snuggle," I say, nuzzling at her nose. "Deal?"

"Deal."

I kiss her chastely and crawl off the bed, heading to the kitchen to fetch some water, scanning the fridge for anything easy to graze on. I pull out some strawberries, fill two glasses, and head back upstairs. She's snoozing when I arrive. Bollock naked. My smile is uncontainable. I place the waters on the nightstand and lower to the bed.

"Baby," I whisper, moving in close to her side, my body spread the length of hers. "Have I fucked you unconscious?" She stretches and moves to face me, opening her mouth when I offer her a strawberry.

Feeding her. Lying here. Just us, no disruptions or outside forces playing havoc with our peace. Only my mind, and I am working hard on controlling that. But it's taken a long day to get here. Monday wasn't much better. And tomorrow? The thought of running the gauntlet again, dodging my past, avoiding interferences, exhausts me here and now.

"You didn't mean it, did you?" I ask quietly, and her chewing slows as she watches me. So I elaborate. "When you said you didn't live here." I can't face another day like today. Uncertain. Dealing with her defiance. If my days are ever going to improve while she's at work, she needs to meet me somewhere in the middle and stop saying or doing things that she knows will send me crazy.

"You want me to live with you, but you won't even tell me how old you are."

"What difference does my age make?" I take a strawberry and sink my teeth in, sucking back the juice.

"Okay." She rids her mouth of food. It doesn't bode well. "What do I tell my parents when they ask about your profession?"

Oh? She's thinking about introducing me to her parents? That's a step in the right direction. What will they think of me? My age? Our relationship? "Tell them I own a hotel."

Ava takes the strawberry I hold out, her eyes narrowing. "What if they would like to see this hotel?"

"Then they can see it. *You* thought it was a hotel." My lips stretch, amused. She's going to have a problem for every solution.

"You had me escorted around the premises by staff and locked me up in your office so no one could talk to me." Her scowl is fierce. "Are you going to do the same with my mum and dad?"

"I'll show them around on a quiet day." Problem solved. Is she really talking about me meeting her parents? Or is she presenting reasons why I shouldn't? The latter is depressing and, even more depressing, so is the answer. She really is worried. About my age, about my manor.

About *me.*

I'd have to control my urges in front of them. Be respectful. Not touch her. I frown to myself. Jesus. Perhaps it's best I *don't* meet her parents.

"What if they want to stay at this hotel?" she goes on. "They live in Newquay so they'll be staying in a hotel if they come to visit."

Another problem. "Should I put them in the communal room?"

She gasps and smacks me, and I cough over a laugh. "I'm glad you find my turmoil so funny."

Turmoil? She's overthinking things. So let me solve all of this for her because, actually, I definitely want to meet her parents. Not because I actually want to meet them, but because of what that means. It's a milestone in a relationship. A serious milestone.

And she seems to be wanting to avoid it.

I get my laughter under control and face her, making sure she sees that I won't accept any bullshit excuses for her to dodge this. It's gonna happen, sooner rather than later. My eyes briefly drop to her stomach. Maybe sooner than she thinks. "Ava," I start, serious, reaching for her pouty lip and smoothing it out. "It would seem you're looking for any excuse to get out of this. If your parents ask how old I am, then make an age up. However old you want me to be, I'll be that. If they come to visit, they will stay here. There are many spare bedrooms, all with bathrooms. Stop fighting it. Now, is that all?"

"Are you going to trample my parents?" she asks quietly.

"If they get in my way." They better not get in my way. How can I ensure that? I'll just have to dazzle them with my winning personality—the easygoing one that's faded recently—and with my wealth. Below the belt? Maybe. But surely all any mother and father want is to know their daughter will be looked after, and I will do that. *If Ava fucking lets me.*

"Why were the police at The Manor?" she blurts, and I scowl at her swift change of subject.

"I told you, some idiot is playing silly games."

"What sort of silly games?"

Good grief. "Ava, it's nothing for you to worry about. End of." I stuff another strawberry in her mouth, my way of ending *that* conversation.

"What about this mystery woman?" she garbles.

God help me. "She's still a mystery." I'm not technically lying.

"So you asked Clive?"

"No, Ava," I breathe, exasperated by the quick-fire round of questions. So apparently, I'm not done dodging bullets today. "I haven't had time. When can I take you shopping?"

Her eyes widen, worry overcoming her.

"I owe you a dress," I remind her. "With the anniversary party coming up, I thought we could kill two birds with one stone." It'll be a lovely day. Just us. Me spoiling her. Plus, I can replace some of the pieces in her wardrobe that send me batty. She needs never know of my ulterior motive.

"I have plenty of dresses."

"Are you going to defy me at every turn today, lady?"

Her nose wrinkles, but she doesn't argue. It's as I thought. She's too beat to challenge me, but not too knackered to find her way into my chest and burrow deeply, her naked skin all over mine, her lips resting on my pec.

I exhale and hold her close, my nose in her hair.

It's complete and utter bliss.

But . . . will the questions ever stop?

18

My lids slowly flicker open, and my eyes battle through the harsh assault of morning light. I focus, finding her directly in my field of vision, and I love the sight of her looking down at my chest, clearly liking what she sees. I don't mind what I'm looking at either. And it's adorned in lace. Straddling me. I start to firm up.

Good fucking morning.

"Hey, baby," I say, my voice thick with a mixture of sleepiness and lust.

"Hey." She sounds perfect too, and in a desperate attempt to get my hands all over her, I shift my arms.

But they go nowhere.

And I hear clanging above my head.

And my fucking wrists hurt.

My eyes are fully open now, all wide and wary, and my sleepy face wrinkles in confusion as I look above my head. I jiggle my arms again, like the sound might confirm what I think I'm looking at.

It does.

"What the fuck?" I quickly search her out, finding her stunning face emblazoned with a look of . . .

Oh fuck.

That's power right there. Power and satisfaction. "Ava," I say quietly, warily, dreading asking. "Why the fuck am I handcuffed to the bed?"

"I'm introducing a new kind of fuck to our relationship, Jesse." Her tone is oozing confidence and evenness but being greeted by her beautiful mouth releasing such vulgar language, especially the moment I wake, instantly heats my blood. Or is it because my hard-on is pushing between her thighs? It could be both.

"Mouth." I lash out, throwing my arms around as I look up to the headboard, my eyes nearly popping out of my head. "These are not my handcuffs."

"No, and there are two pairs. I'm sure you've noticed. So, like I was saying, I've invented a new fuck. And guess what?"

"What?" I honestly don't want to know, but I'm kind of at her mercy right now—not in a good way—and that's a dangerous place to be for both of us.

"I thought of it just for you." She rotates her tiny hips, making me pull in a deep, worried breath. "I love you," she says softly.

"Oh, fucking hell." It hits my waking brain like a brick. I'm being played at my own game, except I fear she's got a different motive. I can see it in the determined edge of her dark eyes. What's she up to?

The delicate flats of her palms plant on my chest, and I watch as her exquisite face nears. I'm fighting to maintain steady breaths. Fuck, I'm struggling to breathe at all. "How old are you?" She skims her lips on mine, and even though that question has just told me all I need to know and I'm more than shocked by it, I can't help being distracted from the clarity of my situation by the feel of her lips on mine. But then she pulls away, and I feel irritation brewing inside. Oh, this could get extremely ugly. I know how stubborn she can be.

With my hands bound, I try to lift my head to secure her lips to mine, knowing that if I can pay some special attention to her mouth, I might stand a chance of getting out of this little situation on top. But I'm denied the opportunity to distract her. I throw her an evil look.

"Thirty-three." I nearly choke on a groan when she rubs into me.

I'm in trouble, more so when she comes in close and starts biting and sucking at me.

"Tell me the truth."

"Holy shit, Ava. I am not telling you how old I am."

Her slender body lifts and she looks down at me, slightly irritated. "Why?"

I have no fucking clue what to say. I know I look good, I know she can't control herself around me, and I know I send her dizzy with lust. But eleven years is a whole fucking decade, plus one! When I was twenty-one, she was ten. It just doesn't sound right. I'm knocking on forty, although I never plan on looking it. And, Jesus, that gap between us is only going to increase come Monday. "Undo the cuffs," I order, my teeth clenched. "I want to touch you." I don't like the delight she displays at my order. She knows she's got me.

"No." The little fucking temptress grinds down hard, sending me wild.

"Fuck." I throw my body around a bit, for absolutely no purpose at all. I'm fucked. "Remove the fucking cuffs, Ava."

She refuses.

"For fuck's sake, don't play games with me, lady."

"I don't think you're in a position to tell me what to do." She's so calm. It makes me freeze . . . and worry more. "Are you going to stop being unreasonable and tell me?"

I'm probably just being difficult now, but if I give in on this, she'll use it against me for the rest of my fucking life. The first thing I'm doing when I get free, *after* I've fucked some sense into her, is buying a bed that has no scope for attaching things to it. "No."

"Fine." She flops down onto my chest, her lace-covered, soft breasts pushing into my hard muscle, and she takes my cheeks in her palms, studying me for a few moments. Then she lowers her lips. I could cry, my cock hardening to exploding point. My tongue leaves my mouth to search her out, but she pulls away. I growl. She should know better than to do this to me. Deny me. Hold me back.

My unease doesn't improve when she moves from my hips and

places her tongue on my aching cock. "Ohhhh, fucking hell." I can't deal with this. "Ava!"

Just when I think she may be taking some notice, she drops me and moves, but then holds something up. I nearly choke on my tongue. I recognize it immediately.

"Oh, no." Should I laugh? Cry? "Ava, I swear to God." My head falls back in total despair, my mind frantically thinking of ways to stop this. The easiest thing would be to just fucking tell her, but what if she really does stop and think for a moment? I'll be fifty when she's just thirty-nine. Fifty! And, again, what about kids? She might not have considered them now, but what if she suddenly does and concludes she wants her children to have a younger, more capable father?

All of that is pointless thinking, bro, because you may have already trapped her into having an old bastard as her kid's father.

Bollocks.

"You can't do this to me," I mumble dejectedly. "Fuck." *Fuck, fuck, fuck.*

I hear the low humming of the vibrator, my head rocking stupidly fast from side to side, trying to blank it out.

"Wow!"

I keep my eyes shut. I can't look.

"This is one powerful machine."

"Ava." I pant and puff, forcing each word past my tight throat. "Remove the fucking cuffs."

The machine stops, and I ease up on the tension that I've injected into my jaw through gritting my teeth. Everything hurts. My wrists, my muscles . . . my fucking cock. I slowly peel my eyes open, wondering whether it's a bad idea. It is. The look in her expressive eyes tells me she's not giving up. "Are you going to tell me how old you are?"

I have the power, I think to myself, like a fucking twat. "No, I'm not." She will not win this. Not in the bedroom. Never. Our chemistry, the sex, my body, her want, it's my only weapon, and I refuse to surrender it. All fucking hell will break loose. I'll be even crazier, and she needs to trust me when I say she doesn't want that.

"Why are you being such a stubborn arse?"

I smile. She's getting frustrated. "Am I not your stubborn god?"

I soon stop grinning like an idiot when I see her start to draw the lace knickers down her legs, revealing the neat strip of hair at the apex of her thighs. My heart rate increases further, my body sweating as she rises to her knees. "Wouldn't you like to help me out here?"

My jaw rolls. I should shut my eyes, not give her the satisfaction that she's driving me fucking nuts, but I can't drag my greedy stare away from the vision before me, oozing fucking power. "Ava, undo these cuffs now so I can fuck you until you're seeing stars."

She ignores my demand, killing me further by touching herself and gasping quietly. "Tell me," she whispers.

"No." She can piss off. There will be no victory for her today. I'm not setting a rod for my own back. "Remove the cuffs." Her lips suddenly land on my stomach, working up my body, until she's at my mouth. I can't help it. Nothing would stop me from responding to those lips, not even my incensed fury at her bravery and nerve. I kiss her, moaning when she teases me with a gentle glide of her body over my throbbing dick. "Oh, Jesus," I mumble, my tone pained. "Ava, please." *Beg*. Just beg her.

"Tell me."

I shake my head, but now I think it's in desolation rather than making a point.

"Fine, have it your way." She repositions her body between my legs and collects the sparkly machine that I'm going to smash into a million pieces once I'm free . . . after I've fucked my angel stupid, just to remind her that . . . well, to show her that age doesn't matter.

"Put it down." I sound deadly. I feel it, not that it makes an ounce of difference. My girl is fearless. "Ava, I swear to God." The vibrating rings in my ears as I watch her take it down to that special place—*my* place. "Don't," I warn. I can't take it. And I can't tell her what she wants to know, because if I confess and it really does hit home for her, I can't stop her if she runs.

"Fuck," I cry, my frustration building with each awful thought. "Ava, fucking fuck, fuck, fuck!"

The sound of a gasp disturbs my cursing fit, and I feel her jerk. "Oh God," she says over a sigh.

My eyes fly open. I'm sweating. Shaking. A mess. "Ava, all of your pleasure comes from me."

"Not today." Her eyes close, robbing me of the stunning shimmer. It's salt in my wounds.

"Ava," I yell, wriggling some more. "Fuck! Ava, you're pushing it!"

"Hmm."

I can't take any more. This is torture at its worst. My head feels like it's going to pop, my hand is fucking killing me, my eyes bleeding, my heart out of control. "I'm thirty-seven," I bellow.

Ava gasps. In shock?

I can see her mentally calculating the years between us.

"For fuck's sake woman, I'm thirty-fucking-seven."

I watch as the vibrator falls to the bed, making a mental note of where it lands so I can destroy the impostor once I'm free.

"Take . . . the . . . fucking . . . cuffs . . . off." I glare at her, not relishing the worried look that drifts across her face.

The warmth of her palms meets my thighs, and I watch as she slowly crawls up my body, resting her lips on mine and threading her hands through my hair. It feels so good, but I can't shake the bubbling anger. What the hell is wrong with me? She's taken the power, and I am not okay with that. "I still love you." Her words ease my trepidation slightly, but not enough.

"Good, now take the cuffs off."

"Are you mad at me?"

"Fucking crazy mad, Ava." She's won. I'll be paying for this eternally.

She sits up on my lap, assessing me, and then forces a cheeky smile. "Can't you be crazy in love?"

"I'm that too. Remove the cuffs."

She goes to move and relief floods me, but then I feel the ready warmth of her entrance brush over me. It sends me over the edge. Tips me. "Damn it, Ava. Take the fucking cuffs off."

"What are you going to do?"

I hate myself for filling her with obvious alarm, but I'm pretty certain she's not as anxious as I am right now. I'm pissed with her for being so crafty, and even more pissed with myself for letting her win this.

"Take them off."

"Not until you tell me what you're going to do."

What I'm going to do? She's worried about the repercussions. Good. "I'm going to fuck you until you beg me to stop, and then you're going to run fourteen miles." I raise my head a little. "And we won't be stopping for a muscle rub or a coffee break."

"I don't want to go for a run," she says coolly. "You can't make me."

"Ava, you need to remember who holds the power in this relationship." I'm surprised by her front, and even more surprised by my continued arrogance. I'm in no position to be throwing such statements around, and her horrified face confirms it.

"I'm sorry, who has the power?" she retorts, resolute and smug.

And there we have it. She knows. She fucking knows what's happening here. I'm powerless, and that is not a place I can afford to be. "Ava, I'm warning you."

"I can't believe you're being so cranky over this. It was okay for *you* to handcuff *me*."

"I was in control," I roar, deranged.

"You're a power freak," she yells back, and I wriggle a little more, just for something to do other than say stupid shit. "I'm going to get a shower."

"I'm only a power freak with you," I shout as she leaves me on the bed. Wait. A shower? Now? What about me? "Ava!"

The bathroom door slams, and I'm alone, simmering with anger and uncertainty. I can hear the spray start, a small whimper escaping me at the mental image of her rubbing soap all over her body. I have issues. Big fucking issues. She loves me, I know for sure, but there's so much that can make her change her mind on that—more important shit than my fucking age.

I slump back, utterly exhausted and wondering . . . what the fuck now? After she's showered, what then? She's got to release me at some point.

Hasn't she?

I narrow one eye on the door. Huff a few times. Slam my head back down to the pillow, and I lie there for what seems like forever, restrained, my mind racing, until I finally hear the door open and look up to see her wander into the room wrapped in a towel. I pout to myself. She's showered without me. I've been deprived of an opportunity to clean her, wash her hair, look after her, and that's plain cruel.

I'm fucked.

My conclusion is a torture session and an age confession too late, but I've finally arrived at a reasonable state of mind. I can't make demands while handcuffed to the bed. I can't enforce them while in this state. So I have no choice but to change my tact. "Baby," I purr softly. "Come and free me, please."

She completely ignores me, settling to dry her hair, leaving me nothing to do but watch her readying herself for work. I've no one to blame but myself. I know I could have handled this better. Yet here I am, still handcuffed to the fucking bed. *Idiot*.

When she's done and looking even more stunning, she wanders over, and I sigh, marvelling at how lovely she is. She dips and kisses me, and I accept, jerking when I feel her lovely palm grasp my still aching arousal. So she's clearly not done killing me softly. "Ava," I say around her mouth, taking everything I can get. "I love you so fucking much." Fuck changing my tact. She's a cruel harlot. "But if you don't undo these cuffs, I'm going to fucking strangle you."

My words have no effect. She just smiles and kisses her way down to my cock. She licks and takes me deep. It's amazing. It's horrific. *Oh Jesus*. "Ava, please." My dick is dropped in an instant, and she's soon walking away. My hope soars when I see her pick up something off the chest of drawers. The key? *Oh, thank God.* Get me out of this hell.

My whole being relaxes when she unlocks a hand, the blood completely drained, leaving it limp and weak . . . and fucking painful. I won't be able to do fuck all because my fucking hands won't work. She puts the key on the table next to the bed, and I look to the small piece of silver on a frown, then to my defiant little temptress, who has never been so worthy of her title. "What are you doing?"

"Where's your phone?" she asks.

My phone? What's my phone got to do with anything? "Why?"

"You'll need it. Where is it?"

"It's in my suit jacket," I say as she backs up to the pile of clothes on the floor. "Ava, just give me the key." She's not leaving me here, surely?

I watch in stunned silence, the crazy building again, not quite believing what's happening. She retrieves my phone, places it just out of reach, and then walks out of the bedroom.

I'm silent for a few moments, struck dumb, at a loss for words. She left me? After the past two days, kicking my boots, searching for distraction in any form, this is bad, bad news. Just lying here, wondering, worrying where she is, who she's seeing, what she's doing. And now also stressing over whether my recently revealed age is going to be an issue. I know Ava. She makes issues out of non-issues. She's a master at it. She's gone, just like I knew she would. And I am *not* okay.

Breathe, Ward. But I feel so powerless. *Do not lose your shit.* The last time I felt so helpless, *she* found me. My scar. It's burning. I close my eyes. Take deep breaths.

She doesn't plunge the knife deeply enough. She doesn't lunge and stab, she swipes and drags, and I'm powerless to stop her, completely paralyzed by the pure, unmistakable intent in her eyes. I've always thought she was unstable. Always questioned if there were issues that she needed help with. Even before our daughter died.

Now? Now she's plain fucking scary, and I have gone out of my way to stay out of her way. I never anticipated she'd come to The Manor. And if she did, security was good enough to alert me of her presence before she actually found me. But I was otherwise engaged. Drunk. Balls deep in a woman.

Lost.

I look down at my naked form, blood gushing from the wound. I inhale and place a hand over it, my palm immediately soaked, slipping across my skin. I swallow. Cough. Blink. "Lauren?" I question, as if asking for a reason for this madness. I look up at her, finding her eyes rooted to my stomach, the knife still in her hand. I move back, and she glances up. And something in her eyes changes, a veil of remorse falling. "What have you done?" I whisper, falling to the couch, the absent pain now finding me.

The knife hits the floor. She flexes her hand, looking down at it, as if she's checking it's actually her hand. "I . . ." A step back.

"Do you want me dead, Lauren?" I grate, blood now pissing all over the couch. "Because you're too late."

"I'm sorry," she blurts, her hands going to her head. "Oh God, I'm sorry. I don't want you to die."

"Then why the fuck did you stab me?" I hiss, my face screwing up, my stomach pumping from my heavy breathing, making my hand slip and slide.

"I need you to love me," she screams, staggering back with the force. "Why can't you love me? Even when I had your daughter, you couldn't love me!" She rushes over and kneels before me, pressing her hand into my wound. "Oh my God." She's panicked, frantic. "Look what you made me do. Don't die, Jesse. You can't leave me. We only have each other."

I stare at her. Just stare, stunned, out of words and out of energy. "I won't leave you," I say quietly, giving her what she wants to hear, and she freezes, looking up at me. I hate the hope I see in her empty eyes. "I think I need a doctor."

"I'll get my dad." Lauren's up fast, running to the phone on the

nightstand. "Dad, dad, Jesse's hurt. I need you to come. I need you to come now!"

She hangs up, just as John bursts into my room. His face when he sees me on the couch, bleeding out, is fraught. And then when he finds Lauren by the bed, it goes from fraught to murderous.

"Don't worry, I've called a doctor," Lauren declares, coming back to me, sitting down and stroking my face with her bloodied hands, whispering words that make me sick to my stomach. I look at John, my eyes warning him.

Tread carefully.

But that plan goes to shit when Sarah breezes into the room. Lauren looks up. A wall of hatred falls. And she's off, flying across the room like a rabid dog. "He's mine!" she screams, charging into Sarah, smashing her up against the wall. I struggle to my feet and get the knife, and John wrestles Lauren to the floor, restraining her, face down, her arms up her back. She's completely immobilized. Except for her mouth.

"He killed our baby," she screeches. "I hate him! He killed our baby. He killed our baby. He killed our baby."

I roar, my head snapping back, my eyes clenching shut. And my heart? The fucker starts to slow. I heave and pulse, blinking the rage from my vision. *Focus*. I need to focus. I turn my head, spotting my phone on the nightstand. My lips press into a straight line, and I wriggle up to sitting, stretching as far as I can, my hand squeezing through the cuff painfully. "Fuck it," I hiss, trying to disregard the discomfort, my fingers skimming the edge of my mobile. "Come on," I murmur, straining. "Fucking hell." My arm feels like it could pop out of its socket. I grit my teeth, cursing constantly, stretching, and wrap my grip around my phone and practically spring back against the headboard, puffing violently. "You are seriously in for it, lady," I mutter, smashing away at the screen of my phone. I dial John. It goes to voicemail. Growling, I dial Sam. It goes to voicemail. "Where the fuck is everyone?" I yell, wriggling for the sake of it, yanking and tugging at the cuff still in place.

Calm down.

I dial John again and get nothing again. I dial Sam again and get nothing again. I dial Drew. Nothing. I yell and slam my head back, looking up at the ceiling, willing myself to calm the fuck down before I break an arm. And I slowly come to terms with my fate. I don't want to call her. I *really* don't want to call her, but she's the lesser of two evils at the moment.

My nostrils flaring dangerously, I dial. She answers in two rings but says nothing.

"Where are you?" I ask shortly, looking up at my hand hanging lifelessly from the bed. The red welts are glowing, the bruising angry, the swelling back.

"Just leaving home for The Manor. Why?"

"I need you to swing by my place."

"Why?"

"Sarah, for fuck's sake, are you going to help me or not?"

"Oh, you want my help?"

I slump on the bed and accept what needs to be done. "Yes, I need your help."

"Okay," she says, sounding all too thrilled about that. "Why?"

"You'll see when you get here." I hang up, refusing to indulge her. I know Sarah better than anyone. If I say I need her help, she'll come running. That won't have changed because I'm in a relationship with a woman she doesn't like or approve of. Would Sarah approve of any woman?

I make a quick call to Clive, telling him to expect Sarah. Then, because of my state of mind—as in, I'm not thinking straight—I try Freja again. *Voicemail.* That she's not answering my calls makes me all kinds of nervous, especially when I'm currently helpless. "Fuck it." I toss my phone aside, closing my eyes and fighting to find that calm. For Ava's sake. *And* for mine.

. . .

An hour later, a whole fucking hour, I finally hear the front door close. I still haven't found that calm I was searching for. "Jesse?"

"The bedroom," I yell, struggling to sit up, my hand throbbing. "What's taken you so fucking long?"

"Traffic." Sarah appears in the doorway, and her curious look soon turns into one of surprise as she takes in my body on the bed, her stare working up from my dick to the headboard where my dead arm hangs. Her mouth falls open.

"Don't ask," I snap, pulling the sheets across my naked lap. "The key's over there." I motion to the cabinet across the room, and she looks, frowning.

"What's—"

"I said, don't ask." I take my hand to my face and scrub down the bristle. "Just get the key, get over here, and free me."

Her head tilts, her indignation fierce. I know what's coming, so I hurry things along.

"Please," I add through gritted teeth.

She walks across the room and collects the key. "Where's Ava?" she asks, coming to the bed.

"At work."

"Oh." I can see the explanation of my situation slowly filtering into her head as she kneels on the edge and leans in to release me. "She left you here like this?"

"Sarah," I say, trying to keep my cool. "I told you not to ask."

She stops just shy of the lock, raising her eyebrows. "Don't be an arsehole, Jesse. I'm here, and she isn't."

"Yes, because she's wise." It would be Ava handcuffed to this bed now if she'd freed me, and I'd torture her until she cried with frustration.

"What happened?"

Jesus Christ. It's clear that if I want to be out of here anytime soon, I need to feed her inquisitiveness. "Ava handcuffed me to the bed and tortured my age out of me." I yank at the cuffs as Sarah recoils. "So, yes, she now knows how old I am."

"And she's gone." She just had to get that in, didn't she? And now the fury and panic are back with a vengeance, not that they left me. My hand drops to the mattress with force, and I wince, having to pick it up with my other to rub some life back into it, pins and needles riddling me.

"Shit," I curse, flexing, rolling, rubbing. It takes a good couple of minutes to work it back to life, and the moment I start to get some feeling again, I shift to the edge of the bed, pulling the sheets with me. My move reveals the massive dildo beneath the tangled covers. It's like a red flag to a bull. I dive at it, swipe it up, and launch it at the wall on a roar. It smashes to smithereens, and Sarah jumps a mile into the air.

I grab my phone and dial Ava, for what purpose I don't know. She won't answer, but she'll know I'm free. I hope she's trembling.

"Is that all?" Sarah asks, failing to hide her amusement and satisfaction.

"Yes." Stomping to the shower, I turn the knob and step under the spray before it's warmed up, hoping the cold might shock away some of this unreasonable rage. Unreasonable? No, it's not unreasonable. It's perfectly reasonable. Ava deliberately put me through hell, forced information out of me, and now she's run. It's done nothing to reassure me that my fear is unfounded, and that's a dose of anger to the melting pot of emotions that I'm way beyond controlling. And, of course, it had to be Sarah to un-cuff me. Sarah to see me so vulnerable because of something Ava did. And Sarah here in our bedroom now? It just feels so fucking wrong.

"Calmed down?" she asks, stepping into the bathroom, gazing around casually.

"Do I look calm?" I turn away from her, giving her the view of my arse instead of my dick, willing on the hotter water to steam up the glass and take her view away altogether. "You can go now." I grimace. "And thanks."

"No problem. I hope you figure things out."

Liar.

I wash my hair, scrub my body and my teeth, all the time muttering and cursing to myself. With a towel wrapped around me, I go to the dressing room and pull out my best gray suit and a blue shirt. My armor. And Ava's downfall. I reach for my chin and feel at the stubble. No time. I have more important things to do than shave. Or pick a tie. I go to the mirror, fastening the cuffs of my shirt before tweaking my hair.

I look dangerously handsome. But I feel dangerous too. "Fuck." I need to calm the hell down before I see Ava.

I strip down and find my running shorts and trainers.

Run.

19

AFTER I NEARLY KILL MYSELF pounding the pavement, I shower again, and get ready again. I feel no better. Unlucky for Ava.

My first stop is her office. I drive slowly past, trying to see through the window. My heart nearly stops when I spy her at her desk. "Thank God." I drive around and around the streets, searching for a parking space. The gods aren't hearing my prayers, so I resort to dropping my Aston off at The Ritz, slipping the valet a few notes. "Make me a reservation in the restaurant. The name's Ward." I say before he can question me. "I'll be back in half hour." He nods, accepting, and takes my keys, and I stride off, checking the traffic before jogging across the road.

I stop just short of her office, looking in the reflection of the shop window next door, fixing my collar. My eyes lift to my hair. And something beyond catches my eye on the other side of the road. I frown, squinting, moving closer to the window. I lose sight of the woman when a lorry rumbles past, and I turn, scanning the pavement on the other side of the street. Nothing.

"Losing my fucking mind." I shake my head, pulling the cuffs of my shirt out from beneath the sleeves of my jacket as I look up and down the road, feeling a little edgy. It's not surprising after the morning I've had.

When I feel composed enough, I enter, unable to stop myself from taking one last look across the street, my shoulders rolling. Ava's voice soon pulls me back round, and it melts into my skin, settling me a little. I tilt my head, admiring her, as the turmoil within calms. Finding her here, however, doesn't dampen the annoyance. I close the door quietly, and I don't announce myself. For now, I simply watch her talking, so animated. Passionate about her work.

She eventually hangs up and swings around.

Freezes.

Eyes wide but at the same time thrilled. It makes me smile. She knew this would end only one way, and that way would never be me letting her keep the power.

"How lovely to see you, Ava." I offer my hand, the one that's sore as fuck, and make sure she gets a prime view of the damage she's done. My hand is only the half of it. She should see the state of my fucking mind.

She stares at the mess, remorse steaming forward. It's a relief, and when she looks up, I nod mildly, relishing her sorrowful eyes. "I'm so sorry," she says as she places her hand in mine.

"I know you are." I'm about to advise her of all the ways she will be apologizing when her boss appears.

"Ah, Mr. Ward."

Ava pulls free from my hand hastily, her discomfort multiplying, but for another reason. It stokes the simmering irritation. When exactly is she going to share our relationship, because I'm so done tiptoeing around her job and her boss?

"How very good to see you," he chimes. "I was just asking Ava if she had heard from you."

Oh? Interesting. And what did Ava say? I can guarantee it wasn't anything to do with being head over heels in love with me. "Mr. Peterson, how are you?"

"Very good, how was your business trip?"

My business trip? She's spun some bullshit about me being away? And if I'm away, she can't crack on with the project. "I secured my assets," I say quietly, flicking a knowing glance Ava's way. She won't be avoiding The Manor anymore, and we need to have a serious talk about hiding our relationship from her boss. "Did you receive the deposit I made?"

"Yes, absolutely. Thank you."

"Good, as I said before, I'm eager to get things moving. My unexpected *trip*"—to heaven and hell and all the places in between—"has put us a bit behind."

"Of course, I'm sure Ava will sort you out." Ava's boss moves in and rubs at her shoulder, and I find my eyes rooting there. What is she, a fucking pet?

"I'm sure she will," I say. "I was going to ask Ava if she would like to join me for some brunch so we can go over a few things." I smile. "You don't mind?"

"Be my guest."

"Actually," Ava interjects, motioning to the open diary on her desk. "I have an appointment at lunchtime."

I swallow hard, my eyes fixed on the *penciled-in* meeting at noon today. With Mikael Van Der Haus. *Oh Jesus.* "That's not until noon." I look up at Ava, making sure she sees the resoluteness in my expression. I try to mask the irritation. And fail. "I won't keep you too long." Fuck, what am I going to do? I'm sure it's no coincidence that Ava's meeting him today, just days after Freja made some indirect threats. *Fuck.*

"There you go." Peterson leaves us. "It was nice to see you, Mr. Ward."

Was it? Fuck my life. Fuck Van Der Haus. Fuck Freja. And fuck *you*, Peterson.

I find Ava again, noting her nerves. Oh, she has no idea. "Shall we?" I slip my hands in my pockets to restrain them from claiming her and carting her out of here, straight back to *Lusso* where there are no work commitments and no Lothario Danes waiting in the wings to snare her.

And handcuffs. No handcuffs.

She starts collecting her things, nervous, and I open the door for her, willing myself to smile. Dazzle her. Make her fall that little bit more. But at the same time, she absolutely needs to know that I will not tolerate behavior like this morning again. I'll keel over.

Ava's work friend, Tom, bowls through the door. "Mr. Ward." His eyes ping-pong between Ava and me.

I clear my throat. "Tom."

"I'm just going for a business meeting with Mr. Ward," Ava says, looking at Tom in a way that suggests he should keep his gob shut. I can't help but laugh. It's laugh or fly off the handle. *Shit*. How the hell do I stop her meeting Van Der Haus?

"Oh, I see. A business meeting, huh?" He winks and Ava rolls her eyes, exiting sharply.

I close the door and join Ava on the pavement. I feel her look at me, wariness leaking from every one of her lovely pores. I know she's expecting me to seize her hand. Maybe even throw her over my shoulder. But no.

I start walking, a nice, leisurely stroll, and she falls into line beside me, constantly peeking up at me as we go. Naturally, I'm itching to touch her, feel her, but with each second I deny us both, her caution grows. And so does her need. I can feel the magnet between us straining to bring us together, and it is taking everything in me and more to resist it. I peek down at her. She's having the same battle. Anger. Desire. It's conflicting.

"Excuse me, have you got the time?" a woman asks.

Why, yes. Yes, I do. *And I bet you're wondering what else I have.* I flash the woman a deliberate, inviting smile, willing her to indulge me. I look down at my watch. "It's ten fifteen," I say, sensing Ava's irritation. Her annoyance. She's jealous. I love it. So I spend a few more moments indulging my admirer, smiling, as she edges past and Ava waits for me to finish proving my point. Happy I have, I slowly carry on, feeling the woman staring at me as I go.

I spot the valet I've not long left my car with, and he tips his hat as the door is opened for us. I swoop my arm out in gesture for Ava to lead on, and she frowns, entering slowly, looking around with an awe she can't hide. Yes, we're having brunch at The Ritz while I make you sweat and then, hopefully, beg for my forgiveness. I'm still thinking of all the ways she can apologize.

We're shown to a table at the far end of the restaurant, and I scan the menu fast and order fast, refraining from sending the waiter on his way when he takes his sweet, motherfucking time dressing our laps with the napkins. He eventually fucks off.

"How's your day going?" I ask, interrupting her taking in our surroundings. There's only one thing in The Ritz right now that should have Ava's attention, and he's right here, brooding as he dumps the napkin back on the table in a messy pile.

She watches me carefully, like she's assessing the merits of bolting and getting out of the firing line. But she won't bolt. And if she does, I'll rugby tackle her to the ground. The Ritz be damned. I'm not cuffed now, and Ava is obviously nervous as shit about my freedom. "I'm not sure," she whispers.

I smile to myself as I contemplate the sparkling silverware. "Shall I tell you how *my* day is going?"

"If you like." Her voice wobbles, her fingers fiddling nervously with the tablecloth. If I *like*? God, she doesn't want to know what I'd like right now. All over this table. Me banging an apology out of her. Showing her that my age doesn't matter because there's no one in this town who can fuck like I can fuck. And though I'm no expert and have screwed it up more times than I care to remember, I need to show her that no one will ever love her like I can love her. But I'm too mad right now, so we'll stick with fucking because, worryingly, I'm apparently better at it.

I nail her to the chair with my laser stare. *If I like?* "Well," I begin, keeping my hands under control, flat on the table. "My morning run was waylaid by a challenging little temptress who handcuffed me to our bed and tortured me for information." My eyes narrow of their own volition, and Ava's lips straighten. I don't know much right now, but I do know that Ava will never handcuff me to a bed ever again. "She then abandoned me, leaving me helpless and in desperate need of her." Is she hearing this? *Desperate*. Judging by her shrinking, seated form, she's taking note. "I eventually got hold of my phone." I show her an inch of space between my thumb and finger. "Which she left just . . . out . . . of . . . reach . . ." My hand throbs, as if to shout its displeasure too. "I then waited for a member of my staff to come and free me." Best not mention Sarah. This grievance is mine and dragging her into it will give Ava a grievance. "I ran fourteen miles in my personal best time to expel some of the pent-up frustrations that she presented me with, and now I'm looking at her beautiful face, wanting to bend her over this wonderfully dressed table and fuck her into next week."

Her mouth falls open. She's shocked? I bet she is nowhere close to the level of disbelief I felt when I opened my eyes this morning. I look down at the lovely, decorated table. And around the restaurant. Why the fuck did I bring her here?

Two coffees appear, and I frown down at the foamy head. That's exactly how my dick probably looks right now. Frothing. I shift in my chair, uncomfortable, as Ava slowly stirs her coffee, looking up at me. "You *have* had quite an action-packed morning."

Action-packed? Fuck me, I must have lost ten kilos, had ten heart attacks, swore more in one day than in my lifetime, and sweated buckets. I never want a repeat. "Ava," I say over a sigh, "don't ever do that to me again."

"You were crazy mad."

"I was way, *way* past crazy mad." I have to start rubbing soothing circles into my head, massaging away the headache that's threatening.

"Why?" she asks, and I stop, frowning.

She needs me to explain? "Because I couldn't get to you," I snap, and she recoils. She really doesn't get it, and that's not good. I can't believe I have to say it, but I will. If it saves me future heart attacks, I absolutely will. "The thought of not being able to reach you actually made me panic."

"I was in the room." She laughs, and then shrinks, making herself small, peeking around nervously.

"You weren't in the room when you left."

Her embarrassment vanishes, and coming up the rear fast, overtaking, is annoyance. I'm staggered. She thinks she's got a right to be mad too? "I left because you threatened me."

"Well," I grate. "That's because you made me crazy mad. When did you get those handcuffs?" I smack the table hard, and the silverware jumps up from the cloth and lands with a clang.

"When I left work yesterday." She snarls. I swear, one more sign of insolence and I absolutely will give everyone in this restaurant a front-row seat to a sense fuck. "You kind of pissed all over my plan with your retribution fuck."

"Watch your mouth," I snap, glancing around, ready to apologize to the lovely people in The Ritz for her disgusting language. "I pissed on *your* plan? Ava, let me tell you"—I lean forward, threatening, and meaning to be—"nowhere in my plan was it written that you would have me restrained and at your mercy. So it is *you* who pissed all over *my* plan." I lean back and hold my hand over my mouth, coughing when the waiter delivers our brunch.

"Is that all, sir?" he asks.

"Yes." *Fuck off.* "Thank you."

Ava wastes no time tucking in, tilting her head as she cuts into an egg. "You should know your temptress is extremely pleased with herself." On a cheeky grin, she pops her fork in her mouth and slips it out on an erection-provoking pop. *Fuck.* I can't be mad with her anymore. It's a waste of our time. She's learned her lesson, I've learned mine. I'll be disposing of all handcuffs at The Manor and maybe sending out a mug shot of Ava to all sex shops. *Do not serve this woman.* Besides, it seems after copping a load of Ava's diary, I have bigger problems on my plate, and since I'm now perfectly reassured that Ava's not skipping town since she found out there's a solid eleven years—soon to be twelve—between us, I should get on and deal with the next shitstorm. I'll start with crowding her.

She has information she deemed vital to our relationship. So, yes, she's pleased with herself. "I bet she is. Does she know how crazy in love with her I am?"

She disintegrates in an instant, her chewing slowing, her eyes shimmering as she admires me across the table. Her view has nothing on mine. "I think she does."

"She had better not just think," I say, finally starting my brunch.

"She knows."

"Good."

"What's the problem, anyway? Thirty-seven is nothing."

What about thirty-eight? Two years off forty. And nothing? She should live thirty-seven years of *my* life. It feels like centuries. A long, painful torture, each day spent in a smog of women and drink to try and make them pass faster and easier. But now I have Ava? I don't want to miss a moment. What I would do to rewind my life and meet her so much sooner. I frown to myself. But if I'd met Ava after Lauren, she would have only been seven. I feel green all of a sudden. Seven? It sounds so fucking wrong. I look up at Ava. The twenty-six-year-old goddess. What's the problem? "I don't know." I shrug. "You're in your mid-twenties, and I'm in my late thirties."

"So?" she says, studying me as I squirm. "It bothers you more than it does me."

Easy for her to say. And how the fuck was I supposed to know that at the crack of dawn when she was getting her kicks out of torturing me? "Maybe," I muse, returning to my plate, my mind returning to Ava's imminent meeting with Van Der Haus.

Your age doesn't matter. She loves you.

It's both a relief and a worry, because if thirty-seven isn't an issue for her, then maybe mid-forties isn't either, and that's exactly where Freja's ex-husband is. Don't tell me Van Der Haus meets with all the interior designers of his projects. No. He has an army of staff to do that and feed back to him. I'm not worrying over nothing. This is something. Van Der Haus knows who I am. He knows his wife has frequented the rooms of my manor. That was enough for him to hold a grudge. Now he also knows his wife was in my bed. If he finds out I'm seeing Ava? His ego would never take it. Or does he already know? Has Freja disregarded my threat? Is that why he's called a meeting with Ava today? These are all questions Freja could answer, if she would only take my fucking call.

My stressed sweat is very real. "So, when are we going dress shopping then?" I blurt after the waiter clears our table, grappling for my coffee to dampen my dry mouth.

"Friday lunch?" she suggests, looking less than enthused.

"That's cutting it a bit fine, isn't it?" She'll find a dress in an hour on her lunchbreak? I remember the last time she found a dress on her lunchbreak. The dress didn't live long.

"I'll find something."

"Put me in your diary for Friday afternoon," I say as the bill lands. "*All* afternoon."

Her frown is so cute. "What?"

I pay, watching her across the table as she slowly figures out what's going down here. Me. Taking the power. She can't deny me. She *owes* me.

"Make Mr. Ward a Friday afternoon appointment," I reiterate. "Say, one-ish. We'll go dress shopping and there will be no rush to get ready for the party." Heaven.

"I can't book out my whole afternoon for one appointment," she protests. And Miss Unreasonable is back.

"You can and you will. I'm paying him enough." I rise from my chair and push it tidily under the table. "You need to tell Patrick that you're living with me." I give her an expectant look. "I'm not pussyfooting around him for much longer."

She accepts the hand I offer, impatience adorning her face. She has absolutely no chance of a win today. "It will make things awkward," she argues, letting me lead her out. "He won't be impressed, Jesse. And I don't want him to think that I'm slacking instead of working if I should have any business meetings with you."

I hope he does give her a hard time. It'll only happen once. She'll quit, I'll set her up in business so she's her own boss with no one to please but me, and all will be right in my world. "I couldn't give a fuck what he thinks. If he doesn't like it, you'll retire."

"You're going to trample him, aren't you?"

I smile but don't answer. I don't need to. I swap a fifty with the valet for my keys and turn into Ava. "Are we friends?"

She melts into my chest, her face nuzzling into my hand on her cheek. "Yes. Thank you for breakfast."

"Anytime." *All* the time. Maybe I could take her for lunch now. Or to The Manor to continue with her work for me. I know I'm hoping in vain. "Where are you going now?" I ask, latching on to my lip. Yes, I saw *who* she's meeting. Problem is, it sent my vision red so I couldn't see *where* she's meeting him.

"The Royal Park."

"Near Lancaster Gate?" I ask, and she nods. "I'll take you." I quickly attach my mouth to hers, kissing her with force, thrusting my groin forward, eliminating any chance of her protesting. I'm taking her. End of. What I don't know yet, though, is what the fuck I'm going to do once I'm there.

Find him.

Kill him.

I laugh at myself, mainly because I'm not joking. I need to be rid of him, and yet I can't do a fucking thing without revealing Ava's and my relationship and that would be a bad, *bad* move. Unless, of course, he already knows, in which case my clock is ticking a lot faster than I'd like.

I pull Ava to my car, place her in the passenger seat, and round the back, searching for an answer to my predicament. There isn't one. I drop into the seat, rev the engine aggressively, and pull off fast. Fuck, this isn't ideal.

"What am I going to tell Patrick?" Ava asks.

"What?" I ask. "About us?"

"No," she sighs, motioning back to The Ritz. "About our business breakfast. What have we discussed?"

"Tell him we've agreed fees," I say. "And that I want you at The Manor on Friday to finalize the designs."

"You make it sound so simple."

I reach for her knee and hold it. "Baby," I murmur, hating seeing her so subdued. None of this needs to be an issue. Another solution. Another problem. "You make it sound so complicated."

And once again I'm considering the merits of buying a private island and taking us there where no one can burst our bubble. Whoever says the past is in the past is a liar. Mine is constantly creeping into my present.

20

It's a short drive to The Royal Park, so any scope to formulate a plan is limited. I feel totally in the dark, so helpless, and helpless feels pretty fucking horrific. If I'm not careful, it could force me into behaving unreasonably. Push Ava away. So my focus is to remind her how damn amazing we are together.

Shouldn't be too hard.

I park outside the hotel and turn in my seat toward her, getting on with reminding her. "I'll see you at home." I pull her mouth onto mine and kiss her slowly and deliberately, and she's all in, finding my flow and following perfectly. The heat of her wet tongue entwining around mine is magic, and she hums, pulling away, her soft lips kissing delicately across mine before she plunges deep again, circling and lapping through my mouth. Yes. Fucking amazing.

"Six-ish." Her whispered words make me smile.

"Ish," I answer quietly, feeling her stiffen, and I know instantly it's because she's building herself up to say something. What now?

"I can't retire at twenty-six," she says with contrived sureness. Sensibility is telling her I'm messing with her over this whole career thing. The huge part of her that knows me inside out—at least, the parts I've *let* her know—is worried I'm deadly serious. I am. But I also know that any insistence will be met with force and, annoyingly, I won't win any approval from my inconveniently ambitious, independent lady if I enforce anything.

"I told you," I murmur. "I don't like sharing you."

"That's stupid," she huffs, and I blink, offended.

Nothing about my feelings is stupid. "Don't call me stupid, Ava."

"I wasn't calling *you* stupid." Her eyes close. It's a sign she's gathering patience. I should follow her lead. "I was calling your ambitious intention stupid. I'm never going to leave you."

I want that signed in blood across my heart. It's an admirable promise. The problem is, she doesn't know what she's promising. I look away from her, my guilt flaring. This is not how I planned for this moment to go. I need her to leave this car more in love with me than ever. *Fuck it.*

I feel her hand rest on my nape and squeeze a little. God love her, here she is trying to reassure me, and here I am hiding a multitude of sins from her. "That doesn't stop people from trying to take you," I whisper, my secrets clogging my throat, desperate for me to spit them out. "I can't let that happen."

"What people?" she asks, my wild, thoughtless statement adding confusion to her concerned expression.

"No specific people." I swallowing down my secrets and battle with the guilt to compose myself. "I don't deserve you, Ava, but by some fucking miracle, I've got you." I can tell her that much. "I'll protect you fiercely," I vow. "Eliminate any threat." Wipe them all out, kill the competition and complications. *Fuck my life.* I look at my hands crushing the steering wheel. Van Der Haus could be my first victim. "Okay, we need to stop talking about this because I'm feeling a bit violent." *Just spit it out. Tell her!* But where do I begin? I draw breath, ready to start talking—though what the fuck I'll say I'm not sure—but she climbs across the car onto my lap, silencing me, holding my face firmly in her hands, looking at me with so much love. This look on her, for me? It's my heartbeat, and it's now my reason to be here. And with a few confessions, it could be stolen from me. I close my mouth, the words retreating, and Ava dips, scanning my face. She rests her lips lightly over mine, and I pull her close, losing myself.

Oh God.

This kiss. It could reduce me to tears. The slow, meticulous, controlled strokes of her tongue, the tender pecks around my mouth, the feelings she's loading it with.

"What's wrong?"

I startle, realizing she's not kissing me anymore. I was in the moment. Then not. I was absorbing the love, and then mentally praying. "Nothing's wrong." I busy my hands, moving a lock of hair from across her cheek, avoiding her probing eyes. "Everything is right."

"You have something you want to tell me," she whispers, tensing all over me. It's a blessing, because she can't feel my body hardening too.

"You're right, I do," I say quietly, scratching through every corner of my brain for the right words. I didn't need to scratch. They're right on the surface in prime position, ready to be said every minute of every day. "I crazy love you, baby."

She withdraws, eyeing me suspiciously. "That's not what you want to tell me."

"Yes, it is. And I'll keep telling you until you get fed up hearing it. It's a novelty to me. I like saying it."

She pouts, her body loosening. It's a narrow escape. "I won't get fed up hearing it," she declares, her nose wrinkling. "And don't be saying it to anyone else. I don't care how much you like saying it."

"Would that make you jealous?"

"Mr. Ward, let's not talk about jealously when you've just vowed to eliminate any threat."

Good point. "Okay, let's not." I grind upward, my dick twitching, coming to life, reminding me of the power it holds. "Let's get a room instead." Perfect solution. No meeting with Van Der Haus, and I get to fully reinforce the scale of our greatness.

Hot and bothered, Ava jumps out of my lap, and I push my lip out, slighted. "I'm going to be late for my meeting." Swooping up her bag, she leans over and kisses me. "I need you waiting in bed when I get home."

"Are you making demands, Miss O'Shea?" Because if they're demands like that, I'll bow to every single one.

"Are you going to deny me, Mr. Ward?"

"Never," I confirm. "But you do remember who has the power, don't you?" I reach for her, not waiting for her answer, ready to show her. But she's out of the car fast, denying me.

"You do," she says, smiling coyly as she stands outside my Aston, leaning down to keep me in her sights. "But I need you. So could you please be naked and waiting?"

Oh, those words. *Need.* It's so much more prolific than want. "You need me?"

"Always. See you at yours."

"Ours!" I shout as the door slams. "For fuck's sake." All that amazing talk and she finishes with something that drains my cup of happiness. It refills somewhat when my eyes find her arse and follow it all the way up the steps until she disappears through the doors.

And then drains once again when I contemplate what kind of reaction Van Der Haus might have to my girl's arse in that figure-hugging dress. It might be the same as the valet whose eyes have just followed Ava into the hotel. I let down my window. "Oi!" I yell, making him jump. "Keep your eyes to yourself or I'll dig them out with a fucking spoon."

The poor kid looks like he could shit himself as I grip the steering wheel. But the kid, who's probably closer in age to my girlfriend than I am, is the least of my worries.

I don't know how long I spend focusing on the air going in and out of my lungs, but my arse is numb.

My phone rings, and the distraction from my low mood is a relief. I release my poor, squeezed steering wheel and click to answer. "John."

"What's up?"

"Nothing," I say, glancing around the street, looking for any sign of the Danish prick, my forehead heavy. "Why?"

"You called. Three times."

My memory is jogged. "Where the fuck were you?" I snap, looking down at the mess of welts on my wrist.

"Do you want to change your tone, or am I beating you when I find you, motherfucker?"

I snarl to myself. "Remind me to remove you from my emergency contacts."

"What was the emergency?"

I don't want to tell him, but Sarah has a big gob, and it's rarely shut. "I was in a bit of a situation," I say, rolling my eyes to myself.

"Standard lately."

I laugh, with no humor at all. "You mean being at a woman's mercy? Yes, I agree."

"What did she do?"

"Handcuffed me to the bed and tortured my age out of me." There's silence. "You can laugh," I grumble, and my car speakers explode with the sound of John's deep, rumbling amusement. If I didn't love the sound of his rare laughter, I'd be pissed off.

"So she's been enlightened," he says, still releasing the odd chuckle.

"Well, she knows how old I am, if that's what you mean."

"And does she know you'll be a year older on Monday?"

"I don't do birthdays," I remind him. I'll be remaining thirty-seven forevermore. "Where were you, anyway? You were supposed to be collecting Ava and taking her to work."

"I'm not doing that anymore."

"Cheers, mate."

"Where are you?"

"I'm outside a hotel deciding whether to ram-raid Ava's meeting with Mikael Van Der Haus."

"Oh, for fuck's sake. I can't deal with your chart-topping stupidity." He hangs up, and I sigh, slipping down into my seat as I look up at the hotel doors and once again think about all the staff Van Der Haus must have to do his work for him.

He wants her. Who wouldn't?

I growl and close my eyes, locking down my body, ensuring it stays in the seat, my mind's eye giving me a recap of the Lusso launch. Van Der Haus's face when he set eyes on Ava.

Jesus.

That was before I was in the equation. Does he know I'm in the equation?

I get out my car and walk to the end of the street, drinking in the fresh air, trying to reason with myself. I'm failing on every level, unable to stop myself wondering what's going on in their meeting. Is he making a move on her? Exacting his revenge?

"Fuck, fuck, fuck," I mutter, pulling out my phone and dialing Drew.

"What's up?"

"I'm about to storm Ava's meeting with Mikael Van Der Haus."

"Why?"

"What if Freja has told him about me and Ava? He already knows his wife's been in my bed."

"Call Freja and find out."

"I've tried. I've burned my bridges there, mate."

"Why would Van Der Haus care, anyway? He cheated on her left and right."

"He cares because his wife *doesn't* care. He never did like me." *Ego.* He tolerated me because I was buying the most expensive unit on his project. "Even *before* Freja discovered The Manor."

"And The Lord who owns it."

"You're supposed to be helping."

"Who cares?" Drew sighs. "They're getting divorced."

"I think Ava might care," I say quietly, stopping at a wall and resting against it, exhausted. "If Van Der Haus tells her I fucked his wife after I met Ava."

He breathes in. "Shit."

"Yeah." Fucking shit. "What should I do?" I cannot believe I'm asking Drew. He's an emotionless freak of nature.

"Mark your territory," he says, simple as that. "Fuck. I'm running over for my next call." He hangs up, and I laugh. Mark my territory? What a stupid idea.

So I pace some more, up and down, spinning my phone. I look at my Rolex a while later. Two hours. She's been in there for two hours. Don't tell me a consultation meeting takes this long. What's going on in there? I dial Freja, pacing again, willing her to answer and not tell me to go fuck myself. Except she doesn't answer.

"Fuck." I get back behind the wheel and anchor myself, giving myself a little therapy session, going over all the reasons why I *shouldn't* storm her meeting.

I can't think of any. All I can think about is Van Der Haus in there getting uncomfortably close to Ava. Leaning in to see the drawings. Sitting close to go over the plans. Borrowing her pen and conveniently brushing her hand as he takes it.

Inviting her to dinner.

Telling her I slept with his wife only a few weeks ago.

I'm out of my car fast, tossing the keys to the valet, and I scan the lobby when I enter. "Excuse me." I stop one of the hotel staff as he crosses the marble floor with a tray of drinks. "If I was to have a business meeting, where would you recommend?"

"The bar, sir. Or if you wanted more privacy, I would suggest the smaller snug." He indicates toward the back of the lobby.

"Thanks," I say quietly, my skin prickling uncomfortably. I don't bother with the bar. I head straight to the smaller snug, where someone would have a meeting if they required a bit of *privacy*.

I reach the doorway and see him immediately. Yet no Ava. But I know she must still be here because there are drawings scattered across the table, Mikael Van Der Haus leaning over them. He's all casual. Relaxed. My hackles rise. In a *business* meeting.

He looks up, stilling when he finds me at the door. Just the slow rise of his body to full height tells me plenty. But not enough. "Mr. Van Der Haus," I say, stuffing my hands into my pockets as I wander in. "Fancy seeing you here."

"Yes," he replies slowly. I detect the animosity. The contempt. *He knows.* "If you don't mind, I'm in the middle of a business meeting."

"I do mind." I reach the table and glance down at Ava's work. As ever, it's spectacular. She should be working for herself. Reaping the benefits, not working herself stupid for someone else's gain. "Very extravagant," I muse, my fists involuntarily clenching in my pockets.

"A little like that sex dungeon you run." His retort is loaded with hostility, and when I glance up at him, I find his expression is too. "Have you fucked my wife there recently?"

He's straight in with a blow below the belt. "I don't fuck *anyone* there anymore." Let's make that clear.

"Oh?" he says, tilting his head. He doesn't believe me. "Anymore?"

"Since I've settled down. I'm a one-woman man, now."

He laughs, and it's like nails across my skin. "You? No woman in their right mind would *settle down* with you, Ward."

I frown to myself, something not adding up. "Well, *one* has."

"Who? I'll pass on the number of a good psychiatrist."

Who? He doesn't know? *Fuck*. I should be panicking, trying to dig myself out of the hole I just put myself in. But instead, I turn my attention to the drawings, running my finger to the bottom right corner where Ava's name is displayed. "This is the woman who designed Lusso," I say thoughtfully. "She's talented."

"Very," he agrees, sounding a little cautious.

"I'd love to meet her." Flicking my eyes up to him, I smile, seeing his alpha ego race to the service.

"She was at the launch." He looks across the pictures, and I know, I just *know*, the fucker is imagining Ava in that red dress. "You should have attended, Mr. Ward, then perhaps you would have had the pleasure."

I laugh to myself, seeing Ava screaming as I slammed her into the tile and fucked her stupid. Oh, I had the pleasure. "Sounds like I missed out."

"Oh, you did."

"Shame," I muse.

"But you're a one-woman man now, as you say, so I hope that one woman is getting what she wants from you."

That's a backward threat if ever I've heard one, and yet it doesn't prompt me to stow away the ego. "Trust me, she is."

"Say hello to my wife if you see her."

"Are you trying to get rid of me, Van Der Haus?"

He starts to shift, and I smile. Bless him.

"I'm here to meet my girlfriend for lunch, anyway," I say, and he laughs under his breath, obviously finding the fact I have a girlfriend funny. My nostrils flare, and I look at Ava's drawings again, talking myself down from punching the bastard.

Then I still, my eyes lifting to the wall before me, feeling Ava close by. Smelling her. I turn and find her motionless in the doorway, looking like a deer caught in the headlights. Her eyes bounce from me to Van Der Haus a few times, then she slowly, tentatively, wanders farther into the room. Her dirty look is mild and brief.

"Mikael," she more or less purrs, putting herself between us at the table. *Bad move, Ava. Don't do silly things like that.*

"Ava," Mikael says, clearing his throat. "Let me introduce you. This is Jesse Ward. He bought the penthouse at Lusso. I was showing Mr. Ward your designs. He's as impressed as I am." He's squeezing every word out, his jaw tight, not that Ava notices. She's too busy preparing to take the power back.

"That's nice." She doesn't even look at me, pushing my buttons further when she gives me her back. "Should we schedule our next meeting now?"

What the fuck is she playing at?

I'm a whole head taller than Ava, so I see the delight on Mikael's face. The smugness. He thinks he has the upper hand. He thinks Ava isn't interested in Jesse Ward, the man who bought Lusso. The man to whom every woman gives a second look. Except, apparently, his girlfriend when she's got the hump with him.

"Yes, that would be good. Does Friday afternoon suit?" he asks. "We can meet at Life and get a rough idea on quantities. Maybe I could buy you lunch?"

"Friday afternoon suits me fine and lunch would be lovely."

Oh, she's gone too far. It's time for a . . . what does she call it? *Trample.*

Both of them.

I move my mouth close to her nape and breathe all over it, delighting in the subtle lift of her shoulders. "I'm sorry to interrupt," I whisper, placing my hands on her shoulders, watching Van Der Haus as I do. He's not copped on yet, not grasped what's happening, his face a picture of blankness. I'll soon fix that *and* my love's obstinacy. I turn Ava to face me, and she peeks up, her eyes round. *Yes, Ava. Yes, I'm doing this.* "Baby," I purr, "have you forgotten I'm taking you shopping?"

She just stares at me, speechless.

"I didn't realize you knew each other." Van Der Haus steps back, his blue eyes squinting, like he's thinking really hard.

"I was in the area." It's time to enlighten the prick; I'll deal with the consequences when I have to. "And I knew the love of my life was here. I thought I would slip in and get my fix." *And you can watch, you womanizing, bitter dickhead.* "I'm not going to see her for another four hours." I keep my warning glare on Van Der Haus as I drop my mouth to Ava's ear. "I missed you." I feel it's not enough marking of one's territory, so I turn her in my arms and pull her back into me, cuddling her from behind, holding her tightly. I kiss the side of her head, eyes still on Van Der Haus.

"I'm sorry," he splutters in disbelief. He better believe it. And he better back the fuck off. "When you mentioned you were here to meet your girlfriend, I didn't realize you were referring to Ava."

"Yes, isn't she beautiful?" I kiss her again. "And all mine," I say, tilting my head, making myself as clear as possible, so if this doesn't stop, it's entirely Van Der Haus's fault when I annihilate him.

He's quiet for a few thoughtful moments, obviously thinking hard about his next move. It better be the right one.

"Mr. Ward," he says, forcing a smile to within an inch of his life. "If I had an Ava, I've no doubt I would do exactly the same." But he doesn't have an Ava. I, however, do. *The* Ava. "Perhaps Monday would be more suitable?" No, not Monday either. But for now, I'll keep my mouth shut. I've made my point.

"Of course, Monday will be fine." Ava rolls her shoulders, trying to break free. It only makes me cling tighter.

Mikael flicks me a cautious look as he holds out his hand. "I'll call you to arrange a time once I've checked my diary."

My rabid stare is telling him to never call her again.

Ava shakes his hand. "I look forward to it."

I flick my hips out, prodding her. There she is. The woman who cannot help poking me.

Van Der Haus slowly and thoughtfully leaves but stops at the entrance. He looks back and our eyes lock. His look darkens, disbelief and anger rolling into one. It tells me this isn't over. It tells me he's retreating to regroup. I silently wish him good luck, my return stare telling him he's a dead man if I see him again.

"I can't believe you just did that," Ava whispers, stock-still in my hold, out of fight. "You've just trampled my most important client."

I turn her toward me, getting up close. "Who is your most important client?"

"You're my lover," she breathes, completely exasperated. She should try living *my* life. "Who happens to be a client."

A person's lover is a person they fuck. She's my life. My best friend. "I am more than your lover." I watch, waiting for her to agree. She doesn't. Instead, she sighs loudly and starts to turn away from me. "I need to get back to work."

I reach for her, stopping her, but she remains with her back to me, making a point. A stupid fucking point. Okay, so I walked into this without really thinking it through. Okay, I marked my territory. Okay, I knowingly put her in an awkward position. But what the fuck else was I supposed to do? Just sit back and let another man, a man who hates me, walk on in and make a move on my woman? My list of transgressions is lengthy, admittedly, but my cause is genuine, and she went one better anyway.

I move, since she's holding her ground, being stubborn, placing my big body before her. "You encouraged him on purpose."

Her eyes close briefly, her cheeks pulsing from her harsh bite. Then she looks at me, and I'm caught off guard by her watery gaze. "Why?" she asks, swallowing.

Oh shit. No, I didn't expect tears. Only defiance. I drop my eyes, shame creeping up on me. "Because I love you."

"That's not a reason."

"Yes, it is," I argue, showing her my outrage. It's the best reason. "And anyway, he's a known womanizer."

"You can't hijack every meeting I have with a male client."

"I won't, just him." Although if he's smart, I won't need to. "And any other man who may be a threat," I add, just to put it out there, just so she's prepared. I'm a tolerant man. I can take a lot, but other men dribbling over Ava isn't one of those things. Never will be, and that's something she has to accept.

"I have to go." She battles in my hold to free herself.

"I'll take you. Collect your things." I help gather her papers from the table, avoiding the incredulous glare coming my way. "These are really very good," I say, peeking over my shoulder, smiling. The glare's gone. She's daydreaming now, lost in thought, looking despondent and sad. I really am my own worst enemy but, again, what the fuck was I supposed to do?

Collecting her motionless form, I walk her out and nod to the valet. I constantly flick my wary eyes to Ava while we wait for my car to be delivered, checking her persona. She's completely withdrawn. I put her in the passenger seat, fasten her seat belt and get in, driving her back to work in silence. She says nothing when she gets out. Not one word. It's kind of worse than being yelled at.

I watch her walk back to her office, looking weighed down. *Fuck.* A car up the road pulls out of a space, so I take the opportunity and slip in. I jog to the florist around the corner and burst through the door. "Mr. Ward," the girl sings, walking straight to the display vases and pulling out some calla lilies. "What's the card to say today?"

My nose wrinkles. "Sorry."

She whirls around. "Oh no." I can see she's desperate to ask what I've done to warrant an apology. I won't entertain her.

"Add an ish on the end."

"Huh?" she says on an unsure laugh. "You're only sorry . . . ish?"

"Exactly." I slap some cash on the counter. "Can you take them over now?" I flash another twenty at her and she beams at me. "Thanks." I leave the florist and head back to my car, slipping in and pulling off.

But I slam on my brakes toward the end of the road when I look up to my rearview mirror and see a woman crossing. "What?" I whisper, blindly reaching for my door handle and opening, my eyes fixed on her, following her to the other side of the street. I jump out and run after her, my heart going crazy in my chest as I dodge cars and people, my eyes never leaving her back. I reach out, closing in, grabbing her arm, and she swings around on a gasp.

I drop her and step back as she looks me up and down. "Can I help you?" she asks, moving back too, out of the reach of the crazy man.

Jesus fucking Christ, what the hell is wrong with me? I shake my head, my eyes dropping to my Grensons and darting. "I'm sorry, I thought you were someone else."

I quickly turn and head back to my car before she can scream for help, rubbing at my stomach, laughing lightly at myself. I really am losing my fucking mind.

Beep!

I follow the sound of the angry horn, seeing a cabbie pulling out and around my abandoned car, shouting some unpleasant shit at me as he passes. It goes way over my head. I look back over my shoulder, shuddering. I would say I need a drink but . . .

Yeah. Can't do that.

21

I SIT AT MY DESK, haunted, unable to shake away the unrest inside. It wasn't her. Just my mind playing games on me. It isn't the first time, and I expect while I'm sober it won't be the last. Can't say I'm a fan.

I look up when Sarah walks in, her heels slowing to a stop when she sees me at my desk. "Okay?" she asks.

"Yeah." I get up and wander over to the drinks cabinet. I stop when I realize I'm working on autopilot, out of habit and nothing more. I stare at the bottles. Bend and open the fridge, pulling out a bottle of water. I twist the cap off, holding my breath through the discomfort in my hand. "I thought I saw someone today," I blurt out, needing to get it off my chest. Unlucky for me, I don't have many people to vent to and Sarah . . . knows. "Twice, actually."

"Who?"

I turn to face her, and she withdraws, her face an unusual shade of alarmed. "You couldn't have."

"I know," I agree, laughing a little. "The second time, I approached her." Or chased her. "It wasn't her at all, just some poor woman with blond hair." I swig some of the water. "I feel like I'm going crazy."

"Well, that's confirmed, Jesse," Sarah says, watching me head back to my desk. She points a look at my hand. "Did you and Ava fix things?"

Why is she asking? She doesn't care. I rest my head back. "What did you want, anyway?"

She sighs, loud and meant to be heard, going to the fridge and the pulling some ice from the compartment at the top, banging it into a napkin and bringing it over. She puts it on my hand, and I smile mildly, silently thanking her. "I have some early meetings tomorrow with suppliers."

"And?"

"I'd appreciate it if you could be there."

"Why?"

She sighs. "The supplies for the new rooms, *when* they're done, are double what we paid last time."

With such emphasis on *when.* But she has a point. The whole project is stalled because my *girlfriend* can't bring herself to face my business. I need to fix that. We have endless members waiting with anticipation for the new wing to be complete, and after the police raid recently, keeping members sweet is quite crucial. "Why are they double?"

"All I keep hearing about is inflation and—"

"Find another supplier."

"I have."

I keep my head back. "And?"

"They're a bit . . . fluffy."

"I hate fluffy."

"I know." Something slaps on my desk and I peek down at it. "The catalogue of fluff."

I reach for the first page and open it, giving the model who looks like a cheap version of our very own in-house dominatrix a dubious look. "Nice."

"Terrible, I know." Sarah plops into the chair opposite me. "Look, I know you're turning all vanilla on us lately and have better things to do than buy stock for your elite sex club, like stalk the young interior designer"—she gives me a sardonic smile, and I give her a curled lip—"but this is important. High membership fees demand quality, non-fluffy equipment. Members don't want cheesy fluff, Jesse. They want quality. It's like putting a stud up against a donkey."

"That's a terrible analogy."

She shrugs. "If the prices rise at our current supplier, we have to raise memberships."

"Then raise them."

"We just did."

"Did we?"

"Yes," John says, wandering in. "We talked about it."

"Did we?"

He lowers next to Sarah. "You need to be at the meeting."

"I can't be at the meeting." I need to take Ava to work. *If she's talking to me.*

"Why?" John asks.

"I'm busy."

"Doing what?"

I look at him, brows raised. *You take her to work for me then.* He rolls his eyes, as he knows what I'm asking, and he doesn't call me out on it, so I'm going to take that as a yes. It's probably safer for all involved if John takes Ava to work anyway. "Fine," I relent. "I'll be here. What time?"

"Eight."

"Eight?" I blurt as Sarah stands and collects the catalogue of fluff.

"Yes, eight. I'm assuming that won't be a problem since your days of nursing a hangover in the mornings are long gone." She saunters to the door, the bitch back, and pulls it open. "And just so you know, Coral's asking if she can come back."

A bark of laughter erupts. "Sure," I sing. "Roll out the red carpet for her, why don't you. And while you're at it, reinstate Freja Van Der Haus's invite on Friday. And any other female members out there who are hell-bent on destroying me."

John smiles a little, rubbing at his top lip with the side of his finger, and Sarah leaves. We both know the only woman in this world who can destroy me isn't a member. And never will be. Might not even step foot in the place.

"All right?" he asks.

"Great." I'm not telling him that I'm seeing things. He'll have me sectioned. "Van Der Haus knows about me and Ava." I can tell him that, though, so then he might appreciate my predicament.

"So Freja *did* tell him."

"Not exactly." I squirm in my seat as John studies me. "I did." I've fucked myself over good and proper.

"Why?"

"Because I'm an award-winning dickhead, John. That's why. Because I can't control my panic or my urges where Ava's concerned, that's why. Because she had a meeting with him today and I spent two hours outside the hotel convincing myself that if I didn't make my presence in her life known, he might try to take her."

"Take her?"

"Date her. Woo her. Whatever. The fact is, I was right to be worried." I sink lower into my chair.

"And do we know if he knows *when* exactly his wife was . . . with you?"

I inhale, regret a vise around my lungs. I'm fucking terrified Freja's given specifics, whether that be in a fit of revenge or just to prove to Mikael that she's not short of male attention. "I don't know."

"Oh dear," John muses, shaking his head to himself. "Van Der Haus already didn't like you."

"Correct."

"And then he found out you slept with his wife."

"Correct."

"And now he's found out that the man who slept with his wife has a girlfriend, and he just so happens to be working with her."

"Correct."

"But he didn't know Ava was your girlfriend until you barged in on their meeting and told him."

I narrow one eye on him, pressing the ice into my hand some more. Whether I stormed the meeting or not, he'd try to take her. Now, though, I've just made the chase a little more exciting for him. Fuck my life. "Are you just going to sit here and state the obvious?"

"Yes, and I'm about to state something else obvious."

"What?"

"You've got to tell Ava." He stands, and I slump some more. Yeah, that simple. Just tell her I betrayed her. Tell her I put my dick in another woman. *Two* other women. The fact that I was ten sheets to the wind and it was brief won't matter. The fact Ava and I were only *seeing* each other, only fresh, new, won't matter. Because it doesn't matter. I've fucked up. Seriously fucked up.

"I can't do that to her, John. Not after everything I've already put her through."

He looks down at my hand. And the welts on my wrist. "You also can't let someone else will do the honors. It has to come from you. You need to get in front of the problem, not wait to see if it explodes."

I laugh to myself. I don't see what other option I have if I want to keep her. I can't get *in front* of this problem. I sigh. "I need you to pick her up for work tomorrow," I say, going to my mobile and texting my regular car valet guy.

"No, Jesse. That is not the answer to your problems—me chaperoning Ava to work."

And all the places in between while I can't be with her. Or, actually, when she won't *let* me be with her. "Her car's being cleaned," I say, holding up my phone. "Nothing more."

"You really are a dick."

My phone dings a message. Car clean confirmed. Perfect. Problem is, I can't have her car cleaned every day. And the reality is, Van Der Haus could call Ava anytime and stir the shit. I can't stop that. But something tells me he might milk this. Leave me sweating. Have fun with it. *Payback.*

Walking to the door, John looks back. "She loves you. You drive her mad, but she loves you."

"And what if she stops loving me?" I ask, hearing the doubt in my voice.

"People can't just stop loving, Jesse," he says, his voice unusually soft. "It's human nature. It's also your saving grace." He leaves, and I reach for my chest, rubbing at the dull ache there. I never anticipated I'd ever feel the pain of true love again. And with the pain of true love comes the potential pain of losing that love. The thought is disheartening. It's also warranted. Because I've lost so many times.

I get up and head upstairs to the extension, walking through the rooms, still shells, poking at the beams, hanging from them, looking out of the windows. It's a beautiful view out onto the front grounds of my manor. The circular driveway. The tree-lined drive that disappears into the distance. The luscious green lawns that stretch for miles.

But people don't come here for the view. No one will look out of these windows and admire their surroundings. There will be curtains up soon, lavish ones, that will block out the world beyond this glass. Because *that* is why people come here.

My phone rings, waking me from my contemplations, and I laugh lightly when I see the screen. "Too late, Freja," I say quietly, answering as I head back downstairs.

"You called?" she says.

"Have you told Mikael about . . ." I stall, wondering how to put it. We didn't really fuck. I barely had my dick inside her for two seconds. But it was still inside her.

"You bending me over the couch in your office a couple of weeks ago?"

My teeth grind. "Yes."

"It may have come up."

I exhale, my body deflating. It won't take long for Mikael to figure there's a crossover. "You're a bitter woman, Freja."

"Jesse, I didn't tell him out of spite for you."

"Sure." I laugh. "Make sure I don't see you again, Freja."

"You won't. I'm back in Denmark, and I don't plan on coming back to London for a while."

I hang up and take the steps down to the driveway on heavy feet, sliding into my Aston, hoping to snap out of this low mood on my way home. It's been a long day, a long fucking week, and I'm only halfway through it. I pull off at an uncharacteristically steady rate, rolling down the driveway, wondering if I'm subconsciously giving myself extra time to pull myself around with a leisurely drive home rather than a hair-raising race to Lusso.

I pass through the gates and stop at the junction of the main road, checking left and right, letting a few cars pass. A BMW slows toward the entrance, indicating to pull into The Manor, so I edge out, ready to pull off. But it doesn't turn, picking up speed and coming straight at me, it's indicator still flashing to turn. "Fuck!" I slam my foot on the brake, bracing my arms against the wheel, flinching, waiting for impact. It misses the nose of my car by a whisker. "Fucking idiot," I hiss, banging my horn. I throw daggers at the driver as he sails past, his attention quickly turning away from The Manor and pointing forward.

"For fuck's sake," I murmur to myself, slamming down on the accelerator and pulling out, fishtailing down the road. I won't have to worry about Ava leaving me if I'm fucking dead. I reach for the screen on the dash and put on some music. Just the radio. Just a bit of background noise to drown out my miserable thoughts.

It doesn't work.

Love hurts.

But losing it is excruciating.

22

Resting against the back wall of the elevator, I gaze up at the ceiling, my hands sunk into my trouser pockets, my body heavy, my heart beating slow and steady, but it hurts. It hurts so much. She's here, Clive confirmed as I passed through the lobby, but I feel no less reassured. Van Der Haus is a ticking fucking time bomb waiting to go off.

The doors open, seeming to slide as slowly as my feet want to work, and I trudge to the door, letting myself in. The moment I lift my eyes, I see her. She's standing on the stairs, her feet bare, her arms full of calla lilies. And even though I know she's had a rough day, she looks fresh. Perfect. I know I look anything but, and I feel less than that. *Inadequate*. *Unworthy*. Ava is without one demon, and here I am loaded with the bastards. The best thing I could do is walk away. Save her the heartache that I'm guaranteed to cause her. Slip back into the shadows with a bottle of vodka and leave her to carry on with her young, healthy life with a man who is as good as she is. I feel my muscles come to life, tightening at the thought. I'm unsure about so much, but one thing I can never question is the level of love I have for this woman. Forever. That has to count for something.

Despondent, I slowly undress, removing my armour, exposing myself, until I'm naked. I finish with my watch, dropping it onto the pile. I see the fleeting look of regret pass across her impassive face when she looks down at the state of my wrists.

I deserve so much more than a few welts.

Ava swallows, keeping her eyes on my body. She's not going to let me near her. Not until I give her something she needs. But what will it be? A reason for invading her day? Or more questions about the mystery woman turning up at Lusso?

"You're not laying a finger on me until you tell me who that woman was," she says, with a strong voice, dragging her eyes from my naked body to my face.

I smile to myself, and there's no humor in it. The irony. To Ava, the woman is more cause for concern than me invading her business meeting. If she only knew the woman's connected to the reason I invaded her business meeting. "I don't know." It's not a complete lie. I'm 99% certain, but that 1%? I should have asked Freja when she called me back. Had it confirmed.

Ava's perfectly smooth forehead wrinkles with a frown. "So you've not asked Clive to stop me from looking at the CCTV?"

Yes, I did that. She knows I did that. Her curiosity might not only kill the cat, it could also kill me. "My beautiful girl is ruthless."

"My god is evasive," she retorts, unmoving.

"Ava, if I didn't need you all over me right now, I'd be challenging you." I'll never tell her that I'm too tired to throw down the countdown.

"But you do," she says, taking advantage of my beaten form. I know she won't like seeing me like this. But she will make the most of my brief exhaustion—because it *is* brief. Touching her is like taking a shot of energy. "So you'll tell me," she adds.

Get ahead of the problem. "I slept with her." I spit the words out fast, praying that will be the end of it. No more pressing. No finer details.

Weirdly, Ava doesn't even flinch. "So why was she here?"

"Because she heard I was missing."

"That's it?" Her disbelief is real and warranted. "She was worried?"

No, that is not it. But it's all you can know. And I'm not sure worried is the right term. If it is, I'm in more trouble than I thought, because you don't worry about someone unless you care for them. And I'm not sure worried is the right term. I'm certain Freja's recent appearance is nothing more than her ego and curiosity getting the better of her. Unlike Coral. I just need them to all fuck off and leave Ava to fucking fix me. "Yes," I confirm. "That's it. Now I get you all over me."

"Why didn't you just tell me this before?"

Why? *Jesus.* "Because it was no big deal until you made it one."

I've answered her questions, more than I would like, and now I need some calm. Some energy. So I collect her from the stairs, forcing her to drop the flowers, and carry her to our bedroom. "*You* made it a big deal by evading my questions," she gripes with little conviction.

I set her down and concentrate on getting her naked, too, taking my time stripping her down, feeling her study me. I like her watching me. Like her seeing the awe that spreads through me each time I'm worshipping her, whether with my eyes or my hands or my heart. Skipping the bed, I lay us down on the rug instead, Ava beneath me, my big body covering hers. And I smell her. Feel her. Take the potent hit of life from her as she curls her arms around me and cuddles me, stroking my hair, both of us quiet. Just being.

Peace. Calm.

I can deal with anything if I always have this. Sex with Ava is out-of-this-world mind-blowing. But cuddling Ava? It's a balm. Restorative. *Essential.* "I've missed you," I say quietly, kissing the hollow of her ear, licking, nibbling, tasting. Every minute feels like an hour, every hour like a day.

"Thank you for the flowers."

"You're welcome." I dot gentle, delicate kisses up her cheek until I have her eyes, spending a moment losing myself further in the dark depths as I brush some hair from her forehead. "I want to drag you to a desert island," I whisper, "and have you all to myself forever." That's a truth I *can* confess. Wouldn't it be perfect? Just us. No drama. No interruptions. Nothing to do but love her. I roll onto my back, helping her sit up. She gazes at me longingly. That look on her will always do it. I've no hope of ever controlling myself. Blood rushes into my dick as her nipples pebble.

"I fucking love you."

"I know you do." She's making a meal of feeling me everywhere she can. "I love you too."

"Even after today?" I watch for her reaction. Wait for the scorn.

"You mean after you stalked me all day?"

I get comfortable, propping my head up on my arms. "I was worried about you." She looks less than convinced. "I was." *Really* was. And for myself. For *us*.

"You were over the top and stupidly possessive," she says, and I laugh hysterically on the inside. I didn't really give myself much choice since I happily threw myself under the bus. "My challenging man needs to relax."

My man? That'll do. Challenging? She's from another planet. "I'm not challenging."

"You're challenging *and* in denial."

"What am I in denial about?" I can assure her I am not in denial. In turmoil perhaps. Not denial. I know I've fucked up. I know I'm a fuckup. I know this slice of heaven could be stolen from me. But it's not stolen if you don't deserve it. So, in fact, it is me stealing something for myself that I shouldn't have. So, no, I am not in denial.

"Being challenging and unreasonable," she tells me. "Your performance today was way off the scales."

She can't be that naïve, surely? Even without all the facts and with me out of the equation, like I was until today when I put myself in the equation—*idiot*—Ava must realize Van Der Haus has a motive. He doesn't only want her talented mind, the womanizing prick. He deserves everything Freja threw at him. I just wish I wasn't one of the things she threw at him. "Mikael would have made a move on you, and then I'd *really* have to trample him."

She laughs again. This isn't funny, and Ava would agree if . . . my thoughts fade off. "Well," she says, all matter-of-fact, feeling my chest. "I think you made your point pretty clear." *I fucking hope so.* "It was embarrassing."

She didn't look very embarrassed to me. Fuming mad, maybe. Frustrated. "It was necessary."

"You should run more. Oh, the bath!" She shoots up and runs into the bathroom, and I crane my head to watch her naked form go. A bath. Sounds fucking perfect.

"No," I say, stretching out my limbs, peeking down at my semi-erect dick. "I need *you* more."

"Don't you have me enough?" she calls.

"Nowhere near, lady," I say to myself, knowing there would be little point ensuring she heard. She doesn't get it. How could she?

She's told you she loves you. What more do you need to do the right thing?

"Oh, bugger off, Jake." I stare at the ceiling. But it's a good question. What more do I need? I need a guarantee. She can throw as many I love yous at me as she likes. They're words. I need a contract. Something unbreakable.

And you're not unreasonable?

"Fuck off."

I hear her feet padding the carpet, and she rounds me, settling back on my lap. "Have you enough?" I ask. "No, I don't. I need you every second of the day, just like you need me. Constant contact." I tweak a nipple, making her jump, and I grin, feeling my semi hard-on firm up, my energy levels lifting. Sex in the bath first? Or here? The bed? The terrace? The office?

"What if you couldn't have me all day?" she asks, bringing me back into the room. Back to reality.

"Are you going to try and stop me?" The whole point of being in this bubble is so that no one can pop it. Ava's come home armed with a bow and fucking arrow.

"No, but there may be situations when you can't have instant access to me. I might be unobtainable."

That sounds serious. Why would she be unobtainable? Even in a meeting she could send a quick, reassuring text. The only time anyone is legally forced to have their mobile switched off is on a plane, and since Ava won't be leaving the country, especially not without me, this shouldn't be a problem.

"Would you make a grab for the vodka?" she blurts out, and I laugh.

Jesus, never again. "I promised you I will never have another drink," I say. "I meant it." I sit up and take her hips, smiling at her flinch. "Bath," I declare. That's enough talking for one session. "I want your wet, slippery skin all over mine."

She doesn't look impressed as she stands, offering me her hand. "Your confidence is commendable."

I move fast, pulling her back to the rug and laying myself all over her, slamming a hard kiss onto her mouth. Maybe this will convince her. "It is all very easy," I say between laps of my tongue, relishing the sound of her want, "because I have you. Unravel your knickers, lady."

"So, tomorrow," she murmurs, kissing me back, indulging me. "I'll be undisturbed all day?"

No. I can't have another Monday or Tuesday. And today was still horrific, despite getting to have brunch with her. And now Van Der Haus is in the picture? How the fuck do I get her back to The Manor to work without us falling out over it? "Lunch?" I ask, knowing I'm clutching at straws.

"I'm meeting Kate for lunch."

"Can't I come?"

"No." She gives me no more. Just a flat, straight no.

"I think you're being unreasonable."

She laughs, her head thrown back, her throat stretched. The sound, the sight, is glorious. The reason? Not so much. I squeeze her tickle spot on a curl of my lip.

"Stop," she yelps, jerking.

"No." I squeeze more, increase the torture.

"Please." Her hands fight with mine, trying to prize me off.

"Lunch."

"Absolutely not." Her laughter increases, her hair flying all over the place, her boobs bouncing. She's leaving me no other choice.

"Maybe a sense fuck will do it." I let go before I bruise her, and she deflates, breathing heavily, shaking her head in despair.

"Jesse," she pants. "I can't be with you every second of the day."

Well, that's not true. I have plenty of money. I want to look after her. Provide. Do all the things a husband—albeit an old-fashioned husband—would want to do. "If you give up work you could be," I say, testing the water.

Her look of horror tells me I have my head in the clouds. There are many women out there who would be content being kept. Ava, unfortunately, isn't one of them. But isn't that a little bit of the reason why I love her? Her passion. Her drive. Her desire to be more than a pretty face. Of course, but I never anticipated being in direct competition for her time. *All* the fucking time. I'm not stupid enough to think she'll really give up her career. My neediness isn't a good enough reason. But the lunch thing? That's plain obstruction on Ava's part.

"Now who's being unreason—"

I roll my hips before she can finish, driving deeply into her, exhaling my relief as I do. My God.

"Oh," she breathes, her whole body loosening, accepting, her hands grappling at my back.

I set the pace, banging in and out of her fast and hard, not leaving any room for her to catch a breath. I take her hands to the floor, holding her down. "Lunch?"

Her eyes widen. Wait, was she expecting me to demand she quit her job? Fuck me, she really does think I'm unreasonable. So lunch should be easy.

But this is Ava.

"No," she yells.

I power on, growling, feeling her body accept my ruthlessness. "You are so receptive to me." And it's beautiful. It's also a really fucking handy weapon.

"Jesse, please."

"Baby, let me have lunch with you."

Her lips seal shut, her head shaking.

"Do I feel good?"

"Yes." Her hips start grinding into every drive, chasing her release. *Oh, baby, you want your cake, huh?*

I can feel my dick swelling more and more, blood surging. I'm not going to be able to hold on for long. "Say yes."

"No!"

Fuck! There'll be no going back for me soon. "Ava, give me what I want."

"Jesse!"

"You're going to come." She looks divine, her face damp, her cheeks pink.

"Yes!"

"Oh, fuck, baby, you do serious things to me." I grind, swivel, retreat, and hit home, watching her, feeling her walls pulsing, the muscles starting to buzz. She's holding her breath. About to come.

I still, swallowing, biting down on my back teeth at the physical pain of stopping pre-explosion. But needs must. She releases her stored air on a gasp. "What are you doing?" she yells, rolling up into me, trying to capture the friction she needs. I don't let her. "You bastard," she seethes.

"Watch your fucking mouth." I strain to keep myself in check too, holding back from doing what instinct and human nature demands. "Say yes, Ava." My body's starting to shake.

"No."

I tactically roll, watching her tense, feeling her greedy hot, wet pussy draw me in. She groans, ordering me to increase my pace, flexing her fingers, her eyes misty with desire. "Say the word, Ava. Say it, and you'll get what you want."

"You don't play fair."

"You want me to stop?"

"No," she growls, her face a picture of frustration.

"I'll ask you one more time, baby," I whisper, continuing to roll, build myself up again. "Lunch?"

I see the fight leave her. *Irresistible. Power.* "Fuck me," she orders, and despite my ears bleeding, I smile.

"Watch your mouth. Was that a yes?"

"Yes!"

"Good girl." I slam into her hard, my jaw tight, falling straight back into a manic pace, thrusting, grunting, gasping. She yells my name, her body tensing in preparation for the onslaught of pleasure as I bang on, and then she screams, and I feel every piece of her jack, her body arching.

I come so fucking hard, I lose all control of my body, the damn thing trembling so much I can't hold my position, collapsing as I pour into her. "My work here is done," I wheeze, fucking beat, but really fucking content.

I take a moment, giving Ava one too, to catch my breath before easing myself up.

"Your hand," she says, worried, and I raise it, showing her how much better it looks.

"It's fine." Not giving me nearly as much grief as it did. "Sarah had me keep ice on it for most of the afternoon."

"Sarah?"

"She was just being a friend," I assure her, but by the look on her face, which has now lost the post-climax flush and is twisted in disapproval, my endeavors are in vain. The last thing I need is Ava adding Sarah to our never-ending list of shit to deal with. Sarah isn't going anywhere, and although I know she loves me, it's not a problem I need to share with Ava. Sarah's loved me forever. It's just life now.

She squirms beneath me and frees herself, and I let her, watching her walk off without a word. *For fuck's sake.* I hear the quiet splashes of her getting into the tub and drag myself up, following her in. "Has someone got a touch of the green-eyed monster?"

"No." She snorts her disgust at the mere suggestion. It's endearing.

I get in behind her, crowding her and easing her back onto my chest. "Ava, you are the only woman for me, and I am all yours." I start soaking her with the sponge, watching the water trail and spread across her flesh, her skin glistening.

"You need to tell me more about yourself."

My working hand falters. "What do you want to know?" I stare down at the back of her head, my mind racing with what she could possibly throw at me next.

"Is The Manor strictly business or have you mixed it with pleasure?"

"Dive straight in, why don't you," I whisper, looking up at the ceiling, maybe for some help from a higher power. But . . . he won't help me. Why would he?

"Tell me."

I draw breath. Denying any involvement in the happenings of The Manor would be idiotic. Divulging the extent of my immersion in the activities would be even more idiotic. "I've dabbled." I'm so fucking glad she can't see my face right now. I'm sure it's displaying all of my sins, my lies, my pain.

"Are you still dabbling?"

I balk, horrified. Is she serious? "No," I snap, insulted, every muscle wanting to tense, uncomfortable, and I strain to stop them, my hand moving the sponge across her torso with a little more vigor.

"When was the last time you dabbled?"

Oh Jesus, someone stop this nightmare. "Way before I met you."

"How long before you met me?"

"Ava, does it matter?"

"Yes."

"It wasn't regular," I spit out, my panic now doing the talking for me, my head scrambled, not giving me any clue how to handle this. I feel cornered.

"That didn't answer my question."

"Is anything I tell you going to change the way you feel about me?"

I feel her stiffen against me. God damn it, I'm making this worse. But I'm not prepared for this. "No," she finally says, quiet and unsure. Suspicious.

"So can we drop it? It's in my past with a whole heap of other stuff, and I would rather leave it there." I'm unwittingly throwing more scraps. More for her to latch on to. "There is only you," I affirm. "End of." I drop my mouth into her hair, silently begging her to ease off. *Change the subject fast.* "When are we moving the rest of your stuff in?"

"I'm here," she says dryly. "I've got to pick up the rest of my stuff from Matt."

Her ex, *Matt*? "No, you fucking won't. I'll send John." Jesus Christ. Does he still have his eye on Ava? "I told you, you won't see him again." She doesn't argue, instead falling quiet, and for the first time since we got in the bath to relax, I actually relax, now all interrogations and talk of exes is done.

"Tell me where you went when you disappeared on me."

Oh my God. Is this punishment for raiding her meeting? "No." I rest my head back and return to silently praying for some mercy as she turns over, facing me.

"The last time you held back on me," she says quietly. "I left you."

The pain is instant. The reminder. The haze of nothingness. Is she threatening me? Her presence in exchange for information? I swallow, fighting to keep my expression soft. "I locked myself in my office."

"For four days?" she asks.

I look away. "Yes, for four days, Ava."

"Look at me." Her voice is loaded with grit, almost angry, and my eyes turn to hers, shocked.

"Excuse me?"

"What were you doing in your office?"

"Drinking." *For fuck's sake.* "That's what I was doing. I was trying to drown out thoughts and images of you with vodka. Are you happy now?" I can't bear this anymore, anxiety rising, and with a lack of Ava to ease it, I can think of only one other way. Drink. *Fuck.* I need to run. Get some air. Breathe. I feel suffocated, and that's not the fucking point of being with this woman.

All my fault.

I take the sides of the tub and push myself up, and water starts splashing when Ava puts up some resistance, fighting to push me back down. I could flick her off me. Get out. Escape.

And then what?

Feeling beaten and so fucking angry with myself, I let her win and rest back in the tub, helping her slide up my body, her face close, her dark eyes scanning mine. "I'm sorry," I say quietly. "I'm so sorry, baby."

"Please, don't be." She kisses me, and I feel like a bastard accepting it.

"When I saw those bruises on your arms, I realized I was in deep, Ava," I try to explain. "Way too deep."

"Shhhh." She crowds me, holding my face, comforting me. "Enough, now."

I hide my face in her chest, ashamed. "It won't happen again," I vow against her wet skin, my eyes clenched shut. "I'll kill myself before hurting you again."

"I said enough, Jesse."

"I love you."

"I know you do," she breathes, almost over a sigh. Like she knows as well as I do that my love for her is unhealthy. "I'm sorry too."

My forehead scrunches as I withdraw from between her boobs. "What have you got to be sorry for?"

"I wish I hadn't left you."

Oh Jesus. No. This is not her fault. "Ava, I don't blame you for walking out on me. I deserved that, and if anything, it will only make me more determined not to drink. Knowing I could lose you is enough of a motivation, trust me."

"I'll never walk away from you again. Never."

How I wish I could have that engraved across my heart. How I wish I could truly depend on those words. "I hope you don't, because I'd be finished." My smile is sad. She thinks she understands the gravity of this situation, of my infatuation, of her feelings for me. The truth is, she has no idea.

She gazes so deeply into my eyes, and I've no doubt I'm looking at a woman who is in love. And when I look in the mirror, I'm looking at a man who doesn't deserve it.

She settles on my chest, and the bathroom falls quiet, leaving me too much space to fill with tormenting thoughts and conclusions. Being with this woman, being a better man, was supposed to be my absolution. A path to a better life. If I was scared of losing her before, now I'm terrified. I could forget my past and move forward with Ava at least with the comfort of knowing that I could be the man she needs. The man she deserves. But still always protective, over the top, and wary of threats. That would never change. But now? This sin is unforgivable, and the guilt is eating me up inside.

Why would she ever stay with a man who would be so careless with her heart?

23

The needle rises, another stitch done. Back inside my body, back up again. Repeat. Every breath I take is painful as Alan carefully stitches me up.

"Nooooo," she shrieks. "Where is he? I hate him!"

The moans start again. A scream. A sob.

"Fuck off. Get away from me. I need Jesse. I love Jesse."

I close my eyes, attempting to block out the tormenting sounds, as well as the unbearable agony of my guilt. I did this. My abdomen barely hurts. But my heart? It beats. It's irreparably broken, but it beats just enough to keep me in my miserable existence.

Just enough to hurt.

The door behind me opens, but I remain in my darkness, avoiding whoever has just entered, and especially avoiding Lauren's father's eyes. I feel Sarah's hand slide onto my shoulder and squeeze softly. "I'm okay," I say for the sake of it. "Where's John?"

"Damage control." At that very moment, the unmistakable sound of glass breaking rings through The Manor, and John's unmistakable low, rumbling curse follows. Sarah's gone in a flash, and I'm quickly following, halting Alan from sewing me up, the needle and thread hanging from my body as I jog after Sarah.

I skid to a stop when I find John with his massive arms wrapped around Lauren's body, restraining her. He has a gash on his bald head, blood trickling down his face, and on the floor, a glass vase is shattered. I step back, shocked by the sight of Lauren bucking and kicking in his hold, thrashing her head back, John constantly dodging her attempts to head-butt him. She looks like a wild animal, her teeth bared, her eyes crazy.

Jesus Christ.

And then she sees me and settles, although her breathing is still chaotic. "Jesse," she whispers, all crazy disappearing and a smile appearing. "You came to save me from this savage." And she chuckles, turning on a dime and laughing like a mad woman, thrashing her head back suddenly, catching John off guard. His nose explodes on a muttered "Motherfucker" and he loses his hold of Lauren. She swings around and cracks him on the side of his head, then grabs anything in sight, hauling at his body, screaming claims of rape and assault, while John deflects the objects coming at him, his nostrils flaring dangerously.

I breathe heavily, stunned into stillness.

"Oh my God, what happened?" Lauren's hands cover her mouth as she takes in my wound, coming to me, taking the thread and inspecting. "Who did this to you?" She looks at John and Sarah accusingly. "Who did it?" she screams. "I'll kill them!"

I see Alan out the corner of my eye looking on, his face a picture of horror.

Of pain.

"She needs help," I say quietly, as Lauren stalks around the entrance hall, arms flailing, yelling.

He can only nod.

"Help?" Lauren grabs the thread that's semi holding me together and yanks on it.

"Fuck!" I double over.

"You crazy bitch!" Sarah is on Lauren like a wolf, dragging her out of The Manor by her hair. "Keep your hands off him!" They struggle, and Lauren grabs hold of an ornament from the side table,

swings, and Sarah yelps as it bounces off her head and blood pours down her forehead.

Fucking hell. I grab Lauren and push her out of the door, slamming it, and I close my eyes, resting my back against the wood. And even though I know it won't redeem me, won't relieve me of my guilt or sins, I apologize.

I apologize over and over again.

One huge inhale.

My chest squeezes, my stomach stings, my head pounds. I open my eyes. I'm sitting up. Rocking back and forth. It takes me a few too many tense moments to realize I'm dreaming. "Jesus." I scrub my palm down my face, wiping away a sheen of sweat. Why? Why are these dreams haunting me? They aren't supposed to happen when I'm with Ava. Is it a sign of the fates not letting me move forward? Trapping me in my misery and self-loathing?

I lie down and reach for Ava, to cuddle her, but I find an empty space next to me. I don't like the cold, hollow sensation that creeps across my skin. "Ava?" I sit back up and scan the bedroom, listening, glancing at the clock. It's three in the morning. "Ava?" I yell, moving to the edge of the bed and going to the door. "Ava, where are you?" I search every bedroom, my heart slowing more with each one I find empty. "Ava!" I run down the stairs. The terrace. The kitchen. The gym. The study.

No Ava.

Racing back upstairs, I go to the bathroom, yelling her name repeatedly. None of her cosmetics are here. I go to the dressing room. None of her clothes. I inhale, shaking, reversing my steps back into the bedroom, looking up at the clock on the wall. The minute hand hasn't moved even a fraction. Stuck in time. And I remember, Ava didn't have a clock put in the penthouse. I swallow, looking at the wall where the photo of the shabby old boats hangs.

There's no picture. The wall is bare. There is no trace of her in this penthouse.

As if she never existed.

As if I dreamt her up.

I shoot up in bed, grappling at the sheets, gasping for breath. Sweat pours from my body.

Ava.

My strung body relaxes when I find her curled up. My exhale is long. My relief unspeakable. But my body still trembles and sweats. I feel like I'm surviving on borrowed time.

I edge to the side of the bed and let my feet meet the carpet, checking the time. It's just past four thirty. I look over my shoulder. She looks so peaceful. So cozy. I'd love nothing more than to cuddle up to her, but I don't want to wake her. I don't want her to see me like this. It'll only spike more questions I can't answer.

I get up and quietly go to the dressing room, pulling on my running kit and trainers, stopping at the door when I leave, watching her for a moment. She's safe in our bed. Safe in our penthouse. Safe from the world.

But the moment she leaves?

I take the stairs and close the door quietly behind me, getting in the elevator and walking circles until it frees me. I break out in a run immediately. It's not dark but not light either, the streets quiet, only the odd delivery van around. It's London at its finest. Quietest. I need my mind to quieten too. The thuds of my strides boom in my ears, and the fresh morning air against my clammy, hot skin, stings. The sky is beginning to glow with the impending sunrise.

I shake my head, my vision distorting, and all I see is me. Me running around Lusso in a crazed state searching for a woman who's not there. Who was never there. I fight to picture Ava, pulling the visions of her closer to me, storing every detail of her features to memory.

Lauren.

My pace increases. "No, not Lauren," I pant. "Ava." I blink, squint, hitting the side of my temple to physically bang away the nightmare memory. But I can't see Ava. I can only see a blade, and it comes at me fast, sinking into my side.

I choke on thin air and stop abruptly just inside the entrance of Green Park, going to the nearest tree and holding the trunk, breathing through the panic. I'm not asleep. I'm wide awake. My nightmares that eased off when I met Ava are back with a vengeance. Why? And why are they haunting me when I'm awake too? Stronger. More vivid. More real. *Why?*

I bunch my fist and hit the tree trunk, cursing when pain shoots up my arm. I'm at a loss. How do I navigate this mess and come out the other side with Ava still loving me?

Marry her.

I laugh at the obscenity, which is a good indication of what Ava would think if I were to ask. There's no way she'd agree. Agreeing to living arrangements was a big enough drama.

I stare at the bark on the tree, my mind circling. And it returns to the same thing over and over.

The natural progression. The right order to do things.

When I get back to Lusso, Ava hasn't moved. I shower and get ready for my early morning meeting, watching her the whole time, wishing I could leave for work and return and find her still here. Instead, I have to let her go out into a world that's hell-bent on taking her from me. I button my black shirt and tuck it into my trousers, zipping myself up as I wander to the bed and lower to the edge beside her, spending some precious time stroking her cheek. How very different this morning is from yesterday. I dip and kiss her forehead, her nose, her cheek, feeling her beginning to stir. "I love you," I whisper, going to her mouth and devoting some time there. "Wake up, my beautiful girl."

Her eyes blink open and she spreads her body out, stretching. "What time is it?" she asks, her voice grainy.

"You're fine, it's only six thirty." She smells so good, like the best mix of her and me all tangled up in the sheets. "I've got a few early supplier meetings at The Manor. I needed to see you before I go."

Hooking her arms over my shoulders, she hauls me down, hugging me, settling, sighing. "My eyes don't have to be open for *you* to see *me*."

No, but I needed to look into her eyes. Hopefully one day she'll understand. "Come and have breakfast with me." I don't give her an opportunity to object, standing and taking her with me, loving the feel of every one of her limbs curled tightly around me. "You're creasing me."

"Put me down then," she says as I carry her down to the kitchen.

"Never."

"I don't need a reminder fuck. You can still come to lunch."

"Mouth." My laugh is light and quiet. She's cute. "I'm sorry. I really needed to see you before I go." I set her on the counter.

"You woke up in the night."

Oh fuck. "I did?"

"You don't remember?"

I laugh on the inside, with no humor at all. Remember? Unfortunately, yes. "No." But I play it down. I have to play it down. I don't know how much she saw. What she heard. Move on. Be cool. It was nothing. "What do you want for breakfast?" I evade her eyes and go to the fridge. "Eggs, bagel, fruit?"

"You said you need me."

I swallow, my eyes stuck on the jar of peanut butter on the top shelf. "And?" I murmur. "I say that when I'm awake." *Please drop it, Ava.*

"You said you were sorry."

For more than she'll ever know. "I've said that when I'm awake too." I face her, and I hate her apprehension. I need to ease that.

I force a smile, and I have no idea how when every fear and feeling I felt when I woke up this morning has returned. "Ava, I was probably having a bad dream," I say, casual. "I don't remember." I quickly turn away before my expression betrays me.

"You were just a bit frantic. I was worried."

God damn me. I swing the door shut, frustrated, not with her, but with myself, and I go to her, wondering how the fuck I ease her worry without somehow increasing it. I get close, nestling myself between her spread thighs and hold her hands. "Stop worrying about what I say in my sleep," I order gently. "Did I say I didn't love you?"

Poor thing looks so confused. "No."

"That's all that matters." My love for her. Love is the answer. I kiss her, breathing her into me, and when I withdraw, I'm quite sure I don't like the expression on her face.

"That wasn't normal," she says with an edge of impatience. "And I'm getting pissed off hearing that tone. You either talk, or I'm gone."

I stare at her, flummoxed.

"What's it to be?"

I have a choice? Because right now it feels like any answer I give will be fatal. "You said you'd never leave me."

"Okay." She scowls, this time to herself, annoyed—I think—that she's been so hasty with her threats. "Let me rephrase that." *Yes, please do.* "I won't leave you if you start answering me when I ask you something. How about that?"

Hmmm. I'm not sure that works for me. "It's not important," I say, and she laughs. Then moves, trying to get down. Oh no. She's serious? She'd walk out because I didn't tell her about a dream? "I dreamt you were gone," I blurt in a panic, and she stills. "I dreamt I woke up and you were gone."

"Gone where?" she asks, confused.

"I don't fucking know." I leave her on the counter, removing my hands so she can't feel the extent of my shakes. "I couldn't find you."

"You dreamt I left you?"

Left? No. It was as if she never existed. Weird as fuck. But, Jesus, it felt scarily real. "I don't know where you went," I explain. "Just gone."

"Oh."

"It wasn't a nice dream, that's all." God, I feel so fucking stupid.

Pathetic. And yet, this fear is not without reason. And I think I have every right to be scared.

"I'm not leaving you, but we've got to talk," she says, her shoulders falling. "I have to torture information out of you, Jesse. It's exhausting."

"I'm sorry," I whisper as she pulls me in for a hug.

"Have you had bad dreams before?"

I cringe into her shoulder. "No." Not bad, terrible.

"Because you drank."

God damn it, yes, being so drunk I'd lose consciousness was helpful. The days were long before Ava, watching the clock, waiting for it to grant me permission to lose myself, escape my past. Escape the flashbacks and dreams. When I met Ava, I suppose she became my escape, which made me crave being with her all the time. Still do. Now, though, the dreams are creeping into my time with her. "No, Ava. I'm not an alcoholic." But I am an Avaholic, it seems.

"I didn't say you were."

She didn't need to. What a shitter of a day so far. Can someone please give me a break? "Can I make you a well-balanced breakfast now?" I ask, keen to move this morning along.

She hesitates, just for a moment. "Yes, please."

"What do you want?"

"Toast."

"Toast? It's hardly well-balanced." a bit like me this morning. I set her breakfast down and collect a jar of peanut butter. I need to know what her movements are today. Where she'll be. Who's she's seeing. I might then settle a little. Not a lot. Just a little.

Not at all.

"So, what's in your diary today?" I ask nonchalantly as I casually dip a finger into my jar and suck off my scoop. Ava coughs and laughs. I pout. "What's so shocking about wanting to know what you're going to be doing?"

"Oh, nothing, if I thought you were genuinely interested and not planning a trampling mission."

"I *am* genuinely interested." Really fucking interested.

"I'll meet you at Baroque at one," she says, evading my question. "I've still got to ring Kate and advise her that you're gatecrashing our ladies' lunch."

"Oh, she won't mind," I assure her. "She loves me." It's a blessing, because I know Kate, despite being a fiery fucker, is also level-headed and logical.

"That's because you bought her Margo Junior."

"No," I say slowly, although I suspect my generosity may have helped my cause. "It's because she told me so."

She frowns. "When?"

"At The Manor."

Fuck. I wasn't supposed to share that, and the reason I wasn't supposed to share that is balking, revealing some half-chewed toast. "What was she doing at The Manor?"

"That is none of our business." I get up, leaving that conversation alone before Ava passes out with shock. "I've got to scram."

"Scram?"

"Skedaddle . . . go . . . leave."

She visibly swoons when I flip her a cheeky wink, but then I see the feistiness rise in her. "I've decided that maybe lunch isn't such a good idea," she says, picking at her breakfast, casual. "I don't want Kate to think we're joined at the hip."

The chance would be a fine thing. And here we have the woman who just cannot help pressing my buttons. She'll learn. One day. I hope. I seize her and get her up against the nearest wall. She's exactly where she wanted me to put her and she's holding back a grin. She thinks she's got the power.

She's right.

I thrust myself against her and relish her sharp intake of breath. If she's craving me, she only has to ask. But I suppose this is more fun. "You didn't mean that." I work my touch down to her pussy, inhaling at the feeling of heat and wetness I find. A given.

"I did," she practically squeaks, stiffening from top to toe.

She thinks she's got the upper hand here. It's almost a shame to prove her otherwise. "Someone is going to be quick." I circle her softly, feeling her beating against my thumb. *Almost* a shame. "Don't play games with me, Ava." I remove my touch and my body from her space, swallowing down my own craving. It's easier than I expect; her shock is quite a vision. "I'm already late because I wanted to make sure you ate. If I knew you were going to play games with me, I would have fucked you first and fed you after." Unable to resist it, I move in, give her one last grind of my hips. "One o'clock," I remind her, looking out the corner of my eye and seeing her toast hanging limply between her fingers. I smile and take a bite. "I love you, lady," I say over my chews.

"You don't," she retorts, short and annoyed. "If you did, you wouldn't abandon me halfway to orgasm."

What the fuck is she on? "Hey, don't *ever* question whether I love you, it'll make me mad."

She blinks, silenced. Ashamed. It's a mild comfort.

"Have a nice day." I kiss her cheek. "I'm going to miss you like crazy, baby." I wrench myself away from her before I cave in to the temptation and Ava's tactics, and depart hastily.

And maybe because I don't want to be around when she leaves for work and finds John waiting for her. I approach her bag that's on the floor and stall, looking back toward the kitchen, pouting as I lower to my haunches and dip into it, pulling out her keys. I see her diary. With my attention split between the kitchen and her organizer, I flick through the pages to this week. I see her appointment with Van Der Haus yesterday, a note to email designs to someone called Ruth Quinn. I scan today's page, then tomorrow's. Nothing for the rest of the week. Or next. This, of course, means nothing. He could call her any time—

A sound comes from the kitchen, and I quickly drop the diary back into her bag and hurry to the door, slipping out quietly. I release air I didn't realize I was holding. "For fuck's sake," I grumble as I go to the elevator, embarrassed and quite ashamed. I stab at the call button and step in, looking down at my Rolex. Where did the last half hour go? Time seems to melt away when I'm with her, and then when I'm not?

Torture.

The doors open and I stride out, stopping at the concierge's desk. "Did a parcel arrive for me yet?" I ask the top of Clive's hat as he rootles through a box under his desk.

"Oh, yes, via courier a few moments ago." He appears, puffing, and rootles through another box, this one, thankfully, actually *on* his desk.

"How long have you been bent over that box?" I ask, alarmed by the sight of his bright red face, all blood having rushed into his head.

He ignores me and pulls out a small brown package and hands it to me, before going back to the other box under his desk. I shake my head and rip it open as I make my way outside, taking the small device over to the gang of men waiting by Ava's car. I toss one of them the keys and pass the device to him. "Fit this on the dashboard," I say, dipping into my pocket and pulling out some cash. "If a woman comes out demanding her car, under no circumstance must you let her take it." I slip one of the guys a bundle of notes, holding it in his waiting palm. "Got it?"

"Yes siree," he quips, tossing the keys in his grasp as he goes back to his van.

I hop in my car and reverse out of the space, pulling up to the opening gates just as John approaches on the other side. I lower my window and slow, and he does the same until we're side by side. "Morning."

He grunts, looking at his dashboard. "You're late."

"And you're early."

"I'll take her to work, but I'm not hanging around all day watching where she goes and who she sees."

Fair dos. I know I'm asking a lot. Hoping a lot. *Praying* a lot. "I'm meeting her for lunch, and I know she's in the office all day."

"And you know that because she told you." He dips, looking over his shades at me. "Right?"

"Right," I say, looking away, ready to drive off before I confess my diary hijacking shame.

"And she knows her car's being cleaned. Right?"

"Right." I flash him a smile, slip on my Ray-Bans and pull off, hearing a few motherfuckers tailing me.

I weave the winding roads through Surrey Hills, my car feeling like it's on rails, gliding. I've been bracing myself for a call since I left John. It hasn't come.

As I near the entrance to The Manor, a car on the other side of the road catches my eye, sitting in a small, overgrown lay-by, and I slow, looking over my glasses as I approach, reaching for my phone. I can't see through the windscreen, the low morning sun reflecting off the glass, hampering my view of the driver. Is there a driver? Abandoned? I frown, splitting my attention between driving and getting my camera on, aiming it at the white BMW. The same car that nearly took me out yesterday when I pulled out of The Manor grounds? I snap a picture of the registration plate, my head craning as I pass, but the moment my Aston is level with the beamer, it pulls off, and I divert my attention to the rearview mirror on a mammoth frown. I'm not being suspicious. In the twenty-one years I've been here, not once has a car stopped by the side of the road just south of the gates. Members pull in and through the gates, and anyone else either drives straight past or pulls *up* to the gates. Then away when they realize it's private property.

Odd.

I turn into the lane and hit the fob to open the gates, humming and tapping the wheel, thoughtful. I go to my phone and log in to The Manor's database, searching for a member and calling the number on his file. "Ward?" Steve says in answer as I crawl through the gates and down the driveway, the sun fighting its way past the dense, lush branches, hitting the ground in peppered, blinding sprays.

I pull the sun visor down. "Yeah, sorry it's so early." I can't say I like this bloke. He's cocky and self-important and, frankly, despite her being somewhat cool with me—or downright rude—his ex-wife seemed anything but.

"No problem, I just got to the station. You calling about Baxter joining?"

"Wh—" I stop myself from asking. *The immigration cop.* "No, actually, I'm after a favor," I say, slowing to a stop and turning off the engine, remaining in my seat.

"Sure thing," he says, quite sure he can help me. "You scratch my back, I'll scratch yours."

I frown. I'm not scratching his fucking back. If anything, I'm watching it. Sarah mentioned he was a bit *loose*. "If I give you a registration number, can you get me the owner of the vehicle?"

"Absolutely. Can I ask if there's a problem? Anything I need to look into?"

"No, just a car I've seen a few times hanging around The Manor entrance. Probably just a random, curious someone." But my gut is telling me otherwise. "I'll text you the registration." I get out of my car as Sarah appears at the entrance, looking impatient. It prompts me to glance at my watch. Five past eight. I'm late. But really fucking early too. "Call me when you have something." I hang up and send the image over to Steve as I walk up the steps and past Sarah. The sound of The Manor in the morning—just staff, no music, glasses and crockery clanging, kitchen appliances buzzing—brings an unexpected smile to my face.

"You're late," Sarah says, flanking me. I ignore her, stopping at the round table in the foyer, looking at the elaborate spray of various stems and bursts of color. They're beautiful, don't get me wrong, but . . .

"Have these changed for callas," I say, getting on my way, leaving Sarah behind, no doubt frowning at the stunning bouquet. "Has our meeting arrived?"

"In your office."

I march on and push my way in, finding a young guy on the couch. He looks like he's just stepped out of Eton. "All right?" I ask, as he looks up, standing, sweeping his floppy hair off his face. Have I got something wrong? I swore we had a meeting with the toy supplier. This kid looks like he supplies to the local plane watchers. I turn and look at Sarah, who's caught up behind me.

"This is Niles," she says, her head tilted, seeing my silent question. "He's new to the company and has been put in charge of our account."

So he graduated from college and steps into the role for account manager for one of the most elite sex clubs in the country? *The fuck?* What the hell did he study? I face him again, taking him in. How? "My father owns the company," he says, obviously reading my interest. "In case you're wondering."

"I was," I confirm, grabbing a water and lowering to the couch opposite him. "So I'm told your prices have gone through the roof."

He smiles. "Not through choice or greed, I assure you." He lowers too, and Sarah joins us, slipping a catalogue onto my lap. I look down.

"Fluff," she says quietly, reminding me of the alternative.

I roll my eyes. "So, come on . . .?"

"Niles," he says, and I smile. "Mr. Ward, your club is the most renowned in England. Probably even Great Britain."

"Compliments will get you nowhere, Niles."

He laughs lightly. "I've done a thorough assessment of the market and the competition."

"Whose competition?"

"Ours and yours."

"Oh? But we don't have any competition, Niles, as you have just pointed out. We are the best."

"Therefore, you must supply the best. It's expected, is it not?"

I inwardly scowl. *Smart-arse.* "It is."

"I have a proposition for you, Mr. Ward."

"And that is?"

"We've signed an exclusive deal with a new manufacturer out of the Netherlands." He passes a file across the table. "The quality is second to none, and I mean *none*."

I open and browse the collection, really fucking impressed. Definitely no fluff. But . . . "It looks expensive, Niles."

"It is, I won't lie. But"—he holds a finger up, eyebrows high—"I would be prepared to sign an exclusive supply deal for The Manor alone, and I'd honor the previous rates plus ten percent."

"Are you saying you'll not supply this collection to any other establishment?"

"That is indeed what I'm saying, but of course, they'll market through other channels."

Just supply to The Manor? "Why?"

"The designer of this collection wants it to remain exclusive. A fat, veiny dildo is ten a penny." He smiles. "If you know what I mean."

Sarah coughs, and I frown. "Why would they limit their supply channels?" It doesn't make any sense.

"The same reason Dior will not sell in Poundland, Mr. Ward. It's simply marketing tactics."

"I feel a catch coming on."

Niles looks down at his file, fiddling with the edge, and I know what's coming.

"How old are you?" I ask.

"Twenty-two."

Jesus. I close my eyes and see me. Young. Reckless. "You're not our usual demographic, Niles." But he's smart. Got his head screwed on. It's more than I can say for myself at that age. Niles seems . . . stable.

"I realize that."

"You like the older woman, then," Sarah pipes in, and I look out the corner of my eye on a smile, seeing the delight in her eyes. Oh, how she will love getting her whip around this boy.

He just smiles. "I handpicked The Manor and presented to the designer. She was impressed."

"Of course she was." I toss the file on the desk. "And your father? I'm guessing he doesn't know about this?"

"I assume members are protected by a confidentiality clause."

"You assume right." I cross one leg over the other, observing him quietly, battling with my conscience. I hate being maneuvered. This infant is cocky, something I also dislike. And yet . . . this could be a lucrative deal. And Sarah could possibly be distracted with an additional, *younger* sub to play with. *Should I?* "We have the annual anniversary party tomorrow. It would be lovely if you joined us. Get to know the place."

He nods, cool as can be. "Thank you."

"There's one more thing," Sarah says, getting up and going to a nearby sideboard, collecting a clipboard. "We have giftbags for members at the party." She smiles sweetly. "A donation will go a long way."

"I'm sure I can arrange something. We have some fantastic new cock rings launching soon." Niles stands and collects his bags. "I'll have the contract drawn up. I assure you, Mr. Ward, your members will be most satisfied with the new collection."

I stand too, accepting his hand when he offers it. Jesus, I bet he's tried everything in the collection, the rampant little fucker. "I'll see you tomorrow." My phone rings, and I excuse myself, wandering across to my desk as Sarah sees Niles out. "Cathy," I sing, settling in my chair.

"My boy," she says. "How I've missed you. How are you? How have you been? Have you settled into your new, swanky penthouse? Oh my, I bet it's a frightful state. I'll be there without delay to get it in shipshape."

I smile, but cringe too. Cathy will be elated when she finds out about Ava, but she'll despair if she finds out about my epic binge and meltdown. Naturally, I'll do what I can to make sure she doesn't. "Welcome back, Cathy," I say. "I have news."

"Oh?"

"I've met someone." My smile is unstoppable, the sound of those words, that statement, feeling so fucking peculiar. But so fucking right. "Someone really special."

"Oh my. Oh Jesse. Oh, my boy. I need to sit down. One moment, let me move the telephone across to the table." There are a few scuffles and knocks, and she's back on the line. "Tell me everything."

I cough a little. Not a chance. "Her name's Ava."

"Ooh, Ava. And how old is Ava?"

My face bunches. Of all the questions? "She's a little younger than I am."

"A little?"

"Yeah, a little."

"How much younger?"

"Eleven years," I say over a cough. *Twelve on Monday.*

Cathy lets out a burst of laughter, and I jump in my chair. "Oh, you little devil, you," she coos. "You're a sugar daddy."

My jaw hits the desk, every inch of me offended. "Seriously, Cathy?" Talk about kicking my ego.

"I've always fancied myself a playboy."

"Behave, will you?" I pull my phone away when another call comes through. It's John. "Cathy, I've got John on the other line."

"Okay, my boy. I'll head to your swanky penthouse shortly. Make you some supper."

"That would be lovely."

"Unless, of course, your new lady friend likes to cook. I don't want to step on any toes."

I smile. "She hates cooking."

"Wonderful!"

"I'll call the concierge and tell him to see you up. Ask for Clive, okay?"

"Clive. Yes, dear, I'll ask for Clive."

"See you, Cathy." I hang up and take John's call, bracing myself for the fireworks.

"How was the meeting?" he asks, and I relax but frown.

"Fine. How was the pickup?"

"Fine."

"No protest?" I ask, surprised.

"No, I think the girl is starting to accept your boundless craziness."

I huff. "If I'm crazy, it's because she sends me crazy. Where are you?"

"On my way." He hangs up, and I relax back in my chair,

chewing my lip, thoughtful. She accepts my boundless craziness. I spin my phone in my hand, my mind spinning with it. *Boundless*.

The natural progression.

I dial Kate, and I can't lie, I hold my breath while it rings until she answers, sounding sleepy. "Morning, Rhino," she quips groggily.

Rhino? *Well, I do ram hard.* "Morning."

"And what can I do for you?"

"Well, since you've asked," I say, trying to calm my racing heartbeat.

24

Surprisingly and most pleasingly, the morning passes relatively quickly and I'm soon heading back into town for my lunch date with my girl. It's the perfect way to break the day into smaller, more manageable chunks, and Ava has absolutely no excuse to not have a lunch break. It's a legal requirement. Both by British law and by Jesse Ward's law. I smile and put some music on, tapping my wheel to the beat of Wonderwall for only a few seconds before the music is replaced by ringing. I scowl at his name on my screen. It's taken him over twenty-four hours to return my SOS call. "What?" I answer shortly.

"You called?"

"Yesterday, Sam. I called yesterday."

"I've been busy."

"You don't work."

He laughs. "I didn't say I was busy with work. What did you want anyway?"

"Nothing." I'm not sharing. I don't feel like being the brunt of his humor today. I'm sure Kate will kindly fill him in on my traumatic experience at the hands of my wicked girlfriend.

Girlfriend. Boyfriend.

I chew my lip, rolling the words around in my mind. Boundless. "So you're still bringing Kate to the party then?" I ask.

"I am."

"And will you be partaking in team activities?" I slow as I approach a roundabout, checking for traffic, waiting with interest for Sam's reply.

"I will."

And there's the difference between Sam and Kate, and Ava and me. Sharing? Not a fucking chance in hell. But something is playing on my mind. "You're spending a lot of time with her, considering all I'm hearing is *casual*."

"She's a good chick."

"And if you hurt her, I won't hear the last of it."

"Don't worry, we're both on the same page," he assures me, although I'm less than assured. "Besides, I get the feeling I'm a bit of a rebound."

Oh. The something she's not telling him? "Has she mentioned an ex?"

"No. No mention at all. I just have a feeling." He pauses a beat. "You could ask Ava."

"I am *not* asking Ava." Let us be clear on that. "And if it's just casual, what the fuck does it matter anyway?" I ask, my head tilted curiously.

"It doesn't. I'll see you soon."

"Actually, I'm heading back into town to meet Ava for lunch."

"I know. Me too. I'll see you soon." He hangs up, and I shake my head, just as Drew calls.

"I'm coming for lunch."

"How very cosmopolitan of you. Are you bringing a date?" I ask, smiling.

"Fuck, no."

"Things didn't work out with Victoria?"

"She thinks I have issues."

I laugh out loud. "We've all got fucking issues."

"You more than any of us."

"What's that supposed to mean?" I ask, my amusement dying. "Go get yourself some feelings, you freak."

"Fuck off. So did you mark your territory yesterday?"

"It was the dumbest idea you've ever had."

"That's not an answer."

I curl my lip at the windscreen. "Yes, I marked my territory. Remind me to never take advice from you again." Truth is, I would have trampled, whether Drew advised it or not.

He laughs. "And did you find out what he knows?"

"He knows his wife and I . . ." I shift in my seat, uncomfortable. "He knows something happened a few weeks ago. He doesn't yet know when Ava and I started seeing each other."

"Shit."

"Indeed." I'm tired of hearing these reactions. I know I'm up shit's creek. "I'll see you soon."

I put my foot down and overtake the lorry, honking my horn impatiently as I do.

Sam's just getting out of his car on the side street when I pull up, and Drew is wandering down the pavement from his office, his mobile at his ear. I zip into a space and go to the ticket machine. "Ladies," I say sardonically as they join me.

"How the fuck can he justify that?" Drew barks into his phone, growling, cursing, then hanging up. He points his phone at me as the machine spits out a ticket. "Just a heads-up," he says, as I lean back, wary. "If I see that prick of an estate agent who sold you the penthouse, I'm going to find the biggest dildo in The Manor and ram it down his throat."

"Yikes," Sam breathes.

"Why the fuck did you let him join?" Drew goes on, getting his waving phone under control and stalking off.

"You want me to pass up revenue because you can't handle a bit of competition?" I slip the ticket onto the dash and lock my car.

Sam coughs, and Drew stops dead in his tracks, his attention still pointing forward. "I can handle competition."

"So what did he do?" I ask as Sam and I join him and the three of us walk in a line down the street.

"Slashed his commission to one percent. It's unheard of in London! The fucking prick has priced everyone out of the race."

"So now wouldn't be a good time to tell you he'll be at the anniversary party tomorrow night?"

Drew's jaw tenses to snapping point. "No, Jesse, now would not be a good time."

"Oh."

"You need a drink," Sam muses.

"No, I need a good fuck, Sam, and that's exactly what I'll get once I've finished lunching with you two girls. I'm fucking starving." Off he goes, every step angry, his pace quite speedy.

"He really is hungry," Sam quips, just as Drew stops again and answers his phone. We pass him, getting the full force of his explicit outburst before he hangs up, straightens his jacket, and follows us.

"I'm over it," he declares, and I laugh as I enter the bar, my eyes, as if they know exactly where to find her, landing on Ava immediately. She has that split expression she often sports, the one that's part delighted and part pissed off. She's happy but not happy to see me.

I look at Kate, and she nods subtlety, telling me silently that she's come through for me. Good girl.

Fucking hell. Am I really doing this?

I give Ava a kiss on the cheek, faltering from pulling away when I catch a whiff of wine. It's hardly past noon. And it's a working day —a working day that we're only halfway through.

Be reasonable, brother. Once upon a time, you watched the clock like a hawk, wishing midday would arrive sooner.

I inwardly laugh. Exactly. It wasn't healthy. Healthy drinking is social drinking, maybe once or twice a month. Definitely not on a lunch break. What would Patrick say?

I pull a chair across and lower, feeling at Ava's thigh, making up for lost time. I can feel her glaring at me.

"You took my car keys," she says, full of indignation.

I ignore her. I didn't come to lunch to argue. "Everyone okay?"

"I'm good," Kate chirps, as Ava fights to withdraw her leg from my touch and I, with little fight, keep it exactly where it is. "And I'm ordering," Kate goes on, grabbing the menu and standing. "What's everyone having?"

"Salad for me," Sam says, settling. "You know what I like."

I raise a brow as Drew scans the menu. "I'll have the club, extra bacon, easy on the pickles, loaded fries, some slaw, and a beer." He slaps the menu on the table. "Please."

"And a side of sex," Sam adds.

"That's for dessert." Drew smiles sarcastically and slumps back in his chair. I look at Ava, finding her watching me, daydreaming.

"You've had a drink." The accusation falls out of my mouth, and she freezes, looking incredibly guilty.

"It was an accident."

It's just a glass of wine. *One* glass. "I don't mind you having a drink if I'm with you, Ava," I say, hoping to eliminate the guilt, returning my attention to Sam and Drew. *One* glass.

"Well, it should be a sport," Drew says, as Kate returns with a waiter who's carrying a tray of drinks.

"What should?" I ask.

"Fucking." Sam smiles up at Kate when she passes him a beer. "Don Juan here thinks he's a pro."

"I am," Drew grunts.

"Wasn't Don Juan famous for seducing women?" Kate asks. "You don't want to seduce, Drew, you just want to fuck. Right?"

Drew points his bottle of beer at Kate, and I look out the corner of my eye, wondering what Ava's making of this. Nothing, apparently. She's still just watching me. I squeeze her thigh, snapping her out of her daze, and she smiles.

"Right," Drew confirms. "And it should be considered an extreme sport."

"So"—Kate's tongue is in her cheek as she lowers to a chair—"How's Victoria?"

I purse my lips and turn my attention Drew's way, along with everyone else around the table.

"Don't ask. She's sweet, but God, she's got to lighten up."

I feel Ava shift under my hold of her leg. "Why did you ask her to go?" she asks, surprising me. How does she know Drew invited Victoria to The Manor? I look at Kate, whose lips form a straight line. Kate told her. Sam told Kate. Drew told Sam.

"It's who I am," Drew says, no apology. "It's what I like."

"Amen." Sam toasts thin air, and Kate joins, hitting her glass against his bottle, both of them smiling knowingly. *Fucking hell.* I discreetly look out the corner of my eye to Ava and find what I knew I would. Wide eyes.

"Anyway"—Drew leans back in his chair, pushing his chest out, stretching—"I've got to make the most of it. Get to thirty-five and it's a slippery slope down to a saggy arse and man boobs." I frown and peek down my front. Is it? My arse cheeks, which I don't mind saying, are like rocks, naturally tense. "I'll think about a woman who loves me for me and not for my body when I need to," he adds, relaxing again, looking around the table at the endless exasperation.

Suddenly, every muscle in my body starts to tense and relax, over and over, my thirty-seven-year-old mind telling me I need to work out more. For fuck's sake. I'm outrageously fit. In incredible shape. But good shape doesn't always mean good health.

Thirty-eight on Monday.

The thought makes me hold Ava's leg tighter. She hasn't asked me when my birthday is. She hasn't told me hers either, not that she needs to. Her driver's license is imprinted on my mind after I had a bad-mannered rummage through her handbag on our first meeting. February 27th. Which sucks incredibly, because she only just turned twenty-six a few months ago. Which means I'm only eleven years older than her for three months. For the other nine months of the year, I'm a whole twelve years older than her.

I grimace and sink into my chair. A birth date is kind of standard information in a relationship.

Boundless. The natural progression.

"Well, I've only got nine years left, so I'd better get my fill." Kate's dry quip wakes me from my silent musings. Nine years until she's thirty-five. God, how I wish I could be young again. How differently I would have done things. But as I look at Ava, who appears to be in a consistent state of shock this lunchtime, I hate the notion that by doing anything different in my life, I might not have met her. And once again I'm mulling over the painful fact that I've had to lose everything I've ever loved to find her. I swallow and drop my eyes to the table. *Anything it takes to keep her*. Because I can't fucking lose again.

"It hits us women worse than you lot."

I look up and see Kate waving a wine glass around in the air, her attention on *us lot*. The men. Though what she's talking about, I can't recall.

"Is that what happened to you, Jesse?" Ava asks, forcing me to push away my depressing thoughts and think really hard about what the fuck we were talking about. My arse cheeks clench again, as if reminding me.

"No." I look at her, relishing her poorly concealed grin. "Do *you* think I'm lacking in the body department?"

"You know I don't."

"So, I'm still your god?"

"You're an arrogant god."

I haul her into me and kiss the daylights out of her. Would she let me be more than just her arrogant god? Like . . . her arrogant husband? *Boundless*. She pushes herself into me, taking everything I'm giving and at the same time begging for more, her tongue greedily dueling with mine. It's a good sign. I hear the mocking sounds of our friends from around the table and release her, enjoying the sight of her flushed face for a few moments.

"Seriously, you guys," Kate moans, and I glance at her. She's smiling. She was half asleep this morning when I called her, but she thinks this rhino's idea is a good one. Great. Me too. "Here's the food, so enough with the sloppy shit."

"Feeling left out?" Sam asks, smothering her, making her push him off. He takes a few French fries and shoves them past his lips, smiling around his chewing when Kate shakes her head.

"Eat up, baby," I say, putting Ava's plate in front of her.

"You eat up too," she retorts, mimicking my move and dragging my plate closer. "Sorry, they didn't have peanut butter."

"Criminal," I mutter, collecting my fork and stabbing at a chip, keeping one hand free and on Ava's thigh. "How's the van?"

Kate sighs and swallows. "Dreamy. If you weren't so stinking rich, I'd offer to pay you back."

"Very honorable of you. Lucky for you, I'm stinking rich." I cast a look across to Ava. "So rich, in fact, Ava could give up work if she liked."

"She doesn't like," she says over a laugh. "Because *she* loves her job."

"Don't I know it," I mumble. "What about your own business?" I ask, casual, feeling three sets of interested eyes bouncing between me and Ava.

"I've never thought about it." She frowns, and I smile on the inside. That's one seed planted. How fast can I make it grow? "Maybe one day. Patrick is a great boss, and I'm not really in any position to take a leap so big. I've not even got my own place."

I dart a stunned look her way, and she flinches, looking apologetic. She still doesn't see Lusso as her home. She still doesn't see my money as hers. For fuck's sake, what will it take?

"I delivered a cake in the shape of a penis today," Kate pipes in, an obvious attempt to distract me from my grievance. "It was massive."

"I got to spread the icing," Sam adds, proud. "I've never seen a cake ejaculate before."

Ava laughs, and I shake my head in dismay while Drew looks plain horrified. "Who the hell orders a penis cake?" He considers the chip in his hand, the tip dowsed in mayo, and grimaces, dropping it to his plate and brushing off his hands. "I'm full."

"Everything set for tomorrow night?" Kate asks casually. I've not known her long, but I can see the effort it's taking her to appear nonchalant, but there's an excited glint in her blue eyes. I hope Sam knows what he's doing.

"All set," I confirm as Ava pushes her plate away. Naturally, I inspect the remains, seeing she's made a good effort. I consider the other half of the sandwich in my grasp, feeling full. I'll never manage the rest. It's nice to have an appetite these days, but my stomach just isn't used to this volume of food.

"I better get back to work," Ava says, standing.

"I'm coming." I get up, casting the rest of the sandwich aside, ignoring Ava's protest. She says her goodbyes while I check the bill and slip some money under a beer bottle, nodding at Kate as I do. "I got it," I say when Sam dips into his pocket. "You can buy me afternoon tea on our next date."

He laughs and shakes my hand as Drew stands. "Thanks, mate. I'm feeling the pinch since that prick of an estate agent moved in on my turf."

"For real?" Sam asks, alarmed.

Drew's pleading fucking poverty for the sake of it. He's minted, and a few lost deals won't change that. "You want me to suspend your membership while things are tight?" I ask.

He scowls, and it's fucking fierce, ignoring my outstretched hand. "Fuck off, Jesse. The Manor is the only thing keeping me sane."

I smile and collect Ava, leading her out of the bar. "Hey," Kate calls, making us both slow. "Saturday night, girly drinks?" Is that a question or a reminder? I pout. I had planned on spending all weekend with Ava. The anniversary tomorrow, vegging on Saturday, maybe asking her something . . . major.

Ava turns to face Kate, and I sense her tension, although Kate's interested gaze aimed my way keeps my attention. What's she playing at? Testing me? Goading me? Her earlier words on our phone call suddenly ring in my head.

Depends? Are you gonna chill the fuck out a bit?

I had laughed. Wondered what the fuck she was talking about. "Depends if your mate persists with the never-ending insolence," I had replied. "So will you help?"

Kate had agreed. Laughed. But she was serious about me chilling out.

This is a test.

"Maybe next week," Ava says, a little high-pitched and squeaky.

I desperately search for the words I need to prove to Kate that I can pass her test. "You can go." I spit it out fast before my mouth seizes shut. She can go out, but you bet your arse she won't be drinking in excess. In fact, probably best she doesn't drink at all, especially if she insists I'm not allowed to go with them. Which she will.

"No," Ava retorts, adamant. "We have The Manor anniversary tomorrow. I'll be knackered." I'd like to think she's dead set on spending the whole weekend with me. Sadly, I realize she's simply trying to avoid a showdown in front of our friends. Kate can go fuck herself if she thinks she's putting me on the spot and I'll bow. Not when it comes to Ava's safety and my sanity.

"Hey, he said it's cool." Kate's eyes remain on mine. She must see the warning radiating from me.

"I'll speak to you later."

"Oh, yes, of course." Kate, her grin impish, returns her attention to Ava, and I appreciate the alleviation of pressure immediately. "Later."

I pull Ava on, keen to get myself out of the spotlight and any further scrutiny, damning Kate's arse to hell. Testing me. I might take that fucking van back.

As we wander side by side down the pavement, Ava tucked under my arm, I feel the familiar sense of despondency creeping up on me. That was the fastest hour in the history of hours. And the next four hours are guaranteed to feel like days. I notice Ava's laser focus stare aimed forward, her face contemplative. And I know exactly what she's thinking.

She stops and looks at me. "If I go out, I won't be drinking, will I?"

"No." I don't beat around the bush. Honestly is the best policy.

I flinch at my own thoughts—I have a nerve—and Ava marches

off, looking quite exasperated. I just don't understand. Why on earth would she want to make herself vulnerable like that? Risk making terrible choices, and then have a god-awful hangover to show for it that'll wipe her out for a day, therefore steal more time from me. "You can have a drink at the party," I call, going after her, hoping to appease her. If she must drink, fine, but we need to come to mutually agreeable terms, and *my* presence in the presence of alcohol seems reasonable.

"Would you get the doormen to spy on me too?" she asks.

She has such a negative perception of everything. "I don't ask them to spy on you, Ava. I ask them to watch over you."

"And call you if I don't follow the rules?"

"No," I say slowly, nudging her, tightening my arm around her neck on a roll of my eyes. "And call me if you are rolling around on the bar floor." I look at the back of her head accusingly. "With your nonexistent dress around your waist." That fucking dress.

She has no comeback, as proven when she remains silent and lets me walk us on to her office. I wonder if today is the day she gets over it and lets Patrick know that we're together.

But . . . no.

"You've got to let me go now," she says quietly, tentatively. We need to fix this. Her parents, her boss. They should know about us. I grumble a protest that she ignores. "What are you going to do for the rest of the day?"

"Think about you."

She sighs. "I'll be back at yours as soon as I finish work.".

My God, what will it take for her to accept where she lives? "Ours," I grate. "What time?" I need specifics. I won't offer to pick her up. I know she'll refuse so, although it kills me, and feels completely fucking pointless when I'm free, I refrain.

"Six-ish."

There's that word again. *Ish*. Translated, vague. "You like that tag on, don't you?" I tilt my head as she shifts uncomfortably. "Ish."

She reaches up, puckering her lips. It's an opportunity I would never pass up. I seize her and get my fix, swooping her over my arm, kissing her madly. "God, I fucking love, love, love you," I whisper, and she smiles, looking up at me as I scan every inch of her face, refreshing all of it in my mind.

"I know you do."

Standing her up, I put my face in her neck, feeling myself swelling up behind my trousers. *Oh dear*. But it's inevitable. *Fucking work.* "I can't get enough of you," I bite at her flesh, sucking, licking. "Let me take you home."

She doesn't have the chance to answer, her phone interrupting us, but I don't let it deter me from my intended persuasion as she rummages through her handbag and I continue ravishing her throat. Which means when she silently groans, I feel the vibration against my lips. I seriously dislike how tense she's become too.

I withdraw, finding her face. Don't like her expression either. "Who is it?" I ask.

Her phone goes into her bag unanswered. "Just a client. I'll see you at your place." She moves away a bit too hastily. Hate that too.

"Damn it, Ava." I grate. "*Ours*." It's *our* fucking place. "Who was it?" Has a stupider question ever been asked?

"It's Mikael." She has the nerve to appear affronted. Inconvenienced. Should I assure her that her feeling of inconvenience has nothing on mine? "*Just* a client." She pretty much wrenches herself out of my hold and marches away, while I watch, astounded at her obstinate reaction. She disappears into her office, answering her phone when it rings again. The persistent fucker. Every muscle in my body winds tight, a stressed sweat breaking out, and my feet are moving before I have a chance to convince them it's a bad idea. That if they carry me into that office, I'll more than likely find myself in Ava's bad books with not much chance of charming my way out of them. I know it better than I know my name. I know I should turn back. Take a breath.

And yet . . .

I catch the door before it closes and follow her to her desk, ignoring her colleagues whose eyes are fixed on my heaving, agitated frame. She sits, spins in her chair, and nearly falls off it when she finds me at the foot of her desk. Her dark eyes widen. Her mouth hangs open. Her stare jumps from the people behind me to the office behind her. And still, she's more concerned about them than the fact that I'm clearly . . . upset.

My eyes narrow, and every part of my brain tells me to seize her mobile and smash it to pieces, eliminating the chances of him calling her again. But he could call the office. Email her. Drop by.

Fuck.

Her phone at her ear shakes. "Mikael," she stammers, trying to gather herself. "I'm sorry." A shake of her head. "Yes, fine." She frowns. "Yes, fine," she repeats. "Thank you." And then she's pushing herself back into her chair, swallowing. "Pardon?" she whispers. Dread fills me, my hands twitching. *What is that fucking bastard saying?*

She just stares at me. Stares, silent, while Mikael says . . . what? She clears her throat, having another check behind her before tilting her head at me in question. I can't talk. Can hardly fucking move, I'm paralyzed by trepidation. "A month-ish," she whispers, uncertain.

I stare at her, in a muddle.

"Why would it be?" she asks, her eyes getting progressively wider. "Okay." She cuts the call, her chest rolling with her deep breaths. I can't move. Can't speak. I also can't read her. She looks pissed, but is that because of what he's said, or simply because I'm standing in her office? I know Ava. She wouldn't want to cause a scene at work, so is she holding out on me until we get home? Waiting to unleash her disgust, really give it to me, before she walks out on me?

"I'm at work," she finally says on a breath of air after what feel like eons of just staring at each other.

"You won't see him again," I grate.

"Why?"

I hold on to my exhale. *Why?* He's not told her? I can't be relieved. He's poking. Stirring. "You just won't," I affirm. "It's not a request, Ava. You won't defy me on this."

"I'll see you at Lusso," she retorts, her words tight. Translated, this conversation is not over. And she didn't say *home*. Our home.

"Yes, you will." I force my dead legs to life and get my arse out of there before any one of my muscles pings and has me bouncing around her office and smashing it up. I make it outside and drink in the fresh air ravenously, leaning on the side of the wall to hold me up. I'm struggling to breathe. Stand. Think.

I stagger to the end of the street and round the corner, leaning my back against a wall, yanking at a tie that isn't there in an attempt to breathe easier. Lifting a hand, I wipe my brow, looking down at my phone in my hand, taking a few deep breaths. "Fuck this shit." I dial him, and the fucker lets it ring and ring, meaning I get more and more worked up. He sends me to his voicemail, and I quickly hang up before I blow the fucking thing up. Be calm. Don't let him know I'm affected by his games.

"Hey!" I look up and see Kate approaching, her smile falling when she sees the state of me. "What's happened?"

Where would I even begin? If I had the energy or inclination, I'd ask her what the fuck she's doing, adding more stress to my life by throwing in girls' night out. Fortunately for Kate, I have more pressing matters to deal with. "Nothing." I make a poor attempt to smile.

"Is this about us going out on Saturday, because—"

"No, Kate, it's nothing to do with you going out on Saturday." I wish it was. "I'm just—" What the fuck do I say?

"Nervous?"

"Yes, nervous."

She smiles and holds up a small pouch, and I accept it, tucking it into my pocket. "I'll see you tomorrow." I start walking aimlessly, feeling her eyes on my back as I go.

I need to ride.

Run.

I'd probably kill myself if I did either right now. So instead, I pass the street where my car's parked and cross Piccadilly to Green

Park. I need to clear my head in a way that doesn't risk my life. Or anyone else's for that matter.

And still, it's not the brightest idea I've had. The moment I step foot into the park, I hear the sounds of a little girl's squeals, and I still, closing my eyes, the noise melding into a familiar shriek of delight. And with it comes pain of excruciating levels. I try so fucking hard to block it out, walking on, sidestepping dog walkers, joggers, mums with prams. Breathing becomes strained. My shirt sticky with sweat.

I come to a stop, realizing I've reached the other side, and look up at Buckingham Palace. I could turn and go back, but as I look over my shoulder, all I see is a gauntlet of triggers that need to be avoided. I've never been in the park at this time. Always at the crack of dawn when there's no one around except fellow runners, or on the odd occasion, late afternoon when mums have taken the kids home for their dinner. I face the palace again, looking left and right, and carry on, just walking, aimlessly.

But not so aimlessly.

I reach St. James Park.

Enter.

Carry on walking, now numb to my surroundings, until I reach Duck Island. I asked for this. For this pain. *More* pain. More reminders. I take the few steps needed to get me to a bench and collapse onto it, feeling so fucking weak. So vulnerable. I close my eyes, terrified about what they might see and the further bedlam it may cause me. And I just sit there, praying the answer to all of my problems finds my sorrowful state here on the bench in a park in central London. Praying for mercy.

"Daddy!"

I snap my eyes open on a crashing beat of my heart. I see nothing —none of the people roaming, the kids playing, the runners running. I see only one thing. My treasured, dearest thing.

"Quack, quack, Daddy."

I get up and go to her, kneeling to help her open the bag of seeds, but her little impatient hands tear it open, scattering the bird seed far and wide.

"Oopsie daisy."

"Oopsie daisy," I mimic quietly on a smile, as a gaggle of ducks waddle up from the water, ambushing us.

"Quack, quack."

They peck, flap their wings, and squabble around our feet as Rosie giggles, flapping her arms, waddling around with them.

"Quack, quack."

"Come here." I scoop her up, out of the chaos crowding our legs, and swing her onto my shoulders. I peek up. She's still flapping, quacking, laughing.

And it's precious. So fucking precious.

"That your phone, mate?"

I look back and find a runner stretching, his foot wedged into a bin, lunging into it. Disorientated, I glance around seeing the low railings that's between us, putting a barrier between the path and the lake, stopping people getting too close to the water. I'm standing on the edge of the lake, and I have no fucking clue how I got here. My heart kicks. I look up, feeling around my shoulders.

Gone.

My breath hitches, still feeling the weight of her there. "Shit." I roughly wipe at my eyes, reversing my steps, and swing my leg over the railings, putting myself on the right side. I go to the bench and drop to the wood. I never dreamed I could feel the same level of adoration again. The peace. The purpose. Could I really have one last chance at happiness? And yet, it's hanging in the balance, the threats to it relentless.

I feel around in my pocket and pull out my phone, along with the pouch Kate gave me.

Whatever it takes.

I wince and check the time. An hour has passed. And then I answer his call. "Jesse Ward," I say coolly. Quietly.

"So when was the last time you fucked my wife?"

I don't answer that question. *Can't* answer that question. He knows, but I'll be damned if I'm confirming. "Stay away from her, Mikael."

"Or else?"

I have no *or else*, and he knows it. "And keep your wife away from me too."

"Ex-wife. She's returned to Denmark to see her mother. Licking her wounds, I expect."

"She meant nothing to me, Mikael," I say, needing him to know that. If that makes me sound like a heartless bastard, I'll take it. If it makes me sound desperate, I'll take it.

"Which time?"

I breathe in, locking down my muscles, forcing calm. "Stay away from Ava. Stay away from me." I hang up, clenching my phone tightly. The space around me is busy now, my eyes allowing me to see real life. And feel it. But I want to stay with my baby girl, listening to her uninhibited giggles. But then I wouldn't have Ava. How can love cause such mutinous conflict?

I consider the velvet pouch in my hand, clench my fist around it, stand, and walk back to my car.

I need to make friends with Ava. And I need to tell her about Mikael.

I just can't go on like this.

25

I'VE SAT outside The Manor, staring at the steering wheel for so long, it's no longer a steering wheel. It's a black blur of nothing. My playlist finished God knows how long ago, and my arse is dead. I'm forced to move when my phone rings in my back pocket, lifting my backside to pull it out. Steve. "Hi," I say, settling back down.

"The white BMW is registered to a Matthew Gary Turner."

Matt. My eyes burn into the glass windscreen before me, every inch of me stiffening. I've spent most of today feeling pretty fucking strung, my whole fucking body is now aching. "Matthew Turner," I repeat, sounding surprisingly calm. Perhaps because I have no rage left inside me. Nothing left to give.

"That's right," Steve replies. "You know him?"

"Yeah, I know him." I hang up, my mind chasing in circles around this new addition to my overflowing pot of shit. What the fuck is he doing hanging around The Manor?

Tap, tap, tap.

"Fucking hell," I breathe, jumping in my seat.

"You gonna sit here all day?" Sam asks, opening my door for me. "You've been here for over an hour."

I exhale and get out, stretching my body as I look up at The Manor, then at my watch. "I need to go," I say, dropping back to the seat and pulling the door shut, starting the engine. It's gone five. By the time I've battled my way back through the traffic to Lusso, it'll be gone six. Ava will be home.

Sam pulls the door open again, and I fight with him to get it shut. "What the fuck's going on?" he asks. "What's wrong?" I turn tired eyes onto him, and he withdraws. "Shit, Jesse, you've got to tell her."

I laugh. Yeah, just like that, tell the woman I love—the woman I'd die for—that I put my dick in two other women. "I might not have to."

"Why?"

"Van Der Haus knows about me and Freja. He also knows about me and Ava. Which means he's currently piecing together a timeline to confirm his suspicions while stirring up a pretty lethal pot of shit."

"Oh shit."

"Yes. And on top of that, I just found out Ava's ex has been hanging around outside The Manor. Call me suspicious, but I get the feeling he's digging for shit on me to feed to Ava." Just another someone trying to stop me remaining in heaven, although heaven feels like fucking hell right now.

"So what are you going to do?"

"Grow some fucking balls and tell Ava about Freja before someone else does."

"Good plan."

"Right after I ask her to marry me." I slam the door and whack my car into gear, but just as I'm about to pull off, Sam throws himself in front of my Aston, slamming his palms down on the bonnet. I flinch, staring at him incredulously, as he stares back with wide, worried eyes. "The fuck?" I yell, getting out.

"Yes, the fuck," he shouts back, marching round to the door. "Are you fucking insane?"

I cock a brow, insulted. "Do you have a death wish? What's so insane about wanting to marry her?"

He stares at me, just stares, and eventually shakes his head. In despair, I think. "You are." He throws his hands up and goes to his Porsche. "You're fucking insane."

"Who's insane?" Sarah asks, strutting across the gravel in her skyscraper heels. I throw Sam a warning look that he can't appreciate because he's not looking at me.

"Him," he yells, firing his fob at his car. "Someone needs to have a word with him."

Sarah looks me up and down. "Why have you been sitting out here in your car for over an hour?"

"I was on a call." I slide back into my car.

"I thought you'd be with Ava, actually."

"Well, clearly I'm not, am I?" And she's probably not talking to me either. I stall, my door half closed, and look up at Sarah. "Why would you think I'd be with Ava?"

She frowns, stepping back, like she could be removing herself from the firing range of something. I'm worried that something is me.

"Sarah," I say slowly, quietly. "Why would you think I'd be with Ava now?"

She looks across to Sam, who's by his car, door open too, but he's not got in. He looks as curious as I feel. And worried. "Well . . ." she says, fading off.

"Sarah, fucking spit it out."

"I overheard her saying she was picking up her things from her ex's. I just assumed you'd go with her."

"Oh fuck," Sam breathes.

My phone ringing screams from every speaker in my car, John's name flashing up on the dashboard. I punch the green button on my steering wheel. "She's been picked up by Kate," John says.

"I know." I cannot fucking believe she's done this. I slam my door and spin away, the back end of my Aston zigzagging across the gravel uncontrollably. "Follow them and tell me where they go," I order.

"Seriously, Jesse?"

"Yes, seriously, John. She's going to her ex's to pick up some stuff, and I've just this moment found out that it's his white BMW that I've seen outside the gates *twice*."

"A white BMW?"

"Yes."

"Motherfucker," he breathes.

"You've seen it too?"

"Yeah, I've seen it." I hear the engine of his Range Rover start. "Can you make me a promise?"

"No." I don't indicate at the gates, hardly stop to check the traffic either, earning myself a few angry horn honks. I look up to my rearview mirror, seeing Sam's Porsche kissing the arse of my Aston. He's waving his arms like a mad man, angry, and a call comes through over John's. "I'll call you when I'm back in the city."

"Wait," John says. "You promise me there will be no physical."

"Promise," I lie, hanging up and taking Sam's call.

"Slow the fuck down," he orders, raging. "You'll get yourself fucking killed, then you'll be marrying no one."

"Yeah, I don't think I'm gonna get a yes from her after what's about to go down." The red in my vision won't shift. It's the final straw. Mikael, Freja, and now Matt? I am so over trying to hold it together.

"Jesse, calm the fuck down."

I hang up, tired of hearing it. *Calm down. Calm down.* They're like broken fucking records. I come up fast behind a Mercedes, a bend in the road up ahead stopping me from overtaking.

It should stop me.

It doesn't.

I put my foot down and zip out, dropping a gear and slamming my foot down, the sound of the Mercedes horn following me as I glide past. I look up at my mirror, seeing Sam close behind, not willing to lose me. And as expected, my phone rings again. "If I make it to the city alive, I'm going to fucking kill you. After everything, Jesse. Jake, Carmichael, Rosie, Rebecca, you drive like this?"

I look at the road, my focus set. Getting behind the wheel has always been dicey. The anger that churns up inside. The resentment that I've driven like a madman for years and am still breathing.

Carmichael was a good driver. It didn't save them.

My knuckles become bloodless around the wheel, my foot heavier on the accelerator, and I drive like a complete arsehole all the way to the city. I call John back when I'm nearing Wimbledon. "Heading west," he says flatly.

West? "Kensington, Holland Park, Notting Hill?"

"Could be any. I'm on Bayswater Road approaching Victoria Gate. Traffic's shocking."

I gage how far away I am from them as I hang up and dial Steve. "Matthew Turner. Is there an address you can give me?" If he talks about scratching backs again, I can't promise I won't turn psycho.

Because you're not already?

"Ladbroke Crescent."

"Where's that?"

"W11."

"Notting Hill." I hang up and enter the street name into my Sat-Nav before calling John. "W11. Ladbroke Crescent."

"You calmed down yet?"

"Nowhere close."

I pull into the street and see John's Range up ahead, as well as Kate's van. Kate looks more than alarmed when I skid to a stop and get out, and John comes to me, hands up, pacifying. Nah. Not happening. "The fuck, Kate?" I yell. "You didn't think to tell me?"

"Tell you?" She laughs, waving her hands up and down my raging frame. "No, I didn't think to tell you. Didn't even cross my fucking mind, because she's *just* picking up her stuff."

"I told her not to!"

"What's your fucking problem, Jesse?"

I feel my nostrils flare, my hand going up and pointing at the row of houses. "My problem is the last time he saw her, he tried to get back in her knickers. My fucking problem is, Kate, he wants her back and he might convince her he's worth a second chance." I breathe out, exhausted, and stamp a few steps away, leaving Kate wide-eyed and wary. After all, Ava must have loved him. "Fuck!" I look at the houses. There's only one with the front door open. Just one. If I go in there, it'll be carnage.

I take a few deep breaths and scrutinize the street, seeing his white BMW. The sly fucker. I snarl, balling my fists, and stalk to the door, following my feet, instinct telling me where to find her. I take the stairs, yelling her name, feeling so fucking out of control. Panicked. Stressed.

I burst through the open door and find them standing close. Face to face. How cozy. I keep my eyes on Ava, truly afraid of what I might do if I look at Matt. She appears dazed. Worried? She should be. She's completely disregarded my wishes. Came anyway, when I overtly told her not to. It's a piss-take. I can't imagine she'd be all too fond of me seeing an ex, lying to her, going behind her back.

I gulp back my anger. Not anger at Ava. Anger at myself. My nerve. My foolishness. My hypocrisy.

"What the fuck are you doing here?" I shout, sounding unhinged. Feeling it. Totally out of control with no chance of getting it back.

She remains silent, unwilling to talk, unwilling to even try and pacify me. Explain. Reassure me. "Answer me!"

She jumps, and I wince, hating the sight of her wary expression. But can I help it? My heart is beating so fast it hurts. It's a sign. It's no longer dead. "I fucking told you," I bellow. "Don't ring him, don't come here. I said John would do it. Go and get in the fucking car," I order, pointing to the door.

The sound of a chuckle foils my plan to *not* kill Matt, and I look at him, astounded, as he tries to get his amusement under control. He's blown it. Asked for it.

Ava hurries out with a box and I turn into him, flexing my fists.

"We kissed," he says, looking really fucking pleased with himself.

They kissed? They fucking *kissed*? Any hope there was of me walking out of here without an assault charge filed against me is lost. I swing at him, delivering an accurate, powerful right hook to his face, sending him staggering back into a wall on a grunt. "You come near her or my manor again, I'll fucking kill you, Turner."

He blinks, part dazed, part surprised. And now I'm going before I end the bastard and am up for murder. I leave him behind, nursing a bloody nose and take the stairs fast, knowing Ava will be making her escape. I discover a peanut gallery of spectators outside, John looking exasperated, Sam looking pissed off, Kate looking wary.

"John!" My fucking hand is throbbing, the damn injury renewed. "Put her stuff in the Rover."

"Leave it, John," Ava yells. "I'm not going with him." The big man stands in the middle of Kate's van and my Aston, palms facing the sky. "Kate, come on." Ava goes to the van and pulls the door open, looking back for her friend who's currently being held back by Sam.

"Get the bags, John." I take the steps down to the street and pace to the van, set to help him.

"Leave them!" Ava screams.

John gives me a look to suggest he'd like nothing more than to get in his car and leave us to hash this out, but he won't. He won't risk the potential backlash. Not from me, but from the law. So he goes to the van and starts taking the boxes out, and Ava, annoyed, hops in Kate's van.

I swing the door open. "Out," I demand, my vocal cords tight.

She fights to close the door again, a fucking pointless exercise. "Just fuck off."

"Mouth!"

"Fuck off," she screams in my face, her cheeks turning pink, her voice breaking.

"Watch your fucking mouth!" I decide physical force is the only way and wrap my arms around her, pulling her out of the van, dodging her flailing arms, manhandling her until I have her secured against my chest.

"Get off me," she hisses as I carry her to my car, squirming, kicking, prying at my hands.

"Shut your filthy mouth, Ava."

She boots me in the shin, and I hold my breath, grunting through the pain. I catch Sam's eye. He looks as disturbed as he should.

"Stop making a scene, Ava," I warn, mindful that the cops could show up at any moment, courtesy of any one of our spectators, and arrest me. And that won't be fucking pretty for anyone. I'm surprised when Ava actually listens and settles. Really surprised. Exhausted?

Me too.

I open the passenger door and put her in the seat, and she can't help but have one more burst of defiance, smacking at my hands as I try to put her belt on. Raging, I take her chin and force her face to mine. She breathes heavily, her expression pure filth. "You had better stay fucking put." She doesn't answer, just yanks her face free from my hold and looks away. I slam the door, take a few breaths, and look up, wiping my nose with the back of my hand. John jerks his head, summoning me, and I wander over, listening for the sound of Ava making an escape. I look back. She's still in her seat, watching. I can see her chest pumping from here.

"Wow," Kate breathes, and I laugh under my breath. I realize my behavior was extreme. Would I do things differently? Can't say I would. "She would never go back to Matt, Jesse. Trust me on that."

I gaze down at the concrete. I notice she didn't say she'd never leave me. I feel something skim my face and see John's boulder fist popping me one on the jaw in jest. I'm in no mood for it. "Don't, John."

"Calm the fuck down."

"Stop fucking telling me to calm the fuck down," I snap. "Everyone, just stop fucking telling me to do that." I stalk off, get in my car, and skid off, my hand screaming when I grip the wheel too tightly.

"How did you know I was here?" Ava asks. She's not done? She wants to fight some more?

"It doesn't fucking matter."

"It does matter. I was fine until you turned up."

I look at her, aghast. Fine until I showed up? "I'm fucking infuriated with you," I yell. "Did you kiss him?"

Her face. How can she appear so stunned? "No! He tried and I beat him off. I was just leaving."

I smack the steering wheel, really fucking hard, and it does my hand no favors. "Don't ever fucking tell me I'm possessive and over the top, do you hear me?"

"You are *stupidly* possessive."

"Ava, in two days I've caught two men trying to get in your knickers. God knows about the times when I've not been there."

"Don't be stupid. You're imagining things. How do you know Mikael?" she fires.

"What?"

"You heard me."

"I bought the penthouse, Ava. How do you think I know him?"

"He thought it was very interesting when I told him that we had been seeing each other for a month-ish. Why would he?"

Jesus fucking Christ. "Why the fuck are you talking to him about us?"

"I wasn't, he asked the question and I answered. Why would he think it's interesting, Jesse?"

"That man wants you, trust me," I yell, at a loss. My time's up.

"Why?"

I'm hitting the steering wheel again. "He wants to take you away from me!"

"But why?" she shouts.

"He just fucking does!"

She withdraws, backing off, settling in her seat, but her eyes remain on my profile, burning into me, her gaze now asking the questions instead of her mouth. I have nothing to offer in this moment. We both need to calm the hell down before we talk, because if I share anything about Mikael now, she'll spin off the handle with me, and this relationship needs only one psycho at a time, or we both might end up dead.

I swallow and force my foot off the pedal, slowing down the car, hoping calmer driving might lead to calmer moods. I glance across to her, seeing her hair in disarray, her olive cheeks tinged pink, her hands twiddling together. What is she thinking?

When I pull up outside Lusso, she's out of my car like a shot. "Ava," I call instinctively, even knowing I should let her go. Let her calm down and take the alone time to calm *myself* down too. My shoulders drop, my hands going into my pockets as I watch her go. Eager to escape me. And no, I'm not surprised.

John pulls up alongside my Aston and gets out, pulling his shades off.

"I'm calm," I say before he can tell me.

"You think throwing your weight around like that is going to help?"

"No, John, I don't, but it's become very obvious since I met Ava O'Shea that I can't seem to control myself and my impulses." Not my love, my desire, my temper. Nothing.

"Well, try."

I sigh. I have. I try every fucking minute of the fucking day. "I'll help you," I say, trudging to the back of his Range Rover as he opens the boot. "You sure you want to come in?"

"It's only you she's angry with, boy. Only you who sends her crazy." He grabs a box and leads the way, and we pass Clive, who looks quite chipper today.

"Mr. Ward," he sings, coming out from behind his desk and joining me.

"You polished the gold on your hat?" I ask, prompting him to reach up on a small grin.

"I met your housekeeper earlier. Lovely lady."

I slow to a stop. *Oh?* "She is." I hitch a brow. "And?"

"And, nothing." He takes the box from my hands and carries it to the elevator, putting it on the floor outside and calling it. "Just my observation." He holds out a set of keys. "I would have given them to Ava but she seemed to be in a hurry." He leans in, one eye narrowed. "And quite unhappy."

"Oh, you sensed that?" I say dryly as I pocket Ava's car keys. "I didn't notice." And shit, Cathy's here. I completely forgot about her return. I look at John. "I haven't told Ava Cathy's back." *Fuck it all.* I pass him and get in the elevator when it opens, and John collects the box Clive set down, joining me, as well as Clive.

I frown at the concierge, but he keeps his old eyes set on the doors, ignoring me. Nosey old fucker. I tap my foot impatiently as the lift carries us up to the penthouse, and I smell it as soon as the doors open. Cathy's lasagna. Something tells me I won't be enjoying a romantic dinner with my girl this evening.

"Hmm, that smell," John says, taking a long hit of it, his big chest swelling.

"Which smell?" I ask, trudging on. "The food or the tension?" I enter the penthouse and find Ava static, looking no less pissed off, and Cathy looking slightly alarmed, a can of some kind of cleaning product and a cloth in her hand.

For fuck's sake. What the hell has Ava said to her? "Cathy, you should probably get off now," I say as gently as I can, trying not to clue her in on the absolute carnage happening. "I'll speak to you tomorrow."

"Of course." She starts collecting her things, all the while flicking cautious eyes both our ways. "I've put dinner in the oven," she goes on. "Give it thirty minutes." She smiles nervously at Ava and comes to me. I kiss her cheek, eyes on Ava, slightly concerned about the remorse on her face.

She catches my eye. Looks past me to John and Clive. Then marches into the kitchen, not just eager to escape *me* now, but eager to escape her shame. The scrutiny. I hear the fridge door open, a huff, and then it slams, followed by her stamping feet again. She emerges and heads for the stairs, making a point of stomping her way up them.

"Jesus Christ," I breathe, dragging my palm down my face and following Cathy out to the elevator.

"Whatever's happened?" Cathy asks, looking quite shook up.

"Just a few words," I assure her, making John grunt in amusement. "I haven't had a chance to tell Ava you were here, Cathy."

"I gathered that." She blows out a breath and tugs her carpet bag into the crook of her arm.

"What did she say?" I ask, not sure I want to know.

"I can't possibly repeat it."

I wince. What a great start. "I'm sorry, she's had a bad day."

"Yeah, a few challenges to deal with," John pipes in, passing me with a box. I curl a lip at his back.

"Challenges?" Cathy asks.

"Don't ask," John calls. "You want a ride home?"

"Oh, yes please, although you'll need to give me a leg up into that big car of yours." She looks at Clive. "He's got a Chelsea tractor, Clive. I need a stepladder to get into it."

"I'll give you a leg up, Cathy." John gives my old housekeeper a rare flash of his gold tooth as he passes me again, collecting another box, and she chuckles. "Let me get the rest of the boxes up."

"I'll help," Clive declares, rolling up his proverbial sleeves and getting back in the elevator.

"Very good of you, Clive," Cathy says.

"He'll probably want paying," I grumble, joining them.

We ride down, and Cathy and Clive chat non-stop, while John and I remain mute, throwing each other curious looks every now and then.

Clive doesn't help at all. He remains in the foyer wooing Cathy with tales of his boxing career in the army while John and I haul the rest of Ava's stuff up to the penthouse. "Is it wise to leave you two alone together?" John asks, setting the final box down.

"I'm calm," I tell him, feeling it for the first time in too long.

"You know what I'm going to say, don't you?"

"Fix it."

"Exactly." He turns and takes his huge body out of my penthouse. "I'll call you later to check everyone's alive." The door closes, and I look toward the staircase. I want nothing more than to go to her, hug her, apologize for ram-raiding her day, if only to get us out of this ugly rut. But I know the wise thing to do is give her space. Time to take a breath and think clearly before she does anything hasty.

Like leave me.

I take one step toward the kitchen, intending on getting some water to ease my scratchy throat, but stop when Ava's handbag on the floor catches my eye. Or, more to the point, what's poking out of it. I crouch slowly and pull out a pot of pills. Vitamins? I turn the white pot in my hand, looking up at the stairs. Why would she be taking vitamins?

There's only one answer.

I inhale, dropping the pot back into her bag. Is that why she's behaving so erratically? Her hormones are all over the place because . . .

My muscles tighten, ready to lift me back to standing, when something else catches my attention. A piece of paper, and on the corner I see a logo from a flight comparison website. The squeeze of my heart? Don't like it at all.

I take the paper and unfold it, finding various flight times from various London airports.

All going to Sweden.

Next fucking week.

She's leaving the fucking country, and she hasn't thought to mention it? I don't—

My thought process stops right there, and the worst realization slams into me, making me reach for the nearby wall to hold me up. "No," I whisper, my eyes going back to the stairs. Sweden. Van der Haus's new apartment block is inspired by Swedish design. "Jesus, no." The fucker. And Ava thinks this is acceptable?

Like a bullet, I take the stairs, flying through our penthouse like a madman. I burst into our bedroom. Empty. Stalk to the bathroom, flinging the door open. She's on the chaise in the window, her eyes glassy. She's upset?

"What the fuck is this?" I bellow, flapping the offending piece of paper around my head.

A fleeting, very fucking telling look of panic washes across her blotchy face before she turns into Hulk with me. "You've been through my bag?" she shrieks. It's fucking ridiculous. I've been going through her bag regularly since I met her. Her bag, her phone, and in this moment, when my fucking life is literally hanging in the balance waiting for some suave Dane to sweep on in and pull the rug from under my besotted feet, I couldn't give a flying fuck. I don't answer her, just wave the paper more, reminding her that this isn't about my bad bag manners and everything about the fact that she thought she could elope to Sweden with an archenemy.

But she doesn't know he's an archenemy, bro. Because you haven't fucking told her.

I mentally tell Jake to shut the fuck up and watch his fucking mouth. The fact Van Der Haus is an enemy isn't the point. I wouldn't be all too tickled pink about her going anywhere with any man. Least of all him. Over my dead fucking body.

Could happen, bro. You're gonna give yourself a fucking heart attack at this rate.

Why the hell does he deem it appropriate to infiltrate my head at the most inappropriate times? If I didn't know him better, I'd think he's sadistically adding to my grievances, purposely reminding me of all the things I have to feel guilty about. But I do know him. He's just trying to be my brother. Jesus, he would have grown into a sarcastic fucker.

I'm suddenly knocked out of Ava's way as she stomps off, and I'm in quick pursuit. I want answers. I follow her down the steps, my lungs screaming for some respite, and endure the filthiest of looks as she swipes her bag from the floor and carries it into the kitchen.

"What the hell are you doing?" I yell, following her. She smashes her bag on the island and starts rummaging through. Is there more in there she needs to hide from me? "It's not in there, it's here. You are not fucking going to Sweden or Denmark or any fucking where, for that matter." Let's be clear on that.

She turns seething eyes onto me, her mouth straight and tight. "Don't go through my bag."

"Why, what else are you hiding from me?" I discard the paper and move away, truly concerned she might swing for me.

"Nothing," she shouts, her fists clenching the leather and squeezing, slamming it down again. She's imagining the bag's me.

"Let me tell you something, lady." I risk getting closer, since she's using her handbag as her outlet for now. I push my face close to hers, hoping she feels the white-hot anger. "I will die before I let you leave the country with that womanizing prick."

"He won't be coming!"

The bag gets another brutal beating, and I laugh on the inside. "Yes, he will. He'll follow you there, trust me. He's relentless in his pursuit of women." Is she that fucking naïve? Clearly she is, which is why it's crucial I keep her out of the reach of that bastard's charms. Next, he'll be inviting her to stay at his swanky Scandinavian home. Taking her skiing. For dinner. Will she try to convince me *he's just a client* then?

"Just like you?" she asks over a laugh, and I frown, rewinding back through the conversation. Relentless. Pursuit. Is she insinuating I'm like Van Der Haus? That I'd cheat on my wife? If I had one.

Jake clears his throat in heaven. *Fuck off!* "That was different." Lord, someone find me some calm before I explode.

"You're impossible."

No, not me. Us. We're impossible, because she will never understand. "And what are you doing taking vitamins?" I ask, keen to get to the bottom of that matter too. "You're pregnant, aren't you?"

She jerks back, like she's been hit with an arrow, her questioning face somewhere between disbelief and rage. She moves fast, hauling something at my head. *Fuck.* I dodge the flying object, looking behind me when it crashes into the wall, missing my head by a whisker.

"I bought the vitamins for you," she screams, pulling my eyes back to her. She's seriously lost the plot.

"Why?"

"You put your body through the mill," she says, breathless. "Have you forgotten?"

Forgotten? No, I'm still fucking suffering for it. I clench my battered hand and scowl. "I don't need pills, Ava," I say, incensed. She thinks a few pills can fix me? How many fucking times do I need to tell her? There's only one thing in this word that can fix me, and she seems determined to break me more. "I've told you." I take hold of her hands, pulling her close, and she breathes into my face, her head retracting back, her eyes darting. "I am not a fucking alcoholic,"

I say calmly. "If I drink now, it will be because *you* make me crazy mad."

"You blame this all on me," she whispers, and I flinch, ashamed, releasing her and walking a few paces away.

"No, I don't." It's everyone, not just her. "What else are you keeping from me?" I ask. "Business trips with rich Danish men? Cozy visits to the ex-boyfriend?"

"Cozy?" She more or less chokes. "You stupid fucking man."

"Mouth!"

"Get lost!" Her words are hissed, her face red, her tone truly venomous. Clearly, I'm not going to get an answer. Clearly, she thinks there's nothing wrong with leaving the country with another fucking man. I can't deal with this kind of irrationality. I feel volatile. Unhinged. It's not supposed to be like this. She's supposed to be my cure, but all I'm feeling is agony again, and I can't even fucking mask it with a drink.

"I can't be around you right now," I yell, feeling helpless. Hopeless. "I fucking love you, Ava. So fucking much, but I can't look at you." I have to leave. Get away from her, and that's something I *never* dreamed I'd feel. "This is fucked up." I walk out, slam the door, and call the elevator.

My foggy vision clears long enough for me to see the state of the man in the reflection of the doors.

Before I put my fist into his face on a roar.

The pain, the noise, the mess of glass spraying, adds that touch more chaos to my world. I abandon the elevator and take the stairs, my fist throbbing, my feet moving fast. Get away. Leave.

As I push my way into the lobby, I find Clive polishing the table between the chairs. Does this guy have a home? A life? "Mr. Ward," he says when he spots me. I keep up my pace, dipping into my pocket and pulling out some notes.

"Don't let Ava leave," I say, slipping a wedge into his hand as I pass. What a ridiculous request. "Or call me if she does."

"You can rely on me, Mr. Ward."

I fall into my car, start the engine, rev it hard, and reverse out of my space, skidding up to the gates that aren't opening fast enough, shaking my damn hand. I only make it to the end of the road before my car starts beeping. Great. Not only is my mood low, but so is my car on fuel. "God damn it," I breathe, turning left instead of right, heading for the nearest fuel station to fill up.

I pull in and stop sharply, sliding out and taking the pump, hissing when I try to squeeze the lever. "Fucking hell." I'm forced to switch hands, and as soon as the fuel starts flowing, I lean back against the car and close my eyes, breathing deeply. Fucked up is right. Stalling going to The Manor would be the wisest thing I could do. Buy myself time to talk myself out of seeking the solace I need.

Don't drink, brother.

I laugh under my breath. "So you're back, huh? Glad you've got something useful to say to me this time."

Do you miss me?

"Don't ask stupid fucking questions, Jake."

You saw Rosie today.

"That's not useful."

You're thinking of asking this woman to marry you, and you don't think you ought to tell her about your daughter? Your brother? She'll understand.

"It's not just telling her about you and Rosie, though, is it? It's about everything that comes with that, all stuff, Jake, I'm not all too fond of sharing."

It wasn't your fault.

"Yeah, it was," I whisper, swallowing. "It's all my fault, Jake. You, Rosie, Sarah, Carmichael, Lauren. I just have a knack for fucking up the good things, don't I? And now I'm fucking up me and Ava."

So you're just going to pretend I never existed?

I flinch, and the pump starts clicking behind me. I open my eyes. Look around me. A woman filling a Fiat 500 across the forecourt is looking at me warily. *Fucking hell.* I pull the pump free and jiggle it before hooking it back in the holder, then walk across the forecourt to the kiosk, smiling mildly at the woman as I pass. She quickly looks away. "Number five," I say, grabbing some gum from the stand on the counter. "And these." I open the pack and slip one into my mouth as I slide my card into the reader and tap in my PIN.

"Receipt?"

"No, thanks." I leave, not bothering to smile at the woman this time, and as I'm lowering into my seat, something across the main road catches my eye, making me hold the top of my car door and pull myself up again. I frown, squint, trying to zoom in. Blond hair. A slight frame. Women with those credentials are ten a penny, but . . .

I slowly shut my door, my feet carrying me to the side of the road. I'm on autopilot. My eyes fixed. My heart thrumming. I really am going fucking crazy. I go to step into the road and get yelled at, and I jump back, just as a van sails past, his horn screaming. "Fuck."

"Hey, mister, are you okay?"

I blink, looking at the teenager beside me on a pushbike. Then across the road again. She's still there. Watching. I check both ways, searching for a gap in the traffic to cross. I can make it after the coming bus if I run.

But when the bus passes, she's gone.

26

I WALK INTO THE BAR, stop, look at the top shelf past Mario, breathe in, turn, and walk out.

"Are you okay, Mr. Ward?" Pete asks, turning as I pass him, his tray balancing on his palm.

Clearly, I don't look it. "Fine, Pete." *Terrible, Pete.* I trudge through the foyer, looking up the stairs when I see someone descending them.

Drew. "Are you okay?"

"Fine." *Awful.* I enter the summer room, frowning at the semi-cleared space, my mind taking its time to catch up. The party tomorrow. Eyes fall on me from various members sitting on various couches, their conversations tapering off as they watch me stalk through.

John's in the corner, wrestling with a tangle of wires and cables. "All good?"

"Amazing." *Horrific.* I make it to the corridor, and Sarah emerges from the entrance that leads to the spa. I'm momentarily bewildered by the height of her heels, wondering how the fuck she walks on them, especially on the tile floor of the spa.

She slows to a stop, her eyes following me as I pass. "Everything all right?"

"Never better." *Never worse.* Although, painfully, I know that's not true. It can get so much worse.

I take the doorknob and curse when a wave of pain shoots through my hand, inhaling a hissed breath as I shake it and use my other hand to let myself into my office. I slam the door. Lean against it. Let the back of my head hit the wood a few times. My eyes fall to the still well-stocked cabinet, casting across the various bottles. I push away from the door with my shoulder blades and walk slowly over, eyes fixed on an unopened bottle of vodka. I stop. Stare at it for a while, then slowly reach out and take it in my grasp, lifting and lowering it, like a dumbbell, getting accustomed to the foreign object in my hold. It's been awhile. But it doesn't take much getting used to. The only difference is the biting pain in my fist.

I turn and rest my arse against the wood, using my spare hand to undo the button on my cuff and roll up my sleeve. Transferring the bottle and repeating, I stare at the couch where Ava sat the day she walked into my office and knocked me on my arse. The couch I bent two other women over and fucked. I drop my eyes to my Grensons, the weight of my guilt becoming too much. Eating me up inside. Making me see things, hear things.

Wiping my brow with the back of my hand, I go to my desk, drop into the chair, and place the bottle on the wood, sinking back into the leather and resting my elbows on the arms, threading my fingers.

Watching it.

There's numbness in that bottle. Escape.

I pull my phone out. Find my most recent picture of Ava. It's this morning. She's asleep in bed, quiet and peaceful. I felt quiet and peaceful too. It was downhill from there. But still, as I stare at the photograph of her, I know I'm looking at freedom. Not escape. Not detachment. I'm looking at feelings. Amazing feelings. I just have to exorcise my demons and release the ghosts. I never imagined how fucking hard that would be. Or what exactly would need to be done to make it happen.

I look up when the door opens. Sarah, her face uncharacteristically soft, holds up a bag of ice.

"Why did you never tell me what a fuck-up I am?" I ask. I admit, I've been burying my head in the sand all these years. Avoiding admitting who I really am. An arsehole. A poor excuse for a man.

"Who you are and what you do never mattered before you met Ava." She shuts the door and comes to me, circling the desk and resting her pert arse down, taking my hand and laying the bag over it. The instant relief is welcome, and I rest my head back, breathing out.

Who I am.

What I do.

Present tense.

Am I incapable of having normality? Unworthy of love? Because Ava just feels like a segue to fucking crazy.

"What's happened now?" Sarah asks.

I laugh, though not in amusement. "You know what happened. I found Ava at her ex's and . . ." I fade off before my mouth runs away with me. Telling Sarah Ava kissed her ex will do their relationship no favors. "My presence went down like a concrete balloon."

"Oh."

"Yeah. Suffice to say, Ava and I have fallen out." Understatement of the fucking millennium. Sarah looks down at my hand. "I punched the elevator," I say before she can ask. "And I stopped at the petrol station to fill up on the way here and . . ." I exhale. "I'm seeing things. Hearing things."

"Not Lauren again?"

I look at Sarah, hardly wanting to admit it. "I need to find her parents. Just check the situation."

"Check if the lunatic bitch is still locked up?" she asks, her hatred as real as it was all those years ago. As if naturally, Sarah's hand reaches up to her head, brushing over the small scar in her hairline. If you didn't know it was there, you'd miss it, her hair styled just right to conceal it. But I know it's there. "Jesse, there is no way on this earth any sane psychiatrist would release that woman into society."

"I know," I breathe, flexing my hand gently under the ice, it feeling a little less swollen.

"And what are you hearing?"

I peek up, my lips pressing together. "Jake." I expect her to laugh. She doesn't. Instead, her shoulders drop, and she gives me eyes full of sympathy. I've just confirmed beyond doubt how mixed up I am, while also proving that the whole Lauren thing really is just my eyes playing tricks on me. And I certainly see the irony that I can share this with Sarah but not with Ava.

You're thinking of asking this woman to marry you, and you don't think you ought to tell her about your daughter? Your brother? She'll understand. Not so sure about that. "Don't look at me like that." I can't stand it. It's exactly how Sarah looked at me for a long time after Lauren tried to rid the world of me. My ex-wife would have been doing the world a favor. I deserved it. She always straddled the line between sanity and insanity. I tipped her.

And now I'm tipping Ava.

The dying anger is resurrected, my fist balling under the ice. "How the fuck did you know Ava was going to her ex's?" I ask, my voice brittle.

Sarah withdraws, and I see her steely defenses rise to back her up. "I told you, I overheard her."

"Where? When? What exactly did she say?"

"Jesus Christ," she snaps, standing. "How the hell did something Ava's done to piss you off become my fault?" Storming away, she wrenches the door open, looking back, ready to fire more words at me. "This thing you've got with her is unhealthy. How she makes you feel, this, this"—she waves a hand up and down my bedraggled form—"the state of you. It's toxic."

"What?" I bark, knowing what she's saying is true, but hating hearing it. I can say it myself all I like. But someone else? No. Sarah and Ava will never be friends. They just need to accept each other's places in my life. Sarah has to accept Ava's place in my heart, Ava needs to accept Sarah's place in The Manor. *And my conscience.* "And being out of my head on vodka and women wasn't toxic?" I stand, furious. "Or are you just pissed off because I'm more coherent these days? Less chance of me bowing to the lure of you and your fucking whip?"

She recoils, injured, and the bastard guilt multiplies. "I've done nothing but be here for you for all these years. Protecting you from the claws of members. Running your fucking business for you. Yes, I may be a bitch from time to time, yes, I may say a few stupid things, but I'm fucking here, despite everything, Jesse, and a bit of fucking gratitude wouldn't go amiss from time to time." She leaves, slamming the door behind her, and I stare at it, a little wide-eyed. Gratitude? It's *how* she wants to express my gratitude that's the problem.

I lower to my chair but freeze mid-sit when door opens again, Sarah clearly not done. "Do you think I'm here for my health?"

I don't answer that, even though I could. It's a rhetorical question. Yes, she is here for her health. Her mental health. I don't know who she sees every time she whips some poor fucker in the rooms of The Manor, but it's what she needs. Like I needed drink and fucking. Escape. Can I hope Sarah finds the one thing that will offer her the peace she needs? The alleviation of guilt?

No, because she can never have what she needs.

Me.

"I'm sorry," I say, making sure I'm looking into her eyes when I say it. I'm not just apologizing for my rant. I'm apologizing for so much more. Most of all for not being able to give her what she wants. Some might say it's cruel to keep her around. Let her see me try to go on and live a normal life. Try to find my peace when she'll never have hers. But it would be crueler to cut the ties. She'd never survive without The Manor. Without me in her life in some small way. It's all she's ever known.

Swallowing, Sarah closes the door softly and comes back to the desk, pushing me down into the chair and placing the ice back on my hand. "Can you be around to help out tomorrow?" And just like that, we're back to business. And this is why it works. She *can* be reasonable.

I look at the couch across the office. My bed for the night. "Sure." Then I look at the bottle. I should ask Sarah to take it. Take it all.

"The gift bags are stored in the room next to the spa. Once the rest of the couches are moved out of the summer room later, we need to bring them through."

"I can do that."

"Remember, black for the men, gold for the ladies."

"Black for the men, gold for the ladies."

"And Drew's asked me to uninvite your estate agent friend."

I roll my eyes. Drew needs to get over Chris. "No. And he's not my friend. What about Niles?" I ask, eyebrow high.

"What about him?"

Look at her acting all nonchalant. "Don't tell me you've not imagined a thousand ways to whip that boy." Poor kid has no idea what he's letting himself in for. "Take it easy on him."

Sarah smiles. It's as salacious as fuck. Her hand rubs mine, and I roll my eyes at her. "You know me. Tender as a feather."

I shake my head, smiling on the inside as the door swings open. I look up, assuming I'll see the big man.

I assumed wrong.

Very, *very* wrong.

Oh fuck.

I feel every muscle in my face give, falling. She came? She came to a place she hates . . . for what? To end things? Tell me she's moved out? My questions, my worries, circle on loop as I stare at her on the threshold of my office looking at Sarah with contempt. Then her dark, troubled, really fucking angry eyes move across to me. She has no makeup on. Her hair is wet. But she's still wearing the blouse and trousers she had on for work today. She's showered but decided to come here. Again, why?

Nervous, I push my feet into the carpet and turn my chair toward her.

Away from Sarah.

Ava swallows. Sarah remains quiet. I'm grateful. This situation does *not* need her input.

"Have you had a drink?" Ava asks, throwing me off. I glance at the bottle on my desk briefly. That's her main worry here? The drink?

"No," I answer quietly. I may have looked at it. Touched it. But I will never let a drop pass my lips ever again. Not after the last time I succumbed to the enticement of escape. Not even after the day I've had today. My gaze falls to the desk, trying to push every shitty thing back so I can deal with the here and now, and I jolt with a start when something connects with my arm. When I realize it's Sarah's hand, I shoot my worried eyes to Ava. I knew Sarah couldn't resist having a fucking poke, even when she knows I'm in absolute pieces over . . . everything.

Things are going to kick off.

"Do you mind?" Ava says, her face a picture of incredulity, and I fold, bracing myself. Two women. Both feisty fuckers. Both in love with me. This is Sarah's domain. She will not take kindly to Ava's frostiness or her claim on me, even though I am irrevocably hers.

"Excuse me?" Sarah asks over a disbelieving laugh.

"You heard me."

Jesus Christ. Ava's nearly frothing at the mouth. She's jealous. It's wrong for me to feel a small element of satisfaction. So wrong, but after today—Mikael, Matt—I can't help it.

I also realize this makes me a monstrous hypocrite.

My hand throbs, and Sarah's fingers curl into my bicep, reminding me that her hand is still there. So I remove it, casting a nervous look to Ava, seeing if she's any nearer to pouncing on Sarah and clawing her eyes out. She's close. And when Sarah, God damn that woman, kisses my cheek, I lock down every muscle, stiff as a board in my chair. I want to tell Sarah to fuck off. *Get* off. Of course I do, but I comprehend that no matter how many times I do that, she will never listen to me.

So, as much as it pains me . . .

Over to Ava.

And, sickly, I quite like green on her.

"Call me if you need me, sweetie," Sarah says. She's fucking asking for it.

Ava opens the door. "Goodbye, Sarah," she says, prompting Sarah to slowly slip off the edge of my desk and walk, even slower, across the office, a certain, aloof sway to her hips, taking her sweet time. Fucking hell, the tension is unbearable.

Ava slams the door behind her, breathes out, and then faces me.

So . . . what now? A hissy fit, I expect. A barrage of questions. A reminder of who actually has the power in this relationship.

If there's still a relationship.

Is there still a relationship?

She nods at the bottle of vodka. "Why is that there?"

I look at it. Frown at it. "I don't know." Maybe I just wanted to torture myself some more. I seriously do not like her disposition. She's together, which is more than I feel. Looks pretty fucking determined. But determined to do what?

"Do you want to drink it?"

"Not now you're here." Cruel. So fucking cruel. And desperate.

"You walked out on me."

"I know."

"What if I hadn't come?"

If she hadn't come, I would have removed the temptation and crashed on the couch. And with that thought, I poke the bottle with my fingers, pushing it across my desk. I don't think I have any right to sound so sure. "I wouldn't have drunk it."

"Then why is it there?"

Because I'm a fuck-up, obviously. Because I am incapable to being in this relationship without ruining it. Because the safety casing around my self-destruct button is broken and I'm scared to death some fucker, probably me, is going to press it and end me. End *us*. "I wasn't going to drink it, Ava."

"Would you drink it if I leave?"

"Are you going to leave me?" I ask, panicked.

"You need to give me some answers." The steeliness is getting steelier. And here come the questions. "Why is Mikael so interested in our relationship?"

Do yourself a favor, brother. Give her the truth or, I promise, you'll lose her and all hope I have of you healing.

"His wife left him," I blurt quickly, praying this isn't the beginning of the end.

She doesn't even flinch. "Because you slept with her."

I swallow, whispering a pathetic, "Yes."

"When?"

Give her the truth. But the truth really could be the end of all hope too. "Months ago, Ava." How has it come to this? Fighting for my life, but in a very different way. "She was the woman who turned up at Lusso," I explain, hoping a little goes a long way. "I'll tell you before you threaten to leave me again."

Her look softens, and the strangest expression makes its way onto her face. One I never expected. Acceptance. "She wasn't worried about you, was she?"

"Yes," I answer, sounding willing. *Feeling* oddly willing too, because with each question I answer, she's settling more, showing less signs of turning and walking out. "Probably," I add. "But she wants me too."

"Who wouldn't?"

You, I think, if you really knew me. Truth kills hope. "I've made it clear, Ava," I add. "I slept with her months ago, and she'd gone back to Denmark. I don't know why she's decided to pursue me now."

She nods, if mildly, absorbing my lie of omission. "So he wants to take me away from you, like you took his wife from him."

Jesus. "I didn't take her away, Ava. She left of her own accord." Because her husband is a lying, cheating bastard. *Like me. And you'll probably leave me when you discover my sins.* "But yes, he does want to take you away from me."

"But you were all friendly," she exclaims, her acceptance making way for confusion. "You bought Lusso."

All friendly? My God, I never truly appreciated how naïve she really is. The tension in that room was so thick I could hardly see Mikael. But she had no reason to believe there was anything in it other than me being . . . well, me. Protective. Possessive. "It was just a front,

Ava." A front as wide as the moon. "On his part. He had nothing on me, nothing he could hurt me with because I didn't care about anything." For a time, he disliked me simply because I owned The Manor. He disliked me because his wife simply looked at me. He disliked me because Freja didn't mourn the loss of her marriage. He disliked me because my manor gave his wife a needed distraction from his wrongs when she finally decided to leave him. Mikael finding out I fucked Freja recently probably wasn't even required for him to retaliate. "But now I have you." I show her the fear in my eyes, praying she sees it and appreciates it. "Now, he knows where to stick the knife in." And he's doing a fine fucking job of twisting it. Worse still, I know he's not done.

Ava's lithe, delicate body shrinks, and she comes to me as I welcome her with open arms, literally, helping her onto my lap and cuddling her so hard. So desperately. She smells so amazing. Clean, pure, untarnished. Good. She's good, levelheaded, and what we have together is making her slightly crazy. Is that what love does? Send you crazy? "I'll die loving you," I whisper. "I can't let you go to Sweden."

"I know." No fight, no protest. Because she understands.

"And you should have let me deal with your things," I go on. "I didn't want you seeing him."

"I know." It's a small win when I feel like I'm constantly losing. "He knows about you."

It's confirmed the fucker has been sniffing around outside The Manor, but I still tense because . . . what does he know? "Knows about me?"

"He told me you're a raving alcoholic."

"I'm a raving alcoholic?" I laugh. And who the fuck has he got that bullshit from? Naturally, I think about Coral's husband, Mike. He's top suspect for tipping off the immigration police too. I've not heard from that bastard since I battered him. Still holding a grudge? I don't know but, thank God, only my closest have every dirty detail of my past.

"It's not funny." She glares at me, unimpressed. "How does he know?"

I'm not mentioning Mike, since he's a link to Coral. "Ava, I honestly have no idea. Anyway, he's misinformed because I'm not an alcoholic."

She bites her lip briefly. "Yes." It's a dreary reply. "I know." She loses her tired expression and finds a worried one. "Jesse, what am I going to do?" she asks. "Mikael is an important client." Important? I'd rather give Patrick a million quid of my personal savings than let Ava work with him. "Did he rehire me for the Life Building just because of you?"

God love her. "No, Ava. He didn't even know about *us* until yesterday. He hired you because you're a talented designer. The fact that you're also stunningly beautiful was an additional benefit. And the fact that I happened to fall in love with you was an even bigger bonus for him."

"You exposed yourself. If you hadn't trampled my meeting, then he might never have made the connection."

Not true. He would have found out sooner or later. I made it sooner. Later would have been preferable. "I acted on impulse when I saw your diary. Anyway, he would have pursued you whether he knew you were mine or not. Like I said, he's relentless."

She doesn't look too sure. Another sign of her naivety. "How do you know?" Her head tilts. "He's married. Well, *was* married."

"That never stopped him before, Ava."

She falls into thought, anxious, no doubt wondering how she comes out the other side of this with a job. I can't lie, I wouldn't mind if she lost her job. I would mind, however, that it would make her sad. I cup her cheeks and aim her face at me, set on distracting her from her woes. "How did you get here?"

My plan works, and she smiles for the first time in what feels like forever. I live for these smiles. "I distracted your appointed guard."

I laugh on the inside. Clive appointed *himself* bodyguard. For a fee, of course. "I shall have to sack him." I'm sure the old boy will be panicking now, thinking I'm going to demand my cash back. I might. He's costing me a fortune in favors. "How did you manage that?"

"Jesse, he's sixty, if a day. I disconnected his telephone system so he couldn't advise you of my escape from your tower in the sky."

"*Our* tower," I correct her. "Disconnected?" I'm worried, even more so when Ava disappears into my body, hiding.

"I ripped the wires out."

"Oh." I can't laugh. Clive will be pissed off. Even more so when I tell him about the elevator doors. This is going to cost me again.

"What are you playing at, getting a pensioner to try and keep me indoors?"

"I didn't want you to leave," I admit, feeling at her damp hair.

"Well, you should've stayed yourself then." She moves, focusing on my torso, yanking my shirt from my trousers and slipping her hands onto my skin before settling again.

"I was crazy mad." I hold her tighter. "You make me crazy mad." Sinking my face into her dark waves, I breathe easy again.

The cause.

The cure.

"How's your hand?" she asks, prompting me to lift it and look at the renewed bruising.

"It would be fine if I didn't keep smashing it into things."

"Let me see." She comes out of her place in my chest and I watch her as she inspects the damage.

"I'm fine," I say quietly.

"You smashed the elevator door."

"I was really mad." It could have been worse. I could have found Mikael or Matt.

"You already told me that." She strokes over my fist, head tilted. "What about the hijacking of my office this afternoon?" she asks, looking up at me, curious. "Were you crazy mad then?"

"Yes, I was." Always fucking crazy. Always owning my crazy. "A bit like you were just now."

"I wasn't mad, Jesse." She's nonchalant as she returns to my hand. "I was marking what's mine." She sure was, and I quite liked it. "She wants you. She couldn't have been more obvious if she'd straddled you and thrust her tits in your face." Fire. Passion. Possessiveness. It tells me she really does love me. Maybe I'll get a yes after all. I smile wide and Ava looks up, catching it. "You look very happy with yourself."

"Oh, I am. I like it when you're all possessive and protective." I have no problem confessing it. "It tells me you're crazy in love with me." And, actually, as I thought before, sometimes it takes a woman to put another woman in her place. Ava's got it in her, and I can see more sass, more fight, rising to the surface.

"I am, even though you are stupidly challenging. And don't be calling Sarah, *sweetie*."

She's so cute. As if. I smother her, kiss her, indulge her, my problems forgotten for today. "I won't."

"You've slept with her."

Or maybe not.

Fuck.

Fuck, fuck, fuck.

I'm trying so hard to look disgusted. Offended. Is this female intuition or Ava intuition? "A dabble," she eventually says when it's obvious I'm stuck for words.

I look away, letting my gaze fall between our bodies. This is one question I've certainly expected. Doesn't mean I want to answer honestly. But . . . "Yeah." I brace myself for a blowback, cringing, wondering if I've just made a monumental fuck up telling Ava about me and Sarah. She's put herself between Ava and me more times than I ever imagined she could. But Ava's reaction?

She doesn't explode. She just looks at me like she feels a little sorry for me. I'm feeling pretty sorry for myself. "I just want to say one thing."

Just one thing? Really? I don't believe her. I've just confessed, under pressure, mind you, that I've slept with a woman who works with me. Don't tell me that will be that, forgotten, never to be discussed again. I don't even want to think about if the boot was on the other foot. Ava would be chained to our bed and he, whomever he may be, would be crushed.

She falls forward and kisses me lightly. "It's all about you."

"It's all about me," I repeat, making her smile. So she'll accept when I propose?

"Good boy."

I absolutely do not deserve this woman. "I love you, Ava."

She settles, peaceful, accepting. "I know."

"Take the day off work tomorrow." I chew my lip for a moment, thinking. She's amenable right now. Accepting. Giving?

There's silence for a moment, while she obviously considers my request. Or demand. "Okay."

"Really?" Wow. That was surprisingly easy. "You're being very reasonable. That's not like you."

She appears outraged for a split second before she curtails it. "I'm ignoring you."

"Not for long." I stand and set her down. *Grace.* This could have all gone a lot differently, but the way Ava came to find *me* and then forgave *me* for something in my past shows true grace. Maturity. I'm taking it as a win. Is it a sign? "I'm taking you home to *our*"—*notice the emphasis on ours, lady*—"tower in the sky. I've not been inside you for way too long. Shall we?" I cock an arm in offer and smile on the inside at her breathless anticipation. *Me too, Ava. Me too.*

"I fancy a bit of rowing."

"We'll row another day, baby. I want to make love." More love. Endless love.

I guide her through The Manor, mindful of the endless attention, the falling conversations, but not paying attention to it. I return John's smile when we approach him at the door.

"I'll see you tomorrow."

"S'all good."

I jolt when his big paw meets my back. I want to ask him why he let Ava in, especially knowing Sarah was nursing my wounds. But, really, I don't need to. He knows, like me, Ava needs to put Sarah in her place. I think she's made her point.

"Leave your car," I say, taking her to my Aston and putting her in the passenger seat. "We'll get it tomorrow."

Again, she accepts. Sucks to think it takes a major blowup

between us, epic meltdowns all round, a smashed elevator, a few crazy episodes of hearing and seeing things to make it happen—but here we are.

The gates up ahead open, clearly by someone else because I've not hit the button yet, and when I see Sam's car, I curse under my breath. His timing is impeccable. Or is it my timing?

"Hey, there's Kate," Ava shrieks, swinging around in her seat as they pass, Kate sinking down, awkwardly waving, Sam bold as brass smiling, his thumb up. I shake my head mildly. "What's she doing here?" Ava asks. I keep my eyes forward. "She's a member, isn't she?"

"I don't discuss members. Confidentiality."

"So she *is* a member?"

I say nothing, ignoring her, seeing the gates closing again, so I hit the button and put my foot down, and as soon as we're on the main road, I tactically put some music on in case Ava gets a hit of inquisitiveness again.

"Who's this?"

"John Legend. You like?" She helps herself to the controls and turns it up. "I'll take that as a yes." The louder the better. Might drown out my niggling conscience. I find her thigh and squeeze, settling in for the ride.

"Is your hand okay?"

"Fine. Unravel your knickers, lady."

"I need to text Patrick."

"Yes, do." That money-grabbing old goat better not put a spanner in my works. "I'm looking forward to having you all to myself tomorrow and all weekend." Oh, God, it's going to be bliss. God help anyone who bursts our bubble. Including me.

"Done." She drops her mobile into her lap and takes my hand, weaving her fingers with mine and gazing out of the window, quiet. Thoughtful. Shit, what I would do to be a fly on the wall of her brain. I could always be prepared for whatever she throws my way. "I can't help but be worried for Kate." Her words are quiet as she keeps her eyes on the countryside passing by.

"Why would you be worried?" I ask, my attention split between Ava and the road. My hand on the wheel is aching like a bitch, but my other hand in hers, warm and tight, is enough for me to endure it.

"I don't know." She turns a half-smile onto me, one I'm not sure I like. She does know why. And suddenly Sam's words are coming back to me.

I get the feeling I'm a rebound.

"The Manor, Kate, Sam. It feels like a recipe for disaster."

"Only if one falls in love with the other," I say quietly, resetting my focus on the road, feeling Ava's gaze boring into my profile.

But she doesn't say any more.

27

I HARDLY HAVE the strength to look at Clive when we enter the foyer. Poor guy looks terrified. Probably thinks I'm going to demand my money back. My thoughts are confirmed when he reaches for his hat where I know he keeps his stash of cash, pushing it farther onto his head . . . a subtle message.

I might take him on if I wasn't becoming more uncomfortable by the second, my trousers getting tighter and tighter. This isn't waiting until we make it upstairs. I peek down at Ava next to me. She's rigid. Fighting the same onslaught of desire. I don't know if she realizes she's done it, but her tongue appears, gliding slowly across her bottom lip.

It's my undoing. *Jesus*. I return my attention to the elevator doors and will them to hurry the hell up before I give Clive a performance that will likely kill him with shock.

"Come on, come on," I breathe, my palms becoming sweaty, my heart battering against my chest in anticipation. There's only one way to end what has been a monumentally shitty day.

As soon as the doors open, I get us in, turn us around, and the moment we meet in the middle, I'm pushing my body into hers, getting her up against the wall. I raise my knee and gently brush it across her front, enjoying the heat of her breath on my face.

"You've upset the concierge."

"Damn." She just gets the word out before I smash my mouth onto hers, grinding myself onto her in an attempt to relieve the painful throb. It doesn't work. Fuck me, I want to spin her, bend her, and fuck her hard.

"Why aren't you wearing a dress?"

She returns my kiss, her mouth hungry, her tongue keen. "I'm running out of dresses."

"Tomorrow, we buy only dresses."

"Tomorrow, we buy *one* dress," she counters, working my belt. I pull back, my desperation advancing into a whole new, knee-trembling territory. Her hand brushes over my cock, and I suppress a groan, naturally pulling away from the friction. The torture. But being drawn to it too. I can do no more than stand still as she licks my bottom lip, mesmerized, every nerve I have buzzing, every drop of blood white-hot, every hair on my body standing on end. And when her hot palm wraps around my girth, I jolt and slam my eyes closed, trying to focus on breathing before I pass out.

"Mouth," I whisper, pretty much signing my death sentence with that one word. The heat of her breath subsides, and I press my hands into the wall, opening my eyes to watch her fall to her knees before me. That sight alone could make me shoot my load on the spot, but my desire retreats when I realize she's not admiring my dick. She's not anticipating the taste of me. She's not considering licking up the bead of pre-cum that's leaking from the tip.

No. She's looking at the gruesome, jagged scar on my abdomen. "What are you waiting for?" I roll my hips forward, regretting the scorn in my tone, not even my throatiness masking it, but I'm in no position to rectify it. She realigns her attention. Takes a stronger hold of my cock. And licks me.

My body folds, shaking, my breathing going to shit. The urge to close my eyes overcomes me, but I resist, watching Ava's tongue work me, her hand thrusting gently, her head moving slowly.

"Fucking hell," I whisper, spasming when the sensation of her tongue meets my balls. *Shit.* She continues her trail down the base all the way to the very end. "All the way, Ava," I order, seeing the doors sliding closed. I hadn't even realized they'd opened.

Absorbed.

I let go of the wall and hit the button to keep the elevator on the top floor, my hips beginning to shake, the effort not to drive myself into her mouth too much, as she laps and licks, peeking up at me every now and then, not looking for approval. She doesn't need it. She just wants to see the state of me. What she does to me. I come from a land where pleasure rules. The Manor is full of men and women who love to give and receive it. They're experts. Ava isn't experienced in pleasure like I know it. And yet it seems she is an expert at delivering it. I wonder if that's what she's thinking. If after today, finding Sarah on my desk, concluding right about me and her, hearing about Freja, Ava feels she needs to mark her territory. Ensure my mind never strays from her.

She suddenly plunges me into her mouth, and I yell out, taking the back of her head, pushing against her advances, losing my fucking mind. I can't hold back anymore, my hips doing as they damn well please, and they want to thrust, over and over, in and out, my face tight, my arms rigid, my legs struggling to hold me up. Blood rushes up through my body into my head, making me dizzy, my vision distorted. Fuck, I'm going to come so hard.

I look down at my big hands encasing her head. At my dick disappearing into her mouth. At her closed eyes. Her flushed cheeks. Her dark, still-damp hair tumbling everywhere.

Her nails stab into my arse. "Harder," I grate, feeling them sink deeper into my flesh. "Oh, fuck." The sensations come on strong, the vibration in my dick, the pounding blood. Then the glorious feeling of her small hand stroking my balls. *Oh God.* And then she grips me hard and my legs give, forcing me to hold the wall. "Holy shit." My other hand automatically goes to my cock and takes hold. I need to see her face. All of it. "Keep hold and open your mouth," I order, thrusting my hand hard and fast, watching her watching me, her eyes drowsy, her skin damp. I hold my breath, chasing the end, tensing everywhere, feeling like any number of blood vessels could burst at any moment. I'm becoming urgent. Panicked. I'm on the edge of release, tinkering there, pleasure teasing me, my balls swelling in her tight hold. And like a boulder, it crashes into me. I clumsily guide my dick to her mouth and watch as it surges, pouring into her and, fuck me, she gulps it down. My lungs scream, and I release my breath, feeling my body deflate, my hand instinctively slowing to a calmer pace. Good God, I'm broken. I pant down at her, my eyes following her hand to mine and watching as she follows my measured, gentle strokes as she continues to lap and lick and swallow.

"I want one of those every day for the rest of my life," I say over fitful breaths. Her eyebrows slowly rise. "From you," I clarify, making her smile before giving my dick one last swirl and a kiss. "Come here." I pull her up, crowding her. "I love you and your filthy mouth."

Her nose wrinkles when I rub it with mine as she pointlessly tucks me back inside my trousers. "I know you do."

I pull her out of the elevator and let us into our penthouse. "That was a complete waste of time," I say over my shoulder. "They'll be off as soon as I get you inside."

She pauses on the threshold, her eyes widen, and I realize why when I catch a whiff of it too. "Dinner," she gasps.

Shit. I take her to the kitchen and pull the oven open, using a glove to get out Cathy's famous lasagna. Sliding it on the counter, I pout at the crusty, burnt top as I throw the oven glove beside it. "I employ a housekeeper and a cook, and you *still* manage to burn dinner." I look out the corner of my eye, expecting complete, warranted indignation, but instead I find worry.

"Will she come back?"

"I hope so." I prod the burnt top. "Cathy's lasagna is delicious." Not that we would have been eating it if it wasn't scorched to a crisp. "It looks like I'll have to find something else to eat." I lift Ava from her feet and walk on, shuddering at the feeling of her fingertips massaging my scalp, marveling at the sparkle in her eyes. Her damp lips still glistening with the remnants of my cum all over them. My feet take me toward the terrace, and I don't try to stop them. I've one memory of the terrace. It's not a pleasant one. Let's change that.

"Where are we going?" she asks.

"An alfresco fuck," I declare, plucking the name from thin air. "It's a pleasant evening. Let's not waste it." I set her down and get straight to work on her clothes, begrudging anything that stands between us, even material. I fight with the annoying buttons, taking forever to simply get her top off. She has my trousers undone, my shirt open, and her hands indulging in my chest by the time I get her blouse open.

"Show-off." I move to her trousers. Front. Back. No zip. No buttons. Are they some kind of brain-teaser? I scowl, kissing her, feeling around, my impatience growing. "Where's the zipper?"

She smiles against my mouth as she leads my hand to her hip, where I locate the zipper. I pull it down, pick her up so she can remove her shoes before I get her out of the trousers and blouse. "Yet another reason for dresses only. Anything that stops me from getting to you fast has to go." I look at her lace-covered boobs. Her lace-covered pussy. Feel my dick rising to attention again. I blow out my cheeks and put some space between us, stripping down. "Lace," I whisper, ridding my tingling body of my boxers, my eyes fixed on her bra.

Suddenly, no bra, the thing falling to the floor. *Lord above*. Her nipples are tight. Dark. Begging to be sucked. I push myself into her and drag a fingertip down her body, inhaling when I push past the seam of her knickers and plunge straight into a puddle of heat. She jolts as I circle her slowly, absorbing her vicious nails clawing at my arms.

"Wet," I whisper hoarsely. "Just for me?"

She accepts and lifts her face, inviting me, so I kiss her, pushing her knickers down her legs as far as I can reach, until I can go no farther. I wrench myself away from her mouth with effort and lower, dragging them the rest of the way, her pussy a magnet to my mouth. I glance up as I move in, seeing the anticipation gazing back at me.

I drag my tongue straight through the middle of her heat, and she sighs, instantly trembling as I lick my way up her firm, smooth skin, finishing at her mouth, kissing her hard. After the day we've had, dealing with what I've dealt with, I feel so fucking lucky to be here now. Reminding her.

I'm compelled to express that, hopefully in a way she'll understand, so I free her mouth and look into her dark eyes, hoping she sees the love in mine. "You are my life," I say firmly, almost angrily, seeing a mixture of satisfaction and worry etched across her dreamy face. God damn it. I kiss her again, hard, pulling her closer, taking her under her knee and holding her leg against me. "Do you love me?" I ask.

"You know I do." I hate the uncertainty. Hate it. Not hers, mine.

"Say it," I demand, squeezing her leg. *I know you do.* It's Ava's way. "I need to hear it."

Her eyes dart across my face, unsure. "I love you." And she kisses me, climbing up my body, holding on. "I'll always love you."

Always.

It's a really long fucking time, but not nearly long enough. We gaze at each other, my cock ready and poised to sink into her. "Do you need me?" I whisper.

"I need you." Need trumps want every day of the week. "I love you." Her eyes shine with a sincerity I've never seen before. I believe her. It doesn't mean I'll ever stop needing to hear it. Doesn't mean I'll ever stop worrying she could change her mind.

"Always." I let her drop slowly onto me, impaling her, my chest expanding with my inhale, Ava's too. I take a moment and a few breaths before risking using my legs to carry Ava to the nearest thing I can lay her on.

A lounger.

Need is more powerful than want.

I need this woman. She needs me. But there's always one person in any relationship that's at a disadvantage. Always one that loves more than the other. This has to be even ground. She hates my protectiveness. I can't change that. She loves my attention. My body. My ability. The explosions of us coming together.

My weapon.

"Feel how perfect we are together?" I push into her slowly, groaning, as she looks up at me, rapt, holding my arms, her body moving with mine effortlessly. "Do you feel it?"

"I do." She nods, biting her lip, her hands caressing my back.

"Me too. Let's make love." I don't take my eyes off her. Can't. And she remains fixated on me. I roll, grind, drive, all slowly, all controlled, savoring every move, as I study the awe on her face. Not awe for me or what I'm doing.

Awe for us.

When we're like this, it's hard to believe there is anything that can tear us apart.

But there is.

If I allow it.

I'm unable to stop my body from moving, from taking the pleasure, and she's not helping, squeezing me inside of her. She tenses, trying to delay the inevitable, but I can feel her going, and then she confirms it, her words urgent.

"Together," I command. She locks down every muscle around me as I fight to remain composed, both physically and emotionally, my eyes stinging, my body shaking violently.

"I'm there, Jesse." She shakes with me, and I see she's gone past the point of return, her hands grappling at my back, her cry high-pitched. It doesn't take much effort to join her. A few thrusts. A yell. A grind. Every muscle gives, and I fall onto her, breathless, as I come again, as hard as I did before, but this time inside of her.

"Fuck," she whispers.

"Mouth," I counter, with no scorn at all. I'm too beat. "Do you think you will ever stop swearing?" It physically hurts hearing such vulgar language coming from the perfect mouth of the perfect woman. Ironic, really, since she's far from perfect. She swears, she drinks, she wears inappropriate clothing. So, yeah, she's far from perfect. And yet perfectly perfect for me.

"I only swear when you challenge me or pleasure me."

Love how she pushes it back onto me. Although, I admit, she's probably right. My shoulder blades pull in, tensing, when her dainty finger glides across my back, and I smile when I figure out that she's spelling something.

Fuck.

I ease up and take my finger to her chest, writing "mouth" across her skin. Then I indulge in her boobs, kissing one nipple, then the other, before latching on with my teeth, looking up at her in warning.

She giggles, freezing, holding her breath, enduring the bite, and I hum, licking some life back into it, the hard pebble against my soft tongue blissful. She relaxes, and after I've played with her boobs a little longer, indulging myself, I glance up and see she's settled, her eyes closed, happy to leave me to lavish her chest with my mouth. But as I work around in circles, I notice her smooth skin becoming bumpy. Cold.

"You're shivering. Let me get you inside." I lift a fraction, but I'm hauled back down, and I laugh at her insatiable need to have me all over her. Shame that doesn't apply during working hours. "Comfy?"

"Hmmm."

"Bed." I stand and lift her into my arms, carrying her to the bedroom, and as soon as I climb in beside her, she's crawling onto me, snuggling deeply. I hold her, looking up at the ceiling, listening to the calming sounds of her breathing changing as she drifts off. This. In our home, in our bed, Ava asleep in my arms, snug, warm, peaceful. It's one of my most favorite places to be. The quiet, the calm, the sense of overwhelming love. It's also a place I'm coming to hate.

Because when I close my eyes, I might not like what I dream. Ghosts. All pointing their fingers at me.

Guilty.

I never appreciated how incredibly hard it is to simply talk. Just talk, tell, explain, beg for mercy. But exposing that side of me, all of my depravities, outright confessing my unforgivable sins to the woman I love? It would be as good as handing her a gun and telling her to put a bullet in me. Offering up endless reasons to walk away.

Why would I do that? I know I'm not good enough for her. I know I don't deserve her. I know she could do better than me. I feel like the serpent in the garden of Eden. Like I don't belong. Like I'm taking something good and ruining it.

My mouth falls to her head buried in my chest. "I love you," I whisper, like it's the answer for all things.

But sadly, love ruins more than it heals.

I have firsthand experience of that.

28

My sleep was broken. It's as if my mind has accelerated into self-preservation mode. Protection. Every time I drifted off, the ghosts came, circling the corners of my conscience, threatening to infiltrate my dreams, and I would wake up with a start. Every hour I found a reason to get up. To use the toilet. To put Ava's phone on charge. To put mine on charge. To check my messages. To get myself some water.

To talk myself out of effectively trapping Ava into being with me.

By 6:00 a.m. I'm out of things to do and I've failed miserably in my attempts to call off my plan. I have had endless opportunities to right my wrongs. Stop taking her pills. Confess. I've taken none. I look around the kitchen from where I'm sitting on a stool at the island, waiting for Jake to appear and throw some hard-to-hear words at me. But none come. Perhaps he's out of sarcasm and jokes.

Perhaps he's given up on me.

"I'm going to ask her to marry me," I say to thin air, hoping to maybe prompt him from his grave. I know he'll think it's a terrible idea. I'd like the opportunity to explain why it's the best idea. I know deep down no ring will secure what I have with Ava. But our vows will mean everything, and she'll know that. She's a fairy-tale girl. Wholesome, traditional. Just as my previous marriage trapped me,

Ava's would free me. *Because I love her.* She makes me want the fairy tale too, and I'll do whatever it takes to give it to her.

I get up and pull my phone off charge, dialing Mikael. Warn him away. Threaten him. Blackmail him. I have to do *something*. It goes to voicemail, so I hang up and dial again. I get his voicemail again. *God damn it.* I end the call and dial yet again, and when it goes to voicemail this time, I talk, despite knowing I should keep my mouth well shut. "I don't know what your fucking game is with Ava, what you're trying to prove, but I'll be dead before I let her get on a plane to Sweden. Find yourself another interior designer, Van Der Haus. I won't ask again." I cut the call, squeezing my hand around my phone with a force I'm sure could crack the screen. "Fuck." I slam it down and push the ball of my hand into my forehead. If I could take that call back, I would. I've just given him exactly what he wants, and it's a sign of my state of mind. "Fuck, fuck, fuck." I slump down on my stool, rest my elbow on the marble and my head in my hand, slowly turning my phone in circles. I should be looking forward to today. I *am* looking forward to today.

Focus on today. I swoop my phone up and dial Zoe. I'm a little surprised when she answers, and even more surprised that she sounds wide awake. "Did you bum dial me?"

"No." I get up and start walking circles around the kitchen, randomly opening door after door, reminding myself of what is kept in each cupboard. "Do you have any available appointments today?"

"On a Friday? No, Jesse. Not in any personal shopper's world would they have an opening on a Friday at this late notice."

"Not even for me?" I ask, ashamed of the coyness in my voice.

"What's it worth?"

I laugh to myself. A few months ago, it would have been *well* worth Zoe's while squeezing me in last minute. Both financially and otherwise. These days? "I'm seeing someone," I blurt, once again ashamed for how I've played that down. "Dating."

"Wow."

"I know." I frown at myself. "Actually, it's more than dating. I'm thinking of proposing."

She laughs, and doesn't that speak volumes? "You? Married?"

"Don't sound so shocked," I grumble, seriously offended, with no right to be.

"I'm sorry," Zoe relents. "It's just . . . well, you're Jesse Ward."

"Reformed."

"And who is the lucky lady who's taken the lord off the market?" she asks. "And is she prepared for the backlash?"

"Jesus, Zoe, I called for an appointment, not an audition for Mastermind."

"And what would your specialist subject be?"

Fucking everything up. I lean back against the counter, looking down my well-formed naked body to my well-formed cock. "I don't have a specialist subject." We all know that's not true. "Can you help me or not? I promised her a new dress for an important party."

"Oh, is this The Manor anniversary?"

"Yes." If she tries to get an invite out of me . . . I'll have to give her one. *Damn it. I'm* the one who has more than used my sex appeal to get things I want, when I want them. *Ava is no exception, it seems.* I'm now banking on Zoe's professional psyche . . . and her love of my pecuniary generosity. "We need a dress and a few other things. But don't mention the other things. She's . . ." How do I put it? "Independent."

"Aren't we all?"

"Ava especially so. Or at least she likes to try and prove she is."

"Ava, huh?"

"Yes, Ava. She's an interior designer. I met her when she came to The Manor to look at the extension." That still hasn't progressed. Do I care? So long as Ava and I are progressing? "Can you help me? I'll be spending an *obscene* amount of money." I can't make it worthwhile for Zoe in one way, so I'll pay her double her normal commission.

"How very Pretty Woman of you."

"Please?"

She sighs. "I'm just getting on the Tube. I'll look at my diary and text you."

"You're a legend. And will you tell Hans in the jewelry department to expect me?"

"Sure. I'll be your PA as well as your personal shopper."

"Thanks, Zoe, I owe you." I hang up and tap my phone on my chin, thinking of the best way to get our day off together to the best start. That's easy. I look down at my dick. It agrees.

I leave my phone and take myself upstairs, and I lift the covers, my eyes taking a long, appreciative jaunt from her shoulder blades, down her spine to her arse. I slide in behind her and spoon her, curling myself around her body, smelling her hair, kissing her shoulder, rolling my groin into her backside, marveling at how perfectly my body cocoons hers. "Wake up, sleepy head," I whisper, reaching for my dick and stroking it to full hardness, slipping it across the crack of her arse, humming as I work my way down to her entrance, rolling the wet, swollen crown of my erection there, preparing her. A sleepy murmur. A mild arch of her body as I slip into her on a suppressed, broken groan, moving my hands to her hips, holding her. God, how she's always ready for me.

She breathes out, her hands coming over her head and resting in my hair, and she cranes her neck, looking back at me with sleepy, half-open eyes as I pump carefully, the pleasure rippling through me calmly. Her mouth opens invitingly, pulling my lips onto hers, and we kiss as deeply as I plunge, our pace becoming more urgent with each drive, our tongues wilder, our bodies tighter.

"Ava, I can't get enough of you," I say, my mouth becoming clumsy, my brain scrambled. "Promise you'll never leave me."

"I won't."

I hiss when she yanks at my hair, as frustrated by constantly reassuring me as I am with myself for asking. She gets us back to kissing, telling me talking isn't on her agenda right now or, more to the point, soothing me, and I'm here for it. But her mouth's suddenly gone from mine and I stare into her eyes, a little surprised, a lot dazed, my hips now working on autopilot, grinding into her, taking all of the pleasure.

"Please believe me," she says, her voice broken and rough.

Oh baby, how I wish I could. Frustration lands, and I try so fucking hard not to let it, but my body has taken on a mind of its own and it wants release. Ava gasps, turning away from me, and I stare at the back of her head, my face strained, as I hammer into her unforgivingly, chasing that release, hoping it releases so much more than the pressure in my dick.

My blood burns, my pace ramping up, my appetite ravenous, my need spiraling. "Fuck," I yell, as it gets me, jerking my body, blowing my mind, squeezing my heart. I come so hard, hissing my way through the sensitivity, pouring into her, listening to the distorted sound of her shout of pleasure. I curse, grabbing at air, drawing it into my lungs urgently as I lose my grip of Ava and flop to my back, closing my eyes and concentrating on finding my breath, feeling her lazily crawl onto my chest.

"That wasn't sleepy sex."

"No?"

She kisses my throat, her wet tongue running over the roughness of my stubble. "No. That was a sleepy fuck."

"For God's sake," I breathe, twitching. Could be her language. Could be her sucking on my neck. "Ava, stop swearing."

"Sorry."

Her mouth latches on to my chest, and I peek down, watching her suck my skin. "Are you trying to mark me?"

"No, just tasting."

I accept, lying still, happy for her to taste me for as long as she likes. I'm good for nothing, anyway. Except the relentless circle of self-torture. *Make today count.* If I can't speak one truth, I should speak another. "Ava?" I whisper as she kisses her way across my heart. It kicks more, like the closer she is, the better it works.

"Hmmm?" she hums, staying exactly where she is, lost in my skin.

"I knew you were the one the second I laid eyes on you," I say quietly, remembering that time. That fateful, life-changing second.

She stills, her lips pausing on my neck. Not surprisingly, those words have her attention. "The one?" she asks, giving up my skin for my face. For the first time, I don't need her eyes to check she's real. I can feel her. So I push her back down into my neck, turning my mouth onto her ear, kissing it, making sure she hears me, making sure my words go straight to her mind and brand themselves there. "The one to bring me back to life." It doesn't get any simpler than that.

She wriggles free, and I let her. "How did you know?"

I love her curiosity. Her need to hear the finer details. I love how I see no fear in her gaze, just wonder. I sit up and get her beneath me, my gaze taking in every detail of her face for a few moments. "Because my heart started beating again," I say quietly, feeling it now, smashing out of my chest. She swallows, clearly at a loss. I've no doubt she must know the intensity of the feelings I have for her. I also know without doubt that she struggles to understand how or why I love her so fiercely.

I wait, pensive and nervous for an interrogation, but she doesn't question me. She simply engulfs me in her arms, wrapping me up tightly like I need protection, and hugs me. It's the best thing she could do. Acceptance.

"Can I feed you?" she asks after a while. I engage my muscles to get up, taking Ava with me, still stuck, every arm and leg wrapped around me. "I'm going to forget how to use my legs." She pulls back, getting my face in her sights as I walk us down to the kitchen.

"Then I'll carry you everywhere."

"You would like that, wouldn't you?"

"I would love it." Naturally.

I sit her on the counter and go to the fridge, feeling her eyes following me there. I inspect the contents. It's more than I'm used to seeing in my fridge. I take some eggs, some butter, some tomatoes, stacking them in the crook of my arm. And a jar of Sun-Pat.

"I'm supposed to be making *you* breakfast." She comes to me, gloriously naked, and nudges me aside. "Sit." She looks stern. It's sexy as fuck. Naked and stern. Telling me what to do, within reason of course. My eyes drop to her boobs. She wants to cook me breakfast? What I'm hungry for does not need cooking. I give her nipple a quick tweak, her chest concaves, pulling away, and I grin, satisfied when it pebbles before I claim my vice and put myself on a stool, happy to watch my naked girlfriend—still hate that word—potter around our kitchen making me breakfast. "What do you want?"

"Fried eggs." I raise my brows, pouting around my dipped finger, as my gaze drops down her naked body.

"I'll cook yours, if you cook mine."

"Savage." I'm about to clean my finger with one more suck and cast aside my peanut butter ready to go in for round two of the day, but the front door closing interrupts me. I look toward the entrance into the kitchen, my brain taking a while to register the impending problem. I look down my body. Naked. Not a problem. Most people in my life have had the pleasure. I look across to Ava. Now that's a *massive* problem. Who the fuck is it? Drew? Sam?

Then it registers who it must be, and I stand, catching the side of the jar and sending it to the floor. It smashes, and I look up at Ava, finding her frozen, eyes round, body naked, waiting for me to enlighten her. She is going to die a million painful deaths, especially after her performance last night.

"Fucking hell, it's Cathy."

Her mouth falls open, her eyes going to the entrance, the information not prompting her to get her sweet arse into gear. I hear the door close and look over my shoulder, silently accepting there is no way out of this. A tea towel?

Ava makes a run for it, her speed quite something, her boobs bouncing, her tight arse not. The look of pure horror on her face, the situation, brings on laughter.

"Shit," she yells, as I finally convince my legs to work and go after her, putting a protective palm over my dick as I run, stopping it from bouncing around and giving me a belly ache.

"Mouth," I say, laughing when I hear Cathy's unmistakable shocked gasp, reaching forward and swatting Ava's backside halfway up the stairs.

"Goodness gracious," Cathy cries. I laugh harder. I'll go to hell.

I look back when I reach the top of the stairs, as Ava runs at full speed into the bedroom. Cathy's at the door, a hand over her mouth, her carpet bag at her feet. I lift my spare hand and wave, smiling like a fool, and get my feet moving again, noticing a spot of blood on the carpet as I enter the bedroom, just as the covers waft into the air and settle on Ava's hiding body. And I realize. She must have stood on some glass. *Shit*.

I go over, riffling through the sheets to find her. "Where are you?" I ask, finally locating her under a pillow. So adorable. "You've upset the concierge, and now you've *really* upset my housekeeper." I roll her to her back and put my face straight between her boobs.

"Don't," she groans, mortified, making me laugh.

"Let me see your foot."

"It hurts." She pouts, that's adorable too, as I push myself up and take her leg by the ankle, scanning the sole of her foot. I see a small bead of blood on her heel and get closer, tracing the tip of my finger there.

"Baby, you've got a piece of glass stuck," I say quietly, cursing myself and my clumsiness, apologizing with a kiss before getting up to go and find something that'll get it out. "Tweezers?"

"Makeup bag," she grumbles, looking plain mortified.

I rummage through her things in the bathroom, until I put my hands on a silver pair of tweezers, returning to the bed. I find her foot and settle on my knees, cleaning up the fresh drop of blood with my tongue, looking up her body when I feel her legs stiffen.

I smile to myself. "Hold still." I'm very aware that me removing this piece of glass isn't the only thing that has her tense. And on that thought, I lick the sole of her foot, watching her stomach harden, all of her abdominal muscles engaging. It's quite gratifying, but now isn't the time, especially with glass in her foot and a traumatized housekeeper on the premises. So I realign my wayward attention and remove the offending piece of glass, putting my lips around the area and sucking. I feel Ava look down at me.

"What are you doing?"

"I'm getting it out." I run my tongue across the area, feeling the shard now protruding from her skin, so I swap my mouth for the tweezers and get up close, pinching at the surface. Two tries and I have it. "There." A quick kiss and I move away, catching a grin on her face. "What are you grinning at?" I ask.

She waves a finger at my face. "Your frown line."

"I don't have a frown line." Do I have a frown line?

She bites her bottom lip. "You do."

Well, that's a kick to my delicate ego. I discard the tweezers and get to my hands and knees, crawling to her and trapping her beneath me. A frown line? "Miss O'Shea, are you saying I have wrinkles?" Do I need to get Sarah's doctor's number?

"No. It only pops up when you're concentrating," she says, her smile not letting up. "Or if you're concerned."

Fuck me, it must be a pretty deep line if that's the case. "It does?"

"It does."

"Oh." I don't tell it to, but my forehead bunches. "Is it there now?"

She giggles, which isn't an answer, but she's happy, and if Ava's happy, I'm happy. I look down at her boobs again and sink my teeth into the flesh, sucking, and she lashes out on a yell.

"Get ready," I order, kissing her forcefully, feeling her open up, inviting me to take more. But . . . urghhhh. "I'll go see if Cathy's run out screaming."

Ava's amusement vanishes, along with her tempting tactics. "Okay," she murmurs, reality finding her, a reality where she's got to face the source of her embarrassment. Maybe apologize too for being a piece of work last night.

"I'll see you downstairs." One more kiss. "Don't be long." I get up, grab some lounge pants and hop into them, pulling them up my legs as I leave the bedroom. I stop at the top of the stairs and smile when I hear the kitchen tap turn on and off. "Here we go," I say to myself, my bare feet quiet on the steps as I take them. I reach the entrance of the kitchen and peek round. She's cleaning up the glass with a dustpan and brush. "Morning," I say tentatively.

"Boy," she shrieks, making me flinch, before she proceeds to dash around the kitchen at a speed that defies her age. She empties the dustpan in the bin, stows it away, grabs her Flash spray, shoots it at the floor, then steps on the pedal of the mop bucket and spins the mop to rid it of excess water before slapping it on the floor and mopping ferociously.

I smile as I wander over to the stool.

"Watch your feet," she barks, shooing me on with her mop. "I might not have got it all." And with that, she abandons the mop and bucket and disappears into the laundry room, returning a moment later armed with the hand-held vac. I can't help but think she's quietly pleased under this fluster that she has something productive to do.

"Cathy—" The vac roars to life, filling the kitchen, making my squint. "I wanted to apologize," I yell over the deafening sound. She doesn't face me. "For the incident yesterday." Is that what I should call Ava's performance? An incident? A showdown? "She wasn't herself." I rest my arse on a stool. "And I may have been the cause for her outburst." This is added quietly as I go to the counter on the other side of the kitchen, looking down at my phone. No returned call from Van Der Haus. No surprises there. I slide it back onto the counter, returning to the island.

"Did you say something, my boy?"

"No, nothing," I murmur absentmindedly, drumming my fingers on the counter, lost in thought. Has he listened to my message?

"Boy?"

I blink and glance up. "What?"

"For breakfast. What would you like? And your new lady friend?"

"Eggs, please, Cathy. And salmon. Ava likes eggs and salmon."

"Lovely." She drizzles some oil in the pan and finds the eggs. "Oh, this mobile telephone thingy is flashing," she says, placing a pan on the hob. I'm off my stool like a bullet, hurrying over. It's Zoe telling me she can make ten o'clock work, take it or leave it, and only for an hour. Also, Hans is expecting me.

"I'll take it," I say to myself as I reply, setting my phone down and going back to my stool. I make it halfway.

"Oh, and again." Cathy chuckles. "I don't know how you kids cope with being available to the world every minute of the day." She cracks some eggs into the pan and stirs them up, humming happily as I reverse my steps, swiping up my phone, my skin chilling at the sight of my sister's name. *Jesus Christ.* I swipe the screen clear and go back to my stool, this time making it.

"So tell me about Ava," Cathy says, distracting me from the impending guilt trip that always comes with a message or call from my sister.

I smile half-heartedly and settle, accepting the fresh jar of peanut butter she slides across to me. "She's wonderful," I say, determined to get my day back on track. "About last night." I unscrew the lid off my vice and have a dip. Cathy turns, armed with her wooden spoon, and raises her brows.

"Well, I see you had a sleepover, so I assume you resolved your differences."

"Yeah." I fill my mouth with my finger and get my first dunk of the day. "She's moved in," I add around my mouthful, and, as expected, Cathy swings around, sending a spray of egg shooting across the kitchen off her spoon. I smile. It's awkward.

"Well, I never," she breathes, abandoning her spoon and coming to me, taking my cheeks between her hands and squishing them. Getting her face close to mine, I find myself leaning back a little, eyes wide. "You deserve this happiness."

Oh no. I can't stand a pep talk right now. "Cathy—"

"You listen to me, my boy."

"I'm listening." I relent, succumbing to the inevitable.

"She must truly be wonderful if you've fallen for her." Her face softens. I can't stand it. "After everything you've been through, I'm so happy you've found the right woman to share your heartache with, someone who can help you heal."

I look away, ashamed. Ava can certainly help me heal. Can she do that without knowing why? "Problem is, Cathy," I say, plucking up the courage to be honest, hoping perhaps that if I say it out loud, I might hear myself. "She doesn't know everything."

Cathy drops me and moves back, aghast. "What?"

"She knows about The Manor," I rush to say, like that might save me from my atrocious crimes. "And that drink and I don't really have the healthiest of relationships. And she knows I've had a colorful . . ." I cough. "Sex life with many partners."

"Your ex-wife?" she asks.

"No," I answer quietly.

"Your brother?"

"No."

"Your uncle?"

I shake my head.

Cathy's shock increases. "Your daughter?"

Another mild shake of my head.

"Oh, Jesse," she breathes. "Oh, no."

"Cathy, I—"

"You've moved a woman into your big, flashy penthouse to share your life, and you're not really sharing your life." She goes back to the pan and stirs some more before putting some bagels in the toaster. "That isn't fair, my boy. She should know those things." She abandons breakfast again and comes back to me, claiming my face, getting closer. Multiplying the guilt. "She should know every detail of what has made you the man you are today."

I smile, and it's so fucking sad. I'm not convinced Ava would want *every* detail. Cathy doesn't even know it all. I take her hands and pull them away from my face. It was pure accident that Cathy learned about my past when she found me on Jake's and my thirtieth birthday absolutely battered on vodka. "Problem is, Cathy, my past is really ugly, and ugly shouldn't feature in Ava's life."

"You're protecting her?"

"Protecting what we have," I confirm. "It's precious. *She's* precious. She makes me want to be a better man, and there are so many reasons for her not to be with me."

"Have faith, my boy." She rubs my cheek. "If she's as special as you say, if she loves you, she'll understand." She whips the jar of peanut butter out of my hand as I hum noncommittally. Her sentiment is sweet, but, I fear, wasted.

Cathy goes back to her cooking, and I return to digging deep for some positivity. "I'm thinking of proposing," I blurt, catching myself by surprise as well as Cathy. *Lie.* I'm not thinking, I'm doing. Am I trying to get Cathy's approval? Just one person who thinks it's a good idea? Kate didn't seem fazed when I told her.

Cathy's mouth hangs open, the spoon limp. "My God, you are besotted, aren't you?"

"Totally. She brings out the best in me." And the absolute worst.

"When?"

I look over my shoulder, checking the coast is clear. Perhaps I should have done that before I mentioned anything about proposals. "It's the anniversary of The Manor tonight."

She bursts out laughing. "Do tell me you're not thinking of asking her at your sex cave."

I roll my eyes. "No, but it will be the first time she sees The Manor in all its glory."

"Well, that's hardly fair." She sniffs, pulling two plates down and putting the bagels on them, followed by the eggs. "I've always wanted to explore the dungeons of The Manor, and you've always insisted I can't."

"I've told you, you won't fit in."

"And Ava will?" She looks up as I jerk on my stool.

"No, she doesn't fit in at all, but if she's going to marry me, she has to see my business."

"So you're confident she'll say yes?"

I jolt again. I love her, she loves me, so any day we don't spend together is a total waste of our times. Of course she'll marry me.

I think.

"Here eat." Cathy puts the plate before me. "You need to build some energy," she says, walking away. "And some balls."

I cough. "Thanks."

"Welcome. I'll keep my fingers crossed for you." She holds her crossed fingers up. "Now, tell me, what happened to the elevator."

I frown as I sink my teeth into my bagel.

"I'm quite sure it had fancy mirrored doors when I was here yesterday."

"Oh, the doors." *Fuck, the doors.* I can't tell Cathy the truth. Seems I'm not very good at speaking the truth of anything to anyone. "I don't know. I've filed a complaint with maintenance. The damn things shattered." I take another bite of my breakfast to halt the lies pouring out. "Obviously faulty glass." *Shut the fuck up, Ward.*

Her eyes drop to my recovering fist. "Fancy that. Glass just spontaneously combusting."

I hum, nodding. Cringing.

"Now, I need to know a few things." She breaks more eggs into the pan.

"Things like what?" I ask, wary.

"Well, if there's a lady of the house, I'm sure there are things she likes doing in certain ways, a particular washing powder to use, cleaning products, towels folded, what shopping and what day."

I blink, taken aback. "You're overthinking this, Cathy."

"Easy for you to say that. You're a man."

"Ouch." I laugh. "Ava isn't pretentious." I smile. "You'll love her." They haven't had the best start, but I've no doubt Cathy will fall in love with Ava as hard as I have. Well, perhaps not that hard, but she'll love her.

"Nevertheless, I should like to know specifics. I can't run a home without the knowledge to do so."

I hear the sound of footsteps behind me and turn on my stool as Ava rounds the corner. My smile drops. Fuck me, was she savaged by dress-eating dogs between here and the bedroom? Where the hell is the rest of her dress? But I hold my tongue and focus on the glorious beauty before me rather than what the glorious beauty *isn't* wearing. Today *has* to be a good day.

"Here she is," I say, inviting Ava onto the stool beside me. "Cathy, this is Ava, love of my life." Poor thing looks so embarrassed as she comes over, her hands twiddling, her moves awkward. I reach for the jug of juice and pour some for her. She won't be lifting a finger today. "I like your dress." *Hate it.* "Too short but excellent access. It can stay." *For that reason alone.* I smile when she glares at me in disbelief, then laugh when she boots me under the island.

"Ava," Cathy coos, taking in my girl, probably thinking how different she looks without a scowl fixed to her face. "It's a pleasure to meet you." I don't miss the quick glance Cathy points my way. Approval. But also disapproval. I can only imagine that disapproval will grow the fonder she grows of Ava, which is a dead cert. "Would you like some breakfast?"

"You too, Cathy." Ava glances at me, smiling nervously. "I would love some breakfast, thank you."

"What would you like?" I don't know why Cathy's asking. She's half made it after I told her what Ava's favorite is. Is this all part of her lady of the house philosophy?

"I'll have the same as Jesse, please." Ava collects her juice, looking over the glass at me as she sips. My smile is unstoppable. I've never seen her looking so awkward.

Ava clearly doesn't appreciate my amusement at watching her squirm. Her hand appears in my lap and disappears past the seam of my lounge pants, and I cough, my eyes on Cathy, who's happily preparing Ava's breakfast. *Fuck.* She seizes my dick, making me jerk, my knee lifting instinctively, hitting the underside of the countertop. I curse, inhaling, sucking my mouthful of bagel back. It hits the back of my throat, making me choke. My eyes water; I can't breathe. What the fuck is she doing?

I suddenly have a glass of water in my hand, and I take it gratefully, supping it back as Ava, the wicked thing, starts stroking my hardening cock. No. Not in front of my lovely, wholesome housekeeper. That's a step too far, even for me.

"You okay?" she asks casually,

"Fine," I squeak. She's getting it. Hard.

My bagel falls from my grasp, I place the water down, and look at the love of my life who seems to have a warped compulsion to send me round the bend. *Breathe. Breathe.* I bite down on my lip, starting to sweat as she rolls the tip of her thumb over the crown, looking smug. So fucking smug.

"Good?" she asks quietly, peeking at me. She's a secret sadist. I puff out my cheeks, planning all the ways I'll get my revenge. But for now? I'll enjoy this addictive torture until I can no longer remain quiet. Then I'll drag her upstairs and fuck her until she begs me to stop.

"There you are, Ava." Cathy presents Ava with her breakfast, she drops my dick, leaving me hard and helpless, and finishes me off by licking what she's collected from my weeping hard-on.

Is she for real?

"Thanks, Cathy." Ava smiles, collects her breakfast, and sinks her teeth in happily, humming her approval, telling Cathy how amazing it is. Oh no. She does not get to do that.

I'll get her upstairs. Gag her.

Ava peeks at me. I hope she sees the disapproval on my face. The disgust. I nod toward the kitchen door, a silent order. "Upstairs, now." I negotiate my strung body up from the stool, looking down at the massive, tented piece of material. "Thanks for breakfast, Cathy. I'm going for a shower." I tilt my head, and Ava nods, watching me shuffle away, trying to hide said tent.

"You're welcome, boy," Cathy sings from the dishwasher, not looking up. Thank God. "Can we go through what you would like me to do today? I'm all out of sync, and I can see that you have done absolutely zero, except break doors and make holes in walls." I see her rising, and I quickly swing away from her before I scar her for life.

"Ava can sort that out with you as soon as she's helped me with something upstairs," I call, rounding the corner and racing up to the bedroom, pulling my lounge pants down as I go. I look down at my cock. It's crying. Literally. "Come on, baby," I say, holding it, applying pressure, trying to stem the incessant throbs. I pace in circles, glancing around, planning my moves. She's dressed. What a waste. But it does mean I get to destroy another non-existent dress.

I look at the door, listening for the sound of her footsteps. Creep closer, listen harder. Nothing. What the hell is taking her so long? My dick twitches as I open the door and peek round. No Ava. "For fuck's sake." I tread to the top of the stairs, my hand still over my groin protectively, and listen. Talking. They're chit-chatting. How lovely.

And then it hits me. "No," I whisper. She's not coming? Her performance downstairs wasn't her punishment for laughing at her discomfort. This is—leaving me here with a raging hard-on, knowing there's fuck all I can do about it without giving Cathy an eyeful, and Cathy has had enough eyefuls. And mouthfuls for that matter. Oh, she's gone too far.

I reverse my steps, my erection now painful, and I will it to stand down, retreat. It doesn't. Instead, it throbs harder. "Fuck," I spit, shutting the door, closing my eyes, and reluctantly accepting what needs to be done. I can't go downstairs with this thing.

Jaw rolling, shoulders dropped, I go to the bathroom and turn on the shower, taking myself to the vanity unit and putting myself before the mirror. Except I don't see me. I see Ava. Bent over, hair a morning tangled, glorious mess, arms braced, body ready, head dropped.

I inhale and circle myself at the root, exhaling from the relief, just from the pressure. And I start to stroke, slowly, imagining it's Ava's pussy encasing me. It's the only way. I haven't wanked off for years, haven't needed to, and I shouldn't need to now. I tighten my fist and increase my pace, resting a hand on the edge of the vanity unit, bracing myself, leaning into it. My breaths come short and fast, the tingles come hard and intense, the blood surges rapidly. "Fuck," I hiss through clenched teeth, the muscles in my arm starting to burn, my thrusts becoming chaotic. I growl, curse, close my eyes, replaying her words, hearing her voice, seeing her eyes.

Take me.

I pump fast, chasing my release.

You weren't imagining it.

My speed increases even more, the end teasing me.

I love you. I need you.

My dick explodes, cum shooting across the vanity, and my lungs drain, my exhale loud and long. "Shit," I breathe, my muscles relaxing, my arm taking the weight of my body leaning into it. I look up at my reflection. Alone. No Ava to smother post-orgasm. No soft skin to kiss. A neck to nuzzle. It's the most unsatisfying release I've ever had.

But it was a means to an end. A lot like my past sex life.

And it won't ever happen again.

I clean up, shower, dry off, brush my teeth, and throw on some old jeans and a white T-shirt faster than Sarah can flick her whip. Fucking fast.

As I exit the bedroom, I feel down my rough face. Shaving feels like a terrible way to spend time these days. I run a hand through my damp hair as I reach the top of the stairs, slowing my pace when I see Ava slumped in a chair. She's speaking quietly. Looks forlorn.

"It's nothing like Matt says, Mum." My hackles rise. Matt? What the fuck has Matt said? And to Ava's mother? My blood starts to simmer, and the only thing stopping it from boiling over is the screaming despondency coating Ava's face. "Mum, listen," she goes on, clearly pacifying her. "I've got to get to work." I feel my shoulders sag, anger making way for disappointment. She's lying to her mother to avoid having *the* conversation. The conversation about *me*. "Please, don't be. Matt wanted me back." Her hand covers her face. "He pounced on me when I went to collect the last of my things and turned nasty when I rebuffed him." Matt turned nasty? With Ava? Fuck me, the emotions in me right now are see-sawing. I'm back to being angry. "Jesse was just protecting me." The mention of my name only alleviates it a teeny, tiny smidge. Has the man got a death wish? Hanging around The Manor, hitting on Ava, *more* than once, calling her parents. Does he know who he's dealing with? I start to shake with rage, and that just makes me all the more fucking angry with Matt. Today is *our* day. Just about us. Can't he just fuck off? "Yes," Ava breathes. "I'm just seeing him." I see her cringe from here. And if she was looking at me, she'd see the steam coming out of my ears. "It's nothing serious."

I cough under my breath. Yeah, that stings.

"He's not an alcoholic, Mum. Matt's being spiteful, ignore him. And don't answer any more of his calls." Fuck me, someone hold me back. Could the arsehole stoop any lower? I watch as Ava continues to pacify her mother. I'm fucking livid.

She eventually cuts the call, blindly discards her mobile, and closes her eyes. Exhausted. Everything about her radiates tiredness. Sadness. *Fucking hell.* There's so much from that conversation that's enraged me, but as I stare at her now, all I want to do is make her feel better. Show her that all this shit isn't for nothing.

I take the stairs slowly, my instinct pulling me to her, demanding I make everything okay. Comfort her. Chase away her woes. Ironic, really, isn't it? I'm the root of her problems, both current and those on the horizon. But isn't that the beauty of horizons? They can never be reached, going on forever, stretching into the distance. Far away.

I can't show Ava my anger, but more than that, I can't show her my hopelessness. So I pluck a smile from nowhere and place a hand on each arm of the chair she's in, towering over her. Yet when she opens her eyes and I see the vast bleakness in them, I can't maintain my false sprightliness. Everything in me sags. "What's up?" I silently beg her not to try to convince me all is well. I don't think I'll be able to hold my temper and stop myself going on a manhunt. But I see her reluctance. Her worry. "Hey, tell me. No more secrets." What a fucking prick I am. Lowering to my haunches, I implore her to share, to be open with me.

"Okay." She looks straight into my eyes, and I take her hands, encouraging her, seeing plain as day her lingering hesitance, as well as I can feel my lingering fury. She inhales, and her words come rushing out with the air. "Matt phoned my parents and told them I'm shacked up with a raving alcoholic who beat him up." She presses her lips together, watching me with wide eyes, moving back slightly, like she's seeing the unbridled rage rising in me and needs to get out of its reach.

Shacked up? He makes it sound sordid. Raving alcoholic? Slight exaggeration. And I beat him up? I punched him. But I'll happily make that part of his pile of bullshit accurate.

"I'm not an alcoholic."

"I know." Her voice is small and timid. "Jesse, how does he know?"

I rise, feeling too coiled crouched on the floor, hoping stretching my body out will release the tension. Good fucking question. "I don't know, Ava." But I will be finding out, as well as teaching Matt a lesson or two in telling tales. First, don't fucking do it, especially when they star me or Ava. Second, if he can't stop himself, at least don't fucking embellish it.

But . . . back to today, which isn't panning out how I hoped. My sole purpose right now is to get on with our day before I let Matt ruin it. "We need to have a chat with Cathy."

"Why do we need a chat with Cathy?"

"She's been away. She needs to know stuff." I get Ava up from the chair, looking down at the half dress she's wearing. Honestly, I want to march her back up the stairs and get her into something far more reasonable, but judging by the look on her face, that won't go down all too well and today has already been too much. And it's only nine.

"Like what?"

"I don't know, that's why we need to talk to her." Specifics, Cathy said.

"No. *You*, Jesse," she counters, removing her hand from mine, stopping me from taking her into the kitchen. "This is *your* place, she is *your* housekeeper."

Really? She's going to do this now? Hasn't there been enough tension for her today? "Ours," I bark, pulling her into me, trapping her. "You really know how to rub me up the wrong way." And the right way, actually. *When* she doesn't abandon me. I subtlety press against her. "Which reminds me. That was cruel and unreasonable. I waited upstairs and you didn't show."

"What did you do?" she asks on a suppressed giggle. This is it. This is more like it. No shit, not today.

"What do you *think* I did?"

Her laughter is life—erection-inducing stuff—the delighted

sparkle in her eyes blinding. *Yes, you have the power, baby.* I roll into her firmly, shutting her up. *But I'm taking it back.*

Unfortunately, she escapes my arms and my intention, grinning as she smiles and pats down the front of her dress. "I'm sorry."

"You will be." I pull her back and kiss her hard. "Don't do it again." And then push her away, relishing the almighty scowl on her face.

"Go talk to your housekeeper," she grates around her rolling jaw.

"Ours," I correct her again. "For fuck's sake, woman." I take her jaw and get nose to nose with her. "You're impossible."

"You go and talk to *the* housekeeper. I need to make peace with Clive." Wrenching herself free, she goes to the front door, calling a goodbye to *our* housekeeper, while I scowl at her back.

"Bye," Cathy shouts from the kitchen, appearing at the doorway armed with a pad and pen. "Now, what milk does Ava like? Skimmed, semi-skimmed, whole?"

"I . . . I think." I frown. "No idea."

"Bread? Whole, granary, white?"

I show the ceiling my palms.

"Brand of shower gel, shampoo, toothpaste?"

I shake my head, lips straight, and Cathy's pad and pen drop heavily with her hands, hitting the front of her apron.

"How am I supposed to know what to buy at the supermarket?"

That's not all she's wondering. She's wondering how I don't know this shit when I'm apparently in love with this woman. She's thinking it's odd. She's thinking I *should* know. "Perhaps it's best if you talk to Ava yourself." I get my keys and phone, checking the screen. Nothing. Running upstairs, I grab what I need and race back down, going to Cathy and dropping a kiss on her cheek. "I expect you'll be gone by the time we're home. Have a lovely weekend."

"You too, boy," she calls to my back. "And try not to break any windows, doors, and walls while I'm away."

I look back, arching an eyebrow at her dry wit, and she smiles sweetly, going back to the kitchen. The elevator doors greet me, and I grimace at them, looking down at my hand. Surprisingly, it looks in a far better state than the doors.

By the time I've made it downstairs, Ava is outside in the car park waiting for me. I can see her past the glass doors, and I smile, pacing through, eager to get to her. My path is suddenly blocked, and I skid to a stop, narrowly missing taking him off his feet. "What are you doing?" I ask, looking down at Clive.

"I just wanted to discuss a small matter with you, Mr. Ward."

"Oh?" I step back, wary. The elevator doors? The vandalizing of his telephone system courtesy of my hot-headed girlfriend?

"I have inside information, you see."

"What's that?"

"The concierge joining us."

"There's a new concierge?"

"There will be. Another one. He's starting in a few weeks. Carl?" He frowns. "No, Colin. Or was it Callum? No, that's it. Casey."

I look past Clive, my patience wearing thin. "What about him?"

"He's a bit straitlaced, if you know what I mean."

I laugh out loud. "Right," I say slowly, tilting my head, narrowing my eye on the old boy. "Are you saying, Clive, that tips might not go as far with the new concierge as they will with you?"

He smiles. "That is indeed what I am saying, Mr. Ward, so please do remember when you need assistance and I might not be on shift, I am only one call away." He winks dramatically as he holds his hand out, and I slowly take it, amused. "Glad that's settled." He pulls his hand out of mine and goes back to his desk, and I notice a piece of paper in my palm with a telephone number. Clive's number.

I laugh as I tuck it in my back pocket and join Ava. "You'll have to talk to her. She's asking about favorite foods, toiletries, and all sorts." I slip my shades on and aim the fob at my Aston, making it blink across the car park, my stride slowing when I catch Ava's smile. "What are you grinning at?"

"Do you not find it strange that you don't know those things?"

Oh great, not her as well. "Your point being?" I ask, pulling her toward my car.

"My point," she sighs, "is that we don't know much about each other."

I slow to a stop, staring ahead. She has no idea. I swallow, shake those thoughts away, and face her, smiling. "What's your favorite food?"

"Smoked salmon."

"I knew that. What deodorant do you use?"

Exasperated, she looks at me tiredly, her eyes looking to the sky briefly when they roll. "Vaseline."

I execute a dramatic phew. "I feel like I know you so much better now." I open the car door for her like a gentleman and smile. "Happy?"

"We're driving?"

I look at my car, my forehead heavy. "Well, I'm not walking, and I don't do public transport, so yes, we're driving." I usher her impatiently into the car, biting my lip, ready to hit her with news I know she won't appreciate. "Anyway, we need to shoot over to The Manor to check everything is in place for tonight." I quickly shut the door, ignoring her sour face as I round the car and slip in. Truth be told, I don't want to waste part of our day doing mundane things such as checking that things are in place, but I also can't leave Sarah and John to deal with the busiest night in The Manor's calendar. Not that I do much, really, but willingness is key. Presence is key. I've never been so present in my life. Besides, we'll need to eat at some point this afternoon, especially if Ava's having a drink tonight, which I know she will be. "Ready?" I ask, starting the engine.

"Why are you even asking me?" She goes into her bag and pulls out some lip gloss, pouting as she applies. "If I say no, will we be staying?"

"No." I pull off, hitting the gate fob and putting on some music. I look across to her in the seat beside me, my mood significantly better than a while ago. I have three whole days with her. It's going to be wonderful.

I grip the wheel with both hands and smile at the road, thinking I need to make some space in the dressing room for her. She can have it all. Every inch of space. Or maybe we could renovate one of the spare bedrooms and make it a dressing room for her. I dismiss that idea. She'd have to leave our bedroom to go there and dress. But we could convert a bedroom into another office. Actually, she can have mine. I only have an office because it came with the penthouse. It was destined to never be used. Now? It could be Ava's. She could work from home. I'd have design tables bought in, computers installed, have every tool she needs to do her work. Filing cabinets, printers, a library for her reference books. It would be amazing, she'd love it, and best of all, she'd never have to leave.

I feel her eyes on me and look across. No doubt she won't like my idea. "What?"

"I was just thinking about how much I love you."

I smile like an idiot. Maybe I'm wrong. Maybe she'll *love* my idea. "I know you do." I squeeze her bare knee, raising my brows when she opens the window. She can't possibly be hot, she's hardly dressed. "Where am I heading then?" I ask for the sake of it, giving the illusion of control, hoping she tells me she doesn't mind and she'll go wherever I decide to take her. Follow me anywhere. Fat fucking chance.

"Oxford Street. All of the stores I like are on Oxford Street."

I sag. Oxford Street? And . . . "All of the stores?"

"Yes."

"Isn't there just one shop you go to?"

"I want some new shoes as well. And maybe a bag. You won't find it all in one store."

"*I* would." *All* of the stores? I'm about to introduce Ava to a new way of shopping. She'll love it. Guaranteed. Anyway, I can't get what *I* need from Oxford Street.

"Where do you go?" She looks at me, curious.

"Harrods. Zoe sorts me out every time. It's quick and pain free."

"Yes," she huffs, laughing but not laughing. "That's because you pay for the service you get."

"The service is second to none and worth every penny. They're the best at what they do. Anyway, you're not buying the dresses, so I get to choose the shopping style."

"One dress, Jesse, you owe me *one* dress."

I'm not getting into an argument over it. Women love shopping. They love being spoiled. She's simply letting her pride and precious independence stop her from making the most of this. On the bright side, Sarah's worry is not a worry, not that I ever feared it was. Ava doesn't want my money. She just wants me.

"One dress," she affirms.

"Lots of dresses." I smile, looking more and more forward to spoiling her rotten. I have never in my life spent any money on a woman. I'm about to make up for it.

"You are *not* buying my clothes," she splutters is revulsion.

"I fucking am," I snap back.

"No, you're not."

I show the roof my eyes. "Ava, this is not up for discussion." I nod to myself. She will let me have this. "End of."

"No, you're right, it's not. I buy my own clothes."

"Why do—"

She reaches for the stereo and turns up the volume, sitting calmly back in her seat, refusing to look at me. *Difficult*. Clinging to her free will like she actually wants to keep it firmly intact. For fuck's sake, she drives me insane. She can let me buy her some clothes and retain her independence. She can indulge my desires and retain her freedom. It's completely beside the point that I want her to wholly depend on me. I know it'll never happen because, like it or not, and I don't like it most of the time, given the circumstances—AKA my history—Ava will never surrender to me completely. Fact. I accept it.

Problem is, Ava's under the incorrect illusion that by creating obstacles such as protesting gifts, she's independent. She's not. She's simply missing out and pissing me off in the process.

I return my attention to the road. She'll relent. I'm not sure how yet, but she will. I start drumming the wheel, thinking, planning, plotting, but by the time we've pulled up outside Harrods and I've parked, I have nothing. Well, I have something, but it's a long shot.

Worth a try, though. "I have a proposition for you," I say, facing her as she collects her bag from the footwell.

"I'm not bargaining with you, and there is no scope for a sense fuck here, is there?" She exits the car, and I curse at her back as I climb out.

"Mouth," I growl. "You already owe me a retribution fuck."

"Do I?"

"Yes, another for your little performance at breakfast."

She sniffs, indignant, despite knowing she wasn't going to get off with that scot-free. "I don't care what you propose." She reaches down to her dress and tugs at the hem, a clue that she thinks it's too short too.

She doesn't care? Hmmm. What does Ava want? My secrets? Nope. My age? She got it. Or—

"You're *not* buying my clothes."

My god, she's stubborn. Immature at times too. So I'll lead by example. I roll my eyes to myself. Like a grown-up. Like a mentor. An older someone for her to look up to. Give me strength. "You've not even heard me out." I soften my voice, hoping to appeal to her reasonable side. I'm beginning to wonder if she has one. "You'll like what I'm going to propose."

I've got her. The curiosity splashed across her face tells me so. "What?" she asks, her chin lifting.

"You let me spoil you—"

"I—"

I shush her, giving her a warning look. "And I will tell you how old I am." I just catch her outrage before I lose her face, closing my eyes and kissing her to death, leaning her back in my arms. It's all I've got, an old card, but one I'm pulling from the pack to play again.

"I know how old you are."

I release her lips "Do you?"

"You lied?" Her mouth hangs open. "Tell me."

"Oh, no," I say over a laugh. "Spoil first, age confession later. You might turn me over. I know my beautiful girl can play dirty."

"I won't," she huffs as I stand her back up, checking her dress hasn't ridden up. "I can't believe you lied to me."

"I can't believe you handcuffed me to the bed." I don't hang around to let the voices in my head call me out. I push into the doors and get us into the store.

29

I HEAD the long way to the elevators to avoid the jewelry rooms and bundle Ava in, hitting the button for the first floor. I see her eyes on the wall, reading the store information guide.

"Hey, I want the fourth floor," she says. I keep my attention forward. "Jesse?"

The doors open and I'm on the move again, pulling Ava past the collections of designer clothes, most, I note as I briefly scan them, a suitable length. "This way," I sing, happy.

I suddenly feel her resistance, not surprisingly since the personal shopping department just came into view. "No, Jesse," she says, adamant, trying to remove her hand from mine, digging her feet in. "No, no, no. Jesse, please."

I focus on pulling her along, working on my speech to talk her round as I do. She'll be fine when she settles down. When she forgets about money and independence. I want her to enjoy this. "I have an appointment with Zoe," I say when we arrive.

"Mr. Ward?" the young chap says, looking down at an iPad.

"Yes."

"Please, this way. Can I get you any drinks? Champagne, perhaps?"

I look at Ava. I'm even willing to let her have a glass if she'll just humor my need to spoil her. But she refuses, shaking her head, now quiet. Apprehensive.

"No," I say to the assistant. "Thank you." We're led into the waiting room and offered a seat, and I lower, pulling Ava down with me. She snatches her hand from mine. "What's up?" I ask tiredly like a dick, reaching for her hand again, holding it.

"Why did you ask me where I wanted to go if you'd already made an appointment?"

"I don't understand why you would want to trail around a dozen stores when you can have everything brought to you here." Ava's version of shopping sounds like hell. Don't tell me she'd prefer that over this. It's easy. Pain free.

"Is this how you shop?"

"Yes." I sigh, done with this debate over fucking shopping. "And I pay for the privilege so just humor me, will you?"

Her lips purse, and I brace myself for the incoming hissy fit but, God love her, Zoe breezes in, her timing perfect. "Jesse," she says, her arms open in invitation. "How are you?"

Stressed. I go to her, letting her say her hello. "She doesn't want to be here," I whisper. "Make this fun." I pull away. "Zoe. I'm good." She doesn't know it yet, but Zoe is helping me in more ways than one, so she's about to be hit with some serious charm because it's going to take longer than she's booked out for me. "You?" I give her a big smile, and she gives me a dubious one, eyeing me with suspicion and confusion. Because in Zoe's world, who wouldn't want to be in Harrods being spoiled? *Exactly.*

"Great," she says slowly. "This must be Ava." Abandoning me, she moves in on Ava, obviously keen to find out what it is about this woman that's got me under the thumb. "It's a pleasure to meet you." Ava smiles, awkward as fuck, and accepts Zoe's hand. It's a step in the right direction. She's not left yet. I'm depending on Zoe now to make sure she doesn't. "So, Ava, Jesse tells me we're looking for something special for an important party."

"Something *very* special," I add, sitting again, helping Ava down too, ignoring her constant, poorly concealed dirty looks.

"Okay, what's your style, Ava?" Zoe asks, and I laugh to myself. *Short things.* "Give me an idea of what you like."

"I don't have a style really."

Lie. She likes anything that'll give me heart failure. "Lots of dresses," I say. "She likes dresses."

"*You* like dresses," Ava retorts quietly. I pout, hitting my knee with hers.

"You're about a ten, yes?" Zoe asks, looking down Ava's frame.

Yes, a perfect ten. "Not too short," I blurt, recoiling at my own words. Did I say that out loud?

When Ava turns a disbelieving look my way, I know I did. I smile, kind of sorry, kind of not.

"Jesse, she has fantastic legs," Zoe pipes in. "It would be a shame to waste them." I glare at her. Does she want this commission or not? "What shoe size are you, Ava?"

"I'm a five."

"Great, let's go." Zoe stands and, surprisingly, Ava joins her without any need for persuasion.

"I can't believe you've done this to me," she moans, and I smile, because I can see she's coming round to this. She just doesn't want to let me have my way.

I give her a quick kiss. "Let me have my fun," I beg. "I get my own little fashion show with my favorite lady modeling."

"Who gets to pick the dress, Jesse?"

That's only a small part of my game plan. "You do." If they're in the acceptable pile. "I'm just observing, I promise." I smile my sincerest smile, willing her to be openminded for the next hour or two. "Go on, knock yourself out." I lower back to the couch and get my mobile out, ready to kick the next part of my plan into action, discreetly peeking up, watching Zoe lead Ava away.

As soon as they're out of sight, I jump up and dash off in the opposite direction through Harrods, racing down to the ground floor. I have no idea how long they'll be before they're back at the changing rooms. Twenty minutes? Half hour? I suppose that all depends on how much *fun* Zoe makes this.

When I make it to the jewelry rooms, I find Hans polishing his glasses. "Ah, Mr. Ward," he says, delighted, slipping them on. "Another Rolex?"

"Not exactly." I take his arm and guide him to a nearby cabinet. "Show me all your diamond rings."

His hands slap over his mouth, his eyes wide. "No."

"Yes, Hans."

"No!"

"Yes, Hans."

His hands move from his mouth to his knees. "Oh my God!"

I look at my Rolex. "Time is not my friend right now, Hans."

"Yes, right. Tell me about the lucky lady," he says, and I frown. "What does she like? What *doesn't* she like? What do *you* like? What *don't* you like? Where will you pop the question? Who will be there? The setting? What time of day? Sunrise? Sunset? The color scheme? Will there be flowers? Water?" He gasps, his hands covering his mouth again. "*How* will you pop the question?"

I stare at him blankly, incredulous. "I just want a ring, Hans."

"Which ring?" He glides a hand across various cabinets, all full of beautiful rings, and I take them all in, even more overwhelmed.

I spot an oval cut diamond on a simple band. "That one," I say, pointing, but no sooner have I uttered the words, I spot another gorgeous teardrop diamond on a slightly thicker, flatter band. "No, that one." Then a square diamond wrapped in a band of tiny diamonds catches my eye. I lower my hand to the glass cabinet and exhale. "Or that one," I say quietly. Fuck, this is harder than I thought it would be. I look up at Hans, lost, and he smiles in sympathy. "I haven't got time to answer your questions, Hans. Zoe is distracting her while I'm here."

"She's here?" he asks, alarmed. "In the store?" He starts looking around in a panic.

"Yes, she's here."

"Why didn't you come alone?"

"This is a spur-of-the-moment thing." *Bullshit. She will say yes, she will say yes.*

"Maybe come back alone next week and we can take the time and consideration this needs."

"No," I say, adamant. "I need the ring today." I'm not wasting another moment. I want a ring on her finger tonight so every man and woman will see it. *Mine.* I pause for thought, reining myself in. But the last thing Ava will want to do is go to my sex club after I've killed her with romance and proposed. *Shit.*

Okay. Maybe tomorrow. I swallow. Or Sunday. I pout. But I'd love to give her *something* special to wear tonight. Something significant. Something every member will see and appreciate.

Mine, mine, mine.

"Mr. Ward?"

I look up at Hans, who has a cushion of rings before him. "One word to describe your love," he says, reminding me of why I'm here.

I smile, prompting one from him. "I have two," I say, every vision of Ava I have stored in my memory coming forward and bombarding my mind's eye. "Understated elegance."

Hans gasps, and he goes straight to the cushion, plucking a ring from the red velvet. "Then you must have this one."

I gaze at his recommendation in his gloved hand.

"This," he says, almost dreamily, pointing at the diamond. "A one-of-a-kind cushion diamond."

I lean in, seeing the edges of the stone are slightly tapered, softening the squarer cut. "It's beautiful."

"Indeed. Two carats. Excellent color, amazing clarity. Like I said, one of a kind."

"It's perfect." I stand, my heart going crazy in my chest. *One of a kind.* "I'll take it."

"It's a very romantic diamond, Mr. Ward. Do you know the lucky lady's size?

I reach into my pocket and pull out the ring Kate nabbed from Ava's jewelry box, a costume piece she used to wear. "Here." I place it down. "Size it to that. How long will it take?"

"Oh, for you, Mr. Ward, we can have it ready by the end of the day."

"Fuck," I curse, making him flinch. "Sorry." There's not a chance I can make it back today to pick it up. "Can you have it delivered?" I ask. "Later today. Leave it with the concierge."

"My pleasure, Mr. Ward."

"Thanks, Hans." I pull out my card and hand it over, and he takes it with the biggest smile. My eyes fall to a necklace, and I slowly move toward it, captivated by the blinder of a diamond. Stunning. Perfect. I just want to buy her everything. "This necklace," I say, my eyes fixed to it. "Do you think she'll like it?"

"How could she not?"

I pout, thinking. It's a whopper of a diamond. Too big? Another catches my eye. Slightly smaller. Less sparkly. Underwhelming, to be honest, compared to the other. Torn, I look at Hans. "I'm going to have Zoe walk past with Ava. Discreetly show her the necklaces." I'm sure Zoe can make an excuse to take Ava back out onto the shop floor at some point during the fitting.

His shoulders straighten. "Oh, Mr. Ward, you are spoiling her."

I motion to the card. "You should probably keep that for now."

He pops it into the machine and I tap in my PIN, looking down at my watch. *Shit*. "I'll be back," I say, dashing off. I've been gone for nearly half an hour. She'll be wondering where I am. I jump on the escalator, run up the steps, and jog through the various departments toward the personal shopping area.

I round a corner.

And nearly barge into the back of Ava.

Fuck.

I skid to a stop, my front literally a hair's breadth away from her back as she juggles a few dresses in her arms. "Fucking hell," she hisses, nearly dropping one of them. I scowl at the back of her head, my lips straight, and reverse my steps, putting myself back around the corner and releasing my held breath. What to do, what to do?

I peek around the corner, spotting Zoe walking toward Ava, therefore toward me. She spots me, frowns, and I quickly put my finger to my mouth to silence her. Her frown deepens, as she splits her attention between me and taking the dresses out of Ava's arms, handing them to a young lad who hangs them on a mobile rail. A *full* mobile rail. I smile to myself. She's having fun.

Ava walks off toward another display, taking in a disturbingly short gray . . . *thing*. Zoe checks her attention is elsewhere and comes over. "What the hell are you doing?"

"I need you to walk Ava through the jewelry rooms. Past Hans. There's a necklace in a cabinet. Diamond. Hans knows the one. He'll give you a wink. Make sure Ava sees it. See if she likes it."

Zoe looks back at Ava, as do I. She's still looking at the short gray thing. "Jesse," she says, looking at her watch. "I allocated an hour. I'm pushing time already."

I point to the mobile rail. "See that?"

"Yes, I see that."

"I'll buy it all." My phone rings, and I pull it out, seeing an unknown number on my screen. Yeah, not answering that. I reject the call, slip my phone back into my pocket, and get back to bribing Zoe. "*All* of it, Zoe."

"Don't be ridiculous."

"I'm not being ridiculous. Every single thing. And the necklace if she likes it."

Her mouth hangs open briefly before she gets it under control. Yes, I'm smitten. "The budget?" she asks.

I say what every commission-based personal shopper wants to hear. "There is no budget."

She grins. "Well, then I guess I need to be getting on."

"Yes, please do." I expect that mobile clothes rail will be loaded to breaking point by the time it makes it back to the personal shopping department. Don't care. "And, Zoe?" I call quietly, making her look back at me. I point to Ava, who is still looking at that offending gray dress. "That dress is *definitely* a no." I need to claw back a little control here. "Anything that short is a big, fat fucking no."

"Then perhaps you should be proposing to a woman more *your* age."

My jaw hits the floor at my feet—the cheeky fucker—and I'm about to retaliate when I see Ava turning. Shit. I quickly disappear round the corner again, smiling at an old couple who are watching me with slightly wary expressions. "Morning," I say, pulling my phone out when it rings again. "Sarah," I answer, wandering away aimlessly.

"I think your card's been cloned. Or stolen. I don't know, but someone's just tried to spend over one hundred grand on it in Harrods."

I stop dead in my tracks. *Oh fuck.* Just one day. All I wanted was one simple, uncomplicated, stress-free day with Ava.

"The bank just called me," she goes on. "They couldn't get through to you. I've told them to freeze your card."

Oh fuck, fuck, fuck.

"Jesse?"

I cringe, looking around me, like a rack of clothes might offer me a way out of this. I have nothing, so I just hum.

"Did you hear a word I just said?" she asks.

"Yeah, I heard."

"Good."

Fuck me, I should have anticipated the fraud department at my bank would flag a transaction of that scale.

"I'll call Harrods," Sarah says. "See if they can give me any details on the person trying to use your card."

Fucking, fuck, fuck, fuck. "It was me, Sarah," I breathe.

"What?" She laughs. "You?"

"Yes, me. I'm in Harrods now, so you can stop panicking. There's no one trying to steal my millions." Somehow, I don't think Sarah will agree with that.

"What on earth are you buying for that kind of money?"

My face bunches, a stressed hand running through my hair. "It doesn't matter." I can't do this now. This whole experience has been a stress-fest already, without Sarah throwing in her thoughts. "I'm not done shopping yet, either, so can you call the bank and tell them to unfreeze my card?"

"I'm too busy getting ready for tonight. You have the number for your personal bank manager in your phone. Call her yourself."

I let out a long, loud sigh. Great. The bank manager who hates me. I bet she's dying to offer her assistance. "Fine."

"And you said you'd be here to help."

"I'm busy right now." I hang up. "Fuck it all to hell," I hiss, scrolling through my contacts, trying to remember her name. Julie, Julia. "Juliette!" I press down on her name and inhale, taking my phone to my ear.

"Juliette Cooke," she says in answer, and I raise my brows. Still going by her married name, then?

I clear my throat and stand taller. "Juliette, hi, it's Jesse Ward."

Silence.

"I'm shopping in Harrods. I believe there's an issue with my card."

"Yes, our fraud department flagged a transaction. Your girlfriend confirmed it was fraudulent and froze your card."

"She's not my girlfriend." I shake my head. "And Sarah, my *colleague*, was mistaken. I have my card and it was me using it. I need you to unfreeze it so I can pay."

"No problem," she replies, clipped. "I'll make a call and have that done as soon as I'm back at my desk."

"How long will that be?"

"I'm just about to go into a meeting with a client, so as soon as I'm finished I'll start the process."

My jaw rolls, my temper flaring. "I need it to happen now. I'm in the store, and I need to pay."

"I'm afraid—"

"Juliette," Fuck this shit. She's being difficult. Obstructive. "I am asking you nicely to unfreeze my card now."

"And I'm telling *you* nicely, Mr. Ward, that I will absolutely do that just as soon as I am at my desk."

"Put the branch manager on."

"What?"

"The branch manager, put them on the phone now."

Silence. Good. We're getting somewhere.

"I'd like to start the process of moving my accounts," I go on.

"Personal *and* company, to another bank. One that appreciates my business, is happy to help, and doesn't use their personal hang-ups as a weapon to hold me to ransom and keep me from *my* money." There are tens of millions spread across those accounts. If Juliette loses my business, I've no doubt she'll lose her job too, because I'll make sure the bank knows why I'm moving my money.

Silence. Good. She's thinking about this.

"I haven't got all day, Juliette."

"I'll postpone my meeting and call Fraud now."

"Very kind." I smile tightly. "And please let me know when the hold has been lifted so I can avoid the embarrassment of having my card declined in Harrods again." I hang up and curse again, then curse harder when a text lands from Zoe, informing me they're heading back to the changing rooms. Fuck, I need to go see Hans. Fuck, I need to be at the changing rooms when Ava returns to them.

"This is not panning out how I hoped," I say to myself, breaking out into a jog, dipping and diving around the various displays on my way back to the personal shopping department.

I spot Ava and Zoe in the distance, ahead of me. "For God's sake." I pick up my pace, round a young couple, jump over a kid, dodge a sales assistant, circling wide around Ava and Zoe.

I'm fucking knackered when I arrive in the waiting area, slumping down onto the couch, fighting to get my breath. It's ridiculous. I run miles most days, and a small sprint across Harrods has me blowing out my arse. It's the circumstances. The stress. My phone rings and I dig it out, seeing Juliette's name on my screen. "Yes?" I answer, as clipped as she should expect.

"Your card is ready to use, Mr. Ward."

Ava and Zoe appear, the rail being dragged along behind them, the young lad in charge of it appearing as knackered as I am. Ava looks delightfully relaxed, and maybe a little embarrassed by the amount of clothes loaded on the rail. I flick Zoe a raised brow, and she shrugs. "Thanks," I say to Juliette, hanging up and rising. "Have fun?" I ask, lavishing Ava, kissing away the blush on her cheeks. "I missed you."

"I've been gone an hour." She laughs as I suspend her in my arms, the sound glorious. This is more like it. This is what I'm here for.

"Too long. What have you got?"

"Too much to choose from." Ava looks at the rail when I stand her up. There will be no choosing.

"Go try," I order softly, swatting her arse, encouraging her on. I give Zoe a pointed look before directing my stare at the jam-packed rail. We're going to be a while. Of course, she ignores me, marching past to the changing rooms, on a mission to bankrupt me.

Ava follows, and when they reach the door into the private room, Zoe invites Ava in, pushing the rail in too, looking back at me.

"She loved it," she mouths.

I put up both hands. All fingers. "Give me ten."

She nods and I leave for yet another sprint around Harrods, arriving at the jewelry room with a sweat. "Hans," I breathe.

"Mr. Ward, I'm afraid—"

"I know, Hans. I've talked to my bank. It's fine, they were being cautious." I can see his relief, his sale saved. "And she loved the necklace, so I'll take that too."

"Mesmerized, Mr. Ward," he sings. "I was quite torn. When your card was declined, I very nearly removed the necklace from the case so she couldn't see it."

"Thank the commission gods, eh, Hans?" I quip, bracing my hands on the edge of the glass counter, probably smearing it to death, trying to catch my breath. "Now, if you could run through the ring and the necklace sharpish, that would be helpful."

"My pleasure." He disappears toward a cash register.

"I bet it is," I mutter, smiling when he returns with the card machine, tapping my PIN in. And we both wait this time, watching for the glorious word *Approved* to appear on the screen.

I breathe out my relief when it does, write down my address for Hans to have them delivered, and call Clive on my way back to let him know Harrods will be dropping off a gift for Ava later today and to keep it in the safe until I collect it from him.

I make it back to the dressing rooms with one minute to spare and drop to the couch, exhausted, just as Zoe peeks around the door to check I'm back.

She smiles. "Ready?"

"Ready." I exhale, getting comfortable, just as Ava breezes out in a beautiful taupe gown. I lied. I'm not ready at all. I stare at her, mouth open, dazzled, as she holds her hands out to the side, like she's scared to touch it.

"What do you think?" she asks, as Zoe stands to the side, smiling.

I blink, shift in my seat, shit happening behind the fly of my jeans that shouldn't be happening in Harrods. "I—" I clear my throat. I didn't appreciate how hard this might be. Watching her try on dress after dress, all of which I know are going to be stunning on her, not to mention sitting here while she's in there undressing over and over again. "It's beautiful."

She smiles, almost shy. "You think?"

Just look at her. Do I think? Fuck me, she's flawless. This is going to be torture.

"You can't buy the first dress you try on." Zoe ushers her back into the dressing room. "Next."

I was right to be worried. It's plain torture watching Ava appear time and again in various beautiful gowns, all fitting her like they were made for her, all absolutely *begging* to be ripped off. Damn, I wish I didn't need to go to The Manor. I want to take her home and hide in our bed until this evening. On that thought, I get up and wander out of the shopping area, calling John. He doesn't answer.

Zoe appears, dragging another trolley along. "You're really pushing your luck."

"It's just a few more things."

"Looks like it. How much longer do you need to bankrupt me?" My phone rings in my hand.

"Only another hour or so," she sings, smiling sweetly. I shake my head at my stupid self. What was I thinking? I answer the unknown number; I won't be making that mistake again.

"Mr. Ward, it's Hans."

"Is there a problem, Hans?"

"No, no problem. I pulled a few strings and had the ring resized so your purchases are ready. I can have them delivered now?"

"Actually, I'm still in the store."

"You are?" he asks, surprised.

I point a look at Zoe. "Yes, I am." Hemorrhaging cash. "I'll pop down and pick them up."

"Excellent."

I hang up. "If she asks where I am, I'm using the gents."

"Whatever you say." Zoe pulls the rail on, and I dash off, wondering when security might show up and find out what the fuck I'm doing running circles around Harrods.

I make it to Hans, who's standing, arm extended, smiling, with two green bags suspended from his finger. I hardly even slow my pace, swiping them from his hand as I jog past, his body turning to follow me. "Good luck, Mr. Ward," he calls with a clap of his hands.

I break out of the store and keep up my pace to my car, opening the driver's door and stuffing the bags beneath the seat. Jesus Christ, this car is currently worth around half a million as it stands. I shut the door and lock it. Walk two paces, pause, and look back at my car. Press the fob to lock it again. Reverse my steps and check it's *really* locked.

When I make it back to the dressing area, Zoe is grinning. "What?" I ask, nervous.

"Nothing," she sings, as a young girl shuffles past with a dress bag laid over her arms, her back purposely turned toward me.

"What's that?"

"Just sit down and enjoy the rest of your show." She wanders off. "It's cost you enough."

I laugh under my breath, lowering to the couch again and leaning back, fucking exhausted. I glance down at my Rolex. I'm sure I said to Ava shopping at Harrods was pain free. Then why the fuck does every muscle I have ache? And my head. I blow out my cheeks and can't even find the will I need to sit up when Ava appears in a lovely blue summer dress that meets my standards. I nod, she smiles, and returns to the dressing room, appearing a few minutes later wearing a spotty dress with longer sleeves. Another nod. Her cheeks are getting pinker, her hair wilder each time I see her. She's knackered too, for very different reasons. A few minutes later, she's appearing again, and suddenly I find some energy. The fuck? I look at the short gray thing with all the disgust I feel.

"She's like a clothes horse, isn't she?" Zoe says dreamily.

I ignore Zoe and give Ava my full attention. "Get it off," I hiss.

For some reason, this amuses Ava, but she backtracks straight back into the changing rooms without protest. I give Zoe my attention. "Seriously?"

"Oh, lighten up. You sound like a dinosaur."

I recoil, my stunned eyes watching Zoe follow Ava. A dinosaur? My disgust multiplies, as do the daggers I'm firing in Zoe's direction. She quickly disappears, dodging them, and I get up, going to the nearest mirror. I sniff, turning my head, feeling at my scruff. Checking my dark blond for grays.

Nothing.

Dinosaur? She's talking out of her fucking arse.

I hear movement behind me and turn, seeing Ava standing stock-still staring at the rail of dresses. "What have we got then?" I wander over.

"Oh, she's got some fabulous pieces," Zoe tells me, shifting the line of dresses along and popping another on the end. "I'm very jealous. I'm just going to get this all wrapped and bagged for you."

"Jesse," Ava says, as I watch Zoe prance off with my card. "I'm really not comfortable with this."

I sigh when I feel her take my hands. "Why?"

She nibbles her lip, looking past me to Zoe, clearly torn. She wants to accept but doesn't think she should. She's worried about what people will think. She's worried about giving people—no names mentioned—ammunition to substantiate their claims that she's after one thing. It's still really fucking insulting, like they're saying I have nothing but money to offer a young, beautiful woman like Ava.

No, you have lies too.

I blink. And devotion. And security. And safety.

"Please," she begs, looking at me with wide, pleading eyes, squeezing my hands. "I don't want you spending all of this money on me."

"It's not all that much." I pout, certain I look as disappointed as I feel. Ava breathes out, her gaze dropping, but her hands remaining clenching mine. I stroke over the backs with my thumbs, wishing she could get past her issues. She can be as independent as she likes. Kind of. Doesn't mean I can't spoil her. Doesn't mean I can't treat her like she's precious. Doesn't mean I can't look after her.

"Just buy me a dress for tonight," she says quietly, her eyes climbing back up my body and landing on mine. "That would be acceptable to me."

"Just one dress?" One measly dress? It can't be like this forever. She's got to get comfortable with my money, or every day will be a struggle. "Another five dresses and you've got a deal," I say, considering the fix I'm in. I have to please Ava, as well as Zoe. I can't take back my promise of extortionate commission, and I can't fall out with Ava. So I'll negotiate for now, show some flex.

"Two," she retorts.

I roll my eyes to myself. Of course she'd counter. "Five. This wasn't part of the deal." She said she'd let me spoil her. The fact I have is beside the point. She doesn't know I've spoiled her, and the deal was that she would *let* me.

"I don't care how old you are. Keep your silly little age secret."

"Okay, but it's still five. I've got to make a phone call. You go and pick five dresses." At least the ones we're taking today. "Zoe has my card. My PIN is one nine seven four."

Ava's eyes bug. "I can't believe you've just told me your PIN number."

"No secrets, remember?" Am I a complete cunt? I quickly turn and walk away before Ava catches my flinch.

"You *are* thirty-seven," she calls, sounding happy. Happy that I'm not older? "Your PIN number. You were born in seventy-four. You didn't lie at all, did you?"

Exactly thirty-eight years ago on Monday. One year closer to forty. And the one woman I love is still on the right side of thirty, by quite some years. How the fuck have I been on this planet for thirty-eight years? And how have I survived them? I honestly don't know, but for the first time in a long time, I'm really fucking happy I did.

I look back at the woman who's changed me—sometimes for the better, sometimes for the worst—blowing her a kiss, before leaving her delighted form and putting myself out of eyeshot.

I dial John. "What are my chances of not coming over this—"

"Zero," he grunts, and my shoulders drop. "A few of the cameras have gone down."

"What?"

"I've called the company. We're on a twelve-hour contract, which means they can come anytime between now and—"

"Early hours of tomorrow morning." I look up at the ceiling. "Fuck."

"Indeed. I'm checking them over to see if it's something I can fix temporarily to tide us over until tomorrow morning. Could do with a hand."

"I'll be there soon."

"Where are you?"

"Hell."

"Still?"

"How's Sarah?"

"Moody. What's gone on?"

Definitely not telling John *that* over the phone. "I'll talk to you later."

"Yeah, we also need to discuss Steve Cooke."

My back straightens. *Loose.* "Why?"

"I'm not sure I like how he conducts himself. He's getting a bit heavy-handed for my liking."

I'll scratch you back, you scratch mine. Fucking hell, is he expecting me to overlook this? "A complaint?"

"Not yet. Give it time."

"We should talk to him tonight." I won't be scratching his back.

"He's not attending. On duty. Tomorrow?"

I inwardly groan. I don't want to do *anything* tomorrow other than worship Ava. I certainly don't want to deal with a *loose* member. "I'm a bit busy tomorrow." I cringe.

"Sunday then."

I grimace. "I'll see you in a bit." I hang up, curse a few times, and return to the personal shopping area, wiping my face clean of irritation. Ava wanders out, her eyes fixed on me, her expression happy. "Thank you." She gives me a kiss, handing me my credit card.

"You're more than welcome." I accept her affection, relinquishing her of the bags. "Do I get another show?" One that doesn't involve me dashing around like a prick in between outfit changes.

"Of course, but you don't get to see the gown."

I laugh to myself. I think I've seen every gown Harrods stocks today. "Which one did you pick?"

"You'll find out later."

A surprise? Can't wait.

"So," she muses, casual. "My man really is knocking on forty."

I pause sucking at her neck and scowl. Jesus, why does forties sound so much older than thirties? Sounds fucking ancient compared to twenties. I get her in my sights, seeing utter delight on her face. I suppose I should be grateful there's not horror. But it would be perfect for me if we never talked about our ages. I take her hand and start leading her on. "Does it bother you?"

"Not at all," she answers quickly, sounding quiet convincing too. So why the fuck won't she stop banging on about it? "Why does it bother you, though?"

"Ava," I say on a sigh, keeping us moving, mindful of the time. "Do you remember one of the very first things you said to me?" *How old are you?*

"Why did you lie?"

"Because you wouldn't have asked if it wasn't a problem." I look down at her, finding a wide, glorious smile.

"It doesn't bother me in the slightest how old you are." She's talking bullshit. Of course it bothers her—as proven with her incessant questioning in that regard. Trying to convince me now that I was worried over nothing is sweet but wasted. "Is that a gray hair?"

I get us on the escalator and turn to face her. She still looks delighted, even if she's trying her hardest not to be. *No, baby, that is not a gray hair.* Because I just fucking checked for them in the mirror. "Do you think you're funny?" I don't give her a moment to answer, dipping and tossing her onto my shoulder.

"Jesse," she shrieks as I turn and walk off the escalator, pacing through the store, smiling at every person I pass who's looking on, some wide-eyed, some turning to mush. Mostly the women.

I pass Hans, whose hand slaps into his chest, love hearts popping into his eyes. I give him a nod. "Good day, Mr. Ward," he calls as we pass.

"So far, so good," I muse, looking up to the sky and throwing a quick prayer out there that it remains this way.

What, until you've got that whopper of a diamond on her finger?

"You got it, Jake," I say quietly.

"What?" Ava says, bobbing up and down.

"Nothing. You okay up there?" I move my hand to her arse and squeeze, and she jolts on a laugh.

"Oh, I'm fine."

I smile. "These knocking-on-forty-shoulders holding you up okay?" My smile widens when her hands stroke over the swell of my backside.

"Perfectly fine."

I lift the bags in my hands for the green-suited man on the door to see. "Hands a little full, mate," I say as I approach, and he laughs, opening the door.

As soon as we're in the sunshine, I lower her, watch as she pulls her dress into place, take her hand, and walk us down the street to my car. I release the boot and pop her bags in there, put Ava in the passenger seat, and kiss her chastely. "We'll grab some lunch at The Manor." I shut the door before she can protest, because I really don't have a choice now but to go help John out. "Enjoying your day so far?" I ask as I slide on my Ray-Bans, looking across the car to her.

"Absolutely."

"Me too." I start the engine. "Put your belt on." Checking my mirrors, I ease out of the parking space and check the dash for the time, cursing when I see it's ticking on. At this rate, we'll get no alone time before we have to be at The Manor again this evening.

I let the windows down and put some music on, stopping at the lights at the end of the street.

"What's up?" Ava asks when I curse.

"Watch," I say, pointing at the lights. "Every single one will be red from here to The Manor."

"We could always just go home instead," she muses, shifting in the leather seat as I turn my eyes slowly onto her, not impressed. Not impressed at all. "John needs a hand with something," I say, my eyes dragging down her front to her boobs.

"Shame," she whispers, gazing out of the window.

Jesus Christ.

"The light's green," she adds, just as a chorus of car horns break out.

I blink and look up, a little disorientated. I can't see her smile. But I can feel it.

30

It's exactly how I predicted. Every single fucking traffic light shone red for me. I pass through the gates of The Manor, the flashes of sun and shade as I drive through the trees casting a pretty pattern across the gravel. The driveway is, as expected, practically empty, all members staying away, all staff vehicles parked around the back. I pull up next to John's Range and Sarah's Audi and see the big guy on the steps, his expression cut with impatience.

I get out and show him my palms, a silent plea not to chew my balls, then open the door and help Ava out. "I want to get done and get home so I can have a few hours of you all to myself." God help anyone who steals anymore time from me today.

She grumbles something under her breath, no longer playful and teasing, but serious. She doesn't want to be here. *Join the club*. I walk us up the steps, frowning at John as we pass. He looks ready to hit something.

"Ava," he grunts, eyes on me.

"Is everything okay?" I ask, wary, looking back at the big man as I take Ava into the bar. I put her on a stool and join her.

"S'all good." He's lying. What the fuck's going on? Whatever it is, he clearly doesn't want Ava to hear. "Caterers are in the kitchen," he says, motioning that way, like I could have forgotten where they are. "And the band will be here at five to set up." His head tilts. "Sarah has it all under control."

Was that a dig? "Great," I say quietly, watching as Ava keeps her attention elsewhere, watching various members of my staff working. "Where is she?" I return my attention back to John.

"She's in your office sorting out the gift bags." He reaches up to his shades and moves them down his nose a tiny bit, looking over the top of them at me. I find myself leaning back on my stool. What the fuck's going on, and why does John seem to be in a foul mood with me?

I order some drinks and lunch, and Mario slides our two waters over. I cautiously turn my eyes back onto a looming John. He flicks his head, an order to get my arse in gear. Looks like it's time to face the music. Would be helpful to know what track I'm walking in on, though. "Are you happy to stay here while I go and check on a few things?" I don't know why the fuck I'm asking. I obviously don't want Ava to hear whatever John has to say.

"Are you going to have Mario guard me?" she asks as I pour her water, a certain edge of sarcasm in her tone.

"No." I throw John a filthy look when the miserable bastard laughs. "There's no need now, is there?"

"I suppose not. Where is everyone?"

"We close during the day on anniversary night. There's a lot to get ready." I return her hands to her lap and drop a kiss on her forehead. "John?" Let's get this over with. Whatever *this* is.

"Ready when you are." The sarcasm in this place today, though?

I curl my lip at John and give Ava a little more fuss, just . . . because. "I'll be as quick as I can. Are you sure you're okay here?" *Please say no. Please insist I stay.*

But she doesn't. Instead, she pushes me off and faces the bar. Just like that. "I'm fine."

"Clearly," I mutter, reluctantly following John out of the bar, looking back, seeing she's already engrossed in Mario's bar skills.

The moment I'm in the foyer, John swings around, and I back up, cautious. He's removed his glasses, a telltale sign that I'm in for it. "What the fuck are you playing at?"

"I don't know," I admit. "What the fuck am I playing at?"

"You're going to ask her to marry you?"

"Oh." I reach up and scratch my head, looking around us, checking for listening ears. And then I wonder— "Wait, how the fuck do you know that?" I step back, getting the whole of his robust frame in my sights, as well as moving out of the reach of his boulder fist. "I've not told you."

"You don't need to when you're spending one hundred grand in Harrods, you stupid motherfucker." He turns and stomps away, and I chase his heels.

"I could have been buying anything. A car, a holiday, a—"

John stops abruptly and flies around, making me back up again. "Were you?"

"Was I what?"

"Buying a holiday, a car?"

No, I was buying a life. I stuff my hands in my pockets. "No," I admit. "I was buying a ring." Just putting it out there. Removing any room for misunderstanding.

I'm a dick.

"And the person whom you're giving this ring to," he says, his voice low. "When she agrees to marry you, it's because she knows you inside out, right? She'll say yes because your relationship is full of honesty and trust and faithfulness."

Well, that's pissed all over my Cornflakes, hasn't it? "I . . . it's . . ." I stall, chewing my lip while chewing over my approach. "I will . . ." I take a few breaths. "It's going to . . ." I scowl. "Oh, do fuck off." I barge past him. "She loves me."

He laughs, and it's torturous, following me through The Manor. "She doesn't fucking know you."

"She knows I love her. Immeasurably."

"Yes, but for a marriage to work, stupid boy, it's kind of essential for each party to know the person they're supposedly loving, or it's technically fucking fraud."

I'm so fucking bored of this conversation. "Fuck off, John, I'm handling this my way."

I'm suddenly not moving forward anymore, courtesy of John's massive bolder fists grabbing my T-shirt and hauling me back. I hit a wall, and he's up in my face, rampant with anger, and I'm wary of it. *Jesus fucking Christ.* "Your way is really stupid, Jesse. You have *got* to see that."

"I don't see anything but her, John." I look away, ashamed, guilty, fraught. But I know he's right. With everything I have, I know he's right.

"Think this through."

"Don't you think I have?"

"No, you couldn't have." His hold of my T-shirt loosens, and he sighs, brushing his palms down the creases he's made in the material. Then he pinches the bridge of his nose on a deep breath before dipping and picking up his shades and sliding them back on. "You think getting a ring on her finger will completely eradicate the risk of her ever leaving when she finds out your truths?"

"No, but when she accepts, I'll know she loves me enough to want to spend her life with me. Have *everything* with me. Forever."

"Jesus Christ," he whispers, turning and pacing. "Why don't you just get her pregnant while you're at it?"

I drop my eyes to the carpet at my feet, shame and guilt flaring.

"And do you think we could go just one day"—he holds up one fat finger—"without you upsetting Sarah?"

"Are we done?" I ask.

"Yeah, we're fucking done." He throws an arm up and snorts, storming off. "The security people will be here within the hour."

"What? So I needn't have come after all?"

"Yes, you fucking needed to come," he yells.

Right. "So you could try and talk me out of asking Ava to marry me?" Doesn't anyone around here want me to be happy?

"No, Jesse, so I could try and talk you into being honest with her." He disappears around a corner, and I clench my head in my hands, growling.

"So it's true?"

I peek through my fingers and find Sarah at the bottom of the stairs. "That wasn't your news to share." My jaw rolls. "Stop fucking interfering, do you hear me?" I stalk to my office and swing the door open. Slam it behind me. Look around. What the fuck am I doing in here? What the fuck am I doing at The Manor? It's the root of all my misery.

I turn, haul the door open, and find Sarah on the other side, her eyes glassy with unfallen tears. "I just have a few questions before you leave," she says, taking her attention to the spreadsheet in her hand. A fat teardrop hits it and splashes, and she quickly swipes the back of her hand across her face, sniffing. "The band will play two sets. Any preference on the time of the final set? Eleven or midnight?"

"I don't mind," I reply softly.

"Are you happy to leave the rooms open indefinitely once they're open at ten thirty?"

"So long as John is still around."

"Would you like to check the party bags? Make sure you're happy with the contents?"

"I trust you."

She looks up at me, swallowing hard. "Do you?" she asks, her lip quivering.

"Sarah," I breathe, walking to my desk and perching on the edge. "You've got to let me have this."

"Have what?" She closes the door, walking into the middle of the room. "A normal life? A younger woman? A—"

"Love, Sarah," I say quietly. "A purpose."

"You have a purpose."

"My purpose for over twenty years has been to get wasted." I wave my hand around aimlessly. "To lose myself in the rooms of The

Manor, a bottle of vodka, and some pussy. Because that is all I deserved."

"But she doesn't know you. Not like I know you."

I inhale, her words hurting. Sarah knows me. Every dirty little secret, and she still loves me. "I can't love you, Sarah."

"You've not even tried."

"You shouldn't need to try to love someone," I whisper. "It should just happen."

She looks away. I take no pleasure from the anguish my truth causes. And I wonder, how can I be so honest with Sarah but not with Ava? Because if Sarah walks out of my life, it would be a blessing. I know that. Problem is, I can't make that happen. She has to leave herself.

And like an iron shield slides into place, hiding her softer side, she sniffs, clears her throat, and straightens her shoulders. "I have way too much to do to stand around chatting. I'll see you later." She leaves, shutting the door quietly behind her, and I look at the ceiling in utter despair, because that there was a woman with no intention of going anywhere. She couldn't survive without The Manor. Has no purpose beyond it. Just clinging to a past that she should let go. Just clinging to a man that she should *definitely* let go.

I breathe out, scrubbing a hand over my face, pulling myself together. Then I return to the bar.

I walk in and find Ava knocking back one of Mario's cocktails. "What have you got there?" I ask, and she whirls around on her stool, all smiles. Oblivious to my turmoil.

"You should try," she says, excited. "Oh my God." She looks in a state of euphoria, something I'm familiar with, but knowing alcohol is the cause?

"No thanks," I mutter, sitting. "I'll take your word for it." I look away. "Don't drink too much."

She throws me an apology, mortified, and puts the glass down, facing the bar again, every inch of her awkward, and I feel awful for it. This isn't Ava's fault. None of my shit is her fault.

Fuck you, Ward. I reach for her, getting her onto my lap. "Hey, it's fine." I peek down to where she's hiding in my chest. "Unravel your knickers, lady." I laugh under my breath. I should heed my own advice and try some unraveling. I lift her face to mine, smiling softly. "Stop it and kiss me."

I don't need to ask her twice. Her fingers feel at my neck, fisting my hair. "I'm sorry," she whispers, indulging in my mouth.

"I said, stop it. I don't know what your concern is." I eye the glass on the bar. It's not my drink of choice, but if she'd had a vodka in her hand? What would I do? Grab it and down it all?

"Did you get everything sorted?"

"I did." I got absolutely nothing sorted. I shouldn't have come here. All I've achieved is upsetting my closest friends, and had it confirmed that I'm reaching for the stars. "Now we eat, and then we go home to bath and snuggle for a while, deal?"

She agrees and we tuck into our lunch when it arrives, a comfortable silence falling between us. Watching her next to me. Just eating, being here. It feels good. Normal.

"Jesse, are you happy for the band to set up in the far corner of the summer room?"

I look over my shoulder and find Sarah. She's reapplied her makeup. Gathered herself. "That's fine. I thought we agreed on that?"

"We did." She shrugs, her eyes looking past me to Ava. "I was just checking. How are you, Ava?"

After much too long thinking about it, Ava turns and smiles. It's fake. "I'm good, thank you, Sarah. And you?"

I move my attention back to Sarah, chewing my way through my steak slowly as I watch her force a smile to within an inch of her life. "I'm fine. Are you looking forward to tonight?"

Oh no, let's not get carried away. A civilized hello is all it needs. "Yes," Ava says, her smile stretching. "I am."

I frown when her fingers slip into her hair and start twiddling. "I'm heading off," I say before throwing a few orders at Sarah, keen to remove us all from the awkward atmosphere. I sound sharp and demanding, and I absolutely didn't mean to.

"Of course." Sarah's a master at delivering looks to kill, and I just dropped dead on the spot. "I'll leave you to it. See you later, Ava."

"Bye," Ava practically sings, and I'm back to looking between them. They both have unnatural smiles in place, neither prepared to be the first to drop it, until Ava relents and returns to her food.

I look at Sarah, like what the fuck? And she mouths, "What?" looking injured, before rolling her eyes and leaving.

"Why are you not looking forward to this evening?" I ask Ava, following her lead and poking at my lunch.

"I am." One hand goes to her hair again and twists a lock around her finger.

"Ava," I sigh tiredly. "Stop twiddling your hair." I'm calling her out. "You did it when Sarah asked you and you're doing it now." She stills when I hit my knee with hers, and I watch as she slowly untwines her fingers and places her cutlery down.

"I'm sorry if I can't get excited about attending a party where every time someone looks at me or speaks to me, I'll be thinking they might want to drag me upstairs and fuck me."

I flinch, dropping my silverware to my plate. "For fuck's sake." I shove it across the bar and wipe my mouth with my napkin, slamming it on the bar. "Ava, watch your mouth," I snap, rubbing soothing circles into my temples. I open my eyes and find her pouting at her plate, sulking. There was absolutely no need for her sarcasm. She thinks I'd allow that? "No one will be doing any such thing because they all know you're mine." And if they don't, I'll make sure they do. "Don't say things that make me crazy mad."

"Sorry," she grumbles sullenly. It's a small relief, her tone and persona telling me she's aware of how unreasonable she's being.

"Please try and show a bit more willingness. I want you to enjoy yourself."

She sighs, softening, and comes at me, climbing onto my lap and smothering me. I take it this means she's sorry. "Forgive me?"

"You're adorable when you sulk."

"You're adorable *all* the time." She kisses me. "Take me home."

Oh God, yes. Let's get out of here. I'm done sharing her for the day. "Deal. Up you get." I rise, lowering her to the floor as I do, our mouths fixed, and I start planning our alone time. Sex, bath, sex, shower, sex, another shower, cuddles, more sex, kisses, more cuddles, more sex, another shower.

And then I might let her get ready.

"Oh, no," Ava blurts, her mouth suddenly missing from mine, her eyes darting, thinking.

"What?"

"I've got to get some whiskey for Clive." She looks at me, a million apologies in her eyes.

"Have you? Why?"

"It's my peace offering. Can we stop somewhere on the way home?"

Is she serious? That old man doesn't want peace, he just wants money. *For fuck's sake.* If we weren't passing a Tesco on route, Clive would *not* be getting his whiskey. Lucky for the old scrounge, there's one ten miles down the road. "Clive's earned well out of this and he didn't even fulfil his brief."

"How much did you pay him?" Ava asks as I walk us out of The Manor.

"Not enough for him to do the job properly." I look back, my brow raised, and she smiles that God-glorious smile, making my dick twitch and my heart soar. "Don't look at me like that when I'm in no position to take you, Ava." I open the car door. "Get in the car."

She stands taller, the signs of a protest coming. *Not now, baby. I'm all out of patience today, and it's a long night ahead of us.* "What about my car?" she asks.

"I'll get one of the staff to drop it off." I help her into my car as I look over the roof, directly down the tree-lined driveway to the gates of The Manor. They're closed, as always, until someone opens them.

How easy it would be to *never* open them again. To never be interrupted. I'm jarred by the thought. But . . . doesn't all my stress, the altercations, my disagreements, lead back to The Manor? The ancient, handsome, sprawling building has always been my life. Like it was Uncle Carmichael's. But he had a woman who welcomed the hedonistic lifestyle he chose to lead. Joined in. I do not, and I don't want one. My purpose and passion now lie outside the gates of The Manor. I'm growing detached, feeling like I no longer need this place. But many do.

So the gates will continue to open.

31

THE TESCO ten miles down the road didn't have the specific whiskey Clive's apparently requested. Neither did the Asda ten miles away from there. Neither did the Sainsburys five miles from there. We're now in a Waitrose three miles from the Sainsburys.

I could have gone to Scotland quicker and picked one up from the fucking distillery. "Just get him this one," I say, holding up a bottle of Glenmorangie.

Ava examines the label, her frustration clear in all the lines on her forehead. "No, it has to be the Port Wood Finish. It's a special one."

Well, isn't that obvious since we can't fucking find it. I sigh and put the bottle back on the shelf, scrubbing my hands down my face and trudging slowly after her as she scans every shelf, high and low. I check my watch. At this rate, there will be no alone time at all. And that fucking sucks. "Ava, baby, I'm dying here."

"I've got to find it," she grates, her fists clenching as she turns a frustrated look my way. "I will *not* give up."

For some reason, her words hit me harder than perhaps they should. She won't give up. Isn't that something I love so desperately about her? Grit. Determination. Commitment. Devotion. Whether that be to find whiskey or stay with me. They're all things I also truly *need* from her. Does that determination drive me completely mad at times? Yes. But it's something so equally beautiful about her as well. She's amazing.

"Jesse?"

I blink, seeing Ava's frustration has turned into a frown.

"Are you okay?"

I match her frown and reach up to my forehead, rubbing the back of my hand across the dampness. A stressed sweat? "Yeah." I gather myself, glancing around. "Come on." I claim her hand and march us out of the supermarket to the car.

"Where are we going?" she asks, pulling her belt on as I reverse out of the parking space.

"To a place where I hope we can find the unicorn of fucking whiskeys," I mutter, and she laughs lightly. "Fuck!" I slam on the brakes, narrowly missing a blue Ford that seems to come out of nowhere.

"Fucking hell," Ava breathes, her arms instinctively braced against the dashboard. I slowly turn displeased eyes onto her, and she smiles awkwardly. "Well, you should watch where you're going."

"I was." I spin the wheel and slam my Aston into Drive, pulling away. "She appeared from nowhere."

"Love how you assume it was a *she*," she muses, reaching into her handbag and pulling out her lip gloss.

"I know it was a woman because I saw her blond hair." I'm not having her peg me as a bigoted pig. Although, to be fair, it would be a flimsy claim from Little Miss Independent. Just because I'm a bit traditional, doesn't make me chauvinistic. "And I'm giving you a fair warning."

"Oh?" she mumbles through taut lips as she applies her gloss. I don't know why, it'll be wiped off soon. "What's that?"

"There are two liquor stores on a street in Mayfair. Old. Traditional. If we don't find it in any of those, we go home and order it online."

"Sounds fair."

I look at her, shocked. "You're being rather amenable." Perhaps today *should* be the day I ask her to be mine forever. *Fuck you, John.*

"I'm tired of shopping," she says over a small smile and a teasing pop of her lips.

"But not tired, right?"

She laughs. "You mean too tired for you to have your way?"

I laugh too, and it's a loud, rich sound, one that I've not heard from myself all too much. Only Ava can spike it. "Have my way?" She's talking like it's not her way too. "What about *your* way?" I ask, splitting my attention between her and the road.

Her eyes drift down my seated form, her body turning a little in the seat to face me. "What about my way?"

Oh, she wants to go into details? "How do you like it, baby?"

She hums, head tilting from side to side in thought, her hand slipping onto my thigh and stroking. I stiffen in my seat. "Old," she whispers, retracting her touch and returning her body forward.

"You think you're funny, huh?" I ask, not insulted, just really fucking happy and content at how easy moments like this are with her. Moments when we simply enjoy being ridiculous because it's safe to be. It's ironic, really. Easy, but the most difficult thing ever. I reach across the car and find her tickle spot, digging in.

"Jesse," she yelps, and proceeds to buck and jack in the seat, laughing uncontrollably. I swerve. It's Ava's saving grace. "Oh God," she puffs, smacking my bicep. "Don't do that when I'm nowhere near a toilet."

I'm laughing again. "Noted. The last thing we need is you having to unravel *wet* knickers."

"If my knickers need unravelling, you should have to do it since you're the one who gets them all twisted in the first place."

"And wet," I say, and she laughs, eyes closed, mouth wide open. I put my foot down and reach for her leg, squeezing. "I love you, lady."

"I know," she sighs, resting her head back on the leather, settling.

"Thank the fucking Lord," I breathe when the owner of the second liquor store we try—our last chance saloon—pulls down a bottle of

Glenmorangie Port Wood Finish from the top shelf and blows off some dust.

"Thank you," Ava says, looking at me. "Lord."

She's so cute. "How much," I ask, pulling out my wallet.

"Oh, no." Ava steps in front of me, like she can block me from the man behind the counter. I'm a head taller than she is. I can still see him, and he's looking between us. "How much?" Ava asks him, rummaging through her bag and pulling out her wallet.

I remain silent and start slowly shaking my head at the man in warning.

"Umm," he says, coughing, torn.

Ava swings around and delivers a dick-slicing glare. "I know what you're doing."

"What?" I say over a laugh.

"Being all passive-aggressive so he won't listen to me."

I snort, insulted. "Me? Passive-aggressive?"

"Yes, you. I'm paying, Ward, and if you be unreasonable about it, there will be consequences."

Consequences? "Like what?"

"You know, I *am* feeling quite tired."

I balk. "That's a low blow."

"But one of the only things you'll listen to." She turns back to the man. "How much?"

"Eighty-nine pounds, dear." He pops it in a paper bag and passes it across the counter, eyeing me as I wander away, relenting, if only because time is ticking and enough has been wasted on other people today. "Passive-aggressive?" I mutter. "She's lost her damn mind."

"Ready?"

"I was ready an hour ago." I open the door for her, unamused. "The question is, lady," I say, catching up with her, getting my mouth to her ear and slipping my hand between her thighs as she walks. She squeaks. "Are *you* ready?"

She doesn't answer, just stiffens from the top of her beautiful head to her cute little toes.

. . .

We leave Clive marveling over his rare bottle, thrilled, and as soon as I get the door to the penthouse unlocked, I hold it open with my foot, letting Ava through. She claims the bags from my hands and carries on her way, leaving me at the door with no bags to hold, and no woman to hold either.

"What are you doing?" I let the door close behind me and toss my keys on the table.

"I'm taking these upstairs to the spare room." She looks back at my pouting face. "You can't see my dress."

"Put them in *our* room."

"No can do," she sing-songs, turning the other way at the top of the stairs. I frown at the now-empty space, hearing a door to one of the spare bedrooms close. The farthest one. The one she retreats to whenever we have words. I hate that room.

I trudge up after her, keen to get our alone time underway before it's too late. I've been waiting all day for this. I approach the door and listen for a moment, hearing the rustling of bags. She's in there, near a bed. Not that I need one. I reach up and purposely, very gently knock the door. It's an effort. I just want to bash the damn thing down, toss her over my shoulder, and take her back to my cave.

"Don't come in," she yells, sounding panicked. I recoil, just as it opens a tiny bit and Ava peeks through the gap. My lips stretch into a killer smile, my hands going into my pockets to restrain them. This is what it will be like on our big day, I know it. Ava in one room, me in another. Her following tradition, me following my instinct. See her. Just see her and ravish her, fuck what tradition dictates.

"Are we getting married?" The words fall out by total accident. Or perhaps not. Perhaps my sub-conscience is curious about what reaction that question might raise. Apparently, no reaction at all. It seems to go right over her head. She thinks I'm joking?

Her hand appears and she flaps it. "I want it to be a surprise. I need to paint my nails. Go."

My bottom lip protrudes. And there I was thinking there couldn't possibly be anything else that could interrupt me. Now I'm losing her to nail polish? "Fine," I relent, being reluctantly reasonable. She's willing to come tonight, we're moving in the right direction, and I need to keep us moving so we're far enough down the road to not turn back when we meet a few . . . bumps. Bumps? Fucking mountains. "I'll wait for you in the bath." I back up. "Don't be long, I've already lost an hour searching for fucking whiskey."

I go to the bathroom, use the toilet and go to the mirror, checking the stubble situation. Shaving is becoming more and more of an effort, time wasted when I could be being more productive. "But she's busy painting her nails," I tell my reflection, opening the cupboard and pulling down my shaving kit before I flip on the bath taps, getting an even flow of hot and cold to make sure it's tolerable once it's full. I add some bubbles too.

While the bath runs, I strip down to my boxers and squirt some shaving gel in my hand, smoothing it all over my cheeks, chin, and neck, feeling the scratch of my bristle as I look into my eyes, turning a few things over in my mind. Will she say yes? What will I do if she doesn't? What the hell do I think I could do? Force her? I laugh at myself, reaching for my razor, pouting. She'd be crazy to turn me down, right? Because while I'm uncertain about much, I know without a shadow of doubt that there is not a man who walks this planet, or ever will, who can or will love her as much as I love her. Okay, so my love comes with a few . . . quirks. But it's rich, pure, and it's real.

I take the razor to my cheek and pause, my eyes widening. "The ring," I whisper to myself. The necklace too. "Fuck." The razor hits the sink with a clang, and I'm out of the bathroom like a rocket, flying down the stairs, grabbing my keys and pelting out the front door. I hit the call button and, thank the elevator gods, it's still on the top floor. The doors slide open and I hop in, walking circles around the small space, watching the floor counter tick down. The moment the gap is big enough, I squeeze through and run through the foyer.

"Hi, Clive," I call as I pass, his startled eyes following me. I make it to my car, not for the first time today blowing out of my fucking arse. I haul the door open and crouch, feeling around under the seat for the bags, my face squished to the side of the leather. I yank them out, stand, and stall shutting the door. "What the . . .?" I reach forward and run my fingers through the white smears all over the seat, raising them to my nose. Then I realize. I shut the door and come face to face with myself in the window.

Bare chested. Boxers. Face full of shaving foam. "For fuck's sake," I mutter, just as a car drives in through the gates—another resident—who pulls up in the reserved space a few away from mine. He gets out. Looks me up and down, pulling his briefcase out behind him.

I nod a polite hello and turn on my bare feet, walking with less urgency back into Lusso. What a fucking day.

I make it back to the penthouse and have a quick listen for movement as I go to my study, hearing nothing. Once I've retrieved the key from its hiding place and opened the safe, I place the two boxes inside before locking it back up. Heading back to the bathroom, I turn off the taps and test the water, then take off my watch and boxers and sink into the bath, without the energy I need to now shave.

I close my eyes and breathe, taking the unexpected time to recharge and give my poor, overused muscles a break from moving. But I won't go to sleep. I can't drift off. *Don't go to sleep.* Not alone in the tub.

I see long, dirty-blond hair on the sweetest, most angelic face. Chubby little hands and legs. Green eyes that match mine and Jake's. I don't think anything in this life will sound as good as the words *Daddy* coming from her little mouth. Will I get that again?

Daddy, Daddy, Daddy.

I inhale sharply and open my eyes. The water is tepid. Probably about the right temperature for Rosie. My heart clenches, and I scrub my wet hands down my face, sighing as I turn on the hot tap and let it warm up the water. The cycle isn't letting up. It's as if the universe deems it necessary and appropriate to ramp up the torture, maybe push me to the brink of despair, forcing some confessions out of me. It's me against my past. My past is creeping ahead.

I reach for my watch, leaning out of the bath, stretching. "Jesus Christ." Two hours have passed. I rest back as I hear a door close in the distance. “Finally,” I say to my darkness, washing the remnants of foam off my face. She appears, a glorious, flustered beauty. She gets out of her dress and lacy underwear, and I sink farther down into the water on a sigh. And then she’s naked, except for her perfectly painted nails.

“Where have you been?” I pout, my eyes following her to the tub, my hands twitching to get hold of her as she steps in and sits between my legs, lying against me.

“I was waiting for my nails to dry.”

I curl my body around her and squeeze. “That’s two hours I’ve lost with you that I’m not going to get back. No more painting nails and hunting down scarce whiskey.”

She chuckles, clinging to my arms, stroking across the hair. “Okay,” she says easily, and I smile. “Clive gave me some post for you this morning. I shoved it in my bag and forgot about it. Sorry.”

“No problem.” I tighten my hold, nuzzling deeper into her neck, relishing the heat and our wet skin rubbing. “I love, love, love you wet and sliding all over me.” I lay a hand over each breast and softly meld the small, perfect mounds. “Tomorrow,” I say hoarsely, sucking at the flesh of her neck, “we stay in bed all day long.” I am *not* leaving this penthouse, be sure of that.

Ava doesn’t protest, so I’m going to assume that’s a straight agreement from her. Then I feel her chest rise on an inhale, and I brace myself for that protest. Or a question. She’s held back on those since last night when we had a little heart-to-heart about a few things. Was it a step in the right direction? Or a leap the wrong way?

“What was the first thing you thought when you saw me?” she asks quietly, making me pause with the attention I’m paying to her neck.

I smile and latch on to her ear. “Mine.”

Water splashes when she jerks on a laugh. “You didn’t.”

“I fucking did.” Among other things. *Like get on my desk so I can fuck you now while I’m sober and will remember every second.* “And now you are.” Putting a finger under her chin, I encourage her head to the side and direct her mouth to mine, pressing my lips to hers. “I love you." I think I loved her then too. Right there in my office, dizzy with uncontrollable reactions, I think I fell in love on the spot.

Ava sighs, indulging my mouth. "I know you do. Did it ever occur to you to ask me to dinner instead of stalking me, asking inappropriate questions, and cornering me in one of your torture chambers?"

I pout, remembering that fateful day, not needing to relive those moments or feelings, because I feel them every day. Between the heart attacks and meltdowns. "No," I reply quietly. "It didn't." I could hardly think at all. "I wasn't thinking straight. You made me crazy confused."

"Confused about what?"

"I don't know. You triggered something in me. It was very disturbing." I look up at the ceiling of the beautiful bathroom that Ava designed, thinking back to those days when she resisted me. It seems laughable now. Look at us. So in love. I was right not to give up, and I'm so thankful I didn't, because fuck knows where I would be now.

Drunk.

Fucking.

Hiding.

Okay, I'm facing some challenges. Terrified of losing again. But, and it's fucked up on so many levels, at least I have something to lose. Which means I'm really quite passionate about keeping it.

"You gave me a flower," she muses.

"Yeah." That was step one of the plan that failed miserably. "I was trying to be a gentleman."

"So the next time you saw me, you asked me how loud I would scream when you fuck me?"

I grin like a dick, but wince at the same time. That should have been game over. Speaks volumes that it wasn't, doesn't it? "Mouth, Ava." I laugh. "I didn't know what to do. I only usually have to smile to get what I want."

"You should have tried to be less arrogant."

"Maybe." Now let's get the nitty-gritty details of Ava's experience that day. I know she was in awe. *Looks*. I know she was curious. *Age*. I know she couldn't string a sentence together without a few deep breaths. *Chemistry.* "Tell me what you thought." I wait, sensing her smiling. "Tell me."

"What?" she asks, laughing. "So your head can swell further?" I make a play for her hip and squeeze. "Stop!"

"Tell me," I order softly. "I want to know."

"I nearly passed out," she whispers, sounding wistful. She's gone back to The Manor that day too. Revisiting our meet-cute. It's a great meet-cute. Someone should write a book about it. "And then you kissed me. Why did you kiss me?"

To this day, I still can't answer that. My brain short-circuited. "I don't know. It just happened." I just needed to touch her. She was the shiny to my magpie. "You nearly passed out?" I smile, despite knowing she was highly affected.

She's suddenly moving, looking back at me. I don't wipe my smugness away in time, not that I was in a rush to. I want her to know how much that pleases me. "I thought you were an arrogant arse, with your touching, tactless comments, and inappropriate manners," she says, and I withdraw but smile harder. "But I was so affected by you."

I was well aware of how affected she was. It made the chase so much more frustrating. I start caressing her nipples, settling back again. "I needed to keep touching you to see if I was imagining things." I know time is knocking on, but I'm without the will to move. This is nice.

"What things?"

"My whole body buzzed every time I laid a finger on you. It still does." *Like now*.

"Me too." She doesn't sound particularly happy about that, more confused. I guess that's to be expected, since this all happened hard and fast and without warning. "Do you realize the effect you have on women?" She's feeling me, stroking my thighs, and I look at her hands moving across my skin, noting that the moment she mentions *other women*, she's got her hands all over me. *Possessive*. Unlike

Ava, I can't say I dislike it. But what effect I have on other women is not something I'm remotely interested in. Ava, though? I want to affect her, consume her, and yet the only thing I truly have to offer her is my complete and utter devotion. My heart. My future.

"Is it similar to the one you have on me?" I ask, holding her hands, needing to feel her. "Do they stop breathing for a few seconds every time they see me?" I take a moment, kissing her hair, feeling her body tighten on mine. "Do they want to keep me in a glass box so nothing and no one can hurt me?" Fuck, I'm not expressing myself very well here. "Do they think their life would be over if I wasn't here?" That's the bottom line. I'd be finished without her. I look down at the back of her head while she remains unmoving and silent, probably absorbing my declaration. It's that simple. Except . . . not.

I begin to get slightly concerned by her lack of a reaction, just lying under her, waiting for . . . anything. She eventually begins to move, and I bite my lip, bracing myself. Will she hit me with more questions? Interrogate me again? Want some context to those words? Because . . . why? Why do I feel like that? Why am I so scared of losing her? Why does she mean so much to me?

Ava looks at me, and I see that curiosity. Those questions. But I also see a ton of love for this fucked-up arsehole. She pushes herself up my body, sliding, and her eyes dart over my face, settling on mine. "You stole my lines," she whispers, her eyes starting to scan my face again, as I release the air I was holding. "I love you so much. You have to promise me that *you'll* never leave *me*."

Fuck, I'm a lucky man. This is why she went to The Manor last night. Despite my anger at her being at her ex's, despite my inappropriate—*for some*—manhandling of her, and our shared volatility, *she* didn't want to lose *me*. "Baby, you're stuck with me forever."

"Good. Kiss me."

"Are you making demands?" Because I like it.

"Yes." There's no apology. "Kiss me."

We really don't have time. But . . . one kiss. I slowly move in, waiting for that moment for when our lips meet and my world goes up in smoke. You'd think I'd be used to it by now. I don't think I ever will be.

It starts soft and slow, unhurried, delicate, until she's forcing herself farther into me, her mouth becoming more urgent. It's an effort not to respond. "I know it would make you very happy to stay here all night," I say around her mouth, smiling at the sound of her humming, making all the right noises at the wrong time. "But we need to think about getting a move on." I tear my mouth away and hoist her up a bit more until my mouth can reach her neck.

"Let's stay." She virtually moans the words, rubbing her boobs into my chest, before slipping back down my body. Her pussy skims my cock.

Fuck. "Oh, you have to let me out because if I stay, we'll be going nowhere." And one thing I can't be is late for the anniversary party. I slam a hard kiss on her lips and, for my sins, push her off me.

I make it maybe a foot off my arse before I'm forced back down and Ava's crawling onto me again. "Stay then." She settles on my lap, her smile poorly concealed. She knows she's got me. "I want to mark you." Eyes on mine, she lowers until she's sucking on my chest. Like a sign of ownership? She already did that. "Ava, we'll be late." She sucks harder, bites a bit, and the blood I've been holding back breaks through the dam and flows into my cock. We're going to The Manor, where endless women will be waiting like wolves to pounce. And she's marking me. It turns me on. "Fuck, I can't say no to you."

Literally.

Physically.

I encourage her to lift, and we both breathe out when she sinks onto me.

Yeah. Can't say no.

32

I'M STANDING, suited, considering the spare bedroom I've stepped foot in maybe three times since I've lived here. All looking for Ava. It would make a wonderful nursery. But maybe a little too far away from our room.

All thoughts for another day, Ward. Let's focus on convincing Ava—and the rest of the world, for that matter—that she should marry me.

I chew my lip, grabbing my tie, vehemently ignoring my subconscience, which is currently reminding me that I have already done things arse about face.

I spray some Aqua di Gio on my neck and go to the mirror, looking at a man I've only recently become acquainted with. A man with clear eyes and a clear mind. Which begs the question why he's having such insane thoughts, given he's lucid for the first time in nearly twenty years.

I slip my Rolex on and fix my collar, get my jacket on, then go downstairs to my study. I stand on the threshold for a while, looking at another space in the penthouse that's under-used. But, again, if Ava set up her own firm? This would be an amazing workspace for her. And in Lusso, a place she designed and executed? Don't tell me that's not the perfect portfolio. To have her meetings with clients and potential clients surrounded by the luxury she created? It makes perfect sense.

Once at my desk, I lower to my chair, pulling my trousers up by the knees and making sure my jacket isn't beneath my arse. I gaze at the wall opposite the desk, my fingers forming a steeple in front of my mouth. It's a little bare. Some art will fix that. Pulling my phone from my pocket, I start scrolling through the images of Ava, marking my favorites. That's all of them.

I get to the most recent image of her in the liquor store leaning over the counter to see the shelfs and smile, head tilted. But I lose the screen when my phone rings. "Clive," I say, getting the key for my safe out of the drawer.

"Mr. Ward, the elevator doors have been repaired."

"Thanks, Clive." I get up and go to the safe in the cupboard.

"Anything else, Mr. Ward?"

I smile a little. "Not now, Clive, but I'm sure I'll require your assistance in the near future."

"Right you are, Mr. Ward." He hangs up, and I tuck my phone away, freeing up both hands to remove the necklace box from the safe. I lift the lid, squinting when the sparkle seems to burst out of the box as if it's been suppressed. I take the necklace and put the box back, shutting the safe, the diamonds hanging from my hand, the spotlights above hitting it from every direction, projecting light beams on the walls. It's quite symbolic. Like Ava, it radiates light. My stomach flutters, and I laugh in response. I'm nervous? I bunch the necklace into my fist carefully and slip it into my trouser pocket, wiping at my forehead without thought. *Really* nervous. I shake my head to myself, checking my watch. "Shit," I breathe, retrieving my phone and leaving my study, dialing John.

"Where are you?" he asks, short and sharp. "It's six."

"I'm on my way." I get to the bottom of the stairs and look up.

"You've left Lusso, haven't you?" John's question is loaded with threat.

"Yeah." I take the stairs two at a time on light feet.

"So you're in the car, aren't you?"

"I am."

"So, Ava can hear me, can't she?"

Fuck it. "All right, Marple. We're just leaving."

"Sarah's stressing about the gift bags."

"Why?"

"No batteries."

"What?"

"Niles provided the toys and no batteries."

I approach our bedroom door. "Schoolboy error," I mutter, which is ironic because he looks like a schoolboy.

"Can you pick some batteries up on your way?"

"Where the hell am I going to get—"

"Fifteen hundred triple A's?"

"Fifteen hundred?" I blurt. "Fucking hell, John. I don't think the local Tesco will have fifteen hundred triple A's knocking around in the stock room."

"I did wonder if I was clutching at straws."

I sigh. No batteries for the cock rings? For fuck's sake. Luxury giftbags that include toys that require batteries but have no batteries. "I'll be there soon." I hang up and get close to the door, knocking gently. "Ava, baby, we need to go."

"Two minutes," she calls as I back away, batteries and lateness forgotten. I'm nervous again, and the anticipation to see her is getting the better of me. I take myself downstairs and put some music on, pace, eyes low, thinking, thinking, thinking. What will her family make of me? It hasn't escaped my notice that Ava hasn't mentioned introducing me to them. And, gutting as it is, I know it's because she's worried about the age gap. She's worried about what her parents will think. And her brother? I cringe. An older brother, though still not as old as me.

I blow out my cheeks, continuing to pace. What does my age matter, really? All any father wants for their daughter is a man who will devote his life to her. Make her his number one priority. I'm that man. If I'm ever blessed enough to have the chance to be a dad again, that's all I'll want for my daughter. A devoted man.

I stop pacing, rubbing my fist into my heart.

She'd be nineteen now.

Dating? Studying?

My lip begins to quiver, and I roughly wipe at my eyes before the tears fall and give me away. I look up and around, at all of the inbuilt speakers pouring music down on me. Moody Blues. Appropriate. My mood has certainly plummeted. I slip my hands into my pockets, feeling the necklace, trying to get my mind back to the present, watching my feet as I wander up and down again. I'm struggling.

What would she have been like?

What would *I* have been like? As a father to a young woman? An inspiration? A failure? A disappointment.

Would I have spiralled if she'd lived? If my actions hadn't killed her, would I be a better man?

"I've never seen him so determined to live," John apparently said to Ava last night. She told me in a whisper, half asleep. Would I have been so determined to *not* live if Rosie had lived?

I take my hands from my pockets and lower to the couch, sitting forward, my fingers fiddling, my body restless. I get back up, pace some more.

And then . . .

I look up and the air I was struggling to find suddenly rushes into my lungs, so fast I can't keep up with the breaths. And there she is.

My reason to breathe.

My reason to go on.

To be the best man I can be.

But is it too late?

It's never too late, Daddy.

I jolt, as Ava grabs the handrail, her eyes full of wonder. Wonder for me? Just look at her. I can hardly take it all in. Not the sight of her in a stunning black lace gown, her long, dark hair cascading over her shoulders. But the sight of her looking at me like I am her be all and end all.

"Oh Jesus," I whisper. I lift a foot, the weight of the love I have for this woman making even the smallest of tasks, like walking, so fucking hard. I take each step with care, slowly, eyes unable to leave hers, and when I've made it to her, I offer my hand. I see her visibly inhale, her arm shaking as she lifts it and gives me her hand. I walk her down the stairs and finally take a moment away from her sheer presence to take in the exquisite dress she's wearing. Fucking hell, it was made for her, the delicate fabric lightly kissing every gorgeous curve. I watch as her shoulders roll with her arduous breathing, and it's such a relief to see. To know she's struggling too.

I walk around the back of her, my eyes up and down, and suck in air when I find her back seriously lacking coverage, the dress plunging to reveal every smooth plane of her skin. I swallow, batting back my knee-jerk reaction, which is to cover her up. Hide her skin from the waiting eyes of the world. Except, I can't. I can't take away something from her that was clearly *meant* for her.

Like I hope no one takes her away from me.

My teeth sink into my bottom lip as I lift a shaky hand and place a shaky finger on the base of her neck, watching her body straighten, the perfect reaction to my touch. Painting a long, slow line down the center of her back, I relish the roll of her body that comes like a wave behind my fingertip. I kiss her skin and round her. "I can't find my breath." I pull her close and feel the inevitable reaction behind my fly. "I *really* like your dress." I look down her front. "You didn't try this one. I would have remembered this one."

"Always in lace," she whispers.

I look at her, stunned. "You chose this dress for me?" I move back, reaching into my pocket, feeling at the diamond. If they don't already, tonight every female member of The Manor will know I'm off the menu. A sharp pain rides through my lip. And every male member is likely to have their legs broken if they so much as peek at her. Fucking hell, I'm at risk of having no members left. Would that be such a terrible thing? I've always thought The Manor would make an amazing hotel resort. Like, a real hotel resort. Maybe a golf club.

I frown and peek up. Ava's quiet and still, letting me have my moment.

I pull the diamond out of my pocket and let it dangle from my finger between us. "Like I chose this for you?"

There is no mistaking the widening of her eyes, her mouth agape as she stares at the fine piece. "Jesse." She's breathless, her troubled eyes coming back to mine. "That necklace was sixty grand."

So she looked closely enough to see the price tag? I circle around the back of her, moving her hair and draping the necklace down her front. The moment the precious stone meets her skin, she breathes in deeply. But she doesn't stop me from putting it on her. I secure the clasp and slip my hands onto her shoulders, kissing her neck beneath the layered chains of the necklace. "You like?"

"You know I do, but . . ." She fades off. "Did Zoe tell you?" she asks, her hand hovering in front of her, her chin dropped, looking at it. Or watching it. Scared of it.

"No," I say, helping her round to face me. I look down at the beauty on *my* beauty, touching it. "I asked Zoe to show it to you." My finger slides from the hard stone onto her soft skin. "You are crazy beautiful." I kiss her, feeling her smile beneath my lips.

"Are you talking to me or the diamond?" She laughs, and it's nervous. I don't want her to be nervous about it. I want her to own it because she carries it wonderfully, and with this dress?

"It's all about you. As it always will be."

"Jesse"—she peeks down again—"what if I lose it, what if—"

"Ava, shut up," I warn softly, brushing her hair back. "It's insured and it's a gift from me. If you don't wear it, I'll be crazy mad. Understand?"

She hesitates, looking unsure, but she softens, accepting, reaching for my chest and moving in, looking up at me. There it is again. Acceptance. I think it's my most favorite look on Ava. I know it's only a necklace, but she accepted it. Because I want her to. This moment feels somehow . . . significant.

"I really don't know what to say."

"You could say you love it," I say. "You could say thank you." *You could say you'll marry me. Have babies with me. Give me everything I never dared dreamed I could be blessed with.*

"I do love it." She smiles. "Thank you."

"You are more than welcome, baby." I accept her kiss. "It's not as beautiful as you, though. Nothing is." Now, we *really* have to go before John kicks my arse and Sarah has a breakdown. "My work here is done." Not quite, but for now. "Come on, you've made your god late." I collect Ava and my keys, and turn off the music, opening the door for her and pulling her into the foyer, unable to stop myself from looking at her constantly, smiling, happy. Again, not because of how incredible she looks, but because she's here. With me. On my arm.

We're a couple.

I feel her watching me too, and I wonder what she's thinking. It's one of the first times in our relationship that I haven't been worried about that. Her eyes sparkling as hard as that diamond around her neck, she rubs at my bottom lip with her thumb. "You're crazy handsome," she says softly, concentrating on her task of cleaning me up. "And all mine."

Something is happening here, and I don't know what. I already knew she loved me. But now, here, it's different. I know The Manor is the last place she wants to be. I know she hasn't been looking forward to this evening. But she's doing it. For me. That's love. Not just adoring but compromising. Maybe the truths I spoke last night have eased her. Reassured her. Even though we barely scraped the barrel of other things I need to render. "Just yours, baby." I kiss her fingers, holding her hand tightly and getting us off the elevator when the doors open. I pull her into my side as we pass Clive, the old boy smiling as we go.

One day, I tell myself, I will share my story with Ava. I could do it now, tell her about Jake and Rosie, smile my way through some of the memories. Problem is, there's no happy ever after for those stories. And I can't tell her the beginning and not the end. But I don't see my family. Don't talk about my family. Don't talk about anything pre-Ava, really. It's only a matter of time before that fact starts spiking questions too.

33

JOHN LOOKS FUCKING furious when I pull up, but he somehow manages to find it in himself to give Ava the cheesiest smile I've ever seen grace his serious face. I laugh to myself. That smile wasn't for Ava, it was for me. A message that I'm the soul focus of his bad mood.

I give him a playful—very real—snarl as I chuck him my keys, and he gives me a look to suggest I'm a dead man. But who's going to kill me? Sarah or John?

"There you are!"

I flinch at the shrill voice of Sarah as I pull Ava along, feeling her hand stiffen in mine. Always does when Sarah's around. I can't hold it against her, especially now she knows Sarah's and I have slept together. But I wish she'd disregard that and listen to me when I tell her there is and never will be anything between us. I suppose it would be helpful to give Ava context but—

Can't do that.

Sarah skids to a stop and looks past me, her eyes going straight to Ava's neck. If she could, she'd frown, but she can't. She can, however, scowl, and she executes that without a problem or fault.

"I'm here now," I say on a sigh, taking Ava into the bar to get her settled before I'm dragged away to deal with the battery crisis.

"Here, sit." I help her onto the stool and take one myself, searching out Mario across the bar, waving him over.

Something is thrust under my nose between me and Ava. "Can we just go through—"

"Sarah, give me a minute," I say, ensuring Ava sees my attention is on her alone. Makes sure she knows Sarah means nothing beyond work. Yes, I care about the woman, but that's simply an unfortunate disadvantage of guilt. "What would you like to drink?"

Ava's gaze goes to the top shelf behind the bar where Mario, the dapper bastard, has appeared, looking chipper, eager to serve.

"I'll have a *Mario Most Marvelous*, please."

"Yes," Mario sings, delighted that someone loves his rocket fuel. Because that's what it is. Highly flammable. Dangerous. I'll be keeping an eye on her. "Mr. Ward?"

"Just a water, please, Mario." I give Ava a quick kiss.

"Sloe gin, Mario." Sarah may as well be on my fucking lap, and Ava pushing herself harder onto my lips, humming happily, is nothing short of pissing up my leg. "Jesse, I could really do with you in the office."

"Sarah, please." She's like a fucking fly buzzing in my ear. I stand, at least showing the signs of my intention to leave, so perhaps she'll shut the fuck up and let me finish what I'm doing. Or actually, let Ava finish what *she's* doing. Claiming me. I ask Ava if she'd like to come, if only to demonstrate who's most important in this situation, and it isn't Sarah or my manor.

"I'm good here," she replies. "You go."

I take my water as Mario sets it down and drop a kiss onto her forehead. "I'll be quick."

I leave fast, Sarah following. "Is it really necessary to show such sickening public displays of affection?"

I stop abruptly, breathe in, and look up to the ornate ceiling of The Manor, making it as obvious as I can that I'm gathering patience. Ripping her head off will only achieve guilt and an earful from John.

"What are you doing?" she snaps from beside me.

"Stopping myself from ripping you a new arsehole."

She pouts. "I might like that."

"Oh, fuck off," I mutter, picking up my feet and breaking into the summer room, weaving through the beautifully dressed tables. Black and gold. I smile. It's brief. What have I got to do to get Ava back in the extension? "What's the deal with the batteries?"

"Well, it's simple. There are no batteries."

I push my way into my office. "How the fuck did he forget batteries?" I pull my phone out and pull up Google. And pause. What the fuck am googling? Where to get fifteen hundred batteries on a Friday night in the Surrey Hills? "You're just gonna have to remove the cock rings from the gift bags."

Sarah breathes in, taking a swig of her drink, looking like she's the one now gathering patience. "I'm going to whip that little prick so hard." She throws the clipboard on the sideboard and paces, and I watch her struggling to walk. Not in the heels, she's a master at walking in heels. It's the red dress. She can hardly put one foot in front of the other it's so tight.

I sit on the couch. "Doesn't look like you can do much in that dress except stand." One swing of her whip might topple her.

"Don't you worry, sweetie," she coos. "With a whip in my hand, I can do anything."

I laugh. It's sardonic. "Have you called the schoolboy?" I ask.

"He isn't answering."

"Probably oiling up, ready for his whipping session."

The door opens, and we both look up, just as the boy himself appears, a box in his hands. "Batteries," he says, looking between us.

"Are you joking?" Sarah slams her glass down and hustles over, opening one of the flaps. "I am going to whip you so fucking hard."

Niles looks at me, somewhere between alarm and excitement, and I raise my brows. "Don't look at me, kid. I've never had the pleasure." I throw a dirty look to Sarah's back, and she turns a wicked smile onto me. "Are we done?" I ask.

"All done." Sarah walks out.

As John walks in. "Nope. Sit your motherfucking arse on that motherfucking sofa, motherfucker."

"That sure is a lot of motherfucking," I quip, cautiously lowering to the couch as instructed. "Am I in trouble?"

"Niles," Sarah hollers. "Get those batteries in the cock rings before I introduce you to my whip."

"Now that's a line I bet you thought you'd never hear," I say, smiling at Niles. "Run along now." He's gone like a shot, and I laugh, but it dries up the moment John sits on the couch opposite me, looking like he's getting comfortable. "Haven't you got valets to direct?" People to scare? Motherfuckers to throw? Anything but hold me here against my will and bring on another barrage of guilt or stress?

"All under control."

"Oh fuck," I breathe as he removes his shades. I'm in for it. I push my back into the sofa. "Come on, then." I hold up my hands, motioning him to come at me like I'm inviting a fight. Obviously, I never would. Not with John. And not because I love him. He's a one punch kind of man. One punch and you're dead. Those spades on the ends of his arms are fatal. "I've not asked her yet, if that's what you're wondering."

"I *was* actually. I didn't see a ring, so thought perhaps—"

"She said no?" I sit up straight. "Do you think she'll say no?"

Those big spades lift and he rubs into his eye sockets. "Do this right, Jesse. Have you met her parents?"

I shrink, not wanting to admit what he already knows. "Why are you so hell-bent on talking me out of this?"

"I don't want to talk you out of this. I want to talk you into doing it right. That means being honest. That means being respectful."

I baulk. "You don't think I respect Ava?"

"Her parents. What are you expecting here? That Ava will finally introduce you to her parents as her fiancé? Or husband?" He laughs. "Even you can see that's crazy."

"Yeah, well, my life is one big crazy these days, isn't it?" Fuck it all. Why'd it take John to make me realize my plan is, actually, really fucking crazy. "They live in Cornwall, John." I frown. "And Ava doesn't seem to be in a rush to make a meet happen." The last time she spoke to her mother, she'd told her I was, in a nutshell, not important enough to mention. *Just seeing him.* "They know about me." I have Ava's ex to thank for that. I'm frowning again. "And think I'm an alcoholic monster who battered her ex." Jesus. They don't even know about my *hotel*. My age. I have red flags all over me for any parent. "God, I hate you," I mutter, rubbing at my forehead.

I need a drink.

Can't have one.

"I have shit to do." John gets up and leaves me alone, and I sink deeper into my chair, running it all over in my head again. Do it right. What the hell is right, anyway? If I ask for Ava's hand, I can't imagine I'll get an excited blessing. Because they don't fucking know me.

And neither does Ava.

"Fuck off, Jake."

"We need help," Sarah says, bursting in. "Guests will be arriving soon, and I have to get all these batteries in the cock rings."

"Right," I sigh, pushing my heavy body out of my chair and following her into the summer room, immediately overwhelmed by a room that I admired when I walked through it minutes ago. Endless tables, a dozen chairs around each, a giftbag at every setting. "Pass me some batteries, then." I hold my hand out and accept the multipack.

"You okay?" Sarah asks, making a start on the next table, Niles going the other way, starting at the opposite end of the room.

"What do you care, Sarah?" I ask tiredly, looking toward the entrance to the bar. I said I wouldn't be long. Not likely.

"You know I care."

Yeah, I know. She just has a really fucked-up way of showing it. I work my way around the table, my big hands struggling with the fiddly task. The tension between us is thick, and it's really fucking weird. "I'm going to marry her," I say, looking up at Sarah, seeing her moves falter. No one will stop me. Not the Sarahs of this world, the Corals, the Frejas, the Mikaels, or the Matts. No one. The only person who can stop me marrying Ava is Ava. Okay, John's stalled me. But only stalled. I'll be pushing to meet the parents tomorrow. Can't say I'm relishing the thought now I'll have to explain myself, because Matt's made that fucking essential. *Dickhead.*

"She can't give you want you need," Sarah says quietly, reluctantly. Reluctant, because she's unsure what I need anymore. I can assure her, it isn't this. "She will never accept you like I can." Her statement is so quiet. Almost unheard. But I hear it.

I toss the empty pack of batteries on the table. "Accept me?" I laugh. "Accept me for being a letdown, Sarah? A total fuck-up? I don't want her to accept me for the piece of shit who lost everything. Who ruined his life. I want her to accept me for being an amazing husband. A wonderful father." I feel my jaw tense, my words becoming hissed, and Sarah steps back, wary. "The man she needs me to be and who I *want* to be." I jab a finger toward the bar. "For *Ava*. For Rosie. For Jake."

"You're delusional."

"You know what, fuck this shit." I flick a hand out and knock over a wineglass. "I don't know why I'm standing here talking about the most pointless fucking thing in the world when I could be out there *with* my world." I stalk off, glaring at John when I find him behind me, warning him not to bother. "Do the fucking batteries yourself."

I stop in the hallway before the bar entrance, taking a moment to calm myself down. Then I slap on a smile and enter, standing tall, confident, when I feel anything but, Sarah's poison making me doubt myself even more. Sarah might think that my relationship with Ava is toxic, but it's got nothing on the one between us, because Sarah knows of all my sins. And she manipulates that knowledge any chance she can get. Yet I have no idea how to stop her.

I see Ava at the bar and relax a little when I note Sam, Drew, and Kate are with her. I also spot Natasha getting up from a nearby table and moving in. "Jesse," she purrs, and I quickly step to the left before she gets too close, making sure I set the tone for the evening.

I smile. "Evening, Natasha."

"Did I see you have company?" she asks over the rim of her glass, looking in Ava's direction.

"No, Natasha, you didn't see I have company, and I'll tell you why."

"Please do," she says, smiling, sultry, as she sips her fizz.

"Well, firstly, this is the first time you've set eyes on me since you arrived."

"But not the first time *ever*, right?"

Unfortunately, yes. In fact, it feels like every other female who has ever laid a hand or eye on me, with the exception of my daughter, of course, has ruined a small piece of me each time. "Right," I say slowly, observing the wolves circling, ready to chase off their competitor. Fucking hell. I take a quick peek at Ava to make sure she's not watching. She's feeling quite possessive today. It's most pleasing, but I don't need a bloodbath in the bar. "Second," I go on, returning my attention to the brazen female who fits in around here perfectly. "I don't have company, Natasha."

Her eyes light up. "No?"

"No." I shake my head, pulling in my suit jacket, backing away. "I have my girlfriend." I flash her a smile that would always usually floor a woman. "Have a good evening."

She grins through a scowl, and that look alone tells me my message hasn't sunken in. I've never truly realized the thickness of the skin around here. It's unreal. I feel like I've just made the challenge more interesting.

I get my arse to the bar before I'm intercepted again, seeing Ava with a full glass in her hand. I look at Mario over her head. He holds up three fingers. I shake my head. "No more," I mouth, and he nods, going on to serve at the other end. My itching palms slide onto the lace at her hips, my chin on her shoulder. "I've neglected you," I say quietly, while also noting that I have very much neglected myself too. No more neglecting. Not tonight. It'll keep the vultures away.

Ava looks back, not looking at all pissed off or uncomfortable. "Yes, you have. Where have you been?"

Yeah, not telling her that. "I couldn't get two yards without someone making a play for me." And I expect that'll be a trend tonight if I stray far from Ava's side, so I'll make a point to remain stuck to her. "I'm all yours now, I promise." Leaning into her, I extend my hand and shake with both the boys, then dip so Kate, who looks really fucking incredible in a green gown, can say hello with a kiss. I glance at Sam when her lips land on my cheek, watching him watch Ava's firecracker of a mate. I'm worried for him. "Is everyone good?"

"We will be when dinner is out of the way." Sam hits his bottle to Drew's, and I look at them both in question. What the fuck's going on? I don't know, but I know I don't like it, and I definitely don't like Ava's tensing body in my hold. She's worried too.

"Ten thirty." I keep my interrogative gaze on Sam as I remove Ava from the stool and sit, putting her between my open thighs, peeking at Kate when I have a quick nuzzle of Ava's neck, seeing the red-headed firecracker doing a terrible job of looking cool, looks being thrown around left and right. Oh God, is what I think happening actually happening? My eyes go back to Drew. His eyebrows rise. *Shit*. I move my eyes to Sam. He's refusing to look at me now. The dickhead. Never in the years I've known him has he spent the night at a woman's house. Never in the time I've known him has he left The Manor to go see a woman who *isn't* a member. And now he's planning on sharing that woman and, worst, with one of his best mates? *Fucking hell.* This stinks of shitstorm.

I shake my head at them, not that they see, and realign my focus on the woman in my arms, licking her neck. "I want to lay you on that bar and take my time peeling all of this lace off." I roll my hips up, like I need to be making my night any harder. Figuratively speaking and literally speaking. "What's under the dress?"

"More lace."

"You're fucking killing me."

"You have to stop."

"Never." I continue with my assault, breathing heavily, increasing the pressure behind my trousers and she lets me.

"You guys."

I jolt with the assistance of a slap on my back, thanks to Kate.

"Put her down."

"Yeah," Sam pipes up. "You're restraining our sexual needs, but it's okay for you to sit there and fondle your girl?"

"Try and stop me." I toss him a tired look. Someone needs to restrain them. This has disaster written all over it. "I'll shut up shop now and take her home."

"You're trampling your mates now," Ava says over a laugh, the others joining her. Don't care. I am very aware of the attention my behavior is drawing. Don't care. Every set of eyes are observing the impenetrable Lord of The Manor giving his soul attention to one woman. Pussy-whipped. Don't care. I get back to *fondling my girl*, biting at her neck, sucking, probably marking her. Again, don't care. *Don't care, don't care, don't care.* And isn't that the beauty of being in love?

"Who's that?"

"Who's who?" I ask, looking up, wiping at my mouth. Ava doesn't get the chance to point her out, because it had to be a *her*, didn't it? I spot Coral by the entrance to the bar, and my stomach turns. *Fuck.* What the fuck are John and Sarah playing at letting her in? But then her disposition registers. She's not drunk. She doesn't appear indignant. She looks lost. Hopeless.

Each one of my muscles tenses as she starts to walk over, and Sam and Drew abruptly shut up when they clock her. This is not ideal, and I have absolutely no fucking idea how to handle it. But I do know I don't need Coral around Ava. Fuck knows what she'll say. So I stand and move out, sitting Ava back down on the stool, feeling her looking at me with probing, accusing eyes. This isn't going to go down well.

But what fucking choice do I have?

"Coral," I say quietly, dodging Ava's eyes. "Do you want to come to my office?"

She opens her mouth to talk, her hands working circles, but no words materialize, so she weakly nods instead.

"Come on." I can't just walk away from Ava, not if I want my balls intact when I return, so I brave facing her. She looks in a state of shock. Disbelief? And no words come to me. Nothing. And even if they did, I don't expect they'd have the desired effect. So I walk away without a word, hoping she'll hear me—forgive me—when I play this down.

Coral turns and I see her wobble, prompting me to instinctively reach forward, ready to catch her. She's not drunk. I know she's not drunk. I've seen her in a state enough to know when she's under the influence. Emotional? Or just plain fucking exhausted by life?

I give John wide eyes as I pass him. He gets my message and immediately announces dinner. I do *not* need Ava sitting there stewing. Who am I kidding? She'll stew, no matter where she is and what she's doing, so John announcing dinner fifteen minutes early is not going to help me out.

I feel Ava's eyes on my back as I walk Coral out of the bar, and I look to the heavens for some mercy. Just a little fucking mercy. What was I to do? Cause a scene? Tell Coral to fuck off? I'm not stupid, and I'm not a monster.

I am, however, fucked.

I guide her through the array of tables in the summer room, and Sarah spots us, her body unbending from over the table, her eyes worried when they land on mine. She knows Coral could kick off. Today, though, I didn't see any fight in her. Just hopelessness and sadness.

"Need anything?" Sarah asks as we pass.

"I've got it." I open the door to my office and apply a little pressure to Coral's back, encouraging her inside, following her in and shutting the door. "Take a seat," I say, going to the fridge. "Water?" I look back and catch a shake of her head as she lowers to one of the couches. I get myself a bottle and put myself on the opposite sofa, and Coral watches me before seeming to measure the space between us, considering the coffee table that's a barrier. I don't relax back, keeping my arse on the edge of the seat. Apt. I feel uneasy. I unscrew the cap of my bottle as I chew my lip, wondering how to approach this. What to say. Pointing out she shouldn't be here seems ridiculous. Asking what she wants seems ridiculous. Truly, I just want to know she's okay, because she seriously doesn't look it.

"It was Mike who told the police you had staff working here illegally," she says, her voice even. I'm not surprised. So I just nod, wondering if she thinks this information will win my approval, as she regards me, waiting for . . . more? I don't give her anything.

"That was her?" she goes on.

My bottle of water pauses halfway to my mouth, and I stare at her, as she stares at me, waiting. "You mean Ava?" I say like a dick, like who else could she mean?

"In the black lace."

All over my lap while I was all over her neck? "Yes, that was Ava." Sarcasm doesn't fit this situation. But facts do. Or do they? I feel like giving Coral any hard-hitting truths might make this situation volatile, and it's currently calm. I need to keep it that way. But there cannot be any room for misunderstanding either. We've got to put this to bed. The last time I saw her, I threw her out of my office. Being cold and hard didn't work.

"She's young," she says quietly, and I hold my tongue, not feeling the need to defend our relationship. "Does she know about us?"

I give her a sharp look, desperate to tell her there is no *us*. "Coral, I'm in love with her."

She laughs, and it's really fucking insulting. Because the Lord of the Sex Manor isn't capable of love. "She can't give you what you need."

Oh Jesus, not her as well. Why the fuck do all these women think they know what I need? I don't entertain her statement. I sit back, crossing one leg over the other, and take some water to moisten my drying mouth. Coral looks at the bottle, where historically a glass of vodka would have been.

"You've stopped drinking," she says.

"Yes."

"Why?"

"Because it was time," I reply, and she nods, dropping her eyes briefly, fiddling with her fingers, before looking back at me.

"So that's it? You're turning your back on everything you were? If she loved you, she wouldn't want you to change." She sits forward more, her hand reaching across the table between us. "I wouldn't want you to change, Jesse."

I smile, and it's really fucking sad. "And that is why you're not the one for me, Coral."

She retracts her hand, her face falling. And I see it finally sink in. "What?"

"The man you've slept with? Got drunk with? Played with? That isn't who I am, Coral. And just the fact you wouldn't want to change me means I could never love you."

Her eyes drop, and she laughs to herself, putting her head in her hands, and I remain where I am, waiting for her next insult. Her next move. A good five minutes pass with nothing, and I start to get twitchy, constantly looking down at my watch. Then she abruptly stands, looking at me, and I see her eyes are full of tears. "I just—" She clears her throat, glancing away, as if she can't bear to look at me. "Do you mind if I use the ladies'?"

"Of course." I slowly lift a hand and point to the door. "You can use the one in the spa. You know where it is." It's a bit farther than the nearest one, but at least she won't have to walk through the summer room with a face stained with tears. Because they're coming.

Her laughter is really awkward. "Yeah, I know where it is." She walks off, and I catch her discreetly wiping at her eyes as she goes.

The door shuts, and I stand, looking at my watch again before I down the rest of my water and throw the bottle in the bin under my desk, stuffing my hands in my pockets and starting to pace, wondering at what point it's acceptable to instigate her departure. I don't know, but she's not thrown herself at me this time, which is an improvement on all others. Tread carefully.

Back and forth I go, for over twenty minutes. I eventually resort to venturing out of my office to look for her, worried she might have relocated her sly side and hit the bar.

I look left and right when I leave, heading away from the summer room and entering the spa area. I pass the pool, the steam rooms, the sauna, and reach the ladies'. I tap on the door. "Coral?" I call, listening. No answer. I push the door open slightly, scanning the space. Empty. "Coral, are you in here?" I hear a snivel and let myself in, walking down the line of cubicles. I find her in the last one, sitting on the lid of the toilet, sobbing her heart out.

I sigh, stepping inside, then back again, not knowing what to do. Then she looks up at me, a wreck of a woman, her body wracked with the force of her cries.

"I'm sorry," she sobs, yanking off some toilet paper and rubbing at her nose. "I've been so stupid."

My face twists, and I lower to my haunches, but I don't touch her. Just pull off more paper and hold it out, and she smiles meekly through her snivels, accepting. "I'm not very good at this," I say like a dickhead.

"What, emotional women?"

"Yeah." I've had the pleasure of a few recently, but Coral doesn't need to know that. It was so much easier to deal with the women of The Manor when I was full of vodka. It never needed to get this far, because the answer when a woman came knocking and threw herself at me was to indulge her. Fuck her.

Build their hopes up.

And now I'm dashing them.

Both unintentional.

"He's taken everything, Jesse," she says, playing with the tissue, looking at me with imploring eyes.

"You have your own money," I say, confused. Coral's parents are very wealthy people. She's a silver spoon child.

She shakes her head, and I withdraw. "What is left is in joint names, and he's frozen it all. Canceled my cards, taken my car." She laughs. "I can't even use my debit card because he's changed the PIN and passwords on all our accounts, so the bank won't talk to me. My parents are abroad and can't transfer me any money because I can't access it. They live in the Lakes District, and I have no money to get there. I used my last fifty pounds to get a cab here, Mike's changed the locks, told my parents I'm an alcoholic, and this"—she gestures to the white dress she's wearing—"is all I have to wear." She bursts into tears again and, God, it makes me feel like shit. What an absolute wanker. And clearly deeply vengeful.

"Come on," I say, rising, offering a hand and pulling her to her feet. I walk her back to my office and pass a box of tissues, then sit down at my desk and open my laptop.

"What are you doing?" she asks.

"I'm booking you a hotel for the night." I tap at the keys, picking the first one that comes up in the search bar.

"Jesse, I—"

I hold a hand up. "Do you have a key to your parents' house?"

She shakes her head. Of course she doesn't. Why would she need a key to a house that's hundreds of miles away? "When are they back?"

"Monday, I think. I'll call them and check." She reaches for her purse.

I change the selection from one night to three. "Let me know. I can always extend it if it's later."

She pulls out her phone and dials, then puts it to her ear but quickly pulls it away, looking at the screen. I don't miss her recoil.

"What?" I ask, naturally standing and walking over.

"It's nothing."

"Coral, what is it?"

She looks up at me. "My phone's been cut off."

I laugh dryly. Fucking hell, he's something else. I go back to my desk, complete the reservation, and book a cab, printing off the confirmation. *Wanker*. Where the fuck is he expecting her to sleep? What the fuck is he expecting her to eat and wear? I growl, incensed. There's a fine line between love and hate, I know that. Can attest to that. My ex-wife loved me so much, she stabbed me because it was unrequited. I suppose I should be grateful Coral's not brandishing a knife.

I rip off the paper from the pad and hand it to her. "A cab's on its way to drive you back into the city."

"Thank you, Jesse. I appreciate it."

"Don't mention it." I open the door, not looking forward to my impending interrogation. "I'll see you out."

I walk her down the corridor and immediately locate John at the table. He doesn't notice me until Ava sits taller in her chair, spotting me. Then he gets up, tossing his napkin down and coming over.

"A cab will be here in a few minutes for Coral." I move away from her.

"Got it."

"Do you have any cash?" I ask, and he frowns. "Mike's frozen everything. Changed the locks. I've booked her a few nights in a hotel until her parents are back, but I can't transfer any money for incidentals because she has no access to her accounts. He's cut off her phone too."

John scowls. "I have cash," he says, tapping his jacket pocket.

"Thanks. I'll pay you back." I look at Coral, hoping it will be the last time. "Take care, Coral."

She nods, lifting her hand to reach for me, but I move back, shaking my head, making myself as clear as possible. This means nothing. I'm just a man helping a woman in need. We're not even friends.

She nods, accepting, moving away, and John walks her out. I search for Ava, finding her looking this way. Her eyes meet mine, and my heart that's been slow this past hour speeds up again to a more comfortable pace. I get my arse across to her, set on making up for lost time. Or I try to get my arse across to her. Every fucker between here and there seems to want to chat.

"The food was sublime, Ward," someone says.

"Thanks."

"It's knocking on ten thirty," someone else says. "You joining us?"

"No."

"Love the giftbags."

"Great night as always."

I nod, not looking, just pushing my way through.

"Who's the hotty in lace?"

I turn my deadly glare on to someone—I've no fucking clue who—and he steps back, his eyes wide. "Off limits."

"Understood."

"Good." I pull my jacket in and take two more steps.

"Jesse, you look dashing this evening."

"Thanks." I dip, letting a woman—again, no idea who—kiss my cheek.

Sam cheers my arrival as I lower to my chair, but Ava does not. I feel her eyes drilling into me as Sarah looks at me in question. She won't be happy that I've bailed Coral out. So I won't be telling her.

Now, I need to apologize to my girl and get on with the night. I squeeze her knee under the table. "Forgive me?"

"Who was that?"

"No one for you to be concerned about. How is the food?" She's barely touched it.

"It's good," she says, definitely short. "You should eat."

The moment she says that, a plate is lowered in front of me. I collect my fork, keeping hold of Ava, and eat with one hand, picking at the salmon, feeling the thorny atmosphere between me and Ava. I keep dodging Sarah's curious looks, and Kate is glaring at me too. *Should I have gotten John to handle Coral?* Fuck, I don't know.

John makes it back to the table and gestures it's taken care of, and I feel Ava stiffen under my hold, taking more wine. Every sip feels like a giant *fuck you.* But I don't bite. Instead, I shower her with attention. She doesn't reciprocate, her mouth tight. Denying me.

I look at her, finding narrowed eyes and a slightly twisted mouth. She's punishing me. "Are you holding back on me?" I helped a woman out. What the hell was I supposed to do? Leave all hell to break loose?

"Yes," she replies, straight-up and curt. "Are you?"

"Hey," I snap before I can stop myself, getting as worked up as Ava. "Who do you think you're talking to?" I realize my hand has tensed, therefore my hold has tightened on her knee, so I loosen it as Ava looks at me in disbelief.

"Let's see what your reaction would be if a mystery man pulled me away from you for over an hour."

Um. Let's not. All the men that could want to pull Ava away from me want to *take* her away from me. Okay, Coral wants me, but what makes Ava's point moot is the simple fact that none of the women who want me could ever turn me against Ava. Sadly, I can't say the same about me. And doesn't that amplify my frustration in this moment when I should definitely be working to ease her worry.

I talk myself down, taking a few breaths, and do something pretty fucking shameful. But as I have said a thousand times, I will wield this power unapologetically. I know this is a conversation we need to have—I can't deflect from who Coral is forever—but now is not the time.

I stroke up Ava's thigh, watching her chest push out subtly. "Ava, please don't say things that will make me crazy mad. I've told you not to worry so you shouldn't. End of."

She snarls, and it's fierce. "Stop kissing all the women," she hisses petulantly, turning back to the table, therefore away from me. But she's not pissed off with me right now. No. She's pissed off with herself because her body is reacting, and she desperately needs to stay mad with me. She'll do her best, I'm sure. As will I to knock her out of her bad mood.

So I continue to play havoc with her senses, stroking her gently over her lace knickers, discreetly watching her battle her instinct to succumb to her desire. *Stubborn woman.* I leave my dessert untouched but down my coffee. I have a feeling I'm going to need some energy to keep my patience.

And I'm right. Ava pretty much ignores me for the rest of dinner, often trying to remove my hand from between her legs. I don't let her. She laughs and talks, but never with me. She's *really* making a point, and unreasonable as it might be, since the reason she's behaving like a brat is because of me, I'm getting annoyed. But an argument isn't going to help. Persevere. I look around the table, seeing everyone talking, but I'm not hearing them. Just observing. In the decades these parties have been held, marking the anniversary of The Manor, I have not once been sober. I was always the first in the bar. Always the first to leave the table after dinner. Always the first to venture upstairs, various eager, female members following me.

Which is why said female members are not pleased. They don't appreciate the changes in me.

And neither in this moment does Ava. I look at her, still defiantly refusing to look at me.

All for you, baby.

Everything I do, every lie I tell, every word I speak, it's all for her. And, selfishly, for me too. Because now, she's a part of me.

"Ladies and gentlemen," John says, winning my attention. He's standing, his shades resting on his shiny black head. "If you could move into the bar area so the room can be cleared, ready for the band to start."

"Fuck, yes, one minute closer to ten thirty," Sam says, helping Kate up. "All right?" he asks her, putting her wine in her hand, like he thinks she might need a little more alcohol in her to take on the rest of the night. She absolutely does not.

I pull Ava up and move in to kiss her, knowing my mouth on hers will almost certainly snap her out of this mood. But I'm given the cold shoulder. She's walking away?

"Oh, fuck this," I mutter, reaching for her arm and stopping her. I am not spending the rest of the night being ignored. I spin her and pull her close. "Are you going to behave like a spoilt brat for the rest of the evening?" I ask as Kev Baxter passes, looking on with too much interest for my liking. "Or have I got to take you upstairs and fuck some sense into you?" I smile past Ava to Kev. It isn't a friendly smile. It's dark. It dares him to look again.

I cup Ava's arse, flexing myself into her lower stomach, making sure she feels me. Every inch of her body locks. Resists. "Do you feel that?" I whisper in her ear, grinding hard. I hear a moan. It's unrestrained, and it takes me back to the day I met her, when she whimpered at the feel of my lips on her cheek and my voice in her ear. She couldn't hide her reaction to me then, and she can't now, so why the fuck we're wasting this time is beyond me. "Answer the question, Ava."

Her hands bunch the material of my jacket at my shoulders, pinching my flesh too, as I nip at her ear. "I feel it," she relents, her voice husky.

"Good," I reply, short and firm. We're getting somewhere. "It's yours. All of it." Every last piece of me. "So stop with the fucking sulks. Do you understand me?"

She swallows, nodding into me, surrendering.

That's that sorted. Now, if we could get on with the rest of our night without any further interruptions or cross words, that would be fucking marvelous. I move back and let Ava gather herself, satisfied by the quivering wreck I can reduce her to with the whisper of a few commanding words and a roll of my hips into hers. She moves into me again with no prompting, taking me by surprise, and looks up at me. She doesn't apologize. But I see it in her eyes. I'm grateful. I've wasted too much of my life already. I don't want to waste more being at odds with her. I dip and kiss her lips gently. "That's better." I collect her and follow the other guests out of the summer room to the bar. "I'm struggling to deal with all of the admiring stares you're attracting," I say, seeing men at every turn admiring her.

"You're attracting quite a bit of attention yourself."

I see Natasha up ahead and see the impending poke coming a mile off. "Jesse," she purrs as I pass with Ava. "You're looking as delicious as ever."

Ava coughs, I shake my head, and Natasha smiles. I won't point out that she's already told me I look delicious. I can sense Ava's claws unsheathing. She doesn't need the extra information that may cause her to actually swipe them.

"Natasha, you are an intolerable flirt as ever." I push Ava on, feeling her resistance, and tuck her into my side, lavishing her with my mouth—a message to both Ava and Natasha. I get her to the bar without delay, mindful of the many women around who could tip Ava over the edge. I truly never appreciated the effort this evening would take. The gauntlet I would be running. I don't know why, perhaps because none of these women ever meant anything to me so I've underestimated how Ava might feel about them. It was only ever sex. Ava would never only ever have sex. Each time, each man, would have meant something to her, so she can't comprehend the concept of meaningless.

And there's just one more reason why I love her.

When we get into the bar, I nod to a guy who's on the stool I need for Ava, and he respectfully gives it up when he sees us approaching. I nod my thanks and put Ava on it. "What would you like to drink?" I ask, willing to show some flex. "*Most Marvelous*?"

"Please, Mario." She smiles his way before turning her attention to Kate who's leaning into me. I pinch my thumb and index fingers, my way of telling Mario to make it a small one.

"I'll have one of those." Kate nods at the jug of pink, holding my arm for support. "These shoes are killing me," she moans, prompting me to look down at the heels gracing her feet. By the sounds of things, they'll be off soon. Everything will be off. "Seriously," she says. "A man categorically devised the high heel, and he did it in an attempt to make it easier for you dudes to rugby tackle us womenfolk to the ground and haul us back to your beds."

I laugh loudly, watching Mario pour the drinks, giving him my fingers again, this time with less space between them. Smaller.

"What's the score?" Sam asks as he eyes me laughing and I wave him off. Kate slaps my shoulder, and I look at her tilted head. The questions in her eyes. There are so many fucking questions. I wouldn't know which she wants an answer to in this moment.

"I'm sorry, drinks?" I ask instead, finding Ava smiling at me fondly. I wrinkle my nose and flip her an endearing wink as she collects her drink, giving one to Kate.

Drew moves in, looking at his watch in front of me, a hint if ever there was one. "All right, rampant pants."

"Not even half hour earlier?" he asks.

"Are you joking? Why would I have a band at the anniversary

dinner if there's no one here to enjoy them?" The moment those doors open, people will disappear.

"You and Ava will be here to enjoy them. And John."

I roll my eyes. "What the fuck's going on, anyway?"

"What are you talking about?"

"I'm talking about you, Sam, and Kate."

He shrugs. "Nothing to tell you, mate."

"Bullshit, Drew. Be careful."

"What's that supposed to mean?"

"It means," I say, moving in closer, checking Sam's whereabouts. "I think Sam has feelings for Kate."

"Of course he has feelings for Kate, you dick."

I recoil.

"But the stubborn fucker won't admit it." Drew shrugs, slurping his beer. "Neither will she. She thinks she wants to dabble." He smiles, a rare, smug smile. "So I'm here to help."

Oh no. "By fucking her?" Makes perfect fucking sense.

"Aren't they pissing you off?" he asks. "All I keep hearing is *just fun*. Give me a fucking break. If there's something there, I'll make sure they both realize."

I laugh, and it dries up when Sam appears. "What's going on?"

"Nothing," Drew and I say in unison, both sinking our drinks. If it didn't sound really weird, I'd say I'd like to be there and watch that happen. Not the fucking. The moment Sam realizes and stops Drew putting his dick in Kate. Jesus Christ, this isn't going to end well.

Ava catches my eye, trying to get my attention. "What's up, baby?"

"Nothing." She motions to the exit. "I'm just going to use the ladies'." She hops down and gets her purse, giving me her hand when I silently ask for it. I kiss the top. "I won't be long."

"Okay." I watch her go with Kate, smiling at her bare back. And growling when I see another member admiring her too.

"Is it ten thirty yet?" Sam asks, distracting me from teaching the guy a lesson on manners when it comes to staring.

"No," I snap, giving him a tired look. Poor fucker has no idea what's coming. "God, you're a dick." I turn to Mario for some more water, hearing Drew chuckle.

"What happened with Coral?" he asks, settling on the stool Ava just vacated, Sam moving in too, eager for the details.

"Mike. It was him who called the police and now he's playing nasty with Coral."

"Fucker," Drew grunts.

"So what did you do?" Sam asks, interested.

"About Mike? Nothing." I'm still considering my options. "About Coral? I've lent her some money and sent her to a hotel for a few nights." Both men recoil, alarmed, and I look between them. "What?"

"And you called *me* a dick?" Sam laughs.

"What the fuck was I supposed to do?"

"Um." Drew starts waving. "Bye."

"Leave a woman to sleep on the street? No money, no food?"

"Jesus, Jesse. I thought you were a smart man." Drew shakes his head and gets down off his stool, joining a group in the corner.

I frown and Sam sighs. "It's commendable, mate, but I think she's leading you down the garden path."

"You didn't see her," I snap, taking my water and drinking. "She was in a state. I couldn't leave her like that, and I definitely didn't want her shouting her mouth off with Ava around. I want to explain to Ava myself, not have her hear it from—"

"*Another* woman who's in love with you?" He shakes his head in despair, and I look over my shoulder, wondering what's taking Ava so long.

"Don't worry," I muse, thoughtful. "They're dropping like flies."

"So you'll talk to Ava?"

"I haven't been given much choice, have I?" My girl might have dropped it for this evening, but you bet the moment she opens her eyes in the morning, the questions will come. I'm just really fucking happy that Freja Van Der Haus is out of the picture, because that shit would stick and never let go. Her husband, however, is another matter entirely. *Fuck.* I get off my stool. "I'm going to find Ava."

"Worried someone's in her ear?"

"No." *Yes.*

I step out of the bar and see her immediately, her back to me. And my heart sinks when I register Sarah with her.

Oh fuck.

34

I CAN'T SEE Ava's eyes, but I can guarantee they're currently looking up and down Sarah's front in a way only a pissed-off woman could achieve. "Less is more, Sarah. Have you ever heard of that saying? You would do well to remember it, especially at your age."

I flinch, as does Sarah. *Jesus Christ.* Those claws are swiping unapologetically. This isn't Ava.

No, you've made her like this.

I'm flinching again. "Ava?" I say quietly, and she swings around. "What's going on?"

Sarah leaves, her face a confusing mix of anger and hurt. Sarah doesn't do hurt. I get nothing from Ava, she just looks around the foyer as members pass, some going upstairs. It's not ten thirty. But I don't have the capacity or inclination right now to stop them. I take a couple of steps toward her, cautious, like I'm approaching a volatile animal. "Ava?"

She looks at me, a swirl of emotions in her eyes, and I stop moving forward when she retreats. "I'm leaving," she says, shaking her head, as if in disappointment, as she turns and walks away from me.

She's leaving? "Ava," I call making chase. Again. Always fucking chasing this woman. Her pace increases, like she genuinely thinks she can outrun me. Not ever, and definitely not in heels. "Ava, get your fucking arse here," I yell at her back, seeing Kate up ahead, looking at us both charging toward her. Ava's approaching the steps, her hands gathering the bottom of her dress. She'll break her fucking neck.

I leap down the steps, missing Kate's static form by a hair's breadth, a cigarette hanging out of her mouth, and get myself in front of Ava, dipping a little to catch her on my shoulder. She yelps as she collides with me and gasps as I hoof her up. "You're not fucking going anywhere, lady."

"Let go of me," she shrieks as I carry her back into The Manor, alarmed looks coming at us from all directions. What the fuck is going on? She went to the ladies', she was fine, and now she's far from fucking fine. Don't tell me an altercation with Sarah caused this severe flip in mood. "Jesse!"

"What's going on?" Kate asks as I march back past her.

"He's an arsehole," Ava spits maliciously, and I laugh sardonically. I'm an arsehole? Five minutes ago, she was sorry. She was all over me. And now I'm an arsehole? It would be lovely to know exactly what has made me an arsehole in the five minutes since she left me in the bar. "Jesse, put me down."

"No," I grunt, jolting a little, getting a better hold of her before she wriggles off. Did Sarah say something? Is that what this is about? I look at Kate flanking me, her face demanding answers. I'd love to enlighten her. "It's fine, Kate." My jaw is aching it's so tense. "I just need a little chat with Ava."

She falls back, and I increase my stride, walking through the middle of endless staff who've cleared the tables in the summer room. For fuck's sake, the band's not even started yet and members are already creeping off upstairs.

I stomp down the corridor as John leaves my office. He laughs. He fucking laughs. I'm in no mood. I pretty much kick the door open, put Ava down, and get up in her face, furious. Walk away. It's what she does, no words, no explanation, she just walks away. I'm so fucking done with her answer to everything. I also realize I'm the biggest hypocrite to walk the planet, because lying and using sex as the answer to everything makes me better, obviously. "Don't you *ever* walk away from me," I bellow, so loud she cowers, and that just pisses me off more, because what did she expect? For me to fall to my knees and beg her not to go? I turn away from her, now frustrated with myself. I've begged her before not to leave me. It didn't work. So, force it is. My physical power over hers. Shameful, yes, but the only way when she's like this. I go to the drinks cabinet and glance across the bottles, my mouth watering. Kill the pain with vodka. Wouldn't that be nice?

I look over my shoulder, set on attempting a calmer approach. My intentions go to shit when I see her running again. Not literally, she's walking, but she's halfway out the door. I fly across my office like I've been launched from a slingshot and get her back inside, slamming the door shut with my foot and looking for something to block it. There's only one thing nearby, a cabinet. It'll do. She's not leaving until we've sorted this shit out, so I heave it into place.

"What the fuck are you playing at?" I ask, trying to stop myself from physically shaking her but being unable to. "What's going on?"

On a look that could turn me to ashes on the spot, she wrenches herself away and turns her back to me. It's all she can do with her means of escape gone, but it has the desired effect. That look was a look that should only ever be directed at a person you hate.

"I can't believe you trample all over any man who so much as looks at me," she seethes, her arms animated, swinging around, "yet you think it's perfectly okay for you to have another woman in your bedroom while you're naked and lying on the bed." She takes a breath, her anger exhausting her, and I step back, momentarily confused. "I thought John freed you," she screeches.

It falls into place. All this because Sarah freed me from the handcuffs? Is she forgetting the small matter that it was her who left me there? She doesn't get to do that and then be pissy with me when I take my only fucking option.

"Well, he didn't. He was at The Manor, Sam was unobtainable, and Sarah was nearby. What did you want me to do?" Lie there all day, my arms dead, my hand throbbing, until she decided she was done playing her stupid fucking game?

"Well"—she laughs in disbelief, and it's a fucking insult—"I wouldn't want you calling another woman."

Typical. She wants to have an omelet without cracking an egg. Women! "Well," I hiss back. "You shouldn't have left me handcuffed to our fucking bed."

Nostrils flaring, jaw ticking, she leans in, and I know her next words are going to tip me. "It's *your* bed."

I hate how well I know her sometimes. "Ours," I yell.

"Yours!"

"Fuck!" I roar to the ceiling, losing my mind.

"And, while we're at it," she goes on, unaffected by the psycho before her ready to tear up his office. *While we're at it?* "I've just had the pleasure of listening to three women compare notes on your sexual abilities." Her eyes harbor an array of emotions—anger, pain, and disbelief. And there we have the true crux of the problem. My past. "That, I really enjoyed." She laughs. It's a demented laugh. She's on the edge with me. "Oh, and Zoe kindly informed me of your busy bed habits," she adds, gasping for more air. "And who the hell was that woman?"

Deep breaths, deep breaths, deep breaths. We need only one unstable person in this relationship at any one time, because two could be seriously damaging. I need to calm things down. Ava knows they mean nothing to me. She fucking knows. "You know I have a history, Ava," I say quietly, going to her. Touch her. Let her feel that she's all that matters to me. *Remind* her.

"Yes, but have you fucked every female member of The Manor?"

"Watch your fucking mouth."

"No," she retorts, pacing to the cabinet and swiping up a bottle. She pours it into a glass with shaking hands, and my eyes fix on it, watching as she takes it to her lips and downs it. Neat. No mixer, no ice. She may as well have swigged it out of the bottle like I do.

Did.

Why? Why would she do that?

Frustration. Hurt. Despair.

And I'm causing it all. I remain quiet behind her, unsure what my next move should be. Worried that if I don't judge this right, it could be the end. She can't deal with this. She can't deal with me, my manor, my history. It's too much for her. *I'm* too much for her. And I can't possibly be mad with her because I'd be so much worse if her sexual history was as colorful as mine. And, worse, that the men she'd been with flaunted that.

I look at my shoes, wondering how we get past that. *If* we can.

Her empty glass hits the wood with force, and I lift my eyes, waiting for her to pour another. She's already had way too much to drink. I've let it slide, hoped it would loosen her up a bit, make her feel more comfortable about being here.

Epic fail.

Ava draws breath, pulling my eyes up her backless dress. "How would you feel if another man laid his eyes all over my naked body while I was handcuffed to a bed?" She sounds calm. It's an act. Her arms are still shaking, even though she has them braced against the wood.

"Murderous," I grate, my eyes narrowing on the back of her head.

She nods. "How would you feel listening to someone voice their opinions on my bedroom manner?" she asks, and my body starts to shake along with hers, the mere thought pushing dangerous buttons. "Saying they were not going to give up trying to get me in bed."

"Don't," I warn, and she turns to face me, taking me in, observing the reaction her questions are getting. Two wrongs do *not* make a right.

"My work here is done." She picks up the bottom of her dress and walks toward the door, and I move two steps to my right, putting myself in front of her, blocking her way, not that she could go anywhere anyway. We are *not* done. We will *never* be done. She stops and looks up at me, and I positively hate the resolution I see in her eyes. "You should know, I'm not leaving, but only because I can't. I'm going out there and I'm going to have a drink, and tomorrow night I'm going out with Kate. And you are not going to stop me."

She's a fucking joke. So now she's going to punish me for something that is way out of my control? No. I am not succumbing to that kind of retaliation. "We'll see about that."

"Yes, we will."

I keep my eyes on hers, begging her to be reasonable. "I can't change my past, Ava."

"I know," she says, simple and accepting, but not accepting. "And it doesn't look like I'm going to be able to forget about it either." She swallows.

She can't forget it. She can't forget about the women who all came *before* her. She just can't. And there's still the one situation that *didn't* happen before I met Ava. Jesus Christ, if this reaction is a measure, I'm truly fucked.

"Will you move the cabinet, please?"

"I love you." My voice is thick, my throat tight.

"Move the cabinet, please."

No acknowledgment. Nothing. "We need to make friends," I say quietly, unprepared to leave this office until we fix this.

"No."

She won't let me touch her because she knows that reaffirms our physical connection, our love, and she needs to stay mad with me. Why? She's made her point. I get it, but as I've told her, I can't change my past. Just like I can't change hers. I can't change that she wants to work, drink, drive me fucking insane either. I can't change the fact that she once loved another man. But would I ever leave her? No. I want her forever. "I'll trample, Ava," I say, moving in as she moves back. "Are you going to deny me?" She retreats some more, until she can retreat no more, her arse against a cabinet. I think she knows she's being excessive, but will she ever admit it? No. *Stubborn.* I dip, getting my face close, resting my hands over hers.

She's vehemently fighting her natural reactions to me. "Tomorrow, I'm going back to Kate's."

"You know that's never going to happen, Ava." And not because

I'll stop her. She doesn't want to leave. She just wants to lash out. Hurt me. "But just you saying it makes me really fucking mad."

"I am."

I get closer. "Crazy mad, Ava," I whisper, wondering if she wants this from me. Unbridled rage. "Look at me."

"No."

"I said, *look* at me." My chest is buzzing against her front, her hands twitching beneath mine.

"Three," I say calmly, and she looks at me. "Kiss me."

She shakes her head.

So I start again. "Three." And move in, my mouth close to hers, breathing hard. She inhales sharply when our mouths touch. I can feel her restraint is about to snap. "Two." She swallows, her eyes falling to my lips. "One." I brush our mouths, and she exhales shakily, turning away.

"No," she snaps, not giving in to the passion that's becoming suffocating. "You're not distracting me, Jesse."

Distracting? No, I'm not. I'm trying to prove that everything in the fucking world is inconsequential. *For fuck's sake.* What does she want from me? I release her hands, and the moment I do, she's shoving me away. I take her wrists, holding her. Her strength surprises me, and I find my hold tightening as she fights to free herself, yelling, lashing out, her hair flying everywhere.

Whoa.

She's losing the plot.

"Ava," I shout, not in fury but so she can hear me over her own screams. *What the fuck?* She's deranged, flinging her body everywhere, yelling. I'm forced to turn her away from me and pin her arms down before she slips free and smacks me or, worse, I inadvertently hurt her. But she doesn't relent, bucking and screaming, while I hold her, shocked. "Fucking stop it, you crazy woman." I've made her crazy. I curse, resorting to getting her on the carpet where there's less risk of injuring herself. On her back beneath me, I hold her arms down by her wrists, straddling her. "Pack it in," I hiss, wincing when her knee catches me in my lower back. "Ava!"

She stills, heaving, her hair in her face, her eyes wild.

And I did that.

I've caused this. *I've* made her unhinged.

I stare at the mess I've made of her. This is fucked up, but more fucked up is my urge to kiss her. Show her I'm worth the heartache and pain. Show her our love will fix it all.

What she knows.

And what she doesn't know.

And as she looks into my eyes, I see the red mist clear from hers. And there's the woman I love. The stable, levelheaded, strong, fierce young woman who's capable of handling me and my love.

I lower my mouth, but not quickly enough. She lifts her head, smashing her lips to mine, and the fire inside rages as hot as her temper. I let go of her hands and feel them immediately hit my back, pulling at my suit jacket, and I clench my fists in her hair, our tongues fighting, our bodies squirming, my dick swelling.

It's mad, chaotic, angry, and just what's needed right now. Ownership. From both of us.

I roll to my back, taking Ava with me, and feel her hands on my trousers, fighting with the zipper. She has me freed in a heartbeat, her small hand wrapped around me, squeezing, as she scrambles down my body and takes me in her mouth.

I buck. "Fuck." I let my head drop to the carpet for a moment as she thrusts a few, merciless times. "Fuck, fuck, fuck." Mustering the strength, I look down my body, seeing her sprawled, holding me, her head bobbing up and down fast, her mouth frantic on my cock, sucking, biting, licking, kissing. Then she grabs my balls with force. Too much force. Pain shoots through to my stomach, and I gag. "Jesus," I bark, tensing, feeling really fucking vulnerable. She's lost her mind. Lost control. And no man wants his dick in a woman's mouth when that's the case. "Ava." I yell her name, reaching down and grabbing the only thing I can reach—her hair—and pulling. "Ava!"

She eases up on my balls and it's a fucking relief. I cover my face with my hands, breathing, catching my breath, unable to stop the blood rushing into my dick and head, my hips starting to circle up into her frantic advances.

The throbs become too much, my teeth clenching to get me through the onslaught of intense pleasure, her mouth getting hotter, her moans louder, my head thicker. I can't catch a breath. Can't breathe. I'm holding on to her hair again for dear life as she ruins me with her mouth, and then one hand is around my throbbing balls again, another on my chest, she squeezes, and I hit the back of her throat. My hips buck, out of control, and I come so fucking hard. Every muscle, limb, and internal organ trembles with the force of my orgasm, and I settle, blinking back the black dots from my vision as she moans and swallows. "Fucking hell, woman," I gasp, reaching down and pulling her up my body, unable to take any more contact down there. "Fucking, *fucking* hell." I kiss her hard. That was an apology fuck, and I both love and hate that I enjoyed it. "I take it that means you're sorry."

"No," she says, and I smile on the inside. Of course she's not. She accepts my kiss and keeps up the momentum, her hands all over the place again, feeling me. But better than lashing out.

Then she grabs my softening dick again, and I choke. *Fuck.* I drop her mouth, but she quickly kills the space between us again. I can't take it, the sensitivity too much, so I reach for her hand, trying to stop her. "Ava," I gasp, forced to turn my head to break our kiss. "Stop." She wrenches her hand out of mine and grabs my dick again, and I wince, avoiding her mouth, turning my head constantly to stop her kissing me. What the hell? "Ava," I say, but she continues to try and claim me, both my mouth and my dick. "Ava, please." I knock her hand away and quickly flip her onto her back, restraining her. Again. I look down at her, withdrawing when I see her eyes brimming with tears.

Oh Jesus. "Baby, don't," I beg, shaking my head, my throat thick as she sobs beneath me, her hair sticking to her face. Despair. Hopelessness. "I understand." Do I? Do I *really* understand? "Don't cry." I kiss her as delicately as she needs to be kissed right now. "It's always just you."

"I'm not coping with this," she says, her voice cracked, her hands feeling at my face. "I feel violent."

Violent.

Makes two of us. And right now, I know, hand on my heart, better than I know anything, violent is not what we need to be. Violent will undoubtedly lead to devastation.

"Mine," she whispers.

"Always just yours." I take her left hand and kiss it. Marriage isn't only what I need. Ava needs it too. I can see that now. "Please, ignore them. They're shocked, that's all." And imagine when I get that ring on her finger because now more than ever, I'm fucking doing it. "Their noses have been put firmly out of joint by a young, dark-eyed, breathtaking beauty. *My* beauty."

"You're *my* beauty."

Not really, but if she needs to believe that, I'll give it to her. "All of me, Ava. Every single piece." I cup her cheeks, getting nose to nose, letting every inch of me cover every inch of her. Protect her. Her dark, watery eyes look up at me, beg me to make everything okay. "Ava, you own me." I close my eyes as I kiss her, keeping it calm and soft. "Do you understand me?" I ask, and she nods, albeit jerkily. "Good girl. You are mine, and I am yours." It feels easy giving her words that will ease her. "I know this is hard for you."

"I love you," she counters, as if worried I might doubt that.

I smile, and I try so hard to make it light rather than sad. "I know you do." *For your sins.* "And I you." It's an effort, my body and my mind exhausted, but I fasten up and stand, pulling Ava up too. "We'll make friends properly later." I turn her in my arms to see the back of her dress. Or lack thereof. "I don't want to trample your dress." I actually do want to trample her dress, as it's been the source of admiring stares all night. But for the sake of peace, I'll stand down. "It looks like it needs a bit of patience, and we all know how little of that I have when it comes to you." I'm ignoring the massive part of my brain that's pointing out that Ava gets admiring stares whether in a couture gown or workout clothes. "Better?" I ask, kissing her nose with the tip of mine when I've returned her to face me.

I move the sideboard as Ava faffs with her hair and face, and we leave the office and the tension behind. But I can't shake the horrible, uncomfortable feeling in my stomach that tells me I'm hoping in vain. Ava's shown how she truly feels about the details of my past she knows. It's not improving my already low confidence. It was a stupid idea bringing her here. So fucking stupid. I'd hoped she'd see the lavish space in all its glory for what it is. An expensive place for expensive people to have their harmless fun. Fulfil their harmless fantasies, all while enjoying the luxurious facilities of The Manor. See it's a business, one that has made me an insanely wealthy man. But more importantly, I hoped she'd see how detached I am from the happenings. I hoped she'd see that I'm no longer interested in anything else but her. I've failed miserably, and it's all down to that shitty past that keeps trailing me and nipping at my heels.

"Motown?" Ava says as we walk through the summer room, where the band have started playing and a few less rampant members have moved onto the dancefloor. Yet their urgency to head upstairs should not be mistaken for a lack of desire. The dancefloor on the anniversary is little more than a prelude of what's to come. A place where foreplay gets underway.

"They're a great band," I say, watching the few people on the floor, wondering if Ava's seeing what I'm seeing. I look back. She's not, her sole focus on me. "You want to dance?"

"Later."

There will be no later. I want to take her home, get us out of this box of triggers. I'm surprised to see the boys are still in the bar when we make it there. Not so surprised to see Sarah with a gin in one hand, a bicep in the other. I put Ava on a stool and let Kate crowd her. I won't want to hear whatever's going to be said, so I move away, waving Mario over.

"You cool?" Sam says, moving into one side.

"Ye—"

"You sure?" Drew asks, putting himself on my other side, both close.

I look between them. "I'm fine."

Drew snorts. "Yes, you looked totally fine as you hustled Ava through The Manor with steam gushing out of your ears and your fists balled ready to punch something."

I roll my eyes and lean over the bar as Mario approaches. "A very small one of your specialties, Mario, and I mean *very* small. In fact, leave the alcohol out."

"You're unbelievable." Sam laughs.

"Fuck off. You want a drink?"

He holds up his beer, and I look at Drew, who starts looking across the top shelf. The hard stuff's coming out. "Glenmorangie Port Wood Finish, on the rocks."

"What the fuck?" I breathe, my eyes going to the top shelf, scanning it. "I have that?" In *my* bar?

"Yeah, you have that."

"Well, fuck me," I say over a laugh, shaking my head. I return my attention to Mario. "Glenmorangie Port Wood Finish for Drew and a beer for Sam." I look between my two mates. "Not heading upstairs yet?"

"No," Sam sighs. "We were waiting to make sure you and Ava came out alive."

"Small misunderstanding." I take the Scotch from Mario and put it in Drew's hand. "And now we're back, so what's stopping you?" My head turns back and forth between them, curious of the atmosphere I'm sensing. "Well?"

"So what was Ava upset about?" Sam asks, a blatant attempt to divert the subject.

I relent, if only to humor him. Is he stalling? "She heard a few members in the ladies' discussing something."

"You," Drew says.

"Me," I confirm. "Then she found out that it was Sarah who freed me from the cuffs. She thought it was John."

"Why'd she think that?"

I shrug, having some water, looking across to Ava and Kate, who are close, talking. "Assumed, I guess." I pull my eyes away from my girl, back to the boys. "Excuse me a minute." I slide the drinks along the bar, pick Kate up, move her to the side, and put a glass of water in Ava's hand. "Drink," I order, jolting when Kate gives me a slap on my shoulder. To my utter surprise—and appreciation—Ava does as she's told and downs the water before holding out the empty, looking at me with high brows, aware of my surprise. I swap it for the fake cocktail. "See how easier things are when you do as you're told?" I don't give her a moment to refute that, turning back toward the boys, unable and unwilling to detach my hand from her knee.

"Sam's right," Drew says.

I frown. What did I miss? "Right about what?"

"Sarah," Drew goes on. "You've got to cut those ties, mate."

"How did we get onto Sarah?"

"She's in love with you," he goes on. "Ava must see it. Women know that kind of stuff. And God help you if she finds out you've slept with her."

"She knows," I sigh, making both men recoil. *Women know that kind of stuff.* Isn't that right?

I leave the boys, turning back toward Ava. Kate's had her long enough. I'm sure she's got all the gory details of our row in my office and why we were rowing.

I kiss Ava, remove her from the stool, and take her place, putting her between my legs, her arms over my shoulders. She regards me, slightly curious, as the rest of the room regards *me*, slightly surprised. Couldn't give a fuck. Ava needs this.

I ask her if she's okay, and she tells me she's perfect. I'll be perfect too once I get her home. Kate aims a camera at us, and it occurs to me that there are no photographs of us together. Not one. Hundreds of Ava on her own, but none of us together. It's not an opportunity I'm prepared to pass up, so I fling Ava back in my arms and ravish her. This picture is going to be one of my favorites. I know it. "Smile for me, baby," I mumble against her throat, but she doesn't smile. She does something even more beautiful than smile. She pulls back and looks at me like I'm the only thing in this world that matters. And then she kisses me, and I get my fill for a few moments before freeing her of my lips, taking a second to appreciate her drowsy eyes and dazed face, before putting her back on her stool, filling her hand with the fake cocktail, and turning toward the boys. "You two still here?" I ask, looking between them.

"Not for long. She wants to dance," Sam says, his eyebrows high. "Before we *dance*." He surrenders his drink and grabs Kate.

"Ava, dance," she shrieks, and I deflate, quite sure I don't want to put myself in the middle of the prelude to Sam, Drew, and Kate's night, and pretty fucking certain Ava doesn't either.

I take one step toward Ava, set on convincing her we should leave, when I spot Chris, the prick of an estate agent, approaching.

Drew groans. "I'm going before I put a stool over his head."

I laugh and hold out my hand. "Evening," I say, watching Drew leave hastily.

"I've gotta tell ya," Chris says, shaking. "It's been a great night." He leans in. "And it's about to get better."

"I'm happy for you."

"So," he says, definitely swaying. I look past him to Sarah, who nods, catching my drift. Watch him. "Who's the beauty on your arm this evening, Ward?"

"That's Ava O'Shea." *Soon to be Ava Ward.* "She's the interior designer of Lusso." He didn't meet her?

"Of course," he muses. "I never had the privilege. I saw her at the launch but didn't get an opportunity to introduce myself. She was there one minute, not the next. I suppose she was busy."

I nod mildly, smiling to myself. "Yes, busy." Being fucked in the bathroom. By me.

"Are you going to introduce me?" he asks as I observe him observing Ava.

"Yeah, I'll introduce you." I see Ava looking this way. "Ava, this is Chris." Let's keep it brief. "He was the acting estate agent of *Lusso*."

I see realization ping into her eyes a moment before she slowly leans back on her stool. *No, baby, I don't like him either.* "Hi," she says politely, offering a hand. I wish she wouldn't. We don't know where Chris has been, and when he accepts, he takes one step closer to her. He's getting this all so very wrong, and as I look at their hands again, I roll my shoulders. "It's nice to meet you." Ava smiles, and as a result, I smile too. *Liar*.

"It's an absolute pleasure." Chris takes another step closer. My smile falls. "I love this dress."

Yeah, that's enough. I grab Chris's shoulder and haul him away, moving in and taking Ava's stool, putting her on my lap. "Chris, you'll do well to keep your hands and your eyes to yourself," I say, seeing John in my peripheral talking to someone but his attention is split, half on me, making sure I'm not about to make a bloodbath of the bar. "Do that and I might not break your fucking legs, understand?"

He looks between Ava and me, his drunk eyes clearing, sobering as he spits an apology. "I assumed she was fair game."

"Excuse me?" Ava splutters.

Fucking hell, mate, shut the fuck up, or it'll be the missus making a mess of you.

But he's right. Historically, every woman to walk the rooms of The Manor are usually fair game. "I suggest you fuck off now," I warn him calmly, working to relax my muscles, at the same time ensuring I keep Ava on my lap for everyone's sake.

I watch as Chris slopes off, tail between his legs, and Ava peeks back at me. "Murderous?" she asks, much calmer than I know she feels.

"Deadly," I growl, worshipping her face, hoping every man left in the bar sees it.

"Are all the women fair game?"

And here we go again. Little Miss Curious who so desperately doesn't want to be curious. "You don't join The Manor if you aren't sexually adventurous."

Her face screws up slightly, her gaze passing across the bar where what remaining members there are downstairs all laugh and chat, kiss and stroke. "How much is the membership?"

I smile to myself. Miss O'Shea is about to comprehend just how wealthy her *old man* is. "Why, do you want to join?" I ask, biting at her neck.

"I might."

"Sarcasm doesn't suit you, lady. Forty-five."

"A month?"

"No," I say, laughing. "Grand a year."

"Shit," she breathes, pushing the side of her face onto my mouth, squirming when I nibble at her ear and flex myself up.

"Mouth."

She becomes stiff on my lap, trying to push back the building lust, like it would be forbidden to get turned on in my manor. It's too late for that. Then she stills, and I know exactly what's coming. "Does Kate pay that?"

"What do *you* think?" It would be anarchy if any paying members found out others were, to put it bluntly, getting their kicks for free.

"Sam. Sam paid."

"At mate's rates, of course."

"I wish you had refused."

"Ava, what Sam and Kate do is their business." *And Drews at the moment, apparently.*

"How many members are there?"

I study the back of her head, amused by her twenty questions. It's a conversation I never dared dream I'd have with Ava and be as comfortable as this. I need to see her face. Her eyes. So I direct her head back to my shoulder, waiting for her to look up at me. "Someone is very nosey, considering they hate the place."

She shrugs as I peck at her cheek. "I'm not nosey."

No, not at all. Just curious, and I like it. Perhaps one day she might even accept The Manor. Perhaps not. Would it be such a terrible thing if she didn't? I consider her flat tummy. This is no place for a child. This isn't even a place for the father of a child, especially one who's married. Or a mother, for that matter. And, as Coral and Mike have proven, it's no place for a couple. So what the fuck am I doing here? I look around the bar. I see Carmichael lounging on a velvet couch in the far corner, a drink in one hand, a woman in the other. He was like a piece of the furniture. Lived the life seamlessly. Except he didn't need to depend on alcohol to do it.

"At the last count," I say quietly. "I think Sarah said fifteen hundred-ish." There were five hundred members when Carmichael died. "But they're not all active at the moment. Some we don't see from one month to the next, some of them meet people and start a relationship, and others take a break from the whole scene."

"Is the restaurant and bar included?"

"No. The bar and restaurant are a separate entity. Some members eat breakfast, lunch, and dinner here four or five times a week. I wouldn't be making much money if I included all meals and drinks in with their memberships. They have accounts they settle on a monthly basis." I'm done talking about The Manor. But I know Ava is far from done. She wants more, but she'll never admit it. "Turn around, I need to see you." I help her to face me, and the moment I have her eyes, eyes that I've always found so expressive, so telling, I see it straightaway. Undisputed interest. "Would you like to see upstairs?" Or have I got this wrong? I don't know. Not even her slight loss of breath tells me. So I wait, pensive and nervous, while Ava stares at me. She's trying to decide—not if she wants to see it, I can see now quite clearly that she does. She's deciding if she should admit it. She wants to know who I was when she walked into my office and my life. I could show her every square inch of this place and she still wouldn't know who I was then. Not until I tell her. Who I am, where I've been, what I've seen.

What I've done.

"Okay," she eventually says, so very quietly, as if ashamed to admit it. I can only nod, wondering if I've made another stupid error of judgment, like bringing her here this evening. This could go one of two ways.

I stand, feeling as apprehensive as Ava looks, and walk us out of the bar, up the stairs, and around the landing. I go slowly, making sure she's got time to change her mind, all the while wondering if I should put a stop to this too. Yet I know if I do, it'll only fuel Ava's curiosity. It'll only make her want to see it more.

I stop at the bottom of the stairs that lead to the communal room, looking down at her. "We need to get cracking on those next week," I say, distracting her for a moment from the engraved wooden doors. "Ready?"

Am *I* ready?

Her mind is clearly going into overdrive. What will she see? What delights await her? I know she'll find some of it filthy. That's good. This place isn't Ava, and that's just one of the reasons I love her so much. I know she'll be turned on by some of it. That's human nature. But what I want her to see beyond everything is that I *don't* want it anymore. I'm not talking gags, cuffs, blindfolds. I'm talking about promiscuousness.

Her. I just want her. I don't want to share myself.

I step into her body, and she looks up at me. Wonder. It's rife. "You're curious."

"Yes."

"You don't have to be so apprehensive. I'll be with you, guiding you through. If you want to leave, say the word and you're out of there."

She nods, returning my squeeze when I tighten my hold of her hand, and I slowly start to walk us up the stairs. I can hear it already. The moans of pleasure, yells of passionate pain. I start to explain what she'll see, preparing her. "It's important for you to remember that everything transpiring is because all parties have agreed. Just by being in this room doesn't necessarily show your desire to participate in any of the acts. Not that you ever will. I'm making it my mission objective to ensure that every man knows what the consequences will be if they approach you." I smile, thoughtful. "I might send a memo."

Her light laugh takes the edge off the intensity, and I'm really fucking grateful. She thinks I'm joking. I'm not.

I reach the doors, placing a hand on the wood, and take a deep breath. I'm about to show the love of my life a huge part of who I was before she found me, no holds barred. This is The Manor, and under the impeccable facade, it is sex personified.

The sounds become richer, louder, more passionate. I close my eyes and inhale, ready for it. This is one part of me I can give to her. This is a question I can answer. This is for her to get out of her system, and for me to reinforce that all of it means nothing to me. Never did, really, only escape. And now I don't need to escape.

I pull her closer to my side and watch as she starts the daunting task of taking it all in. The décor, the people, the lack of clothes, the weird ease of everyone, some chatting, some laughing.

The music.

Her hold on me becomes tighter, and I take my eyes off her briefly, saying a few hellos, seeing the women look down my fully clothed body, see their eyebrows rise. See the men eye Ava. I ask her if she's all right, bringing us to a stop, getting closer, making sure the men understand the situation. She nods, quiet, and I wonder what the hell is going on in her mind. I want to say she hasn't lived. Truth is, it's me who hasn't lived. Despite being considerably older than she is. Despite being immersed in the world of sex and kink. Despite being a multimillionaire.

I haven't lived. Just slowly died.

That's changing now.

I look to our left and see Caitlin, one of the younger members of The Manor, a lawyer from aristocracy who has an edge about her—something that's obvious when she's blindfolded and tied to a St. Andrews Cross. She's a keen horse rider. Loves a whip or two. And isn't that obvious as Wesley, a barrister from Kent, teases her skin with the tip of a crop. She chose that crop. It's the best. The one with the sharpest bite.

Ava begins to fidget beside me, and I smile to myself, taking a quick peek of her, seeing her eyes darting, as if she thinks she'll be judged for watching. Admiring. Enjoying.

No one around here will judge her.

Wesley pleasures Caitlin, she whimpers, writhes, he moans and growls, and between them they entice the interest of many. I gaze around. How many times have I been in this room in the past twenty years? How many times have I woken up in here trying to recall the night before? Who it was. What we did. I have never been in here and been lucid. Not even when I found Ava in here that horrific day she discovered what The Manor truly is. Because I was crazed with worry. Out of my mind. I saw nothing but the horror and disgust on her face.

Now, though? I don't see horror or disgust. I see inquisitiveness. Fascination. When she found this room, her horror and disgust was all for me. Not my manor. It was because I'd deceived her.

I shy away from those thoughts and squeeze Ava's hand when I see her looking around the room again, and I nod toward Caitlin and Wesley, encouraging her to watch.

Just as Wes twirls Caitlin's favorite crop. I'm very aware that this is where I might lose her fascination—where desire ramps up and turns into a cocktail of pain and pleasure. Wes starts to trace the contours of her body, working her up, getting her impatient. This room, the people in it, the acts in progression. They're the clearest they have ever been. But nowhere near as clear as the woman beside me. I cock my head to myself in curiosity when Ava's hot hand in mine stiffens, and I'm pretty fucking sure I just heard her moan. I look down at her as she peeks up at me. She's turned on. Does she know what's coming?

When Wes brings that crop down on Caitlin's arse, I flinch, and Ava swings round, putting her face in my chest, hiding. I hold her there, looking down at the back of her head as another crack of the whip penetrates the air. She burrows deeper, I hold her tighter. The pain side of The Manor has never been my thing. I've always tortured myself enough, I didn't need the help of others for that, and by others, I mean Sarah. And giving in to Sarah's whip would be as good as telling her I could love her back.

"This is not your thing," I say quietly, seeing various ladies of The Manor looking this way. "Let's move on." I collect her hand and walk away as she asks me what track is playing.

"Enigma." A regular in the communal room on anniversary night.

"Is it making you horny?"

Ava snorts, denying it, her cheeks taking on a deep shade of red and her fingers plunging into her hair. She's hilarious. I knock her hand away from her head, smirking when she realizes she's given herself away. "Just for the record," I say, bending to get up in her face. "None of this will ever happen with us." I flip her a cheeky wink when she looks me up and down, considering my body, as I consider hers.

"What about the other stuff?" she asks, and she quickly has my sharp attention again. I knew it. She's turned on. But what exactly is turning her on? The atmosphere? The music? The audience?

"I don't share you with anyone, Ava," I affirm. "Not even their eyes."

She smiles, and I absolutely do not know what to make of it, before she faces Marcus, Paco, Tim, and Marina. All exhibitionists, all city traders, all brash. And as if backing up my silent assessment, Marina, sprawled out on a fur blanket, eyes me, licks her lips, and I shake my head, laughing under my breath. Her eyes are inviting me. Her body is inviting me.

They all move in, her worshippers, and start pleasuring her, themselves, the audience. I press my lips together, leaning back on my heels, looking down at Ava, but quickly look away when she catches me observing her. This is strangely fascinating, seeing her react like this to something she apparently has an aversion to. Which circles me round to her disgust again. *All for me.* I split my attention between Ava and the scene, just to see what she's seeing. Marina's eyes catch mine often, and each time, I pull Ava closer. A message. Problem is, women around here are as bold as women can come. They know what they want and are not afraid to express that.

Things begin to get urgent between the group, and as Marina's visibly starts to tense, I feel Ava tensing too.

Marina is kissed, licked, sucked, every part of her body being subjected to some kind of touch, and she's out of her mind, fighting the bonds. She comes hard, and I can feel everyone holding their breath with her and releasing it when she explodes. Except me. And

Ava. I smile to myself. But my smile waivers when a small frown worries its way onto Ava's forehead and she glances around the room. It's one of the only times I've known exactly what's running through her mind, and I suppose it was inevitable if I was going to bring her in here. And, really, one of the reasons I did.

This is not Ava. I get her attention, and she gazes up at me as I take her hands and face her. "You're not an exhibitionist, Ava," I say, nodding to the various naked people surrounding us. "And I love you all the more for it. You are mine and mine only, and I am only yours. Do you understand me?"

Her lip wobbles a fraction, emotion getting the better of her, but it means so much too. It means she's as mad about me as I am about her. It means she is as passionate about exclusiveness as I am. Possessive. Protective. I just wish neither of us had previous lovers, boyfriends, fucks. I wish there was no need for possessiveness. I wish we were both invisible to the entire world except each other.

I pull her into me, hugging her, not only because I need her close, but because I don't want her seeing the anguish on my face. "Fucking hell." *Get a grip, Ward.* "I can't tell you how much I love you." I bury my face in her hair and get a solid hit of Ava to see me through the next . . . few seconds? "Come on, I want to dance with you." Do something relatively normal, like normal couples do, even though we're far from normal. I lean down, face close, and her head retracts. "I bet if I checked, you'd be wet." Her lips press together, holding back a confirmation. She's embarrassed. "Only for me." Biting her lip, she looks back again, eager for more, just as Marina is flipped onto all fours and pounded into by Paco while Tim rams his cock into her mouth. Ah. Foreplay is over. I tug Ava's hand—she doesn't need to see what's coming—but she's unmoving, and I wince when Marcus shoves a larger than average butt plug into Marina's arse. The worshipping's over. Now, she's an object. Now, it's raw, carnal fucking, and there will be no holding back. Marina's had her release. It's the men's turn. All three of them.

I look down at Ava, cringing when I see the horror and disgust has returned. "Come on, you've seen enough." Get me the fuck out of here before she asks exactly what I know she's going to ask. Dance with her. Remind her that what we just left behind is not what I want anymore. It didn't turn me on before, it doesn't now. All I've ever seen when I've walked the rooms of The Manor is opportunity. I've never looked at any of the women and been turned on, although they undoubtedly thought I was when I regarded them with hungry eyes. The hunger was for the escape, not for their bodies.

"Jesse?" Ava says as I pull her out of the communal room, her voice small and nervous.

I close my eyes, breathing in, gathering myself, telling her not to go there. Once again, I'm regretting my moves. I thought bringing her in here wouldn't only kill her curiosity but also enforce my feelings toward her. I never intended for her to feel inadequate. I don't want to hear her tell me that she can't give me this. I don't *want* this. "I just need you."

"Have—"

"I said, don't." I walk on but stop abruptly when a pair of familiar tits block my path. *For fuck's sake.*

"You're a bit overdressed, Jesse," Natasha says, looking me up and down.

And I've had enough. I won't have this a moment longer, the snide remarks, the goading, the sheer lack of respect for the woman I love.

I sidestep Natasha's naked body and pull Ava on. "Have some fucking respect, Natasha." I take the steps as fast as I'm comfortable with, knowing Ava's in heels.

"I would like to send a memo too," Ava mutters behind me, and every tense muscle loosens immediately. Sarcasm actually suits her right now.

"Whatever you want," I say on a small laugh. And I mean it. I will give her whatever she wants. We round the landing, and I see John up ahead, running a routine check. "Sam? Drew?" I mouth, and he points downstairs. Fucking hell, they're still abstaining? I look down at my watch. It's gone eleven.

I take the steps down to the foyer, the space now sparse of

members. "Do you want a drink?" I ask when we near the bar.

"Please."

I detect melancholy and study her face, trying to read her thoughts. It's a constant challenge.

"Why did you take me up there?" she asks. I can suddenly read her. Not her thoughts, but her expression. Accusing.

"You want me to be more open with you," I say quietly. And I don't want her constantly wondering about the infamous rooms of The Manor. Rooms I'll never step foot in again.

"I never want to go up there again."

"Then you won't."

"And I never want you to go up there either."

And there we have the true issue. It's me. Just me. How the fuck can I reassure her if she doesn't hear me? "I've no need to go up there," I say gently. "Everything I need is standing within touching distance, and I plan on keeping her that close."

She nods. Swallows. Blinks. "Thank you."

Why the hell is she thanking me? "You find Kate, and I'll get the drinks," I tell her, feeling at her face. She needs distracting. "Go." I guide her to the door and watch her walk toward the summer room, willing every female member of The Manor to be wise. Be wise or die.

I turn toward the bar and exhale loudly, and Mario's bushy Italian eyebrows lift. "Don't ask," I say, rubbing at my cheeks. "Can I get a water?"

One lands in front of me the moment I utter the words. "And for Ava?" He measures a small space between his fingers. "A *very* small one?"

I laugh, downing my drink, moistening my parched mouth. "Not even very small, Mario." I slide the glass toward him. "And if she asks for another one this evening, leave out the . . ." I trail off, frowning. "What do you put in those things, anyway?"

"Ah," he sings, laughing. "That is secret. Like Luigi and his lemon pasta." He taps his nose. "Secret family recipes."

"Right," I say, pulling my phone out when it vibrates in my

pocket. "Well, whatever it is, leave it out." I look down at the screen and a message from Coral telling me she's arrived at the hotel and checked in. I spin my phone in my hand, thoughtful. I thought she'd been cut off?

"Hey, Jesse."

I turn and find Niles slumped on a couch, looking slightly roughed up. "All right?" I ask.

He grins, and when I look over my shoulder, the reason for his chirpiness becomes clear. Sarah, clad in leather from her tits to her toes, snaps her whip, making me flinch. "I'll leave you two to it," I say, skirting past her and heading for the summer room. "Enjoy."

"Oh, we will."

I stop and turn back, remembering I have a bone to pick with her. A whole fucking graveyard of them. "Why the fuck did you tell . . ." But . . . what's the fucking point in calling her out? She doesn't give a fuck, and I'm long past trying to make her care. I just need to make sure I don't give her any ammo. I back away, Sarah watching me, her head tilting, a fraction of smugness being lost. "Never mind," I say. "Have a good night." I walk away and make it to the edge of the dance floor. The music is booming, and I spy the boys. I smile. What the fuck is wrong with those two? I see Kate and Ava, dancing like normal girls would dance in a bar. In the whole time I've owned this place, I don't think I've ever seen two women dancing together like friends. Only perhaps with a man wedged between them. *Foreplay.* That was me once. Searching for anything that would make me feel . . . empty.

I shuffle my way through the crowds and make it to them, cocking an interested look at the boys that goes over both their heads. Has there been a change of plan? Kate's bailed? Sam's admitted he's catching feelings? Drew's told them to go it alone?

I move in on Ava and plaster myself to her back, greeting her, feeling her. "I'm going to dirty you up," I declare, lowering and taking her dress at the knees, lifting it a smidge so she can stoop with me, and when I start circling my hips into her arse, she's right there with me, laughing, comfortable, and happy.

Just us, the music, our moves, how easily my body moves with hers, and how effortlessly she follows. How perfectly she fits against me. Simply . . . dancing. "Oh God, I love you." I drown her face with kisses, noting the track coming to an end, so I send her out on a twirl before pulling her close again, gently swaying us. "More dancing?"

"Drink," she says.

"You can't keep up with your god, sweet temptress." I keep us exactly where we are, hardly moving, just touching, while the rest of the floor go wild for Stevie Wonder. "Are you happy?" I ask, wondering where that question came from. Unease? Worry after taking her upstairs? She's happy now, dancing, being relatively normal, being swooned all over, and I take immense comfort from the fact that I, Jesse Ward, Lord of the Sex Manor, can give her that. I can give her anything.

"Deliriously," she says, hauling me into her.

"Then my work here is done."

She lets me snuggle for a while in her neck, holding me like I need to be held, and I feel comforted by that. Her holding me. "Your temptress is dying of thirst."

"God forbid," I whisper, tearing us apart. And isn't that apt? Because nothing could tear us apart. Only me. "Come on, I don't want to be accused of neglecting you." I put her in front of me and guide her off the floor, making it only two paces before I feel someone's hands on my shoulders. I tense. *Oh no. No. Don't do it.*

I'm hauled back onto the floor, with what feels like dozens of hands on my body, all dirty hands, all not meant to be there. "For fuck's sake," I mutter, trying to see who's ambushed me. "Get the hell off me." I wriggle and writhe, my ears bleeding, caused by the sounds of their delighted cackles. One's Trisha. One's Mandy. I look to my left, spying Marina too. Jesus Christ, she's barely over her orgasm and searching for her next. "Get o—" I still when I see Ava coming toward us. "Oh fuck," I breathe, feeling the hands still grappling at me. She looks livid. Disgusted. I expect her to lash out. She doesn't. I don't know if it's a message or something, a lesson perhaps, one Ava wants me to take note of, but she simply offers her hand, looking at me to take, which I do. Of course I do. And she gently pulls me toward her.

Mine.

She leads me away, confident, owning it. Owning *me*. And it's sexy as fucking hell. I swoop in and sweep her off her feet, ravishing her. "I love it when you're all possessive." I'm ignoring the fact that she did that without any bloodshed. It was definitely a message to me. "Kiss me." She shakes her head, rolls her eyes, but she indulges my demand and lets me indulge her mouth as I walk blindly back to the bar with her in my arms.

"There." I sit her down and give Mario a look, *the* look, as he wanders over, smiling, getting two bottles of water and passing them over with a ready prepared glass of his specialty. Minus the alcohol.

"Mario, how's the stock?" I ask, taking a seat and watching in astonishment as Ava downs the water ravenously before I check the shelves and fridges.

"Ah, Mr. Ward, you have thirsty members this evening. I'll do stocktake tomorrow. We have a delivery arriving on Sunday."

"Good man." I return my attention to Ava and the glimmering diamond around her neck. She looks tired, has lost some of her sparkle. It's been a tumultuous day. "Are you okay?"

"Fine," she says over a yawn as I tweak the diamond.

"I'm taking you home. It's been a long day." Of which we could have saved a few hours looking for a Scotch that was at The Manor the whole fucking time. I jolt when the unmistakable hand of the big man meets me shoulder.

"You good, girl?" he asks, as Ava yawns again, nodding. She's hit a brick wall. God, I cannot wait to spend the rest of the weekend without any interruptions. In bed. The bath. The kitchen. Eating, kissing, cuddling, vegging.

"I'm taking her home," I tell John. "Everything okay upstairs?"

"S'all good. I'll call for your car." Going to his phone, John looks at me, nodding, peeking over the top of his glasses. Talking to me without talking to me. And I hear him, loud and clear. *Do this right.* Fine. Tomorrow, I'll push to meet her parents.

"I need to see Kate," Ava mumbles, slipping down from her stool. Fucking hell, she'll face-plant if she walks anywhere. I quickly reach for her and stop her going, and John laughs.

"I think I may have just seen her disappear upstairs with Sam."

Oh, so the arrangement is going ahead? He didn't mention Drew, and something tells me not to either. "Do you want to go and say goodbye?" I ask, and she shudders.

"No." She frowns and peeks past me to the foyer where the stairs lead to all things hedonistic. "Take me home."

"With pleasure," I say, seeing her now practically falling asleep where she sits. I turn to John. "I won't be in tomorrow."

"Because you're meeting her parents, right?" he says quietly.

"They live in Cornwall, John," I reply on a whisper, looking back at Ava. "I can't just pop by for a cuppa. But I promise I'll meet them before I ask Ava."

"Make sure you do."

I look at Ava on the stool, checking the distance. "It was Mike who called the police," I say quietly, and John nods, looking pretty fucking savage. If I were Mike, I wouldn't only be avoiding *me*.

"And Steve Cooke," he says, reminding me of that problem to deal with.

Fuck it all to hell. Can't I have just one day away from shit? But a loose member isn't the kind of member we should have around. "Tell me what you're thinking."

"Talk to him. If he doesn't listen, he goes."

"Right. Let me know when he's next in." *Please don't be tomorrow.* "We'll have a chat with him."

John nods, reaching past me and knocking Ava from her semiconscious state. "Night, girl."

"Night, John," she mumbles, flopping down from the stool. "Night, Mario." She falls into my side, and I pluck a giftbag off the bar as I lead her out, the first to leave the anniversary party in . . . ever. Because I have something to go home to, and it beats the hell out of this place.

I get her into the car, her body now useless, all her energy spent on fighting off the women of The Manor. And God, did she do me proud. I shut the door and look up at the front of the building, the old, limestone bricks illuminated, every window glowing. It looks so beautiful. Full of beautiful people doing not so beautiful things. Love is beautiful. And there is none of that within the walls of The Manor.

Only unrequited.

Only unhealthy love.

Only momentary lust that can't truly satisfy lonely hearts.

I always felt like I needed this place. And now I feel like I'm growing detached. It's something in my way, along with all the other things in my way. And I could be rid of it.

I nod, thoughtful, surprised I'm having these thoughts as I round my car and slip in behind the wheel. But The Manor was Uncle Carmichael's baby. He turned an old, dilapidated manor house into a luxurious resort for the sexually adventurous, and all it's really brought is heartache and pain. I realize that now.

"I've had the best day," Ava slurs, part tiredness, part drunkenness.

"Baby, I've had the best day, thank you."

"Why are you thanking me for?" she asks.

"For letting me remind you." I start the car and drive slowly down the driveaway, beneath the trees, between the spotlights that light the way. I look up into my rearview mirror, watching The Manor get farther away. Until I pass through the gates and it's gone completely. At least, gone from sight. From my life? I've clung to The Manor all my life. It's oddly been a lifeline and at the same time, my absolute downfall. I can feel my hold on it slipping, and I'm doing nothing to stop the detachment setting in.

I absentmindedly reach for Ava's hand and clasp it, entwining my fingers with hers, holding on.

I would sacrifice anything in this world for her.

Even The Manor.

I look across the car and see her eyes are closed. Snoozing.

I feel like I've wasted too much time. No more. But like John has said, and for which I am grateful, I must do this the right way.

35

I PULL through the gates and park up, turning off the engine and looking at her. Absolutely dead to the world. Has been since we pulled out of the gates of The Manor.

Ejecting myself, I round the front of the car and gather her into my arms. "Jesus fucking Christ," I whisper, trying to get her limp body out of the seat without disturbing her.

"Watch your mouth," she mumbles, circling her arms around my neck and holding on.

"Or else what?" I ask over a light laugh as I walk us into Lusso. But my amusement dies when the hairs on the back of my neck stand on end, and I stop, turning to face the glass doors with Ava in my arms, scanning the darkness outside. "What the fuck is that?" I ask quietly, a coldness creeping through my veins, cooling them.

"What?" Ava murmurs sleepily.

"Nothing, baby. Go back to sleep." I feel like a fish in a bowl standing here, exposed. So I step outside again, scanning the car park, listening. The odd car, a few joyous yells in the distance. My eyes naturally dart as I reverse my steps, backing up, and I turn, constantly looking over my shoulder as I walk to the elevator.

"Evening, Clive," I say, having one last look, not that I can see anything out there in the darkness. Paranoid? Making nothings into somethings. Again?

"Mr. Ward," Clive says, coming out from behind his desk, eyeing Ava in my arms. "Need any help?"

"No." I'm looking back over my shoulder again. "I've got her. Thanks." I step inside and lift a knee to rest Ava on while freeing a hand to punch in my code. "Good night."

He tips his hat and the doors close. I feel like I'm going crazy. *Ironic.*

I get us into the penthouse, lock the door, something I rarely do—don't need to, because the concierges *and* the private elevator—and wander around the floor, checking each room, carrying Ava as I do. Why? Who do I think I'll find? "*Really* fucking losing my mind." I head upstairs, feeling Ava stir in my arms. I look down as I carry her up and see her fighting to open her eyes.

She smiles, clinging on tighter. "You're so handsome, Jesse Ward of an age I now know."

I chuckle. "And you're so fucking amazing, lady."

"Watch your mouth."

"No."

"Okay."

I place her carefully on the bed and reach up to yank my tie loose and release the top button of my shirt as she rolls onto her side on a grumble. "Come on, you." I discard my tie and pull at her hip. "Let's get you out of that dress."

"Leave it."

"I am not sleeping with you fully dressed, lady. Not ever. Come here." I take her limp hands and hoist her to the end of the bed, kneeling, removing her shoes, before getting her to her feet. I inspect the dress, the front, the back. "How do you get this thing off?" I start feeling around the lace, not finding anything that indicates a zip, until Ava points it out.

I unfasten her, and the moment the dress hits the floor, I gulp. Jesus Christ. More lace. Sexy lace. Delicate, tasteful lace. She hits my chest, falling into me. "I think I might just leave you in this," I say, my hands falling to her waist. I'm having a serious mental battle to stop myself from getting too carried away. She's good for nothing.

Except just . . . being here. And that will do. It'll always do. I take her to the bathroom, and she watches me with drowsy eyes as I brush her teeth, taking my time, making sure I do a thorough job. She spits when ordered to, leaving a trail of paste across her bottom lip that I am more than happy to mop up. Mistake. The moment I suck my thumb, her tired eyes win back their sparkle and she's hauling me into her.

"Has someone woken up?" I ask, pushing my lips onto hers, tasting the mint.

"It's you. It's instinctive." Her hand feels down to my dick and strokes me, but it's slow, languid. Tired. We've got all weekend to make love, and I'd prefer it if she's fully awake when we do.

"I never in a million years thought I would ever say this"—I stroke her hair out of her face, smiling at her struggle to appear alert when she's on the verge of passing out—"but I'm not going to take you tonight." Her answer to that is a lethargic flex of her hips into me. "No." I look to the window in the bathroom, not that I can see outside. "Do you want to wash your makeup off?"

"Are you denying me?" she asks.

Oh, the irony. "I guess I am. Who would have thought?" I grab a face cloth and wet it, taking it to her cheek. "Show me that beautiful face." And let's see if we can wash away the indignance.

"But I thought we were going to make friends properly?"

"Are we not friends?"

"No, we're not."

"Oh?" This is news to me. "Would you snuggle with someone you're not friends with?"

Her hands land on my arse, hauling me in again. This time, I don't stop her. Her head drops back, and she looks up at me. My smile. It's unstoppable. Just . . . look at her. Mine. All fucking mine. And best of all? She wants to be. "I might," she says sleepily, "if my non-friend promises to make friends with me in the morning."

It's an easy deal. I take her off the unit and carry her into the bedroom, stripping her down to nothing and gesturing for her to climb in as I undress, leaving my clothes in a pile with Ava's and getting in with her. She crawls onto me and settles. Never too tired to find her place. On me. Close to me.

I blow her hair out of my face and hold her, stroking, kissing her head, breathing her into me. "Tomorrow," I whisper, "we get all your things from Kate's." She doesn't protest. "On Monday, we tell Patrick, and I think you should be letting your parents know I'm more than just a friend." I wait for what she might say to that.

I get nothing.

I'm not surprised. She's dragging her feet, being non-committed on that front, and it isn't because she's dog-tired right now. So in the morning, we'll talk about it. Make a plan. I need to meet her parents before I ask her to marry me. And if Ava blocks me meeting them, I'll take matters into my own hands.

John will be delighted.

I peek down at her, seeing her face squished into my chest, her mouth open, but I don't move her. Not yet. I wait another five minutes—five minutes that feels like five hours, before I start to peel her arms and legs away from me, taking the utmost care not to wake her, and remove her necklace carefully before I grab my phone from my suit jacket and head downstairs, stopping off at my study to put the diamond in the safe.

Leaving the penthouse, I lock the door behind me and go down to the foyer. "Mr. Ward." Clive looks at me tiredly when I reach his desk. "May I recommend clothes?"

I laugh mildly at the old goat.

"What's that on your chest?"

I look down, to the bruise Ava has put there. Marking me. "Nothing, Clive." I look over my shoulder to the darkness outside. "The security is all working fine, right? The cameras, the alarms etcetera?"

"Always, Mr. Ward."

I nod, turning back to him, but something catches my eye, moving outside. "What was that?"

"What?"

I'm off, running out into the darkness.

In my boxers.

"Fuck!" I yelp, as I crash into someone.

A cart.

A fucking shopping cart.

"Dude," someone yells, as it topples onto its side and bedding, bags, and fuck knows what else tips all over the car park.

I gather myself, shaking my head, taking in the scene. "Sorry," I splutter, wincing at the pain in my shin, taking in the hairy man before me, his clothes big and utterly filthy.

"Mr. Ward." Clive darts out, looking between me and . . . a homeless man? I scan the ground around me. His worldly possessions are strewn everywhere. "Oh no, not you again." Clive grumbles.

"Who again?" I ask, looking between them.

"He keeps sneaking in when residents come in and out of the gates. Making a home for himself by the trash cans."

"You folk sure do throw out some decent rubbish." The guy starts picking up his things and I set his cart back on its wheels.

"For fuck's sake." I dump his duvet in the cart. "You shouldn't be in here, mate."

"Yeah, well, you do what you have to do to survive, *mate*."

"I'm sure," I say, going for my pocket for my wallet. Frowning.

"You supposed to be wearing clothes?" he asks, taking the handle of his cart.

I laugh under my breath and scrub a hand down my face. "Goodnight." I leave Clive to see off the vagrant, wandering back into the foyer and returning to the penthouse, unlocking the door and letting myself in. And I stand there, laughing to myself. So fucking paranoid.

I look up the stairs, where she's tucked up cozy and safe. Without me wrapped around her. I need to fix that. I also need to stop letting my imagination runaway with me.

I lock the door. Check it. Then go to join Ava in our bed.

36

I SLEEP LIKE A BABY, our warm, naked skin touching all night. To think I can have this every night for the rest of my life? *Someone*. Someone who's mine. Someone *no* one can take away from me. I reach for my phone and seize the opportunity to catch another picture of her sleeping, her rich, dark hair fanning every inch of my chest.

I wake up the screen and point the camera down at her, smiling as I take a picture of her on me, then settle back and browse through my building collection of pictures. There's nothing else on my phone since I met her. Just Ava. Ava walking, Ava running, Ava showering, cleaning her teeth, sleeping, eating, lost in thought. She's beautiful in every single one.

Beautiful and mine.

Do it right.

I look at the time. Six thirty. I could call Kate and get Ava's parents number. But I'm pretty sure I won't win any brownie points if I call them at this time of day and introduce myself, then follow it up by advising them of my intention to marry their daughter. "Fuck it." I wouldn't win any brownie points if I did that at *any* time of day.

Doesn't matter. I don't want brownie points. I want Ava. They have to like me because Ava loves me. It's the rules. I can win them over. No sweat. So why the fuck am I actually sweating? And my heart's beating way faster than normal? Asking her dad? It's a bit traditional, and Ava and I aren't traditional. I pout. We're better than traditional.

I don't want to wait. Now feels . . . right.

So fuck you, John.

I start the delicate task of peeling Ava off me, holding my breath when she stirs, breathing again when she settles and I'm free from beneath her. Then I stand by the edge of the bed staring at her, for the first time wondering how the fuck I'm going to do this.

I think back to the barrage of questions Hans hauled at me. When, where, and how?

Now.

Here.

But the how? Fuck, this is harder than I anticipated. And what if she says no? What if she runs away, scared? Because that's what Ava does. Especially when she doesn't want to face facts. Face the truth. And the truth is, she wants to spend her life with me, which means she should want to marry me. But I can see it now. Resistance. Other influences getting in her way. So, yes, asking her parents would be a bad idea. She's too young. The age gap. The whirlwind romance, although *romance* is a stretch. Ava will overthink this. Moving her in was a task. Every step of our relationship has been a mammoth effort. This is going to be no different.

I need to stop her running. Make her hear me.

I think for a moment, considering my options. And then I smile, my eyes falling to the bedside table and the drawer where those handcuffs are kept.

Memorable, to put it mildly.

Perfect.

So *us*.

I creep to the bedroom door and hurry down to my study, going to the safe and pulling out the ring. My stomach flips. *Fucking hell.* I open the box and stare at the diamond. The damn thing sparkles, even without light to bounce off. I pull it from the cushion with delicate fingers and snap the box shut again, blindly putting it back in the safe as I study the showstopper. Simple. Elegant. Perfect.

Heading back upstairs, the ring firmly in my clenched fist, I mentally practice my proposal. "I adore you. Will you marry me?" I stroke my chin, pondering the words. "You're my world. Will you do me the honor of also being my wife?" I stop at the top of the stairs. *Will you promise to be mine forever and never break that promise?*

In a nutshell.

Tick, tock, tick, tock.

I enter the bedroom and find Ava's rolled onto her back. "Handy," I muse to myself, setting the ring on the bedside table next to the giftbag I brought home from the party. Because I know she was curious about that too and, actually, it's going to be useful. I retrieve the cuffs from the drawer and gently, holding my breath, stretch her arm to the headboard, looping the cuff around her wrist and securing it, taking the weight of her arm as I lower it until I'm sure it's not going to jar and wake her. I repeat on the other side, gingerly kneeling on the bed, my attention constantly split between Ava and the cuffs. I secure her other hand, gently releasing my hold as I pull away, watching her, arms spread, eyes closed, lips parted just a fraction.

And . . . breathe.

I step back and admire her as I drag my boxers down my legs, kicking them off, then take the ring and slip it onto her left finger, watching her oblivious face as I do. Perfect fit. My moves might appear confident. It's a front. I'm just covering all my bases, making it pretty impossible for her to say no. And what Ava and I both know is that she can't say no to me when she *wants* me. So I'll ensure she wants me.

Smiling, I take a picture of her in all her glory, then put on the track that was playing in the communal room last night.

I crawl onto her, not taking as much care now because it would be really handy if she's awake and alert when I pop the question. She stretches, rolling her entire body into mine. I quell a groan, lifting my hips when her groin presses into my cock, which is also now waking up. Stirring. "Lord above," I whisper, talking the rampant fucker down. Not now. I never dreamt I'd think it, but there's something I want to do more than have sex with Ava.

Ask first, fuck her after.

Celebrate.

Because she will say yes. She *will* say yes.

I get her lips close to mine, circling our noses, scanning her eyes, waiting for them to open. I see a small flicker. "Good morning," I whisper, pulling back a fraction to get her entire face in my sights. She squints, and a slow smile pulls at her lips when she finds me gazing down at her. It falls the moment she attempts to move and the clang of the cuffs sounds.

I hold my breath, waiting for it, trying so fucking hard not to smile at her expression as she slowly fathoms what's going on.

She looks above us. Exhales.

"Were you planning on going somewhere?" I ask, bringing her attention back my way. Her eyes are no longer drowsy with sleep. Her face is no longer peacefully unaware. She knows what's coming.

But, also, doesn't.

"What are you going to do?" The graininess of her words does not assist with the situation growing between my legs.

"We're going to make friends. You want to make friends, don't you?"

She pouts. It's adorable. "Sleepy sex?"

"No, not sleepy sex," I muse. "I haven't thought of a name for this one yet." I have. I just can't tell her what it is without giving away my intention. This here, ladies and gentlemen, will be The Proposal Fuck. It's in pole position to being my favorite. Her answer, of course, will dictate that. So let's get on with it.

Her eyes follow me as I reach for the gold giftbag on the bedside table, and I sit astride of her, peeking inside. "What have we got in here then?" I have a rummage, as Ava has a pointless wriggle, and pull out the first thing I lay my hands on. A vibrator. "We don't need that." I still have war wounds, and I doubt the mental scars will be gone anytime soon. I toss it aside and dive back into the bag. I know what I'm looking for. Where the fuck is it? "What else is there?" I pull out a box of condoms, snort, and chuck them over my shoulder. "We don't need those either."

Ava's head lifts from the pillow, trying to see what it is exactly we don't need. I should watch my words. "What?" she asks.

I bite at my lip, mentally scolding myself, and ignore her, my eyes drifting onto her stomach beneath the bag as I pull out a scrap of silver material. "Not lace," I muse, thoughtful, blindly dipping into the bag again, my eyes still on her tummy, not the bag. Not that she'd realize, since the bag is on her tummy. Is she still taking her pills? Remembering?

My teeth sink in a little too hard, and I scowl at myself, resetting my attention on the bag before Ava notices I'm distracted. I pull out a voucher for Botox. For God's sake. I rip it up and throw it.

"What was that?" Ava asks.

I look up to the smooth, young skin of her face. "Nothing you'll ever need."

But she wants to know, of course she wants to know, pressing me.

"A voucher for Botox."

She laughs.

I finally find what I want and toss the rest aside, unimpressed with the contents. But this? I study the cock ring, pouting, feeling Ava's wary curiosity studying it too. "This looks interesting."

"What the hell is that?"

She doesn't know? God love her, I'd say she's led a sheltered life, but it's me who's led a debauched life. I reach forward and plump her pillow, giving her a quick kiss. "I want you to have a good view." I raise to my knees, and the smooth skin of her forehead becomes creased as she watches me start to slip the cock ring over my dick.

"Oh, no," she blurts, horrified, my intentions slowly becoming clear. Kind of. "If I don't get battery-operated devices, neither do you." She bucks beneath me, forcing me to move or risk her catching me in the bollocks. I focus on my task, tweaking the metal piece into position as she makes her displeasure known, defiantly looking away, like she can escape.

"Look at me," I say through my teeth, being forced to take her jaw and direct her face downward. Her gaze drops to mine. She can't hide the glimmer of lust. The sparks of hunger. I'm going to make her want me so badly, she'll do anything to get me. "Kiss me now, Ava." I drop my mouth a fraction, invitingly, and she doesn't let me down, lifting and catching my lips, kissing me hungrily, and I indulge her, sweeping my tongue through her mouth, relishing her moaning, increasing the pressure, ravenous. "You will watch," I pant, wrenching myself away.

"Turn the music off," she yells, bucking, knocking me off balance on my knees, and very nearly catching my fucking balls again.

I grab her hip bone to still her. "Why?" I ask, as she pants up in my face, her cheeks a beautiful shade of flushed. "Are you feeling horny?" I drift down to her boobs and take a nipple into my mouth, sucking hard, forcing her spine to bend sharply and her eyes to close.

No escape.

I order her to open her eyes through my mouthful of boob, squeezing her hip until she obeys, looking at her looking at me as I worship her body. She stiffens, relaxes, stiffens, relaxes.

"You're cruel," she breathes, squirming, hating the pleasure, loving the pleasure.

I rise to my knees and circle my girth, turning on the cock ring. The intense vibration catches me off guard. "Wow," I whisper, almost silent, as Ava hides from me again. I grab her hip, she jerks, opening her eyes, and I start stroking my dick as she reluctantly admires.

"Oh God," she whimpers, shaking her head, now fixated on my dick, which is throbbing against my palm, weeping with want, pulsing with need.

"This feels good, baby. Do you want to help me out?"

She looks up at me, her lips twisted. Not happy. "Fuck you."

"Mouth," I breathe, my hand working faster. It's the final straw for Ava. She explodes, throwing her body around, shaking her head, sending her hair wafting around. "You'll mark yourself, Ava." I grunt, forced to slow down or shoot my load too soon. I'm enjoying this too much. Her blatant need. Fuck, it looks good on her. "Stop fighting."

She doesn't listen. My defiant little temptress, who isn't even trying to be tempting now. But fuck, I'm tempted. I'm tempted to abandon my torture and give her what she wants.

Me.

I gulp, jolt. *Fuck.*

I pass the point of no return, my vision becoming cloudy, my thighs starting to ache, my biceps, my jaw. Everything hard.

"Please," Ava begs. But I'm in no position to stop myself now.

"It's not nice, is it?" My eyes fall to her boobs. "Think of this the next time you stop me from touching you."

She cries out, slamming her eyes closed, escaping the sight of me on the cusp of ecstasy, begging me to stop teasing her.

"Open your fucking eyes," I yell, my fist working fast, the pressure building, my release coming.

"No!"

Fuck.

I slip a hand between her legs and slide my finger through her pussy, and she screams, her eyes opening and narrowing. She looks like she wants to fucking kill me.

I'll take my chances. "You'll watch." The blood surges, the sensitivity jarring me, and I curse loudly as I walk on my knees up her body and straddle her face.

Her lips are parted. Her tongue traces the bottom one. Hungry. Inviting. It's my undoing. And really fucking ironic that even though she's tied up, powerless, she still holds all the power. "Open your mouth." My hand shoots out to the headboard to hold myself up, and I glance at her hands held in place by the cuffs. "Oh, Jesus." My chin hits my chest and I come hard, all over her mouth. She swallows ravenously, gulping it all down, and then she takes me deep, cock ring and all, sucking me gently, licking softly.

Oh. My. God.

I'm a quivering wreck, short of breath, and she's beneath me, worshipping me, looking at me with adoration. *Fucking hell.* I pull off the ring, toss it aside, and fall onto her, her legs cradling my body, her eyes fixed to mine as I watch her, wondering if I could adore this woman any more. And yet each day, I do. "I might keep you like this forever," I whisper, kissing her deeply, moaning when she moans. "This way, I will know where you are all the time."

"I think that might be falling dangerously close to sex slave territory," she whispers, not relinquishing my mouth, just talking around it.

"And that's a problem because?" I ask, turning my head, taking a different angle, humming my pleasure.

"Because I would like to think that you want me for more than my body," she replies, now turning her head, making sure there's not a tiny bit of my mouth she's not explored.

I'm lost. So lost in this kiss. "Oh, I want you for more," I whisper, leaving her lips for a moment to spread kisses up her cheek, her forehead, and back down the other side, plunging my tongue back in, shifting, feeling blood starting to creep back into my dick. "Like my wife."

I frown into my darkness, and Ava stills beneath me, her tongue slowing, where mine continues its sweet assault on her mouth until the sudden awkward atmosphere can no longer be ignored. Shit. That was *not* how it was supposed to happen.

I sigh, giving up on the kiss too, and brave facing her. I hate the look of pure shock staring back at me. But I'm in now. No going back. Not that I want to only, perhaps, to think before I fucking speak.

"Marry me." I internally flinch the moment I demand it. *Ask, Ward. You're supposed to ask.*

Her eyes look like they might fall out of her head. "You can't ask me that when I'm handcuffed to the bed," she gasps, jiggling the cuffs, as if to remind me that I do, indeed, have her handcuffed to our bed.

"Does someone need some sense fucking into them?" I need to shut the fuck up, regroup, and start again. But I can't. So I kiss her instead, reminding her of how amazing we feel together, how much love we create. But she doesn't return my gesture, her mouth, lips, and tongue remaining unmoving. Bollocks. I give up on the kiss and try to recover the situation before I completely lose her to my apparent craziness. I'd have to succumb to her constant, ridiculous claims that I'm ridiculous, because I really am being ridiculous right now. Demanding. I look up at the cuffs. Restraining. What was I thinking? Have I completely blown this?

Standard.

"That was a joke, a very badly timed joke." How the hell do I pull this back? I suddenly can't look at her, can't face the unwelcome disbelief. And the silence? It's fucking screaming. Even the music has stopped, as if it's sensed the atmosphere and wants out too.

Talk, brother. Talk with words from your heart, because she's proved you have one and it is far from black.

Jesus.

I swallow, blinking back the tears prickling the backs of my eyes, and listen to my little brother.

For the first time in your fucking life. Well done.

Her gaze is fixed on me, her expression completely blank. She's wondering if she's dreaming. Or having a nightmare. "You completely consume me, Ava," I say quietly, more nervous than I've ever been in my life. I know this woman inside out. She's currently assessing every inch of me, our relationship, the circumstances. She's searching for a reason to say no and, frighteningly, there are plenty. But I hope she bypasses all of that and thinks about the one thing that truly matters. How much we love each other. "I can't function without you." My fucking voice is cracking. "I'm totally addicted to you, baby. You own me. Marry me."

She's like a statue, unmoving, unresponsive. Frozen by shock. Is it that shocking? Me wanting to make her mine officially forever? God damn it, she's still searching for the reason she needs to say no. Or maybe deciding which reason carries the most clout. My age, her age, my way with her, the fact we've only been together a matter of weeks, that I haven't met her parents, her brother.

I've blown it. I've made a mess of this like I've made—

"Okay."

I withdraw, looking at her lips, wondering if I heard that in my head.

Did she say *okay*?

"You're my life," she adds, simple as that.

"Yes?" I ask, shocked.

"It's instinctive." She smiles mildly, not looking unsure, but definitely shaken. Because her instinct is to marry me. "No sense fuck required," she whispers, jiggling her wrists, making me blink rapidly and look up to the headboard. "Can you let me go now?"

I shoot forward and grab the key, my shaking hands not helping me with the fiddly locks. I release both hands and haul Ava up, dropping my arse to my heels, hugging her hard as I turn and drop to the bed, so fucking overwhelmed. "I'm going to make you so happy."

She tries to fight her way free, but I hold firm, needing these tears to fuck right off before she clocks them. I need to be nothing but strength for her. A rock.

But she doesn't give up. I, however, do. I release her and let her see me, and the moment she does, she visibly deflates, her eyes softening along with her body. "You already make me happy," she says, her voice soft too, as she feels at my face. That's also gentle. She's treating me like I treat her. With the utmost care. Like I'm delicate. I hate that I am. This woman is the beginning and the end of me. "Why are you crying?"

Why? Because I'm so fucking happy. Overwhelmed. "See what you do to me?" I roughly wipe at my face and pull her closer. "I can't believe you're in my life," I admit. "I can't believe you're mine. You are so, so precious to me, baby."

She lets me take in every inch of her face, watching me. "You're precious to me too."

I truly hope I am. My God, she said yes. I can't even believe it, even though I imagined. Hoped. She said yes. "Are we friends?"

Her accepting, soft smile puts a lump back in my throat. "Always."

Not true, but I appreciate her sentiment. I'm sure she'll defy me again sometime soon. I'm sure she'll accuse me of being overprotective. Unreasonable. I'm sure I'll laugh at her claims. "Good, my work here is done." My dick disagrees, starting to pulse, telling me there's still unfinished business, and I am not about to argue with that. I roll us until she's beneath me and shift my hips until my cock skims her waiting entrance. One thrust pushes me inside her to the hilt, and I exhale, taking a moment, as does she. "Now, we have sleepy celebration sex." I register the music's playing again, like it's sensed the atmosphere has improved and it's safe to return to the room. No. I turn it off and get back to business. "I only want to hear *you* when you come for me." I close the gap between our mouths and secure her hands above her head, and I remember as I thread our fingers and feel it. The ring. She's not registered it's there?

"That was a proposal fuck." She smiles around our kiss, meeting every advance with a roll of her hips, taking me deep. Deep but slow.

And it is glorious.

"You'll be Mrs. Ward," I whisper, abandoning her mouth for her eyes, pumping slowly into her.

"I will."

"You'll be mine forever," I tell her, as if subconsciously ensuring she realizes what she's agreed to.

"I already am."

Good God. I'm forced to take a moment, breathing through the pleasure and contentment, feeling her squeezing me. "I'm going to worship you every day for the rest of my life." I lose control of my hips and buck, feeling my cock expanding, throbbing, screaming for release. "Jesus."

Her fingers clawing around mine, her head shaking, she cries out, and I catch her lips and increase the pace, taking us to the edge, our kiss clumsy—teeth clashing, tongues dueling, lips everywhere.

Her heels dig into my arse, holding tight.

And I'm gone.

It takes me out completely, bends my body, burns my blood, fogs my brain. Fucking hell. I vaguely hear Ava's yell past my bellow, and I collapse, twitching, Ava's breathing loud, mine strained. "I can't breathe," I gasp, my body limp and heavy, my sweaty hands peeling from Ava's. She hugs me. I don't know where she finds the energy, but then like magic, perhaps because I know I must be a weight on her, I find some myself and kiss my way up her neck, her cheek, to her lips. "I crazy love you, baby." More every second. "I'm glad we're friends."

I heave myself off her with effort and fall to my back, grateful for the shot of cool air to my chest. I smile at the ceiling, not quite believing what's happened, as she sits herself on my stomach and her hands land on my chest. I glance at the ring that she *still* hasn't realized is there and rest my big hands over her petite ones, ready to point it out. God, it looks so good on her.

But she speaks as I draw breath, affirming, as she does, that she knows fine well that I love her. Then she eyes me in a way that tells me I'm about to be interrogated. I'm not worried. Not at this particular moment in time, anyway, because she's about to ask about Coral. I knew it was coming. "If I'm going to marry you, you have to answer some questions." She finishes and clears her throat, her back straightening in a show of fortitude.

Here we go.

37

A DISCUSSION about Coral was inevitable, but not ideal after the blissful moment we just shared. But Ava looks rather adamant. I *have* to answer some questions. "I do, do I?"

"Yes, you do."

Very adamant. "Come on then, spit it out." I know I sound tired. Can't help it. "What do you want to know?" I raise my brows as Ava lowers hers, unimpressed, and I apologize for appearing bored.

"Who was that woman last night?" she asks.

"Coral."

Her level of unimpressed increases. "I know her name is Coral." Head tilted, she looks at me with a warning look. "*Who* is she?"

"She's the wife of the nasty little fucker who got ejected from The Manor the day you found the communal room." I'll let Ava conclude the rest based on what she heard on the day I'd rather forget. She doesn't need explicit details.

She's silent, tying up all of the ends, piecing it altogether. "You had an affair with her?"

"No, they came to me to source someone to participate in a threesome."

She withdraws, and I immediately wish I could take those words and ram them back in my mouth. Because she looks disgusted. "You?" Ava asks, as if she needs to. I still nod, feeling shame creeping up on me. I don't want her to be disgusted with me. "Why would you do that?"

Fucking hell. I did it because I could. I did it because I was a hedonistic playboy with not one care in the fucking world. I did it because I was reckless and fucked up. "She asked me to."

She sucks her bottom lip in briefly, doing what I hoped she wouldn't. Making a big deal of it. I fucked Coral. She mistakenly thought it meant more. The end.

"She fell in love with you," Ava says.

I can't say I wouldn't have accepted Coral and Mike's offer had I known Coral would fall in love with me, because . . . well, I just didn't care back then. Didn't think about the bigger picture. "I guess she did."

She nods, and on this occasion, I really fucking hate the look of acceptance on her, because I will never accept another man loving her. "What did she want yesterday?" she asks, and I inwardly groan. We're not done. "You were gone for a long time."

"She left Mike . . ." I reach for the strength to give her honesty. "For me," I add, and I detect another small, accepting nod. "I don't know why. I never gave her any reason to believe I wanted her like that." I wait for a reaction. Nothing, which surprises me. "He's thrown her out, took her car, and seized her cards. She has nothing."

And then there's something. A frown. I'm not sure I like it. "She came to you for help?"

"Yes," I reply, slowly and warily.

"And what did you say?"

"I said I would do what I could." Why do I have a horrible feeling that *that* was the wrong answer? I feel a bit strung all of a sudden, and it's not a welcome feeling so close off the back of complete bliss.

"Has this got anything to do with the police?" Ava goes on, her brain working overtime.

"Mike's playing games," I say on an unamused laugh. I'll finish the job if he comes close enough. "He advised the immigration police that half of my staff are illegal immigrants. It was cleared up quite quickly, no harm done. It was just a bit inconvenient."

"Why didn't you just tell me all of this instead of letting my mind race?"

"Why would I trouble you with that trivial shit?"

She eyes me, her bottom lip slipping between her teeth, looking thoughtful. I don't like it. "So, you took part in the threesome and that was it?"

Really don't like it. "Yes."

"You're lying to me," she grates, trying to remove her hands from beneath mine. *Oh, here we go.* "That wasn't it, was it?"

Why the hell does she want all the dirty little details? It's maddening, and it won't change a thing. I love her. I want to marry her. Coral means nothing. *For fuck's sake.* "Not exactly, no." I can't look at her right now. Not with that disgust plastered all over her face. "Do we need to go on with this? She was under the wrong impression that I wanted more, I didn't. End of." I am in no position to be irate, and yet here I am. Irate.

"So you *did* have an affair with her?" she asks quietly.

Jesus Christ. "Yes." Fuck me. If having sex with Coral while Mike wasn't there and was unaware, then yes, I had an affair. I didn't' even consider that at the time, though, because, again . . . I didn't care. Now? Oh, how I'd change so much. I growl, frustrated. "Okay, yes, I did, but it was just sex, nothing more." To me, anyway. We fucked. I left, or I asked her to leave. "Now, let's drop it."

"You told me once that you've never wanted to fuck a woman more than once, she says quietly, her eyes darting across my chest briefly. "Only me."

God love her, she sounds so disappointed. "I never said I didn't have a woman more than once," I reply gently, hating having to explain this. Hating bursting her bubble. "I said I've never *wanted* a woman more than once. It was a means to an end, that's all. She offered it on a plate."

"So, you haven't only fucked me more than once?"

I flinch, cringing, so fucking uncomfortable. How did we get here? "Ava, watch your mouth," I say, if only to buy myself some time.

"No," she snaps, startling me. "Not when we're talking about you fucking other women." Her nostrils flare, her jaw rolls. "You've not just fucked me more than once, have you?"

What is she trying to achieve, except severe annoyance on my part and hurt on hers? She's like a dog with a fucking bone. "No, I've not, but you have to understand none of them meant anything to me. I used them, treated them like objects. I'm not proud, but that's just the way it was. They would take me whatever way I came, Ava." *Drunk, heartless, emotionless, cold.* "They all wanted more, but they certainly never expected it. Now, though, they've seen I can be a one-woman man." I fucking hate myself right now. Everyone around me keeps harping on about my past being in my past, all facets of it. And here we have a perfect example that it doesn't matter. It can still hurt Ava, and that's what I want to avoid at all costs. *Want* to. Don't know if I can.

"She's still in love with you," Ava whispers, her voice trembling with her lip, her hands gripping mine hard. "She can't have you. None of them can."

My stress and irritation subside at the sight of her . . . fear. She's scared of losing me. I can relate. It's my greatest fear. "She can't. I told her that." Numerous times, and now I finally feel like it's sinking in. "None of them can. It's all about you."

"I don't want you helping Coral either. It's unfair for you to expect me to be okay with that."

Whoa. "Ava, I can't turn my back on her." She's acting on impulse. She doesn't mean that, surely? I'd expect coldness from Sarah, yes, but Ava? She's not heartless.

"Okay, I'll keep working for Mikael."

I stare at her, aghast. If she ever tells me I'm unreasonable ever again . . . "You had better retract that statement." What the hell is wrong with her?

"No." Her look is pure defiance. She knows she's being selfish. It doesn't matter the circumstances, only that she's acting with spite.

Fine, have it your way, Ava. It looks like this morning's going to the dogs, anyway. "Three," I say calmly, and she laughs without humor as I feel her muscles engaging, prompting me to lock down my hold.

"Oh no, you don't," she hisses.

"Two," I continue, giving it to her, fierce, my hold *and* my expression.

"No! You are not giving me the countdown on this." She wriggles and squirms. "No way, Ward. You can take your zero and shove it up your fucking arse!"

"Mouth," I bellow, manhandling her onto her front before she knocks either of us out with her flailing arms and legs. It's not easy, her strength's surprising, and I'm short of breath when I finally have her pinned on her front. "One," I wheeze.

"Get lost," she gasps back. *So* stubborn. This is ridiculous. We're at odds over something that is so fucking unimportant.

"Zero, baby." I go straight for her weak spot and tickle the hell out of her, determined to get some lightness back.

"Jesse!" Her scream of my name is ear-piercing, could probably be heard as far as The Manor. I don't stop. Not until she promises to drop her issue that isn't really a fucking issue. I'm never seeing Coral again. Don't need to.

"Okay," she shrieks. "Okay, I'm sorry." I ease off the pressure, watching her squished face in the sheets, her mouth open, gasping for air as she apologizes repeatedly.

I stop torturing her and turn her over, swathing her and lowering my mouth. "Kiss me."

She pounces like a lion, attacking me insatiably, her mind distracted, her grievance forgotten, just as I planned. But when her mouth gets firmer on mine and she bites at my lip and whips her tongue around my mouth, I realize it's not forgotten. She's marking her territory.

Me.

"Just you, Ava," I affirm. "I love *you*."

"Just me," she says quietly, sounding unsure. Telling herself.

I pull back and smile mildly down at her. "Good girl. I've fucked you, and now I need to feed you."

"Is Cathy coming in?"

"No, weekends are her own. Up you get." I pull her to sitting and get up, picking up all the things I tossed on the floor and taking them to the dressing room, shoving them in the wardrobe and slipping on some lounge pants. I enter the bedroom and find Ava's made no attempt to get up. In fact, she's lying back down and looking quite smug about it. I eye her as I tie the string on the waist of my lounge pants, and her smile widens. "Are you going to lie there all day?" I ask as she blatantly admires me.

"You promised a lie in."

Of which you've just wasted bellyaching over something irrelevant. I'm fast learning when to talk and when to keep my mouth shut. *Happy wife, happy life.* I wander over, and her eyes follow me to the end of the bed. She can't restrain her grin. She's asking for it, and I'll happily give it to her. I grab her ankle and she yelps delightedly as I yank her down the bed to me, caging her in with my arms. "Tell me we're friends."

"We're friends."

"Tell me you love me." I get temptingly close, nose to nose, breathing across her face.

Her smile is life. "I love you."

"Tell me you'll marry me."

"I'll marry you."

"And I can't wait." I look at her lips, the draw strong. "Kiss me." I groan as she locks our lips and wraps her limbs around me, clinging to my front as I stand up straight and meet her swirling tongue, carrying her to the bathroom and setting her down outside the shower. Or trying to. She's not letting go willingly, so I help her along, smiling when she protests. "You brush your teeth, I'll start breakfast."

"Do I *need* to brush my teeth?"

Always reading between the lines. "No, I just thought that maybe you would like to." I put her in front of the mirror and take in the sight of the couple before us. There's no escaping it—they're a really good-looking couple. I hold her eyes as I kiss her shoulder. Then smack her arse and leave, a shit-eating grin on my face. I collect my phone, get Ava's from her purse, and take the stairs, collecting my laptop from my office on my way and taking it to the kitchen. I put Ava's phone on charge, go to the fridge, have a few finger dips of my favorite stuff, and then settle at the island and open the lid of my laptop.

My fingers don't even meet the keys, pausing when I hear Ava shriek in the distance. "What the hell?" I'm off my stool like a bullet, my heart clattering, and I fly back up the stairs three at a time and fall into the bedroom. I hear terribly strained breathing coming from the bathroom. "Ava?" I gasp, rushing that way. I find her on the chaise in the window, her head between her legs. Fucking hell, what's happened? A dizzy spell? *Why would she have a dizzy spell?* I gasp to myself. Is she pregnant? "Ava, baby. What's wrong?" I hurry over and collapse to my knees, rubbing at her legs, willing her to speak, tell me, but all I get is overwrought, labored breathing. Jesus, have I ever felt so scared? I shy away from that thought quickly. Yes, I have. Once before, and my life quickly fell apart. "Ava, God help me, what's happened?" I can't stand it a moment longer. My heart is about to break out of my chest and land on the bathroom floor. I encourage her face up and find toothpaste smeared around her mouth. "Please," I beg, wary of the tears pouring. "Tell me."

Her mouth opens, closes, opens again, yet no words come out, but her hand appears, and that confuses the fuck out of me. Until I see the ring. *The ring?* Is she kidding me? All this over a little diamond? "You found it then?" I sigh, my heart settling to a less dangerous pace. "You took your bloody time. Jesus, Ava. I had a thousand heart attacks." She looks at me like I've just landed from Mars as I kiss her hand, smiling up at her. "Do you like it?"

"Oh God." She looks down at the sparkling gem, then gasps, reaching for her neck.

"It's in the safe," I say quickly, seeing panic flare. I bring her hand back down. "Tell me," I push. "Do you like it?"

Ava shakes her head, frowning. It's not a no. It's disbelief. "You know I do." She admires it for a moment, and my heart sings with joy. She loves it. It's hard not to, really. "Wait there a minute," she says. "When did you put this on my finger?"

"Right after I cuffed you."

"That's rather confident of you."

"A man can be optimistic."

"You call it optimistic; I call it pigheadedness."

I am many things, but I am not pigheaded. Quite the opposite in fact, but if it makes her happy . . . "You can call it whatever the fuck you like," I say, claiming her and taking her to the bathroom floor. "She said yes." I get her on her back and lose myself in her naked chest, wriggling my face, like some fifteen-year-old virgin who's just encountered his first pair of tits.

"Stop!" She giggles, making no attempt to stop me at all.

"No. I'm marking you." I suck her flesh into my mouth and peek up at her, seeing a woman in her element, calm and relaxed. Happy. I smile around my mouthful of boob and get back to my task, sucking the blood to the surface of her skin. And she lets me. It's beautiful. "There." I release her and check the perfect dark circle. "Now we match."

"Happy?"

"I am." On cloud nine. "You?"

Her smile lights up my world. "Delighted."

"Good, my work here is done. Next job, feed my temptress. Up you get." I stand and get her off the floor. "Are you coming down anytime soon?"

"I'll be five minutes . . . ish."

"Ish," I whisper, nipping her ear and smacking her bum. "Be quick." I'm looking forward to being stuck to her for the rest of the weekend. No interruptions, no outside forces infiltrating our bubble, nothing.

I'm smiling again as I head down the stairs, but my contentment is short-lived when I arrive back at the island, my stomach dropping when I'm greeted with a text message from Mikael. "Fuck," I whisper, reading Van Der Haus's words—a reply to yesterday's barrage of warnings I left on his voicemail.

Now why would I do that?

Fuck.

38

I SWALLOW, looking at the ceiling. Why should he back off? "Because I'll be up for fucking murder if you don't," I growl, forgetting myself for a moment, looking over my shoulder. "Shit." I drop my phone on the counter, losing my face in my hands. The anger is brewing. I'm keeping a lid on it, and it's an effort, but if I release the pressure, I'm going to fucking explode, and I can't have that while Ava's around.

I swipe up my mobile and stalk into the laundry room, releasing a suppressed yell the moment the door's closed behind me. "Fuck," I hiss, my fist balling, crushing my mobile in my hand. I read the message again, like it could have morphed into a different *message*. Anything non-threatening. Anything that'll lessen the fury.

Nope.

He's still telling me that he's about to ruin me. Ruin Ava. Ruin *us*.

I rest against the washing machine, concentrating on getting my temper under control before Ava comes down and detects something's wrong. Sweeping a stressed hand through my hair, I check the time as my mobile rings in my hand. *Sam*. I take a few needed, calming breaths and answer as I leave the laundry room, going to the fridge and plucking my peanut butter from the shelf before settling back on the stool.

"Worst thing I've ever done," he says, sounding fraught. It brings a small smile to my face, my own woes lifting for a moment to listen to Sam's.

"So you did actually do it?" I ask. Interesting. I was putting my money on it being halted before Drew had a chance to make Kate privy to his famous piercing.

"Yes, we did it. And you know what?"

"What?"

"I could tell she didn't want to, not that Drew's not sex on legs, obviously, but because she likes me."

I pause with my finger in my mouth. "And do you like her?"

"Don't ask me stupid fucking questions, Jesse. Whenever have I stayed at a bird's place? Whenever have I had lunch with one? Gone out on the town with one? Baked fucking cakes with one? Of course I like her. She's a cool bird."

"Don't ever let Kate hear you call her *bird.*" I laugh to myself as I plunge my finger into the jar of peanut butter. He's such a knobhead. "So she likes you but she didn't call a halt on it, and neither did you?" And neither did Drew?

"No, and you know why, don't you?"

"No, Sam, I don't. This whole fucking situation is burning my brain, if you want the truth."

"She didn't stop it because she's stubborn."

I raise my brows to myself. "And why didn't you stop it?"

"Oh, fuck off." He hangs up on me, and I flinch, insulted.

"Charming," I mutter, pulling up Drew's number, worried this might cause a problem between my mates. Why the fuck didn't Drew put a stop to it? He's a knobhead too. He answers, sounding tired and groggy. "Where are you?" I ask.

There's a brief silence, and I know it's because he's currently looking around trying to figure that out for himself. "What the fuck are you doing calling me at this time?"

"Why the fuck didn't you stop it?" I counter, and then inhale. "Oh my God, you couldn't, could you?" This is bad news. "Because you were enjoying it."

"Chill out, Judge Judy. I thought one of those two idiots were going to stop it."

"And then suddenly your pierced dick was in Kate?"

Drew laughs. "Ever seen Sam look like he wants to kill someone?"

"No."

"It's priceless."

"You're fucked up."

"Whatever. I had a nice time and now hopefully those two will admit what we all know."

"Sam already did."

"Well, my work here is done."

"That's my line."

"God, you're being a bitch today."

"Fuck you. Things won't be weird, will they?"

"No, they won't be weird. Kate's cool, but she's not my cup of tea."

Now *there's* the million-dollar question. "What's your cup of tea?"

"Gagged and heartless." He hangs up, leaving me shaking my head to myself, and my phone is quickly ringing again.

Fuck me, here I was thinking of having a nice, quiet weekend. "John?"

"I brought Ava's car over."

"I didn't ask you to."

"I brought Ava's car over," he repeats, sterner, lower, moodier.

I frown down the line. "Thanks."

"Open the motherfucking door, you stupid motherfucker."

I get up and go to the door, swinging it open, my phone still at my ear, finding John on the other side. He tosses the keys at me, and I catch them. "This feels like an intervention."

He looks past me, searching for Ava no doubt. Or for the signs of something on her finger. "You did it, didn't you?"

I press my lips together, not prepared to rat myself out. I can keep Ava away from The Manor for the next few days. Tell John I've met her parents. I can't imagine Ava will be rushing to share the details of my memorable proposal. "Did what?"

He takes off his glasses and looks at me. *Really* looks at me. "You can't lie to me."

Fuck, he's right. Never could. "How the fuck did you know?"

"Because I woke up this morning and had this funny feeling in my gut that you'd done something stupid." He turns and walks away. "And my gut when it comes to you is always right."

"What does your gut say about me marrying Ava?" I call after him.

"You're a first-class, professional cunt, Jesse."

I recoil. "John?" I say, wounded, but he flaps a hand irritably, dismissing me, and carries on his way, getting in the elevator. And he doesn't look up as the doors close.

Cunt? *Definitely* prefer motherfucker.

I shut the door and lean against it, sighing, trying not to think about the fact that John is always right. And back down the pan goes my mood as I trudge to the kitchen and toss Ava's keys on the side.

I settle at the computer and stare at the blank screen for a few moments. Then wake it up and type something into the search bar, scrolling through the results. And every place I click on tells me it's not available until next year. Some even the year after. "Fuck me," I breathe. At this rate, I'll be drawing my pension before I get my girl down the aisle, and that won't do.

Make it official.

Get on with life.

"Here, I forgot to give you these."

I look up from my peanut butter and find Ava holding out some post. "You open them," I say, and she frowns, thrusting them forward, obviously not comfortable with that. Damn it. She's leading by example. Teaching me some manners. I take the envelopes and toss them aside, going back to my screen, frowning. Churches, manor houses, town halls. Where do I even start?

"My car's back?"

"John dropped it off." *And joined Van Der Haus in ruining my morning.* "Are you religious?"

A small hesitation, and for a second I'm worried she'll hit me with the news that her parents—whom I am yet to meet—are church goers. "No," she eventually says.

"Me neither." That's helpful. The churches seem to be the busiest, and I doubt I'd be accepted into the house of God anyway. "Do you have any preference on dates?"

"What for?"

Her obvious confusion pulls me away from a viable option—a country club on the outskirts of Kent. "Is there any particular date you would like to become Mrs. Ava Ward?" God, that sounds amazing.

Recognition dawns on her, and we're quickly both on the same page. "I don't know, next year, the year after?" She plucks some bread out of the toaster, happily slapping some butter on, and I stare at her, alarmed, oblivious to the jar slipping out of my hand. It hits the marble with a clang, getting Ava's attention and knocking me from my inertness.

"Next year?" I splutter.

"Okay, the year after." Sinking her teeth into her toast, she smiles. She fucking smiles like waiting two years to get married is something to celebrate.

"The year after?" she adds tentatively.

"We get married next month." And that's going to be a painful wait. "Next fucking year," I say in disbelief, getting more peanut butter. Apparently, we're not on the same page. Not even the same book. Hell, she's in a completely different genre to me.

"Jesse, I can't marry you next month," Ava says, laughing.

"Yes, you can and you will," I grunt when the lovely country club just outside Kent shows there's nothing available for the next eighteen months. This is ridiculous. Why the hell would anyone wait so long to tie the knot? So much can happen in that time. For example, one person could change their mind.

"No, I can't." Ava's still laughing. Like . . . this is funny?

I put my jar down with a heavier hand than intended, and Ava jumps. She can't? No, she *won't*, and that's different territory. "Excuse me?"

"Jesse," she says, exhaling, and I can see she's falling into a pacifying state. "My parents don't even really know about you. You can't expect me to call them up and break this sort of news down the phone."

Fuck it all. The parents. If John was here, he'd smash my head onto the counter. I'm tempted to do it myself. "We'll go and see them. I'm not pussyfooting around, Ava." God, listen to me. Yes, I am hearing myself. No, I can't help it.

I stare at her, as she stares at me. I hate that she's so worried about me meeting her parents. What the hell does she think I'll do? Bang my fists on my chest, toss her onto my shoulder, and steal her away from them? I'm a rational man. I would never come between Ava and her parents.

"You're being unreasonable." She looks at me with too much disdain for my liking, nibbling at her toast.

"Do you love me?" I ask.

"Don't ask stupid questions."

"Good." So let's get on with this. "I love you too. We get married next month."

Her toast hits her plate, her eyes closing briefly to gather herself. She's digging her heels in, and that's not what I need right now. I need acquiescence. "Jesse, I'm not marrying you next month." She takes her plate to the bin and drops the rest of her toast in there. I can see what's coming a mile off. She's going to walk away.

"Come here," I say, feeling my heartbeats quickening. It's unstoppable. Annoying. Almost like an alarm bell that's goes off inside me to warn me shit's about to go down, or, in other words, Ava is leaving.

"No," she says simply, facing me, her determination worrying. So perhaps I need to fuck some sense into her. Convince her in a way we both love. "And you are not going to be fucking an agreement out of me," she fires, reading my mind, making me recoil. "Forget it."

"Watch your fucking mouth, Ava," I grumble, going for the jugular. It's not failed me yet. "Three."

Poor thing, her eyes nearly pop out of her head. Why's she so stunned? This is what we do. Spar with words. Then with bodies. Ava says no to something she wants, and I convince her I'm right and she's wrong. "Oh no." She laughs. "Don't even think about it."

Too late. I've thought about it, and it's happening. "Two."

"No," she warns.

I smile to myself as she scans the space, searching for an escape. I get up and brush off my hands, getting ready to catch her. The countdown. Best invention ever. It takes a heated discussion to heat of another kind. It's our way of resolving our differences. And best of all, I always come out on top. Literally. "One."

"Jesse, you can fuck right off!" She flinches herself this time, a sign that even she hates her swearing. And another clue, if ever I needed one, and I don't, that she's in it to wind me the hell up.

"Mouth," I yell, not wasting anymore time. "Zero." I round the island, and she goes the other way. "Come here."

"No." She switches directions, as do I. "What's the rush? I'm not going anywhere."

"Damn right you're not. Why are you delaying it?"

"I'm not delaying," she argues. "It takes a good year to organize a wedding."

"Not our wedding." I feign breaking out in a run, stopping when she yelps and dashes off the other way. "Stop running from me, Ava. You know it makes me crazy mad."

"Then stop being unreasonable." She yelps again when I make a dash for her, but she somehow manages to keep the distance between us.

She's in control.

"Ava," I warn.

"Jesse," she sings, sarcastic as fuck, mocking the hell out of me.

"Right." I break out in a sprint, and she squeals, laughing as she runs out of the kitchen. I'll have her in my arms by step five, easy. But she doesn't go up the stairs. She dashes into the gym and slams the door, and I wedge a palm into the glass just before it meets the frame, my jaw tight as I look at her on the other side, merely an inch away, so close. But I can't reach her. I'll put her on her arse if I barge in. Maybe shatter the glass. *Fucking hell.* All I can see is Ava in that dream. Within reach but not reachable. "Let go of the door."

"What are you going to do?" she asks, and I freeze, registering her worry past my own. What am I going to do? Love her. That's what I'm going to do. With everything I have, I will love her, and I need her to let me do that.

"What do you think I'm going to do?"

"I don't know."

Her answer pains me, and I loosen my hold. It's the small window of opportunity she needs, and she takes it, quickly slamming the door and locking it. *The fuck?* "You didn't just do that." I take the handle for what it's worth. This door isn't opening unless I smash the fucking thing down. Panic. It's brewing. "Ava, open the door." I can't control my breath, and Ava must see that. But she still refuses. She leaves me suffering. "Ava, you know how it makes me feel if I can't lay my hands on you. Open the door."

"No." She stands her ground, but I can see it's hard for her. I can see it's going against the grain for her too, which makes it all the more pathetic that we're here. "Tell me we can discuss *our* wedding reasonably."

"We were. Ava, please," I beg. "Open the door.'

"No, we weren't discussing it, Jesse. You were *telling* me how it's going to be." Her head tilts and shakes mildly too. "You've really never had a relationship, have you?"

"No." This isn't breaking news. "I've told you this."

"I can tell," she breathes, looking increasingly exasperated while I'm becoming increasingly stressed. I look at the lock on the door. Wonder if Clive has a toolbox. "You're shit at it."

I snap my gaze to hers, insulted. I'm shit at it? "I love you," I say, wounded. Am I terrible at that? "Please, open the door." How did we get here? Not half hour ago we were making love after taking the next step in our incredible relationship. Consummating. Loving. Now we're a million miles away from each other with a barrier between us. I see myself, feeling at the never-ending pane of glass stretching out into the distance, looking up and seeing it stretching up to the sky. No way round. No way over. No way through. Ava is on the other side. The side where I can't be. The side where everyone I've ever loved can be found. I blink, wince, shudder.

"Do you agree?"

I stare at her, annoyed, powerless, scared. "I agree. Open the door." We both lift a hand in turn and reach for the handle, but Ava retracts hers, and I frown. What now?

"I'm going out with Kate later," she declares with a strong voice.

"What?" Don't tell me she's going to harness this power for as long as it takes for her to get every little thing she wants while I sacrifice every big thing I want?

"Last night, I told you that I was going out with Kate."

"And?" She was pissy. She said all kinds of things she didn't mean, all meant to rile me or hurt me. I assumed that was one of them. "Open the door."

"You can't stop me from seeing my friend," she says. "If I'm going to marry you, it's not so you can control my every move. I'm going out with Kate later and you're going to let me . . . without a fuss."

Control her? Yeah, fucking likely. And I would never stop her seeing her friend. I'm not a monster. But I had very detailed plans about how we'd spend this weekend together, and Ava going out on the town without me, drinking, didn't feature in those plans. What the hell am I supposed to do? "You're pushing your luck, lady," I grumble, making her blink, before she turns away and sits herself down on a bench. I shake the door handle. "Ava, what are you doing? Open the fucking door."

"I'm not opening that door until you start being more reasonable. If you want to marry me, you need to loosen up."

"It's not unreasonable to worry about you."

"You don't worry, Jesse," she says, laughing, although it's exasperated. "You torture yourself."

I can't dispute that. I do. And now she's torturing me because I torture myself? Yes, that's perfectly reasonable. "Open the door."

"I'm going out with Kate later."

Should I agree? I don't have much fucking choice, do I? "Fine," I hiss. This weekend is slowly going to shit. "But you're not drinking," I add, making sure *that's* clear. "Open the fucking door."

Her sigh is so loud and exaggerated, I highly expect the force of it to shatter the glass door. She wanders over like she has all the time in the world, like I'm not standing here about ready to burst with stress, and maybe a little anger now too. She's taken advantage. I'm annoyed.

The second the door's unlocked, I push my way in before she has a chance to recant and slap some more conditions on me, and claim her, getting her on the floor and smothering her entirely. "Please don't do that to me again. Promise me."

"It's the only way I can get you to listen to me."

"I'll listen." Is this what they call compromise? I don't like it. "Just don't put anything between us again."

"You can't be with me all of the time."

"I know." And doesn't that suck gravely? "But it will be on my terms when I can't be." I need to have warning. Be prepared. Plan how I might kill the time. It's not very reasonable to land it on me at the eleventh hour and expect me to be cool with it.

She laughs. "What about me?"

"I'll listen," I say, flipping her a quick half-hearted scowl before resuming my place in her neck. "You're being very challenging, wife-to-be."

She doesn't retort, and it's a novelty. She doesn't even want to go out. She just wants to demonstrate independence. Call the shots. Show me how it's apparently going to be. I'm not overreacting. Each and every time Ava has gone out without me, she's got too drunk to look after herself. We've argued. This time won't be any different. Plus, she's vulnerable when she's drunk. Exposed. An easy target. She should trust me, I know. Why can't she see this from my perspective instead of using it as a tool against me, and for what?

I sit up and pull her onto my lap. "Why don't you go to The Manor for a drink?" Problem solved.

Her face twists. It should be unattractive. Not on my Ava. "Absolutely not."

"Why?"

"So you can keep an eye on me?"

Why does she have to word things so they make me sound like a neurotic twat? No, it's so I can take care of her. Simple. But clearly, she's in no mood to listen. "It's logical," I say instead. "You can have a drink, I can make sure you're safe, and then I can bring you home." Be at her beck and call.

"No," she says, shaking her head at the same time. "End of."

I try jutting out my lip, being all adorable and irresistible. Doesn't work. Ava is developing a bad habit of resisting me. "Impossible woman." This isn't the end of it. I'll convince her, just watch me. I stand up, putting her on her feet and brushing her hair off her cheek. "I'm going to get a shower." I hitch a brow. "You'll come."

Leaning back, she maintains her unwavering firmness. "I've had a shower."

"Well, you'll have another with me."

"I'll be up in a minute." Breaking free of me, she heads out of the gym. "I need to call Kate. Where's my phone?"

I'd love to hear what Kate's got to say about last night. "Charging on the side." I trudge on heavy feet upstairs to the shower. "Don't be long."

39

I GET in the shower and make fast work of it. I'm an optimistic man, but I know she won't be joining me this morning. But this afternoon? I get out and brush my teeth, my mind cluttered with so much, then throw on some clothes before heading back downstairs to find her.

I pause at the top when I see her lost amid piles of clothes. "Oh," I say to myself. Zoe sure did work fast. Will this be another trigger for us to have words this morning? Something else I have to relent on? I take the stairs as Ava crumples to her back on a huff, overwhelmed. "Hey, baby," I say, looking down at her. "I've been waiting for you. What's up?"

She motions to the clothes surrounding her, like I could have missed it all.

Admittedly, there's a hell of a lot more than even I expected. "It arrived then?"

Ava huffs and puffs, and I roll my eyes, joining her on the floor, not crowding her, but just lying with her.

"Look at me," I say gently, and she does, albeit on a sigh. "What's the problem?"

"This is too much," she says. She's wrong. It'll never be enough. "I just want you."

I laugh to myself. Then why the hell is she so fixed on delaying making me hers officially? "I'm glad, but I've never had anyone to share my money with, Ava." I pout, trying for adorable again. "Please humor me."

"People will think I'm marrying you for your money."

Yes, because I look like a shipwreck. For fuck's sake. "I couldn't give a fuck what people think. It's all about us." I roll over so I'm facing her, tugging at her waist impatiently to join me. "Now, shut up." She's talked about a whole load of irrelevant things this morning. Enough.

"You won't have any money left if you spend like you did yesterday."

I'm laughing to myself again. I couldn't spend my millions in twenty lifetimes. I struggle to spend the interest. "Ava, I said shut up."

Her dark eyes sparkle, and I see her softening. "Make me."

No problem. I roll onto her and plunge my tongue deeply into her mouth, starting the first phase of my plan to keep her at home with me tonight. And she reciprocates beautifully, giving me all of the sounds.

"Hmm, you taste good," she says as I roll us onto a pile of likely obscenely expensive dresses. She bites my lip and straddles me, pushing her palms into my pecs and rising to sit, glancing around at her new wardrobe. She's smiling. "I guess we should move this." She quickly looks overwhelmed again. "Where am I going to put it all?"

"In the dressing room."

"The dressing room is full of *your* clothes."

"Then I'll make room." I sit up and slap a kiss on her lips, taking her hips and lifting her off my lap and standing. I strip out of my clothes under her curious eyes, all the way down to my boxers.

"What are you doing?"

"Preparing to work up a sweat." I silently delight at her inability to *not* take in every glorious piece of me. "Earth to Ava," I whisper. She looks up at me. "Okay there?"

"I know what you're doing."

"What am I doing?"

"You're starting the process." She stands and gathers up a pile of clothes, turning and walking away.

"What process?" I call to her back.

"The process that you *think* will mean I will stay home with you tonight." She stops at the bottom of the stairs. "It won't work." I scowl, and she smiles. "Besides, I have a ton of new outfits to try out." She takes the stairs. "I might go out tomorrow night too."

"You're fucking not," I say, my bubble burst.

"Come along now, dear. Make yourself useful."

I dip to scoop up some clothes, thoroughly pussy-whipped—couldn't give a fuck—and smile, but it falters, my body half bent. Ava called Kate and she hasn't mentioned anything about last night. Which definitely means Kate has not told Ava.

I abandon her clothes and go to the kitchen, finding my phone, stalling when I see it's moved. I look back at the door.

"What's taking you so long," she yells. "I'll be here a whole year."

"Hopefully," I grumble, returning my attention to my mobile. *Definitely* moved. I scoop it up and go to my call history, withdrawing when I see one from Coral twenty minutes ago. And it wasn't a missed call. "What the fuck?" I whisper, opening the details. Forty seconds. It's not long, but really fucking long. A lot can be said in forty seconds. So what was said, and why hasn't Ava mentioned it? I bite at my lip, looking at the doorway when Ava appears, smiling, her cheeks flushed.

"Come on, muscles, I have half of Harrods to get upstairs."

I force a smile and discard my phone, moving in on her and tossing her over my shoulder, slapping her arse. I don't know what was said, but she's still here and she's still talking to me, so I assume Ava was the one to speak the most, and after this morning, I can't imagine it was all very pleasant. She's trampling. Fine. I'm done with Coral. Ava can have at her. But she's got a nerve being in my phone when she's kicked up such a stink about me playing with hers.

"Carry the clothes, not me," she says, laughing. I dip, Ava still on my shoulder, and grab a few bags, passing them back to her before getting some more. Then I take the stairs up to the dressing room and lower everything to the carpet, Ava last. She blows her hair out of her face and starts walking up and down, scanning the rails, and I look around my feet, lowering to pick up something familiar. I frown at the dress. The *very* short, *very* skimpy gray dress. This was a no. *What the fuck, Zoe?* I'll be calling her. And this dress will be disappearing the moment Ava's not here. I drop it on a snarl and look up, finding Ava looking overwhelmed again.

"I don't know where to start."

"It's easy," I say, stepping into one section and gathering the row of suits, unhooking them and carrying them to the end section, looping them over the rail. "Done."

"What about them?" she asks, pointing to a pile of stonewash jeans.

"What about them?"

"Can you move those too?"

I shrug and take the neat stack, putting them on the top shelf, stretching. Smiling. Because she's admiring me. I peek over my shoulder. Smirk. For someone who opposed moving into Lusso at every turn, she seems quite settled in. "Anything else, dear?" I face her, giving her my chest, and take the time to admire her legs. She has the most amazing legs. Even better when they're wrapped around me. So I take her waist and lift her, and they automatically curl around my hips, her arms around my neck. I look up. Wrinkle my nose. She kisses it.

"It'll take days at this rate," she says.

"And that's a problem because?"

"It's a problem because I am going out tonight." Lowering her mouth, she drops the gentlest kiss on my lips, and I'm done for. Fuck the dressing room, the clothes. Now this is the kind of perfect day I was hoping for, and as I deepen our kiss, so does she, humming her pleasure, pushing her chest into mine. "I want you," she whispers.

Of course she does.

I walk us out of the dressing room, lay her on the bed, and watch as she wriggles free of the shirt and I drag my boxers down. I crawl my way to her, my eyes dragging over every inch of her skin until I make it to her eyes. Her lips twitch, her hands on my shoulders, her breathing becoming rushed. Anticipation.

I kiss her gently, swivel my hips, and we both breathe out as I sink into her.

40

SHE'S DOING her utmost to ignore me as she gets herself ready for her night out, but I'm strategically placing myself in prime spots and my body in prime positions—showcasing my physique, acting casual—so she can't. It's highly amusing, observing her playing tug of war with her resistance.

I watch her hurry out of the bathroom, escaping the temptation, lifting my head off the chaise to watch her go. Then dropping it in exasperation. She's a determined little thing today. It's time to pull out the big guns.

I get up and go after her, catching her wrist as she's entering the dressing room. She doesn't show enough surprise for me to think she's actually surprised. She's been expecting this. *Begging* for this. I tug her towel off, toss her on the bed, and flip her onto all fours, gazing down her spine to her arse, smoothing over it with my palm. "You won't come." Not unless she gives me what I want. I slip my fingers into her, inhaling, seeing her back arch like a cat and her head drop, her beautifully blow-dried hair fanning the sheets. "This is for my pleasure, not yours." I stroke the warm, soft walls of her pussy, my mouth parted, the sight quite something. But she's tense. Tight. She knows what's coming.

"Oh God," she moans.

"Relax," I say, holding my cock, slipping the head over her pussy, feeling her tightening, making it difficult for me to enter her. "Damn it, Ava, stop fighting me."

"You're going to desert me, aren't you?" she asks, breathless, smacking the mattress with a balled fist. "You're not going to see me through."

"That's my call, baby." I deliver a stinger of a slap to her arse and caress the instant blemish, growling when she refuses to relax, taking my hand beneath us and slipping my fingers through her saturated pussy. She moans, softening, and I slip straight into her on a strangled groan, my shakes instant. She starts moving immediately, trying to seize the pleasure. Not today. I pull out.

"No," she yells.

"Oh, yes." I slip my fingers back into her, making sure I add some friction to her buzzing nub of nerves. She tries to grab it again. I withdraw. There will be no orgasm for my lady this time, unless, of course, she surrenders. I guide my dick to her opening.

"No, Jesse. Please." She pushes back, and I pull away, denying her.

"You love it, Ava." The push, the pull, the desperation. I wait for her to still before advancing, slowly plunging into her, hissing my way through the sensitivity, watching her head turn from side to side. I curse when she slams back onto me, a move made from pure frustration. So she wants it hard? I'm here for it. I start banging into her, my eyes spoiled for views: my dick plunging in and out, her hands bunching and relaxing, her head thrashing. She yells constantly. I have to stop for a moment, or I'll be a goner, and I am far from done with her. "You feel fucking amazing, baby. Brace yourself on the headboard."

She obeys immediately, whimpering loudly as she rises, and I grunt, gritting my teeth, concentrating so fucking hard on holding back my release. "Do you have a good grip?" I ask, drawing a perfect line down her spine, watching her hands flex around the wood.

"Yes," she replies, short and curt.

I smile as I slip out, slap her arse, and slam back in. "Brace your arms, Ava." I drive forward again, hard and fast, hissing as I do, and she yells, telling me it feels good, accepting the pleasure, screaming. The walls of her pussy start to pulse, her hips shooting back to catch each thrust. She's going to come. "Oh, no you don't." I pull out and get her onto her back, kneeling over her, taking my dick in my fist and thrusting. "Open your eyes, Ava," I yell when she defiantly slams them shut.

"You're a bastard," she yells, furious. "I'm going to get *so* drunk tonight."

"No, you're not." I swallow, my focus becoming hazy, as Ava, battles with her impulse to watch me pleasure myself all over her. I watch her boobs bounce, her eyes betraying her, sparkling delightedly, admittedly with a hint of anger mixed in there. Here it comes. *Fuck.*

I fall forward, taking the headboard for support, and roar when the pressure becomes too much, right before the tip of my cock detonates and shoots cum all over her boobs. I gasp, my heart hammering, my brow wet, as I slow my strokes and breathe through the toe-curling pleasure. Sated. Ava, however, and quite ironically, looks fit to burst. "Do you want to come?" I ask, breathless.

Her jaw twitches, no doubt from the force of her bite. "I'm going out."

"Stubborn woman." I rub myself all over her chest, admiring my work and her tidy bruise as I tuck myself away. "My work here is done." I slam a hard kiss on her lips, smiling when she accepts my tongue. I indulge her for a few seconds, kissing her as desperately as she's kissing me, moaning as indulgently as she does.

Then I deny her again, pulling away, smiling down at her when she completely loses the plot and screams, thrashing around. I laugh and get off the bed, slapping her arse one last time. "Don't shower."

"I've not got time!" she shouts, followed by a few more shrieks of displeasure, as I smile my way out of the bedroom.

I make it to the kitchen and call Sam, dropping onto a stool. "Busy?" I ask, and he laughs. I roll my eyes. "I'm not happy."

"No shit, Jesse. They'll be fine."

"Sam, the last time you said that I found Ava pissed up on a bar floor wearing next to nothing." I go to the fridge and yank the door open, scanning the contents. "Also, is last night classified information or—"

"Let's never talk about last night ever again."

"Are you at Kate's?"

"Yes."

"And Drew? Where's he?"

"I don't know, why?"

"I called him. He sounded worse for wear, and he didn't answer when I asked him where he was."

"I'll find out. So, did you do it?"

"Do what?" I take my peanut butter and go to the island, waking up my laptop.

"Ask Ava to marry you."

I smile. "Yes."

"And her parents? They're happy?"

"Have you been talking to John?" I unscrew the cap of my jar and poke a finger in aggressively. "I'm meeting her parents this weekend." Ava just doesn't know it yet.

"That's great."

"I'll call you when I've dropped Ava off." I hang up and think about how I can subtly hint to the parent situation again without it resulting in Ava evading and me being pissed off. It shouldn't even be a situation. Maybe I *should* take the lead. Call them. Yes, I should call them. Explain. Explain what? I frown as I suck my finger clean, seeing something out the corner of my eye.

Ava.

Creeping through the lounge.

Wearing the gray dress that puts the one involved in the dress massacre to shame.

What the ever-loving fuck? I very nearly bite my fucking finger off. "You're not fucking wearing that!" I yell, taking her in, top to toe, my eyes wide, my mouth hanging open. *Jesus fucking Christ.* "A—"

She's off like a gazelle, making her escape, and I flinch when the front door slams, shaking the penthouse. "Ava," I bellow, going after her. "She'll be the fucking death of me," I hiss, flinging the door open, just as the elevator doors meet in the middle. I catch a glimpse of her. Smug. Waving. I'll kill her. Slowly. And that dress is getting shredded while she watches. I look between the elevator and the door that leads to the stairwell, torn over which will get me to her the fastest. "Fuck it." I head for the stairwell and punch in the code to let me through, flinging myself down the first few flights before I meet another door with another code. "Fuck's sake," I hiss, fumbling with the keypad. As soon as I'm through, I race down like a whirlwind, breaking out into the foyer and sprinting through, catching Clive's alarmed face, his hand in midair holding a phone.

"Mr. Ward," he says, following me as I tear past. "No clothes again today?"

I break out into the low evening sunshine, spotting her running toward her car. "Get your sweet fucking arse back inside," I roar, not slowing my pace, racing toward her. She stops and pivots. Could be me, but she looks amused. Not for long. I dip as I approach, tackling her low, flipping her up onto my shoulder, and turn and walk her back toward the privacy of our home. Of all the dresses, of course she chose this one.

I snarl at thin air and grab the hem, yanking it down her thighs, not caring how rough I am. The damn thing will be in a million pieces soon anyway. "It's just my fucking luck that I go and fall crazy in love with most impossible woman in the fucking world," I grumble as she chuckles, bouncing up and down on my shoulder as I stride back into Lusso. "Evening, Clive."

He doesn't even look up from what he's doing this time. "Mr. Ward. Hello, Ava."

"Hi Clive," she chimes, as happy as a pig in shit.

"I'm at a fucking loss," I mutter, wondering how I knock this irritating bad habit out of her. I enter the code in the elevator. She'll put me in an early fucking grave.

"Have you still not got that code changed?"

I scowl at the doors as they close, feeling her small hands sliding past my boxers. She thinks that's the end of it? "Shut up, Ava."

"Are we friends?"

"No." I smack her arse hard, jolting her on my shoulder, making her squeal. "Don't fuck with me, beautiful girl," I warn. "You should know by now, I always win."

"I know," she sighs, accepting what we both know is bullshit. "I love you."

"I love you too." I smile a little, turning my face into her thigh, breathing her skin into me. Soothing. A balm. "But you're a fucking pain in the arse." The doors open, and I pace out, taking us back into the penthouse and setting her on her feet.

Flicking her hair out of her face, she turns and struts away with extra sway, my eyes stuck to her arse as she takes the stairs. I definitely caught the terribly concealed smug look on her face. She knew the outcome of this whole situation. She knew I'd chase her down. And she still put the dress on anyway. Anyone would think she likes it when I'm . . . assertive.

"I guess I'll go find something more suitable to wear," she says as she reaches the top, looking over her shoulder, coy. Teasing. What the fuck is she playing at? "By sir's standards."

I lower my head, looking at her through slightly narrowed eyes. "I think I'll come and supervise."

She smiles, all wide and bright, reaching behind to unzip her dress and watches as I follow her up the stairs into the bedroom. She isn't playing fair. She tosses her clutch on the bed and disappears into the dressing room, and I dump my arse on the edge of the bed, feeling moody, listening to her huff and puff her way out of the gray dress. I eye her purse, listening out for her, as I pull it close and get her mobile out, set on texting her parents' number to my phone. Except I can't. Because it's asking me for a PIN. "The fuck?" I whisper, tapping at the screen. She locked her phone? Why? "You really piss me off." I slam it back in her bag, just as she appears at the door, half out of the dress, grinning. Of course, she thinks the dress is still my issue.

"I do?" she asks, letting the material fall down to her stomach, revealing lace-covered boobs and a beautiful bruise skimming the seam. I pout as she backs up.

"Don't bother hanging it back up," I grumble, shifting on the bed, uncomfortable. I hear her laugh, then a few clangs and clatters, a few more huffs and puffs.

My eyes fall to the bedside table, seeing something that shouldn't be there. My forehead heavy, I look away when Ava appears in a lovely pink dress, which is of a far more acceptable length.

She looks down her front, patting down the slightly puffy skirt. "Is this okay?"

"It's fine." I point at the nightstand. "What the fuck is that doing there?"

She looks to where I'm pointing. "Oh."

Jaw ticking, I reach for her ring. "Come here," I order, and she does, immediately holding out her hand. I slip it back on her finger. "Never take it off again."

"I was moisturizing. I forgot to put it back on, that's all."

"Yes, because you were too busy plotting how you were going to send your husband to the brink of insanity." I look up at her, finding one of her perfectly plucked eyebrows arched.

"You're not my husband."

"Just getting used to it." I grin. "Wife." Fuck, that sounds good.

"I'm a bit young to be a wife." She circles the bruise on my chest, admiring it.

"But I'm old enough to be a husband?" I ask, insulted.

"There's eleven years between us." She dips and kisses my nose. *Soon to be twelve.* "Like it or not, you're much older than I am."

"Not," I breathe, pulling her between my legs and tilting my head farther back, silently telling her to kiss me, exhaling happily when she does. "Are you sure you want to go out?" I ask around her mouth, certain this kiss could sway her.

She cups my cheeks and slows the swirl of her tongue, pulling back and dotting a few lovely pecks up my nose to my forehead. I've got her. I hum, happy, and squeeze her arse. "You'll crease my dress," she says quietly.

"Doesn't matter if you're not going out."

I feel her smile where her mouth is on my forehead, and she pulls back, my cheeks still in her palms, and scans my face. "I'm going out."

My face screws up, she removes herself from my arms, and I fall back to the mattress on a grunt. "I hope you have a wonderful time without me."

She laughs and goes back to the dressing room. "I'm sure you have things to catch up on with Sam and Drew."

I hitch a brow, looking at the entrance of the dressing room. "Like what?" Am I wrong? Did Kate spill the beans?

"I don't know. Man stuff."

"Your new necklace would look lovely with that dress." Load her with diamonds. Tells potential creeps there's a very wealthy, very territorial man in the wings waiting to rip their heads off. Ava appears with some heels on, and I groan, looking up at the ceiling.

"The weight of this diamond is enough responsibility."

"Fine." The ring is the biggest sign. "It's really not fair for you to look like that when I'm not with you."

"Worried some younger, hotter, less complicated man will come along and steal me from you?"

I blink. Yes. That's exactly what I'm worried about. But instead, I say, "Hotter?" And complicated? She doesn't know the half of it. "Baby, there is no one hotter than I am." I rise to my feet, and her gaze follows me up. I motion down my front. "I might be thirty-seven, but I'm a banging thirty-seven. And don't say shit like that." I go to the dressing room and pull on some jeans, now even moodier, buttoning the fly as I go to the doorway, finding her fluffing her hair in the mirror. "And for the record, I will kill any unfortunate fucker who thinks they can have you."

She looks at me in the reflection, a small smile tickling her lips. "You mean anyone who takes me away from you."

"Or that," I agree, reversing my steps and grabbing some boots and a T-shirt, slipping them on.

When I'm ready I get some cash and motion to the door, but she doesn't leave and instead comes to me, hands on my chest. "No one is going to take me away from you."

I take her hand and kiss the sparkling gem on her finger as I look into her eyes, nodding mildly, feeling more in love with her than ever before. "I suppose we better get going," I say, hitching a hopeful brow.

"We had." She removes herself from my space. "I just need to change my handbag and earrings."

I trudge off, grumpy. "I'll wait for you downstairs." What the hell am I going to do all night?

41

KATE IS full of beans when she hops in the car, gushing all over the Aston. I pull out and look up at my rearview mirror when she wedges herself between the seats, a shock of red blocking my view out the back window. “Come on then, let’s have a look.”

“What?” Ava looks back at Kate, and Kate looks at me, cursing, her eyes wide.

“It’s fine.” I put her mind at ease, turning onto the main road, feeling Ava’s incredulous stare on my profile.

“She knew?”

“I needed one of your rings to make sure the size was right.”

Ava lets me off the hook and aims her grievance on her friend. “You *knew*?”

“Yep.” Kate makes grabby hands at Ava. “Was it romantic? Show me.”

Ava obliges, but she’s laughing, accusing eyes on me. I ignore her. I thought it was *very* romantic. And, like I said, memorable. “Yeah, it was romantic,” Ava says, her voice breathy with the tail end of her laugh.

“Fucking hell,” Kate blurts, her nose nearly touching the diamond. “That is some serious special.” She flips me an impressed look, and my chest swells with pride. I did good. "So, when's the wedding?" she asks, sitting back and faffing with her handbag. *Next month.* "Shit, Ava." Kate looks up again. "Have you told your mum and dad?"

Very good question, Kate. The atmosphere between Ava and me has just dropped to sub-zero temperatures, and I peek out the corner of my eye, interested, seeing her eyes fixed forward. "Don't know and no," she says off-hand as I slow at some lights. I narrow an eye, unhappy. I'm giving her a pass for tonight. Tomorrow, we're dealing with parents and dates. No excuses. And if she fights me, I'll do what I've been silently threatening. Call them myself.

Ava, still avoiding my eyes, turns in her seat to face Kate. "Did you enjoy your evening?" she asks.

"Yes, it was fab," Kate says, cool as can be, pouting into a small mirror.

I look at Ava. She's scowling mildly at her friend, contemplating her next words. "What time did you wrap up?" she asks. I smile and pull away when the lights change to green.

"I can't remember. Is there a point to this line of enquiry?"

For God's sake, why the hell are they being so coy? "I think Ava would like to know if you enjoyed yourself upstairs after I took her home," I say, smiling at Ava's gaping mouth as Kate hits my shoulder.

"That, my friend," she muses, still coy, still casual, "is none of your business. Well, it is, but it isn't." She chuckles, going back to her mirror. I can't claim to know Kate very well, but I know someone who's feigning coolness, and she's definitely feigning coolness. What the fuck happened between those three?

The girls chit-chat about anything and nothing for the rest of the drive, and as soon as we pull up, I check to see if Jay is on the door. I spot his shiny bald head first as he steps out onto the pavement in his customary black suit. I nod as I let Kate out the back, and he nods in return, stepping aside to let Kate pass.

Ava is out of the car before I have a chance to be a gent and open her door, putting herself in front of me. "Don't drink," I say softly as

I take her in my arms, hoping every man in the bar and beyond is watching.

"I won't."

She's giving me lip service. I don't know who of the two of us is the biggest idiot right now. Me for expecting her not to drink, or Ava for promising not to. "I mean it."

"I won't drink."

"I'll pick you up," I tell her. "Ring me." I swoop in and kiss her, hearing Jay snort his tiredness.

"I'll ring you." She looks at me with soft eyes. Pacifyingly. "Go for a run or something." She rips the plaster off and leaves me on the pavement, feeling like she's taken my arms and legs with her.

"Fuck me, Ward." Jay comes over, looking up and down the car. "Where's this paranoia come from, anyway?"

"I'm not paranoid," I mutter, dipping into my pocket and pulling out some notes, thumbing a few off the wedge of cash. "Just reasonably concerned for her safety."

"Like a father would be if his teenage daughter just discovered alcohol, short dresses, and male attention?"

My thumb falters, and I hit Jay with a glare. "Fuck off, Jay." I thrust the money into his chest. "Make sure she stays safe."

"You got it." He tucks the money away. "Try not to worry."

I scoff and drop into the driver's seat, drumming the steering wheel.

Now what? My phone answers that question, an unknown London number dominating the screen on the dashboard. "Hello?" I answer, quiet and wary.

"Mr. Ward, it's Julian from the Connaught."

"Okay," I say, my frown huge, no doubt. "And what can I do for you?"

"I have Mrs. Seymour here."

"Coral?"

"Yes. She'd like to extend her stay for a few extra nights, and I need the cardholder's authorization."

I slump down in my seat, wincing. *Fucking hell.* I feel like I'm between a rock and a hard place. Don't rock the boat with Coral. But don't upset Ava. How do I achieve both?

"Mr. Ward?"

Torn, I try to weigh up my options, feeling like I'm being held to ransom. "Fine," I snap, agitated.

"I can charge it to the card we hold on file?"

"Yes," I hiss. "Is she there?"

"Mrs. Seymour?"

"No, Pussy Galore."

"Excuse me?"

"Yes, Mrs. Seymour, Julian. Is she there?"

"Yes, sir."

"Put her on." I think I could burn holes through the glass of my windscreen with my hard stare.

"Hello," Coral says, soft and unsure.

"Why did you call me this morning?" I ask shortly, starting my car and pulling away before Ava clocks me loitering outside the bar and accuses me of crowding her again.

Coral stalls, silent, shocked by my question. Because she obviously thinks Ava's told me and is also obviously wondering what Ava said. "Your girlfriend told you?"

"No," I say, turning into a side street and pulling over. "My fiancée did." I am a classified dickhead. For sure.

"Fiancée?" she breathes as I rub at my forehead. "You're getting married?"

Cringing, I shrink into the leather of my chair. "Why did you call me, Coral?"

"To thank you. For the hotel."

"There's no need to thank me." I never want to speak to her again, and I won't after this call. "I've authorized the hotel to charge my card, but you need to find somewhere to stay."

"I will. Just as soon as my parents are home."

I nod, checking my mirrors and pulling out. "I wish you the best, Coral." I hang up and put my foot down, heading back to Lusso, and the second I pull through the gates, I hear a horn sounding. I look up at my rearview mirror and see Sam in his Porsche behind me, Drew in the passenger seat.

I park and get out as Sam pulls into the space next to me. "We're here to save the day," he declares.

I snort and throw Drew an accusing stare. "Where the fuck were you when I called this morning?" He freezes, the door of Sam's Porsche half closed, looking between us.

"Why the fuck is everyone so concerned by where I've been?" he snaps, slamming the door and storming past me, heading into Lusso.

Call me suspicious, but I get the feeling Drew was somewhere he shouldn't have been last night. I look at Sam, tilting my head, and he shrugs. "Spoke to Kate?"

"Yes, I've spoken to Kate."

"And?"

We start to tail Drew as Sam considers me for a few moments. "There's definitely something she's not telling me."

"So ask her."

He laughs. "You think I'm gonna take relationship advice from a man who's convinced by marrying a woman she could never leave him, no matter what he's done or what she finds out?"

"I'm marrying her because I love her."

"I've no doubt," he muses as Drew hits the call button for the elevator blindly, frowning to himself. He doesn't look his usual self. It's weird. I look at Sam. He's a bit off too.

We all get in when the doors open, and I punch in the code. "You know," Sam says. "I don't think I'll have that beer after all." He steps out, leaving me and Drew in the elevator.

I'm done with this. I look between them but settle my stare on Drew. "Why the fuck did you have to go and put your dick in Kate?"

"Me?" he blurts, his hand indicating to his chest. Then he settles his stare on Sam. "Because he said it was cool."

"Me?" Sam asks, laughing. "When did the word, *I'm cool with you putting your dick in Kate* come out of my mouth?"

"When you *didn't* oppose my offer to join me at The Manor."

"*You* instigated it?" I look at Drew like he's stupid, because he obviously fucking is, stopping the doors from closing.

"I was trying to help," Drew says, laughing, his voice high-pitched.

"Well, can I suggest you don't?"

"Absolutely."

"And can I suggest you don't put your dick in Kate again?" Sam adds, pretty much kicking the door open when it tries to close again.

"You can." Drew sighs. "Mate, I honestly thought one of you would stop the whole thing before it got to anyone's dick being in anyone. Turns out you're both stubborn fuckers. On the plus side, though, Kate seemed to have fun."

Sam launches at Drew, and I quickly get between them before blood is shed, holding Sam back while looking at Drew in warning. "May I now suggest you shut the fuck up?"

"You may." Drew sighs again, putting his life at risk by putting himself in front of Sam, taking his shoulders. "Mate, she clearly has feelings for you and is clearly trying to hide them. I don't know what else to say."

"How about we never mention this ever again?"

"Fine."

"Fine."

"Fine," I add, making it a full house of *fines*. "Beer?" I ask, stepping back inside the elevator.

Drew joins me and Sam backs up, thumbing over his shoulder. "I think I'll go meet up with Kate."

I frown. "But she's with Ava."

"And?" He turns and walks off, and I'm quickly going after him. If he can meet up with Kate, then surely it's acceptable for me to meet up with Ava.

"What about me?" Drew asks. "I don't want to meet up with anyone."

"Not even the person who you weren't supposed to meet up with last night?" I call back.

"Definitely not," he grunts. I was right, but his expression right now and his response are clear signs that he's full of regret. Can't lie, though, I'm really curious. "Fuck this, I'm going to The Manor. You can drop me back at my place so I can get my car."

"No problem." I'll just pop by to see Ava. Make sure she's okay. She can't possibly protest that. Hopefully, with Sam there and Kate welcoming him, I might be invited to stay too.

Doubt it.

42

Jay's face is a picture of warning when I appear outside the bar. "It's been a quiet night," he says as I pass. "Let's keep it that way."

I ignore him and enter, scanning the bar for them. Sam spots the girls first and moves in, and damn if Kate isn't delighted to see him. I can't say with confidence that Ava's going to feel the same. I stand behind her for a time, building up the courage to make my presence known, bracing myself for the backlash. My time is up when she stands, turning this way.

Staggering.

What the actual fuck?

This is *not* a good start. She's staggering all over the fucking place. If anyone ever wondered where the term legless came from, they'd only need to look at my wife-to-be right now. I am fucking livid. No drink, she said. Fair enough, I knew she was lying, but to get completely shitfaced? She's hung herself. Gone way too far.

I roll my shoulders, trying to shake off the untamed rage before it has me exploding and doing more damage, my brain telling me to go to her quickly before she face-plants and breaks something, but my legs aren't listening.

Then she spots me, and she has the nerve to looked pissed off. Oh, there's going to be one hell of a showdown, and I can't bring myself to try and stop it. I draw breath, ready to silence the bar with my rant, but she staggers again, and I march forward, set on taking her home this minute. But then her expression changes, the anger for me falling and confusion embedding itself on her face. And she sways, reaching for the nearest table. Fuck, she's going to pass out. "Ava?" She blinks, shakes her head mildly, as if trying to shake away the fog. "Ava!" I yell, breaking into a run as I watch her body tilt forward, plummeting headfirst toward me. Toward the floor. "Fuck." I catch her in the nick of time, and she's a dead weight in my arms, floppy and completely out of it. I see Kate and Sam looking this way, alarmed. "If either of you say this is fine, I will lose my shit." Because I'm not there already. I carry her to a nearby chair and sit down, getting her on my lap, holding her limp body with one arm, trying to direct her face to mine. "Ava?" I wriggle her but she's completely unresponsive.

"She wasn't drunk," Kate says, falling to her knees in front of us, assessing her friend.

"Don't, Kate," I warn, in no mood for bullshit, as I pull back one of Ava's lids, recoiling when I see her eyes rolling. "This is fucking ridiculous." I stand with her draped across my arms and start walking out of the bar. "I'm taking her to a hospital." Did she eat? Have enough water today? Jesus. Could she be pregnant? I grit my teeth, unable to accept that she'd get herself so drunk if she knew she was. So perhaps she doesn't know she is. *Fucking hell.*

Jay flanks me as I carry her out, clearing the path. "What's happened?" he asks, naturally alarmed.

"She passed out. How much has she had to drink?"

"I'm not her personal bodyguard, Ward. I do what I can, as I have explained endless times. Do you want me to call an ambulance?"

"I'll get her there quicker myself." I open my car door and get Ava in the seat, tapping her cheeks a few times, trying to bring her round. Nothing. I take her wrist, feeling for her pulse while I watch her chest. *Fuming.* She has drunk herself into a fucking coma. "I am never letting you out of my sight again." I put her seatbelt on and shut the door, the agony and fear of seeing her like this very real, but there's anger too. How irresponsible she is. How inconsiderate. How fucking reckless.

Kate rushes out the bar carrying Ava's bag. "We'll follow you," she says, letting Sam pull her to his car.

The drive to the hospital gets me even more riled, the stench of wine on her potent. I know I have a sensitive nose, but this is absurd. I park illegally and haphazardly and carry her into A&E, yelling for assistance.

"Has she been drinking?" a nurse asks as she shows us to a private room.

"Yes," I grate.

"How much?"

"Too much." I lay her on the bed and reluctantly move back, letting the nurse start taking Ava's observations.

"Her name?"

"Ava," I answer shortly as she pulls her lids back, shining a light in them. "Is she okay?"

"Just give us space, Mr. . . ."

"Ward."

"And you are?"

"Husband."

I look at the door when another nurse joins us, pulling in a machine. "If you wouldn't mind waiting outside," she says, not physically moving me, but not far off, and short of physically moving *her*, I have no choice but to leave or get myself arrested for alleged assault. The door shuts in my face, and I stare at the blue glossy finish, feeling at my chest, my heart slowing down. *Jesus fucking Christ.*

I stride up and down, for what feels like forever, and Kate bursts through the door and spots me, slowing her pace. "She's in there," I say, motioning to the door. "With nurses."

"Do they know what's wrong?"

I shake my head, my eyes on my feet, walking up and down, up and down. "Fuck," I yell, my fists balling. "I fucking knew I shouldn't have let her out." I'm so fucking angry with myself for going against my gut. It won't happen again. I look at Kate accusingly, and she looks away, appearing pissed off. She can fuck off. I'm savage and, actually, I'm pissed off with her too, and I'm just about to tell her when the door opens, shutting me up. A nurse steps out, and I step forward, firm in my stance but cautious. "How is she? What's wrong with her? Hav—"

"Mr. Ward." She raises her hand to silence me. "She's okay. Still unconscious, however. Her heart rate is a little fast. We've called for a doctor," she says, looking at the watch attached to her pocket.

"Then where the hell is he?" I ask, feeling a hand land on my bicep. I look to my side and find Sam. I shrug him off. No, I won't calm down. Can't.

"On his way, Mr. Ward." She holds out her hand. "Her jewelry."

"You removed it?" I ask, accepting the earrings and her engagement ring.

"It's standard practice. Just in case—"

"In case what?"

"In case we need to take Ava to theatre."

"Why would you need to do that?" I ask, my vocal chords straining with the effort not to shout.

She motions to the door, not answering, because she doesn't have an answer. "You can sit with her while you wait."

"Thanks," I murmur, dragging my heavy body to the room. I wince when I see her on the bed, looking washed out.

"Give me your keys," Sam says, holding his hand out. "Your car's blocking one of the ambulance bays. They're calling a tow truck."

I pat at my pockets, frowning. "I left them in there."

Sam leaves me and Kate alone, and I keep pacing, fighting to keep my temper in check. I know it's fear fueling it. The longer the silence stretches, the higher the tension gets, Kate constantly flicking me cautious looks, me constantly cursing under my breath, raking a hand through my hair so much I'm sure I won't have any left by tomorrow. The pressure inside is becoming uncontrollable.

"This," I say, finally bursting, jabbing my finger toward Ava. "Is the very reason I do not want her drinking. I know all of you think it's just because of my toxic relationship with drink, but it's not. It's this."

"So you admit you had a toxic relationship with drink?" Kate asks, as if that's appropriate right now.

"Fuck off, Kate."

She closes her eyes, guilt finding her. "Jesse, calm down. She had three glasses of wine. She wasn't drunk."

"Sure," I grunt, dropping to a chair and taking Ava's hand in mine, clenching it hard, willing her to open her eyes.

Wake up.

But she doesn't, and my heartbeats become duller by the minute.

43

Hours pass. I check every inch of her, more than once, looking for cuts, bruises, blemishes, marks, any injuries that may need looking at, despite knowing the nurses did that when we arrived. A doctor comes, assesses her, and leaves, asking the nurses to monitor her heartbeat and blood pressure, and they come in every half hour to check Ava's stats, reminding us each time there's only supposed to be one person in the room, so Kate and Sam tag team, dipping in and out when they can, bringing coffees, asking if I need anything, telling me they've checked in with John and Drew. Kate mentions Ava's parents. Fuck, no, I am not calling them, not yet. What will they think of me?

I glance down at my Rolex. Three thirty. Kate's snuck back in. My arse is dead, my heart slowing more with every minute that ticks by, and the pressure inside is becoming unbearable. It needs to release or I'm going to implode. I look at Kate. "Why were you testing me?"

"What?"

"When you invited Ava out tonight, you were testing me." I saw it in her eyes when she asked, her attention fully on me, watching for my reaction.

"You can't control her."

"I don't want to control her. I want to keep her safe."

Kate leans forward on her chair, her attention acute and all on me. "What from, Jesse?" she asks. "What the hell are you so scared of losing her to?"

I shy away from her question. "I know I'm a little over the top sometimes," I say quietly.

"Passionate," Kate says, almost correcting me, surprising me too. I look at her, and she rolls her eyes, sitting back again. "She'll always fight you because your expectations are fucking ridiculous."

Nice. I thought she loved me. "There's nothing ridiculous about being worr—"

Ava murmurs, her hand moving, her face screwing up. "Ava?" I breathe, too much air leaving me, my relief immeasurable. "Ava baby, open your eyes." I take in her pasty complexion, her usually olive skin gray, her lips dry. Dead. It's taking too much energy to be patient and calm. "Will someone tell me what the fuck is going on," I yell.

Her eyes open.

"Ava, baby?" I get close, smelling her, watching her, feeling her.

"Hi," she says, one eye open a little, her face cut with pain.

"Oh, thank fucking God." I kiss her forehead, her cheek, and she grumbles, squirming away as Sam enters, obviously hearing us.

"Ava, chick, are you okay?"

Is he fucking blind? "Does she fucking look all right?" I ask, my voice strained, trying to keep the volume down and failing miserably. "For fuck's sake."

"Calm down," Kate hisses.

"Where am I?" Ava scans the room, confused.

"You're in hospital, baby." I can't keep my hands off her. It's as if my subconscious is telling me not to let her out of my hold. Don't lose her again.

She tries to sit up. Oh, no. "I need the toilet." She slaps my hands away, irritated, and sits up. I can tell she regrets it when she clenches her eyes closed, hiding her face in her hands. Why the hell does she fight me at every turn?

"I'll take her." Kate gets up. "Ava, come on."

"No fucking way," I scoff, looking around the room for a bedpan. She's not leaving this bed until the doctor tells me why the hell she's in it in the first place.

Of course, Ava protests, insisting she's fine, and tries to get out of the bed. God help me.

"I don't think so, lady." I collect her, grumbling my disapproval, with Ava and the lack of adjoining bathrooms, carrying her out of the room. She doesn't fight me this time, without the energy, and that's fucking worrying in itself. I stand outside the room looking for a sign to the nearest toilet, but instead I find a nurse who sings her delight to see Ava in my arms.

"She's come round."

I see a sign at the end of the corridor pointing to the toilet. "I'm taking her to the bathroom." I get moving, the nurse on my heels.

"Sir, please, we need a urine sample."

I stop and hold out a hand from under Ava's bent legs, taking the thick cardboard container.

I place Ava down as soon as I get her inside, holding her with one hand as I lock the door with the other. Then I wriggle her dress up, draw her knickers down, and ease her down to the seat with the pee pot underneath her. Her eyes remain closed, her body deflating, as she pees for bloody England. That'll be all of the wine she apparently hasn't drunk. For fuck's sake.

"No stage fright then?"

"You've fucked me up the arse," she says, opening an eye. "I'm coping."

Sarcastic Ava. Because now is the time. "Ava, will you watch your fucking mouth?"

Her eyes close again and quiet falls, the pee still coming as I remain crouched in front of her. I can tell she's trying to piece together the night. It's worrying that she can't, or if she can, she's remaining quiet about it, and that unsettles me more. "I'm done," she breathes. "Did I pee on you?"

"No." I help her up a little and negotiate the cup from beneath her, placing it on the back of the toilet and squirting some anti-bac onto my hands and rubbing it into hers. I stand her up and pull her dress into place, carrying her back to the room via the nurses' station so I can tell them where to find the pee.

"Ava, what happened?" Kate asks as I lay her back down on the bed.

"I don't know."

I laugh, not in amusement. "*I* do."

"I *wasn't* drunk," she grates.

"You pass out from being sober often, do you?" I ask, my voice raising unstoppably. Jesus Christ. I can't release this tension inside me, even though I know she's okay. Kind of. Because things between us will be even more strained now. Me more protective, more anxious, Ava fighting me harder as a result.

"Don't shout at her," Kate hisses, making me wilt slightly. Walk. Just walk in circles. Focus on breathing. "She had a few glasses of wine. She's got through two bottles before and not passed out." Yes, but emotions dictate levels of intoxication. I've had two bottles of vodka before and remained conscious. On a bad day, one bottle could knock me out. "Did you eat?" Kate asks, getting up and going to Ava.

"Yes."

Or . . . "Are you pregnant?" I blurt out, and Ava recoils, horrified. By the question or by the answer?

"No," she says, looking away from me. Her eyes dart. Uncertainty engulfs me.

"Are you sure?" I ask when she looks at me again. I can't read her. Is she looking at me accusingly, or is that guilt?

"Yes." She flinches, a result of her high-pitched squeak, I think. Or was it because of something else? Realization? Comprehension? Fuck, I don't know. Has she replaced all the pills I took? Has she been taking them if she has replaced them? Because now I'm thinking about it, I can't recall seeing her take any pills.

"I'm just asking," I say, feeling all eyes on me, all eyes except

Ava's, who suddenly can't bring herself to look at me. This is fucked up, and despite wanting to press, I don't.

"What do you remember?" Kate asks.

I pace as I watch Ava avoiding me, shaking her head, not sharing anything that might tell us why she collapsed. Sam tries to jog her memory. It doesn't work, Ava constantly and consistently tells us she can't remember anything. I don't like this. None of it.

"Why is everyone making such a bloody fuss?" She's getting frustrated. *She's* getting frustrated? I muscle my way past Sam, fuming, and take her hand. "Ava, it is four o'clock in the fucking morning." Fuck me, I feel like I could pop. "You've been out cold for nearly seven hours, so don't you *dare* tell me not to make a fucking fuss."

Her widening eyes is a sign of comprehension. Good. Maybe now she'll understand why I'm fit to burst.

The nurse enters again and gives all of us a tired look. "It's one visitor in the room. You need to leave."

I feel Kate look at me, assessing the pros and cons of leaving me to be the one visitor. Like she has a choice.

"We'll go and get something to eat." She and Sam leave together, and the nurse gets to work on taking Ava's blood pressure once again. I'm tempted to ask her to check mine, because I'm sure I'm in heart attack territory.

"Would you like a cup of tea?" she asks as she leaves. Ava accepts. I decline, sitting beside the bed and clenching Ava's hand, dropping my face. The room is silent. But so loud, with so many questions screaming to be answered. The only sounds are my heartbeats and Ava's breathing, which changes. I peek up, finding her snoozing again, and then to the door when it knocks. A doctor appears, a different one than who's stopped by a few times in the night. He nods at me, and I'm about to start demanding answers when Ava stirs, and his attention goes to her.

"I was told you were awake."

Ava looks between the doctor and me, probably checking my current state. *Still stressed, baby. Still stressed.*

He introduces himself and asks how she feels, his full body and attention facing Ava's way, and I can't help but wonder if he's had a warning about me. I'm pretty sure there were a few times in the night when staff thought they might have been forced to call security.

"I'm fine. My head is banging," she says, her voice tired. "But other than that, I'm fine."

Fine? She is *not* fine, and neither am I.

The doctor smiles, friendly, checking Ava's eyes with a pen light. "I'm glad. What do you remember about last night?"

I watch her, my patience fraying even more when she shows intolerance. "Not a lot," she says, sounding bored. I squeeze her hand, trying to encourage more from her, but only get another harsh look thrown at me.

"You are?" the doctor asks. I feel him studying me.

"Husband."

Ava's gaze becomes questioning as the doctor looks at his notes. "It says *Miss* O'Shea."

"We get married next month." Ava doesn't protest. Whether that's through lack of desire or energy, I couldn't give a fuck.

The doctor accepts this and gets back to what's really important here—why Ava has been unconscious for over seven hours. "We ran some routine tests on your urine." He pulls a chair toward the bed and sits. "When was the date of your last period?"

"A week-ish ago."

He nods, while I observe how uncomfortable Ava is, my mind fogging, my head bending, my body becoming stiffer by the second as the doctor talks. I hear nothing. Then I hear . . . something.

"You're not pregnant."

"I'm not?" Ava blurts. She's surprised. She thought she was?

"Well," Doctor Manvi says, casting a glance my way. "I say you're not, but if it's only been a week since your period, it may be too early to tell. Do you use the contraceptive pill, Ava?"

Fucking hell.

Surprise has gone and nerves are here.

"Yes."

"Then I think we can safely say you're not pregnant."

Her eyes widen. She shifts. Refuses to look at me, which is probably a good thing right now. My hand around hers must be a sign of my tenseness, though. She's thinking about all of the pills she's missed, and I'm thinking about how guilty I must look. *Too early to tell.* "Ava, it's important that you try to remember anything of last night, who you spoke to, who you met."

"What?" I ask, sounding impatient. What the hell has that got to do with anything? "What are you trying to say?"

"We proceeded with a further test." He eyes me with caution. "Your symptoms prompted it."

"Symptoms?" Ava whispers. "What symptoms?"

I do not like the way he keeps looking at me. Like he's bracing himself for a blowback. "We found clear evidence of Rohypnol in your urine."

I feel like someone just stabbed me in the heart, twisted the knife, and pulled it beating from my chest. "What?" I stand abruptly, my chair flying back, my hands starting to shake. Rohypnol? "As in date rape?" I ask, now not bothering to even try and control the volume of my voice.

The doctor confirms I heard right, his regret obvious.

"Jesus fucking Christ," I look to the heavens for help. No help. They don't see me. I walk on shaky legs across the room and hold whatever I can find to keep me up, breathing heavily, head dropped.

"Ava," the doctor goes on, leaving me to try and shake this unshakable panic. Date rape. Someone wanted to take advantage of her? Violate her? Hurt her? Who? "I would advise you notify the police. You need to tell them everything you remember. Sir, can you confirm whether she was alone at any point?"

I think he's talking to me now, but I can't speak. All I can do is walk my way through the horrid moments when I arrived at the bar and watched her collapse. What would have happened if I hadn't been there? I shudder, losing my breath.

"We need to do an examination to determine whether you were raped."

My blood feels like ice. "She wasn't alone," I say quietly, seeing her in the bar, her eyes on me, rolling, her body crumpling. "I watched her hit the deck. I was there in a split second." Catching her. Saving her. From what?

Every fear, every worry, every minute of stress I've ever felt since meeting Ava has been validated, and I dare anyone to tell me I'm neurotic now. I fucking *dare* them. I look at Ava. She looks in a state of shock, whereas I'm so fucking angry, my body doesn't know what to do. My mouth doesn't know what to say.

"And you are sure of this?" the doctor asks.

"Yes." Only sure of what I saw when I got there. But she was conscious. Any sexual predator would wait until she's not. Until the drug had worked. The doctor pushes, insisting on the examination. "I've checked every square inch of her." I can hardly breathe. My heart hurts. "There isn't a mark on her." I go to the door and fling it open, calling Kate before I see her on a chair up the corridor. I meet her in the middle. "Before I arrived," I say, as Sam joins us. "Was Ava ever alone? Even for just a minute."

"What? Why are—"

"Just answer the question, Kate. Was she alone?"

Kate's face bunches, trying to remember, obviously sensing my urgency. "Um, I can't—" She curses. "I went for a smoke but she was with Tom."

"Tom?"

"Yes, Tom."

"I didn't see Tom in the bar."

"He left."

"When?"

She's getting frustrated by my quick-fire, endless questions. "I don't know, Jesse. What's going on?"

Sam moves in and puts an arm around Kate protectively, looking at me in question. *Keep it together, keep it together.*

I return to the bed. "Baby," I breathe, my temperature spiking. "Kate said she went for a cigarette, but Tom was with you. Can you remember that?'

She nods. "Yes." But then frowns. "But Tom went to the toilet while Kate was having a cigarette."

She was on her own. Fuck me, a sitting duck, just waiting to be . . . what? "Okay." *Breathe.* "Do you remember what happened during the time you were on your own?"

"Yes. Why?"

"Because, Ava, I don't want anyone poking you about unless they really need to, so please, think hard. Before I turned up, were you okay? Do you remember everything?"

"Yes," she answers, getting worked up. "I do."

"Ava, I would be happier if you would consent to the examination."

Jesus Christ, won't he listen? Does he think I would obstruct him if I knew she could have been—

My stomach turns.

"No," Ava says, resolute, more worked up, motioning down her body. "I know nothing happened. I have no bruises, no cuts."

"If you are one hundred percent sure, Ava," the doctor relents. "I can't force you."

"Damn right you can't fucking force her." Hasn't she been through enough without being poked and prodded at?

"Nothing happened." She clenches at my hand, holding me tightly, as if she's worried I might let them take her away from me. No. Never. "I remember everything until Jesse arrived." Her eyes find mine, full of tears and distress. It's hit her. How this *could* have been. "I remember everything," she says, whimpering, gripping me harder.

"I know." I swallow and nod, forcing a smile, here for her, because that's what she needs right now. Like I need a stiff fucking drink. "I believe you."

The doctor doesn't push anymore, accepting and ordering her discharge papers.

"How long will that take?" I ask.

"Sir." He laughs, and I could punch him for it. "We are in the aftermath of a Saturday night in central London. How long is a piece of string?"

I am not sitting around here waiting indefinitely. "I'm taking her home now." I collect Ava's shoes as he leaves the room, and I make it to the side of the bed just as she starts sobbing. If there was ever a way to increase the unrest within me, it's Ava's tears. I drop her shoes and hug her. "Baby, please don't cry. I'll get really crazy mad if you cry." She works up into a full-blown sobbing session, bursting into tears, clinging to me. "God help me," I mutter. "God, *fucking* help me."

"I'm so sorry."

"Ava, please shut up." I don't want her apologies. I want her to bloody listen to me. Hear me.

It takes some time, me just holding her, Ava clinging to me, but she eventually calms down and lets go of me, roughly wiping at her face, as if mad. With herself? "I'm fine. I want to go home." She kicks her legs over the side of the bed, like she thinks she's walking out of here. Give me strength. I pick her up and carry her out, asking Kate to grab her things as I pass.

"What's going on?" Sam asks, his worried eyes on Ava in my arms. Kate rushes into the room and reappears with Ava's purse and shoes.

"She was drugged." I swallow, trying to quench the anger from pouring out of me.

"Oh shit," Sam breathes.

"What?" Kate gasps. "Like date rape?"

"Yes." I turn and push through some double doors with my back, catching their eyes. Both shocked. Both concerned. Both knowing exactly what this means. "I'm taking her home." *And never letting her out of my sight again.*

It's daylight when we get outside. Fucking daylight. I get Ava in the car and shut the door. Kate hands me her bag and shoes. "Thanks."

"Please, Jesse, do not do anything stupid," she says, reaching for my arm and rubbing. She sees the pressure in me.

"What, like drink?" I ask, looking up at her. I hear Sam curse under his breath. "I don't want a drink," I lie. "I'll call you later." I round the back of the car and get in.

Thank God, she sleeps the entire way home so she doesn't see the turmoil I can't hide. The conflicting emotions inside me are taking their toll, and I'm forced to constantly wipe my eyes clear of fury and tears so I can see the road.

I don't want a drink.

I want a *lot* of drink.

Something to crush this awful ache in my chest.

But I can't have one.

Won't have one.

44

I PUT HER IN BED. I couldn't bring myself to get in with her. I was shaking too hard. Sweating too much. So I left her, placing her ring on the nightstand. I showered, half dressed, and put myself on the chair in the lounge, staring out at the London skyline for hours, the penthouse quiet. My mind loud. I've called Jay and asked for the footage from last night. I started to call Steve Cooke but decided against it. I don't want the police taking care of this. *I'll* take care of it.

My way. It won't be pleasant. It won't be clean.

Who the fuck did this?

Ava's phone rings, interrupting my mental warpath, and I look at it next to mine on the table in front of me.

Dan.

I slowly lean forward, watching it ring until it rings off. Her brother. I chew my lip, thinking, as it starts ringing again. I look up the stairs. Pick it up. Connect the call and rest slowly back.

"Hello."

There's a long pause before he speaks. "I suppose you're this new man we keep hearing about." He's hostile. I guess I can't blame him. But if he's expecting pleasantries from me, he's called at the wrong fucking time. Not that he knows. Not that he *can* know.

"You suppose right." I won't ask what they've heard. I know.

"Where's Ava?"

No introduction. No hello, how are you? Nothing. I already don't like him, and I sense the feeling is mutual. But for the sake of Ava . . . "She's sleeping. I'll get her to call you when she's awake. It's Dan, isn't it?"

"It is. And you're . . ."

I shift in my chair, uncomfortable. Don't tell me that with the information of my friendship with alcohol and my fist's friendship with Matt's face, they didn't get a name. "Jesse Ward."

"It's late for her to be sleeping."

"She was out with Kate last night."

Silence. A long, lingering silence. "Right. Since Kate is single these days." That hostility just grew.

"But Ava is not," I add, making that clear.

"So she was out with Kate but she stayed at your place? Doesn't make much sense since she's living with Kate."

"It makes sense because she lives *here*."

"What?"

"With me. In my apartment. She lives here."

A light laugh comes down the line with a puff of disbelieving air. "She's moved in?"

"Yes."

"How long have you been dating?"

"A while."

"Right." He doesn't sound impressed. Expected. "We made plans to do something today."

"I—" I don't have the capacity right now to stroke his ego. Answer his questions. And I know the last thing I should do is piss off her brother. *Too late, Ward.* But before I do any further damage . . . "It was nice chatting." *Lie.* "I'll have Ava call you when she wakes up." I hang up and clench Ava's phone in my fist, gritting my teeth. The need to go on a rampage until I find out who did this to her is fierce.

I get up, needing to move, going to the kitchen, shaking away the visions of a bottle. Clear liquid. The relief after just one swig. I swallow and get a glass, my hand shaking as I fill it with water and guzzle it. My eyes fall to the post Ava gave me. Distraction. I swipe it up and tear the envelope open, scanning the text.

No.

My breath comes in short, sharp bursts, my mouth watering as I read at the invitation to my sister's wedding. The RSVP details, the date to reply by, which has passed, the address to reply to. "Fuck." I move across the kitchen fast and toss it in the bin, scrubbing down my cheeks. Run. Work out. I need to do something because I'm spiraling, and it's beginning to panic me. But I can't leave her.

Returning to my chair in the lounge, I lower and pick up my phone, spinning it in my hand. I drop my head back, staring at the ceiling, making sure I don't close my eyes, scared of what I might see if I do.

Jake. Rosie. Carmichael.

Vodka.

I shift, uncomfortable. My mobile ringing is a godsend. I answer to John, smiling at the irony of his timing. He knows. He just knows. I look down my bare chest, chewing my lip, the finger of my free hand gripping the arm of the chair. Holding on. Or holding myself back.

"How is she?" he asks, his voice deep and grave.

"Sleeping."

"And you?"

Unhinged. Struggling to see reason. Violent. Fucking terrified. I laugh under my breath. It's all the answer he needs. "Jay's getting me the camera footage from the bar."

He hums, thoughtful. "I'll ask around too. Any ideas?"

"I don't know," I answer, blinking, my eyes dry and scratchy from being forced to remain open. "I swear to God, I'll claw their fucking eyes out."

"You need to keep it together. Do *not* turn to the drink, Jesse."

"I'm close, John," I admit, needing him to know my state of mind. "I really need it. Fuck, it's a mess." I suddenly feel Ava's presence and look up to see her sitting at the top of the stairs in her underwear, looking small and timid. To think she might have been preyed upon. Hurt. Taken away from me. "See what you can find out, John," I say quietly, watching her. "I won't be in for a few days."

"Call me if you need anything."

Talking down from the edge? "Yeah, thanks, big man."

John cuts the call and I remain in the chair, searching for the energy to stand and the words to say. How the fuck do I approach this without it blowing up in my face?

She looks at me, looks away, looks at me again, as if checking I'm still watching her. She's getting more fidgety. More worked up. I don't like the thick atmosphere. I need to fix it. Don't know if I can.

It takes both hands wedged into the arms of the chair to push me up, and I go to her. She follows me all the way to the top of the stairs. I can see it in her eyes. Rebelliousness being located. Fight rising. She knows I have every reason to be fucking mad, and now she's mad with herself for proving my worries are justified.

"If you are going to shout at me, I'll go now," she says, confident but not. She doesn't want to leave. But she's threatening it anyway. Pulling her ace card. But I keep my cool. Keep my head.

"I've shouted enough." I look her over again, from top to toe. "How do you feel?"

"Fine," she bites back, astounding me. She's waiting for my fury? For me to yell and demand compliance? I haven't the energy. She's here. She's okay.

". . . Ish?"

"No. Fine."

In body, maybe. In spirit? She's channeling her anger in the wrong direction. I lower, getting closer to her, crowding her. My hands rest on the step on either side of her. She peeks up at me.

"I'm crazy mad, Ava." I don't sound it. But, God, I feel it.

"I wasn't drunk."

"I told you not to drink at all," I counter. "I knew I shouldn't have let you go out."

Nostrils flaring, she glares at me with angry eyes. "I'm curious as to why you think you can dictate what I do. I'm a grown woman. Do you expect me to live a life with you where my every move is controlled?"

Controlled? Her mind always defaults to that one, undesirable word. "You are mine. It's my job to keep you safe." And I'm not being allowed to do my job.

"You said you were close. Close to what?"

"Nothing."

"Nothing?" She practically laughs over the word. "You want a drink, don't you? That's what you need to deal with this *fucking mess.*"

She's right, of course. But instead of admitting it, I tell her to mind her fucking language. "We would not be in this situation if you'd fucking listened to me," I grate.

"I'm sorry! I'm sorry for not listening." She stands abruptly, nearly knocking me back down the steps. And now she's going to do what Ava does best. Walk away. Hide. "I'm sorry if you feel the need to drown in vodka because of me," she hisses. I flinch, not only at the words but at the venom in them. "I'm obviously bad for your health. I'll put you out of your misery."

I stare at her naked back as she walks away, hurt mixing with the anger. She'd leave. She thinks I might have a drink, and she'd leave anyway? "Crazy mad, Ava," I breathe, getting up and going after her. She looks back, sees me coming at her, and faces me, her eyes dropping down my chest as I approach. And as if she's realized she's lost her focus, she stands taller. Challenging.

This is going to blow up.

"Kiss me," I say in desperation, hoping the flames of our passion win over the heat of our anger.

"No," she yells, disgusted. So she'd rather argue? Tear each other apart?

"Three." I have no idea what I'm doing. I don't know why the fuck I'm giving her the countdown now. It's so fucking inappropriate. Maybe because I desperately need something close to normal back, and the countdown is normal for us.

"Are you mad?"

"Crazy fucking mad, Ava," I confirm. "Two."

Her eyes go round, her head shaking.

"One." Her mouth opens to protest, her body engages to run. "Zero." I catch her before she gets two paces away, walking her to the bed and trapping her beneath my body. The moment my naked chest meets her lace-covered boobs, my heart calms. My world stabilizes. I can see the peace coming into her dark eyes as I stare at her, drawing soft lines around her stomach. But there's still that tenacity lingering. "I'm putting your resistance down to the drugs. I'm giving you another three seconds to make the right decision. Three." I put my mouth close to hers, begging her to embrace one of our strengths. Give herself to the chemistry. Her nipples are hardening. Her body heating up. All good signs.

But she fights it, her shimmering eyes narrowed.

"Two."

She licks her lips, her body talking, and mine is listening.

I swallow, watching, feeling, hearing, smelling her desire. A second later, she rises and presses her mouth onto mine, and everything is right again, if only for a few moments. I'll take it. Any scrap of calm, I'll take it. Her hands clench at my shoulders, then move to my nape, feeling.

"Please don't have a drink," she whispers.

I hate myself for inadvertently revealing my weakness. "I'm not going to have a drink, Ava." Not now. Half hour ago, though? I release her lips and sit up, helping her onto my lap. I spend a few needed moments feeling her silky, dark hair, looking into her expressive brown eyes, stroking her smooth olive skin that, right now, is too pale. "Last night in the hospital when you wouldn't come round," I say, my throat thick. "I felt my heart getting slower by the minute. You will never know how much I love you. If you were ever taken away from me, I wouldn't survive it, Ava." It's the truth. I'm barely surviving now, when we're at odds and there are so many question marks hanging over us. "I want to rip my own head off for giving you room to defy me."

"I'm okay," she says, her voice small.

"But what if you weren't?" I ask. "What if I didn't come when I did?" Jesus Christ, God knows what could have happened. "I just came to the bar to check you were okay, and then I was going to leave. Can you imagine how it felt to see you collapse like that?" It's all I can see. Her body failing her. Me catching her.

"It was a freak incident," she protests, but I hear the doubt in her tone. "Someone playing stupid games. I was in the wrong place at the wrong time, that's all. You'll put yourself in a stress-induced coma at this rate." She squeezes my hands, looking at me sorrowfully. *Wrong place, wrong time.* "Then what will I do?"

Then you'll be free of my shady past. Free from my demons that are threatening to pollute you. I drop my eyes, shame engulfing me. I've done everything I can to ensure she can't leave me. I realize nothing will be one hundred percent effective. But each and every thing I've done is something to help me prove I'm worth it. It will show me I'm still worthy of such treasures. But, and I keep going back to it, her face when the doctor asked her if she could be pregnant. Horror, disgust. It was rife. She doesn't want kids. What I haven't yet established is if that is now, never, or that she simply doesn't want them with me.

"You looked relieved when the doctor said you weren't pregnant."

She stares at me in stunned silence for a few telling moments before she looks away. "I missed a pill," she says quietly, and I'm thrown by it. She thinks she needs to prepare me for this possibility. *Jesus, this is so fucked up.* "I missed a few," she adds. "I lost them again."

"You've not replaced them?"

"I forgot."

"Okay," I say slowly, probably wrongly surprised. "So when did you last take your pill?"

"Only a few days ago."

Her hand moves in mine. She's lying. My heart starts to beat faster. How long has it been? "So you'll replace them?" If it's been a *few days,* although I expect it's been longer, she really could be pregnant. I subtly breathe in, willing my racing heart to calm down.

"Tomorrow."

And will she remember to take them? *If you don't steal them, yes.* There's nothing like a pregnancy scare to get your contraception on track. I don't know what the fuck I'm thinking. Am I actually trying to justify my behavior? Pass the blame? I look up at her, right into her eyes, and I see it.

Questions.

Sudden comprehension.

"Jesse?" she says, her teeth sinking into her lip.

"What?" *Fuck, she's onto me.*

Her eyes narrow as she regards me, definitely searching for guilt. "Nothing," she eventually says, relaxing. But something tells me I'm not off the hook. Or maybe she thinks it's so outlandish, she's dismissed her suspicion.

"Your brother rang," I say quickly, and it has the desired effect. She looks very worried all of a sudden.

"Dan?" she asks. "You spoke to him?"

"Well, I couldn't leave it ringing constantly. He would have been worried." I scowl. "And why is there a lock on your phone?"

"It didn't stop you answering, though, did it?" she retorts, amused but not. "What did you say to my brother?"

"I didn't tell him what had happened. I don't want your family thinking that I can't look after you. He said you were supposed to be seeing him."

Her expression is all kinds of worried, suspicious, and impatient. "You told him I'm living with you, didn't you?"

"Yes."

If her popping eyes are a measure, she obviously wasn't expecting honesty. "Jesse," she moans, collapsing into my body. "What have you done?"

I've started moving this relationship along at a reasonable rate, and it's time to meet the parents. "Hey, look at me." I force her face up. "Don't you think he would've been worried if I had left your phone to ring off continuously?"

She has no answer to that. She knows I'm right. She still sighs, though, as if I'm the exasperating one. I can't be bothered to argue anymore. I'm so fucking exhausted. But still, the toxic energy inside lingers, and I really need to be rid of it. My legs are itching to move. My heart itching to beat fast and hard. "I'm going for a run," I say, feeling her stiffen in my arms. She thinks I want to drag her along. As if. Her body needs some recovery time and, actually, I need some alone time. *Is she pregnant?* "You take a shower. I'll get something to eat while I'm out."

"Can't you stay?"

"No." I stand her up and take her into the bathroom. "In the shower." I get out of there feeling forlorn and deflated, wondering why today I'm taking running over being close to Ava.

I hate the answer.

Guilt.

I run like a crazy man. I still feel like one. She's definitely suspicious, and for the first time, I consider what she might do if she finds out she's not mislaid her pills on those few occasions, but they were instead taken. I also never considered she'd forget to replace them. I also never considered that I'd reach a point of complete regret and remorse. I felt guilty. I knew what I was doing, but I still felt guilty. It's being superseded by regret now. All I've achieved is giving her one more reason to leave me. I have to stop this madness.

My pace slows when I see a Starbucks up ahead, until I'm jogging, sweating, every muscle screaming. Alive. I stop just shy of the door and look back down the street to the store I passed, and my steps reverse. I walk in and up and down the aisles until I find what I'm looking for. I take all of them off the shelf and juggle the boxes to the checkout. The young girl behind the counter raises her brows at the piles of pregnancy tests before her.

"Would you like a bag?"

"I'd say so, wouldn't you?"

On a small, unimpressed scowl, she rings through my purchases, I pay, bag them up, and get my arse into Starbucks, ordering some drinks and some breakfast for Ava. Me? Not hungry. As I'm leaving, my phone rings. I have to stop and place everything down to take the call from Jay. "Hi."

"I have something you should see."

45

I PUT the full bag of pregnancy tests on the shelf in the laundry room and go straight to the fridge, pulling out the peanut butter and diving in. My body's strung, my foot's tapping wildly on the floor, and my mind's racing. The run was fucking pointless.

Ava walks in, and I force myself to smile. I can tell she's not buying it. I hold up her drink and something to eat, and she accepts, lowering to a seat beside me. Too close. She must be able to feel the tension on my skin. I look down at her jeans and tee, which look three sizes too big, searching for something normal to say. Anything. *Speak!* "I hope you've got lace on under all of that baggy shit." Normal for *us*.

"I have," she replies, showing me. Usually, such a move would have me off this stool and throwing her over my shoulder. Now, I can only nod. "I thought you were getting dinner?" She inspects her choices and settles on a croissant.

"Technically, as you have been asleep all day, it's breakfast time." I offer her some peanut butter when I see her nose wrinkle. "What do you want to do this evening?"

"I get to pick?"

"I told you, I have to let you have your way some of the time. I'm all for give and take." She laughs as I brush some pasty away from her lip. "Something funny?"

"No, nothing," she says, coughing, forcing me to pat her on the back. Is she choking? My pats become firmer, until she swallows, smiling her thanks. "It went down the wrong way."

I exhale, relieved, wondering if the world could stop throwing me challenges, and look at the phone on the wall when it rings. My heart turns in my chest as I abandon Ava and my peanut butter to answer. "Mr. Ward, there's a . . . man here to see you." I can see Clive in my mind eyeing Jay with suspicion. I can't blame him. He looks like he could play the role of any skinhead gangster in any Guy Richie movie.

"Clive, yes, see him up." I stare at the wall for a few moments, feeling Ava's inquisitive stare on my back. "Jay," I say in answer to her silent question.

"Jay?" she questions. "Who's Jay?"

Hopefully the man with some answers. "The doorman." I collect my jar and put it back in the fridge, feeling the atmosphere thicken. "He's got the CCTV footage from the bar." I leave the kitchen and walk on slightly wobbly legs to the door, taking a breath before I pull it open, just as Jay steps off the elevator. He looks as impressed as always as he holds up some kind of disc. What's on it that warrants a visit? What do I need to see? "Come in," I say, opening the way for him.

The moment we enter the kitchen, Ava looks at Jay, drops down from her stool, and walks out, not even saying hello to him.

"Where are you going?" I ask as she passes us, frowning at her back.

"Toilet." She disappears, and I look at Jay. He shrugs, but something tells me he's a man in the know. I look around the corner and up the stairs, just catching sight of her before she goes into the bedroom. She looked in a rush. What the fuck is going on?

"Use the TV in the lounge," I tell him. "I'll be back in a minute." I leave Jay and go after Ava. The bedroom is empty. She's in the bathroom. Door closed. I try the handle. Locked. "Ava?"

"Yes?"

I frown at the wood. She sounded . . . worried. "What's up, baby?" I keep my voice gentle. "You okay?"

"Yes, fine. I'll be down in a minute."

"Why is the door locked?"

A beat, just a beat, but quite a telling beat. "I didn't realize I'd locked it. I'm having a wee."

I step back, suspicious. "Okay," I say quietly. When has she ever locked the bathroom when she's used it? We were past shyness on the first . . . *date*. "Don't be long."

"I won't," she sings, as I back up, my mind racing, my eyes on the wood. I don't like this, not at all.

When I make it downstairs, Jay's in front of the TV, a remote control in his hand. "What am I watching for?" I ask, joining him, looking back up the stairs. Is she throwing up? Morning sickness?

"Just watch," Jay says, pulling my attention round.

I squint, focused on the TV as Jay speeds up the footage, seeing the comings and goings of a London bar on a Saturday night. Then I see her. It's grainy, blurry, but I'd know my girl anywhere. "Slow it," I say, and he does. "That's it, leave it playing."

I study the screen, Ava and her friends huddled around a table, each of them coming and going, but Ava remains on her stool for the duration. Then, suddenly, all of them are gone and she's alone. Alone until a man approaches. I exhale, leaning in, squinting harder to see the blurry footage better. "Pause it." The screen stills, and I wander closer, eyes on the man by Ava's table. *Turner*. She never mentioned him. Why? "Keep it going." My eyes travel around the TV, then down to the bar floor when Ava starts picking things up. "I need another angle."

"There's another camera."

"Get me it," I order shortly, looking at him. "Did you see her talking to him?" The burn in my gut is intense.

Jay shakes his head, frustrated. "Ward, I do what I can," he says, like cut him some fucking slack. "But if I'm called away to deal with some drunken twat or a few catfighting girls, I can't watch her."

"I don't need someone watching me." Ava's voice pierces the thick air, and I turn to find her sitting at the top of the stairs, looking wary and nervous. Her firm tone isn't fooling me. Why the hell didn't she mention Turner? To protect him?

"Did you leave your drink unattended at any point?" Jay speaks up, filling the horrible silence. He thinks Matt is responsible too. Is this some kind of sick retaliation after I punched him? I'll fucking kill him.

"No."

"When did you start feeling strange?" I ask, my body tightening everywhere, engaging, getting ready to let loose, trying to hide my balled fists from Ava.

"I had a little stagger at the bar," she says, her eyes flicking constantly from me to Jay. She shakes her head. "But I put it down to my heels."

"Did you speak to anyone at the bar?"

She stares at my heaving form, silent. Guilty. How much exactly has she withheld from me? What hasn't she shared?

"Answer the question, Ava."

"There was a guy at the bar who offered to buy me a drink." She rushes over her words. "I refused."

So now we have two potential culprits? Any more?

"It was fine," she says with absolutely no conviction. "I left the bar and returned to Kate."

It's fine. It's fine. Nothing about *any* of this is *fine*. "Stop saying it's fine," I snap, louder than I mean to, but the strength required to remain *fine* is more than I have. She looks at me, and I see it on every inch of her. She knows that this is not good. She knows this will send me over the edge. She knows every reason why I'm so fucking protective is happening on the screen behind me. She can't even look at me, her eyes instead on the TV. Then I catch a slight recoil before she can rein it in. What was that?

I face the screen, the turmoil within flaring, the pressure in my head building. And then I see what she's seen. *The fuck?* A man, suited, tall, light-haired, is at the bar. *Van Der Haus.* My stomach turns as I watch him come on and off the screen, as Ava orders drinks a few meters up the busy bar, and another man moves in, talking to her. She's on the floor again, picking something up before she staggers away. *What was Van Der Haus doing when he was off the screen?* What was he doing before this footage captured him?

I can hardly see now through my rage, so I turn away from the screen—I've seen enough—and look at Ava. My beautiful, young, *careless*, fiancée. The odds have always been against me but, truly, I never ever considered that someone would act so callously to exact their revenge. Never. I protect her from my past, from alcohol, from accidents, the leery eyes of other men. But this?

"Have you seen enough?" Jay asks, uncomfortable.

"Yes."

I hear the front door close a few moments later, and the silence screams as I lock every muscle down, coiled, tense, and fuming. She's quiet. Guilty. "You didn't mention Matt before." My throat hurts, the muscles there tense too.

"I didn't want to upset you." She can't even look at me.

"Upset me?" This isn't me being upset. This is me being on the edge of something really fucking dangerous. I am so far out of control, I'm scared. More scared than I ever have been, because everything I dreaded is happening. All because of me and my fuck-ups, she could have been hurt. Or worse.

"Okay," Ava retorts, braving facing me. I hate to think what must be staring back at her. I can hardly see through the red mist. "I didn't want to piss you off. It was a chance meeting."

A chance meeting that she didn't think was important after she was fucking drugged? And not only that, clearly more was said than a polite hello. What shit was he spilling about me this time? "But you had a few minutes' conversation. What did you talk about?"

"He apologized."

"And that took a few minutes?" Why the fuck am I so focused on Matt? A regrettable ex is the least of my worries. A scorned husband of an ex-fuck is where my focus should be. "I told you not to see him again."

She looks insulted. Rightly so, I realize there's nothing in it for her, but if I don't focus on Matt, I'll have to focus on Van Der Haus, and that shit's gonna be messy. "Jesse, I didn't plan on it. I told you, it was only by chance. I wanted to know how he knows about you."

Knows about me? "Do you care?"

"No, I don't."

Calm. Please, give me calm. "Then leave it." I need to get the fuck away from her before she sees the need in my eyes. Not need for her. Not even need for vengeance.

I need a fucking drink.

I need to escape this new nightmare. *Shower.* Cold water on me. Anything to shock me out of this spiral. "I'm going for a shower." I climb the stairs, eyes on my feet, and pass her static, sitting form.

I flip on the spray, wrestle my way out of my running clothes and step into the cold rain, looking up at the ceiling, willing the madness to retreat.

Drink. Drink. Drink.

Numb.

"Will you please just rant at me and have it over with?" Ava says from past the glass.

I can't rant. Dare not. Every scrap of anger inside me is being reserved. I let the freezing water keep my mind clear before getting out and drying. She's sitting by the sink. But I can't look at her, so I leave the bathroom and go to our dressing room, pulling on some jeans and a T-shirt absentmindedly.

"Jesse?"

I pass her standing in the middle of the bedroom, her fingers twiddling, and go to brush my teeth. I can taste vodka now. Crave it. I look past me in the mirror and see her looking lost and uncertain. The emotions inside me are winning. I'm about to blurt out my whole horrid history, give her all of my sins, tell her why Van Der Haus is so hung up on me and Ava. It'll be the end if I do that. She isn't prepared or equipped to take it.

Drink.

She begs me to talk.

I can't.

I wash my face, needing another shock of cold on my skin. A few deep breaths. A small shake of my head to try and keep the impending flashback at bay. My hands clench. I breathe in deeply.

She produces a bottle of vodka from her bag. Unscrews the cap. Takes a glug. My face remains impassive, but when she holds it out, I find some strength to take it and sit up. And I down half, forcing myself not to gag. The burn in my throat is welcome. It's something else to focus on. Something other than my unrelenting pain. I don't hand the bottle back. I work my way through it under Lauren's watchful eyes until it's empty, before slumping back to my mattress and closing my eyes.

I lose my breath for a moment. *Leave*. Get out of here. As I pass Ava, she comes after me, panicking. I'm panicking too. "Where are you going?"

I stop dead in my tracks, swallowing, my skin clammy. I need to reassure her. Give her some comfort. I look back. Hate the distress on her face. "I need to sort some things out at The Manor."

"I thought we were doing something this evening," she says, the edge of desperation in her words sharp.

"Something came up."

"You're mad with me," she blurts.

My voice is suddenly gone, so I can only shake my head. I know it's not convincing. I'm mad with her, yes. I'm mad with the world, with everything, but I'm mostly mad with myself, and the need to be punished is unshakeable.

And that need becomes even worse as I take the stairs fast, hearing her crying.

I look back when I get to the door, my hand on the handle, my heart in my throat.

I did that to her.

And I must pay for it.

Problem is, if I have a drink, it'll be Ava paying for it.

46

I REMEMBER nothing of the journey to The Manor. I'm too lost in memories and regret. I walk into the busy foyer and see John first. I shy away from his questioning face, passing him and going to the bar. I get three offers from various female members before I make it there.

"Mr. Ward?" Mario asks, as he polishes a glass, my eyes fixed on the top shelf.

John's massive hand appears on the bar next to mine, his mobile placed down more calmly than I know he's feeling. I leave and go to my office. I slam the door and walk to the drinks cabinet. Pick up a bottle. Roar at it and slam it down.

Never again.

I walk circles, heave, hit anything that I pass, my heart beating a mile a minute. I sit down. Get up. Pick up the vodka. Stare at it. Set it down. Walk some more.

For over an hour, I go round in circles. Walk. Sit. Stand.

And repeat.

My eyes are constantly being pulled toward the relief. I fight it. With everything I have, I fight it.

Until I can fight it no more.

I pick up the bottle and stare at the clear poison inside. *Escape.* I start to unscrew the bottle, sniffing, blinking back the sting in my eyes.

Drink.

Don't drink.

Drink.

Don't drink.

I languidly look over my shoulder when the door opens, finding Sarah dressed to the nines in leather, her whip limp, her face maddeningly interested.

Punishment.

Punishment.

Punishment.

Pay for your wrongs and hope that somehow I'm offered a little mercy, some strength to get through this. I set the bottle down, swallow, and pull my T-shirt up over my head, dropping to my knees. I hear her inhale. Sense the thrill.

Fucking punish me!

Hit me until I can't take any more.

I look at her. She's caught in a trance, but I see the exhilaration she's trying to hide. I know she won't like seeing me like this. But I also know that her sick mind has wanted to do this to me since the day I killed our daughters. This could be the closure Sarah needs. I can't consider that I'm succumbing to her. I'm actually succumbing to the booze.

"No," John gasps, bursting into my office. He finds me on the floor. "Get up, motherfucker," he seethes, coming to me and manhandling me to my feet. "Put your fucking shirt on and go back to your girl."

I flip, losing all reason, finding strength in my chaos, anger fueling me. I wrestle him off me, shoving his big body away. "Get the fuck out," I order.

"No."

"Get out!" I bellow.

John finds Sarah, yanking off his glasses and pointing them at her. "If you truly love him, you won't do this."

She remains silent as John looks between us, and I look at Sarah, my eyes demanding her to whip me until I bleed. She might love me, but she definitely needs this more.

"You're both as fucked up as each other," John growls. "I'm fucking done with you." He leaves, slamming the door with force behind him, and I drop to my knees, drop my head, and close my eyes. I hear her breathing become heavier. I hear her walk around the back of me. I smell her desire.

I close my eyes and watch as every person I've ever loved parades through my memory.

"Happy birthday for tomorrow," Sarah purrs.

Crack.

I grunt, my spine snapping violently. "Again," I order, rolling my shoulder blades, straightening, the biting sting very fucking real.

Crack.

"Again," I say.

Crack.

"Again."

Crack.

"Again!" I roar.

And then—

Numb.

I'm numb, the pain of my memories, my sins, superseding the pain caused by the whip. There's no stinging or stabbing anymore as the leather connects with my back. The only pain I feel is in my heart. It's the crippling agony of failure—failure to protect the only thing left in my life that means something to me. Drink would've numbed this torture. But it also would have caused more pain . . . more failure. More reasons to drive the only beautiful thing in my life away.

But, I realize now, I don't need alcohol to drive her away.

Even stone-cold sober I'm poisonous.

A failure.

I could smell the ignorance and escape that bottle of vodka would provide, but I could also smell the remorse that would follow.

Punish myself.

That's my only option. And here on my knees, I can pray too. And yet I know this won't make me miraculously worthy of her love.

Crack.

Because I'm wired to always fuck up everything good that comes into my life.

Crack.

Maybe this is my penance—God giving me a brief perception of how my life could be, knowing I'll screw it up.

Crack.

Leaving me hollower and more lost than before.

Crack.

Or, maybe one day I might get something in my life right. I won't ruin the people I love.

Maybe.

Who knows.

Crack.

My back bows sharply, my head flying back as the leather meets my flesh, and there's pain again. An inferno blazing across the flesh of my back. *Fucking hell.* Distant yells, cries, sobs reach my ears, and I search in my darkness for the source. Is it Jake yelling at me? Rosie crying?

No . . .

A scream, loud and frightened. A yell, angry and stressed.

Ava.

John.

My head whips up, finding them in a physical struggle. She's screaming, thumping, and hitting him. He's cursing, yelling, trying to catch her flailing arms.

What is she doing here? What's happening?

Where the fuck am I?

"Ava?"

She stills at the low husk of my voice, turning toward me. The distress and pain etched all over her beautiful face cripples me, brings my reality crashing back. I'm on my knees, The Manor, Sarah, the whip, my sins. And then Ava releases a pained sob, and it kicks some life into me. My legs are like jelly as I try to stand, reaching for thin air for support, my mind still partly fogged. I shake my head harshly, seeing beads of sweat fly off me.

"Ava?" I finally convince my legs to play ball and stand. Staggering, swaying, disorientated. Fuck, I feel more pissed than any amount of vodka could achieve.

Ava can't be here. She can't. I shake my head again, closing my eyes, hoping that when I open them, we're not here. We're in bed. Cuddled up. Loving. I open my eyes, and my heart splits. She's on her knees, sobbing, looking at me with nothing but pure agony gushing from her dark eyes.

"Jesus, no." I go to her but get pulled back, and the feeling is like one of the awful dreams I have, when I am reaching for her, seeing her, but I can't get to her. "Get the fuck off me!" I shove Sarah away. "Ava, baby." I go to her, joining her on the floor, scanning every broken piece of her. "What are you doing here?" I pull her face to mine and recoil when she looks at me. Pain. It's intensifying the closer I get, the more I look.

She pushes me away, doesn't want me to touch her.

"Ava, please."

She gets up and barges past John, and I'm quickly following. I can't feel my legs, but they're moving fast. She disappears into the ladies' bathroom, and I steam in after her, John in tow.

The sound that greets me punches a hole in my gut.

Retches.

She's being sick.

I've made her physically sick. That's how disgusted she is by me.

"Ava!" I yell, banging on the door. I should be gently coaxing her from the cubicle, but my fear is growing by the second. "Ava! Open the door. Please." I let my head meet the wood, my palms and chest pressed into it, like it makes me that little bit closer to her. "Ava, please. Open the door."

Nothing.

"Who let her in?" I don't mean to punch the door in anger. "Fuck! Who the fucking hell let her in?"

"I didn't let her in," John says, sounding mystified. "I would never have let her in." His big palm meets my shoulder, rubbing soothing circles into a piece of flesh that isn't welted. I don't need to look at his face to know he's being honest.

We both look toward the door when Kate flies in, her pretty face looking back and forth between us. "What's going on?" she asks. Her eyes widen. "Fuck, Jesse, what the hell happened to your back?"

"Nothing," I snap. My fucking back is the least of my worries right now. *Fuck.*

"Don't fucking talk to me like that. Where's Ava? What the hell is going on? Ava?"

"She's in there. She won't come out. Please, Kate, get her out." I bang the door again for no purpose at all. She's not coming out while I'm here. I know that.

"Hey," Kate snaps, forcing me back from the door, looking up and down my pathetic form. "Tell me why she's locked in there and why you're out here bleeding all over the place?"

I look away, so fucking ashamed. "Ava walked in on something she shouldn't have seen." I'm vague. "She's freaked out. I need to see her."

"If you've fucked her over, Jesse," she seethes. "Ava?"

"It's not like that." My hands find my hair and yank. What the fuck have I done?

"Well, what is it like then? She's in there throwing up. Ava?" Kate starts a gentler tapping of the door. "Ava, come on. Open the door."

"Ava!" I yell.

"Jesse, just go."

I snort my repulsion. "No." So she can walk out of my manor and never return?

Kate shoves me back, resorting to brute force, hissing words at me I'm struggling to hear, and John starts pulling at my arm, his rumble of my name softer than usual, but there's an edge of *don't fuck with me* in his tone. I look at the door again. It's not opening while I'm in here.

"Let's get you sorted out, you stupid motherfucker."

Reluctantly, I let John lead me from Ava, hoping my absence will encourage her out. I give Kate a pleading look, anything to make her see my turmoil. She'll never understand, but worst of all, I know Ava won't either.

John guides my useless body back to my office, and I can feel the stares of the members, the men probably smug to see me in such a fucking state over a woman, probably thinking I've got what's been coming to me for many years. They're all right. The women are probably itching to comfort me, to take my mind off things. It'll never work. If I lose this woman, there's only one thing that'll take away the pain. And it isn't Sarah's whip.

John lets loose once my office door is closed, and I stand before his hulking frame and accept the rant I deserve. "For fuck's sake." His loud boom knocks me back a step. "Of all the fucked-up sorry shit you do, this takes the fucking cake!" He prods me in my shoulder, only lightly, but it's enough to make me stagger. "I fucking told you! Stay away from the fucking drink. That didn't mean exchange it for the motherfucking whip!" I glance up and watch as he removes his glasses. "You are your own worst enemy, Jesse."

"I know." I have no defense, nothing that'll make this acceptable. I'm going to try, though.

Sam's head pops around the door, disturbing us, and once he's taken both of us in, he smiles a nervous smile, apologizes for the interruption, then quietly leaves again.

John's attention is fired straight back at the sorry state of a man before him.

Me.

"I told you to put your shirt on. I told you to go back to your girl and make things right, not wallow in your own self-fucking-pity and join Sarah in her fucked-up sadistic shit. Be a fucking man, you stupid motherfucker."

"I—" Sam's random visit to my office quickly registers in my screwed-up brain. He didn't ask how I am. What's happened. Why the fuck my back's bleeding. "Fuck," I breathe, barging past John and thundering down the corridor. I burst through the doors of the ladies' and halt when I find her. She locks eyes with me, calm, like she fully expected my arrival.

There's a silent understanding that passes between us as we watch each other, Kate remaining quiet to the side. Hoping I'm not reading it wrong, I go to Ava and pick her up, carrying her back to my office. Having her in my arms, holding on to me, is beyond what I could ever describe, and in this moment, I realize that every word that comes now has got to count.

I settle on the sofa, keeping her close, trying hard not to flinch at the contact of leather on my raw flesh. The numbness is fading, being replaced with a sting to accompany my tormented heart. My face instinctively finds the soft skin of her neck, the smell of her hair easing me a little. Her tears, however, don't. "Please don't cry. It's killing me."

"Why?" Her soft question catches me off guard. It's a question I should have expected and it's one that now needs answering.

"I promised you I wouldn't have a drink."

"You wanted a drink?"

"I wanted to block it out." Translated: yes.

"Look at me," she says harshly, but I can't face her. I can't confront the hurt I've caused. "Damn it, Jesse, look at me." She's moving, attempting to drag me from my hiding place. My hiss of discomfort stops her. "Three." Her calm voice makes me go rigid. That and the one word that will lead to the answers much quicker than I'd like. I need to piece this together, make the most of the words I'm about to say. She's using my own manipulation against me. "Two."

"What happens on zero?"

"I leave."

I raise my head fast. "Please don't."

Her face drops, all resentment seeming to fall away at my words. I didn't intend to make her feel guilty.

She moves to sit astride me, her arms carefully enclosing me in hers. "Tell me what you were blocking out."

"Hurting you."

"I don't understand," she says, her face so expressive, so confused. "I would rather you had a drink."

"You wouldn't." My small, ironic laugh isn't stoppable. She really has no idea.

Ava sits back, determined to have my eyes. I could never deny her. So I face her. "I would rather face you with half a vodka distillery inside you than see what I just saw."

"Trust me, Ava, you wouldn't."

"Trust you? Jesse, I feel sick with betrayal." Suddenly, she's removing herself from my body, the loss of her touching me unbearable. I try to reclaim her but get shrugged off. "I'm not leaving," she snaps, making me retract my hand in shock as she starts a dogged march around my office. My unease doesn't improve when she lowers herself on the opposite sofa, making a point of keeping out of my reach. I'm slowly forming words in my head, words to explain or make her feel better, but they're not in order yet. I'm not sure where to begin.

She sighs and starts rubbing comforting circles into her temples. I want to do that. I want to do anything I can to make her feel better.

"Is there anything else I need to know?" she asks, watching closely for my reaction to her question.

I try to hide my unease. "Like what?"

The look of disgust on her face is warranted. "I don't know, you tell me." Her arms catapult to the ceiling. "Why would I prefer this to drunken Jesse?"

Gritting my teeth, I move forward, trying to close the space between us. My elbows hit my knees and I mimic Ava's attempt to soothe my brain ache by rubbing circles in my temples too. "Drink and sex go hand in hand for me." I say the first words that'll commence the unraveling of my secrets.

"What does that mean?"

Jesus Christ. How do I explain this? "Ava, I inherited The Manor when I was twenty-one. Can you imagine a young lad with this place and a whole lot of women ready and willing?"

"You mean the dabbling?" Her voice is quiet and cautious. She's starting to work this out.

"Yes, the dabbling, but it's all behind me." I move farther forward. "Now, it's all about you." I need her to understand this. It might make the rest easier for her to come to terms with.

"You drank and dabbled?"

"Yes, like I said, drink and sex go hand in hand. Please, come here."

My request is ignored. "So you didn't have a drink because you would have wanted to have sex?"

"I don't trust myself with alcohol, Ava."

"Because you think you will jump the nearest woman?"

Another ironic laugh falls unwittingly from my lips. "I don't think so. I couldn't do that to you." I should stab myself for my nerve and save her the trouble of dealing with this fucked-up arsehole any longer.

"You don't *think* so?"

"It's not a risk I'm willing to take. Ava." *Again.* "I drink too much, lose reason, and women throw themselves at me willingly. You've seen it."

"You didn't look very capable of anything last Friday," she shouts incredulously.

"Yeah, that's not my normal level of intemperance, Ava. I was on a mind-numbing mission."

"So, you usually maintain a steady level of drinking and then have lots of sex with lots of willing women?" she asks, her thirst for clarity strong. And really fucking dangerous. "You've never had a drink when you've slept with me?"

I can't do this without contact, so I shove aside the table that's blocking my access to her and fall to my knees before her. "No, Ava. I have never been under the influence of alcohol when I've had you. I don't need it. Alcohol blocked things out for me, made me forget how hollow my life was. I didn't give a fuck about any of the women

I slept with, not one. And then you fell into my life and things changed completely. You brought me back to life, Ava. I never want to touch the drink because if I start, I might not stop, and I never want to miss a moment with you." I'm a bastard. A desperate, hopeless bastard. I can see the tears forming in her eyes. I'm not sure how this can get any worse.

"Have you had sleepy sex with anyone else?" she asks, her voice brittle, ready to crack.

I do a shit job of hiding my exasperation at her silly question, sighing loudly. "No."

"What about a sense fuck?" She looks fierce.

"Ava, no. I've never cared about anyone else enough to need or want to fuck any sense into them." Jesus Christ, what the hell do I sound like? I find her legs and squeeze some reassurance into them. "Only you."

My hands are pushed aside and she's on her feet quickly. "So on Thursday in your office, are you telling me that if you had drank the vodka, I would've found you nailing Sarah on your desk, not just looking cozy with her on your desk?"

Good Lord, someone stop this horror movie. I jump up and stalk over to her, taking a firm hold of her small body. "No, don't be so stupid." I wouldn't touch Sarah with a pole, not ever again, and I would never let her lay a hand on me.

But a whip?

"I don't think I'm being stupid. It's bad enough worrying about you drinking." She starts quietly, quite calmly, but her voice rises toward the end, and her next words are yelled. "I don't know if I can cope with the additional worry of you being drunk and wanting to fuck other women." She's losing control, her scathing words making me jump back, injured, even though I have no right to be.

I also have no right to reprimand her on her foul language . . . but. "Will you watch your fucking mouth? It doesn't make me want to fuck other women. It just makes me want to fuck."

"So I had better ensure that I'm with you when you have a drink then, hadn't I?"

Oh God, yes, she had. But it's too late already. "I won't be having a drink. When will you listen to me, woman?" I'm losing control now, too, the plan to try and make these words count failing terribly. "I don't need a drink." I fear I might tighten my grip too hard, so I release her, removing myself from her space and taking a walk across my office to try and gather some calming thoughts. It's no good. Nothing will work. I jab my finger in her face. "I need *you*." It's quickly brushed aside.

"You need me to replace drink and screwing."

Where the hell did she get that from? I need her to breathe, it's simple.

"You manipulate me," she yells.

"I don't manipulate you," I protest, but I know I really do. Constant contact, making unreasonable demands, and blowing her mind with our chemistry is a way for me to control her. Control my fear.

"Yes, you do," she screeches. "With sex! Sense fucking, reminder fucking. It's all manipulation. I need you, and you use it against me." Her jaw twists, anger crashing in to join her shock and devastation.

"No." I lash out, sending the poison that has brought me to this hideous place in my life crashing to my office floor. The loud smashing of bottles and glasses recedes, and I find myself holding her arms firmly again. "I need you to need me, Ava," I pant, exhausted. If she'd only depend on me, not for everything, but just listen to me when I make my so-called unreasonable requests. "It doesn't get any simpler than that. How many times have I got to tell you? As long as you need me, I look after myself. Simple." Not so fucking simple at all.

She bursts, my stupid words, and I know they're stupid, tipping her. "How is having yourself whipped looking after yourself?"

Fuck, I'm messing it up more with every word I say. "I don't fucking know." My hair takes a severe punishing when I yank at it violently. I have no answer to that. Desperation? Hopelessness? Desolation? Fear? There are four reasons, and I'm not finished yet.

"I do need you," she says, calming a little. "But not like this."

Her defeatism worries me. I'm losing her. Talking, speaking, giving her words, is only making things worse.

I take her hands gently. "Look at me."

She breathes in, gathering energy to obey my desperate order, and looks at me. There's no denying, she's the strong one right now. The more stable one of us.

"Tell me, how do I make you feel?" I ask. "I know how you make *me* feel." And it shouldn't be like this. "Yes, I've had a lot of women, but it was all just sex. Mindless sex. No feelings." She has to believe that. "Ava, I *need* you," I whisper, my voice breaking.

"How can you need me if I make you do this to yourself?" she asks. "You're more self-destructive now than you were before me. I've made you *need* alcohol, not want it. I've made you into an unreasonable, crazy man, and *I'm* certainly not stable anymore. Don't you see what we're doing to each other?"

What? No, no, we're amazing for each other. "Ava—"

"And for the record, I hate the fact that you've put it about."

I take a deep breath. I hate that too. With a vengeance. How do I pull this around? *Can* I pull this around? I'm silently pondering that, digging deep, when Ava gasps, her eyes filling with dread. With realization. The sound, the sight, pumps fear straight into my veins and freezes them.

"When you disappeared for four days." Her words catch in her throat, trepidation splashed all over her beautiful face.

Oh fuck, no. No, no, no, I am not prepared for this. But my time is up. This whole fucking mess is about to get messier. "They meant nothing," I say clearly. "I love *you*. I need *you*."

Her mouth widens. Like she's asked but didn't believe, but now I've confirmed it. "Oh God." She folds to the floor, sobs spilling out of her. "You were fucking other women."

I fall to my knees, taking a firm but gentle hold, shaking her a little, for what purpose I don't know. "Ava, listen to me. They meant nothing. I was falling in love with you. I knew I would hurt you." I hold on to her for dear life. "I didn't want to hurt you," I grate.

"You said you couldn't do it to me. You forgot to add *again*. You should have said you couldn't do it to me *again*."

"I didn't want to hurt you," I murmur pathetically.

"So to remedy that, you fucked other women?" Her reasonable question leaves me without an answer. I ask myself the same thing every day, ten times a day, since that day I walked away from her outside her office and drowned myself in vodka. "How many?"

I wince. "Ava, please don't. I hate myself."

"I hate you too! How could you?"

"Ava, why are you not listening to me?"

"I am, and I don't like what I'm hearing!" She's moving, taking herself away, and I make a panicked grab for her hips, placing my forehead on her stomach, my emotions completely taking over.

My body starts to jerk. My eyes burst with tears. I've lost. *Pathetic*. Nothing like the man she needs and deserves. "I'm sorry," I whisper, broken. "I love you. Please, I beg you, please don't leave me. Marry me."

"What?" Her tone is shocked, disgusted, everything I don't want it to be. "I can't marry someone I don't understand." And those words finish me off, making me slump before her. Ruined. "I thought I was working you out." Her voice is trembling. "You've destroyed me again, Jesse."

"Ava, please," I beg. "I was a mess. I lost control. I thought I could fight you out of my head." *Because I knew I could do this to you!*

"By getting pissed and fucking other women?"

"I didn't know what to do." It's all I have in this moment. The truth for once. My overwhelming anxiety, fear and dread at her being hurt hasn't improved. It never will. Neither will my dread of losing her. It will always be with me, whether the ghosts of my past follow me or not. My excuses for leaving her for those four days will never be good enough. Fear in a man like me is laughable, but that's what this woman reduces me to. A wreck. A tragic excuse of a man. I really don't deserve her love. But I'm far too selfish to give it up easily. Because where I will be without her is not a place I want to go again. And deep down, I know she doesn't want me to go there either.

"You could have talked to me."

Talk. It's easier said than done when you've spent a lifetime being silent. Hiding. "Ava, you would have run away from me again."

"All of the apologies you've been giving me were because your conscience was eating away at you. It wasn't because you were drunk, or because of The Manor. It's because you screwed around on me. You said you hadn't dabbled since way before me. You've lied to me. Every time I think we've made progress, more bombshells. I can't cope with this anymore. I don't know who you are, Jesse."

"You *do* know me. I've fucked up. I've really fucked up, but no one knows me better than you. No one."

"Sarah might do. She seems to know you *very* well." Her tone is flat, almost resentful. "Why?"

My body gives, my arse hitting my heels. If Ava doesn't leave me, if we can get past this, I might explain that to her one day. She deserves to know . . . but only if she stays. For now, though, I can only explain this with how my spiraling could have ended. "I've let you down. I wanted a drink, but I promised you I wouldn't, and I know what's likely to happen if I do."

"So you had yourself whipped? I don't understand."

"Ava, you know I've led a colorful life. I've broken marriages, treated women like objects, and taken what's not mine. I've damaged people, and I feel like all of this is my penance. I've found my little piece of heaven, and I feel like everyone is going out of their way to take it away from me."

"*You* are the only one who's going to fuck this up. Just you. *You* drinking, *you* being a control freak, *you* fucking other women. You!"

Yes, me. Always me. "I can't believe I've got you. I'm terrified you're going to be taken away from me."

"So you ask a woman I despise, a woman who wants to take *you* away from *me*, to whip you?"

"Sarah doesn't want to take me away from you." Why the hell am

I protecting her? *Because I owe her.* Sarah is just one more person in this world who I've let down. Because by giving myself to her that one time, caving to the pressure, I let her down. I let us all down.

"Yes, Jesse, she does. You doing this to yourself is agony for me. You are punishing me, not you. I love you, despite all of the shit you keep landing on me, but I can't watch you do this to yourself."

What does that mean? What's that resoluteness I hear in her voice and can see on her face? "Don't leave me." My voice has taken on an unwarranted demanding tone, and I grab her hands. "I'll die before I'm without you."

"Don't say that," she yells, furious. "That's crazy talk."

Can't she see? I pull her to her knees. "It's not crazy. That nightmare I had when you were gone. Just like that—gone. It gave me a clue of what it would be like without you." The reminder brings all of the tormenting images back. Blackness. Emptiness. Pain. "Ava, it killed me."

"If I leave, it would be because I can't watch you hurt yourself. I can't watch you torture yourself anymore."

"You could never understand how much I love you." I've tried to show her and failed. I clasp her face, but she fights me off again. "Let me touch you."

"I do understand, Jesse, because I feel the same. Even though you've fucked me over completely, I still fucking love you, and I fucking hate myself for it. So don't you dare tell me I don't understand."

"It's not possible." Anger surges through me, and I reach forward, yanking her to me on a sharp intake of breath. "It's just not fucking possible."

She doesn't fight me off this time. She's given in, letting me feel and hold her for a short while. I've reduced her to this.

Exhaustion.

"I'm going to get something to clean you with," she says, trying to break away. I'm not prepared to let her go, but she finds strength from somewhere, managing to shrug me off. "I need to clean you up."

"Don't walk away from me."

"I said I would never leave you." Her words are calm and even. "I meant it." She walks out of my office, leaving me on my knees a broken, pathetic excuse of a man. I slump down, my muscles done.

My heart done.

My mind done.

And Ava, despite her promise, looked done too.

47

It feels like hours I'm on my knees. Pins and needles have found me, but I can't find the will to get myself up. I can't find the will to be strong. Can barely find the will to breathe. Full control—I never felt like I've had any, and now, suddenly, with Ava in my life, I crave it. Need it. It keeps me . . . stable. And isn't this proof? Here, now, what I've done, my back shredded, it's all proof.

I grab fistfuls of my hair, pulling. I betrayed her. There are so many people who could take away my newfound utopia, and the most likely person is me.

Hopelessness isn't a feeling I'm used to. Now, it seems to rule me. Along with guilt. Along with self-loathing. Every undesirable emotion is now blanketing the other more incredible feelings. Happiness. Contentment. Pure, undying love.

I glance around my office. Can I have freedom? Freedom from all of my sins? And forgiveness. Can I have that too? Will she ever forgive me? Because my failure to keep her safe isn't the only reason to bring me here. It was the breaking point for me, yes, but truly, it was the guilt that sent me to Sarah and her whip.

My head drops, the backs of my damn eyes pinching, and that wretched hopelessness steams forward, inflicting its usual agony. I feel like I'm asking for the world. I glance up to the cabinet across my office that stores my vice. Then to the floor where smashed glasses and bottles litter the carpet. My lip curls in contempt—contempt for me and for the poison that's ruled my life for so long. I won't be wasted anymore. My love won't be wasted.

"You doing this to yourself is agony for me. You are punishing me, not you. I love you, despite all of the shit you keep landing on me, but I can't watch you do this to yourself."

She's right. She shouldn't have to watch me do this to myself. That's not how love works.

I push myself up from the floor, hissing my way through the flaming stings across my back. Reaching over my shoulder, I swipe a hand through one of the lashes, feeling the warm wetness of the weeping wound.

Ava's gone to fetch some things to clean me up, to tend to my wounds. *What kind of man are you?* She shouldn't be taking care of me, although, ironically, she has since we met, whether she realizes or not.

Stalking to the door, I yank it open and immediately hear a commotion in the distance. I frown as I pace through the summer room, and when I round the corner into the main entrance hall of The Manor, the sounds get louder. I look up to the gallery landing, taking in the scene of dozens of people all crowding around . . . what?

Taking the stairs fast, I reach the top in a heartbeat and push my way through the throngs of people, not at all fazed that I'm still shirtless and giving members of my club a good eyeful of my messed-up back. I spot Sarah propped up against a wall, her hand resting on her throat, her eyes a little glazed. Then she sees me. Swallows. And quickly looks away.

"What's going on?" I ask, looking around at the many faces, searching for an answer. But they all back away, wary. So I return my attention to Sarah, my face demanding an answer. She closes her eyes, and I reach forward, tugging her hand away from her neck. A scattering of faint blemishes greets me, and I recoil. "Who did this?"

I don't know why I'm asking. I know damn well, and the longer I'm standing here waiting for the answer, my fear is spiraling unstoppably. "Where is she?"

Sarah says nothing, but she glances past me, and I turn to follow her stare, finding she's looking toward the staircase that leads up to the communal room. Something shifts in my gut—something I don't like. And before my brain can engage and tell me it's terror, I'm flying up the stairs like a man possessed and bursting through the doors.

I stagger to a stop, breathless, as I scan the space before me. Naked bodies. Everywhere. Moans of pleasure, of pain, of complete and utter ecstasy. And I hate that I'm looking at each woman, searching for my girl, the thought of her with another man paralyzing me. I understand. She wants to punish me, to give me payback for betraying her. God help the man who has accepted her offer. I'll crush every bone in his fucking body.

But I recognize none of the bodies. I recognize none of the moans. And then like a poorly timed showreel, images of Ava's body, every limb and every curve, pass through my mind, reminding me of her perfection, reminding me that she doesn't belong in this dark, decadent world.

I jolt forward when John collides with my back, the force knocking me out of my trance. "Fuck no," he breathes, and I instinctively turn my head slowly to my right.

And I see her.

Dangling lifelessly from some shackles, her head heavy and limp, her eyes closed. And then her body swings a little, and her back comes into view. "No," I whisper, grabbing John's shoulder to hold myself up, my legs losing all feeling. The mess of her back. The sight of her barely conscious, her head limp. A strangled whimper escapes me, just as a crop whips the air and lashes her back on a deafening crack. Her head flies back, and for the first time I see the pain in her expression.

It causes me more pain than anything physical could. God help me, I feel like someone just reached into my chest and ripped my black heart out. I look to the man holding the whip. Steve Cooke. *Jesus Christ.* The pleasure on his face has me blinking back my rage. Then he raises his arm again.

"Nooooooo!" I roar, forcing my legs to cooperate, running to the other end of the communal room as Ava jerks, the metal of the shackles clanging loudly. People jump from my path—all sick motherfuckers enjoying the show. They'll never step foot in this place again.

I reach her, and my useless hands go on a feeling frenzy across her skin, my mind not giving me the instructions to free her. "Jesus. Ava, no. John!" I shout. "Release her hands!" I hear John cursing, feeling the pound of his boots beneath my feet, as I spew constant words of utter disbelief, of despair. "John, fucking hell, get her down." I stroke and feel, scan her face, say her name, my heartbeats becoming faster and faster as John works quickly to release her. She drops into my arms like a stone, limp and lifeless. What has she done? How could she? "Ava?" I negotiate her in my arms, trying my hardest not to touch the welts on her back. It's impossible. She flinches, chokes. *Fuck!*

I cast my eyes around the silent room, seeing disturbed expressions on the faces of all the members standing motionless, watching this horror show. The sick thing is, I know they're not horrified by what they've witnessed happening. They're disturbed by my reaction. This is just a normal day in the office for these hedonistic, twisted fucks.

My eyes land on Steve. He's a dead man walking, and judging by the wideness of his eyes, he knows it. "Don't let him go anywhere," I growl, making sure he sees the psycho in my stare before I stride away, my focus forward, ignoring the constant gasps of shock as I go.

Kate rounds the gallery landing, racing toward us. "What the fuck?" she breathes, taking in Ava's lifeless body in my arms before looking at me in question.

I flick John a discreet look over my shoulder, knowing he'll be tailing me, and he intervenes, blocking Kate from coming after me as I pass her. "Give him a chance," John says quietly.

I pace through The Manor to my office, people moving out of my path, giving me space, or a wide berth, and kick the door of my office open and shoulder it shut. I go to the couch, keeping Ava close to my chest as I lower to my arse. "You stupid, stupid girl," I whisper raggedly, burying my face in her neck and breathing deeply. "You crazy, stupid girl." I've felt a pain so intense before. A hopelessness so debilitating. I'm back to where I started.

For the life of me, I can't fathom her reasoning or process a revenge so cruel. My head is in disarray, nothing making sense to me. All I know is the woman I love with a power even I find difficult to comprehend, is in my arms, weak and bleeding. Because of me. And I have no idea how to fix this mess.

I lift my eyes but not my head when the door knocks. "What?"

John enters, takes in the scene, and starts to shake his head in despair as he strides over, placing a bowl of liquid and some pads on the table. Ava's clothes are placed carefully on the back of the couch before he leaves quietly, and I swallow, finding the strength I need to face the results of Ava's recklessness.

I shift, only a fraction, and she immediately hisses in pain, so I still, clenching my eyes closed. "Oh, Jesus," I breathe. "Baby, I need to move you, I need to see your back."

She starts to protest weakly, and I exhale, gingerly dropping my lips to the back of her head. "Why?" I ask. What is this madness? "I don't understand."

She doesn't speak, and I don't know if it's because she can't or simply doesn't know why herself. It has to be the latter. I've sent her crazy. "Ava, I need to see your back." I move again, and this time she lets me position her upright on my lap. She seems okay for a moment, and then quickly she's far from it.

Catapulting forward, she starts to retch, yelping in between her heaves. "Oh, God, Ava." *Fuck.* I instinctively place my palm on her back to rub and she jerks.

And vomits everywhere.

I curse and apologize, over and over, doing my best to pull her hair back, feeling utterly useless. "What have you done?" Her retches continue, as well as her cries. I can't stand this. "I'm going to move you now, okay?" I take her gently under her arms and start to lift, but a pain-filled yelp halts me, and I growl to myself. "I can't lift you without touching you," I say, gingerly negotiating her body, wincing every time she cries out. "Get on your front." I gently help her down, the full, brutal mess of her back coming into view. I have to swallow to stop myself from throwing up too. At least a dozen lines span her back, all straight, all evenly placed, all red raw, but only one has broken her skin. This is the work of an expert—the work of a man who knows what he's doing. None of the lashes lap, and none will leave permanent damage. Not that these trivial points dilute my fury or lessen his punishment. He won't be able to hold a whip again by the time I'm done with him, let alone thrash it.

"I can't believe you've done this." I drop to my knees and reach for the bowl of water John delivered, pulling it closer. I soak some cotton wool as I warn her quietly of the coming sting. "I'll be gentle." I drop forward to find her eyes, to check she's hearing me. It's all I can do not to sob at the sight of her looking so vacant and hollow. The eyes that possess me, the eyes I can read like a book, are empty. So I lean in and kiss her gently, hoping for the usual heat that any one of our kisses stokes.

Nothing.

God damn you, Jesse, you twisted, fucked-up piece of shit.

You. Did. This.

I tentatively reach forward and unfasten Ava's bra, flinching when she hisses, and then gently swipe the cotton wool across the angriest of the lashes. I quickly withdraw when she cries out and apologize again, getting more stressed, shakier, and angrier.

It's a few minutes of cursing and whimpers, and when I've done the best I can and am no longer able to stand the constant flinches of her body, I toss the cotton wool in the bowl and push it away. I jump up, sidestep the vomit on the carpet, and grab a bottle of water off my desk. "Can you sit up?" I ask as I lower to my haunches by the couch again.

She starts gingerly moving. "Shit," I mutter. "Fuck. God damn it." I squeeze my eyes closed and try to get myself together, knowing I'm of no use flapping like an old woman. Her unfastened bra drops, and she feebly attempts to cover her dignity. "Leave it." I brush her feeling hands aside and place the water in her grasp. "Open your mouth," I order, slipping two painkillers past her lips. "Drink." I help her get the bottle to her mouth, feeling her shake as I do. How the hell did I let it come to this?

I need to get her home. Away from here.

I go to my desk and collect my things, yanking my T-shirt on as I go back to Ava and snatch her clothes off the back of the sofa. "I'm taking you home," I say as I crouch before her, indicating for her to step into her jeans. I pull them up and reach for her top, knowing this part of dressing her won't be so straightforward. I glace at her exposed breasts. This is going to sting like a bitch. "Can we try?" I ask, pulling at the neck, trying to make the opening larger. I start to ease it over her head, but the moment she tries to lift her arms, she sniffles, shaking her head, and I plead with her not to cry, kissing her forehead and pulling away, seeing rivers of tears streaming down her cheeks. I curse and discard her top. "Come here." I feel only mildly consoled that it's her back that'll be exposed to dozens of curious eyes, not her front. "Wrap your legs around my waist, arms around my neck. Be careful," I order, lifting her, making sure I avoid her back. "Are you okay?"

Her nod doesn't comfort me. She's not okay. I'm not okay. Can we ever be okay again? I shake my head and hold her nape as I walk to the door, taking deep breathes, preparing myself to face the spectators. I'm also trying to calm the rising anger. My emotion, my despair, my fury, it's all mixing up, my head feeling like it's going to detonate.

I stride out of my office, and when I round the corner, I find members still hanging around, gathered in small crowds, whispering and talking. "John," I call, and every set of eyes turn our way. I ignore them, as well as the unwelcome intakes of shocked breath.

"How's the girl?"

"How does she fucking look?" I snap, irritated, although that irritation is all for me. And my friend knows that, which is probably why he's not calling me out on it. "Get a cotton sheet from the cleaning quarters."

"Ava?" Kate appears, her eyes nailed to the wounds, her mouth hanging open. "Oh, fucking hell. What have you done, you stupid cow?"

"I'm taking her home." I pass quickly. "She's fine, I'll call you."

"Jesse, she's bleeding."

"I know, Kate. I fucking know." Does she think I'm fucking blind? "I'll call you."

I walk on, my face tight, everyone moving out of my way. Good, because the urge to set Ava down and annihilate everything in my path is strong. I could easily sweep through The Manor with an ax and destroy it room by room.

I close my eyes and refocus on my breathing, but when I open them, all air disappears from my lungs along with my words of reason. I see Steve visibly swallow. "Jesse, mate, I didn't know."

Kill him. I stop in my tracks and stare at the man who violated Ava and, in the process, signed his death sentence. "You want to be thanking all that's fucking holy I've got my girl in my arms, because if I didn't, the cleaners would be scooping up your remains for a fucking year."

"I . . . I . . . I didn't know."

Is he for real? "No one told you she was mine?"

"I . . . I assumed . . . I . . ."

My control is gone. My sense gone. "She's mine!" I bellow, needing the world to know it. I'm done with life without her. I'm through with being the predictable man I've always been. Now, I'm unpredictable. My feelings are unpredictable. My reactions unpredictable. These days, I don't even know what I'm doing myself until I've done it. Don't know what I'm saying until I've said it.

But it all comes naturally, and I'll be damned if I can stop it. I'm a madman, and as I gaze around at the people staring on, watching me heaving with Ava clinging to my front, I realize they're all thinking I'm a madman too.

I feel Ava shift slightly in my hold, registering a mild whimper. "I'm sorry," I whisper, not knowing what I'm apologizing for. Everything? "You're a fucking dead man, Steve," I growl, the seesaw of emotions inside me tilting back to murderous. How easy it would be to let loose and crush him. Would I feel any better? After all, is there really anyone to blame here except me?

John steps forward, obviously wary, obviously sensing the beast is about to be unleashed. "Jesse?" he says, extending a raised palm, like, *cool down.* "S'all good. Priorities, yeah?"

Priorities. I push on, walking to the car, Kate tailing me, fussing and faffing, to the point I have to tell her to back off.

She's suddenly in front of me, her look fierce. "Stop being such a pigheaded twat and accept the fucking help." She thrusts her hand forward. "You're not the only one who cares about her."

I breathe in my patience, relenting. "My keys are in my back pocket."

Kate's behind me quickly, rummaging through urgently. I can feel the sea of curious eyes behind me, and I turn to find some members have followed us outside.

"Everyone needs to fuck off back inside." I'm not even attempting to move Ava until the peanut gallery has pissed off. Not just to save my sanity, but to save her dignity.

John starts shooing people away, tossing lethal glares here and there, and as soon as everyone is back inside, I start the painful task of getting Ava in my car. Her grip of me relaxes, and I take my time, watching for signs of pain as I give her instructions, before I grab the sheet from John and lay it over her. Fuck the seat belt. I shut the door and hurry around, settling in the driver's seat. Her eyes are closed. And then . . . not.

Fuck me, just look at her. My defiant, savage beauty. Her dark eyes are brimming again, mirroring the hopelessness in mine. "Stop,"

I demand, my voice strained, my eyes stinging. I can't stand to see her crying anymore. But I'm not just telling her. I'm telling myself.

I can't marry a man I don't know.

You are punishing me, not you.

Her words play on repeat.

She said she'd never leave me, but now?

Is this where it ends?

48

I LAY with her for a while, touching her face, until she dozed off. Then I went downstairs, only mildly aware of all the things littering the bedroom floor, clothes, shoes, cosmetics. It looks like she started to pack, to leave, but there's some of my stuff too. I haven't the capacity to wonder why.

I settle on the chair on an uncomfortable hiss and text John, Kate, and the boys to let them know we're home. Resting back, I close my eyes and try to straighten out my mind, try to fathom why she's done this. I have no idea. I'm stumped. Angry.

Ava's mobile rings, pulling my heavy head down, and my slowing heart picks up a pace when I see her mother's calling.

I can't marry a man I don't understand.

I swallow and take a few deep breaths, collecting it off the table and answering, clearing my throat first, hoping I sound . . . sane. "Mrs. O'Shea?"

There's a brief pause before she speaks. "Yes."

I swallow again and clear my throat. Fuck me, I'm nervous. Better than being raging mad. "My name's Jesse W—"

"I know who you are." She doesn't sound all too impressed. I don't suppose I can blame her. Everything she knows about me isn't exactly glowing. "Where's Ava?"

I look at the stairs. "Sleeping."

"Did you punch Matt?"

I recoil. To the point. I want to say he deserved it. I want to give her every detail that led me to socking him in the face. God, he deserved so much more. "I don't know how much you know about their breakup."

"I don't care about their breakup. He's in her past, and I have no doubt he'll stay there. She was too good for him. My question is, are *you* good enough?"

Wow. Brutal. I'm nowhere near good enough. Not as I am. But I'm working on it. "I adore your daughter."

"You hardly know her."

"Trust me, Mrs. O'Shea. I know her." It's Ava who doesn't know me. "She's stubborn," I say, and she snorts. Laughter, I think. "Driven. Has sass for days. Is annoyingly but admirably independent. Beautiful. Passionate." I shift in my chair, wondering if any of this is landing. It's not bullshit. Not lip-service. I mean every word. But I could never blame Ava's mother, a woman who's never met me and only ever heard negative things about me, for being skeptical. "I could never even begin to describe the level of love and respect I have for your daughter."

"Try."

I blink. She's going to make me work hard for this, and while I'd usually dismiss such demands, this is Ava's mother. "She's very quickly become all I want to live for," I say, and she inhales. Only subtly, but I catch it. "Believe me when I say, she is all that matters to me. I know she cares about your opinion. I know she's nervous for you to meet me."

"Why?"

"Well, I'm older," I say, laughing under my breath. "I'm sure you've heard."

"How much older?"

"Eleven years." I peek down at my phone when another call comes in. I reject John and get back to Ava's mother. "I was wondering how you would feel about visiting?" I'm being smart.

Any offer to drive down to Cornwall will be met with suspicion. They'll want to see my home. See where I live.

"Let me talk to Ava's father."

Her father. Another obstacle. Someone else to sweeten. "Okay. Will you text me to let me know?"

"Yes. Let me get a pen. What's your number?"

I reel it off, repeating it when she asks, and listening back as she replays it to me. "That's it," I confirm. "It was good talking to you."

She hums, and I'm not sure what to make of it. Is she always so reserved, or is she just treading carefully?

With me.

She hangs up, and I sit in the quiet for a while, my back stinging, my muscles aching. She's not sure about me. I blow out my cheeks. Makes two of us. This is an unexpected turn. I don't know where I stand with Ava, what's happening from here, where we're going. Is she pregnant, is she not, does she still want to marry me? Be with me at all?

How much older?

Eleven years.

I breathe in and out slowly, relaxing back in the chair, my eyes on my wrist. On my Rolex. And I watch the hands glide around the face, ticking down to midnight.

The moment it hits twelve, my phone chimes.

Happy birthday, big brother. I love you. Amalie xxx

I swallow. Let my head fall back. "Happy birthday, Jake," I whisper.

Happy birthday, Jesse. Miss you, bro.

I don't try to stop the tears rolling down my cheeks.

49

THE FIRST THING I see when I open my eyes is Ava. The first thing I think is . . . why isn't she spread all over me? Then my brain wakes up and I remember . . . everything. She's watching me. Quiet.

She's still here.

I shift forward, getting as close as I can to her. It's not close enough. She moves, slowly and on endless winces, onto her side, and I help her shift closer until our chests are pressed together and her breath is my breath.

"It is possible," she says, her voice cracked and sleepy. "To understand how you feel about me, it is possible."

Is she saying what I think she's saying? "You did this to yourself to prove you love me?"

"No, you know I love you," she answers, and I can't lie, it's a relief. She loves me. *Still* loves me. "I did it to show you what it feels like."

"I don't understand," I admit, confused. "I know what it feels like to be whipped." It's currently throbbing on my back, and it won't be happening again.

"I don't mean that." She appears to get a little frustrated, struggling to explain her point. "I mean the agony of seeing the man I love hurting himself."

Confused, I scan her eyes, taken aback. She had herself whipped because I did?

"Nothing will ever hurt me as much as seeing you doing that to yourself. That will kill me, nothing else." She strokes at my face, incredibly together and lucid. "If you punish yourself again, I will too."

Well, that's a threat no man could ever ignore. "You love me." I need to hear her say it again. I feel like we've come back from war and everything has changed since we've been away. The weight that was on my shoulders seems to have lifted.

"I need you," she says, forsaking love for need. "I need you strong and healthy. I need you to understand how much I love you. I need you to know I can't be without you either. I would die before losing you too."

I can't believe this. What she's saying, her resoluteness, her incredible strength. *Her forgiveness.* "I don't deserve you, Ava." For the first time, she will understand why I believe that. "Not after the life I've lived. I've never had anything I've valued or wanted to protect . . ." *since I lost my brother and daughter.* I swallow. "Now I have, and it's a bizarre mix of total happiness and complete fucking fear." I'm talking, and I can't stop myself. She hasn't left me. I should be able to tell her anything and she'd still love me. But there's still a chance she could doubt me. There's a chance she's pregnant, and if she knew I lost my daughter because I was careless, reckless, and so fucking weak?

"I've made you like this," she whispers.

No, I have made myself like this. "I crave control with you, Ava." I say it how it is. How we all know it is. "I can't help it. I really can't."

"I know. I know you can't." She comes closer, cuddling into me, but my hands remain under control. Not touching anywhere it could hurt.

"You're hurting because of me," I say quietly.

"And you are because of me. We deal with the past," she says, and I'm fucking flinching again. "As long as I have you, the *strong* you, we deal with it. It's not your history that's hurting me. It's you. The things you are doing now." She sounds so fucking together. So reasonable.

"You're crazy mad." I gently ease her out of my chest and kiss her softly. "Crazy, crazy mad."

"I'm crazy in love with you," she says around my mouth. "Please don't do that to yourself again." A jerk, a flinch. "My back hurts."

God damn it. I break our kiss. "I'm still furious with you."

"I'm not very happy with you either."

Thrown right back at me, and I can't say a single thing. "I can't touch you." Not anywhere but her face, and my hands are twitching like mad.

Her face screws up as I smother her cheeks with my lips. "How's your back?" she asks.

"Fine. I'm just pissed at you." Yes, we've moved mountains. Yes, we're okay. Does this mean Ava will have suddenly become completely submissive? Give me a break. I need to make sure I only fight her on the things I'm passionate about, or we'll always be fighting. "We need to get you moving or you'll seize up."

"I'm happy to seize up."

"Not a chance, lady." Not an option. "You need a lavender bath and some cream on your back. I can't believe out of all of my members, you picked the most unstable one."

"I did?"

"You did. John and I were due to have a meeting to discuss revoking his membership. We've been monitoring him for a while. His behavior has become a little erratic lately"—*loose*—"and while some of the women welcome the rough side of his sexual exploits, others not so much. He makes some women uncomfortable and that's a problem." God damn it, I should have acted earlier. "He hadn't done anything to warrant us getting rid of him until last night."

Her lips form a straight, guilty line. "I asked him."

"There are rules, Ava." I get close to her face, nibbling her lip, letting it slide through my teeth and pop out. "Did he give you an out?"

A frown. "No."

"The list of his offenses goes on and on. He's broken a lot of rules. He's got to go."

"I don't remember him," she says. "He wasn't at the anniversary party."

"No, he was on duty."

"Duty?"

"He's a cop."

"What?" She chokes over the word.

"He's a copper."

"You threatened to kill a cop?"

"I was crazy mad." Understatement of the fucking century. When John and I spoke about meeting with Steve, I felt quietly torn, since he'd helped determine Turner had been harassing me. His talk of scratching backs has taken a whole new meaning. He's a cunt. End of. Back to Ava. I consider her for a moment as she watches me play with her hair. "I've been thinking," I say.

"What about?"

"Well, about a lot of things. But the first thing is that I need to talk to Patrick about Van Der Haus."

Ava's face screws up. Then is quickly uncreased. "It's Monday," she shrieks, moving, like what? She's going to work? She can hardly move, for God's sake, as proven with the accompanying yelp.

"Do you honestly think I'm letting you go anywhere?" It doesn't take much force to get her to lie still again. "Listen, that's not the only thing I've been thinking about." How do I put this? How do I explain that I'm fully aware of my . . . quirks, while also pointing out hers. Ava's right. We need to communicate more with words.

Sometimes.

"What?" She looks so nervous.

"I can't ever be without you."

"I know that."

"But it's not because I'm worried about reverting back to my old ways. I love you because you give me purpose. You've filled a massive hole with your beautiful face and your spirit, and while I might be making your life a little more difficult with my challenging ways, I want to throw that right back at you."

I expect her to swoon, given I was rather eloquent. She doesn't. She chuckles. I'm offended. "I am not challenging, Jesse Ward." She's deluded. I could give her endless examples of her challenging ways, and she must know I'm about to because her hand covers my mouth to stop me from speaking. "You just said that I've filled a massive hole with my spirit—"

"And your beautiful face."

She looks momentarily flattered. "Part of that spirit is my incessant need to challenge *your* challenging ways," she goes on. I try not to roll my eyes. Fail. "You'll never get rid of that tiny part of me that rebels against you and you wouldn't want to. That's what makes me different from all the women of The Manor who've licked your boots for far too long." They never licked my boots. They licked everything, but never my boots. "I've given myself to you completely. Every part of me is yours. No one will ever take me away from you. Not ever. And I know part of your issue is keeping me as far away from what the other women in your life represent."

"There have been no other women in my life," I mumble, outraged. Fucks, yes. Flings, yes. But nothing substantial enough to class as *another woman*. Not even my ex-wife.

"But I need to know something."

Oh shit.

"You want to keep me as far away from the women of The Manor," she says, looking almost embarrassed. "But what about the sex?"

Her question *and* her disposition make me smile, but my amusement is short-lived. Ava gasps and then quickly looks disgusted. What did I do? "You don't like me drinking because you think I'm going to do what you used to do when you were drunk," she blurts in a rush. "You think I'm going to want to fuck everything in sight."

"Will you stop fucking swearing?" I fall to my back, annoyed. Because she has me pinned. A little. I scowl when she appears on my thighs. And also because it fucking hurts my back to lie on it.

"It is, isn't it?" she presses. "That's the reason."

Again, I'm wondering how to put this. "It's not just that, Ava. You're vulnerable when you're drunk."

"But it is part of the reason, isn't it?"

"Yes, I guess so."

"Okay, what about the sex?" She's all coy now. It's adorable.

"I already told you this. I can't get close enough to you."

"Sleepy sex achieves that." And now she's aloof. Give me a break. She loves me having control in the bedroom. She loves my moves. It's why she persistently defies my reasonable requests.

"Yes, it does," I agree. "But we have an incredible chemistry. I've never felt it before."

Happy Ava. It's my favorite, along with Insatiable Ava and Acceptable Ava. "What feelings?"

She wants more words, and I'm thrilled to give them to her. "It's pure bliss, baby," I start, stroking her thighs, feeling her weak, battered body respond. "Total gratification." I hitch a brow, watching as she breathes through the contact, her eyes back to the usual, brilliant sparkle. "Absolute, complete earth-shifting, universe-shaking love."

"Yeah?" she asks, doing a terrible job of holding back her satisfied smile.

"Oh yeah," I whisper. "Complete heaven."

Letting her smile loose, she forgets herself for a moment and plummets to my chest. "Ouch."

"Careful," I moan, helping her to sit up again. God, this sucks. "Does it hurt bad?"

"It's fine. What am I going to do about work?"

"Unravel your knickers." I start to gingerly move us to get up. She needs that bath, loads of lavender, and I've got to keep her moving or she'll seize up. "I've spoken to Patrick." I embellish the truth. I couldn't talk to him because I couldn't get into Ava's phone to get his number, so I was forced to leave a message on the office answering machine.

She groans, clinging to me. "Is there anyone in my life who you haven't trampled?"

She has no idea. "Don't be cheeky. There are no whip marks on your arse, lady. Anyway, why does our home look like it's been ransacked by burglars?" Everything is everywhere.

"I was looking for something."

"What?"

She looks at me through one narrowed eye as I lower her to her feet, and it hits me. *Oh fuck*. "Nothing," she says slowly as I turn her toward the bathroom and away from me, looking up at the ceiling. *Fuck, fuck, fuck.* Was she looking for her pills?

"What did you tell Patrick?"

I lift her up onto the vanity and start running us a bath. "I told him you passed out on Saturday and put your back out."

"Did he not think it strange that you called him?"

I don't know, because I didn't actually *speak* to him. "I don't know, and I don't really care." I return to Ava, pouting at her back in the mirror. "Look what you've done to your beautiful body. I won't be taking you on your back for a while."

Her pout matches mine as she peers over her shoulder to inspect the damage. "Is that it?"

"What do you mean, is that it?"

"Turn around." She's quickly forcing me around in front of her, and she inhales when she has my back. "See, yours are better than mine."

The fuck?

I'm moving before I think better of it, taking her from the unit and putting her on her feet, shaking some fucking sense into her, since I can't currently fuck it into her. "Shut up, Ava."

She wilts, remorseful. "Sorry, it just hurts so much. I thought it would look a lot worse than that."

"It's fucking bad enough." For the love of God. I go back to the bath, incensed.

"I said, I'm sorry."

I leave Ava to think about how ridiculous she's being while I fix our bath and pick up the various things scattered around the floor, wondering if she's going to ask me if I've been taking her pills. Quite honestly, I think, and hope, she's telling herself not to be so crazy. Because who would do that? Me, that's who. I regret it, yes, and I definitely won't be doing it again. Because that's crazy behavior. The question is, though, have I succeeded in my crazy endeavor?

I try to help her off the unit and get snubbed, and she goes to the bath and lowers herself in, slowly, cautiously, her face pained. She eventually opens her eyes, and I motion for her to move down to make space, which she does on a few mumbles.

I get in and ease her to my chest. "Don't fight me," I order, nipping at her ear, smiling when she squirms before she settles and sighs. I watch the water lap over her flesh, the air quiet, the atmosphere easy. It's a stark contrast to the horrors of last night, and somewhere I didn't think we'd be this morning. I'm grateful. So fucking grateful.

"So, Steve is out on his arse?" she asks, her toes slipping across my shins.

I sigh. I don't want to talk about Steve, The Manor, or last night. "Gone."

"No questions asked?"

"Not one," I confirm. "Except whether he would prefer burial or cremation. Am I hurting you?"

"No, I'm fine."

I settle, my own back burning, but I sustain the pain. It's the least I can do.

"So, does the same apply to Sarah?" Ava asks, at the very moment I lower into her neck to kiss it.

I freeze. "What has Sarah got to do with this?"

"She hurt you."

"I asked her to."

"I asked Steve to."

"Yes, but Steve knew you were off limits, that you are mine. He crossed a clear line that I drew and not just with who he practiced his shit on, but also *how* he carried it out, although the former is my ultimate bone of contention." I devote some time to her ear, licking and kissing and biting. Pacifying? Fuck me, I do not want to have to deal with a demand to fire Sarah. "He accepted a whip from someone he hadn't met before and never even clarified the limits. You could have been mentally unstable for all he knew."

"I probably was at that specific moment. And anyway, you're mine. You're off limits too, you know."

"I know." I relent, sighing. "I know, baby. Never again, but I think you've demonstrated your grievance with Sarah." I bet her neck does *not* look pretty this morning.

"So you're not getting rid of her?" she asks, sounding . . . shocked?

Ava can't appreciate it, but Sarah cannot leave The Manor, and not only because I couldn't run it without her. "She's an employee and a close friend. I can't sack her for doing something I asked her to, Ava."

"She planned it, Jesse."

"What do you mean, she planned it?" Planned what? Me being pathetic? Me cheating?

"The text that I got from John."

"What text?"

"The one she sent from John's phone saying I should go to The Manor."

What the hell? Wait— "You think Sarah lifted John's phone and sent you a text?"

"Yes."

I laugh, and it's a nervous laugh. "Don't be daft."

"I'm not being daft. I have it on my phone, I'll show you."

"Ava, Sarah wouldn't do that." Fuck me, she totally would. And yet, I can't confess that. I can't open *that* can of worms.

"Do you think I imagined it?"

"No, I'm thinking that you were drugged on Saturday night and maybe you've made a mistake." I am absolutely begging the gods that hate me that she made a mistake, because that is *not* a problem I want to deal with.

"I'll show you. She wants you."

"Well she can't have me, she knows that. I belong to you." Ava accepts my lips on her cheek when I kiss her.

"You do."

So we're clear. Good. Enough about The Manor and the people who walk the rooms. "Lean forward so I can bathe your back." Easing her forward, I flinch at the sight of her maimed back, my cheeks blowing out, my heart hurting. "I'll be gentle." *So gentle.*

"I like you rough."

My smile is small. Her lightness is needed when I feel heavy with regret. "Ava, don't say things like that when I'm in no position to violate you." Her shoulder blades pull in a tiny bit when I rest the sponge there, and I immediately replace it with my lips, feeling her relax under them. So that is what I do. Squeeze warm water over her, kiss her, squeeze, kiss, over and over, her quiet murmurs of contentment welcomed as I focus on that—and not the damage before me—before moving on to her hair. I let her slip down into the water between my thighs, holding her shoulders, and she looks up at me as I gently tend to her. A small smile tickles her lips.

"What?" I ask, and her eyes light up. My dick is literally tickling the top of her head. "Stop it," I warn. She pouts. "Stop that too." She's insatiable. I wish I could indulge it. "Come on, out." I help her up and lift her out, ignoring her grumbles of protest, wrapping her up in a towel while I dry myself and then gently dabbing at her back to dry her.

I scoop her up and carry her to the bed. I feel her eyes on my profile. Watching me. Enjoying me looking after her. Of course, it's my favorite job too, but not under these circumstances. I wasn't the man she needed last night. Broken, a mess, angry, and out-of-control desperate.

My back twinges. Never again.

I lay her on her front and pull the towel free, putting myself on her undamaged, pert arse, losing my own towel as I do. Just look at the fucking state of her. *Breathe.* I reach for the tub of cream on the nightstand. "This might be a bit cold." The moment the cream meets her skin, she hisses, going stiff beneath me. I hush her gently, gritting my teeth too, like I can help her through it. One thing's certain, though. *I hope.* "You won't be doing this again, will you?"

"I will if you do." She sucks in air as I start to pat in the cream, turning her face into the sheets, her shoulder blades pulling in. Then she definitely won't. My dick twitches. Inevitable. I'm touching her, after all.

I work over every inch of her back, five times over, and with each minute that passes, a little more blood drips into my cock. Fucking hell. Ava's about to get her way.

I start to lower my lips to her shoulder but stop when I hear someone downstairs calling a *hello*.

Oh fuck. I remembered to call everyone . . .

Except Cathy.

Ava lifts her head and looks toward the door, and my dick wilts with sadness. I curse and get up, heading for the dressing room. "I forgot to call Cathy." I go to where I keep my jeans and find a pile of female clothes. "Shit." Where did we move them to? I open a few more doors until I find a pair, pull them on, grab a T-shirt, and hiss as I pull the fucker down my torso. "Up you get, I need to feed you." I take her hips and lift her from the bed.

Her nose wrinkles. "I'm not hungry."

"You will eat. Your stomach must be completely empty after you released the contents of it all over my office floor."

Embarrassment moves in. It's ridiculous. "I'm sorry."

"Don't be sorry." I push her wet hair over her shoulder. "Get some clothes on. I'll meet you in the kitchen." I leave her with a quick kiss and go down to see Cathy.

50

BUT I FIND the kitchen empty. "Cathy?"

"In here, boy."

I look toward the laundry room as I go to the fridge. "Morning." I pluck down a jar of peanut butter, settling on a stool and diving in.

She appears at the doorway, a bag in her hands, her face wrinkled in question. "What's this on the shelf, boy? It's blocking the washing powder." She peeks into the bag and pulls out a box, and I still on my stool, my finger hanging out of my mouth. *Please don't come downstairs yet, Ava.* My brain's yelling at me to get up, go to her, take the bag before she has a chance to figure out what those boxes are. "Damn it," she curses, squinting at the label. "I need my specs."

I drop my jar and dash over, swiping the bag from one hand and the box from the other. "Just some meds," I say, smiling like a dickhead, instinctively putting the bag behind my back.

"*Some* meds? You going into the pharmaceuticals business, boy?"

I laugh, harder than it's funny, and scoot past her, opening a cupboard and shoving the bag inside.

"Oh, I see," she muses as I shut the door and stare at it. She sees what? "Well, I suppose going cold turkey might have its side effects."

What the fuck is she talking about? I turn with a monster frown as she opens the dishwasher. And it clicks. She thinks I need meds to help me give up the drink? I laugh to myself. The irony. I probably do. "They're just a backup," I say, taking my stool and my jar again.

She looks up and smiles. Not at me, but past me, and I turn to see Ava in the doorway, her body swathed in baggy clothes. "Good morning, Ava," Cathy says.

Ava sits, and my nose moves in, smelling her. Clean. All poison washed and rubbed away. "Hi, Cathy," she says, flapping her hands at me. "How are you?" She looks at me, scowling at me crowding her. We have some making up to do. I dip my finger and rub it across her lip, and her face twists with disgust. She's adorable, her chin smeared in my vice. Let's not waste it. I lean in and lick it off.

Ava and Sun-Pat. "Yum."

"I'm very well," Cathy says, as Ava bats me away. "Would you like some breakfast? Salmon?"

"Please." Relaxing, she watches Cathy faff around our kitchen, looking content. Happy. Everything she said to me this morning rings in my head. We're back on track. Finally. "We have some news, Cathy," I say, feeling Ava's curious eyes fall onto me. "Ava will soon be Mrs. Ward."

Cathy looks directly at me, and I realize I might have just made a huge mistake. Fuck, will she assume I've told Ava *everything*? "Oh, how wonderful!" She drops everything in her hands and makes a beeline for Ava, and I wince when she hugs her, rubbing at her back. "Oh, I'm so happy." Finally releasing Ava, she looks at her with so much appreciation, I hope Ava sees it. "I can't tell you how happy that makes me," she gushes, feeling at Ava's cheeks, while Ava looks at her, a little shook. "He's a good boy." And now she's kissing her. *Jesus, Cathy, too much.* I fear the worst when my lovely housekeeper turns her attention my way. I slowly lower my peanut butter in preparation of her attack. I'm forced into her chest, powerless to stop her, as Ava looks at me, mystified. By Cathy or me? "My boy is finally settling down." She frees me. Oh no. Her eyes are tearing up.

"Cathy, stop that," I warn gently, praying there is no mention of the part of my past that Ava still doesn't know about.

"I'm sorry." Flapping a hand in her own face, like she's flapping away the tears, she returns to making breakfast. "So, where and when?"

"Next month at The Manor," I say, relaxing a little, looking at Ava when the coffee pot she's just picked up clangs against something.

Her eyebrows shoot up as she looks at me. "Really?"

"Really." I've searched high and low for a venue. There's nothing. Not until next year or the year after, and I can't wait that long. I'm impatient. Excited. I appreciate The Manor isn't her favorite place, but I can change that. Make her see it in a different light. The building, the decor, the architecture, the grounds. Not what happens upstairs, but the beauty of the building and its surroundings. I've only recently started appreciating it myself.

"How lovely," Cathy sings. I agree. Lovely.

"It will be." I'll shut The Manor down. Decorate the entire place, make the private suites actual suites, have all of our guests stay. It will be amazing. But something tells me Ava doesn't agree. My cheek is burning from her hard stare, and I slowly screw the lid of my jar back on, pondering how I can convince her how wonderful it would be. I don't know why I didn't suggest it before. Why the hell would we pay to hire a lovely manor house in the countryside when I own a manor myself? Probably one of the most prestigious and well-kept. It's a wedding planner's dream. And I can only imagine Uncle Carmichael smiling down as he watches me start a new life—a life he wanted for me—surrounded by the beauty he created.

I look out the corner of my eye when I see Ava move. She gets down from the stool, plucks up something from the worktop, circling behind me. I sit up straight, nervous, but then warm and fuzzy when I feel her breath close to my ear. "Who are you marrying?" she whispers.

My secret smile drops like lead, my disbelieving eyes following her to the bin. Did she say that?

"Compensation," I mutter like a twat, like she owes me, and

follow it up with, "I'll trample, Ava." Because I'm not being unreasonable enough.

I glare at her as Ava glares at me. She's going to protest for the sake of it? After everything she's said this morning, all of the reassurances, she's going to take this away?

Stamping on the pedal of the bin with a little too much force, the lid flies up and Ava finally frees me of her filthy look. My fucking face is aching by the time I relax it. I rub at the muscles on my forehead. This morning was going so well. No sex, granted, but all things considered, we've made serious headway, and now she's going to put the blockers on for . . . what?

Part of that spirit is a need to defy you.

"Ain't that right," I mutter, looking up. Ava is engrossed, reading something. My blood cools. *Oh shit.* I fly across the kitchen and pluck it from her hand, dropping it back in the bin and taking her elbow, guiding her back to her stool. "Sit." *Fuck. Fuck, fuck, fuck.* What the hell is wrong with me? I'm leaving evidence of my arseholery all over the fucking place—pregnancy tests, invitations.

"Your sister?" Ava asks, her voice small, when, really, she should he throwing her sass my way, because my behavior right now warrants it.

"Leave it." *Please, leave it.*

"Here you are." Cathy, oblivious to the change in mood, places a plate in front of each of us then excuses herself to go do some polishing. I stare down at my breakfast, as ever trying to figure out how to explain myself. What to say that will make things better rather than worse. I'm no expert at talking. That's been proven a million times over. Hence, I drown her with physical affection.

I look across to Ava's plate. Untouched. She slips down off the stool. "Where are you going?" I ask, panicked.

"Upstairs." She doesn't even look at me, so she can't appreciate the fear I'm feeling.

Always fucking running away. "Ava, don't walk away from me," I shout at her back. "Ava!"

"You are more than crazy mad if you think I'm marrying you,

Jesse," she says as she swings round, faster than her body should allow. It's a sign of how mad she is. But her words are even. Resolute. And they fucking hurt. She leaves and I push my plate away, slamming my balled fist into the marble. "Fuck." Will I ever get anything right?

I get up to go after her but think better of it and quickly sit back down. I'm clearly crazy mad because I *do* think she can marry me. I get up again. Sit back down. Up, down, up, down. "For fuck's sake." I drop my head in my hands and fist my hair. Talk to her.

Tell me we can discuss our wedding reasonably.

Okay, so she doesn't like being told what to do and what is happening. Unless she's under me. I roll my eyes and grab our phones, making my way upstairs, but I'm pulled to a stop when mine rings. "Hello?"

"It's Elizabeth," Ava's mother declares.

I backtrack and take myself into my study, shutting the door quietly. "Hi," I say, sitting at my desk.

"We're here."

I sit up straight. "Where?"

"In London."

"What?" *Fuck.* "I mean, that's great." I laugh like a dickhead. "You didn't waste any time, did you?" They must have left Cornwall at the crack of dawn.

"Strike while the iron's hot," she says.

Or turn up and try to catch me . . . what? Drunk? Punching Matt? "Where are you staying?" I ask.

"The St. James's Hotel and Club."

"Nice."

"So, your address? We'll head over now."

Oh Jesus, this is not ideal. "Actually, I was heading out for a run shortly. I'll be around the royal parks—seems crazy not to meet up."

"And Ava?"

I look at the door. "She has some work stuff to catch up on." I slap my forehead with my palm. "Truth is, Mrs. O'Shea, I was hoping to meet you and your husband before I tell Ava you're here."

"Why?"

Lord, she's hard work. "I wanted to talk to you about something."

She gasps. "My God, she's pregnant, isn't she? That's why she's moved in."

I balk. "God, no." Someone slap me. Dan's obviously spoken to his parents about Ava's living arrangements. *Fucker*. "Would you mind? Meeting? I'm sure you've got plenty you want to know about me, and I know it'll make Ava uncomfortable if you're firing your questions at me while she's there."

She laughs. "God, you do know her well."

I smile. That feels good. "About an hour?"

"Call me when you're nearby."

"Thank you." I disconnect the call and stare at the wall. It really is quite bland. Needs . . . something. I tilt my head. Look down at my phone, thumbing through the pictures. All Ava. I smile, put Ava's dying phone on charge, and head up to the bedroom. I find her dressed. For work? *Shit.* She looks at me in the reflection of the mirror briefly before going back to applying her makeup. "Where are you going?" I ask, nervous.

"I'm going to work."

"No, you're not." I flinch. *Dickhead.*

"Yes," she counters, calm and collected. Determined. "I am." She brushes at her cheeks, and I don't miss the slight jar of her body as she stands tall again. Her back hurts. Another reason for her to stay home. But she would never admit she's uncomfortable.

"How's your back?"

"Sore."

I sink my teeth into my lip, searching for the words. God damn it, Amalie leads to my parents, my parents lead to Jake, Jake leads to Carmichael, Carmichael leads to Rosie . . .

I can't tell her about Amalie without turning out the whole dirty story.

"Where's my phone?" Ava asks, looking at me for an answer, her head slightly tilted.

"It's charging in my office."

"Thank you." Collecting her bag, she leaves, and her walking out on me feels so much worse than telling Ava about Amalie. I rush forward and jump in front of the doorway, blocking her escape, and she gasps, stepping back, looking up at me. I can see her body bracing to be manhandled.

"Let's talk," I blurt. "Please, don't go. I'll talk."

She can't hide her surprise. "You want to talk?"

Yes, and I'm as surprised as you. "Well, I can't fuck any sense into you," I say, moody. "So I guess I'll have to *talk* some into you."

"That is the conventional way of dealing with things, Jesse," she says on a sigh. Conventional? Since when have we been conventional?

"Yes, but my way is much more fun." I smile when I see her holding her own back. But she won't release it. Trying to be a grown-up, I expect. Or demonstrate control. Whatever. I absolutely cannot go back to fearing if we have a relationship left to salvage.

I get closer. It's tactical. And I hold her hands. That's tactical too. But I give her words to go with our super-charged energy. "I've never had to explain my life to anyone, Ava." Never wanted to either. "It's not something I relish the thought of talking about."

"I'm not marrying someone who refuses to open up," she says, soft but firm. "You keep holding information back then we end up in a huge mess."

"I didn't tell you things because I was scared you would run." And she did. Endlessly, and she's doing it now.

I'm not helping. Her sigh tells me so. "Jesse, I've found out some pretty shocking stuff," she says. "And I'm still here."

"Ava, you know more about me than any other living soul. I've never been close to anyone, not like you." And I've definitely not *wanted* to be close to anyone. "You don't tend to get caught up in conversation and life stories when you're just fucking someone." Did I say that out loud? Her flinch says yes.

"Don't say things like that."

I shouldn't talk at all. It doesn't get me anywhere. Someone wise once said actions speak louder than words. I like that someone. But I reluctantly accept that Ava is actually right. I don't want her to be, but she is. I've got to open up about that part of my life. It just hurts. It hurts so bad.

I take us to the bed and sit us down. "The last time I saw my parents it didn't go particularly well," I begin, trying to lock away the emotions and give it to her as it is. "My sister was a bit underhanded and set us up to meet. My father had a rant, my mother got upset, and I got very drunk." My go-to solution at the time to escape. "So you can imagine how it ended." Messy. Really fucking messy. From what I can remember, anyway. Which is a lot of swearing. A lot of accusations. A lot of truths. I yelled at them, and they yelled back. Actually, Dad yelled. Mum mostly cried.

Ava's expression harbors sympathy that I just don't deserve and feel guilty accepting. "So your sister obviously wants you to make amends."

"Amalie is a bit stubborn. She won't accept that too much has happened, too many harsh words exchanged over the years." In truth, she was too young to see how things were when Jake and I were teenagers. Shielded by the friction, by both of our parents, and by us. "It's not fixable, Ava," I say, the very words crushing me. To them, I'm a huge disappointment. I can't be that to Ava. I can't ever have her look at me like they looked at me. Like I'm a letdown. A failure.

"But they're your parents." She looks so sad. I could hug her for it. "You're their son."

I stopped being my parents' son the day I took Jake drinking and they lost him. And that was half the problem. *They* lost him. It only compounded the fact that I wasn't good enough. It should have been me under that car. I know they agree.

"That invitation only arrived because my sister sent it behind my parents' backs. They don't want me there. Their address was scrubbed off and replaced with Amalie's."

She thinks for a moment, her eyes darting across her thighs. "But Amalie obviously wants you there." She looks up at me. So keen to fix everything. "Don't you want to see her get married?"

God, I'd be a mess, so it's probably best I'm not there. My little sister? I can't promise I wouldn't be throwing out a few warnings to this Dr. David too, which, of course, I have no right to do. "I would love to see my little sister get married, but I also don't want her wedding ruined. If I go, it will end only one way. Trust me." And while Ava keeps me relatively stable and away from the booze, I'm terrified my parents could be a trigger, and then *nothing* could hold me back.

"What happened to make it like this?" she asks, holding my hands tighter. Encouraging me?

God, what can I give her? "You already know that Carmichael left me The Manor when he died. Of course, when I told you that, you thought it was a hotel." I show my lingering amusement at that fact, and Ava grimaces. "Things were already strained after they moved to Spain and I chose to stay with Carmichael." Because . . . Rosie. "I was eighteen, living at The Manor, and I understand that it was any parents' worst nightmare." I laugh, uncomfortable, but I push on, spilling my past. Or as much of it as I can without talking about Jake, Rosie, and Lauren. The former two, dead, the latter locked up somewhere safe where she can't try to kill me again. "I slipped into a playboy lifestyle and fell harder when Carmichael died." And Rosie. And Rebecca. I swallow down the lump in my throat and look at my thumbs rubbing fast circles across the tops of Ava's hands. And I notice . . . her lack of ring. I look at the nightstand and see it is still where I placed it when we returned from the hospital. She hasn't put it back on?

I ease off before I give her friction burns. There are enough welts on her body right now. "If it wasn't for John, there probably wouldn't be The Manor." I don't mention Sarah. That would be fatal. "He practically ran it while I gorged on too much drink and too many women."

"Oh." She blinks, her long lashes fluttering in surprise.

"I calmed it down"—when Rosie was born—"but my parents offered me an ultimatum; The Manor or them. I chose The Manor." I chose Rosie. "Carmichael was my hero, I couldn't sell up." And then it all went to shit.

"Your parents knew you were carrying on . . ." Ava fades off, thinking how she should word it. There's no way to sugarcoat it. "Well, like you were."

Fucking. Drinking. Debased hedonism. "Yes, and they predicted it so, you see, they were right, and they've never let me forget it." Ever. It's their ace card, the one that's drawn and wielded like a weapon. Nothing's ever mentioned about my time with Rosie. The relationship I had with my girl. She was everything. A reason. And then there was no reason. Only regret and pain. "I've lived a pretty sordid lifestyle," I whisper, seeing it's hurting her to hear this, but knowing it's what she needs. What *we* need. "I admit that. Carmichael was the family black sheep. No one spoke to him, and the family disowned him. They were embarrassed of him, and then he died and I filled the shoes of the black sheep. My parents are ashamed of me. That's it." *And please, can we now stop talking about it?* I've never heard myself say those words. I'm sure if I had gone to therapy like John demanded, it would have come up. But my therapy was liquid.

"They shouldn't be ashamed of you."

"It's just the way it is." I stole their son.

"So you've known John a long time?" she asks, and I feel the pressure lift, her focus now on the big man. My fucking hero. I'll talk about that miserable motherfucker all day long.

"Yes, a long time." I smile. "He was great friends with Carmichael."

"How old is he?"

Good question. I have no fucking idea. Birthdays in our relationship simply don't exist. But I know he and Carmichael were on the rugby team together at college. "Fifty-ish, I think."

"Well, how old was Carmichael?"

"When he died?" Too young. "Thirty-one."

Her big brown eyes become even bigger. "That young?"

"There were ten years between my father and Carmichael. He was an afterthought on my grandparents' part." And the bane of my father's life. Smarter, better looking, more popular.

"Oh, so, there was only ten years between you and Carmichael too?"

I smile. "He was more like a brother." An older brother to me and Jake, although I was arguably closer to him. Jake was too busy being controlled by our parents.

"How did he die?"

The pressure is back. I can't lie about this. "In a car accident."

Her whole body deflates, sadness dragging it down. Then her eyebrows pinch and her eyes drop to my stomach.

To my scar.

Oh.

And yet, I don't put her straight. Instead, I let her believe what her imagination's telling her, because it's a fuck load better than the truth. I get her onto my lap. Enough talking. "Don't go to work." Pushing my nose to hers, I give her pleading eyes. I've talked. Told her so much, way more than I ever thought I could. She can't possibly claim she doesn't know me now. "Stay at home and let me love you. I want to take you out for dinner this evening." *With some special guests.* "I owe you some special time."

I've got her. She swoons, gets closer to me, smells me, feels me. "I go back to work tomorrow."

"Fine." Now, onto the second part of my plan. But there's not a chance in hell she'll let me get away with leaving Lusso after I've made such a fuss about her staying home from work. "Right, I'm going for a run"—she will never stop me running—"to alleviate some of the pressure that my challenging temptress presents me with." I smile wide. She looks at me like I'm mad. "And then we snuggle all afternoon and go out for dinner. Deal?"

"Deal, but I challenge the middle part of that statement and trump it with a deluded god."

I'll be her god all day long. Deluded or not. I drop to the mattress, taking Ava with me, and give her a demand she doesn't mind. To kiss me. And she does. Of course she does. Sweet thing, she likes me to be bossy when it suits her. I relinquish her lips—it's really fucking hard—and ease her onto the sheets beside me before I get carried away. I have some parents to pacify.

I go to the dressing room, getting into my running kit. Not ideal for meeting the parents, but I can hardly go running in a three-piece. I do go to the bathroom, however, and check my hair.

"Have a snooze," I say, going to the bed and dropping kisses all over her face. "And if you're lucky, I might indulge you later."

"Indulge me now." She grabs my T-shirt and hauls me down, and I bury my fists in the mattress, stopping her.

Fuck. Me.

"Later," I promise, wrenching myself away and turning her onto her front. I swat her arse, relish her squeal, slip her engagement ring off the nightstand, and head out, swiping up my keys from the table as I pass.

Nervous.

As.

Shit.

51

I DON'T NEED to worry about identifying her mother. She's the bloody spitting image, just older. But not that much older. Jesus Christ, she looks mid-forties, perhaps. It's a kick in the gut, because there are clearly less years between Ava's mother and me than there are between Ava and me. I blow out my cheeks, reality hitting hard. No wonder Ava was so reserved about me meeting them. *Cradle-snatcher*.

I walk through the long, narrow café just off Bury Street, my eyes trained on Ava's mum. I can't see her father as his back's to me. When I reach the table, I swallow, clear my throat, and take a breath. "Mr. O'Shea. Mrs. O'Shea." They both look up from their menus and then down at my shorts. I feel like a total tit. "Your daughter's smart," I rush to explain. "It was the only way I could sneak out and not raise suspicion." Ava's mother just stares at me, and I can't help but think that she's wowed. Standard. Just not ideal when it's your soon-to-be mother-in-law. But, shame on me, it's an advantage. I motion down my front. "So excuse the state of me."

Ava's mother's eyes bug a little. "Excused."

And her father's eyes climb my body to my face. "You're quite an impressive specimen, aren't you?" he says dryly, and I laugh, while Ava's mother gasps.

"Jesse Ward." I extend my hand.

"Joseph O'Shea." He accepts, giving it a firm shake. "And this is Elizabeth."

"Pleasure."

"Please, sit." He motions to a chair next to him, and I lower to it. All eyes on me. "Coffee?"

"Sure." I wave a waiter over and order the first thing that rolls off my tongue. "Cappuccino, please. No chocolate." I frown at myself.

"Oh, that's Ava's go-to." Elizabeth smiles. She's far warmer in person than she was on the phone. "I'll have a latte, please, and Joseph will have a flat white." She hands the waiter the menu on a smile and looks straight at me. "So, what do you do, Jesse?"

I own the most elite, exclusive sex club in the British Isles. I'm clearing my throat again, resting my elbows on the table. "I own a hotel."

They both sit back, interested. "Here in London?" Elizabeth asks, and I just know she's also silently asking how much that must be worth.

"In The Surrey Hills, actually. It's a manor. Been in the family for many years."

"A manor?" She looks at Joseph, seeing his reaction. He doesn't have one. He's a quiet man. Only speaks when he has something worthwhile to say. I like him. Elizabeth? She's high-maintenance. Endearing, but I can tell she's going to have an opinion on a lot. It's fine. I'll humor her, so long as she humors me.

"So how did you meet Ava?" Joseph asks, turning slightly in his chair, not facing me, but making sure I know I have his attention. I expect he vies for attention a lot when his wife's around.

The waiter returns with our coffees and I smile my thanks, stirring. "She designed my penthouse."

Ava's mother's cup clangs. "You have a penthouse too?"

"Elizabeth," Joseph sighs.

"I'm just getting the facts, Joseph."

I smile into my cup as I take a sip. "I have a penthouse too," I confirm.

"You're wealthy."

"Jesus Christ," Joseph breathes, shaking his head. "You'll have to excuse my wife."

"Loaded." I don't beat around the bush, and Ava's dad laughs at my candid reply. "I don't mean to be blunt, but you're here to find out as much as possible about the man your daughter has moved in with, and time isn't exactly on our side." So let us get to the point. I lean forward, serious, looking between them. "I love your daughter. I don't know what you need from me to prove my intentions are honorable, but whatever that is, I'll give it to you."

"I'd ask if you can look after her," Joseph says, laughing. "But that's been proven."

I inwardly flinch, seeing the mess of Ava's back in my mind. Seeing her in a hospital bed. "It would be easier to look after her if she didn't insist she *doesn't* need looking after."

"Ha!" Joseph looks at his wife. "Not like her mother then."

"I'm sorry, you've lost me."

"Elizabeth doesn't mind being kept at all, do you, darling?"

She scowls. "You're a traditional man, Joseph. Don't tell me you don't like me being at home keeping the house, raising the children."

"Our children left home years ago."

"You want me to get a job now?" She looks plain horrified.

"God, no. You're too busy with you endless ladies' lunches."

I chuckle, and Joseph looks at me out the corner of his eye with a small smile. I *really* like him. Traditional. "I will look after Ava, Mr. O'Shea."

"Joseph, please. Call me Joseph."

"Joseph," I say, looking at Ava's mother. She nods. Elizabeth it is.

"So Ava's moved in with you," Joseph says, turning his coffee cup.

"Made sense, since she doesn't have her own place and I have . . . well, two."

"A hotel and a penthouse," Elizabeth says quietly, so obviously mentally calculating how much that must equate to.

"Everything I have is hers."

"Everything?" she asks.

Heart, body, soul, and money. But we all know Elizabeth is talking about money when she says everything. "I don't need money," I tell them. "I need your daughter. I've spent many years alone, lonely, getting unsolicited attention that money brings. All I want is Ava, so if I had to give away every penny I have, I would if it meant I could just keep her."

"Don't do that," Elizabeth blurts, and then recoils, as if she can't quite believe she's said it. Joseph shakes his head in despair. "I mean, it's not necessary."

I smile down at my cup. "She's my world. I don't know how else I can express that."

"You don't need to." She swoons, hand on chest and all. If only her daughter was as reciprocating.

I look at Ava's dad. His eyebrows are high, as if he knows what's coming. "Joseph, I . . ." My eyes fall to my coffee and dart. How the fuck do I ask this?

"Yes."

I look up. "What?"

"I said yes." He reaches for my hand and pats it a few times before returning to his coffee. And that's that. I have his blessing. I'm floored. Thrilled too, naturally, but really fucking floored.

"Oh my God, our girl is getting married," Elizabeth sings, silencing the café.

"Well, let's be quiet, shall we?" Joseph says. "Since our girl doesn't know it yet."

I refocus on my coffee. Guilty. She knows . . . but doesn't know. "I'd love it if you would come to dinner at ours tonight."

"The manor?" Elizabeth asks, and I cough.

"No." Jesus Christ. "The penthouse." I need to clear out The Manor before Ava's parents come within a mile of it. "We'll get married at The Manor."

"Oh my," she breathes, relaxing back in her chair. "What a treat."

I smile. She has no idea.

. . .

I leave Joseph and Elizabeth to finish their coffees and head back to my car, an unstoppable grin on my face. Everything's coming together. Everything will be okay.

I cross the road and find a traffic warden standing beside my car taking a picture of the registration. I look down at my watch to check how long I've been here. Barely over an hour.

"I paid to park," I say as I approach.

He hardly looks up. "Only for an hour." He peeks at his watch. "Your ticket expired at twelve fifteen."

I look at my own watch. "It's twelve eighteen."

"It's twelve twenty, according to mine."

"What is that?" I ask, trying to see his wrist.

He looks up. "What?"

"Your watch. What make?" It looks like it came out of a Christmas cracker.

He peeks down at it. "A Casio, I think."

"Well, mine's a Role—" What the fuck am I doing? "You know what, give me the ticket." I hold out my hand on a smile, and he cocks a brow that's definitely wary. "Can you speed things up?"

He goes back to his little computer, and I sigh, resting my arse on the bonnet of my car and sending a few messages about tonight's plans. I smile while I do that too.

"Sir."

I look up and find the warden looking past me on a furrow of his brow. "Do you know that woman?"

"What woman?" I ask, looking around. I see no one.

"That woman, there. She's . . ." He pouts, stepping to one side then the other, searching the street, and I find myself mirroring him, my cheerfulness fading. "Oh, she's gone."

"She was looking at me?" I don't want to sound like a dick, but many women *look* at me.

The warden looks me up and down. "I expect you're used to it."

He holds the ticket out and nods to my car. “Young, fit”—he waves at the Aston—“rich.”

I laugh and take the ticket. “I’ve never been issued compliments at the same time as a parking fine.”

“First time for everything, sir. Have a good day.”

“You too.” I hop in my car and pull out and, naturally, I have another scan of the street, my skin prickly. It’s as if my mind can’t allow me to have this newfound freedom from the shit that’s always held me prisoner in guilt and grief.

52

She sleeps for England, all day long. Cathy's left one of her famous lasagnas on the counter with a note to freeze it if we don't eat it today. My stomach growls at the sight of it. I'm hungry, but we have dinner plans tonight, so I serve myself a small portion and put the rest in the freezer. I go to my office and sit at my desk while I eat it, running over my words, my plan, but I'm constantly distracted by the bare wall before me, and not for the first time I wonder why Ava never had anything hung there when it so obviously needs it. I open my laptop, smiling, and google *Bespoke Wallpaper*.

A few hours later, I've uploaded all of my favorite pictures of Ava and I have what can only be described as a masterpiece on my screen. Happy, I order way too may rolls. Then I search for a wedding planner while I eat. We're going to need one if I'm going to turn this around as fast as I want to.

After I've put my plate in the dishwasher, I head upstairs, brush my teeth, strip down, shower and shave, and by the time I'm done, she's *still* asleep. I stand at the end of the bed, watching her as I dry off. "Ava, baby, it's time to wake up." Her forehead bunches, her lashes flutter. "Good morning, baby."

She looks around the bedroom a little disorientated. "It's not, is it?"

"No, it's five o'clock." I drop the towel and join her on the bed. "You've been asleep all afternoon. How does your back feel?"

"It feels okay," she says, rubbing into the sheets. "I'm a lazy arse, wallowing in bed all afternoon on a workday."

"Just think"—I welcome her into my chest when she shuffles closer—"if you gave up work, you could do this every day. How perfect would that be?" I look down at the back of her head on a smile, feeling her hot breath on my chest.

"For you. Perfect for you because you'll know where I am all the time." She kisses my pec.

"Exactly. You could come to work with me, and we would never have to be apart."

Another kiss. "You'd get sick of me."

"Not possible." I suppress a groan, trying to contain myself. She's far from ready for me to have my way. But didn't I promise her earlier? Yes, but . . . parents. "Are you going to let me take you out for dinner?"

Her hand drifts down my torso, and I know I am absolutely done for. "Or we could just stay right here."

"Nothing would please me more, but I would like to take you out." Time isn't on my side. "Do you mind?" Poor thing looks completely mystified, and my dick is bereft. It's been two days since I had her, and I don't mind admitting I'm getting a bit desperate. My balls swell, agreeing. "But then again, I've not been inside you for way too long. That is not acceptable." I take her to her back, watching for any signs of discomfort. Nothing. Only signs of want and lust. "Baby, sleepy sex is off the menu for a while, so I'm just going to fuck you. Any objections?"

"You're asking if you can fuck me?"

She's definitely suspicious. "Watch your mouth." I devote some attention to her face, kissing away her frown. "I'm trying to be reasonable."

"Don't be!"

I smile into her skin but make sure it's gone when I pull back to look at her. "You don't want me to be reasonable?"

She shakes her head, hardly able to admit it. "No."

"So, let me clarify this"—I push my hips forward; she whimpers —"I'm a little confused. You really don't want me to be reasonable?"

"No," she yelps, biting down on her lip.

I walk my fingers down her skin to the crease at the top of her thighs, stroking across the lace of her underwear, relishing the feeling of her becoming stiff beneath me. "I see." I bite my lip, pushing past the material and slipping through her drenched pussy. "Carte Blanche?"

"Yes!"

The power is mine again, and it feels so fucking good. It feels like us. "Well, now you're just giving me mixed signals." I feel her desperation as well as I can hear it. "I love how wet you are for me."

"Please, Jesse."

And she begs. Yes, she begs.

I push my finger into her, inhaling with her as I do. "Soft, hot, and made just for me." I pull the cups of her bra down. "My mark is fading." I latch on and start refreshing the bruise. "We don't want you forgetting who you belong to, do we?"

"Ohhhhhh."

"Do we, Ava?" I work her, bite at her boobs, at her flesh, and she gives me all the sounds as I give her all the words she craves when she's at the mercy of our passion. Perfect. She comes hard, all over my hand, her fingers digging into my shoulders, her mouth hungry for mine.

I don't give her a chance to recover, my own blood raging, my dick painfully hard. Not ideal when we're seeing her parents. I need a release.

I help her off the bed and lift her to my chest, and she wraps her arms and legs around me, clinging on, avoiding the center of my back. It doesn't hurt. Nothing hurts right now. It's a first.

"Where are we going?" she asks as I walk us out.

"My office." I'm yet to have her on my desk, and since I can't have her on her back, it's the perfect opportunity.

"Wait," she blurts.

"What's the matter?" I stop at the door, looking at her in question.

She points back at the dressing room. "Take me to the wardrobe."

She wants me to fuck her in the dressing room? "Why?"

"Because we need a condom."

My recoil is unstoppable. "What?"

"We *need* a condom."

"I don't have any."

"You do. In the wardrobe."

Oh fuck. She knows. Or is she just suspicious and hoping I'll confess? Never. I'm struggling to believe I did it myself. She's not taking her pills right now. She's missed plenty over the weeks. But a condom? "Ava, I don't do condoms with you."

"Then we don't have sex."

Say what now? "Excuse me?" Why the hell does she look so amused? *Jesus Christ.* Was she searching for her pills or condoms? Does she think I took her pills, or doesn't she? She doesn't appear all too mad if she thinks I did. Does that mean she's open to babies? I am so fucking confused. And now she's saying we're going to abstain. Because, assumingly, she doesn't want to get pregnant. "You heard."

And what did I hear, because I'm getting all kinds of mixed messages here? "For fuck's sake." I go back to the dressing room and get the condoms. "This is ridiculous." A fucking condom? I would say I'd pull out, but I could never deprive myself of the incredible feeling of coming inside her, and then she'd be pissy. Or would she? I don't even fucking know anymore.

"You know, my mark is fading too," she says as I carry her down to the study.

"It is?"

"It needs freshening up." She's trying to appease me. God love her, it's working.

"My girl is possessive. Knock yourself out, baby." I grunt when she bites at me, letting her make her mark. "I want to take you right here so whenever I have to work, I will see you spread naked on my desk." I laugh to myself. Whenever have I *worked* in here? That's about to change. I lower her and take a seat, pulling her knickers down and dropping them into my top drawer. She raises a brow. "You've just come all over them. I want to be able to smell you too. Spread your legs."

She opens up and I stare at her pussy—her wet, throbbing pussy. My cock lurches as I remove her bra and put it with her knickers. "Lean back on your hands." I relax in my chair and Ava follows my instruction, although with some reluctance. What is that? "Why are you nervous?"

"I'm not."

I look up at her. She's definitely nervous. Is she worried about having sex with me? Is that because of her back? The protection situation? "I love you," I say, and she visibly softens. Like she needed to hear it?

"I love you too."

"Don't ever doubt it."

"I won't." A swallow, a quick glance down my body. "Have you finished with your observations?"

"No." I spread her legs farther. "I'm evaluating my assets." I get comfortable again, like I have all the time in the world. Which I don't.

"I'm an asset?"

"No, you're *my* asset." I know she's admiring her asset too. "Would you like to hear my verdict?"

"I would."

"I'm a very rich man." I give her a cheeky half-smile and take her ankles, putting her feet on my shoulders, improving an already incredible view. "Don't hold back on me." I kiss her ankle and she jerks.

And I make her watch me as I make her come again, her body beautifully receptive to my touch. "There it is." She gasps up at the ceiling, her chest heaving, and I'm out of the energy and patience I need to continue proving who has the power right now.

Her.

Always, her.

"Come here." I pull her onto my lap and hold my cock. "Lift."

"Condom."

"Ava." I strain out her name, my dick pulsing in my hold. "Don't ask me to wear a condom."

She pants, holding firm, refusing to sink down. I don't know where the fuck she's getting the strength. "Jesse, do you realize how lucky we are that I'm not already pregnant?"

Lucky? And it isn't yet confirmed beyond doubt, is it? And now I'm thinking about it, as I stare at her boobs, they look a little rounder. And this feeling I have in my bones? I can't shake it. My gut is telling me she's pregnant. So what does it matter if we use a condom or not?

My dick weeps, it screams, begs for contact. She doesn't give in, and I look at her. Something passes between us, a silent message.

She knows.

She knows what I've done.

She takes a condom and kneels between my legs, holding me as she slides it on, glancing up as me every now and then, expecting me to halt this. I can't. I need to be inside her too bad.

I help her back onto my lap, and kiss her chest, her nipples. Her body is tightening again. "Lower gently." I take her arse and encourage her down. We both moan. Both shake. She brings her forehead to mine and pants in my face.

"Hold still." I could come at any moment. "You feel so perfect around me." Even with a condom between us. "How long do you think you could stand this without responding?"

I kiss her. She kisses me back. I turn away. "Not long then."

"You're denying me."

"It's a challenge."

"*You're* a challenge." She tries to capture my lips again. I deny her. She tries to move on me, I hold down on her hips firmer. She growls and gives up.

"You need me," I whisper.

"I need you." She swoops in and tries to kiss me again. I'm

having none of it. "How would you feel if anyone stopped you from kissing me?" she asks.

"Deadly."

Her eyes sparkle triumphantly as she thrusts down. "Me too." Circles.

Fuck. Every muscle quakes, every vein throbs. "Who has the power, Ava?" I ask, my voice hoarse, my throat tight.

"You." Another subtle grind from her, another hard swallow from me.

I love how she humors me. "Do you want me to fuck you?"

"Yes," she whispers, raising slightly in invitation, and I smash upward, meeting her as she comes down. "Like that?" I don't give her a chance to recover, hitting her hard again.

And I fuck her, in full control of her pleasure, and she obeys every order. Takes every pound. Holds back when I tell her not to come. I push her boundaries, and she takes it all.

"I love you," she says, drowsy, exhausted, as I thrust on, watching her on my lap, her boobs bouncing.

"I love you too, baby." I slow my pace, easing off on the power, seeing she's reached her limit, and hold the back of her head, feeling her breathlessness on my skin. "Shall we come together?"

She nods and drags her mouth across my cheek to my lips when I demand her to kiss me, and I roll myself into her, tussling with her tongue as she adores me with less vigor. I hum. "You're delicious. I can feel you tightening around me. It feels so good."

"*You* feel good."

Shit. "Come for me," I order, grinding into her, and she instantly jerks and goes stiff in my arms. My dick bursts, tingles riddling my body. "Oh, Jesus." I have to stop, the sensitivity too much, my body trembling to deal with it. "You're amazing," I pant, shuddering, my cock lunging inside of her, filling her. But not filling her.

"That was so good." She kisses me, but I'm too wiped out to respond. "It wasn't so bad, was it?"

"No, it wasn't," I admit. "But it's still something between us."

"You want to trample the condom." She smiles against my mouth. Cheeky.

"I do." At least she's still talking to me. "You need to get ready or we'll be late."

"Where are we going?" She locks down on my lap, becoming heavier. "I'm comfy."

If I didn't have to move, I wouldn't. But I have to. "For dinner. I made a reservation." I pull her lips off my chest and her face up. "Shower."

"Let me love you."

"Ava," I groan, as she disappears back into my neck, and I pull her out before I succumb and hold her on my lap with firm hands. The bruise on her chest glows at me, fresh and bold. "You'll always have this," I say, tracing the edge. "Always."

"You should have your name tattooed on my forehead." She smiles as she studies her own handiwork on my pec. "And then there will be no mistaking who I belong to."

"Not a bad idea. I like it." I get up and she clings on, letting me carry her to the bedroom. I get her on her front ready to rub some more cream into her skin. I'll do it again after her shower. And then before bed too. I pull off the condom, throw it away, and sit myself on Ava's backside. Her skin's dry, no doubt from rubbing into the sheets. I squeeze some cream out and she gasps, her head snapping up.

"Sorry, this might be cold," I say, smiling when she throws a dirty look over her shoulder before settling and getting comfortable. I'm having a lovely time, looking after her, listening to her tell me how much she loves me, how attracted she is to me, how she'll keep me forever. Then like a bolt out of the blue, "Where are you hiding my pills?"

I freeze, my satisfied smile dropping, my eyes shooting up her skin to the back of her head. "What are you talking about?" Thank God she can't see my face right now. My heart starts pounding nervously.

"I'm talking about the fact that my contraceptive pills have recently been growing legs and running away and it's only been happening since I met you." She sounds so calm and together. It's more than I deserve, and yet I can't bring myself to admit it.

I start to move my hands again, realizing they're still motionless on her skin. "Why would I do that?"

"I'm not going anywhere, if that's what you're worried about."

I laugh, a laugh of rich humor. "No, you're not." I don't know how I should take this whole, odd interaction.

"It's fine," she sighs. "I'll go to the doctors to replace them. You'll just have to wear a condom until I can restart my course."

I scowl at her back. "I don't like wearing condoms with you."

"We won't be having any sex then."

"Watch your mouth," I grumble, and a silence falls, while I massage her back and Ava stares across the room, quiet. Fuck me, my head could explode. So, so calm. Accepting. Is she now owning my crazy too? "You okay?" I ask, and she blinks, coming back into the room.

"Fine." Flexing her shoulder blades, she groans. "How long has Cathy worked for you?"

She wants to change the subject? Fine by me. "Nearly ten years."

"She's fond of you."

"She is." Probably through sympathy, I expect. She thinks I need looking after.

"Does she know about The Manor? Ouch!"

Shit. I lift my hand from the particularly angry welt, apologizing repeatedly, kissing her between her wounds, feeling fucking awful.

"It's fine." She strains the words. "I'm fine. Unravel your boxer shorts."

I raise my brows. Sarcasm. I lift off her arse and slap it. "Don't be clever."

She accepts my scorn and proceeds to pick my brain about Cathy, The Manor, whether she knows about it. "Yes, she knows. It's not some secret society, Ava. There are no cloak and daggers. You're done. Up you get."

"You kept it a secret from me." She sits on the edge of the bed and rolls her shoulders.

"That's because I was falling hard and fast in love with you, and it scared me to death to think you would run away from me if you found out." I rub the cream into my hands. "And you did."

"It was a bit of a shock. I knew you were experienced, but I didn't anticipate it was because you owned a sex club that you utilized excessively." Her face screws up, her disgust back, and I wonder if she'll ever get past that part of my past.

"Hey." I crowd her, pushing her down to the bed and reminding her that I am a different man now. One that's hopelessly in love with her. "Let's not revisit old news. It's all about us now, and tomorrow, and the next day, and then the rest of our lives."

"Okay." Her smile is glorious. She likes that plan. "Kiss me."

"I'm sorry. Who has the power?"

"You do."

"Good girl." She lurches up, and with one swirl of her tongue, I'm hers and she proves who, in fact, has the power. But, fuck it, I'm pushing time already. I rip our mouths apart. She moans. "I'm ignoring you." It'll be game over if I don't, and I can't have us both anything less than perfectly together when we see her parents. And, preferably, dressed. "Wear your new cream dress." I go to the dressing room and find my navy suit and ponder for way too long over what color shirt to wear. I decide to go bold. Not in color but in choice. Pink.

I get dressed and leave Ava in the bedroom. By the look of her current state of readiness, I have a good half hour to make the calls I need to make. Starting with Jay. I want to see the other footage from the bar.

It rings and rings and rings, and I check the time, accepting he's probably at work. So I leave a message to call me back. I can't go throwing accusations around, can't annihilate Van Der Haus, without solid proof. I call John to check in, and to also check something else. "Will you do me a favor?" I ask.

"Depends what it is."

"Check your phone and see if any messages were sent to Ava last night."

"What?"

"Ava said she got a message from you saying she should go to The Manor."

"I sent her no message." He sounds defensive. "Why the fuck would I tell her to come to The Manor when I know you're about to either drink of get your sorry arse whipped?"

I tilt my head, palm up. "Exactly."

There's a brief silence. Then a rush of air. Realization. "You think—"

"Ava *thinks*. Did you have your phone with you?"

"I can't fucking remember. It was a bit of a stressful day. She thinks Sarah texted her from my phone?"

"Do you think she would?" I ask, hating that my gut says yes. I don't want to believe her cruelty could dip to such lows. I also don't want to consider the repercussions if it turns out she has.

"I don't know," John admits.

"Me neither."

"Have you seen the message?"

"No. I'm wondering if Ava's got mixed up." Like John said, the past day has been a blur. Fuck, the whole weekend. And there's no denying my head's spinning—seeing things, hearing my brother. "If it turns out it was her, John, that will be the end, you know that, don't you?" I've given that woman the benefit of the doubt too much. Let things slide because of my loyalty to Carmichael. I can't leave her with the freedom to destroy what I have with Ava.

"I know that," he admits reluctantly. I don't know how we always manage to feel sorry for Sarah. She's a vindictive bitch. She's also deeply broken. And that's probably why I've put up with her over the years. Because it was me who broke her.

"Okay, I've got to go, I've got dinner with Ava's parents."

"No shit."

"Yes shit." I smile, big and wide, though the miserable fucker can't see it. "I'm taking your advice."

"What advice?"

"Doing things the right way."

"You already did the thing."

"I'm re-doing it." I go to hang up and quickly put the phone back to my ear when I remember something. "Hey, John, how old are you?"

"Fuck off." He hangs up and I look at my phone incredulously.

"Charming." I lower to a stool and try Jay again, and this time he answers. "Anything?"

"The camera's down," he says, and I roll my eyes. "I've asked the barmen who were on that night if they saw anything untoward."

"And?"

"Nothing."

I deflate. "The guy at the bar."

"In the suit? I assume he's the problem here. Who is he?"

I laugh. "I haven't got time to explain." Just thinking of that snake brings on a murderous sweat. Not tonight.

I'm nearly knocked off my stool when Ava walks into the kitchen looking like a gorgeous, shimmering goddess. *Fuck . . . me.* That beauty will soon be my wife. And judging by the way she's taking me in with delighted eyes, she'll be absolutely fine about me being her husband once she sees her parents are fine with it.

I invite her onto my lap, her face now curious as she walks over and puts herself between my legs. "So, what can you tell me other than that?" I ignore Ava's interest and kiss her frown away. "It's fucking convenient that the other camera's broken. Have you checked the footage from outside the bar?" Ava stills and scans my face, her look telling me to calm down. I'm calm. Perfectly calm.

"The one camera that's working is the footage you saw. Maintaining CCTV is expensive. Cameras break all the time. Some have glasses thrown at them. The manager can't afford to replace them constantly. I'll keep digging."

"Fine, let me know what you find." I cast my phone aside, scowling, thinking, wondering. "It's a fucking joke."

"You think it was Mikael in the footage, don't you?" Ava says quietly.

"Yes, I do."

"Do you think that Mikael drugged me?"

"I don't know, Ava." I sigh. I *need* proof.

"It's a bit farfetched, isn't it?"

"He hates me. He knows you're my Achilles heel. He's been waiting for this."

"Should we go to the police?" she asks, facing me. She looks so worried, finding it hard to comprehend. Me too, to be honest. It's the lowest of blows, unbelievable, and yet I saw him with my own eyes.

"No, I'm dealing with it."

She doesn't argue with me, and it's a fucking novelty. Because she's scared. God, how simple her life would be without me. "I should be walking away from you." I let my thoughts roll out of my mouth. "If I could bear it, I would."

She looks at me in horror. "What?"

Her aversion is a small consolation. "I've upset a lot of people, Ava." Jesus, the reality is, the weight of my guilt is lifting, but now I may have to deal with the repercussions. Ava's my weak spot. And she hasn't led the life I have. She's been sheltered to an extent. I've seen what people are capable of, therefore my worry is warranted.

"Shut up, don't say things like that."

"Ava, the drink, the women—"

"I said, don't. I don't need a reminder that there have been other women since I've met you."

I match her wince, apologizing. "I wish I could change everything, except you. You're the only right thing in my life, and I'm even making that all wrong."

My face is grabbed and pulled up. She's fuming. Really, really mad. "Don't."

"I don't know what I've done to deserve you."

"You reminded me."

Reminded her. God, the strength, the determination. It's potent. Why am I ruining what should be a wonderful evening? Dwelling on . . . everything. Surely now we're stronger than ever. And I'm about to make us even stronger. And Ava's flushed cheeks need to be flushed for another reason. *Get us back on track.* So I feel up her leg to her lace knickers. "I like your dress."

"I like my dress too." She holds my shoulders, and I jolt when I hear something hit the floor. Her bag.

I smile and collect some of her wetness and wipe it across her lips. "I'm a very lucky man." And then I kiss it off, tasting her gloss mixed with her desire.

"That color doesn't suit you," she whispers, wiping my mouth.

Puckering my lips, I feel the sticky remnants of her lip color. "No?" Her laugh is pure joy, and it brings untold joy to me too. "I want to dance with you," I declare as I turn on some music, totally random, quite inappropriate, but the upbeat tempo is perfect.

She smiles, unsure, questioning me, as I pull her close. And then she says, "You make me so happy," and I just know in this moment that she'll never leave me. I don't know whether it's just this moment, I truly hope not, but the feeling inside of completeness is strong, and I can see it in her too. Regardless of my transgressions. Regardless of her suspicions about her pills. She's here, and she's loving me with a fierceness equal to mine.

"I'm going to make you happy for the rest of my life, baby," I promise, because from this moment forward, I'm going to try my damned hardest to be more reasonable. Less crazy.

As soon as I know exactly what the deal is with Van Der Haus. Naturally, I'm making no promises on the reasonability vow. I won't get hung up on it, because I bet my gorgeous wife-to-be couldn't promise to be less defiant.

"Let's dance." I guide her out of the kitchen into the lounge, and I dance with my girl, twirling her, holding her, turning her, and her smile pumps me full of life. There's not a square inch of our home I don't dance her through, even out onto the terrace where London is happening down below. And we are happening up here, high above the city.

"What are we doing?" she asks, continuing to humor me, following my random steps.

"I don't know," I admit. "Something between a waltz and a quickstep, I think." Could be some tango in there too. Can't be sure. What I do know is that we're not winning any ballroom dancing competitions. But we're definitely both still *winning*.

Ava chuckles as I work us back into the kitchen, widening my smile, my eyes set firmly on her looking up at me. "I think I enjoy this just as much as being buried inside you."

"Really?" she gasps, shocked.

"No." What the fuck am I saying? "That's probably the stupidest thing I've ever said."

Her throat comes into my sights when she falls apart laughing, losing all strength in her muscles so I'm practically holding her up. It's too much to resist, and I home in on her, lifting her to me, relishing the feeling of her locking my waist in her curled legs. Then I just stare at her. I think about our journey. How fucking lucky I am. How I can't screw this up. She's given me a second chance.

I sit her on the counter, marveling at her small, unsure smile. Holding her face, I get as close as I can. "Who has the power, Ava?" I whisper.

My question exasperates her. It won't when she sees my point. "*You* do."

I shake my head mildly, and she withdraws slightly. "You're wrong."

"I am?"

"You are. *You're* the one with the power, baby."

She doesn't look like she agrees. "But you always insist it's *you* who holds the power."

Yes, and just the mere fact I bang on about it so much should be a clue. "I like you stroking my ego," I quip flippantly, and she's laughing again, filling my heart with happiness.

"Are you joking?"

"No." Her amusement disappears, and she's quickly mystified, scanning my face, waiting for what comes next. "I hold the power over your body, Ava," I say, not quite believing I'm exposing my weakness. "When those beautiful eyes are full of lust for me, *that's* when I hold the power." And to demonstrate, I touch her gently on the inside of her thigh, and as predicted, her back straightens, desire floods her eyes, and she's clinging to me. Perfect. I kiss her gently. "See." And step back, losing all contact. "The power's yours again."

I watch as she slowly comprehends what I've said. As she finally understands. I'm at her mercy. And I absolutely do not mind telling her. "That's why you fuck me senseless," she says, biting down on her lip. "Give me the countdown and demand I kiss you when I'm mad."

I laugh under my breath. Bang on the money. "Watch your mouth," I say softly, with no scorn at all, smiling like a crazy man. Because, and it's been proven endless times, when it comes to this woman, I am definitely, certifiably fucking crazy.

"You've completely exposed yourself." She laughs over her words. "I'm never going to let you touch me again."

My body folds in an instant, and the laughter that comes out of me is the richest, most genuine laughter I've ever heard from myself. My eyes pinch with tears, my stomach aches, and when I've finally composed myself, I find her watching on, delighted. She loves me laughing. And I fucking love *her*.

"Well, Mr. Ward," she says, casually. "Given how much sex we have, I'd say you're the majority shareholder of power in this relationship."

"Baby." I chuckle, off again, fighting for breath through my amusement. "We will *never* have enough sex."

She grins. "That makes you a very powerful man then." And she seems absolutely fine with that.

I sigh, lost in her beguiling brown eyes. "Oh Jesus, Ava. I love you so fucking much." I cup her cheeks in my hands. "Kiss me."

"Feeling weak?"

Oh, the sass. "I am." I tempt her, moving closer, a miniscule dash of contact, and she folds, kissing me deeply, giving me back the power, if only for a moment.

"Better?" she asks.

"Much." I have never been so content. "Come on, lady, we have a date." I get her down off the counter and quickly check my watch. *Shit*. They'll be waiting in the stairwell. I rush to get her bag and turn off the music, and it occurs to me that I haven't thought about how the hell I get Ava to come back up to the penthouse once we're downstairs. Maybe I leave something behind. Ask her to come get it? *Stupid.* I would never do that. I'd put her in the car and come back myself. "Ready?" *Think, think, think.*

"Oh, let me show you the message." Ava starts rooting through her bag.

"What message?"

"The one sent from John's phone." She quickly has her phone facing me, and I can see she's holding her breath. Nervous. I look at the screen. And withdraw. She wasn't imagining anything. She wasn't mistaken. That's definitely John's number. And the message?

He's fine, but you should probably come.

I was definitely not fine. Ava definitely shouldn't have come. John would agree on both counts. *What the fuck?* "I'll be dealing with this," I say reluctantly. Fuck, this isn't good. I don't even want to consider the carnage on the horizon. I put Ava's phone down, feeling my mood dipping. I mustn't let it. Not tonight. But tomorrow?

I'm about to walk us out when Ava's mobile starts dancing across the marble, and I instinctively look. Ruth Quinn. "Who's that?" I ask. It's a knee-jerk question, because Ava looks complete exasperated as she collects her phone to answer.

"A new client. A pain in the arse new client."

A client? No. I'm not about to let more clients get in the way. It's her day off. I take Ava's phone from her and put it back on the worktop. "No work today. Are you ready for our date?"

"Yes." Her smile, her delight. She is so ready, in her element, happy we're doing normal couple things. Except we'll never be a normal couple.

I link our arms and smile to myself, looking back at her phone on the counter. She'll need to come back to get it.

When we get to the elevator, I peek toward the door to the stairwell, then down at my watch, making sure there's not a chance of us bumping into her parents sneaking into the penthouse. It's close. I silently will the elevator to hurry the fuck up, feeling Ava's hand slip onto my arse under my jacket. She wants constant contact too. I bet that changes when she finds out her parents are here. And that sucks. But, I will be setting the standard. Making sure everyone in our lives knows the deal. "I should make you give me an apology fuck here and now," I say quietly, definitely not wanting her parents to hear that if they happen to be close enough to listen.

"Do I owe you an apology?"

"You do."

"What for?" I see her thinking hard, searching for her crimes. There are plenty, and I'm sure more to come.

"You owe me an apology for making me wait too damn long for you," I say, and she moves in closer, humming her happiness, as we step into the elevator when the doors open. I can't lie, the urge to have a quick fuck against the wall is fierce. Her parents are already getting in my way.

Unreasonable?

Not at all.

But I resist, and we reach the ground floor with both our clothes intact.

Clive kills me as we walk through the foyer, nodding like he's on some covert operation, avoiding Ava's eyes. And now . . .

"Oh, Kate rang," I say, pointing the fob at my car. "You should probably call her back."

"You answered my phone again?" Ava asks, going to her bag where her phone *isn't*. "Jesse, I've left my phone in the tower."

The tower? That makes me a knight in shining armor. Now, as I said, I would usually be a gent, put her in the car, and go get it for her. But today, I can't be a gent. I huff and puff and pull my car door open and, bless her, she looks apologetic. I'm such a dick. I give her my keys and tell her to hurry up, and as soon as she's back in the elevator, I go to Clive's desk. "You can come up now, Clive," I say over a laugh as he peeks around, checking the coast is clear. I slide his compensation across the desk, and he slips it straight into his hat. I look over my shoulder when I hear voices. Sam and Kate, but no Drew? "Where is he?" I ask, looking between them.

"A deal's gone south," Sam says. "He'll be late."

"Where is she?" Kate asks.

"She forgot her phone. Or, I made her forget it."

"Crafty. Are Elizabeth and Joseph up there?"

"Yes, waiting for her in the kitchen."

"Oh, I love it." Kate claps. "She's gonna shit her knickers." And then she launches herself at me, hugging me to death.

"Fuck," I blurt, my damn back exploding into flames. "Kate." I reach back and disconnect her vise-like arms from my back. "Ease up, for fuck's sake."

"Shit, sorry." She frees me. "You've done some crazy—"

"Okay." I hold up a hand. "Today is a good day. Yesterday never happened, okay?"

Sam smacks my arm. "Congratulations, mate."

I should rip him a new arsehole for being Kate's bitch yesterday, checking the coast was clear for Ava to escape The Manor, except I don't, because everything was okay in the end. "Thanks." I go to the elevator and hit the button, pulling in my jacket, taking a breath. "Let's do this."

"I spoke to Elizabeth earlier." Kate is like a jack-in-the-box. "She said you asked Joseph."

I smile. Not really, I didn't have to. "Listen, Ava's brother will be here soon."

"Dan?" Kate blurts. I look at her, curious. "I mean, sure, of course he'd be here."

Odd. "You okay?"

"Fine." She gives me a toothy smile as I step into the elevator.

"Will you give me fifteen minutes?" I ask. "Cathy and Luigi will be here soon too."

"Sure." Sam puts himself in a chair and pulls Kate down onto his lap, and the doors close, carrying me up to the penthouse. I check myself in the mirror. Fix my hair. Smooth down my suit. And then walk up and down the small space, one hand in my pocket, feeling at her ring.

Praying.

53

I TAKE the biggest breath when I leave the cart and before I walk into the penthouse. The first thing I hear is crying. Ava. Is that good or bad? Fuck, I don't know. I wander to the kitchen and find Elizabeth embracing her in a hug. She's smiling into her shoulder, looking far from worried. It's a relief. So why is Ava crying? I ponder that for a moment and come back to the same thing.

Emotion.

She's pregnant.

Elizabeth releases Ava and looks at her fondly. "You have sent me and your dad wild with worry these last few weeks," she scorns gently.

"I'm sorry." Ava rubs at her face. "I've had a crazy few weeks."

I laugh to myself. Crazy indeed.

"Hold up." Ava looks between her parents. "How did you really get in?"

She's only just wondering that? "I invited them," I say quietly, and all three sets of eyes come at me.

Ava looks pretty freaked out. Unsure. "You never said," she says, nervous, looking between her mum and dad and back to me.

"I didn't want to row over it," I tell her. *Because you would have found a way to stall again.* "They're here now."

I catch Elizabeth's eye, and I know, just by the way she's looking at me, I've won her over. It could be the penthouse. The Manor. My wealth. It could be Ava's dad having a word. It could be me looking dapper in my suit. Couldn't give a fuck.

Ava, completely blindsided, starts stuttering and stammering over her words, motioning to her parents. "Jesse, this is my mum and dad. Elizabeth and Joseph."

"We've met." She's about to have kittens, I just know it.

"What?"

"We've met." I can't help my smile, the questions flooding from her eyes as she looks at me with fear too. It brings home just how concerned she is. If they'll like me. Approve. I go to her, but I'm respectful and don't completely smother her, which is alien to me. "I didn't go for a run this morning."

She still looks shell-shocked. "You didn't?" she asks, and I shake my head. "You had your running kit on."

"I know." I look across to Elizabeth and Joseph, smiling, remembering both of their looks when they took in my shorts. "It's not what I would have chosen to wear to meet your parents, but desperate times."

"You're making up for it now, Jesse," Elizabeth says, reaching for my arm, rubbing it reassuringly. *Definitely* won her over. It's probably the money. Again, couldn't give a fuck. And what Elizabeth here is failing to realize is Ava is way more valuable than manors and penthouses.

"I'm sorry," Ava breathes. "I'm confused."

"Sit." I lead her to a stool. "I spoke to your mum late last night," I explain as I lower next to her. "She was understandably worried about you and asked me lots of question." I peek at Elizabeth, and she laughs, flapping a hand, like I'm being dramatic. I'm not. I'm so glad I took the reins on this. I would have hated Ava to have faced Elizabeth's initial coolness toward me. It would have made things so much harder.

"Nosey, isn't she?" Joseph says, finally speaking up.

"She's my little girl, Joseph."

"Anyway, I thought it was best for them to come and see for themselves that I'm not a raving loon, keeping you captive in our tower." *Go fuck yourself, Matt.* And, obviously, I didn't plan on them turning up so soon, but it's all worked out in the end. "So, here they are."

"Here we are!"

Ava looks at her mother, a little exasperated, a little alarmed. "So, you met them this morning?" she asks. "Why?"

Yeah, I can't tell her that right now. "I felt I needed to explain myself. Ava, neither of us anticipated each other, and for very different reasons. I know your parents' opinion counts for a lot to you, and as it means so much to you, it means a lot to me too. My priority is you. You're all that matters to me." I squeeze her hands. "I love you."

She looks at me with wide eyes. Speechless, I think.

"All any father wants is for their daughter to be taken care of," Joseph says, offering a hand. "I believe you'll do good."

I shake, firm and manly, making sure he knows how dedicated I am. I read him well. "It's my full-time job." I blink, surprised, when Ava bursts into laughter, and I turn an interested look her way. She knows I'm serious.

"Come here, you silly sod." Elizabeth claims Ava, pulling her away from me, and hugs her. I grit my teeth for her, feeling her pain, as her mum whispers in her ear, words of encouragement and support, I hope.

I look at Joseph. He rolls his eyes. "Right, are we eating or what?" he asks. "And I'm gagging for a pint."

"Do you mind if I use your bathroom, Jesse?" Elizabeth asks. I don't know her well, but I can see she's just gagging to look around. I'll indulge her.

"Sure." I motion to the doorway. "Do a right and an immediate right again. Knock yourself out."

"Pardon?"

I smile when Ava laughs, thrown back weeks to that Friday she walked into my office. "I'm sorry. Go for it. Like I said, right and right again. By the gym."

"Oh, thank you."

"So, what do you drive?" Joseph asks as I get Ava back, closer, putting her between my legs. I watch for Joseph's reaction and get nothing. It's a good sign.

"A DBS."

His eyes light up. "Aston Martin?"

I nod, storing the information away for use later. He's a petrol head. "That's it."

"Nice. And the hotel is in The Surrey Hills?"

"It is." I look at the back of Ava's head when she solidifies in my arms. "I'll show you one day, perhaps on your next visit." *Like in a few weeks when we get married.*

"Sure," he muses, looking around the kitchen. "Elizabeth loves anything luxury." Which is a massive advantage for me. "It's a nice place you have here."

"Thank you, but your daughter is responsible for that. I just bought it."

"So, this is the big project that stole all of your time?" he asks Ava. "You did a good job."

"Thanks, Dad." She's not relaxing in the least, so when I hear the door, I send her on her way to answer it, and she seems quite content with that.

"Who is it?" she asks, looking at me as she wanders off.

"I don't know. Go and see." I give my attention to Joseph. "That'll be Kate, Sam, and Dan."

"Oh, Kate. It will be nice to see her. Who's Sam?"

"One of my best friends."

He nods, taking another look around. "Ava designed all this?" he muses, clearly impressed. "I knew she was a talented girl, but this is something else."

"Talented and *really* driven."

He laughs. "And stubborn?"

"Yes," I gasp, so relieved to hear he's aware of the challenges I face.

"Well, you're in for a ride, let me assure you of that."

I laugh as a guy wanders into my kitchen, and I discreetly weigh him up. Ava's brother. Older than her. A good-looking bloke. "Dad," Dan says, bypassing me on the stool and greeting his old man.

"Hey, kid." Joseph gives him an affectionate hug and then motions to me. "This is Jesse."

Dan turns to me, all smiles, and offers his hand. "Nice to meet you."

"Face to face," I say, making sure it's remembered we've spoken, and Ava's parents clearly know because they knew Ava had moved in. Fuck, not liking her brother isn't ideal. But I've got to try. I take his hand and smile mildly when he holds it with a firm hand. He's not going to be the first to release. For fuck's sake, I'm too old for this game. He can have the win, but only because I know Ava will freak the fuck out if she smells some animosity between us. So I smile, pulling back until he releases me.

"My man," Sam's voice is a godsend.

"This is Sam Kelt," I say, motioning to Dan. "Ava's brother."

Sam nods, Dan nods. I get the feeling Kate's already introduced them. And I get the feeling Dan's not all too keen on Sam either. Does he like *anyone*?

"Hi, Joseph," Kate says, moving in on Ava's dad and giving him a hug he's not all too comfortable with.

"Her brother's a bit hostile," Sam says, moving into my side.

"He doesn't like me." It's a fact. "Want a drink?" I go to the fridge and pull out a bottle of champagne and some beers, making sure one lands in Joseph's hand first and Ava's brother's hand last.

"You're not drinking?" Dan asks.

"I want a clear head," I reply, offhand, smiling, relishing his obvious displeasure.

"For when you propose," he says, too loudly for my liking.

I grit my teeth discreetly and find Ava with Kate and Elizabeth across the kitchen looking more relaxed. "Look," I say, moving a little closer to him, making sure I'm out of Joseph's earshot, and everyone else for that matter. "You've made it clear you don't like me."

"Have I?"

"Come on, Dan." I'm being more than reasonable here, and it fucking kills me. But the last thing I need is another obstacle. "It will crush Ava if she senses bad feeling between us."

He looks past me to his sister. "She's a good girl."

"I know."

"Deserves the best."

"I'll give her the best."

"Don't fuck with her."

I smile, but it's mild, maybe even guilty. "If I hurt her, I give you full permission to gut me." Dan doesn't need to know that I'll have gutted myself before he gets to me. I hold my hand out, and he looks down. "Truce?"

He nods, accepting, as Cathy wanders in, all smiles, followed by an energetic Luigi. "Excuse me a moment." I head over and relieve Cathy of her bag, letting her hug me, enduring the pain, *again*, before shaking Luigi's hand. "I can't thank you enough for this." I know Cathy will be in her element. She refused payment. So I bought her some Air Miles instead. She often goes to Ireland, so she'll have no choice but to use them or waste them, and Cathy doesn't waste anything.

"I'll clear the kitchen so you can get on."

"The tables are being laid on the terrace," Luigi says. "You can move the party out there."

"Thanks."

"Now go," Cathy says, virtually pushing me back over to a curious Ava.

"What's happening?" she asks.

"We're having dinner."

She cranes her neck to see the hive of activity breaking out. "Here?"

"Yes, I arranged for Luigi to come in and do the honors. We'll eat on the terrace. It's a nice evening." I pull her closer, scanning her face as I clear her eye of a strand of hair.

"I can't believe you did this." She doesn't shy away from my affection. Another good sign.

"Whatever it takes," I say. "You know this."

"You might get the loving brother speech." She feels at my arms, looking so awkward. *Too late.* "Do you think you could humor him?"

"You mean another man telling me how to look after you?" I ask. "I don't think so." It's bad enough I've bent to her brother's ego already. If he starts throwing his weight around, I can't promise I won't help him take the weight off his feet and put him on his arse.

"Whatever it takes?" she says despondently, worried.

I can't stand it. So I bend again, kissing her sweetly. "Whatever it takes. Come on."

I herd everyone out of the kitchen to make way for Cathy and Luigi, watching, interested, as Ava's mother swoons all over the penthouse. It's a bit of a reality check. I've spent my life immersed in luxury, became a multi-multi-millionaire at twenty-one, and I've only recently come to truly see what I've got. Because for the first time in years, my vision is clear and so is my mind, letting me process my life. My world. A world that I want to be in now, because I'm with this woman.

This incredible, graceful, sometimes challenging, woman.

I watch her as she takes a seat along with everyone, smiling, relaxed, and I take the bottle of white, working my way around the table, pouring wine for all.

Except me.

And Ava.

She doesn't acknowledge my move, helping herself to a bottle and pouring herself. It's another challenge. Should she be drinking? Do I have a whole new other reason to curb her alcohol intake?

I sip my water, trying to distract myself, running over my proposal repeatedly, except now, I'm not nervous. It could be because I've got Joseph and Elizabeth's blessing. It could be simply because Ava looks so content in this moment. I smile, continuing to watch her, as she chats, laughs, completely at ease. With her parents and me in the same room. Or on the same terrace of my ten-million-pound penthouse above the dazzling, bright lights of London.

"Dan, come on," Ava drones, looking a little uncomfortable. It pulls me back to the present, and I follow her attention to her brother opposite me.

"I mean it," he says, relaxed back in his chair. "You're my baby sister." He points his bottle at me. "You've had your warning."

"Daniel O'Shea," Elizabeth snaps on a hiss. "That's enough."

I smile on the inside and raise my glass to my lips. "It's fine, Elizabeth," I assure her, taking a sip. "He's just being a big brother." *And a cunt.* I smile across the table at him, all friendly. I have a feeling it's going to get harder and harder to keep this front in place. But for Ava? I'll manage. I look away from him before we get into a staring deadlock.

"Kate's not her normal self," I say to Ava as I watch her friend chat with Elizabeth. "Is she okay?" I refill Ava's water, a silent gesture to drink up. Hopefully it'll balance out the wine, which she's having far too much of. When should I intervene?

"She and Dan have a bit of a history." Ava looks at her brother. "It's complicated."

Oh? A history as in, *a history*? And is it really history, because the vibe around the table tells me not? "I see." I look at Sam. Has he sensed it? I need to dig on that. Ava's brother does *not* need to be giving me another reason to dislike him. "Did you enjoy your pasta?"

Her joy is infectious. Her plate is empty. An appetite? She's definitely eating more. "It was lovely. Thank you."

"You are more than welcome." I take her hand that's on my knee and squeeze. "Nothing stands in the way now, does it?" No scorned exes, no scorned fucks, no parents or brothers, or too-familiar clients.

"No," she agrees, looking as light as I feel. "The path is clear."

Good. Let's get this over with. "I'm glad you said that." I stand and get a startled Ava up. "Excuse us for a few minutes."

"Where are we going?" she asks as I lead her away from the silent table.

I smile at thin air before me, taking one last deep breath before I stop, turn, and drop to my knee. Her face. God, I wish I could take a picture of it and add it to my bespoke wallpaper. "Shall we try this the traditional way?"

"Oh God." She looks over her shoulder. *Yes, baby, they're all looking at you.* I can feel her fear through our joined hands. Her nerves. Her worry. I'm quick to ease it.

"I've trampled them all," I say when she's back facing me, to check I'm really on my knee. "Delicately . . . ish." Very fucking delicately. I don't want to even consider where we'd be if her parents had hated me and insisted Ava walk away. I shudder at the thought. "I've even asked your father," I add, knowing that's the biggest hurdle for her. She jerks on a sob. A happy sob. "You must know how hard that was for me." I gaze up at her, her hair cascading over her shoulders, creating a kind of veil. A barrier. A private space for us in this moment. I take my other knee to the floor and hold the backs of her thighs, applying a little pressure, telling her I want her closer. She obliges, feeling through my hair. "Anything it takes, Ava." I want a picture of this expression too. It's the best kind of acceptance. "Marry me, baby," I whisper, and she shakes her head mildly. It's not a refusal, I know that. It's awe.

"You're crazy mad." She chokes, her emotions falling past her lips and creeping into her eyes as she dips and places her lips on mine. "You crazy, crazy man."

"Will I be crazy mad and married? Please tell me I'll be crazy mad and married to you." She's not said yes. I want a firm *yes*. So I pull her to the floor, and she blinks back her tears. "It's all about you and it always will be. For the rest of my life, it's only you," I promise her. "I love you, beyond crazy. Marry me, Ava."

She collapses into my arms, the moment overwhelming her. She's not alone. My damn throat has closed up on me, and my eyes are burning. "Is that a yes?"

"Yes." She sobs over her answer, laughs a little too, and I tumble back to the decking, taking her with me. "I can't breathe." I kiss her like we always kiss, with passion and power, and I could not give a flying fuck who judges. "I love you so much." I find her ring in my pocket and slip it on, while Ava remains hiding in my neck.

"I love you too."

"I'm so glad." I give her one last gift. "You're the best birthday present I've ever had."

She's never moved so fucking fast. She's out of my neck in a heartbeat, looking at me with a mixture of delight and surprise. "It's your birthday?"

The first one in many years that I've acknowledged. "It is."

"Today?"

"Yes." So now she will ask how old I am, and I will tell her the truth.

"How old are you?" she says, her lips stretching, the corners quirking. It's the best sight, because she fucking knows, and she doesn't give a shit.

"I'm thirty-eight." Thirty-*fucking*-eight.

"Happy birthday," she says, so thrilled, her beam so precious.

My grin hurts my face, and my eyes finally release the building tears of true fucking happiness.

"Don't mind us." Sam's voice penetrates our moment, and Ava starts laughing in my neck. I brush her hair out of my face and drop my head to the side, where our table full of guests all look on.

"I forgot we had company," I say, getting to my feet, pulling Ava up and helping her straighten her dress out. She looks at me, and I just catch a flush of embarrassment creeping into her cheeks as her mother ambushes her from the side, throwing her arms around her. Ah, fuck. Ava's shoulders shoot up, and she doesn't conceal her hiss very well. Not that Elizabeth notices. I take my life into my own hands and muscle my way between them.

"Excuse me, I'm not finished with her yet," I say, placing my palm over Ava's nape—not her back—and leading her into the penthouse. I hear Elizabeth's indignation before I turn and see it.

And so it begins.

As soon as I have Ava out of sight, I turn her, walk her to the nearest wall, and gently ease her up against it. My kiss is anything but gentle, though. I slam our mouths together, hungry for her, and she's right there with me. "We're getting married at The Manor."

She moans, grappling at my shoulders.

"In two weeks," I add.

"Okay," she says, biting at my lips.

Whoa.

I tear our mouths apart and look at her. "We're getting married at The Manor in two weeks," I repeat, leaving no room for protests when I remind her that she agreed to this in the throes of passion.

She smiles. "And I said, *okay*."

I smile. I smile so fucking hard.

And then haul her back onto my mouth, kissing her to death, and her hand squeezes me past my trousers, massages, strokes my raging hard-on. I'd love nothing more than to take her upstairs. Can't do that.

Fucking hell.

"Take me upstairs," she mumbles around my tongue, rolling herself onto me.

I groan, mentally crying my eyes out. *Really* can't do that, I tell myself over and over. I have to stop this before I ruin everything I've painstakingly built with her parents. *Respect.* So I rip myself away, panting, and shake my head.

"Please," she begs.

"No." I wipe across her mouth, dragging her lip. "Go reapply your lipstick," I order, turning her by her shoulders. "We'll have celebration sex later."

"Sleepy celebration sex?" she asks, looking unimpressed.

"There will be nothing sleepy about it. Go."

I watch her climb the stairs to the bedroom and quickly go back to the terrace, just to show my face—and only my face, because I must hide my groin area—so I poke my head around the open doors, just so everyone knows I've not dragged her upstairs, out of respect for her parents and nothing else. "Anyone want a beer while I'm in the kitchen?" I see the relief on Ava's father's face. He thought I had.

He holds his glass up that has an inch in the bottom, and I nod, looking at her brother. He raises his wine glass. Sam holds a hand up.

I spend a few moments waiting for my dick to deflate, then I go to the kitchen and give Cathy and Luigi all the praise they deserve. The kitchen looks like nothing's happened. It's astonishing. Then I go to call John.

"What's up?" he asks in answer.

"Nothing's up."

"What did she say?"

"What do you think she said?" I roll my eyes, a bit too cocksure. "Yes, of course."

"Any news on Van Der Haus?"

"Nothing. The other cameras are out of action so there's still a massive question mark over who that was in the footage."

"It's London. There are a million blond men in suites."

I scowl as I look up the stairs. I don't want to talk about Van Der Haus. "We need to send an email out to all our members."

"Why?"

"Because The Manor will be closed for the weekend in a few weeks."

"Why?"

"Because there's going to be a wedding." I press my lips together, waiting for it.

Silence.

"John—"

"In two weeks?"

"Yes."

"Does Ava know this?"

Grinning, I look down at my shoes, scuffing the soles across the wood. "She absolutely knows."

"Jesus Christ," he grumbles. "Sarah won't be happy."

I come crashing down to earth. Speaking of Sarah . . . "John, I saw the message on Ava's phone from yours. She wasn't mistaken at all."

"Fuck," he curses, and I have to agree. But I'll add a few more fucks. "What are you going to do?"

"I have to let her go." Or, more to the point, Sarah has to let *me* go. She has to let me live.

I hear his inhale, feel his dread. The blowback could be really ugly. And once again, I'll protect Ava from the poison coming. I look over my shoulder, seeing her coming down the stairs. "I have to go." I hang up. "Hey."

"Is everything okay?" she asks, unsure.

I pluck a smile from nowhere, facing her, summoning her with my arms. "Everything is fine, baby." I welcome her into my embrace, putting an arm around her and walking her out onto the terrace. And suddenly everything is far from fine. My peace was really short-lived.

And I'm back to protecting Ava from something that could hurt her.

And now, that something is Sarah.

Because she is the key to every last one of my dirty secrets and painful sins.

Jesse's side of the story continues in This Woman Forever Coming May 2024

ALSO BY JODI ELLEN MALPAS

The This Man Series

This Man

Beneath This Man

This Man Confessed

All I Am – Drew's Story (A This Man Novella)

With This Man

The One Night Series

One Night - Promised

One Night - Denied

One Night - Unveiled

Standalone Novels

The Protector

The Forbidden

Gentleman Sinner

Perfect Chaos

Leave Me Breathless

For You

The Smoke & Mirrors Duology

The Controversial Princess

His True Queen

The Hunt Legacy Duology

Artful Lies

Wicked Truths

The Unlawful Men Series

The Brit

The Enigma

The Resurrection

The Rising

The American

The Belmore Square Series

One Night with the Duke

A Gentleman Never Tells

This Woman Series

(The This Man Series from Jesse's POV)

This Woman

With This Woman

This Woman Forever

ABOUT JODI ELLEN MALPAS

Jodi Ellen Malpas was born and raised in England, where she lives with her husband, boys and Theo the Doberman. She is a self-professed daydreamer, and has a terrible weak spot for alpha males. Writing powerful love stories with addictive characters has become her passion—a passion she now shares with her devoted readers. She's a proud #1 *New York Times* Bestselling Author, a *Sunday Times* Bestseller, and her work is published in over twenty-five languages across the world. You can learn more about Jodi & her words at: www.jodiellenmalpas.co.uk

Milton Keynes UK
Ingram Content Group UK Ltd.
UKHW040753170324
439572UK00001B/4

9 781957 597508